I0708608

I conceived this project in Boston during the summer of '92 while producing my first Shakespeare (Romeo & Juliet). It was staged at the Huntington Theatre Studio and sold out before we opened. That was when the notion of a prequel was born that would reveal how the famous families came to be at each other's throats, and how the associations between so many characters were first formed. The full story frame of Capulet (6 books) was written over 4 years writing 7 days a week 7 hours a day with just a few exceptions.

For the trivial record, my first experience with Shakespeare was as a punishment in my last year of high school. I was given a detention for fighting (a bully was harassing a friend and though I'm no hero I intervened). The English Mistress who caught us made me memorise the 'quality of mercy' monologue from *The Merchant of Venice*. It had to be word perfect to avoid another stay. She told me it wasn't word perfect. But she said I was 'good' and would let me off if I agreed to audition for the play. I did. Somehow I managed to get the lead.

That led me to a BA in Drama at the University of Queensland. UQ led me to a BFA in Acting at Cornish College in the USA. That led to specialised study at the National Shakespeare Conservatory in NY (closed after 9/11) and finally an MFA scholarship to study Directing at Boston University. Fast forward 25 years. I began this project in earnest during the last few months of the pandemic.

I hope their tale moves you.

I found it very moving to write.

Marcus Hogan

Capulet

a novel series by Marcus Hogan

Inspired by the source material from 'Il Novellino' (33rd Section) by Masuccio Salernitano 1476
and all subsequent iterations thereafter until the play by William Shakespeare

Book 1: Fate

Book 2: Verona

Book 3: Justice

Book 4: Ambition

Book 5: Retribution

Book 6: Folly

ISBN: 978-1-7643534-8-9 (Paperback)
ISBN: 978-1-7643534-9-6 (Hardcover)
ISBN: 978-1-7643534-7-2 (eBook)

Published by Poquelin Press
Copyright © Marcus Hogan 2025

Copyediting and proofreading completed by Katie Lowe
Typesetting and layout completed by Essential Self-Publishing
(www.essentialselfpub.com.au)

Capulet

Book 4: Ambition

a novel by Marcus Hogan

Chapter 1 fall from Disgrace

It was Saturday still, yet the sun was finally setting. Upon the previous Sunday, Esmeralda Montecchi's incarceration had begun after she fled Verona's ancient arena, the scene of a duel where her husband Onorato was slain. She had plunged through the streets in a fit of desperation, stormed wildly into the cathedral to accuse the Capulets of treachery. In her spitting vehemence, she invoked a pagan curse of retribution down upon their heads. In the wake of all her actions, two trials erupted.

By Friday her civil trial was already complete, aided by her unmitigated confessions. As you'll recall, just one day later the Ceremony of Disgrace held in the old castle's marshalling yard had stripped the Montecchi prima donna and her dead primo don of their honorific titles. That grisly ritual had begun at midday. Before Verona's civic tower bell had chimed again it was done. As she was escorted away in dread silence — watched from the battlements above by every valued peer in Verona — the fallen prima donna could no longer count herself among the elite, let alone the exalted.

You'll also recall that when Esmeralda was first taken into custody, the personal guard of Prince Escalus ushered her afoot, in all her finery, from the cathedral to the castle and placed her in an underworld cell. Shortly thereafter, at the intercession of Princess Florentia, she was brought above ground and held in a sunlit bedchamber until the prince arrived with disturbing news. The dread Holy Office of Inquisition had been stirred into motion.

Esmeralda was shunted back to the dungeon, stripped of all possessions. Then, thanks to the spectre she met in the form of a newly appointed Inquisitor Brother Eustace — and the warnings of her fond confessor Friar Lorenzo — the prima donna was plunged into a dazing consideration. She was forced to accept that a power she could not exert control upon might alter the quality of her life forever.

A week later, still reeling after the Ceremony of Disgrace, what began as a dazing consideration had become a desperate reality. From one moment to the next until then had been a span of six days, barely a blink of the eyelash of time. Her next sunrise would usher Sunday in again. Then, with or without Esmeralda in it, life in the world beyond her captivity would not cease its motion. And so in less than one week, Esmeralda's entire world appeared to have been vanquished.

At least, as you'll finally recall, after the ritual she was returned to her confinement in a less squalid cell. She was also fed, then offered the lure of an extended rest. But her keeper, Sister Boniface, whose hard demeanour appeared to be softening to her predicament, had quietly warned her to be wary of the inquisitor's promises. Yet given the harrowing experience Esmeralda had just endured, given she felt she had done all Brother Eustace had asked of her, she assumed he would expect no more from her that day.

Esmeralda drained the bowl of thin leek soup. She gulped down a vial of water. Then exhausted to the point where even the loss of her luxurious hair — cut to shards before the ceremony began — no longer mattered, she fell into a deep slumber. It was the first time since being arrested for heresy that Esmeralda Margherita Rossana Montecchi, the woman who was no longer a prima donna, allowed herself to do so.

That was half an hour after the tower bell struck one. The door lock rattled after her keeper stepped out. And despite the sunlight still streaming in, her heavy lids shut. Settling against her thin mattress of straw above the stone slab as she did so, Esmeralda felt assured by the inquisitor's comment that she would not be interrupted until *much later*. It suggested her eyes need not open again until later that evening and perhaps, blissfully, not even until the next day.

Yet before the tower bell had struck four that same day Esmeralda was nudged persistently. Then bleary and blinking she rose from her slab. She tried to lay back again. Wiry hands gripped her shoulders and drew her up.

'Up woman.' snapped Sister Boniface. 'Up now.'

Esmeralda lifted again. Eyes opened again. There before her, the door hung open and two militia guardsmen stood waiting. The sister's anxious expression was foreboding.

Esmeralda squinted. 'Is it Sunday already?'

'Saturday still. Not yet four.'

'Not yet ...' Esmeralda faltered 'but I thought —'

'No more prattling woman. Inquisitor Eustace awaits. Hurry. Hurry.'

'Get her on her feet!' came a grumbling voice beyond the door. 'Or we'll do it for you.'

'Yes. Yes. We're coming.'

'Water please,' Esmeralda croaked. 'Water.'

Wiry hands filled a bowl from the vial. A grunt of exasperation sounded from the hall. Heavy boots shuffled. Suddenly the bowl that had lifted for parched lips was snatched away. Water smacked hard into Esmeralda's face, drenching hair, shoulders and arms.

'Get up BITCH! I won't be late for the likes of you.'

A massive hand gripped Esmeralda's arm, hauled her to her feet and dragged her beyond the threshold. Barefoot still, she stumbled through the close corridors to descend to the former level she had occupied. Despite her realisation that Apollo's fiery chariot still hadn't left the sky, the world she descended into seemed to belong to an eternal night.

Finally, a turning revealed an open door ahead and walls beyond it, bathed in the pallor of flickering light. Esmeralda recognised the interview chamber. Since her incarceration, she had attended it more than once a day, at any hour of the day or evening. By then she felt she knew the method of enquiry — what to expect. Yet as Friar Lorenzo attested to me many years later, the treatment she received on that occasion was unlike any other.

From Esmeralda's first bald interview with Brother Eustace until her final appearance at the Civil Court — Sunday to Thursday — she'd been made to stand for hours, wearily responding to droning questions put by her inquisitor or listening to his scribes repeat responses she had already given. Over the course of five gruelling days she heard them repeated ad nauseam.

The great sticking point Brother Eustace held her on during that time was with respect to the chief accusation —evidence suggested the accused had kept up an *enduring* practice of black witchcraft. That suggestion had been made clear from the start, framed by his very first question when her inquisition proper began in that bleak stone chamber chosen to serve for it.

'Esmeralda Montecchi.' he stared calmly. 'If, as you contest, you are *not* a black witch of *enduring* practice —'

'I am not —'

'Silence.' Brows lifted. 'You understand the rules as I explained them. You may *only* respond if I *invite* your response. Is that *finally* clear? Or must I instruct the gag be applied to ensure compliance?'

That instrument had been laid in readiness upon the scribe's table. Esmeralda couldn't help but glance at it.

'No Brother Eustace. I understand.'

He pouted in thought.

'Brother Simone where was I?'

The shuffler's eyes lurched then leapt to his parchment. 'Umm ... ahh ... "*not a black witch of —*'

'Yes, yes. Not of *enduring* practice, then how do you *explain* having learnt the pagan curse *by rote* which you uttered so foully in God's sacred house?'

It was a critical point to ascertain, of course. Her apparent familiarity with such an incantation appeared to evidence her guilt against that portion of the charge. Yet if conceded, that first sticking point would become a mechanism to unleash an avalanche of associated points designed to suffocate her ability or will to respond.

It took less than ten minutes in that first interrogation for Esmeralda to gain a grim sense of what lay ahead.

'Read my enquiry back again.' he instructed.

Friar Lorenzo and the shuffler were seated together at a broad table. Their scribbling halted. Their heads lifted.

'And ... *alternate* each question between you.'

They blinked in confusion, not understanding the inquisitor's method, yet not willing to question it.

'Yes Inquisitor.' the shuffler bleated.

Too nervous to locate his place, the shuffler glanced at Friar Lorenzo, urging him to start. The Inquisitor shut his eyes as the Friar's eyes widened and he cleared his throat to repeat the first question.

'What *other* conjuring spells have you learned?'

The friar glanced at the shuffler as the alternating repetition began.

'*Who* taught you that first and any others?'

'Have you ever measured or mixed potions for a *maleficent* purpose?'

'Have you ever *purchased* potions for a maleficent purpose?'

'If so, *where* and from *whom* did you obtain these?'

'Have you ever *administered* potions for a maleficent purpose to your *enemies?*'

'Do you keep congress with *accomplices* to black arts such as these?'

The inquisitor nodded his affirmation.

That had been the first volley Esmeralda endured and it had served as a portent for what followed. Brother Eustace had intended to leave her in no doubt she was facing a dogged interrogator. For three days and nights thereafter he had pressed on with relentless vigour, pursuing his quarry again, again and yet again over a bewildering list of obscure queries and suggestions.

Throughout Friar Lorenzo's attendance as a scribe, he felt the inquisitor was never satisfied by any first response from Esmeralda. Every query, claim and reply had been dissected time and again to grind her will in the hope she may reveal untold secrets. But three days on from their starting, no such result was forthcoming.

At the end of that first portion of his *enquiry*, as Brother Eustace described it, he confided to his scribes.

'For the sake of *valid* evidence, I've come to the conclusion her foreknowledge of that curse amounts to a *very small* token.'

Friar Lorenzo blinked in surprise at the frank admission. He had expected a far more prejudiced response. Yet he feared eager agreement might perversely affect the inquisitor's instincts. And so, without resorting to falsehood, Friar Lorenzo innocently questioned the surety of it.

'Do you feel certain Brother Eustace?'

'Yes. Though she repeated it more than once during her outburst in the cathedral, the incantation is just a *single* utterance, drawn from the Lusitanian mythology of her Portuguese homeland.'

'And what does that suggest to you?'

The Inquisitor pursed his lips. 'Just as she insists, Friar Lorenzo, any child as they grew, might retain such a phrase if uttered repeatedly by a doddering grandmother.'

'That does seem a reasonable assessment.'

'There can be no other for the sake of her soul.'

Friar Lorenzo nodded. 'Of course brother.'

'Our time is of the essence in this matter and we must get to the truth of it. There's nothing to be gained from pursuing flimsy evidence beyond its value. To do so would be to risk the time it may take to uncover what is tangible.'

'Yes. I see.' Friar Lorenzo pouted in thought.

'Only from that discovery will it become clear to me how to save her. That's my prima mission of course. To save her soul at any cost.'

With that purposeful summation he led them away through the bleak corridors to ascend back into the light. And so yes, the heretical incantation that Esmeralda had used to curse the Capulets was brief. Moreover sweet friends, it was certainly something that could be learnt as a child by rote with little attempt or intent to do so.

I submit it here below in English for your own consideration. Yes, I sound rather legal.

With all her will and power, may the potent force of Atégina strike them down as payment in blood for my cost.

That was the forbidden curse uttered by Esmeralda in front of the archbishop, Prince Escalus, Princess Florentia and a cathedral full of elite witnesses. Her claim to have learnt it from her grandmother as a child seemed credible. She explained the use of it began as a game. And in her Portuguese homeland, a version was also used by children before bedtime to ward away evil night spirits.

Repeated in ignorance so often, that pagan chant had lodged in her memory. Her brothers knew it. Many children of noble rank knew it and used it as a prankish jibe. Often, they'd utter it in anger to one another, exchanging *them* for *thee* in jest, never truly meaning or understanding.

However Friar Lorenzo believed it was something else Esmeralda revealed which had finally swayed the inquisitor. When she married Onorato and came to live in Verona, he faced constant peril as an active soldier. More and more openly, he began to discuss the dire aspects of his work and the dangerous trials he faced during combat.

Yet it was all for a purpose. At that time, Verona was threatened from more than one side and some rival factions within Verona schemed against his faction. Onorato's mercenary reputation as the Black Wolf began to rise, yet so did the count of his enemies abroad and within the vicinity.

As a result, during his absences Onorato feared attacks from outside upon Verona and attacks upon his faction from within. And so, quite early in their marriage, he insisted Esmeralda undertake martial training to help ensure her safety. A grim veteran was assigned to tutor her in personal combat. She had explained that during those gruelling sessions her tutor encouraged her use of the chant.

'What possible purpose could that incantation serve?' spat the inquisitor.

'My tutor said that in times of dire crisis, ordinary soldiers used personal incantations to steel their resolve or stir up their blood.'

'To motivate their anger? A personal battle cry?'

'Yes Brother Eustace. He said boys learnt such things when still young. He wanted me to fashion my own, but it must be something I'd recall instinctively. I told him I knew a fiery incantation. He suggested I try it. It seemed to rouse my ire in the manner he wanted.

And so …'

'And so …' Eustace shut his eyes 'it became a private affirmation you chanted in dire moments to summon the resolve to face an enemy without fear.'

'Yes. But without any intention to …'

'Yes … I see.' His eyes remained shut. 'I see.'

Listening on, Friar Lorenzo not only saw, but began to feel what had transpired in the cathedral may be entirely forgivable. Yes, after the disaster at the arena, when she'd seen Onorato cut down by crossbow bolts, been struck in the face herself, Esmeralda had fled in chaos. Then in grief and anger she had uttered the curse at the height of her panic. But surely every erratic reaction was triggered by the most overwhelming moment of despair her life had ever known?

Moreover he was finally convinced Esmeralda regretted that rash utterance and comprehended how misguided it was to use such a phrase for such a purpose. Finally, she agreed without question, that if she ever felt the need to do the same again, to summon resolve against such bitter hardship, she must only do so by invoking God's protection or Christ or the saints or angels.

It occurred to her wily inquisitor, of course, to summon that martial tutor who had trained Esmeralda to ratify that portion of her claim. Sadly however he was killed during the season before in the war against Padua. Despite that lack, Brother Eustace had drawn his conclusion.

'Although, as a Christian woman, your testimony reveals unwise behaviour to choose such an incantation for such a purpose, for the sake of the question put to yourself by this inquisition — *Why was it known by rote?* — I find your explanation to be credible.'

'Thank you Brother Eustace.'

'What's important now is that you *forswear* the black name of Atégina.'

'Yes I do. I foreswear it with all my heart.'

'Moreover you must denounce as impure, that childhood utterance which glamourised the ill-bred thought of an infamous Portuguese witch.'

'I *do* denounce it. It *is* impure. The thought of it now makes me feel greatly ashamed.'

Esmeralda frowned, clutched her hands and bowed her head. The beady eyes in the Inquisitor's boyish face scanned for any hint of insincerity. That was just the start of her avowals. By that evening Brother Eustace declared himself satisfied of her earnestness. What remained was to apply a *remedy* against the *sickness* of her memory of it.

'That trick of your childhood learning must be purged from your adult mind.'

The gruelling session which followed that declaration lasted three more hours. Esmeralda remained standing throughout. By its end she was utterly spent from more questioning, responding, foreswearing and denouncing. And through it all, the silent form of Sister Boniface had loomed at her shoulder.

The grim prioress refused to rest whenever her prisoner was not permitted to. It added to Esmeralda's sense of oppression. But after that gruelling session she was finally relieved to feel she'd gained some shred of victory. Barely able to stand, she listened as the notion of a remedy for her wayward learning was discussed. The inquisitor seemed inspired by a suggestion of the shuffler to replace her *dirty* incantation with a pure affirmation that mimicked it.

'Bravo Brother Simone.' he agreed enthusiastically. 'A *holy affirmation* to replace that *heretical incantation*. We must choose one that affirms a venerable saint to replace the former image of that dark apparition. An alter ego to envision when chanting it in recitation. A saint who invokes the power of light rather than darkness.'

'Why yes Brother Eustace.' said Friar Lorenzo. 'Yet which one to choose?'

Many venerable saints were considered. Then Sister Boniface suggested a recitation that novices used to call on the power of *Saint Agatha* the Virgin of Sicily.

'Lord of all you know my heart and desires. Possess all that I am. Fortify me to slay the Devil.'

In the same manner Esmeralda had used the former incantation, this prayer was used to fortify the strength of holy women in moments of peril or weakness.

The inquisitor proclaimed that notion to be inspired!

'The saintly name of *Agatha* is so very like the sullied name of *Atégina*.' He declared. 'Whose words could be better to summon in an effort to purge that dark image?'

The shuffler scowled at his praise for the suggestion. Esmeralda spoke the affirmation, agreeing it was simple to recall. The inquisitor insisted Boniface take charge of her practice to ensure a firm result. She must be made to recite until it became instinct to speak it. That result must be accomplished before he could consider his work to be done.

'The affirmation must be practiced so doggedly Sister that she begins to recite it in her sleep. I shall hold your efforts solely responsible for her progress.'

'I understand Brother.'

'I hope you do. For I'll have occasion very soon to put her result to the test.'

Listening on, Esmeralda pressed her lips. Despite any victory she felt she may have gained up to then, that warning sounded dismal. Over her shoulder the prioress stared.

'Of course Brother Eustace.' she droned.

'And remember Prioress ...' he added 'in the lower recesses here, none above ground can hear the wildest screams of disorder.'

Esmeralda and Friar Lorenzo both froze to hear that suggestion. Sister Boniface blinked in confusion.

'Yes Inquisitor Eustace.' she replied. 'Yet may I ask ... what's that to the point of my task?'

The inquisitor glanced at Esmeralda. Friar Lorenzo now felt sure the remark was calculated to unsettle her.

'I mean Sister, that for the sake of your task, you may monitor the penitent's chanting at any hour of the day or night for as long as you require and allow her to shout in full voice without any need for restraint.'

'Oh. Yes Brother.' she droned . 'In the Abbey's confinement

cells, novitiates are often compelled to learn such things by rote in the very same manner.'

'Of course.' Brother Eustace agreed as his eyes turned to Esmeralda. 'From this moment until her Inquisition is concluded, you will instruct her for half an hour upon every third hour of the day and night.'

It was clear to Friar Lorenzo that order had withered Esmeralda's spirit and failed to excite Sister Boniface.

'It shall be done. Trust me to see to it Brother.'

That was agreed upon Wednesday and it immediately led to Esmeralda's confession to all the remaining charges and an unmitigated promise to repent. From then until the Ceremony of Disgrace was conducted, Sister Boniface had compelled her, every three hours day and night for at least half an hour, to shout the affirmation in full voice. It was relentless and utterly fatiguing for both women.

From that point, the momentum of both trials gathered pace. As you know, Esmeralda agreed to make an early payment of penance, which included her appearance in the Civil Court on Friday to make full confession and seek atonement from the Capulets. Finally you'll recall, she agreed to pay her debt further, by participating in the Ceremony of Disgrace at noon upon Saturday.

And so, just a few hours after that grim ceremony was completed, Esmeralda entered the interrogation chamber yet again. Now she was in a state of higher anxiety, fed by the shock of her awakening and by her stalwart keeper's anxious demeanour. Remarkably however, when both women stepped inside the broad chamber, it was empty.

Both blinked in confusion. Sister Boniface stared at their escort. The guardsman announced that if the inquisitor wasn't yet returned, the prioress must take her prisoner to a holding cell nearby and practice recitation until called. All at once Esmeralda was returned to the hideous cell she thought she had left behind.

'In the interim' the guard grunted locking them both in together 'she mustn't be allowed to sit or lie down.'

Insidiously both were made to wait two hours more.

Yes, during that time Boniface ensured the affirmation was recited for half an hour as originally instructed. But this time when it was done, she doused her lantern to plunge them into darkness. Boniface feared the chamber held hidden passages behind its walls used for observation. Instructed not to allow Esmeralda to sit or lie down, under the cover of pitch darkness, she guided her gently back to the wall to rest.

In the swallowing gloom, Sister Boniface heard Esmeralda shivering. She laid herself against the wall next to Esmeralda and reached across her chest, turning her shivering form as she went to draw the penitent over to lay against herself. The warmth rising through the sister's robes must have felt like a furnace to Esmeralda. A hand moved behind her head. For an instant her instinct drove against the pressure of it until another palm pressed upon her forehead. The effect was irresistible and she gave into the guidance.

Esmeralda's head was turned as their cheeks met in the darkness: one like ice, the other fire. Fingertips grazed down her forehead and eyes, urging them to close. Hands gripping folds of heavy fabric lifted to embrace, as an angel from the blessed order of Saint Clare defied the spirit of her instructions to wrap her warm wings around the fallen prima donna in comfort.

'Thank you.' Esmeralda rasped in the darkness.

Fingertips pressed upon cracked dry lips.

'Hush.' came the very faint whisper. 'Rest.'

Unlike Dominicans such as the shuffler and Brother Eustace, Franciscans like Friar Lorenzo and Sister Boniface were not obliged to blindly follow a superior's instruction if it spurred against their conscience. Esmeralda thanked God for the inspiration of Saint Francis to insist upon that rule and his devotee Saint Clare for upholding it too.

It was ironic that Esmeralda had only met Friar Lorenzo because when he first came to serve in Verona she was a patroness of the Poor Clares. Sister Boniface served in Bussolengo of course. She had not met Esmeralda before. Yes, Boniface knew Esmeralda had a reputation for being a haughty prima donna. Yet she also knew Esmeralda's support for the abbey in Verona had begun when she first arrived from Portugal, and had remained unwavering since.

In truth, Esmeralda showed little interest to support any other order. The greatest irony was that independent aspect of the Franciscan's creed — the right to question a command — had made her feel the Poor Clares to be more akin to herself. Dear Heaven sweet friends, fate seems to move in such meandering ways.

By the time the inquisitor did return, night had fallen. Friar Lorenzo felt that each session he attended until that day was an unbearable torment. Yet on that occasion, he felt hopeful. The inquisitor had confided to his scribes that if all went well in that critical session, Esmeralda's torment would finally be ended. After the profound humiliation she had suffered over the previous two days, Friar Lorenzo couldn't imagine Esmeralda's plight could become any worse.

Yet when he followed the inquisitor into the interrogation chamber, he was surprised to see the Captain of Militia. Then as each man entered the ghoulish room, their eyes widened. Set in the open space, where Esmeralda was usually made to stand, stood a foreboding device. The Friar looked upon it with a very dark sense of misgiving.

Chapter 2   Pool of the Gods

Just at the time Esmeralda, so deep in the bowels of the old castle, was forced to awaken again, the Capulets and their new allies were still in Verona citadel and not far away. As agreed upon the day before, when they'd met for the first time outside the Civil Court, Armand and Ilaria were escorted by Duchess Yolanthe de Paris, her associate Sieur Auguste Nobel and her French Majesty's ward, Eloise du Marche, to an exotic domain of pleasure where water was to be their main source of indulgence.

Within an hour of departing the Ceremony of Disgrace they were relieved and relaxing together. At that grim ritual before, to which their attendance had been invited by Prince Escalus on behalf of the inquisitor, you'll recall all four factions — Capulet, de Paris, Cortellani, Nobel — had stood in their finery looking down at the spectacle, united in a show of elite force. Their attendance, coordinated by Duchess de Paris, was meant to defy threats made against the Capulets by the Montecchi upon the day before.

At that dark ceremony, perched above the marshalling yard on a private balcony, yet again they had found themselves surrounded on all sides by the Montecchi, but that time in the protective presence of Prince Escalus and Magistrate Pasqualie. As the lurid ritual ran on before them, the dire faced Montecchis, all clad in black and grey and humiliation had remained deathly quiet.

Once that duty was completed, the Cortellani faction — Don Sabatino and Donna Aurelie — resisted the temptation to join the relaxing celebration thereafter. With so much time lost to the trial that week and much to do before we returned to their estate in the northern hills, they announced their intention to return to their citadel apartments and prepare.

'Thank you Duchess.' said Aurelie kissing her thrice. 'Another time. However my big brother and new sister must return to enjoying their marriage tour.'

Don Sabatino felt Aurelie's hand reach for his arm. 'Whilst we, mia cara ...' he began 'must check upon the state of our world.'

'Yes.' agreed the young Duchess. 'Despite the disastrous events of this week for you all, I'm so very glad they've had the effect of bringing us all together.'

Sieur Nobel beside her gave an affable smile. 'And in a week or two, when we return here from Venice, I very much look forward to discussing our plans with you both.'

'Meanwhile' Yolanthe cast a mischievous glance at Armand and Ilaria 'we'll begin with this victorious couple.'

'Of course.' Aurelie agreed. She leaned to kiss her brother's cheek fondly and squeezed Ilaria's hand. 'Yet perhaps for now, given what they've been through, both should pursue a little more pleasure than business.'

And so, lacking the Cortellani's secure company to help protect us, yet escorted by a full complement of Duchess Yolanthe's mercenary Scots warriors, we entered her glamorous conveyance again. The transit was short, just four blocks to the south-west, not far from the ancient arena where the drama had begun.

Knowing an elegant bathhouse was to be our destination after the ceremony, my ebony lute hung upon my back and my battered Irish harp was tucked under my arm. A gaudy thought occurred to me then as we clattered away. What a caustic jibe it would have been during the Ceremony of Disgrace to strike up a lively air. Cupid's Balls! I never would have left it alive. But that thought made me smile.

Less than an hour later my eyes beheld the revelation of alluring bodies emerging from cocoons of exquisite attire, preparing to immerse into steaming scented water. When we arrived at *Piscinia Degli Dei* – the Pool of the Gods – Sieur Nobel embraced our hosts. Linus and Penelope Kazan reacted as if they were of his famille. Nobel introduced them to the duchess, du Marche and the Capulets.

Although our own giant warrior Caspar, young Squire Fabrizio and my sweet Maxine hung back with me hesitantly, Armand and Ilaria were quickly assured no personal guards or servers would be required, nor indeed were permitted to follow them into the exclusive establishment. Sieur Nobel himself assured them that all their personal needs would be accommodated within and all who entered would remain safe and well.

It seemed even I was to be left at the threshold. Then Nobel responded to a whisper from Eloise to Duchess Yolanthe that ran from the duchess to himself, from himself to Signore Linus and from Linus to his wife.

Signora Penelope turned politely to Duchess Yolanthe and curtsied. 'I understand your Grace, yet we retain fine musicians of our own to play for your pleasure?'

My expression was crestfallen. I saw Eloise frown. 'Do you retain any who have played for the French monarchs at their personal insistence?'

The Capulets, Caspar, Fabrizio and Maxine either turned their eyes to Heaven or shook their heads in disbelief.

Signora Kazan blinked at Eloise. 'Well ... no.' she confessed, turning to the Duchess. 'In that case your Grace, by all means, we shall happily allow it.'

No, I didn't smile. Yet I lifted my nose to appear aloof. Eloise thought that was antic. Maxine did not. And so, with yet another backward glance to my sweetheart left behind once again, I departed in the wake of elite company.

Despite the hour on a hot summer's day, from the moment we entered the atmosphere was shaded and intimate. It also offered a wonderful scent, a stark contrast to the glare and public exposure we'd experienced at the *disgraceful* ceremony. We were informed that one prestigious bathhouse in Verona, the most ancient of all, was still fed by a thermal spring. Interesting. Yet that was also a favoured haunt of the Montecchi, making it less interesting.

Pool of the Gods however had been recently acquired by the Kazans. I presumed Nobel held a stake in the venture. At ground level, it housed a drinking hall for the citizenry. For elite clientele, access to the bathhouse was only available through a separated entry and then above stairs.

At such a height, its pools were fed with water from a tower, built for purpose, that stood hard by the building. The massive oaken barrel was masked to put it out of sight and fed water through a metal trough, heated by a mighty furnace anchored between itself and the bathhouse. That clever arrangement was causing similar establishments to become popular in the Germanic states, where the presence of thermal springs is less frequent.

After introductions, the men and women of our party were ushered into separate *preparation* chambers. Yes, I went with the men. Yes, I attempted to follow the women! Oh yes, they thought I was amusing, even the flame haired, blue eyed duchess. Both Ilaria and Eloise suspected I would attempt it however. That felt like some kind of portent to me.

Once I found my way, those entering were assisted, one servant to each patron, to shed their garments. Depending on the nature of its fabric, clothing was hung or else folded and shelved. Knowing that I would *not* be immersing in a pool of any kind, hot, cold or otherwise, yet anticipating warmth ahead, I doffed my outer covering.

Nobel and Armand shed their garments completely to don open robes of shining amber silk. We were warned portions of the floor in each chamber surrounding the pools could warm up rather intensely from the latent heat. And so fetterless sandals were offered to protect the undersides of feet. I made a mental note to be cautious of that danger. My skin's rather sensitive you know. Well no, you don't know, as I've not said so before. Yet now you do know.

Oh ... just pay attention.

After being attended to individually, a single usher led the men through to the next chamber which had two entrances and a single exit. One glance revealed its intended use for massaging, oiling and scraping any patron who sought such comfort before entering a pool chamber beyond to plunge and soak.

It was in that second chamber that our entourage was reunited. We heard them chattering together before we saw them. Elegant feminine headpieces had been removed to reveal loosely bound locks, drawn down seductively, yet still held above shoulders to resist the coming touch of water. A parade of lustrous colour leapt for admiring eyes. Ilaria's golden hair contrasted with Yolanthe's carotene tresses and Eloise's dark chestnut locks.

Dear Heaven I tell you, from my work in Paris I'd been present among gatherings of scantily clad women before. Yes, I considered myself fortunate in that respect. Some I counted as sirens with great allure. Yet nothing prepared me for the sight of those three extraordinary women entering together. I was utterly mesmerised.

Now in the absence of more distracting couture, the effect of arched brows, curled lashes and lacquered lips seemed accentuated, along with necks, ears, wrists and fingers still adorned with jewels, pearls, silver and gold. All showed starkly against the elegant simplicity of their ankle-length robes of shining pearl silk and fine gauze. The latter was so sheer that the nails of a hand held under it could be seen through the surface.

Entering to greet us came a new pair of servers, one male and the other female, both clad in Grecian style thongs with nothing more above the waist. Their single garment was of fine twisted linen, wrapped about their waists and drawn firmly between their legs. At a glance I suspected both were chosen for the attractiveness of their physiques and poise.

My cathouse experience also caused me to suspect both would possess the ability to resist responding too generously to patrons. Particularly any — male or female — who sought to converse with them too long or engage them too intimately. They ushered our ensemble through to rejoin our hosts who awaited in the bathing chamber.

Penelope and Linus smiled again, embracing and kissing the members of our party once more, yet now as if all were long lost friends. No, there was no fond reception for me! Yet I paid little heed to that lack of attention for the chamber we stood in was a marvel of restful decadence. Hefty shutters darkened the windows and were hung over with thick, colourful tapestries. Together, they blocked virtually all daylight from penetrating at any hour.

Penelope explained, however, they could be drawn away upon request when patrons sought, in the ancient Roman style, to warm their bodies in the morning or afternoon sunlight. And for any who wished to lay out of the water at noon to expose their bodies to the most potent glow from Apollo's fiery chariot, a quartet of large ceiling panels directly overhead could also be drawn back.

But the darkened effect that greeted us that day, with the chamber bathed in fluttering light made it feel like a blissful sanctum of seclusion. The ceiling and every wall were draped with soft shining fabrics, their textures catching the glow of dozens of oil lamps and candelabra which illuminated the chamber.

Dominating the centre of course was the surface of the pool, held in a vast wooden tub, its rim fashioned flush to the hardwood floor surrounding it. The pool was deep enough for a man of moderate height to stand in the centre immersed up to their chest. And it was broad enough to allow a generous number — at least a score — of bodies to sit at their ease or lounge together around its generous circuit.

From where we had entered, a path of exposed flooring offered one the chance to walk without hindrance up to the watery edge. More of the same around the pools circumference gave access to stroll around the full circuit. Intrigued by the warning we were offered, I reached down to touch it. Yes it was palpably warm, almost hot. Elsewhere however, soft furs were laid on the floor and strewn with decadent cushioning to shield against that effect.

Every spare portion was covered to allow patrons to walk beyond the rim on bare skin or sit or recline without any need to cover one's body. The exception was a second pathway that led from the watery edge into another chamber. Before I could consider any more, Nobel led by example being first to disrobe and wandered to the edge.

Before entering the clear scented water, which exhaled wisps of steam here and there, he gathered a wide glass of their potent hazel liqueur. Unlike some merchants I knew, who tended to taste their own fare and become large about the middle, the fabric merchant showed a trim figure. He was covered from chest to waist with dark woolly hair and hung under all that was a modest manly endowment.

Oh yes, I noticed it. Well I'm sure all young men feel compelled to compare their own to another's. As the water rose above his thighs Nobel released a groan of pleasure, drawing more attention to himself. The pool held two ledges below its surface to step down onto before one's feet felt the bottom. Both ledges underfoot were wide of course, so as not to be easily tripped upon.

Nobel lowered to the first step with a smile. Then raising his glass, his ass descend below the steaming waterline as he stepped down again. Taking one more step immersed him to the base of his chest. He waded to the further side, dipping his head under before rising again.

His bare ass lifted. He turned with a welcoming smile and lowered to sit upon the first ledge, facing us all. The water lapped at his waist as the female server stepped down beside him, lowering to her knees to present a salver of morsels to tempt his interest. One had ventured in, four were left to follow. All at once I became mindful of my task.

As soon as the Duchess came to understand I possessed musical talent which Eloise suggested Queen Marie had praised me for, she insisted on judging my skill for herself. Not knowing what the ambience of this destination may be however, I had brought both my lute and harp to fit the tone of my offering to whatever I may find.

Indeed, while they had greeted each other again after we entered, I wandered about to find myself a vantage. I was settled by the time Nobel had sauntered into the water. As I watched his server kneel I was minded to begin tuning both instruments, a subtle way to draw attention to myself. Naked bodies can be difficult to compete with in that regard, yet working in the cathouse had taught me a trick or two.

My eyes rested upon the duchess as I began to play and hum a romantic lament. It was just a taste, to see if I could lure her interest. The quartet still stood together with the hosts. The Capulets were hand in hand, looking a little protective of each other. As soon as I began tuning however, Ilaria smiled at me. I felt she was proud to show me off in front of such a potent clutch of new associates.

Moments after I began the Duchess and Eloise were approached by the hosts who began to peel their coverings away. Oh for the love of folly, it was impossible to keep my mind upon my work as soft silk slid from two pairs of flawless shoulders, offering up the sight of their forms to all. Penelope hovered about their hair, tucking loose strands away. Neither woman seemed abashed by the revelation of their bodies. I suspected the presence of Armand standing opposite may have had something to do with that.

Each reached for a glass of liqueur. Long lacquered nails — bronze for the duchess, scarlet for Eloise — gleamed around rims of finely cut crystal, etched with acorns and filigree. A salver of morsels in the male server's hands was lifted to tempt them. They pretended to be distracted by his offering and himself. Yet as Penelope stepped behind Ilaria and drew the robe from her shoulders, neither could resist the temptation to watch.

If they hoped to be encouraged by the sight of some imperfection, I can only say that when the silk fell away, any such hopes must have been dashed. Yes, Duchess Yolanthe de Paris and Demoiselle Eloise du Marche were both very alluring. Yet so was their rival. Since that time I've come to the conclusion of course, there is no such thing as physical perfection.

Every person — more or less — is drawn to others by the vagaries of their own preferences. What's alluring to one may not seem alluring to another at all. Yet only a fool would fail to acknowledge the presence of God-given beauty where it was so evident, as it was on that day. I glanced discreetly, then began to sing, pleased to notice it distracted that smouldering young duchess.

'Dear Heaven Eloise you're right. What an *exquisite* voice.' I inclined my head in thanks as she used her comment to close upon Ilaria. 'Oh darling he's *very* good. How much do you *want* for him?'

Eloise had followed her of course.

'Yoli!' she huffed. 'Not *every* person is for sale.'

Ilaria grazed her eyes over the salver between them, then met Yolanthe's gaze. 'You want our *squire*. You want our *musician*. I suspect you also want my *husband?*'

Armand shared a self-deprecating glance with Eloise who smiled.

But Yolanthe matched Ilaria's gaze with a look of penitent confession.

'Darling it's true. I do want them all.' She glanced at Armand. 'So ... don't treat any of them poorly *or else*.'

Eloise tilted her eyes to Heaven, hoping to ensure Ilaria understood that was nothing but a tease. But before Ilaria could respond, Yolanthe turned to evade her reply.

'Auguste darling?' she called. 'How do I look?'

'Yoli you know you look as beautiful naked as you do in the finest couture.'

'Hmm?' she turned back to Ilaria. 'That's a *clever* thing to say. *Liar!*' she called to Nobel with a smile.

'Not at all Yoli.' he protested. 'Penelope! Linus!' The hosts were replenishing the liqueur. 'Dame Capulet's the daughter of mercantile *royalty!*' Swishing to stir, Linus handed a glass to Ilaria. 'Treat her like a queen!'

Penelope reached to tuck a loose strand of Ilaria's hair. 'Oh Auguste, every woman to *Piscinia Degli Dei* is treated like a Queen.'

Yolanthe pouted. 'I don't like the sound of that at all. I need to feel *special.*'

'Then you Duchess ...' Linus announced 'shall be treated like a Goddess!'

'Yes that sounds better.' Yolanthe smiled. 'And speaking of Goddesses.' Her eyes turned to Ilaria. 'Armand, your wife's body is divine. Even I want to make love to her.'

Ilaria all but spurted her liqueur.

'Leave the poor woman alone Yoli!' Eloise scolded as she sipped delicately.

Yet just as she said so Penelope drew Armand's robe away to reveal the contours of his hardened physique. If it was done in an effort to distract them all it had the desired effect.

'Oh dear God!' shrieked Yolanthe. Her hand fell onto the swell of his chest to trace a livid scar. 'Is this where that *bitch* ...?'

'I'm very glad to hear someone *else* call her that.' said Ilaria. 'But no —'

'No Yoli.' Eloise interrupted Ilaria in turn. 'That's from an English archer in Carentan.'

With the excuse of explanation at her disposal, Eloise sidled in too and laid her fingers on the scar. Ilaria betrayed a grimace of frustration that Eloise shared enough intimacy to know so much. All at once, Armand was at odds about which direction to look. I didn't know whether to be amused or concerned for him. Everywhere his eyes sought to stray, feminine eyes caught his own and drifted over his form as they grazed with fingertips and discussed him together.

Armand seemed to suffer it silently, or perhaps he enjoyed it silently. Either way, it were as if my handsome young master was a gorgeous statue brought along for their personal assessment and admiration.

'You're right Eloise' Ilaria conceded 'that was the English arrow. The *bitch* shot him in the *back*.'

Yolanthe's eyes lit with interest. 'Oh gorgeous man, turn around and let me see.' Armand began to turn but paused when she cried again as her fingertips leapt to trace a scar below his rib. 'Dear Heaven Ilaria what's *this* one?' Then she reached for his thigh. 'And *that?*'

Armand explained for himself. 'Those were taken at Formigny your Grace.'

Ilaria touched his rib with a frown. 'That was a *pike*.' She touched his thigh. 'This was a *dagger*.'

Yolanthe's brows suddenly knit in anger. 'Oh those ... *fucking* English bastards!'

Eloise widened her eyes. 'Hold nothing back Yoli.'

'Oh Eloise don't be absurd! It burns my blood to think —' her eyes filled with passion as she checked herself. 'At any rate, I'm sure Ilaria has said *worse* when occasion demanded. I'm pleased to now know we share the want to call that Montecchi *slut* what she is!'

'Like my husband Yolanthe, upon rare occasions, I've been known to allow my language to flare.'

That was a coded reprimand for Armand of course, who had not shared with Ilaria what both women had revealed the day before. As you'll recall, both had known about Armand's use of crass language in his most passionate moments at Carentan. Now he wore a sheepish look. I thought Ilaria's poke of revenge was justified and amusing.

'Oh my love.' Yolanthe clutched Ilaria protectively. 'When you saw him with *these* you must have felt —' She embraced her impulsively. 'Oh you *poor* thing.'

It was already clear the Duchess was prone to emphatic displays of passion. Yet it was also clear she could be manipulative. At that moment however, even I was convinced her empathy was genuine. Then I found myself questioning, was she really imagining what Ilaria must have felt, or simply imagining how she would have reacted herself if Armand belonged to her.

As Yolanthe drew back she glanced at Armand. 'Now ... I *must* see the others. *Turn* for me Adonis.'

Like a slave in the market he revolved at her bidding. I couldn't tell whether the sight of his wound or the play of the muscles in his back and ass drew her greater attention. I could tell that now the wound in his back was clearly revealed, Eloise was staring too.

'Armand!' she spat, seeing it for the first time. 'Merciful Gods she *must* pay for that!' Eloise stared hotly at Ilaria. 'No *wonder* you made her kneel in the court.'

'Thank you Eloise. I didn't think it too much.' Armand suffered a second glance of reproach and seemed to feel he deserved that too.

'No I should say not.' Yolanthe agreed. 'However Ilaria I must confess something to you.'

Ilaria blinked innocently. 'Yes Yolanthe?'

'The sight of it makes me want to *kiss* Adonis where he was hurt —'

'YOLI!' Eloise snapped hotly.

'Yes! Yes! Yes however Ilaria darling ... for pity ... I'll kiss *you* again instead.'

Ilaria seemed surprised to feel the press of sincerity holding upon her cheek. She withdrew it and their eyes met. Ilaria smiled, seeming to lose her last shred of impatience with the prankish pair. 'Such *restraint* Yolanthe?'

'Oh fuck it all woman. You must call me *Yoli!*'

Eloise spurted her own liqueur in surprise. The sparring duet were now staring at each other.

'*Well* Eloise?' huffed Yolanthe. 'Oh for the love of mercy. We're standing here *naked* with our *hands* all over her naked husband. I'd hardly call this a *formal* interaction!'

'And ...' Nobel called 'you're all standing *outside* the pool which is not what this chamber was created for.'

Looking very much at his ease, Nobel raised a glass above the steaming water with beckoning intent. Yolanthe kept her eyes on Ilaria for a moment.

'Call me Yoli.' she repeated. Then she puckered her lips slowly, looked down and lowered them onto the scar upon Armand's back. Lifting she patted it gently. Her eyes met Ilaria's again who frowned in mock reprimand as the Duchess drew away to sashay around the rim of the pool.

My voice became lost as my eyes followed her. I watched her hips swaying gracefully as she went. She halted to step from her sandals and accept Nobel's reaching hand. Then lowering herself with a sigh of relief, Yolanthe de Paris leaned back to display her chest and the play of carotene hair above the perfection of her neck and shoulders.

I hummed gently and began to wonder how I became so blessed as to be granted admission to such extraordinary situations in the company of such extraordinary people. Clearly the elite didn't live as the rest. Perhaps one day I'd sit in a pool with such people rather than just play for them.

'Ilaria come in!' Yolanthe insisted. 'It's blissful. Hurry Eloise. Stop showing yourself off! He's *spoken* for!'

'I'm sorry Ilaria' Eloise began quietly 'but it's true. I *do* like to show off.'

'Yes so I'm told' Ilaria glanced at Armand 'in manly attire, and on horseback no less?'

Eloise grinned. 'Manly attire. Womanly attire. No attire at all!'

'No attire at all?' Ilaria lifted her brows and bent a questioning glance at her husband.

'Yes.' Eloise added. 'But I'm sorry to confess, this is the first time he's seen me naked.'

'Is that reassuring?' Ilaria asked stoically.

'Dear Heaven but you're patient.'

'Am I?'

'Yes.' Her brown eyes stared frankly. 'I can see why he loves you. He knows I'm fickle. But like a good friend he tolerates that with patience.' Her hand reached for Ilaria. 'I hope we can be friends. You must grow used to me. Heaven knows you'll never grow used to Yoli and her flirting.'

'She is ... relentless?'

'With men *and* women. Be warned. If she can't have Armand? Consider yourself a target.'

Normally, I would have considered such a remark an antic quip. And although it was said in a moment of subdued conviviality, it seemed clear Eloise was attempting to be candid. Ilaria and Armand shared an interesting look.

Eloise sipped, turned upon her heel and began to sashay around the pool too. Yes, that distracted me. Both women seemed beautiful to me. Both had captivating eyes and hair. Yolanthe was tall, while Eloise was middling in height. Like a sensual siren, Yolanthe was full breasted and curvaceous yet Eloise was trim, firm and pert breasted, like a female athlete. Ilaria's own figure and height stood somewhere between both descriptions.

When Eloise reached Nobel and Yolanthe, she lowered herself on the other side of him. He appeared far too nonchalant for a mature man who sat between a pair of a such beautiful younger women. Deciding to enter at the pools nearest point, Armand and Ilaria finally approached the rim facing the trio opposite. Armand stepped onto the second tier and offered his hand to Ilaria. Now like mischievous children together, Yolanthe, Auguste and Eloise watched on with interest.

From across the pool at that distance of course, it was impossible to avoid a view of his masculinity; a fulsome endowment that hung to suggest intimacy with Armand would not be a disappointment. Nor could they fail to notice the hair between Ilaria's legs was as fair as the hair above.

As Ilaria stepped into the pool beside Armand, he lowered himself down then slid back to offer her room on the wide seating ledge in front of him. She stepped onto the second ledge before him, then revolved and lowered herself between his muscular thighs. For a moment, the allure of her lovely form raised brows and smirks from the other side. Facing all three with a smile, Ilaria wiggled back to nestle in, leaning her back onto his firm torso, laying her head upon the swell of his chest.

A server had held their glasses while they descended and returned them to each. Sipping to taste the liquid, Ilaria watched the others still. Slowly, her free arm lifted from the water, reaching up and behind to lay her fingertips against Armand's neck and head. She tilted her head back to draw a kiss from him. Her eyes shut as his lips descended, creating the image of a languishing God and Goddess. After taking their time, Ilaria settled again and gazed at them all.

'Oh Auguste you were right!' she purred, inhaling the scent rising upon the steam. 'This is what we needed.'

'Ilaria?' Yolanthe smiled.

'Yes … Yoli.'

'Ah. That's much better, darling. Do your close friends have a pet name for you?'

'My famille and dearest friends call me *Ria*.'

'Oh I like that. Yet Adonis doesn't call you Ria.'

'No. He only calls me —'

'Angel.' Yolanthe sighed. 'Yes darling we know but that's not for me. *Ria* sounds just right. Well then Ria, you will let me know if you ever require *assistance*.'

'Assistance for?'

'Oh Ria, no matter how irresistible a *man* may be —'

'Yoli! Whatever you're about to say —'

'Hush Eloise.' Yolanthe frowned with mock concern. 'I mean to say Ria, though you're newlywed, even at the start, there can be moments when a woman is simply too *spent* to summon the passion her husband may need to be —'

'Yoli ...' Ilaria frowned quizzically 'I think I can already feel some of the passion that I've summoned.' Her eyes shut again as she smiled. 'And I don't *believe* I shall require any assistance to attend to it.'

Armand's knee was bent. Ilaria drew her hand drew provocatively across his thigh. Yolanthe and Ilaria's eyes had become locked together, light blue blazing into green. A moment of restraint hung in the balance, then Yolanthe, Eloise and Auguste all burst into a fit of infectious laughter.

Although he had stoically averted his eyes again, even Armand was smiling. It seemed he was becoming used to being the centre of such flirtatious attention. It caused my mind to cast back to the attention Esmeralda Montecchi lavished on him when we first met with her, and how quickly that changed when her foul husband had arrived. Thank God that beast was gone, I thought, and that nightmare was finally ended.

Ilaria opened her eyes, grinning at their enjoyment.

'I know I *should* apologise Ria. But you can tell how much I love to flirt.'

'*Do* you?' Ilaria sipped. 'Mmm. Auguste this liqueur is exquisite.'

'*Love* to flirt?' Eloise huffed. 'It's a *compulsion*.'

'Well yes.' Yolanthe purred. 'But only when I'm so far from my gorgeous *Reynard*. Which is too often.'

'The duke?' Armand was happy to alter the subject.

'Oh Adonis, he doesn't *mind*. Heavens, he's older than Auguste! We married for convenience darling, *my* convenience. It's why he was contracted to take my name.'

'Oh?' Ilaria murmured. 'Who was he *before*?'

'*Bouchard*. And Ria he's very, very handsome.'

'He is.' Eloise agreed.

'And ... I *love* the way he makes love to me.'

Ilaria stared and pouted with a frown. 'Yoli do you always discuss *intimacy* so ...'

'Scandalously?' Eloise insisted, bulging her eyes.

'Candidly.' Yolanthe corrected. 'Yes of *course* I do darling. The two of you are just getting started. Wait 'til you've extended your circuit, particularly beyond borders. *You'll* see. Without Reynard's intimacy for my comfort, flirting is a lovely diversion.'

'Forgive me for *diverting* the subject.' said Nobel.

'Oh yes you would!' she huffed in mock protest.

'But Yoli that theme, that they're *just getting started*, tweaked my mind to our business.'

'*Everything* tweaks your mind to our business.'

He ran on as his eyes settled on Armand. 'By the civil court's ruling, you've been granted *unencumbered* —'

'Really Auguste' Yolanthe interrupted 'who utters a word like *unencumbered* in such a seductive setting?'

'Oh? I think that's a very alluring word Yoli. I'm interested in the allure of *enlarging* our fortunes. And *unencumbered* title to a prestigious holding such as *Sycamore Hill* ...'

Yolanthe frowned at herself. 'Yes Auguste, you're right darling. That *does* sound seductive.' she purred.

Nobel ran on. 'Armand please correct me if I'm wrong. But I'm given to understand that as well as their holdings in the citadel, your sister's faction controls the connecting estate?'

Armand raised his brows, nodded his assent, and wound his arms firmly around Ilaria, now more attentive to Nobel than Yolanthe.

'Ah then, with blood relations hard by who also hold titles in the citadel, that unencumbered holding at Sycamore Hill would appear to offer you both safe roots if ...'

'If?' echoed Armand.

'If you were both minded ... perhaps ... to stay here for a time and try your luck in the local market.'

The duchess appeared to have sobered to Nobel's effort. 'Yes, pretty people.' she agreed. 'Have you considered the prospect of *settling* in Verona? Or do you intend to hold this new asset at a *distance?*'

'Or ...' added Nobel 'perhaps you plan to sell it and be done before you return?'

'Oh no.' Ilaria surprised him with her decisive tone. 'I'm sure the latter's no option for us. Is it, my heart?'

'No angel.' Armand agreed.

'We'd sooner offer it *gratis* to Aurelie than sell. But in truth Auguste, the question you ask is one of those *things* Armand alluded to yesterday — things we're *yet to decide.*'

Ilaria's lack of denial toward any interest to stay in Verona however, simply triggered more interest. The Duchess frowned thoughtfully.

'Then Ria ... that would suggest you are *considering* the prospect of settling?'

Hearing that question was the very first moment I realised for myself that may be a possibility. Ilaria leaned her head back in response and turned to look at Armand.

'Considering it?' she said as his brows lifted. '*Yes.*'

Armand kissed the corner of her forehead in agreement. Feeling his touch, Ilaria turned to kiss him again. Yet she did it so possessively I felt sure she was signalling to her rivals how much they belonged to each other.

'Oh.' said Yolanthe glancing at Nobel.

'That's very good to hear.' he added with a smile. They seemed to speak fluently in tandem on subjects that shared their interest. 'No matter whether you stay *or* return, now that you hold a significant local asset, we wish to sound out your interest in an enterprise of ours.'

Ilaria pouted in consideration. The look on her face began to unsettle me. I knew from Maxine that, due to Ilaria's anxiety over the last two days, she had eaten very little. And as her glass was filled again, the glint in her eye made me suspect their liqueur was beginning to affect her.

'I can disclose to you both that, as an agent for Marchand & Quenneville abroad ...' she offered rather too casually 'we *do* have mercantile ambitions in Verona.'

'And *beyond* Verona.' added Armand.

He squeezed his embrace about her shoulders. A glance between Yolanthe and Nobel urged them to compress their smiles. Yet it gave the impression of a pair of ragamuffins who contemplated mischief.

'Why are we *not* surprised to hear it?' Nobel's tone was convivial. 'Well, your *own* designs notwithstanding, I can disclose we have a *substantial* venture afoot here already that may be aligned to your own interest.'

'And during this first tour, we've made a *great* deal of progress toward it.' added Yolanthe.

'Before departing Lyon' Nobel ran on 'our factions entered into a long-term partnership which, as a starting point, has committed us to a *decade* of working together.'

Ilaria's eyes widened. 'You have a *firm* agreement?'

'I consider it a *marriage* darling.' purred Yolanthe.

'That sounds ... intimate.'

Yolanthe laid her hand on Nobel's and wound her fingers through his before kissing his bearded cheek.

'A partnership of such length is of no less importance.' she purred. 'Reynard's my husband at *play*. Auguste is my husband at *work*.' She stroked his beard. 'Were he not a Jew I may have made him *both*.'

Yolanthe's eyes were beginning to fire with intensity. Her potent charisma, well known to her famille as the undisputed matriarch of their powerful House, was finally beginning to emerge beyond her mask.

'*Madame* Nobel may object to hearing you say so!' Eloise said with a smirk, patting Nobel's other hand with a playful, yet questioning glance.

'Perhaps.' said Yolanthe. Her eyes hung on Armand. 'Yet if I had needed to, I would have found her another husband. One less occupied with servicing my own needs.'

Yolanthe's glance shifted to Ilaria as she smiled. She slid like a serpent from her seat and slithered through the steaming water to turn and nestle in next to the fond pair.

'However Ria, she can have Auguste as *her* playmate. I love him for his devoted attention to the rises and falls in my *ledger*.'

'Yoli, you manage to make even the keeping of *accounts* sound seductive.'

The sultry young duchess drained her cup, reaching out seductively to place it on the floor. The Grecian clad male lowered to his knees to collect it. Yolanthe smiled at him then caught Ilaria's eye.

'Oh I think that kind of devotion is *very* seductive Ria.' She glanced at Ilaria's hand entwined with Armand's. 'A marriage needs seduction.'

She laid a fingertip on Ilaria's wrist to graze up the length of her arm, tipping off the crest of her shoulder to move onto Armand's bicep, grazing down until it rested on their hands.

'And in return for that devotion Ilaria —' Nobel lifted Eloise's hand in turn '— I expect Yoli will deliver a *faithful* term of partnership to me.'

He pressed his lips upon the back of her hand. Eloise seemed to accept it without any show of interest or dismissal. That startled me. I felt certain it startled Armand.

'Truly Auguste ...' Ilaria replied calmly, though I felt sure these revelations were startling her too 'it seems Yoli and yourself are a match made in Heaven.' She turned her face to stare into Yolanthe's pale blue eyes. The flame haired siren was now hovering in their company as intimately as an additional lover.

'Oh we *are* darling. However ...'

Cautiously but unstoppably, Yolanthe held Ilaria's gaze and slithered out a hand to reach behind the heft of Armand's broad neck, leaning her breast against the edge of his shoulder.

'Ilaria.' she whispered. 'Armand. We can think of an even *better* match. One truly made in Heaven.'

'Can you?' said Ilaria quietly.

Had I not still been playing but softly, I would have said at the moment one may have heard a feather float.

'Of course darling. Our mariage de *deux*, could be a marriage de *trois*.'

'Hmm ... de trois?

'De trois.'

'Let me guess ... Paris?'

'Yes.'

'Nobel?'

'Yes.'

'Hmm ... Capulet?

'In time darling, to satisfy its need, who knows how many may enter our menage.'

'More?' asked Armand, drawing her fond glance.

Yolanthe had drawn so close to him I felt sure he could smell the sweetness of her breath and noticed the smattering of light freckles that dotted her shoulders, clavicle and the swell of her chest.

'Perhaps Ria ...' she whispered '*Cortellani* too.'

'Ahhh yesss I see.' Ilaria purred, rolling her cheek to face her. 'Interesting.'

'Perhaps even ... *Orlandi?*'

'Hmm? Yoli who is that, pray tell?'

Yolanthe glanced at Nobel. He nodded assent. Her tone became conspiratorial. 'Oh he's a very, very, very wealthy count from the south who now resides in Verona.'

'A count?' said Ilaria.

'Yes Ria and ... through a powerful intermediary —'

'My good friend' Nobel put in 'Enea Piccolomini who serve's up north in the Emperor's court, my very good friend Count Orlandi is connected to the service of his Holiness in Rome.'

Yolanthe smiled as Nobel finished his affirmation. She nodded her agreement, reaching out a fingertip to gently trace Ilaria's brow.

'Indeed Ria, after Auguste shows off his flourishing assets in Venice to me over the next few days, I'm headed onto Rome to meet the count who has...' She traced the other brow. 'promised to introduce me to Piccolomini.'

'Oh? And how will that assist you?'

'I hope it will assist us all darling. For if all goes well with both men, we may secure a *bottomless* fund of local support for our Italian enterprise backed by his Holiness.'

'That sounds very ...' began Ilaria.

'Political.' Armand finished with a frown.

'As trade expands Adonis' even Ilaria now smiled at her use of that sobriquet 'it becomes impossible to separate business from politics.'

'Hmm.' Armand pouted. 'I'm not a political person.'

'Fortunately gorgeous man, in our company, you wouldn't *need* to be. Oh honestly darling, politics *bores* me too. Yet I do have a *talent* for it. Don't I Auguste?

'A very *great* talent.' Nobel smirked.

'And ... in order to secure such a boon for our enterprise darling, I'll be as political as that *need* requires.'

She said it so blithely, yet to me it sounded ominous.

'We've already begun to lay our foundations without such help of course.' Added Nobel. 'And if we so choose, we can forge on entirely without it.'

'En route from Lyon Ria ...' Yolanthe reached to dip a finger into Ilaria's liqueur 'Auguste and I secured assets in both Grenoble and Milan from our joint fund.' She parted her lips, pushed her finger in to taste and drew it out slowly.

'Grenoble.' said Ilaria. 'I think it's a *very* interesting location.' She dipped her own finger in and offered it to Armand who seemed to enjoy her attention. I began to suspect the potent concoction was affecting him too.

'So do we Ilaria.' said Nobel with a grin. 'We leave for Venice tomorrow. My emporium there is thriving beyond all expectation. It's been open for two seasons.'

'Does trade in Venice *have* a season?'

Nobels eyes leapt open. He tossed his head to laugh.

'Oh Yoli she's a clever woman! In Venice, Ilaria, every month is the season for something.' He was suddenly enraptured. 'For one cut from the right cloth, such as yourself, a mercantile port of such stature ... truly my dear, Venice is intoxicating.'

'Yet Verona is crucial to our interest too Ria.' Yolanthe added. 'This visit is just a *preliminary* assessment. We've inspected several sites already. Yet we —'

'Hadn't planned to action another purchase' Nobel put in 'until we had returned.'

'Howeverrrr ...' Yolanthe purred 'We didn't expect to find the daughter of my partner's greatest rival here.' Her eyes met Armand. 'Let alone to find her on the hand of a feted Chevalier, or see them locked in a trial to decide the ownership of such a formidable asset.'

Nobel was animated. 'Ilaria for years I've hoped to find a potent excuse to approach your parents with a venture to end our rivalry. You say you harbour an interest *here*?'

'Yes Auguste we certainly do.'

'Then may I ask what *particular* interest draws you?'

A smile creased Ilaria lips. Drawn on by the haze of drink and surging with confidence in her pedigree, she stood slowly, dripping water, and stepped down to draw on through the wide basin. Lowering and rising again she turned to settle where the duchess had been perched next to Nobel. Clearly Yolanthe, her arm still cradled about Armand's neck, hadn't expected Ilaria to do so and appeared to wonder why she would leave him in her close company.

Then with no hint of irony or sarcasm, the dimples on Ilaria's cheeks perked, as she offered them her answer.

Chapter 3 the Ordeal

On a fateful day in our future, these words will be uttered by Esmeralda Montecchi —

After suffering an ordeal at the hands of an inquisitor I feel compelled to lack mercy for all.

Inside the interrogation chamber, the device that Friar Lorenzo had found himself staring at so gravely, was not unlike a child's seesaw. Yet it wasn't as long as a seesaw and the stout board above was wider than any used for a prankish teetering device. It was suspended over the same style of fulcrum below, similar in appearance to a carpenter's horse so often used with a plank to improvise a seesaw. This fulcrum was not made of stout wood however but stout iron and sat higher from the ground at waist height.

And so the make of that mechanism seemed simple, yes. But as the Friar stared, the manner of its use remained uncertain which made the tall man shudder at its sight. More foreboding still was the image of what was affixed to each corner of the board, wide belt leathers with receiving buckles anchored by them. Next to the device sat a wooden pail, large enough for child to bathe in, and indeed, it brimmed with water. A smaller bucket beside it was filled with torn strips of gauze, and a hard, tallish stool sat next to all.

Behind that worrying display — more foreboding than all else — two grisly new characters to the drama stood in wait. The pair appeared to be some manner of master and apprentice. Friar Lorenzo assumed the taller man might become the occupant of the stool? Or was that finally a modicum of luxury provided for Esmeralda to sit on?

The eldest of the grim pair was of middling height, wiry, muscular and wore no upper covering save a thin shirt of impoverished linen. His drawn sleeves were held above his elbows by makeshift garters. Friar Lorenzo felt that for all intents he looked as if he may be a smith. He wondered if either were the same men enlisted to officiate at the noon day fiasco. He recalled the grim faces of those smiths from earlier — felt he may never forget them. Yet at that moment he couldn't be sure if either were those, for each wore a close-fitting hooded mask to obscure their identity.

The taller apprentice, younger by perhaps ten years or more, judging by the less weathered shine of his skin, appeared more warrior like, bulging with muscle from calf to neck. Ominously Lorenzo thought the hooded masks may identify both as servants to the Office of the Public Executioner. He felt certain however such a grave task as an execution, even under such circumstances, could not be undertaken so peremptorily that night. And so the humble friar surmised that the kind of men usually employed to conduct executions, might also find employment in the kind of role he now feared himself about to bear witness to.

It wasn't regular practise for executioners to conduct their work in anonymity. Yet it wasn't unheard of. Particularly so if the threat of retribution from a powerful faction against the conduct of their work, incited fear to perform it unveiled. This donning of masks suggested to the Friar that fear of a Montecchi response to whatever was about to occur, had prompted that need to be disguised.

Many of the men — and in some cases women — of that craft, were considered *noble* by the grant of their profession. Yet the nature of their profession was considered to be so *ignoble* that few in exalted society would willingly engage with any of their ilk. Ironically therefore, their station was politically exalted, yet their faction was socially outcast.

Exalted or otherwise, both menacing forms stood impassively in wait upon their need. From behind the safety of his station — an oaken table in the shadowy recess at the rear — Friar Lorenzo feared what impact the sight of them, and the mechanism they stood by, would have on Esmeralda. With nothing upon her feet to announce her footfall, a click at the latch from the door and the subsequent heave of it, were the only warning he had of her entry. Her hang-faced keeper, Sister Boniface, was following behind.

Esmeralda dared not halt as she came on before she turned to face the Inquisitor's table, even though her eyes met the lurid sight of that device and the masked men behind it. By the time she did turn, despite her firm intent to reveal no fear at all, her eyes were already brimming with tears. Her Inquisitor, Brother Eustace sat next to Don Elio Lanza, the Captain of Militia, whose appearance on that occasion seemed as surprising to Esmeralda as his blank expression.

Halting behind Esmeralda and already gulping in shock, Sister Boniface turned to face them too.

'Good evening Esmeralda Montecchi.'

The Inquisitor's manner was cordial. The table he and Captain Lanza sat behind was a mimic of that for his scribes who were located behind and offset to the their right. Friar Lorenzo sensed Captain Lanza was very ill-at-ease to see at close range the result of Esmeralda's recent treatment.

'The hair of a novitiate becomes you.'

Friar Lorenzo bent his brows at the extraordinary remark. Yet a twitch in Esmeralda's eye, of something akin to relief, made him wonder if the inquisitor always began at such moments with an attempt to lull. The inquisitor ran on.

'I say so because I feel your submission to that need, without protest, is firm evidence of your willingness to endure the penance you must pay. Congratulations.' Her jaw hung in disbelief. 'I hope you're *thankful* for the chance to sacrifice your hair as a token of repentance? I know the sight of you at the ceremony had a great effect on your *peers*.'

She pressed her lips to swallow.

'Yes Brother Eustace ... I'm ... thankful.'

Her voice croaked from chanting. And this time, unlike every time before, Esmeralda hadn't glanced at the friar to look for guidance before her response. She knew what the little despot wanted. Until she was finally free, she could no longer see any other course than to give it to him.

'You've been offered rest. Allowed to slake your thirst. Even to break your fast.'

His brows lifted as if expecting a reply. The gesture was a confusing contradiction, flying in the face of the stern protocol he had insisted upon to only respond if requested to.

'Thank you — Brother Eustace.' she stammered.

'You performed that portion of your penance today with fortitude.' She smiled weakly. 'You also received *two* boons today Esmeralda, an *end* to your Civil Trial and no further cost to acquit. The Capulets showed great mercy in that regard. Don't you *agree?*'

Though her eyes were still wet from her tears of despair, a spark of something else lit them to hear that name.

'Esmeralda.' His brows lifted. 'I *asked* if you agree?'

Her stare became vacant, her mind seemed lost again. As during previous interrogations, Sister Boniface reached to prod her shoulder and solicit a reply. That seemed to nudge Esmeralda's feeble senses yet still no reply was heard. Captain Lanza glared at the inquisitor who leaned forward.

'Esmeralda I asked if you agree that the Capulets have shown you great mercy?'

'Amen Brother Eustace.' she croaked in a whisper.

'Hmm.' He leaned back. 'Sister Boniface reports you've been practising your affirmation.'

'Yes Brother Eustace.'

'Tell Captain Lanza which one we chose for you.'

Her dead eyes met his stoic stare. 'An incantation used by Holy Saint Agatha for her protection.'

'Agatha?' said the Captain. 'I don't recall her.'

'Esmeralda, recall the elements of Saint Agatha's inspiring story for the Captain.'

She gulped to prepare as Lanza turned with a frown.

'That won't be —' he began.

'Yes Brother Eustace' she interrupted.

Sister Boniface grimaced. Esmeralda licked her lips. Her nostrils flared for breath.

'During the Christian persecutions of the Emperor Decius, a Roman Governor sought to compel Agatha to revoke her vow of chastity and marry him.'

'Did she submit?' asked the inquisitor.

'Agatha refused. The Governor had Agatha imprisoned in an effort to compel her. She refused again. He had her enslaved in a bordello.'

'Did she submit to him thereafter?'

'Even after being compelled to lie with so many men, Agatha refused to marry him still. To compel Agatha, he ordered her torture.'

'Did she submit?'

'Still Agatha refused. Spiteful at her devotion, the governor ordered Agatha's breasts to be cut from her body, then brought her before him again to renounce her faith.'

The inquisitor opened his eyes. 'Did the stricken Agatha renounce her faith?'

Esmeralda met his stare. 'No.' she croaked stoutly. 'No she did not.' Her lower lip trembled. 'Agatha refused.' A glow kindled in her dark eyes. 'And so that vile...' Brows before her lifted in warning. 'And so *he* ... ordered for Agatha to be burnt at the stake.'

Eyes shut again. 'Yes. He did so.'

Sister Boniface reached to tap. Esmeralda inhaled.

'Yet on that dark day God shook the ground in anger with a mighty earthquake. The Governor relented in fear, yet still ordered her eternal imprisonment. Holy Agatha died in prison, a blessed martyr.'

'Jupiter's Balls!' spat the captain. 'Is all that *true*?'

'Indeed.' muttered Brother Eustace. 'It's a tale of the worst and best of humanity wrapped into one. The vicious savagery of a lustful pagan beast. The inspiring strength of a Christian woman of grace. As Sister Boniface reminded us, that story gave rise to the use of an incantation Agatha created to fortify her strength in moments of dire sufferance or whenever she felt tempted to weakness.'

'Esmeralda. Recite the incantation for the captain.'

As the Friar listened he couldn't help but consider a dark parallel between the pagan beast mocked by the inquisitor and his treatment of Esmeralda. She moistened her lips again, gulped to fill her lungs. Then, as if warding off an assault by the Devil himself, she screamed into their eyes.

'LORD OF ALL! YOU KNOW ...'

'HALT!' cried the little despot. 'Speak it *softly* now Esmeralda, as if in a private utterance to God.'

She nodded with relief, then shut her eyes.

'Lord of all, you know my heart and desires, possess all that I am, fortify me to slay the devil. Lord of all —'

'Halt! Very good Esmeralda.' His interest in her display seemed to have vanished. 'And so now I will begin what I hope may be the final phase of our work together.' Her eyelids fluttered. 'You understand that I'm compelled by the rules to *test* all that you've uttered in confession.'

'Yes' she croaked.

'If I can ratify the sincerity of your words under the test of an *Ordeal* ...' Her face blanched like a child that hears a surgeon tell he must make an incision. 'then I can complete my work with you.' His eyes lifted. 'The men behind you attend by order of Verona's Podesta Prince Escalus de Treviso. They shall conduct your Ordeal on behalf of that office, and so fall under Captain Lanza's command not my own. Do you understand?'

'I understand.'

'I attend only as a witness to their conduct, not to personally inflict any physical duress. However, their orders allow them to be guided in what they do by my instructions. And at all times my instructions must be guided by the strict code of rules for inquisitional process. Esmeralda Montecchi do you understand *everything* I've explained to you?'

Lost in a haze, her eyes had begun drifting about the chamber. She scanned Friar Lorenzo's face in the torchlit shadows. He thought she may seek the mute interaction of his counsel, yet this time her gaze hadn't held him at all. Given the accumulation of all she had suffered, he could no longer be sure how well Esmeralda's mind was functioning.

When the inquisitor asked her for that final confirmation, as subtly as Friar Lorenzo had dared, he nodded his affirmation. Yet despite taking that risk, Esmeralda showed no sign of observing him. Then finally, vacantly, she responded.

'Yes ... I understand.'

'That is well. And do you *agree* that both the offices of law represented here, Spiritual and Civil, have a *right* to proceed with you in this manner?'

A whimper sounded from behind as Sister Boniface stifled a desperate want to object. That sound pricked the Friar's conscience too as all eyes locked upon the stricken prioress, all but the prisoner standing before her.

'Amen.' Esmeralda whispered.

'Brother Simone. Friar Lorenzo. Record the prisoner's acknowledgment of our *right* to proceed.'

'Yes Inquisitor.' the shuffler bleated from his seat next to the friar.

The sound of quills dipping and tapping then scratching and scribbling pervaded for a moment. Silence.

'Esmeralda. The apparatus behind you is a *new* device for this purpose. I acquired it especially to ensure we accord with the *altered* rules for conducting *tests of veracity*. I've never seen it in use. For your sake however, I'm *grateful* we've secured it and have this chance to test its value for myself. It comes to us from the French.'

'The F-French?' she stammered.

'We believe it to be a more merciful means by which to conduct an ordeal.' His tone was like that of a parent attempting to assure a fretting child. 'No blades, no points or heated elements. No incisions are required. No drawing of parts of the body to inflict pain or damage to joints or muscles at all.' He turned to the captain. 'All such methods are now forbidden by the Holy Office.'

Esmeralda's brows lifted, sensing the promise of some sliver of relief.

'Your description makes it sound ... merciful.' droned Captain Lanza.

'I believe it is. I hold great hope it shall become our favoured method to conduct these final sessions in a more *civilised* manner.'

That description sounded so earnest on his thin lips, even Friar Lorenzo took heart.

'Now we will begin Esmeralda. Prioress.' Sister Boniface glanced. 'Remove the prisoner's garment.'

The sister entered into a dutiful trance.

'Arms *up!*' she snapped.

It appeared Sister Boniface knew this would be done, for she bent to grasp the foul garment's hem without hesitation and lifted it high. Yet it seemed to Friar Lorenzo that Esmeralda was given no warning at all.

In an instant she was naked before them. Her mind seemed to reel, hands quivering, lifting and dropping and lifting again, thoughts flailing about whether to cover her exposure. Then suddenly her hands stopped and fell limp. Perhaps it was a decision to submit. Perhaps body and mind were simply too taken with fatigue to resist any further.

Friar Lorenzo lurched in horror. It was far too much for him to bear. His conscience screamed at him — *For once in this despicable proceeding I must intercede.*

'Brother Eustace!' He attempted to stand in protest, yet due to his height, his head smacked the low, angled ceiling. 'Is this *truly* required?' He bent awkwardly to avoid the slope. Moreover, his abrupt motion to stand had disturbed a brimming ink pot. The shuffler beside him muttered his frustration as he launched an antic yet vain attempt to rescue the precious liquid.

Eustace turned and glared at him. 'The requirements of this Inquisition are *not* answerable to you Friar Lorenzo. However ... with deference to your *mis*understanding, I will explain. Indeed this measure is *required* by the rules.'

'I *understand* —' he spat.

'Moreover Friar' his beady eyes bulged 'this measure is often undertaken from the *very start* of an interrogation. For the sake of mercy in this case however' he caught Esmeralda's eye 'I've refrained from its use until now. You also seem to have forgotten that I could have made this entire proceeding *public*.'

'Oh ... yes.' stammered Lorenzo.

'Yet I have *not*. That means I could have compelled her to endure it before all in the Civil Court yesterday or even at the ceremony today. Yet I did *not*.'

The friar was surprised to hear the little despot confess so much. Esmeralda's expression revealed she hadn't expected to hear him say anything like it at all.

'I *cannot* withhold from it now. However —'

'Yet Brother if mercy allowed you *before* —'

'FROM THIS MOMENT ...' he snapped with impatience 'to *ensure* the results of our final test *cannot* be questioned by any who investigate hereafter — which is usual practice and always painstaking — I simply *cannot* afford to forego this measure now. For the love of mercy Friar would you have me risk her being made to endure *all this again* at the hands of another?'

Esmeralda's eyes shut in pain at the thought.

'Against a record that would clearly show this *strict* measure was *dispensed* with altogether?'

The friar's eyes met Esmeralda's. For once in their entire time with this dread man, she counselled his reply, with a silent nod of her head.

'No Brother Eustace.' He gulped. 'Certainly not.'

'Then Friar please control your outbursts and allow me attend to my work. *All* of us stand as if naked before the eyes of the Almighty. The rules stipulate that before I apply the *final* test, I must make *every* attempt to ensure all pretence to a penitent's *pride* has been stripped away.' He swung about to face forward. 'Esmeralda Montecchi. You've been made to stand naked before us as God first made you. Do you *object* to this treatment?'

She didn't shift her eyes to observe Friar Lorenzo.

'No Brother Eustace' she croaked 'I do not object.'

The friar lifted his eyes at the sound. What he saw seemed bitterly ironic. Now divested of her filthy smock, Esmeralda appeared more formidable. Even the lack of her hair seemed to add potency to the strong lines of her face. Though fatigued to the point of collapse, her naked form rippled with the muscularity of an exhausted athlete rather than the excess of an overindulged aristocrat.

'Sit down Friar. And ensure your question, my reply and the prisoner's response to my *following* question, are all recorded faithfully in *your* register.'

Lorenzo sat quietly.

'And now Captain, if *you're* satisfied, please instruct your men to prepare my prisoner.'

Without a word, the Captain caught the eyes of both and nodded. The shorter master came forward to stand before Esmeralda while the larger apprentice stepped up behind to tip the empty board against its fulcrum. It became vertical in an instant, leather straps and buckles hanging against their weight.

'Step back.' the master instructed. Esmeralda flinched but then shuffled back. His emotionless voice was unnerving. 'Again.' She did so. 'Again.' She complied.

Her ass and shoulders pressed against the vertical board. She flinched to feel the surface, then inhaled in shock when hands touched her body, gripping her ankle.

'Do *not* resist us' the master forewarned.

Snap! The apprentice's hand hauled at the leather and struck the loose end home through the buckle. Tug! Rattle! The strap pulled tight, shunting her foot and tipping Esmeralda's balance.

'Arms!' snapped the master. She lifted. 'Higher!'

The other strap wrapped her loose ankle. Snap!

The master stepped in so close she reacted to the smell of his breath. He gripped her hand, lifted further, drew the thick leather across her wrist. Tug! Rattle! He fastened quickly, before moving to the next. Snap! Tug! Rattle!

In a moment both wrists and ankles were strapped tight against the board, forcing Esmeralda to drive her weight onto the inner edges of her feet. She squirmed to adjust her posture, straightened her head for comfort. Yet as she did so, to the friar's horror, the hooded men moved to stand at either side. TILT!

Suddenly the pair had tipped Esmeralda back. She spurted a gasp. Her feet were facing the tables, her head was cut from their view. Then UP! The muscular pair lifted it all at once, the tilting board and body above it, its fulcrum anchored by some kind of mechanical sorcery, all came off the floor completely.

'Uggghhh!' Esmeralda's gasp filled the chamber.

Strapped to the board, in a macabre dance a trois, they rotated a quarter circuit then set down! The feet of the fulcrum thumped upon the floor. TILT!

'Ugghoooz!' Esmeralda spat out a wheezing grunt as she lifted again.

Her arms flexed by instinct, jaw and stomach clenching hard, holding against the strain. Now almost vertical, without the floor to stand on her body hung by the wrists against her full weight. From the front table's vantage, by virtue of her rotation, she was draped in lurid profile like an image of crucifixion, yet with her feet lashed to spread them apart instead of being nailed in the centre together.

The master held, tilting her aloft while his apprentice stepped off to snatch up the stool. The loud scraping scrawl of hardwood on stone as he dragged it to one side had frightened Esmeralda. Without warning — TILT! Her eyes jumped as she tipped back again, hauled over by the master while his apprentice, unseen by her, guided the stools placement under the head end to arrest its fall. Finally it was lowered to lay firmly on top of it.

Now it was clear, the stool was used as a leg to brace the lie of the tilting table. It was clear to the friar too, unlike a seesaw, the head end was overweighted to lure its balance in just one direction, head down. Secured there, the final alignment saw Esmeralda's head falling on a slight angle, perhaps five points below horizontal.

Friar Lorenzo assumed those first cavortions were to position all so those seated at the fore could observe Esmeralda's face and hear any responses. Seated in his dark recess as they watched, he was already muttering furious prayers for the protection of his dearest friend. Now understanding what lay ahead for them to witness, he promised he would never agree to assist an inquisition again. Yet he also feared that now, having been inducted to all its grim parts, his experience may be summoned in the future.

Friar Lorenzo perished that thought to focus on the ordeal unfolding before him. Esmeralda's breath was erratic, her torso lifting and falling at the base of her ribs. Her dark nipples were stiff with cold or fear or both. And under the play of flickering light, despite the chill in the that deep stone chamber, her skin gleamed with perspiration.

Silence reigned for a long moment. Then with no warning at all, the inquisitor rose to his feet and unleased a hideous scream.

'ESMERALDA MONTECCHI! You recanted your former worship of that black witch, the goddess Atégina! Yet I believe you LIED! Your recant is UNFAITFHUL.'

She turned her head to see him. His brows were knit, eyes brimming with accusation. From the moment her garment had been lifted, it seemed she'd been shocked into realising resistance would purchase nothing but lingering sufferance. Desperately now she sought any means to avoid a protraction.

'NO!' she rasped. 'I DO renounce her!'

'Renounce WHO Esmeralda?'

'I *can't* speak her name!'

'I attest you do NOT truly recant. CONFESS it!'

'I *cannot* do so!' Her voice was failing. 'I'm a *true* daughter of the church!'

'I know you are not! You're *false* Esmeralda. Confess to me. Your recant was a LIE! Confess it NOW and spare yourself the pain of what's to come.'

The inquisitor knew that was true. A single word of recant would have instantly halted him. Yet it would also see Esmeralda's journey of suffering start over, only to lead her back to this treacherous moment.

'Confess you've been FALSE Esmeralda!'

Her head shunted in protest. She glared at the dark stone ceiling. Clenching her eyes shut Esmeralda sucked in air to fill her lungs and summon the will to chant for her saviour's protection.

'Lord of all you know my heart and desire!' Gasp. 'Possess all that I am!' Gasp. 'Fortify me to SLAY —'

'SILENCE!' he bellowed.

Instinctively Esmeralda obeyed, snapping her head to see him. Their eyes locked for a moment. The little Dominican knit his brows and looked to his right.

'Captain please instruct your men they're now at *my* disposal to command.' His head turned back to gauge the effect of that instruction on Esmeralda. 'Your power will of course *remain* to call a halt at any moment you may see fit.'

Captain Lanza reached beneath the table and lifted to reveal a gavel in his hand. He held it for the henchman to see. Esmeralda saw it too. His eyes fell on the masked duet. The wiry master nodded in comprehension.

'They're at your service to command Inquisitor. Signal with one strike when you wish them to *apply* the device.' SMACK went the gavel. Esmeralda jolted. 'Signal with a burst of three or four when you wish them to *relent*.'

SMACK! SMACK! SMACK!

'Very simple Captain. Thank you.'

'No matter *what* you command however, the master has been instructed to relent if he feels that he *must*.'

'As it should be.' the inquisitor agreed.

Captain Lanza's eyes were empty as he set down the gavel. Esmeralda watched her tormentor grasp the blunt tool and lift it. In the shadows behind him she could see Friar Lorenzo. He was transfixed with fear. Now the little tyrant had a new bauble to wield.

Her eyes stretched wide as a torrent of chanting BURST from Esmeralda's lips, hoping to appease him or incite another question, anything to delay her fate. Glaring in panic to assure him of her conviction she chanted in an intimate whisper, just as Brother Eustace had requested, as if her calls were for the ear of God alone.

His boyish face watched in wonder for a moment, then he squinted petulantly, lifted the gavel and THUMPED it down on the board. Esmeralda's heart leapt.

She screamed her incantation to Heaven.

Unseen by her, the master reached into the smaller bucket to gather a clump of gauze strips. He dumped the handful into the vessel that was brimming with water. Both buckets now sat on the floor directly below Esmeralda's head. The apprentice moved behind her head, sliding his huge hand along her cheek. She flinched at the touch. A second hand drew up under her chin. Both gripped firmly.

SNAP! Her head jolted up to face the bottomless dark of the ceiling. Her senses seemed to reel feeling that anonymous brute could compel her with so little effort.

Her tongue licked parched lips, she gulped to prepare as her lips parted, allowing her chanting to explode in defiance and chase away her helplessness. Mouth open wide, Esmeralda shouted to Heaven when heart-stopping panic assailed her senses. SHOVE! SHOVE! SHOVE!

Clumps of wet wadding drove into her mouth, smothering her words. Fingers pushed the fabric into her throat, leaving the fore-end shards jutting out, overflowing from her mouth and dribbling foul water down her neck.

Unable to breathe, Esmeralda's nostrils flared to suck air in through her nose. PRESS! The massive hand of the masked apprentice had clamped against her mouth as his master lifted a pewter ladle from the bucket.

The wicked spoon lifted into view. It was large, nearly as broad as Esmeralda's face, with a wide spout to its rim. The fingers clamped above her fabric filled mouth began to separate. The ladle's wide base lowered, spilling droplets at the edges. causing her eyes to twitch closed.

In a flash of sudden terror Esmeralda seemed to grasp the ghastly nature of her ordeal. The ladle mouth tipped, drizzling water over the fingers that smothered her.

Pour! Slosh! Trickle. Trickle. Trickle.

Her throat was filling. Water poured into her mouth, filled her nose. Eyes bulging in desperation, Esmeralda's head and neck began to shunt violently. Her chest, arms and legs heaved, shuddering and bucking in wild resistance.

Friar Lorenzo clutched his rosary. His eyes shut tight. The sound of Esmeralda's wild protest, rising and catching in her throat, wracked his mind. Her shuddering and twisting to escape suffocation churned his guts. Face wet with tears, he gripped his huge head in hands, pleading to Heaven in desperate whispers to stop her insidious torment until the master relented and he heard the fulcrum bend as they tilted Esmeralda up and over to drain the killing fluid.

Dear God have mercy. That was only the start.

Aided by the hideous recurring torture that new *civilised* method – dripping suffocation – inflicted upon Esmeralda's body and mind, her Inquisitor continued to direct the application of his penitent's *ordeal*. As he did so, time and again the wincing Friar and bulging-eyed shuffler recorded her wild refusals to recant.

In time Friar Lorenzo would learn that, while it was true the *method* used on that occasion was new to Brother Eustace, long before Esmeralda's ordeal began the little despot had understood the precise manner of it. Far more importantly, he understood it was extraordinarily effective. Even before the device had been brought to the castle the master who applied it had informed Brother Eustace he believed no man or woman – elite or common, warrior or peasant or religious fanatic – could withstand the suffering of that simple yet brutal regime.

The Friar would also learn that, before Brother Eustace decided on its use, he queried a fellow inquisitor who attended several cases in France where the method was first applied. That brother held the firm opinion that, within the strict guidance of their new rules, that mechanism was *proof* against any chance of *failure*.

Of course the little despot was determined to see such proof for himself. Moreover he felt at that time that he – *may never find an adversary more formidable to test upon the new device, than that fallen prima Donna of Montecchi. There was an intensity about her sense of conviction that I had rarely seen* – he admitted in his later summary. Perhaps he could have added – *save his own image in the mirror.*

But that was to come. And Esmeralda's ordeal had only just begun as Friar Lorenzo now struggled to hold his quill steady in his hands.

Time and again he watched Esmeralda being drawn back down to have water ladled into her mouth, dripping and filling and spilling ,each time to reignite that panicked sensation of suffocation. Time and again her eyes bulged as she lay close to death, until the master signalled his apprentice to lift, drain and revive her. On more than one occasion he drew a vial of foul-smelling paste from a pouch, smearing it under her nose to revive her. Yet as each brutal bout was completed, the results of that remedy began to lag.

As the ordeal wore on, each time the pouring ceased and she was lifted, dripping, draining, sputtering and sucking for precious air to regain her wits and refuse to recant — Esmeralda did so with less and less vigour. During each respite — after her mouth was unpacked and the inquisitor conferred — the chanting erupted again. Yet no longer did her eyes spit wild defiance at her tormentor. Bleary eyed and barely conscious, Esmeralda stared into a dark abyss of rock hanging above her, appealing through the floor of that Hell to the hidden mercy of Heaven above.

It was becoming clear that the strength of her body was nothing compared to the strength of Esmeralda's fiery will. Through all her suffering Friar Lorenzo wept like a child, fearing it would be too much, fearing she would finally recant and set the brutal cycle of another inquisition into motion. Then he began to feel the Portuguese aristocrat would not be broken by that little tyrant and his borrowed henchman. At least, he desperately hoped so.

Finally however a dark new thought began to trouble him. He suspected Esmeralda may now prefer death by misadventure at the hands of that zealot rather than recant her confession. In the history of the inquisition such tragic outcomes were not unheard of. Some penitents perished while their sincerity was being *tested*. If one died before a result was *determined*, refusal to recant until that moment was seen as a torch that would light their way to Heaven.

In such cases an inquisitor would still be held to have fulfilled the primary task of saving their soul. Friar Lorenzo watched on with new eyes as that terrible thought took hold. He understood the new rules of conduct for a *Test by Ordeal* would only allow Eustace to submit Esmeralda for a *limited* time. That limit remained somewhat at the discretion of each inquisitor. The duration could be one hour or many, yet usually was *not* more than a day. However if an inquisitor could fitfully argue a dire case warranted an extension a test, it *could* last more than a day or even two.

Cupid's Balls! Imagine the foul wretches in a chamber in Rome who discussed and decided such things.

Moreover, regardless of *length of period* applied, Friar Lorenzo understood inquisitors were also at liberty to conduct ordeals *with* or *without* any pauses for relent. No, the little despot hadn't shared with his scribes just how long he intended to submit Esmeralda to her ordeal. Yet one thing was already clear — he had decided to conduct it relentlessly.

For more than two hours from her first submersion, Friar Lorenzo waited for an end to be declared. By then the inquisitor was no longer seated. With gavel in hand he leaned over the penitent as she suffered. Every time she was lifted to hang from the board, convulsing, gasping and retching, the despot stood before her. Then leaning close as she was lowered back again, hand beside her head, he implored her to admit to the falsehood of her confessions. His stale breath blasted into her eyes.

'DO IT Esmeralda!' he screamed. 'Invoke the dark deity you TRULY worship in the recesses of your heart!'

Her eyes lit again. Lacking for breath and faltering for voice, her incantation croaked out in reply.

Eustace winced in frustration. SLAM! The gavel smacked hard by her head. TILT!

She was tipped. She was suffocated. She was lifted. Again and again and again.

Impotent with rage in his corner, more than once Lorenzo tried to summon the will to intervene. More than once his ass lifted, his mouth opened yet each time he wavered. He knew that once the final step was begun, any stop may imperil her chance for absolution. Moreover, he knew the office represented by the inquisitor held such dread sway that none in the chamber, not even Captain Lanza, would dare intervene until the despot was done.

When she had barely a whisper of voice left to claim her innocence, the friar heard the gavel smash by her ear yet again. By that point he felt sure Brother Eustace lacked any modicum of control. Even the harsh Sister Boniface, though still standing mute, had shed all pretence of sobriety. Long before then she began to weep openly at the cruelty displayed by her monastic kin and groaned in protest at the unbearable sufferance it inflicted on her ward.

Then in a moment that defied all the friar's past knowledge of the hard woman, Sister Boniface finally snapped and fell to her knees at the little demon's feet. Begging him to halt, she clutched at the hem of his robe. Beady eyes blazed with resentment as he bent to smack her hands away. The barbaric gavel rose and fell. Boniface cried in torment as the board lowered again. The ladle was lifted. Water was poured.

But after so much duress, the human reflex to react, even against that life-threatening sensation of suffocation, had become so drained from Esmeralda's body that she barely responded. Lorenzo sat frozen. In a livid moment, the shuffler leaned in to reprimand his failure to continue recording. The friar's eyes bulged. He snarled and snatched the shuffler's quill, snapping it and tossing it down. Sister Boniface's defiance had stirred him. He opened his mouth to shout in protest. To lend his voice to hers and demand a halt!

Yet before the enraged friar could utter another sound the unthinkable happened. Just as the ghastly ladle lifted from the bucket to hover once again, the *apprentice* thrust out a palm to halt its progress. Not stopping at this, his broad fingers gripped the rim to snatch it from his master!

Clank! Clatter! Clang!

The muscular man hurled it across the chamber.

Boniface, Lorenzo and the shuffler all stared in utter disbelief. Mouths hung open, uncertain just what in the name of all Heaven was happening! Still not done the terrifying apprentice shunted his boot against the wide bucket's rim and shoved hard. The hefty pail spun and smacked, drenching the stone floor with a wash of foul water. The inquisitor straightened in shock to glare at the wilful man.

Yet the brutish rescuer had more. He closed on the inquisitor who recoiled as they met. Looming over the little despot the apprentice SNATCHED the token of power from his sweaty paw. Brother Eustace gulped. Remarkably then the bold apprentice turned to toss that foul little mallet right into the captain's lap! More remarkably still Captain Lanza merely caught it with tired ease and calmly stowed it away!

Friar Lorenzo stared wide-eyed in astonishment, feeling as if he sat in a dream, for it seemed that quite literally, God had answered his desperate prayers to end Esmeralda's suffering. Then the unwieldy apprentice turned his attention upon his own master. The younger man signalled to his elder to raise up the board. More stunning still his elder complied without protest.

Esmeralda hung limp. The apprentice rushed in to draw the wadding from her mouth, motioned for her to be lowered and bent to see. Her mouth was clear. He turned his ear and pressed it to her chest.

Her defiant heart was still beating.

He lifted and looked. She breathed. Esmeralda was alive but wholly incoherent. Slowly she began to mutter then babbled her chant. Taking heart and feeling compelled Friar Lorenzo came forward. Buckles were unfastened. Limbs were freed. Leaning in a daze against the board, bereft of any will to continue, the inquisitor stepped away. After a moment he drew back to assist the effort to revive her.

The apprentice — turned new master — signalled for Sister Boniface to approach. She came forward cautiously, as if approaching a vision of Christ on Calgary. Boniface couldn't tell by what authority the man had taken control, but her need to tend Esmeralda, and the response of her betters to the man made sense of her want to comply.

After whispering to the sister the apprentice drew off his large shirt and handed it to her. He turned back to the board, ran his hands under Esmeralda's limp body, head and back, to draw her collapsed form upright. Boniface lifted the broad shirt, then drew it down over Esmeralda's head. As it was shuffled to her waist, the anonymous saviour laid her back down while the prioress shunted its hem further along.

Esmeralda was tall, but the generous garment was large enough to draw beyond her knees. As the friar watched that mute spectacle of emancipation run on, it began to dawn on him that, during all the hubbub, other than the inquisitor's surprised glare, neither he, nor the Captain of Militia or Master Executioner had uttered a single word to contest him.

So far, it had all been remarkable.

Then a more remarkable moment followed.

Stripped of his shirt — yet still masked — as if he were a bother tradesman the apprentice laid a hefty arm about the inquisitor's shoulders to draw him away. While they conferenced in the dim recess of a corner he beckoned for Captain Lanza to join them. For a moment, the trio stood together. Friar Lorenzo watched in confusion as, first Captain Lanza, then Inquisitor Eustace, nodded affirmations.

Finally the rescuer separated from that pair to return to Esmeralda. Then like an athlete who's completed a trial of endurance, the apprentice stretched for his comfort, paused a moment and scanned the makeshift table. Drawing in to stand by Esmeralda, he whispered to Sister Boniface again. She nodded in compliance. Gingerly, his arms slid under Esmeralda's back and knees, this time to lift her up and free.

To Friar Lorenzo it seemed that his dearest friend, the woman he loved, who he felt may indeed love him, was unwitting of her saviour's assistance. In quiet protest the fallen prima donna still whimpered her chant, apparently unaware that her ordeal had ended.

A groan drew her saviour's attention. He shuffled her form in his muscular arms to gain a firmer hold. Then he turned and vanished, Sister Boniface trailed in his wake, leaving Friar Lorenzo to wonder *who* in Heaven that man may be.

Only a downward glance by the friar — to avert his eyes for shame as the rescuer passed — allowed him to notice a unique ring worn upon her saviour's finger. It was a wide band of gold that splayed into an oval. Inscribed upon that oval was a winged lion. Suddenly, it all made sense. Friar Lorenzo now understood that the torment of Esmeralda's Inquisition had indeed ended.

Moreover he now felt assured that, whatever else may happen, however many more trifling chores may remain to complete in this matter, no dungeon cell would ever hold Esmeralda again. Captain Lanza whispered to the Master Executioner, glanced at the inquisitor and also departed.

The inquisitor glanced at the shuffler, and not waiting for either that minion or the Friar, departed alone. The shuffler opened his boiled leather case. The seal of the Holy office of Inquisition was impressed on it. Carefully he stored his parchments and inkwell within, then stooped with a glare to retrieve the shards of his broken quill.

'Brother I feel obliged to inform you' he drawled 'I was compelled to record your behaviour and destruction of this!' His drooping eyes opened wide in punctuation.

'As you will Brother Simone. Do you know the identity of her saviour?'

'It's not my place to conjecture on such things Brother.' He huffed. 'Nor to *discuss* them. Should Inquisitor Eustace see fit, he may tell us in his good time. For now, we must return to the scriptorium, compare our records and copy all for safekeeping. I shall await you beyond.'

'No need to wait for me Brother. I'll need more than a moment to collect my thoughts. What I've witnessed today has famished my mind.'

Brother Simone shuffled away in the desolate silence. The tall

Franciscan watched the Master Executioner draw off his hooded mask and continue to dismantle his infernal machine. A moment later the man appeared to realise he required something more to complete his task and exited the chamber. Finally alone, Lorenzo dropped to his knees to offer thanks to God for Esmeralda's deliverance.

There was no way the humble Friar could comprehend of course, that with an end to Esmeralda Montecchi's ordeal, the ordeal of Armand and Ilaria de Capulet at her unforgiving hands, had just begun. For you see my solemn friends, the premiere son of a House aligned to the *Guelphs* had vanquished the primo son of a House aligned to the *Ghibellines*.

Armand de *Capulet* had slain Onorato *Montecchi*. Montecchi was vanquished by Capulet ... for now. But to tangle that web further, a new Emperor was coming who would revive the Ghibelline's hopes for new power and their dreams of submission. Many in Verona, such as Prince Escalus, feared that if the Capulets chose to stay, lasting peace between these new rivals would not be possible.

When the challenge was sent by Onorato to Armand to engage in a fight to the death over the possession of Sycamore Hill, it was delivered by Aldobrando Montecchi who offered some customary words in parting:

The victor shall harvest fame and spoils.

Yet by the time such a deadly contest comes to an end — in one fateful moment — by declaring triumph for a victor one must also declare devastation for the vanquished.

The Civil Trial that followed their fatal result was declared by Prince Escalus to have been *fairly* decided. Moreover Don Pasquale, Verona's magistrate, had declared the Capulets must be allowed to inherit the Montecchi's estate — *unencumbered*. To myself at that time, a grave chapter in the Capulet's story seemed to have ended.

But from the reaping of those blood-stained spoils, the seeds of a reverberating legacy of retribution had been planted. And now it was set to rise at the cost of a more potent harvest — innocence. For as that mired legacy begins to grow, children on both sides will inherit a will to hate and pursue violence against each other.

I mention this now sweet friends, for as this milestone in the Capulet's tale is reached, children such as Romeo Montecchi — now the primo son of his faction — are barely beginning their lives. And soon a son, daughter and niece for the Capulets will also breathe their first — oh yes, Thibault, Rosaline and Juliet are coming.

But for now, there's more to tell of this fated first crossing of paths between the Houses of Capulet, Montecchi and Paris. For at the very moment Esmeralda Montecchi's Ordeal began in earnest, as wadding was shoved in and the water poured on, elsewhere in Verona, immersed in the Pool of the Gods, discussion among those latter players had arrived at a critical moment.

Ilaria was considering just how to answer that fateful question posed by Yolanthe de Paris. Her answer had the power to change our lives. For you know what they say —

The victor shall harvest fame and spoils.

The vanquished shall harvest ruin and toil.

But there are fights and battles and wars. And if a fight is done but a battle not won or the war yet complete ... who can tell which side will be declared the victor?

Chapter 4 Sirens

'Why ... ' Ilaria paused for effect as her green eyes hung on the provocative sight across the steaming water of Yolanthe's naked form languishing next to her husband 'we're interested in silk of course.' Ilaria glanced at Nobel, now next to herself with Eloise at his side. The look on their faces revealed all. 'Among *other* fancies.' Ilaria added.

The duchess arched a brow in anticipation.

'Such as?'

As I played softly I felt sure she must have been intoxicated by the thrill of having her body immersed next to Armand's and be leaning against him. And so I was surprised anything Ilaria may say at that moment would distract her attention so completely. Yet it did so.

'Such as the *rarest* dyes that may be sourced to *soak* it and *fashion* it to my will to create new styles of couture that may draw the interest of a legion of new patrons.'

Nobel's brows lifted and he grinned, then laughed. 'Oh that's *ambitious* young Marchand.'

'Ambitious young *Capulet*.' Ilaria purred and blew a kiss to her now smiling husband.

That seemed to remind the flame-haired young duchess just where she was and who she was there with.

'He stands corrected' said Eloise. 'I think ... may I also call you Ria?'

'Yes Eloise. Of course you may.'

'Then Ria I think your ambitions are inspiring and ... that you have finally have Yoli's undivided attention.'

'Yes she does.' Yoli glanced at Nobel. 'You must know darling that we are *very* happy to hear you say so.' She drew her arm from Armand's shoulders.

For a moment it seemed the siren had relinquished her provocative claim to him as she fixed her stare across the steaming surface towards his wife. Instead, she turned her hips over to nestle in more, drawing her hand through the loop of his arm and resting her fingertips down upon his thigh. I gulped in anticipation and began to hum. Cupid's Balls! I couldn't risk the folly of attempting to recall lyrics.

A heartbeat followed, then another and another.

Though Armand's eyes lifted to Heaven and back again Ilaria didn't flinch or lose any warmth in her smile. I couldn't tell if the liqueur had taken a firm grip on her senses or whether she'd begun to accept Yoli's posturing intimacy as little more than a game — or perhaps a screen to distract her in the midst of their rising negotiation. If it was the latter, then the real task for Ilaria would be to see beyond it.

The flame-haired duchess was thinking too. For the sake of her trade ambitions this intimate tete-a-tete was critical, yes. But she and Nobel were departing for Venice next day and declared that time was of the essence.

Just one day earlier — two hours before the prince declared the trial to be over — the surgeon also declared Armand was recovered well enough to travel. With the trial complete, the Capulets were no longer compelled to remain in the citadel, risking close company with so many local strangers who may be Montecchi famiglia or associates. Armand and Ilaria were finally free to leave Verona or stay. They could take time to enjoy the rest of their tour or, for the sake of safety, be done and depart next morning for Lyon.

But the trio in their present company no longer felt like strangers. Not only were they Français but Yolanthe's faction were now based in Lyon; Nobel had known Ilaria's parents for many years; even Eloise — despite Ilaria's right to be wary of her history with Armand — had an unexpected value for Ilaria to nurture through her relationship, as a ward of the French Queen. Finally, Nobel's confession of their interest to include the Cortelannis was also significant.

One thing however that Ilaria felt she knew for certain was that no one in this flirtatious company was a friend of the Montecchi. Not only did they now share their dislike for that faction, they had shared the danger of facing the Montecchi together. Oh yes, I had begun to suspect that was just as the duchess had intended. From our time at war in Normandy I had learnt such interactions had a way of creating fast, firm bonds among people who may otherwise discover nothing in common to tie them.

Finally I also suspected that for Ilaria, since their shared experiences had begun, she was starting to enjoy the manner in which those unpredictable women, and the charming Nobel, were wooing her own interest so playfully. And so at that moment Ilaria decided, if the fleeting attention of this exalted young duchess was lured, under the purging influence of that sumptuous chamber, the exotic liqueur and their entertaining company, to nestle with her husband? Then she was feeling bold enough to unwind her leash.

For not only did Ilaria allow it, in return she decided to be even more provocative. Indeed I felt sure at that moment, even the risk of doing so seemed attractive to her. It were as if Ilaria felt compelled to test her new husband's boundaries. I noted a look rising in her sparkling green eyes that worried me. She was becoming much too confident.

For the love of erotic folly! Most women I knew would never have remained in that setting in such company with the man they loved, let alone the man they'd only just wed! That first approach at court would have been enough contact for most women and also the last. But Ilaria was not like most women, nor was Yolanthe, nor Eloise. Each was extraordinary in their own way.

Years later Ilaria confessed she felt that day *as if a twist of pure fate had led her into elite kindred company* — the kind she may not find again easily if she let that chance to secure it slip away. Yet as piqued as Ilaria's interest had become, her instinct for caution was not entirely bereft. She wanted more information. She intended to extract it.

That look in her eye sparked again. Just as the impulse gripped her at the first sight of *Sycamore Hill*, now a compulsion to gain — or at least investigate — something she desired while it still lay within reach, took control of her.

'And now *if I may be so bold*' she mimicked Nobel 'what special interest draws your menage here by way of Grenoble and Milan to Venice? As if it's any wonder.'

Nobel grinned and loosed a good-humoured laugh. 'You're certainly your mother's daughter! *Silk* is our interest too of course!'

'Imagine that angel?' said Armand.

He risked turning his head to look at Yolanthe. Her pale blue eyes lit with hunger. Her hand lifted slowly as she ran her fingertip over the scar on his chest again, now very thoughtfully. Ilaria watched calmly, wondering if — now their discussion was wandering to the point of it all — that provocation was an attempt to distract her?

'Yes my heart, I do imagine it. I also imagine it's not merely sales in silk that encourages such a grand enterprise. Consider it, the *mighty* merchant house of Nobel —'

'Joined with the *exalted* house of Paris!' Armand pouted in mock confusion. His playfulness made Yolanthe smile. Totally unexpected — though given the circumstances perhaps it should have been — it also became clear her broad nipples were hardening. If Yolanthe did hope to distract Ilaria, I felt that change would do so. I saw Ilaria glance. How could she not? Yet so did Nobel and Eloise too.

Totally unnoticed, I simply stared.

Ilaria ran on unperturbed. '*Either* player alone could stand to risk the investment needed to make a play to dominate rivals in those markets.' she added thoughtfully, as if completely immersed in the discussion of business.

But she couldn't help but also be mindful that Yolanthe's finger still grazed Armand's chest, while measure for measure, the sight of her nipples declared how much that intimacy affected her. Ilaria stood again, water dripping down her distracting body. The finger halted.

Ilaria stepped down and down again to glide back through the steaming water. Then she rose up and up again, before turning to sit. This time she rested on the other side of Armand, looping her arm through.

'Yet they'd accomplish much more *together?*'

Ilaria leaned to whisper into Armand's ear.

Puzzled by them, Yolanthe shared a look with Nobel. Armand knitted his brows, then nodded his agreement. Eloise flitted her eyes in anticipation from one to another about the circuit. It was highly unusual to see her vaulted mentor and the wily Nobel being played by a pair of *naïve* gamesters.

'Oh yes, my handsome.' Ilaria agreed.

Suddenly I noticed, though Yolanthe's finger had ceased to graze, mischievously she had left her hand at rest over the older wound upon Armand's muscular chest. Ilaria lifted a hand to rest it over Yolanthe's. Their eyes met, pale blue blazing into bright green.

'Yoli it's clear that you and Auguste — perhaps her Majesty too — seek nothing less than ... *control.*'

The flame haired siren blinked in confusion. For the very first time Yolanthe appeared to hang on the verge of something akin to poor humour. I guessed she was not used to being outfoxed, let alone having it happen in the company of familiars such as Nobel and Eloise, nor to have her plotting revealed with so little effort by one she considered to be a relative youth and amateur.

What's more, to my dismay, her nipples began to soften. Who was distracting who?

'*Control?*' Yolanthe lifted her brows in innocence.

Ilaria leaned across Armand's chest, and in a mimic of Yoli's former treatment of herself, reached a fingertip toward her cheek, lifting to trace along her perfect brow.

'*Complete* control of *all* silk supply.' She stretched each clarifying vowel as she spoke and hung upon every consonant. 'Ten years together Yoli?'

'Yes darling.'

Ilaria's finger fell to trace her cheek down and up again to the trace the other brow. 'Mmm. Half that is enough time to establish holdings in *every* citadel from Venice to Lyon.' Ilaria glanced at Armand. 'Perhaps, my heart, all the way to *Genoa?*'

Armand looked at Yolanthe. 'Your Grace I confess, had that been left to myself to surmise, I would never have fathomed it.'

Yolanthe continued to stare. For a moment, it was clear that despite the fact he had spoken, like a stricken paramour she was desperately lost in his eyes. Yet Ilaria knew how to break that spell, reaching to turn his head.

'That is why ...' *kiss* 'your clever parents ...' *kiss* 'married you' *kiss* 'to me.'

'And you're a formidable pair.' Nobel added. 'Aren't they Yoli?'

The duchess wore a sobered look.

'Clearly.' Her eyes searched from one to the other. 'Oh gorgeous people ... I *don't* want to be your rival.'

'No?'

'Of course not Ria. No Adonis. You know I adore you. *Both* of you.'

'And therefore ...' Nobel purred from the opposite side, lifting an arm with a glance to summon Eloise 'why be *rivals* to such an undertaking?' She settled in snugly beside the elder merchant. The sight of their casual intimacy unsettled me. 'Until today, Yoli and I planned to lay our foundations in Verona a little more cautiously. However —'

Ilaria cut in. 'Now that a rival is *awake* to your —'

'A *potent* rival' Nobel corrected 'who *should* be capable of recognising the true value of the gifts we bear.'

'Oh my heart, what's the phrase Maman loves to say? "*Hostium munera, non munera.*" '

'Angle my Latin is scarce but I know it — A *gift from an enemy is no gift at all.*'

'Ah no Armand. Don't speak of us as enemies.' Nobel insisted. 'Spirited rivals in trade until this moment, yes. But please understand, they're not the same thing at all.'

'No, beautiful people, they're not.' Yolanthe agreed. 'Speak of *partnership.*'

She drew her hand away and swirled about to kneel before them both. Her ears, neck and wrists sparkled with diamonds and pearls. She laid a hand on each of theirs. Her pale blue eyes were filling with a fire that commands the attention of all who see it.

'People like that Montecchi bitch are your enemies, not Auguste and I. And darlings be warned, despite the fact she knelt to beg your forgiveness and swore her contrition, with that lacerated face and disastrous hair, I'm firmly convinced she remains your enemy still.'

Ilaria scowled. 'I don't doubt it.'

'*Never* doubt it Ria. And so Adonis, if you do settle *here* the power of her faction will be a continuing risk to both your sister and yourself.'

Armand knit his brows.

'And ...' Nobel added 'to any in Verona you may seek to hold an alliance with.'

'Armand you're a soldier.' Yolanthe said soberly. 'Many hidden enemies stalk about our world. I know you *know* it.' His eyes lit with comprehension. 'Auguste and I ... we are *not* those. We see the *magnificent* potential for the rising House of Capulet in Verona.

'It's true Armand.' Nobel pleaded. 'But that potential would grow more safely, become more vast, with longer term alliances that offer more formidable support against the reach of enemies like the Montecchi.'

'Yes!' snapped Yolanthe on fire. 'Yes beautiful people we're admirers who want to be your lasting allies, an *alliance Français* forged in Italia.'

Her mask of frivolity was completely swept aside, replaced by the spellbinding image of a supplicant prophetess who warned against a want of ambition.

Ilaria tilted her head thoughtfully, considering this version of Yolanthe. Another version of her had made Ilaria laugh and feel anxious in a moment. This version made her wonder if the world lay at their feet. Safety, wealth, power, promise, even friendship could be created for herself and Armand through Ilaria's ability to expand their circuit of association. And it all seemed to hang like ripe fruit for the taking? All this sat woven in one passionate offering.

Nobel was illuminated. 'Consider it my friends, the *lasting* benefit to all. The vast security that may come from such a mighty alliance for the future of both your *familles*.'

The wily merchant was attentive, but Nobel was also a master negotiator. Yes, his affable manner and sincerity engendered trust. But for those with a talent to sell, the real cleverness lies in knowing the genuine value of a product. With such knowledge, all one need do is reveal that value to those who desire it and have the ability to recognise it.

Once revealed to the right person, such an offering will draw their interest onto itself.

Moreover, a man of Nobel's experience understood it wasn't wealth or power that appealed to the newlywed Capulets, still reeling from the danger of the world they had launched into. It was *safety* they now longed for, safety for the long road they now realised lay ahead of them. Yolanthe understood the same. Yet she understood one thing more. With a woman's insight she could tell how the possibility of forging of an *independent* path to their future appealed so much to Ilaria.

Indeed both Capulets were the kind of confident young people who longed to prove they could make their way without familial guidance. They were a pairing of bold independents. And they revelled in the notion that both their familles would admire any ability shown to grow their fortune from alliances formed by the cleverness of their instincts. Yolanthe felt sure that lure, perhaps more than any other, had the power to draw Ilaria in.

The young Duchess de Paris was already dangling an irresistible prize, yet just to be certain, she dangled another.

'Darlings. When Auguste suggested we approach you, I agreed you may prove a formidable couple who may kindle our real interest. Now we've met, even after such a short time I confess, we can see so *much* more. If you stay in Verona, you'll have *children* of course.

Ilaria looked puzzled.

'Yes of course Yoli. God grant it be so.'

'Perhaps a *daughter?*'

Ilaria flushed. 'I dearly hope for sons *and* daughters.'

'So do I darling. And I'm willing to reveal ... that we've determined my little brother Astor will be married to one from among Verona's elite.'

'We intend to entrench Astor here' Nobel added 'in service to our long-term plan.'

Ilaria's brows lifted. 'You've decided already?'

'If such decisions aren't made well ahead of time Ria, they're often *never* made. I'm now Duchess de Paris. By that time Astor will be nothing less than *Count* de Paris. That's the kind of stature our faction can offer to an ally with his marriage. Is it *not* Auguste?'

'Why yes. Beyond all doubt. ' Nobel agreed. 'He'll become Count de Paris at *least*.'

'To bind Astor to a pedigree such as yours beautiful people, I'd love to promise him to your daughter. Think of it Ria. At the very least she would begin her married life as *Countess* de Paris.'

Cupid's Balls! My own mouth was agape to hear it. The offering was as unexpected as it was beyond the stars. And I had to admit, I felt the move was a master stroke of negotiation.

'Oh ... good Heaven,' stuttered Ilaria. 'I've never even considered such a thing.'

She stared in bewilderment at Armand. He was equally surprised.

'Well consider it now. By your own telling darling, your match with Adonis was made before your own birth.'

'Well ... yes. Yes it was.'

'For that to happen your parents had to consider — more importantly had to *act* — just as we do now. Imagine if they'd *never* done so? In that case my love you'd have no *rivals* for Adonis, because he'd be married to *another*.'

Suddenly, I heard the echo of that speech made to Armand on his wedding night. I knew at that moment, that he and Ilaria heard it too. All at once, their minds were swimming in deep consideration.

'To ensure the security of our children's futures, these compacts must be made *long* before time. We could begin with a betrothal for your first child — a premiere daughter or son — *whichever* it may be, that would bind the fortunes of our *familles* in marriage. And *then* pretty people, when they have children of their *own*? When the blood of our *familles* is fully mingled together ...' Yolanthe paused.

Ilaria was speechless. Armand pushed his lower lip to his upper in thought.

'I must say ...' Armand began 'that's much *more* than we expected to hear you propose ... Yolanthe.'

Ilaria glanced in surprise at his use of her forename, then back at the duchess. A glint lit up in her pale blue eyes.

'Mercy Adonis, if it accomplished nothing more than to hear my name pass your lips, it was worth the offering.'

Suddenly the enigmatic firebrand became the most charming person in the chamber. Somehow she managed to mimic the sincerity of Eloise's heartfelt confessions. It was like watching an acrobatic maestra perform astonishing feats of physical skill, nor was she yet done.

'Armand. Ilaria. Come what may we can always become partners in an *enterprise*. I certainly wish us to be. But I'm also suggesting, if you enter an alliance with us, I'd consider your value important enough to offer *this* too. The Houses of Capulet and Paris, not merely in an enterprise compact, but a *familial* compact.'

Ilaria found her voice. 'Yoli *both* offers are ... very generous and very attractive.'

'I'm so glad to hear you say so.'

'And of course, we shall consider them both.'

'Yes darlings you must. You must.'

'For today however ... for the moment ... given we've *only* just met you ...'

Yolanthe gripped their hands more firmly.

'Oh Ria I know it's insanity. I know darling. Yet it's also perfection! I'm so very sure of it.'

'And ... given we've not even finished our marriage tour, then first and foremost, I'd like to consider your offer to assist *my* ambitious plan to control the flow of silk from Venice to Lyon.'

Ilaria pressed a wry smile, then Nobel burst into a fit of hearty laughter as Eloise smiled broadly too.

'By the Gods Armand!' huffed Nobel. 'You've married a woman of exceptional vision.'

'I'm happy for her to raise a trade empire — despite my own lack of ability to assist.'

'Armand! Don't say so!' Ilaria pleaded. She buried her forehead in his cheek.

'No.' Armand insisted to Nobel. 'A man must know his limits. As long as I remain sole conqueror of her heart.'

Yolanthe lifted her hand to her heart and flung her head back with a gasp. 'Oh for the love of pity Adonis, no more. Ilaria! Your husband makes me wet.'

'YOLI!' hissed Eloise.

'Oh hush! I'm sure you've lost all control!'

An awkward silence reigned. Nobel feared his brash partner had finally talked the sale to death when a roar of laughter burst from Armand. Until then he had managed to quell his response to every jibe and quip with a sober countenance or a retiring blush. Yet somehow the persistent, sultry young duchess had finally managed to find his limit.

A cascade of smiles set every face bubbling. Yoli pressed her hands for joy then reached for their hands again.

'Apologies Ria. I said *too* much ... again. I say too much.' It seemed the blitherer had returned.

'Amen!' cried Eloise tilting her eyes to Heaven.

Ilaria frowned. 'Yolanthe de Paris you are the most *forward* woman I've ever encountered.'

'Ah!' She grinned. 'I'm so *glad* to hear it.'

Ilaria glanced at Armand. 'When I married him I expected to encounter rivals among new peers. Yet what am I to make of a woman as exalted and beautiful as yourself —'

'Oh. You think me *beautiful!*' She used the moment to slide herself between them and wiggle in comfortably. She flitted her glance to Armand then returned to Ilaria.

'You *know* you are ... a woman who not only throws her interest so *wantonly* at my husband, but does so before my very eyes.'

'Well I ...' Yoli's eyes lowered for an instant then lifted in mock exasperation. 'Oh Ria for the love of mercy keep him on a leash. Tits of Venus! I'm a woman after all. Du Marche is a woman too ... I *believe*. Adonis is ... well I'll speak *no* more of him. I'll *look* no more.' She covered her eyes. 'Yet that's hard to do when I know he's right there. And so naked. And —' she separated her fingers to peek. 'Oh now I'm being pathetic. Like Thisbe peeking at Pyramus. I missed my calling darling. I should have been a —'

'Yoli!' snapped Eloise.

'Yes darling?'

'For the love of peace. Tais-toi!'

'I will. Except to say' Eloise rolled her eyes drastically. 'that it's my hope you both know that I'll never shrink from speaking the *truth* to you.'

'I believe you've convinced us that's true.'

'You praised my *beauty* Ria and I thank you. But I know it doesn't hold a candle to yours darling.'

'Yoli?' Eloise warned again.

'Ah no hush, let me finish. And Ria it's clear there's far *more* to you than that. Oh yes, one may fail to see it at a distance. But up close, any ninny can tell. I fear that I've met my match in you darling. But I *like* that. If you swear right now that we shall at least be friends ... and to consider the rest 'til tomorrow morning to give us your answer —'

Ilaria laid a fingertip to her lips.

'Yes Yoli we *shall* be friends. And yes, you'll have our answer for the rest tomorrow.'

'Perfection.'

The Capulets watery encounter with the House of Power left me in heavy thought, wondering just how clever this dithering duchess may be. For the love of folly, her bold tactic, to ask *so far beyond* the target of their stated ambition toward the Capulets, seemed clever. And though at the time it appeared *impetuous*, I felt certain she and Nobel had considered every aspect in advance. I thought back to seeing herself and Nobel the day before we met them. Then next day, almost from the moment they came forward, the couple alluded to their interest in offering a *merchant* proposition.

Thereafter we discovered Eloise travelled in their company. That factum suggested that, from the moment they knew of the trial, at the very least, the Duchess and Nobel would have been learning more about Armand from Eloise. Then I recalled Yolanthe had also mentioned her little brother before we left for the burial. Finally, in the seductive comfort of the bathhouse, it had emerged she sought not just a short-term traders agreement to test a relationship with the Capulets, but an enduring factional alliance.

That first would have been a daunting prospect for the newly-weds to decide alone. Yet to offer so far past that goal — a familial compact — the betrothal of an unborn child? To me the tactic seemed to ensure Armand and Ilaria would feel pressured to accept the lesser offering, merely to make the greater seem possible. Perhaps more cleverly, the second offering made the first seem much less imposing — ten years compared to a lifetime.

Moreover Yolanthe had dangled her bait to a young, inexperienced, yet much too confident French couple, who had wandered far from home and still felt the war behind them remained a hovering threat. To crown it all, the Duchess's pending departure to Venice next day put the requirement for a final response upon a very short leash. Particularly so, when coupled with the suggestion she was moving onto Rome before returning to Verona, and that once complete, her negotiations there may extinguish any chance for new players to enter the alliance thereafter.

Every aspect of the situation appeared to ensure that the pressure to not only consider, but to act at once, with no chance of sending to Lyon for mature guidance, was inescapable. And finally, given the Capulet's harrowing experiences caused by the war — experiences Eloise knew so much about and may have shared before their approach — in such insecure times, what young elite couple would not want to secure such a future for their unborn daughter to become a Countess, perhaps in time, even a Duchess? Cupid's Balls!

Such an offer was not tantalising but breathtaking.

And beyond every other aspect, I realised that to the Capulets, the Duchess de Paris and Nobel were no longer just a pair of luring merchants, but guardian angels who sought to protect them — and Armand's sister — from the reach of the Montecchi. That appealed to our chevalier's sense of protection. Yolanthe de Paris was appealing to them both but with quite different lures.

As I thought it all through I began to understand that Yolanthe de Paris didn't barter in *fortunes*. She bartered in *trust* which allowed her to form alliances that *grew* fortunes. I decided that despite her lack of years the young duchess was clever, far more clever than I. And the more I considered her cleverness, the more that attempt to insert herself into the Capulet's lives began to concern me.

Outside the bathhouse, Caspar, Maxine and young Fabrizio awaited us. The sun was lowering. We had enough time to rejoin the Cortelannis, exit the citadel and travel safely into the northern hills, back to the comfort of *Hazel Wood*. Later that evening, before Maxine fell asleep in my arms I told her all. Yet before I shut my eyes, I thought of the Duchess de Paris. Yes, I felt sure she was trouble. Yet I also felt she was a marvel. An intoxicating marvel.

Chapter 5 So be it

Esmeralda awoke in a sunlit bedchamber. It was the same room Princess Florentia had removed her to one week prior, before she was made to return to the dungeon and began her gruesome descent. Yet now that nightmare had ended. After her rescue by the mysterious apprentice she was deposited into the comfort of that soft bed and slept through the night. Though instinct had drawn her awake as the first light of day crept into that chamber, within moments Esmeralda fell back into slumber and didn't reopen her eyes again until nightfall.

How could I know so much now that Friar Lorenzo had exited her drama? Time will reveal that soon enough. For now, hold such impertinent questions and pay attention.

Though her eyes did open for that brief moment in the lamplit bedchamber, barely long enough for Sister Boniface to realise she had stirred, Esmeralda remained incoherent. Almost at once she began to babble and turn and toss, at moments clearly imagining herself to still be strapped to the board. Yes she was free but didn't yet comprehend it.

Nor did Esmeralda yet recall that she had fallen from grace. Indeed she'd fallen as far from grace as one may fall. So far that, within another day, her faction would arrange, not just to withdraw their battered prima donna from that castle, but away from Verona altogether. They wanted to ensure she vanished from sight in that citadel for a very long time, perhaps forever more.

Before the Capulets arrived in Verona, for nearly two decades Esmeralda Montecchi had been prima donna of her powerful House. She and Onorato were known to the newly elected Emperor. They were also known to his Holiness in Rome. Yet after Onorato's death, a spate of more dire events unfolded which had led to her utter ruin. What's more, after seven generations of proud possession, the Montecchi's familial estate upon Sycamore Hill had now passed into the hands of a foreign rival.

For her mighty albergo it was a disgrace, a bitter, humiliating, lasting disgrace. No, I didn't feel sorry for them. No, I did not feel sorry for her. Yes, I know scripture tells us all to forgive and to forget. Yet I've learnt that some things are not always forgettable. Nor are the people who do such things always forgivable.

Oh bite my bare ass! That's still how I feel.

At that time however, to some souls more charitable than myself, or to any in Verona who still stood in fear of her faction's powerful reach, some began to refer to Esmeralda as the *Black Widow*. Yet since her inquisition, some less sensitive souls dared to call her the *Black Witch*. Yet I confess, rarely did I hear that last said upon the street or in the marketplace, any louder than a fretful whisper.

More important than whispers however, were *thoughts*. For thoughts lead to *decisions* and the Capulets now had an important decision to make. And for Ilaria, despite the rankle of potential romantic rivalries that may stem from embracing a long-term association with Yolanthe and Eloise, all the other benefits to gain from it seemed to be so potent that their value couldn't be ignored for the sake of a that single point of *personal* reluctance.

Not least considerable among such benefits was that if a marriage match to Ilaria's first daughter was forthcoming from that association, she would be guaranteed to begin her life bearing the title of *Countess*. Needless to say, as her fond mother, Ilaria would know her daughter enjoyed the security that such a start to adult life may bring.

For myself — watching the newlyweds wrestle with that decision after we arrived back at Hazel Wood — my sense of foreboding prevailed despite the opportunities being dangled. And mostly for Ilaria's sake. In truth I no longer fretted any impact from Eloise upon Ilaria as a romantic rival. Yet I did fret the impact of a lasting association with this clever young duchess and perhaps even Nobel.

I was glad the Capulets were spending that night before the morning of their decision in less volatile company with Don Sabatino and Donna Aurelie. If anyone in Verona could have a stabilising influence on them both, particularly Ilaria, it was their powerful sister.

'Before any of her offerings are decided on darlings' Aurelie began 'for a pair of newlyweds who are yet to complete their marriage tour, your most pressing priority is to put the distress of that trial behind you.'

Sabatino embraced her. 'Yes mia cara I agree.'

'Of course you do Sab. We must all move on and out from under the pall left behind by these dreadful events.'

'And perhaps before morning' Sabatino added 'we can help you both think of a strategy that will allow you to placate the duchess, yet without acting too rashly.'

'That would be wonderful.' Ilaria sighed and kissed Armand's cheek. 'Yet I don't wish to lose sight of the fact that these opportunities could be life changing.'

'It's true darling.' Aurelie's brows lifted. 'Even I think they sound rather ... breathtaking.'

'And so I wouldn't wish us to forego them for the sake of being too cautious.'

I was perched upon a stool and had only just ceased playing my lute as I began to stow it.

'My grandam use to say' I announced uninvited 'a *cautious* woman thinks upon her *feet* with her eyes *open*.' I lifted my battered Irish harp. 'Yet an incautious woman thinks upon her *back* with her eyes *shut!*'

The prima Donna turned her attention to me.

'That homespun wisdom is quaint Marcel. Yet I doubt Ilaria is likely to fall pregnant as a result of any interaction she may have with the duchess in the morning.'

'Having met her prima Donna ... I'm not so certain!'

A hand smacked my shoulder! 'Imbecile!' snapped Maxine. 'This is serious. Stop sharing your antic opinions.'

I poked my tongue at her which drew smiles from all.

'No Maxine.' Aurelie insisted. 'His grandam has a point. The narrow aim of her adage may seem wide of the mark, yet it's broader warning is not.'

'I concur mia cara.' Sabatino turned thoughtfully. 'And ironically Ilaria, you say they spoke of their own association as a *marriage?*'

'She did so.'

'Which then led to a discussion of a betrothal that would lead on to children and so ...'

My own eyes lit with recognition. 'And so my grandam was wiser than I knew to warn me. Even though I am *not* a woman or ... *remotely* cautious.'

Aurelie rolled her eyes leaning into Armand.

'Thank Heaven big brother he's your musician and not your legal advocate.'

'Is he our musician?' Armand stared doubtfully. 'After four months of service I still don't know what to make of the rogue.'

Into the night, and rather casually, Sabatino and Aurelie helped Armand and Ilaria prepare for their meeting next morning.

In stark contrast a more dire meeting of mentors had convened in the citadel that evening at the Palace of the Podestà. Prince Escalus de Treviso, Magistrate Pasquale, Captain Lanza and Inquisitor Eustace were considering the finale of both trials and what the results may portend.

'The *Black Werewolf of Verona* and *Black Witch of Montecchi.*' said the magistrate.

'That's disparaging.' replied Captain Lanza. 'They're not going to like hearing that.'

'The new faction leaders must be convinced to remain calm.' added the magistrate. 'And *patient.*'

Captain Lanza furrowed his brows. 'I rarely hear that word used to describe the Montecchi.'

'Well Onorato is gone' said the Prince 'and Brando's agreed to take Esmeralda away.'

'Perhaps it's better Highness' said the magistrate 'if she appears to vanish entirely. At least for some time.'

'Agreed. Yet their names remain on everyone's lips in the citadel. And now their faction's boiling with rage.'

The magistrate sighed. 'They'll boil over if they ever learn how much other forces came into play.'

The comment drew every eye to him.

'Within Verona's walls only those in this chamber understand that much.' the Prince replied quietly. 'Between you magistrate, Captain Lanza and Inquisitor Eustace I feel secure. The only two I can't feel certain for ...'

The Prince paused as his gaze rested on a silent duet.

'Highness my scribes are bound by their oath to the Office of Inquisition.' Brother Eustace insisted. 'That faith's never been broken by any Holy Officer or his attendants.'

The tall muscular form of Escalus lifted from his chair to punctuate his intent as he glowered in the direction of both men. 'Friar Lorenzo. Brother Simone. You both understand what's at stake in this matter?'

'Yes your Highness.' said Lorenzo calmly. 'As you know I am also an ordained priest. This confidence is as sacrosanct to me as any offering in confession would be.'

'Brother Simone?'

'Is a Dominican Highness' the inquisitor answered for him 'sworn to absolute *obedience*, which in these matters he owes directly to *me*. To break that vow would be to cast his soul beyond the reach of redemption into damnation.'

Prince Escalus narrowed his eyes. 'Is that how you feel Brother Simone?'

'Your Highness I would much sooner die than breach the Inquisitor's confidence in me.'

'If you do so ...' Escalus added 'I'll see you die so slowly and painfully that you'll wish you were never born.'

'Threats are unnecessary Highness. Yet I'm sure he understands it was not offered idly.'

'Very well. Unless the seal of our secrecy's broken beyond these walls by the few in Venice and Rome who've played a part, the Montecchi should remain none the wiser.'

The Inquisitor lifted his brows. 'You're Montecchi by marriage

Highness.' He said bluntly.

'At a distance, yes. But I have no ties of blood with them to shake my resolve. I belong to Venice.'

The humble Friar Lorenzo said no more during that dark conference before he was finally relieved of any more duty to his brief term of service to the Inquisition.

Alone and in silence that night, he returned to his quiet cell on the north riverbank to contemplate what he knew. Laid out on his stone slab in the darkness with his eyes wide open, he understood Esmeralda would be taken away the next day. He didn't know if he'd ever see her again. He now felt sure, beyond any doubt, that he loved her. He found it very hard to accept what he now understood about her fate and that he must keep the secrets of it all.

Oh yes, he knew some folk from outside her faction felt sympathetic toward the dire outcomes that had overtaken her life. Sister Boniface had become one such. In their view, through no fault of her own but marital loyalty, Esmeralda had become embroiled in the shame of her husband's wrongdoing. Then her sympathisers — after watching a widow who had witnessed her husband's death suffer such a momentous public fall — felt the relentless effort taken thereafter to shame Esmeralda, had *exceeded* the boundary of what she truly deserved.

Yes, that's what *some* thought.

Yet none but a select few — Friar Lorenzo now among them — understood those relentless efforts against herself and her husband's memory, had been quietly manipulated by political forces bent on making an example of them both. Indeed, all that followed had been managed by two powerful and collaborating parties, in an effort to send a potent message to the political faction they represented.

As you now understand, the House of Montecchi belonged to the Ghibelline faction that supported the Emperor. The Houses of Capulet and Paris belonged to the Guelph faction that supported his Holiness. That last is the same faction which Yolanthe de Paris intended to seek a deeper alliance with during her visit to Rome.

Rome understood the power of the new Emperor was rising. Frederick was soon to be crowned and that coronation would threaten the balance of power between Italy and Germany. Some Italian powerbrokers hoped his coronation could be halted, yet that was not certain. And so despite any outcome that may eventuate thereafter, any chance that arose before that time for the forces that opposed Frederich — Rome and Venice — to make an example of two strong Ghibelline leaders in a vital citadel like Verona, was seen as too great an opportunity to let slip by.

Even Brother Eustace, the doggedly spiritual inquisitor, had understood from the start of Esmeralda's trial, that his effort to pursue her was expected to serve the interests of two political powers that he couldn't resist — his Holiness in Rome and the powerbrokers of Venice. The latter of course were represented in Verona by Prince Escalus and Princess Florentia de Treviso.

When Armand and Ilaria first arrived they discovered that Venice not only controlled Verona, it had remained neutral between the Emperor and the Pope for many years. But at that moment, with the power of a new Emperor rising, Venice became concerned that both sides of the ancient feud needed a timely reminder that, inside their own domains — in citadels like Verona — the power of Venice to defend its neutrality would remain unshakeable.

And so Venice was determined to demonstrate to both sides they would not hesitate to tear down the local leaders of either faction — in any citadel — if such people appeared, because of the Emperor's rising, to think it may be time to begin stirring the political pot again. Then at their fatal first meeting, Onorato Montecchi knowingly stirred that pot against the naïve Capulets, and suddenly the time was ripe for Venice to teach the arrogant Ghibellines a lesson.

If the final result was to be that a pair of the Emperor's most entrenched allies were turned into a scalding example, then so be it. To ensure future peace, Onorato's dishonour beyond his death and Esmeralda's living torment and disgrace, were worth the price of their purchase.

Of course it had suited his Holiness in Rome at that moment to allow Venice to gain such a result. And so it suited Venice to cooperate with an inquisition controlled by Rome's powerbrokers in Verona. Rome was eager to ensure that Venice gained the harsh result it desired.

You know I'm no historian, let alone a politician. Yet now I realise that in the elite game of balancing political power, when one side among three is *rising*, and one sitting between two is claiming *neutrality*, often that neutral power will aid the side whose power is *reducing* in an effort to restore their fragile balance.

Oh my sweet friends, despite every saint who prays and every angel who sings in Heaven, I confess that I've hated the Montecchi. But now, so long after these events unfolded, to know that truth makes me fear for us all, innocent and guilty alike. It even makes me question how guilty Esmeralda may have been, not thereafter, but at that critical moment at the beginning until her inquisition ended.

At the time it was all happening to her of course, Esmeralda understood none of this. Years later Sister Boniface told me there were moments during Esmeralda's confinement when she blamed her brutal husband's impulsiveness. There were moments when she blamed herself. Yet by the time her torturous ordeal had been endured she blamed the Capulets, fixating in particular upon the part Ilaria had played.

Many times as Esmeralda was being drowned relentlessly, she recalled the image of them at the Ceremony of Disgrace, watching from above, so visible in their finery. At that time she didn't know who the strangers were that stood by their side in support, a man and two women. Yet she remembered them too, would never forget their faces.

After they were identified Esmeralda swore to hold the French Duchess and her associates to account.

'I'll strike at that slut so deeply she'll cry for the rest of her life.'

And guilty by association of course, in Esmeralda's torn mind, were Aurelie and Sabatino. She had shared a lasting friendship with both until her fatal transgressions. Now she blamed all these and swore to find ways to make them all feel the pain of her cost.

Yet not for a single moment did Esmeralda suspect that, in an effort to keep the political peace, her own kin by marriage — Escalus and Florentia — had been forced to help to ensure her destruction. Oh yes, in time she would begin to piece it all together.

But at that moment what she knew of Prince Escalus for a certainty — from the reassurance of Sister Boniface who now understood — was that when the inquisitor confided to the Prince he was ready to submit Esmeralda to an ordeal, to ensure her safety Escalus installed himself there in disguise.

It was the Prince who had intervened to end her suffering, covered her naked body, lifted her in his arms and carried her up to safety. He also made it clear to the little despot that his work with Esmeralda was done. For the few who were present in that chamber of her horror, who saw the ghastly sight of her broken form thereafter, mind bereft of sense, muttering like a dullard, the halt Escalus called had not been ordered soon enough.

In the trials aftermath, none of Verona's citizens who harboured pity for Esmeralda understood the dark politics involved. Nor did it seem there were any witnesses to tell of the torture she had suffered. And so nothing was learnt of the mysterious circumstances by which it had ended.

Yet after Esmeralda was taken far away and began to recover, to recollect fragments, some among the Montecchi in Verona began to sniff and scratch at the puzzle in their minds. For when her inquisition was declared to be over, almost immediately her sympathisers began to hear the degenerate whispers that followed —

She-Devil. Goblin. Montecchi Witch.

Snipes to spite her fallen name and her husband's memory were uttered smugly by the lofty and low.

Many among her famiglia, particularly those who now controlled their mighty faction, began to consider if Esmeralda's misfortune may yet be repaired. Some even began to wonder if, despite the effort to erase them, the public memorials that honoured Onorato's service might also be restored. Indeed many among the Montecchi felt that restoration must not only be secured, it must be done with all haste and at *any* cost.

To the Capulets however, particularly Ilaria, the feeling was very different. One Montecchi was dead in shame, the other now lived in shame. She felt that for both, that result was deserved. Now it was over, the thought of either vile creature, was a bleak spectre to consider.

And so ... on the morning after the Ceremony of Disgrace and their seductive sojourn in the bathhouse, the travelling entourage of the Duchess de Paris was halted in the broad turning circuit at Hazel Wood. After wandering together in the gorgeous, manicured gardens, Yolanthe and Ilaria returned to the train to part company.

If Esmeralda Montecchi was still lurking down in the citadel, Ilaria's great hope in that regard was summed up to her new friend as they halted to say farewell.

'I hope never to encounter that *fucking* bitch again.' said Ilaria, linked arm in arm with Yolanthe.

Though she had whispered that spirited word, I heard it quite clearly. Because the duchess had shown an interest in acquiring my talent, I still considered it wise — against unexpected future need — to make myself more conspicuous to her rather than less. And so, as they had approached, I approached them too, turning to trail along behind.

No, I wasn't surprised to hear the noun that followed, but it was the very first time I had heard Ilaria use that lively adjective to embellish it.

'Oh darling I understand that hope.' purred Yolanthe. 'I do. But I also understand people like the Montecchi. And so while I'm away seeking to expand our alliance, by all means beautiful girl, attempt to relax and enjoy yourselves. Yet stay *alert* and —' the siren hesitated.

'Yes Yoli?'

'Oh well darling, fuck your Adonis day and night if you must. I know I would.'

'Hold nothing back Yoli.'

'Oh now you sound like that hussy Eloise. And you know I wouldn't hold back. However Ria ...'

'However?'

'You *must* come to a decision on whether you intend to stay or leave. I *need* to know.'

Ilaria arched a brow. 'I *must* decide?'

'Oh you know I love to order you about. It makes me feel powerful. But I do need to know. Time is of the essence. And truly Ria, I don't want to press on without you both.'

'We *will* decide.'

'And by the time I return, as well as that answer, I also expect to hear that my new best friend is *pregnant*!' Yolanthe grinned as Ilaria sighed. 'Well I want the chance to marry your gorgeous daughter to my little brother.'

'Go.'

'You know, if you're simply not up to servicing Adonis's needs at present —'

'Go.'

'He's welcome to come with us to Venice. Perhaps I should ask him.'

'Go now.'

'Perhaps Eloise should —'

'Go before Dame Capulet is compelled to issue a challenge to Duchess de Paris.'

'Oh Ria I wouldn't want to hurt you. But we *could* have a friendly competition. Between the three of us —'

'Three?'

'We can't leave *Eloise* out. To see who can make your Lion —'

'Yoli go to Rome! Find your Count Orlandi and his powerful consort.'

'Piccolomini!'

'Yes. He sounds very musical. I'm sure in the company of two formidable men, you'll manage to find more distraction.'

'That sounds saucy!' I cried to amuse them both and make the duchess mindful. Ilaria glared.

'It *wasn't* intended to be, you rascal.'

'Oh Ria I like him too. If I can't take Adonis to Venice, then at least let your skinny man —'

'No Yoli! Now go!'

'So be it. Wish me *bonne chance.*'

The duchess did go, with a lascivious grin. Then we watched the smiling faces of Yolanthe, Eloise and Nobel recede into the distance as they stood together, lifted through the gaping void in the roof of her extraordinary conveyance. I did wonder what it would have been like to go along.

We expected her to return quite soon, within at least a fortnight. Yet she didn't at all. Indeed Yolanthe's absence continued to extend although Ilaria received messages from her. It made the itinerant nature of her circumstances more apparent. In pursuit of power and perhaps more distraction, the young duchess was living her life, flitting from exalted pillar to post, from Venice to Rome and beyond.

She seemed to be a whirlwind when we met her. She continued to be. When she departed that first time, within just two days of meeting the Capulets, she had managed to coax them to sign a *formative* agreement. It bound their initial interest. Yet that morning, thanks to a suggestion from Aurelie the evening before, Ilaria insisted they be granted an extension of time to consider things more fully before making an *irrevocable* commitment.

Just when Nobel was wavering, a stern look from Armand to the duchess seemed to sway the result. That had been Aurelie's suggestion too. Having heard how Yolanthe behaved in the bathhouse, she felt certain his quiet influence upon her would be potent. She was correct.

No mention of a marriage pact had been made in the document they signed that morning. For although, if it came to pass, it would help bind all parties in the alliance, it would also require a separate agreement between the Houses of Capulet and Paris.

And so as their train departed for Venice and Rome thereafter, the decision left before Armand and Ilaria was whether to finalise a long-term trade pact. It would last a *decade* to begin, in active partnership with Nobel and Paris and in silent partnership with her French Majesty of course.

Moreover, the Capulets must also agree, for a minimum period of *five* years, to remain in Verona to oversee the growth of their interests. And though my employers were still left with that weighty issue to consider, from the blithering advice that *Yoli* had offered *Ria* in parting, only one thing hung heavily upon my own mind —

her warning against the threat of the Montecchi.

Chapter 6 Possession

Two weeks after the Duchess departed, no word of her impending return had arrived and the Capulets remained at Hazel Wood. Yet the early harvest season had begun and so, with the Montecchi estate now rightfully theirs, Armand and Ilaria announced an intention to re-enter the gates of Sycamore Hill. They must inspect the asset more closely to decide what work may be required to take up possession.

Though their decision on whether to remain in Verona was still pending, they had decided, even if we were to leave — at least for a time before we did so — we must occupy the ancient villa. That would ensure they learnt as much as possible about their new hold-ing before determining how to deal with it thereafter.

We arrived in Verona a little past mid-summer. The Capulets had planned to stay perhaps a week — not more than two — before returning along the silk road and through the same alpine passes. Yes, a turn in Venice had originally been considered, yet now seemed too much to contemplate. For you see, by the time that decision to take possession of Sycamore Hill was made, autumn was looming.

And if after all, a final decision was made to leave? Any return to Lyon would require us to reach the alps before winter's approach made the way too harsh to travel. I was heartened by Armand's recov-ery. He could walk for longer periods though hadn't yet recovered enough to ride.

On the day we entered Sycamore Hill however, he stubbornly insisted Ilaria and himself — with Caspar going before of course — must walk up the steep rise from the gate together until they stood beneath the ancient tree which gave the estate its lyrical name.

'Call it a rite of possession.' Armand smiled to his unconvinced bride.

'Armand you're still much too —'

'In love?' Kiss. 'With my wife?' Kiss. 'To want to miss this chance to share it together?' A lengthy kiss. 'Yes.'

Yet I too was mindful of his tender condition and Ilaria's reluctance for him to test it. So I offered the use of my ass to ferry them both. Oh the sight of them aboard that farting she-devil *would* have been priceless. But Armand would have none of it. And so, taking Ilaria's hand, they ventured on afoot. He reached the crest with a little assistance from his beautiful bride, having waved all other help aside. That *was* priceless to see.

Failing for breath, they faced each other as the rest of us — Maxine, Fabrizio and I — straggled in and ranged about to join them. It was a moment of quiet triumph. Caspar returned from his scouting foray to consent to a lowering of vigilance. Armand was smiling. We all vividly remembered the terrible suspense of the last time we stood there together, waiting to know our fate.

'If I had to lean on someone for support' Armand began 'it may as well be an angel.'

'That's sweet my heart. But I know Caspar's shoulder is too tall for you to lean on.'

'It's true. Nor does he smell as sweet. Nor do I have any inclination in his company to do this.'

Beneath the spreading sycamore, Armand lifted Ilaria in his arms and crushed her to him as they sealed their breathless homecoming — of sorts — with a loving kiss. Finally their lips parted. Blue eyes gazed into green. Their entourage stood about them, quietly watching and waiting. Oh I wished Liberati and Boccolo had been there to share in that moment, but they were gone to Lyon to fetch assistance.

Ilaria turned from Armand's embrace. 'Well Caspar, I should hope he doesn't feel inclined to do that with you.'

For the love folly we burst into a chorus of antic laughter. Even that giant ninny grinned like a child.

Of course, Armand refused to set Ilaria down until he had carried her — with some level of discomfort it must be confessed — up the wide casement of marble stairs and over the stately threshold. And I must confess, that despite our intimate number — swelled by a pair of Cortellani guards who remained at the gate and a pair who followed Caspar forward and now became sentinels on either side of the entry portal — the occasion had a grand sense of accomplishment.

The House of Capulet had claimed a stake in Verona.
One question hung in the minds of us all?
Would its young leaders be inclined to stay?

Thereafter the work of assessment and some hasty preparations began. By the time everything that was required to allow us to occupy had been done — a week and odd days — we had remained in Verona longer than first anticipated. Yet since the trial's conclusion, nothing had presented as too great a surprise or appeared to threaten our chance to return to France before the approach of winter.

Soon after that first week of possession however, a worrying problem began to emerge. Yes the estate felt like a paradise. Yet it was meant to be a *working* paradise. And though Sycamore Hill wasn't as vast as some like Hazel Wood, it wasn't small either and needed labour to run it. Virtually all who had inhabited it were gone. What the Capulets discovered was that, thanks to a fear of Montecchi retribution, few would risk enlistment to work there now.

But the time for the main harvest of grapes and olives was looming as Montecchi intimidation began to confound the need to ensure it would be managed. Solving that difficulty threatened a greater delay of course. And at that moment, even if the Capulets managed to gain the upper hand on that setback; even if they made a decision to leave before winter — which they *still* had not — we couldn't yet consider departure because they still awaited the arrival of one who was expected.

No, I'm not referring to the Duchess. She would come in her own sweet time. And in truth, three weeks after her departure, Ilaria still had no word from Rome of her success or failure, or when to expect her return. Beyond her return, we awaited the coming of another Capulet. For as you may recall, within two days of the arena disaster, Aurelie had sent for her brother Tristan to come urgently.

Our stalwart veterans, Liberati and Boccolo, had ridden posthaste for Lyon to fetch him and request Sieur Olivier to allow him to bring reinforcements. For security against the threat of Montecchi retaliation of course, that summons had been sent at the start of the trial. None had expected the trial to be ended so quickly.

Yet once it was done — and since the dangerous confrontation in the western borgo — the Capulets still anticipated more men would be needed, to secure our safe journey home when we departed. Now it suddenly seemed, they might be needed beforehand in Verona itself.

By the time Armand and Ilaria crossed the threshold of Sycamore Hill, we judged that Tristan would just be setting forth from Lyon. It should take him at least a fortnight more to complete the journey to join us. Based on that calculation, and in consultation with the Cortelannis, the Capulets made a decision.

'Sab ...' Aurelie frowned in thought. 'I think you're right. I can't see another alternative.'

'Nor can I mia cara.'

It was Ilaria's turn to frown. 'But Armand this feels wrong. I don't want to resort to such a thing.'

'Nor do I angel. Yet ...' He felt lost for words.

'We understand Ria. But it's more common in Italy. Particularly in citadels close to the ports. What else can be done? The Montecchi have made it clear to all hereabout.'

'And you both must realise' added Sabatino 'the harvest in olives, wine, pomegranates and tomatoes from Sycamore Hill are depended on by a great many interests. Saint Peter's nearby for one. The Abbey of Saint Clare just beyond it is another. The loss of that harvest in fine weather is just too much to contemplate.'

'Sab's right darlings. For the sake of your goodwill, it would be an unmitigated disaster. At the very least Ilaria, let's hasten abroad to see. No need to decide 'til we arrive. But we must go while there's still time and you must arrive prepared to do what may be necessary.'

Aurelie's bright blue eyes, the mimic of Armand's, challenged her soberly. Ilaria glanced from one to the other.

'Oh dear my stomach's turning. Yes then, very well.'

'It's the only way darling. And I'm coming too.'

Ilaria's eyes lit with relief. 'Oh would you Lee Lee? Yes thank you.'

'We're famiglia now. We share every burden.'

And so while we waited for Tristan to arrive, the trio hastened to Venice in an effort to solve our deepening crisis. If Ilaria did finally agree, the solution would allow them to reap a first harvest at Sycamore Hill, but more importantly, to trade the result. It was the first merchant responsibility she would attempt to undertake without the aid of her parents.

While they were gone Sabatino had agreed to make a start at Sycamore Hill with labour drawn away from Hazel Wood. Yet even with that assistance, splitting his own force between both estates, left both desperately short to manage the scale of their work. And though he went into the citadel to try for himself — thanks to the Montecchi still — none who weren't already in their employ were willing to risk working that season for the Cortelannis either.

And so as a last resort, yet much against their want, Armand and Ilaria had hastened to Venice to consider the purchase of enough slaves to make up for their lack. Though some in France still purchased slaves regularly, the grim practise had become far less common. In Lyon, it had fallen out of favour many years before.

The Church had rules and advice about the use of slaves of course. Mostly, it frowned on the use of Christian slaves within the borders of Christian kingdoms. Yet it also frowned upon owners who failed to induct non-Christian slaves into the fold after purchase. Why should a Christian, they argue, purchase a pagan to work in a Christian kingdom if they have no intention of attempting to redeem them?

Cupid's Balls! Imagine the diabolical discussion that flowed when that rule was debated. I knew very little of such things of course. Yet I did know, from former slaves I had associated with in the cathouse — some I had fond and intimate relations with — that Christian slaves who were traded in Egypt and Africa, were not always compelled to renounce their faith. Somehow to me, at least upon that level, the heathens seemed more Christian-hearted than Christians. Yes, that seemed confusing.

Despite that confusion, when we first entered Italy we quickly discovered the will to purchase slaves there ran on unabated. Particularly so in citadels like Milan or Verona which sat so close to the mighty port citadels of Genoa and Venice. Indeed, as we had travelled east from Turin, drawing closer to Milan and then Verona, we had seen more and more slaves in each citadel we stopped in. Since Milan however, Verona had held the greatest number so far.

Most of the slaves we'd seen thereabouts appeared Slavic or Nordic. I learned they were sourced through Venice from ports upon both sides of the Black Sea. That meant most who were purchased or taken from the northern Black Sea coast were Pagans or Christians, while those from the southern shores were Moslems. I say *purchased* or *taken* because some were indeed abducted, and so sold without consent. Yet we were led to believe that most were not.

And so with the harvest in wait upon *the Hill* — as we now referred to it — and Montecchi agents lurking in the citadel, threatening any who showed interest in working for *the foreigners*, the Capulets agreed they could see no other alternative. While in transit to Venice they vowed that whoever they may purchase would be granted their freedom at once in return for a single season of labour before having the chance to be replaced, unless they agreed to remain.

The journey to Venice — which can be made in a day by a single rider at pace yet was covered in two by ourselves — offered our trio a chance to visit Nobel's *Grand Emporium*. And though Auguste, Yolanthe and Eloise were absent in Rome, our trio were received by Nobel's charming nephew and mesmerised by the scale and opulence of his enterprise.

I had no doubt, despite how glamorous the young Duchess de Paris may be, it would have turned her own head to see it all too. And our own merchant princess Ilaria — quite apart from their urgent task of averting a disaster in Verona — was also smitten by the dazzling port citadel of Venice. At least she was, until Armand and Ilaria finally laid eyes upon the wretched conditions of those held in the slave market.

Mercy dear friends, they simply couldn't believe what they saw. Nor could I. Naked wretches of both sexes and of every age and condition were tethered in chains to holdfast iron rings anchored onto the hard dockyard timber. Most wore iron collars about their necks and ankles. All were unshaded and so exposed to the remorseless heat.

Soon after we entered, a newly docked pair of ships began to unload its human cargo. We saw the miserable sight for ourselves as more than four hundred slaves were disgorged between them in a single delivery. Aurelie had seen it before of course. Yet for Armand and Ilaria, Maxine and myself, we'd never experienced anything like it. Nor do I ever hope to see the like of it again.

Oh my sad friends, had I not seen the horror of it for myself I could not have imagined the nature of how such people were brought into our world. Never in my life have I been so glad to be living free. Never have I felt so ashamed of our culture. Greatly we feared that most we set eyes upon would soon be at the mercy of much harsher treatment than anything the Capulets would offer, hauled away by masters and mistresses who cared nothing for them.

Knowing Armand and Ilaria as we did, it seemed to Maxine and myself, that any poor wretches they chose to take away from that harrowing place, would be better off in their employment than any other alternative. From the moment Ilaria saw them her eyes began welling with tears. Then, as we began to walk among them, led on by an agent, she couldn't stop weeping. Armand looked grim-faced as she held his arm tightly. I believe the agent touring them through misunderstood Ilaria's reaction.

'If what you see here seems unsuitable for your purpose Madonna' he began casually 'you may purchase a token to attend the more exclusive auction held for our more discerning clients.'

He promised that offering, conducted away from the grime and inhumanity of the open market, would show off the healthiest and most alluring new arrivals.

'The inhumanity is not in the location Signore.' Armand replied soberly. He turned to Ilaria. 'What do think? Shall we attend this other auction or —'

'Oh no. No, no, no. Let's do something for these poor people here. I'm sure they stand in greater need of fair treatment.'

The agent tilted his eyes to Heaven. 'They're slaves Madonna. And not our prima stock. Treat them as you will.'

Ilaria narrowed her eyes at him but Aurelie noticed her reaction and replied.

'We're not here to discuss morality!' she snapped. 'You know the name Cortellani?'

The agent scowled petulantly. 'No Madonna.'

Aurelie stared without a hint of reaction.

'Then I assume you know the name Nobel?'

The agent's well-fed face lit with interest.

'Of course Madonna. Who in Venice does not?'

'Then man you would do well not to trifle with three of his close associates.'

'Of course not Madonna.'

'That's prima Donna to you.'

'My deep apologies prima Donna. Please let me know what you require.'

'That sounds more like it. The primo Don of Capulet ... you'd best recall that name hereafter.'

'Capulet? Yes I will prima Donna.'

'Needs ten to a dozen. For some he needs particular skills. Here is a list. Show us the worst you have that fit the need for each.'

'The *worst* prima Donna? But for an associate of Nobel —'

'Do as you're told man. And hurry.'

'Oh yes Monsieur please hurry.' Ilaria added. 'The sooner we're done the sooner we can relieve the discomfort of at least some of these poor people.'

'Ah you're Français? I too am Français. For *you* I will hurry.' He turned to Aurelie. 'And with you prima Donna ... now I must haggle.'

'We're both Français by birth you rogue. What's the difference ?'

'I mean no disrespect prima Donna, yet clearly she's the *nice* one. Of course if you wish me to haggle price with Madame Capulet?'

'Oh no you don't. That's what angry prima Donnas are for.'

'Then follow me prima Donna. And mind your step.'

In less than a week, we had returned to the Hill with ten new people — including a cook. From the estate's former retinue, only two stalwarts and their families had remained. One was the game warden, Guilio. His wife Dulcet was Français and served double duty as the butcher. The other remaining tenant was Clario, the master vintner, along with his wife Micola, and their rather large family.

I wondered of course why these two dared to stay when all else had fled. It seemed neither famiglia feared retribution for doing so. Eventually, we discovered their lodgings sat upon plots that lay within the estate's boundary, but were also owned outright by each. Not even the seething Montecchi expected such well-anchored folk to leave their own land or give up the right to ply their ancestral trade.

Thankfully, we returned to them from Venice with help to remedy our labour shortfall. Within ten days of our return, each slave we brought with us had been granted their freedom and told, any who wished it, could leave without further burden on their time. Yet all who decided to stay were offered a single season of service to begin. When that was rendered, each would then have the right to stay longer or go without hindrance — unless the Capulets decided their service was not worth retaining.

Somehow, despite our gruesome experience at the slave market, that mission to Venice seemed to fortify Armand and Ilaria's spirits. I think that despite their reluctance to purchase human beings for labour, they ultimately looked upon it as chance to attempt a charita-ble rescue. All but one chose to stay for the season. And that last returned to the Hill two days later to see if they could still take up the offering. That was permitted of course.

As a daughter of merchants herself, when that last was agreed,

Ilaria summed up the bittersweet nature of it all.

'Given the state we found them in' she said vacantly 'I believe everyone in our care will be better off for it.'

'As do I.' Armand replied.

'Yet every purchase we've made of their human cargo offers those merchants and slavers more incentive to continue with their hateful trade.'

'It's true.' Armand agreed. 'How can such a circuit of misery ever be broken?'

I wondered the same for myself. Yet there was little time to ponder such questions. For having returned, a great deal of work began to consume them both. Soon however, with Sabatino and Aurelie to guide their efforts, in little more than a fortnight thereafter, the Capulets felt the harvest would be safe. And so at last, they turned their minds to finalising an answer for the Duchess.

As fate would have it, the sight of Nobel's operations in Venice had impacted them greatly. And what's more, the Capulet's need to solve that first conundrum had offered them a chance to interact with the Cortelannis on something more meaningful than the pursuit of social distractions.

All in all, their fleeting visit to the port citadel with Aurelie, their consideration of how enjoyable working with Sabatino and herself had been thereafter — indeed all the Cortelanni's unwavering support lent by since our arrival — had become impossible to ignore. The elite duet, Sabatino and Aurelie, seemed unflappable. If the Capulets decided to stay they began to understand what it may really mean to be able to count on the Cortelanni's continuing support.

Then one morning, just as I began to wonder how the pair may be feeling about the momentous decision, I heard Ilaria announce to Armand they must inspect the dove house. That caught my attention. It sat outside of course, beyond the rear of the villa's vast kitchen. As they made their way through towards it, Ilaria directed Gianna, our new cook, to follow them. I followed them all with my lute on my back.

Oh yes, Maxine glared in an attempt to drive me away. But I was hungry and hoped that proximity to our new *maker of meals* might yield me a morsel or two. As they went along, Armand and Ilaria were deep in conversation about their need to answer the duchess. We stepped beyond the kitchen threshold to halt in the yard that separated the kitchen from the dove house.

'Marcel start from that end to count the dove holes.'

'Yes Madame.' I bowed superciliously.

'Maxine start from the other and count how many birds we have.'

'Yes Mistress. Doves or pigeons or all?'

'Hmm. A separate count for each? Yes.'

To gain attention I began to count aloud and pointed with different parts of my body. 'One.' *Finger.* 'Two.' *Elbow.* 'Three.' *Nose.* ' Four ...'

'Rascal ...' Ilaria frowned 'count silently so none else lose their place.'

'That's a smart notion.' Armand smiled.

He pressed a palm against the ageing structure, leaning to test its firmness, yet didn't smile at the result.

'And Maxine when you're done ...' Ilaria added 'count again to be sure and once more.'

Ilaria turned to Armand who already held an egg in his hand. She took it to place in Gianna's outstretched apron. The shy cook said nothing and seemed unwilling to take her eyes from the ground for more than a fleeting second.

'Now angel what were you saying?'

'Oh just that ... it's become a point of interest to me that, although both are established in Lyon, Nobel now appears to be more tied to his holdings in Venice.'

'That's food for thought.'

'And the scale of his enterprise there was ... unexpected.'

'Yes. Had we not seen it, I would have held other accounts to be exaggerated.'

'As would I. And so surely my handsome —'

'I'm handsome this morning?'

'Armand ... I won't let you distract me so easily.'

'I'm *not* handsome this morning?'

'Hush you're always handsome. We must be ready with a decision.'

'Haven't you already come to a decision?'

'No my heart. I want us to decide together. I just feel each point
speaks to the potential of —'

'I don't disagree.'

'Oh what a silly way to say you *do* agree.'

'Well ... and I suppose, quite by accident, if we did choose to
stay, the support and goodwill of our famille here has been tested
convincingly.'

'Oh they've been so wonderful. Sabatino and Aurelie are such a
dear couple.'

Ilaria peered and reached into a dove hole. Her eyes lit up as she
drew out an egg. 'Gianna?'

Shy eyes lifted. Without a word, Gianna stepped closer. Her
small hand reached to take it and place it in her apron gently. Eyes
lowered again.

'And with such clear evidence that our potential allies are committed to the region ...'

'Yes I *agree*. A future in Verona is becoming a little easier to imagine.'

'Easier to imagine. But it's not quite so easy to decide once and
for all.'

'No. And now angel ... I promised Sab to accompany him to the
vintner.'

'Oh yes you did and I'm coming too.'

'Are you?'

'I'm anxious to meet his wife. Aurelie says she has many daughters. Gianna?'

'Yes Madonna?'

'Please collect the rest. And make a list of what you'll need to
run the kitchen properly.'

'Pardon Madonna?'

'Yes Gianna?'

'But you mean ... collect them *without* supervision?'

Ilaria blinked in surprise and looked to Armand who bent his brows in confusion.

'Why yes Gianna. Collect what you need and note it in the kitchen ledger. We need to gain a sense of how many eggs this number of birds can produce. Do you understand?'

'Yes. Yet Madonna ...' she hesitated.

'Gianna is something the matter?' Suddenly Ilaria felt she had guessed what the problem may be. 'Oh dear. If you can't write Gianna then Maxine can stay to assist.'

'I can make a mark Madonna. Yet aren't you afraid?'

Armand and Ilaria frowned with concern.

'Afraid of what Gianna?'

'Aren't you and afraid that I'll steal your eggs?'

Ilaria repressed a smile. 'Oh. Do you intend to?'

'Why ... no Madonna.' she pleaded. 'It's not only Christians who're forbidden to steal.' Her eyes lowered.

'Gianna please look at me.' Her eyes lifted shyly. 'After what you must have been through, we'll trust you completely until you demonstrate that we can't.'

'Don Capulet is in agreement?' She began to cower. 'I don't wish to be punished.'

'Gianna ...' Armand began softly. 'Don Capulet is in agreement that ... whatever Donna Capulet needs from you ... is what you must do. And Gianna?'

'Yes Signore?'

'If there's any need to punish for you for anything, which I do *not* anticipate, then it will be for Donna Capulet *alone* to decide and to administer.'

'Oh. Yes Signore.'

'Unless you hurt my people or possessions Gianna, I'll never lay a hand on you. And Gianna, if anyone ever threatens you ... you must tell me at once.'

'Yes Signore. Because I'm now your possession.'

'No Gianna you're free now. Your paper's signed and being kept safe in the citadel bank for you to present as proof. Do you understand?'

'I'm really free?'

'You are. But you've agreed to serve here for one season. To cook.'

'Yes Signore.'

'After that you're free to go. If Madame likes your work, she'll ask if *you* wish to stay. Until then, while you remain here I'll protect you and every person in our care.'

While Gianna had stood listening without a sound, tears began to rise and then fell from her eyes. Maxine stopped counting to cry too, then lifted her own apron to wipe Gianna's cheeks. Ilaria lost all control and hugged our new cook impulsively. Yes, she destroyed every egg they had collected. And so Maxine agreed to stay to assist her.

As we left them to their task, I glanced back, wondering at how little kindness so many people seemed to know in their lives. Yes, just as the harsh agent in Venice had suggested, Ilaria was the kind one. But so was Armand and so, I hoped, were we all. Yet, I can't include myself. That must be for others to judge.

By that day, every important delay and task had been managed and Armand had regained his health substantially. Although he had only just quit the consistent need to take a portion of rest each day. There seemed no doubt that after our return from Venice, his improvement was hastened by how Aurelie and Ilaria took so many matters into their own hands. They conspired to ensure he wasn't burdened too quickly with too much.

A few days before, I had stood with them both as they oversaw the start of the olive harvest. Ilaria was paying close attention as Aurelie reached into a basket to test the fare for smell and taste.

'Oh you know what he's like Ria. When you told me he walked up that hill and carried you up those stairs, I could have throttled the imbecile.'

'Yes. But he's my imbecile. And I enjoyed feeling like he couldn't climb the hill without my assistance.'

'Only you could convince him to accept such help. Stupido!'

'Ah. That's what my mentor, Countess de Viviers, loves to say.'

'I remember him serving as her page when I was a girl. She's a very glamorous woman. I watched our maman and her going at it one day, screaming like two alley cats. I thought the countess was in for a thrashing.'

'Dear mercy Lee Lee what was that about?'

'Your imbecile of course. Nearly killed himself leaping onto a bear.'

'I heard tell of that incident. I'm sure your maman was beside herself.'

'For a time. Yet after threatening to kill the countess, in several different ways, if anything like it should ever happen again —'

'Oh no.'

'Oh yes. Then they got rolling drunk and ended up in the bathhouse together!'

Both women laughed and and tested more olives.

'I've been to that bathhouse. There's nothing like the push of firm fingers through oil on your body. And a plunge in hot water to soothe away raw nerves.'

'Not to mention more drink. They both left together less sober than they arrived.'

'It's all a potent combination.'

That conversation was overheard a few days before the dove house encounter with Gianna. The morning after the Dovehouse encounter I was standing idle near the stable house. Armand's mighty warhorse Victoire — the dark dappled grey beast with its black mane and tail — stood out of his stall in the care of Adolphous, our new ostler.

Just one week before, and rather unexpectedly, that Germanic horse master had wandered up the hill in search of employment. He presented a parchment: a note of introduction from Gunter von Hartvigson — the man most referred to simply as *the Viking*. You may recall he served as marshal to Armand's infamous duel. Hartvigson was well known in the citadel as a giant bruiser who kept order at a drinking house and bordello called *The Dragon*. No the Viking may not have been considered an auspicious man to recommend anyone, yet with respect to our new ostler, given the Montecchi threats, Armand was surprised to find anyone come calling in search of any style of employment.

However we quickly learned that any associate of the Viking, like the bruiser himself, cared little for the Montecchi and this new man appeared to show no trace of fear in the face of their threats. Certainly the grizzled horse master didn't seem to fear them at all. Yet he did seem to know his business around beasts of the stable.

And so, with a ripe red apple in hand, I watched him inspect that stallion's nearside forehoof. As I plunged my teeth in for a satisfied bite, I watched Armand too. He stood at a near distance to the new man, looking as if he may be considering whether or not to ride his tall battle horse again. The air was still warmish but autumn had arrived. And so as I munched, the smells of final harvest had filled my nostrils.

From the entry road at the base of the hill, bordered either side by the now-yellowing sycamores, all the way up to the crest, the mighty hillside showed a patchwork of russet tones that made the estate more enchanting to behold. Over the last few mornings as I stood on the hilltop under the ancient tree, I had begun to feel a new chill in the air.

Upon that morning, before I'd noticed the ostler and Armand together, that chill had made me mindful. If we were *not* going to stay, but waited too much longer, the path along which we came hither from Lyon, through the alps beyond Grenoble, would be too grim to contemplate. What's more, even if we departed very soon and attempted to return at the same leisurely pace we had come hither, stopping at the points of interest Ilaria would insist on? By the time we reached the alps, it would still be too difficult for a mixed company to make the crossing back into France.

Just as I contemplated that, I saw Ilaria exiting the villa. She descended the wide marble casement of stairs and headed towards the stable. That was when I decided to enter the stable and poke my nose in, as they say. I continued to munch after she arrived. Then, almost as if my own thoughts had willed it, they entered a discussion on the need to *hasten* if they finally decided to return, rather than stay.

Ilaria patted the muscular neck of the great dark-grey beast. No not Armand! Victoire.

'Haste would spoil the *social* nature of our tour.'

She rubbed Victoire's cheek and smothered the massive nose with her delicate hand. As she felt the stallion push against her palm, Armand drew in behind to wrap her in his muscular arms.

'Compared to some angel, we've already had more than our fair share of —'

'You only marry *once*. And so my heart —' she whispered to forestall him.

'Amen.' he whispered to forestall her.

She turned in his arms. They were both smiling.

'And so I'll only have *one* marriage tour to enjoy.'

'Amen.'

'And so if we do return this season, I don't intend to allow these delays forced on us by that ... *bitch* ... to spoil my single chance to enjoy our promenade.'

Though she had hesitated to say it, he frowned a little to hear it. The frown melted.

'That seems reasonable.'

His lips pressed her forehead.

She lifted her chin to kiss him.

'Amen.' said Ilaria as their lips parted. 'We must only return when we can do so at a *leisurely* pace.' She was decisive. 'If we discover that we must remain here until the winter's passed, thankfully we now have a lovely villa, high on a hill, to bide that time in comfort.'

'And *safety* Madonna.' said Adolphus in his Germanic thick accent. He was wiping the flanks of the great dappled beast with a handful of fresh straw.

'Yes Adolphus.' Ilaria smiled. 'With Liberati and Boccolo still absent, I feel safer with you here to assist Armand and Caspar.'

'I'm grateful for the chance to serve. And never you fear Madonna. This villa is lovely, yes. But as Don Capulet knows it's designed for security too.'

'And soon ...' Armand added 'my little brother shall arrive with some assistance.'

'Yes my heart. I'm looking forward to meeting Tristan. Aurelie's very excited. I'm sure we'll all be safe enough until he arrives.'

I cleared my throat. 'I feel safer here than if we had remained in the citadel.' I presented what was left of my apple to the mouth of the grey beast.

'For once rogue, I agree with you.' said Armand.

'I'm gratified.'

'Are you rascal?' Ilaria lifted her brows.

'Oh yes Madame.'

'You won't be so gratified when I tell Giana where all her apples have gone.'

Though tempted to retort, I bit my tongue. And despite what I'd said, I still pondered our safety. The Montecchi still worried me. Yet I understood that for our greater safety, beyond the stout quartet of Cortellani men-at-arms who remained temporarily in our service, Hazel Wood sat just two miles to the north, home to two dozen more.

Until the younger Capulet arrived, who I was also yet to meet, it was good to know the considerable support of Sabatino and Aurelie was so close at hand. I felt the cool breeze upon my cheek again and noticed the stall beside Victoire's was empty. Every day since we had taken possession of the Hill, our giant squire Caspar had mounted Loki at first light. That painted beast was large enough to carry three ordinary mortals or one lumbering dunderhead. Now with Fabrizio serving as junior squire they rode out together — four times each day yet at staggered intervals — to patrol the unfamiliar perimeter.

Caspar was scouring for trouble of course. But he was also learning the lay of the land. During the first week he had wisely invited the game keeper to lead them and counted on his guidance. Giulio was born at Sycamore Hill and knew the lay of it — and every other estate in the northern hills — like the back of his own hand. Several times, our new ostler had joined in. Adolphus said that in order to tend our beasts properly, he needed to understand the manner of terrain they were being navigated upon.

I knew when I saw Armand in the stable that morning, gazing at Victoire, that he was wondering whether it was time to join the next patrol himself. Seeing him still there with Ilaria by his side, I felt that, despite the burden of recent experiences, the rhythm of wedded life for the Capulets seemed to be settling at last. She wove her arm around his waist. Their eyes met.

Armand was a chevalier of twenty-one years, beginning to stir again in the company of a lovely bride four years his junior. They were still so deeply in love and so new to marriage that, despite his injuries, they lusted for each other as only new lovers can do. Fortunately, after the trial, the beauty and privacy of Sycamore Hill offered the perfect setting to rekindle that interest. And so, very soon thereafter that morning, and for the very first time, I watched them mount Victoire together without a saddle.

After Armand had gingerly raised himself aboard, Ilaria reached her left hand up to his right, then placed her left foot upon his own. He leaned away to lever her up and onto the broad back of that mythical beast. Once aboard — still seated in side-saddle posture of course — she shunted her ass with a smile to settle in closer behind him.

I felt sure she hadn't noticed how the brawny ostler, hidden on the far side, discreetly reached an anchoring hand to grip Armand's elbow as she swung herself into position. He'd never usually require assistance of course. And I saw him wince a little and pat the German's broad shoulder for thanks. But then, I saw the fond kiss Ilaria put on her husband's back, and the look in her eyes as she laid her cheek down, and I realised she knew.

Oh dear Heaven, I tell you sweet friends, such rare indelible moments are the stuff that love is truly made of. What an incredible joy it is to be in love, to know you're loved, to want to create such heartfelt memories together. I feel as if every moment of torment experienced in our lives is erased by that enduring legacy, the comforting recollection of their love in tandem.

Out they went to walk that gorgeous monster over the estate they now owned together. As they emerged from the stable, Caspar arrived with Fabrizio in his wake, insisting they must follow for safety. But Ilaria waved his care away and simply looked at our giant with a mischievous smile.

'If we're not back in an hour Caspar ... it shall be because we're hard at work upon a secluded hillside ... attempting to summon an heir to inherit this prize.'

Even I was forbidden to follow.

And so no, you have no firsthand account of how they attempted to summon anything!

More is the pity, as they say.

We watched Victoire carry them away.

I knew they were happy.

Unknown to us at that moment, yet greatly suspected, the Montecchi were down in the citadel, seething with anger.

Moreover they had sent their spies into the hills to watch us. It galled them to know the haughty French interlopers had taken possession and sat in high comfort on Sycamore Hill.

It galled them more to hear they were seen on a secluded hillside of their stolen estate, naked and fucking like fancy French rabbits, or to imagine them free every night to indulge their appetite for each other in the sumptuous bed chambers of their ancestral villa.

They whispered in hot anger. *He* was merely an exalted French pimp. *She* was no more than a glorified French whore. The murdered Montecchi primo don Onorato, the respected Black Wolf of Verona, had been right to treat those crawling Capulets as infesting vermin.

I could tell you the text of those whisperings are drawn from my potent imagination. Yet the source was a pair of Montecchi rustics we encountered in the citadel soon after. We had descended with Caspar for an unescorted visit to gather supplies from Herb Market Square. Maxine and I had heard them by the fountain, ranting away.

Those ranging about us didn't recognise Maxine or myself from the trial. Yes, they knew we were strangers. And yes, the giant ninny was easy for all to identify. But almost at once after we arrived, Caspar had stalked away to some distance, too far for my comfort at the time. And so for safety we pretended to be Germanics, just passing through.

Maxine seemed to enjoy the ruse as I began to engage that antic pair. Then my sweetheart warmed up to it, enquiring more secretively if the rustics had and spicy morsels of local gossip to share. Cupid's spicy balls! She got what she asked for. What's more, it became clear from the content of their sniping the Montecchi weren't just livid at the mere *thought* of us, but from that snide account of Armand and Ilaria upon the hill, they were *watching* us too.

Suddenly, the two miles of distance between Sycamore Hill and Hazel Wood seemed much further for safety. Suddenly, the continuing absence of our people and the impending arrival of more, seemed much more pressing.

All at once my fears, which had abated that day when the loving couple rode out together, came flooding back to me.

Now the decision to take possession of Sycamore Hill seemed far more dangerous.

Chapter 7 Foreboding

We returned on from Herb Market Square that afternoon under a cloud of foreboding, knowing without doubt we were being watched by the Montecchi. As soon as we had boarded the wagon to make our way back, Maxine and I alerted Caspar. Upon our return to the Hill we hastened to report it to the Capulets. That evening they gathered us all together to announce a crucial decision. Given the first hint of winter would soon be upon us, given our help from Lyon had still not come, even if that help arrived the very next day we would now remain in Verona until the start of spring.

Oddly to me, it seemed that decision had been made as a result of Ilaria's singular insistence, rather than a shared consideration of what may be safer for all. However, our shy Moslem cook Giana was very relieved to hear it. She had dreaded the thought of working under the threat of the Montecchi without Armand close by to protect her. I can't say I blamed her for that.

And though the announcement felt confounding to me, now so alert — knowing Montecchi eyes were watching us — I didn't probe the sense of it any further that night. Yet as I considered our predicament again the next morning, it set me to wondering. Had anything occurred recently, something I had overlooked, to sway Ilaria's mind so firmly?

I began to wonder at it because ... I realised there was a risk for the Capulets associated with staying that I hadn't reckoned on before. It regarded their status as the *newly nominated heirs* to their faction. More precisely, it had to do with how this decision may impact on that status.

If you cast your minds back you'll recall how the declaration of their inheritance was signed, sealed and announced by Armand's parents on the morning after their marriage. Indeed it had occurred, with quite a flourish, just before we set out upon our tour. Yet by now, the new premiere couple of the warrior House of Capulet should have returned to take up their new responsibilities.

Moreover, they had agreed to do so within a certain frame of time. Ilaria was expected to proceed, under the close tutelage of Armand's parents, to learn to fit into her new role as the new premiere dame. As that began, Ilaria's parents would finally begin to mentor Armand into the fabric trade, opening his way forward for a very different future.

From their recent scraps of conversation I had gleaned that Armand hoped the acquisition of a valuable estate — so close to Aurelie's — would cause his parents to feel such a delay was justified. And Ilaria felt — for the sake of placating her own parents — that if the pact with the Duchess de Paris and Nobel was pursued, they would also agree that any delay was justified. Hmmm?

Having met both exalted couples I wasn't sure just how reasonable either pair would be of this delay. Nor how they may react to any potent risks that Armand and Ilaria had run together without prior consultation. Oh yes, there may be a dazzling result to show in each case. Yet the final result of both still remained unsure. Yes, they now possessed Sycamore Hill. Yet the Montecchi seemed to hope to make them pay a steeper price for it. Cupid's Balls!

And not only had the agreement with Yolanthe de Paris not been finalised, her own whereabouts could not even be accounted for. What's more — for Armand and Ilaria both — there seemed to be the issue of a *reckless approach* to gaining these results that, for the sake of establishing what style of leadership was expected in future, may require a deeper discussion with their betters.

Still, now with a little more time on their side — but expecting Yolanthe to return at any moment to hear their final decision — the Capulets must finally answer the most important question. Just how lastingly did Armand and Ilaria wish to remain at Sycamore Hill?

Would the coming spring see us return to Lyon?

Or would they agree to stay for at least five seasons?

Paris and Nobel, strong advocates for the latter, had certainly gone to Rome to enlist more formidable support for the enterprise. For an ambitious young couple to fall in so soon with allies of such far-reaching influence — willing to support them closely in Verona and link them to a port such as Venice — was very impacting. More-over, the support of that duet alone suggested this venture may bring a sense of financial security with it that could mitigate any risk they may run by staying abroad longer and trying their luck.

And my sweet friends, that was the whole point of course, that notion of their *luck*. A wily merchant doesn't want luck to matter too greatly in any undertaking. Yet so far there was no doubt, the young Capulets had been lucky. Armand's challenge to Onorato Montecchi in a moment of wild passion — to risk their estate in a game of chance — was *one* thing. Ilaria's decision to risk the lives of all to deliver a clutch of flowers to a poor boy's burial was *also* one thing. Well yes, that's now *two* things!

But the more I came to know Armand and Ilaria, the more I realised they seemed to manage to do all things — even undertake their most dire follies — together. However, what should now follow for them as a couple, as a pair of responsible new leaders, should be *entirely* different. The should begin to count less on risk and luck and more upon prudence and strategy. Oh yes, now I sound wise.

Yet it's easy to sound so in hindsight.

That evening I stood with them upon the landing above the broad entry stairs. As we watched the fall of another sunset together, I plucked at my battered Irish harp. Somehow it reminded me of that moment in Carentan when Armand stood on the ramparts with Eloise. At that time Eloise had been anxious of pouring her heart out to him. Now, after relaying what we had heard in the market, Ilaria seemed anxious too. Yet her anxiety was about discussing our *longer-term* safety, and of how much the *lasting* support of strong allies may make all the difference.

'Not to mention ...' Armand said quietly 'her aggressive nature.'

'Yoli is *not* a shrinking violet. Nor is Nobel.'

'No. We saw how that agent in Venice reacted to his name. And Cortellani's a very potent name in Verona, yet he didn't blink an eye at it.'

'The mention of Nobel snapped him to attention. As if the new Emperor himself had arrived in that foul market.'

'It did angel. Hmm. And so, if we *do* still remain at odds with the Montecchi —'

Ilaria lifted her brows. 'Well, judging by their threats to any who showed an interest in working here ...'

'Yes I know. Then finalising an alliance with the Houses of Paris and Nobel ...'

'And the Cortelannis too ...'

'Yes. That would harness a potent force to balance against a local threat like the Montecchi, no matter how powerful they may seem.'

'Armand. There is ...'

'Oh!' Armand glanced at me. 'Did you hear *that* rogue?'

My eyes lit up and I understood in an instant.

'Oh yes I heard it. Brace yourself brave chevalier.'

Ilaria rolled her bright green eyes, glancing back and forth at us. 'What are you both gabbling about?'

'The portent of hearing you address me so formally.'

'*Armand* means she's contemplative.' I added. '*Armand Gabriel Felix* means she's angry.

'Or frustrated!' he put in with a smile. 'But *my handsome* always seems to presage a weighty request.'

'Or an *intimate* request!' Now Ilaria was blushing. 'And *my heart* seems to mean ...' I faltered. 'Well ... it just seems to mean that ...' She was glaring right at me.

'I love him. And truth be told I *always* love him. Even when I'm angered, frustrated, in great need or — but listen to me both of you. Well perhaps not you rascal, just play.' I did so. 'There's something *else* to consider — a matter of *conscience* and ... well I feel *very* responsible for it.'

My ears pricked to hear it. Armand's smile softened. 'W h a t ' s that my angel?'

'If we did leave here, and the Montecchi remain so bitterly opposed to the Capulets? What of *Aurelie's* safety? She was a Capulet and now they know it plainly. Without us here to act as a shield I fear that she and Sabatino ...'

'Would be left alone to fend off a danger that we laid at their door. Yes I had considered it. Even my *own* insistence to fight Onorato has put her in —'

'Armand!' Ilaria scolded him. 'You would have had no need to do so if *I* hadn't —'

He reached for her hands. 'Oh angel, angel, angel let's ... let's just agree that together —'

'Surely' I blurted '*both* your rash decisions have laid this danger at her door!'

Oh yes, they stared. But in truth I had heard as much as I could take from them.

'Well rascal, I may not have said it so bluntly.'

Ilaria stared.

'No Madame. But that's part of my purpose.'

'Is it indeed?' Armand replied.

'I hope so for both your sakes. Well? If I can't bleat out the truth when you're both being so foolish ... who else shall do it? And before either of you insist, yet again, that it's your *own* fault or agree on a suicide pact of shame that would leave me unemployed —'

'Mercy knave! You don't lack for —'

'Oh hush for a moment Madame Capricious and just let me finish!'

Ilaria opened her lips to rebuke me but Armand clamped his arms about her. 'No, no, no angel. Let him spout for a moment.'

'Thank you Master, because you must both consider one *very* important factum.'

They glanced at each other sceptically.

'Yes rogue I'll bite.'

He stared with mock impatience.

'What factum pray tell?'

She stared with real impatience.

'You both forget that I was there *too*!'

'He was there angel.' He frowned knowingly.

'Oh yes and so?' She frowned impatiently.

'And so ... I saw that vile dastard enter into your lives! Never has my mind been more made up in an instant. The loathsome primo don of Montecchi — may the Devil take his filthy mouth to the end of his own large cock and spurt fire down his throat for all eternity!'

'Marcel HOLD your tongue!' Ilaria spat hotly.

Her eyes were wide with utter surprise.

'NO MADAME! I can't apologise for disparaging that lecherous beast! From the moment he saw the icons on your wagons that wolf was spoiling for a fight. Don't you remember? Even before we laid eyes on him, he vented to his lackey outside — *Yes! I saw it!*

Armand nodded. 'Those *were* the first words I recall hearing him say.'

Ilaria shuddered. 'I shall never forget them.'

'Nor will I Madame. Yet by the time *we* saw him, that brute was a volcano of lewdness just waiting to erupt. And he finally did so. With his shame-faced wife, rigid by his side as you descended these very steps, he made that vile boast to ...'

'Marcel!' Armand hissed. 'That's enough.'

Ilaria erupted. 'UGGGHH that was detestable. I can't forget how humiliated I felt.'

I gripped my harp angrily. 'Nor can I forget his promise to do the same to the woman I love. In my opinion Madame, some things must never be forgotten or forgiven! Remember Chevalier? Remember when Toulon said that?'

A distant look overcame Armand.

'Yes, he said it often. Yet I can't say that I have ever agreed with that sentiment.'

'Nor did I *before* we met that dirty beast. Now I do. I'll never forget or forgive!'

Ilaria glanced at me, her eyes filled with bitterness. 'Scripture says that we must.'

'Well I say' I began to rant wildly 'I hope that beast is BURN-ING in Hades RIGHT now — receiving the same treatment he threatened to give Maxine with a burning hot poker up his —'

'MARCEL!' Armand bellowed. 'By thunder hold your tongue or

I'll smack those words from your mouth!'

I glared like a mad man. My jaw fell agape. 'Hold MY tongue Master? That tyrant promised to whip me to an inch of my life and I STILL didn't hold my tongue!'

'Mercy he's out of control!'

'Out of CONTROL Madame!' They stared in astonishment as I held for a heartbeat then began to restrain myself. 'No Madame. I *was* out of control then. Yet now ... I have my wits about me ... even if the Capulets do *not*.'

Ilaria looked at me, beginning to suspect at least some of my tantrum was for show.

'Rascal what are you aiming at?'

'Perhaps' Armand said soberly 'it's time we ended this discussion.'

'No please Master ... let me say one thing more to your own point at hand?'

'I think I've lost track of any point.'

'That you both say ... you hold *yourselves* to blame for your brave sister's danger.'

'Yes. It still seems hard to deny.'

'But think carefully, both of you. No sooner had we met that vile cretin and escaped his clutches, then we learned that he had recently clashed with Don Sabatino!'

'That's true rogue. At the horse auction.'

'Well yes rascal and so?'

'And so clever woman perhaps, just perhaps — for I put nothing past that demon's capability for wrongdoing — that earlier clash with Don Sabatino was incited as a prelude to a *larger* confrontation he planned for *later*, well before he ever discovered your sister was a Capulet.'

Both began to stare in deeper consideration.

Brows bent. Glances were exchanged.

Ilaria frowned. 'You mean that —'

'Perhaps Madame that dead dastard had a *longer* plan in his sights. To secure —'

'Hazel Wood?' Armand cut in.

He and Ilaria turned to each other.

'Dear Heaven, my heart. Knowing the man as we do now, it sounds very plausible.'

'Knowing the *cretin* Madame, it sounds probable!'

'Well rogue. I don't disagree.'

Ilaria shook her head in mock dismay at his signature manner of perversely expressing agreement.

'Then *pretty people* — as the duchess loves to say —' that made them smile 'consider this. Had you not met him that day, had you met him *next* day in the citadel instead, perhaps at the cathedral or some such ...'

'Indeed we already discussed meeting the brother next day to see his child.'

'Yes. And given the dastard's wife and Donna Aurelie were close friends, that meeting was bound to occur. I feel sure the *eventual* result would have been the *very* same but simply secured upon a *different* pretext.'

'Hmm.' Armand glanced at me. 'That may be so.'

'For even if he had met you *later* ... once he realised your connection to the Cortelannis and your allegiance to the Guelphs, he still would have invited you here to ensure the same result, to ensure his ill use of you Madame, could be used as a more likely pretext to expand a rift he had already attempted to ignite.'

'But rascal, could he have been *so* calculating?'

'Ask yourself, after such a long time in the Cortellani's company, would a man like him suddenly risk the ire of their well respected faction, just for the sake of a single horse?' I lifted my brows like a demanding tutor.

'Even as volatile as he appeared to be' said Armand 'given his station, one wouldn't think so.'

'Nor Master, from what we know, did his past behaviour suggest it. What changed more recently however, indeed not long before the auction, was the arrival of important news.'

Ilaria lit with comprehension.

'That the new emperor had finally found a bride?'

Armand stared for a long moment. 'Angel I wouldn't have suggested it before. But now I believe it's true.'

'And so pretty people' I attempted to mimic the sultry voice 'decide to *stay* or *leave* as you will. But don't believe for a moment that the Cortellani's trouble with the Montecchi ... has been of *your* making.'

I began to strum softly, still shaking with passion, yet pleased with my result. Then to my utter surprise, I felt the sacred touch of an angel's lips upon my worthless cheek.

'I fear that from the mouth of our fool —'

'Oh I often spit pearls of wisdom Madame. Yet sometimes they're smeared with a coating of grime.'

By then, Apollo's fiery chariot was all but gone from the sky as his afterglow painted the horizon.

Maxine appeared bearing a taper to attend to the entry lamps and perhaps investigate what we had been up to. I was glad she hadn't witnessed my tirade.

'Angel this has all made me wonder.'

'Yes my heart.'

'If we did return to Lyon we could always leave stout people here to protect our interests. Perhaps even *Caspar*.'

'Cupid's Balls!' I spurted. 'What a notion!'

Armand's hand hefted onto my shoulder. 'If I were the Montecchi I wouldn't want Caspar for an enemy, allied to the Cortelannis, Paris and Nobel.'

'Heavens Armand. That's a wonderful idea.'

'I won't say it's my *preferred* solution. But if we did return to France, we don't need to leave insecurity behind.'

'Yes. And I know many like Giana, now fear the prospect of our going.'

The mention of Gianna made Armand thoughtful.

'Hmm. Given they're all strangers that we've brought here too ... their safety is a large responsibility.' He gazed at Ilaria. 'I'm beginning to realise why my father was frustrated when I treated our succession so casually.'

'I feel that too. Last spring I was still unwed and fretted your return. I couldn't see an interest in my world beyond the want for us to be reunited. Yet since then?'

'Yes.' Armand agreed. 'A great deal has happened. And we've seen so much more of the world.'

'And so many who are suffering. I know they were always there, of course. But since we left Lyon I feel as if my eyes are seeing things more clearly. Those poor wretches trapped by the plague in Brescia. That woman at the lake —'

'Fausta?' I recalled.

'Yes with her daughter. Not to mention the poor Grisantis who lost their son.'

Maxine sighed. 'Oh Madame that was so terrible.'

'And now seeing those slaves in Venice. Hundreds of women, children and men chained to the docks like livestock. So many people are suffering so gravely.'

'That was the most disturbing.' Armand replied. 'I've never seen anything like it. At least those we've brought to Verona are free.'

'Yes. But now their safety rests in our hands, along with Fabrizio and Maxine ...'

'And me.' I bleated.

'And all the rest here on the Hill, old and new, whether we stay or go. Oh my heart.'

'I know Dame Capulet. Our lives are changing ... rather quickly.'

'And our responsibilities, Sieur Capulet, are growing just as quickly.'

'They are. Yet this is just a *fraction* of what my parents have been responsible for all this time.'

'And mine.'

Armand's blue eyes opened wide. He huffed in bewilderment and shook his head. 'Angel how did they manage to do it?'

'Together my heart. They did it together.'

'I hate to think of facing it any other way.'

I looked them over thoughtfully for a moment.

'My *maman* was alone.' I mumbled. 'And only responsible for me. Yet I fear I was too much for any parent to handle, alone or together.'

'I'm sure that was true!' Maxine agreed with a wink.

Armand turned his attention to me. 'Moreover wise counsellor, with respect to your sage advice —'

'Offered from my heart for the sake of your sanity.'

'Yes. But despite the grimy pearls you threw in our faces to offset our guilt, now that I know Aurelie's safety *continues* to be threatened, I still feel obliged to secure it.'

'Oh so do I.' Ilaria insisted. 'We must at any cost.'

And so despite our lively conversation; despite having a chance to speak my unfettered mind; both still felt anxious for Aurelie's safety. I believed however, they now felt less guilt for her predicament. I also felt certain I had reached the bottom of my question that pre-cipitated it all.

Why did I feel Ilaria was behind the decision to stay 'til spring?

At that point, it seemed clear to me, the matter of her guilt over Aurelie's danger had been the major issue. Yet I couldn't have been more wrong!

For you see, in addition to all I thought I knew — but didn't — even before the autumn had come, indeed as soon as the trial had completed, Ilaria sent word to her parents to explain every twist and turn to them. She had also included the prospect of striking a pact with Nobel. Then by the time it was decided they would remain until the spring, just one day before, Ilaria had received a reply.

I knew it had come. I didn't know her parents had offered their firm support.

'Sweetheart you must consider, how remaining in the Italian market

would allow you to forge new enterprises in Verona. Those would enjoy the significant advantage of lying so wonderfully close to a port citadel such as Venice.'

That note of support had affected Ilaria's thinking.

And though I knew nothing of that, I was certain Armand felt strongly that Lyon was their home. He and Ilaria had grown there together, grew to love each other. Yet there they were in Verona, living on a bountiful estate in a lovely Roma villa — the first signifi-cant possession they had gained together. And so despite all foreboding, having agreed to stay a few months longer, they seemed to begin to enjoy their time at Sycamore Hill.

For a week after their announcement I watched them closely, anxious to gather some sense of what fate had in store for myself through their final decision. Yet I still couldn't glean which way they were leaning. Did they feel they had merely extended their tour? Or were they trying to test how much they may wish to stay? Would they make Verona their home, our home? Or would they finally decide Sycamore Hill was no more than an enchanting summer residence and still depart in the spring to settle in Lyon?

Every next day I heard them consider and reconsider every issue and question. Autumn was ending. Ever more fretfully the return of the Duchess de Paris was looming. Yet still it seemed they couldn't agree upon a final answer.

'Yes I know my heart. Lyon is home to us both.'

Ilaria frowned as her eyes scanned the hogs in the pen before us. She was looking for a sacrifice to send the game keeper's wife in to fetch. The stout woman hung impatiently.

'Oh this is difficult.' Ilaria bleated.

Armand took his eyes from her to glance in the pen. 'Angel you must choose one.'

'Yes I know. I know.'

'Would you like me to choose?'

'No I must do it.' Her eyes narrowed. A lacquered nail extended.

'That one Dulcet!'

'Yes Madonna.'

Ilaria's brows knit in consternation as her instruction sent Dulcet, knife in hand, hurtling about. The condemned snorter fled and squealed of course. Armand open his eyes as if to suggest he waited on a response.

'Oh yes, Lyon is home. But the interests of both our *familles* there are well established.'

Armand pouted in thought, as if his mind ran ahead of her intention. 'Yes. And I agree as you said. There's no shortage of siblings or duets of uncles and aunts to recruit against the need to replace our leadership.'

'Your maman said it herself Armand, they have far more candidates than they need.'

'However angel, none of those are the *declared* Premiere Sieur or Dame of Capulet.'

She began to smile as she watched Dulcet wrestle with the lively hog. 'No. But my handsome ...'

Armand glanced at me. I shrugged and turned my eyes to Heaven.

'I saw that look rascal!' she reprimanded. 'Armand how much is our impact there *really* required for the sake of their future? Perhaps if our efforts are focused elsewhere ...'

'In Verona?'

'Or perhaps Milan. Even Genoa. Then we may have a more meaningful impact.'

As I heard her say so, I realised that was indeed a potent point. Perhaps at that moment for them both, it was the *most* potent point. For they were not merely deciding where to plant their roots. For the sake of their faction's future, they must consider where those roots might generate the greatest benefit for all.

Armand look fuddled. Perhaps not from confusion, yet in an attempt to put the point Ilaria had raised more plainly, I offered some unsolicited assistance.

'Madame, if I may, I think you mean to put the question that —'

'Rascal I mean to make myself watch Dulcet kill that poor beast!' She narrowed her eyes and clenched her hands.

'You could look away Madame. I suspect she'll do so whether you're watching or not.'

'A premiere dame must face reality.' She turned, grim faced, as Dulcet wrangled the beast into position.

'Yes Madame. But I think the important question you're trying to put is, will the House of Capulet in *Lyon* stand to benefit as much from your leadership *there* as it may from an effort here to create a House of Capulet in Verona? Or in Milan. Or in Genoa. Or some such?'

'Yes interloper *and*' She squinted in anticipation. 'Oh mercy here it comes!'

Just as she said so, the air was rent with an extraordinary squealing cry that chortled and then suffocated upon its own utterance. All eyes turned on the wild image of Dulcet, poised like a spectre, having sliced the neck of that upended beast. She gripped it harder as its death throes shunted and bucked it in her strong arms. Her expression was like cold stone.

Ilaria stared. Maxine stared. I stared. Armand had little reaction at all. Dulcet relaxed her grip, her hands smothered in steaming blood that flowed like a river. Somehow, despite the theatre of Dulcet's antics having warned us before, I had expected her to haul the captive into the haunted slaughter shed — and so out of our sight — before murdering it!

'With your permission Madonna.' She huffed. 'I'll take it within for butchering?'

'Of course dear Dulcet. Please tell Giulio —'

'He *traps* the game Madonna. I butcher it all.'

'That's a handy skill to have.' said Armand.

'It keeps me busy Don Capulet. With respect, if yourself or Madonna Capulet ever wish to learn a handy trick or two, don't hesitate to ask me.'

'Thank you Dulcet.' Ilaria said awkwardly. 'Yet I've found on the hunt my heart's too soft for such things. We're just very glad, after all the others left, you've both stayed on to do such important work for us.'

'This is our land too Madonna. We won't leave it or you. But soft heart or hard Madonna, my offer remains. You'll be surprised what you can become accustomed to and learn. The world outside our gate can be dangerous for a woman. Even for a prima donna.'

'We saw proof of that' I blurted 'on the day we came *inside* the gate.'

'Rascal tais-toi.' Ilaria insisted. 'Thank you again Dulcet. And ... I'll take it under advisement.'

I walked from the bloody scene feeling that — despite the lingering image of a squealing hog dying in the grip of a deadly woman — Armand and Ilaria had finally plumbed the depths of every major issue relating to their decision. At least I hoped it may be so. For I knew the duchess was no longer expected to return at any moment, she was overdue.

By that time I thought that I knew *every* question that should matter on that weighty subject to the Capulets. Yet there was one other question looming for Ilaria that I knew nothing about at all. And for the love of folly, it was a more potent question than any other. When and how would she tell Armand that she was carrying their first child?

Chapter 8 More to Love

No, I had not notion Ilaria was wrestling with that question. Cupid's Balls! I'm a man. At that time I was a young man, not even married. All I had ever considered about the intimacy between men and women that creates a child was the important question of — how could I enjoy it as much as possible? Well bite my bare ass, yes I did!

In hindsight I realise that by the time we reached Verona, Ilaria had already suspected her condition. Yet she showed no evidence of it at that time, at least to my ignorant eyes. Thereafter of course, when Armand was wounded next day in the duel and during the week of the trial that followed, Ilaria continued to say nothing. Her intimacy to comfort Armand was fervently indulged, yes. But due to his fragile condition, their romantic intimacy was not.

Then on the day the trial had ended, the day we met the duchess, though Armand's convalescence continued, their sexual antics had resumed and still Ilaria remained tight-lipped. Even the next day in the bathhouse, when she had bared her body before all, we didn't suspect it. Perhaps in hindsight the duchess may have detected it. She was said to have three children of her own, left in care in Lyon. And one day before Yolanthe had announced to Ilaria and Aurelie that she was *enjoying a hiatus* from having more children.

As you know, Aurelie didn't attend at the bathhouse but Yolanthe did and knew more of such things than myself. I believe she noticed subtleties that Armand and myself failed to observe. Next day Yolanthe's parting words to Ilaria amounted to a directive to bring forth a child to enable further discussion of a betrothal.

Then we took possession of Sycamore Hill, and with Armand's health restoring, their passion had ignited again. You now know of their frolic upon the hillside. Perhaps by then she was hoping the daft oaf — I mean my gracious employer Chevalier Capulet — might glean the truth for himself. Or perhaps in anticipation of what was to come, Ilaria had simply decided to enjoy as much intimacy as possible before her altered state made that less possible.

No, in all this time since I've never questioned her directly about it. To this day, I remain confused about some of her behaviour that followed. You know it was already their custom to have me play in their chamber before they slept, particularly after drinking together when their passion was rising. No, the signs of that were not hard to detect. With each next rising step the merry couple took together upon the casement of stairs, their hands became busier, lips reached further, hair became wilder.

And so, thanks to my close proximity at such moments, I feel certain that for a fortnight thereafter, Ilaria was attempting to sustain their intimacy — whilst managing more and more precariously — to keep that secret from Armand. Looking back now, I realise during that time that, subtly, the nature of her intimate ritual began to alter.

For instead of removing each layer, slowly or wildly, to expose bare skin before consummating their effort, bits and pieces began to remain in place for her but not for him. At first she retained the inner layers below the chest. But towards the end, her chest remained covered too.

Oh yes at the time, those variations made me wonder a little. Yet I decided she was just being impulsive, no longer willing to wait for the final unveiling to consummate their union. Now I understand that her breasts were swelling and nipples darkening, signals that may — even by flickering lamplight — have given up her secret too soon. The most telltale sign I should have woken to was when — as they became more engaged — Ilaria began to extinguish the lamps herself and finally began to insist that Maxine reduce the number of lamps laid out when she prepared the chamber.

Now of course, I also know why Ilaria had waited as long as she did. But now you must wait a moment too. Oh, be patient. You know I'll tell all. And so finally, by the time the imminent return of the duchess was overdue, the question of when to reveal the surprise was begging to be answered. By then it was clear to Ilaria the swell of her form, above and below, would soon betray her too openly — at least to Armand. And she didn't just wonder *when* to tell him, but *how* to tell him. For she wanted the moment to be more than just memorable.

Then upon the day after Dulcet had done her duty with the squealing hog, an answer to both questions emerged in a single moment. Just after midday, when Apollo's fiery chariot hung high above us all, eleven warlike horses came cantering through the sycamore grove at the base of the hill. They were challenged at the gate. The bell below rang out a coded alarm. The bell upon the crest rang out in reply.

Shortly thereafter a cavalcade of battle horses ascended the entry path and halted before the ancient villa. With the welcome sight of eight formidable men-at-arms at his back, followed by our own Liberati and Boccolo, Chevalier Tristan de Capulet had finally arrived.

As Armand hugged his brother and introduced his bride, he still remained oblivious to Ilaria's condition. Maxine stood quietly behind her. As her close serving woman she knew Ilaria's secret before any other of course. Indeed Maxine has always sworn to me that she knew it *before* Ilaria did so! What's more, Maxine was the reason that secret was held back so long. She had counselled it was better to wait until a certain moment, whereafter the likelihood of losing a child before it was due, had passed.

My sweetheart is full of mysterious knowledge and ways in relation to many obscure things. For the most part, her *powers* in that regard remained hushed to ears beyond our close company. Given we had recently witnessed the result of an inquisition, she was disposed to be more cautious than to discuss such things openly, or among unfamiliar people.

After Maxine, Armand's sister Aurelie came to know before any other. Following their visit to Venice, Ilaria and Aurelie worked closely together to make ready to reap the harvest. Then the stern prima donna and mother of three became wise to the issue rather quickly and rather bluntly, I'm told, confronted Ilaria to confess.

'You think I *haven't* noticed?' Aurelie said casually.

Ilaria halted for a sliver of a moment.

'Noticed what Lee Lee?'

'Ria I have three of my own and the last is still coddled by his wet nurse.'

'Your last?' She shot a glance to Maxine. 'Oh yes little Pietro is so lovely.'

'Come now woman. Stop this pretence.'

'Pretence? I'm sure I don't know —'

Like a vixen to a hen Aurelie latched her bright blue eyes onto Maxine. 'Did *you* put her up to this?'

'Pardon Prima Donna? I put Madame *up* to something?'

'Oh stop this at once. Both of you being so evasive.'

'Stop what Aurelie?'

'Yes, perhaps my maternal instincts have jilted me? Or perhaps I should summon my oafish brother over here to ask him some questions?'

'Oh leave him be. He seems so content stomping in the tub with Clario's daughters.'

'His giggling daughters Madame.' Maxin added. They all think the master is humorous.'

'I prefer they think him humorous to handsome.'

Aurelie huffed. 'He's an ignorant imbecile.'

'Oh Lee Lee what's he done now?'

'I've heard how amorous you've been since you came to the Hill.'

'You've heard ...? Well yes, I confess we may have been. Is that so wrong?'

'Half a year after he's wed, what manner of husband makes love to his wife so frequently and still fails to notice?'

'Oh Lee Lee please hush. Yes it's true. But please don't tell Armand. Not yet.'

'No darling I won't tell him ... yet.'

'Thank you. Thank you.'

'First I have to clout the both of you for attempting to keep it from *me*.'

'Yes I'm sorry. But I'm so happy you know finally.'

'Finally? I've known for ... oh darling I'll just say congratulations.' Her brows lifted. 'What wonderful news!'

All at once they were embracing and crying together. Until a voice startled them.

'Lee Lee what's wrong? Angel what's the matter?'

'Well I —' Ilaria stammered. 'That is my heart, Lee Lee and I were just ...'

'Yes?' he said awkwardly, shirt spattered with pulp and dripping from the knees down.

'I was just telling Ria' Aurelie cut in 'that little Pietro took his first steps this morning.'

'Oh. That is something to ... cry about. Yet doesn't that seem rather sudden?'

Aurelie, Ilaria and Maxine blinked in surprise.

'Stupido.' Aurelie retorted with a huff. 'What would you know of such things?'

Armand kissed them both and wandered away to restore his appearance to some semblance of dignity.

From the moment Ilaria's secret was shared with Aurelie, they began to forge the kind of bond that only women who have had children seem to experience. As you know, before we met Maxine, she was a wet nurse. She had borne a child herself and though, very sadly he didn't survive long, she too understood the experience very deeply.

Between the practical Maxine and strong prima donna Aurelie, Ilaria was flanked by good company, able to assist her with any challenges that lay ahead. And once that trio put their heads together, Aurelie brought her husband Sabatino into their confidence. As soon as he knew, both Cortelannis began to visit the Hill much more frequently.

Which brings me back to the long-awaited arrival of Tristan. For that band of conspirators had drawn together just days before his arrival. And before the saddle weary second son even had time to smack the dust from his boots, they drew him into their conspiracy. Indeed Aurelie was so desperate to ensure Tristan didn't accidentally surmise the truth and tip Armand off to the secret — no that wouldn't have been likely yet she didn't want to take the chance — that she rushed to embrace the unsuspecting fellow before anyone else could touch him.

'Ah Tristan!' she cried. 'Long lost favourite brother!'

She ran to him like a lost child to a parent, took him in her arms and smothered him with kisses. Then for the love of folly, the moment they came together Tristan did exactly as Armand had done before, sweeping Aurelie off her feet and crushing her to him. They were spinning for joy.

Suddenly she whispered. 'Ilaria's pregnant! Armand knows nothing! Don't tell!'

When Tristan laughed so uncontrollably before he set Aurelie down, I should have realised something more was afoot. I didn't of course. Nor did Armand.

Tristan and Aurelie hadn't seen each other in more than four years. As you know he was absent when Armand and Ilaria were married, engaged as a senior squire to a mercenary knight who entered the civil war in Milan. During that adventure however — just as Armand had experienced against the English — Tristan was granted ascension to the rank of chevalier *before his time* and *in the field* for conspicuous bravery. And despite the grave circumstance which had brought him hastening to our aide, hearing such intimate and welcome news so suddenly, seemed a wonderful way for Tristan and Aurelie to rekindle their acquaintance after so long.

Oh and yes, on that day I was finally allowed to share the secret too. Then just hours after Tristan arrived, I was recruited to act as a lure to draw Armand away upon a ruse. The conspiratorial quintet — Ilaria, Aurelie, Sabatino, Tristan and Maxine — needed time to put their heads together. For as you can imagine, time was now of the essence.

Over the previous few days, Ilaria had feigned illness in an effort to resist any more intimacy with Armand in the bedchamber. That was ironic, for she had been suffering from morning sickness for some time already and had been feigning *wellness*! Yet she knew the time had come. All they needed was a little more to prepare.

Urgently they gathered to devise a plan of how to — with great surprise — disclose Ilaria's condition to the man who had contributed to it so willingly. In their hushed and hurried conference, they discussed hosting a soiree in honour of Tristan's arrival. He revealed that, in just two days, it would also mark the anniversary of his birth.

'Oh how could I not have recalled that?'

'I did not 'til you drew me into this antic conspiracy. Based on the news we received in Lyon, I was expecting to leap off my horse and run straight into the battle!

'You are darling. Against our big brother and his lack of awareness.'

'I can't believe he suspects nothing!'

'I can't believe you believe that!'

Ilaria smiled. 'Oh be more kind to the man I love.'

'I love him too Ria. Yet in matters beyond bloodsport and war I don't underestimate his capacity for oversight.'

As they attempted to laugh more quietly together, the conspirators agreed that a dual celebration, hosted at Hazel Wood, would be a fitting device. They would celebrate Tristan's arrival in tandem with the day of his birth. Before then, they would finalise the finer details of how they intended to spring their trap.

That evening, before the Cortelannis left Sycamore Hill, Aurelie reminded Armand that two days hence, upon Friday evening and — for safety — well before sunset, the Capulets must venture along to Hazel Wood. There in the chateau wing of the villa Sabatino had built for his French bride, as temperatures in the vale began to cool with the coming of winter, all would attend an intimate feast.

'And bring' Sabatino added 'several casks of the early corvina.'

'Oh yes.' Armand said proudly. 'You must all try it.'

Two days later, toting my battered Irish harp and black ebony lute, our party departed for Hazel Wood well before sunset. The *declared* guest arrived with the *unwitting* guest. Both feasted on salt bream boiled in orange juice and much more. I could see Armand's health had returned with gusto for he was displaying a hearty appetite. And now with Tristan arrived, he seemed more relaxed than ever before. After dining, as they munched on warm hazelnuts, a beaker of the early vintage was offered to all.

In the cool of the evening all sat lounging apart, yet together, as I hummed and plucked softly. Then when the Cortellani children — Angelique, Vincenzo and little Pietro — were ushered out by their nurse Luchia, the conspirators all sat smiling and were ready to spring the trap.

Armand held his beaker aloft as a server filled it.

'Tristan.' He smiled. 'Our early harvest vintage? As good as any in Lyon?'

Every ear appeared to hang upon the verdict. Yet undetected by Armand, Ilaria had winked to Sabatino who sent that sly signal around to all except their victim.

'Big brother ...' Tristan glanced about uneasy at the thought of passing judgement on a local standard 'ask me again when I've sampled *several* more.'

Gentle laughter rose to admonish him as he rested back with a smile, stretching his long legs against the fatigue of having spent so many days in the saddle. His ears drank in the dulcet tones as I plucked upon my harp. From experience I understood that in the cusp between feeding and drinking, a harp's the wisest instrument to set a restful tone. My lute sat close by however, against the coming need to rouse the mood when the wine's effect had a chance to accumulate.

'To want to taste so much? It *must* be to your liking!' Armand replied.

'Armand!' Ilaria replied. 'Leave our newly arrived saviour alone.' She smiled at Tristan.

'Our saviour? Yet *I'm* the wounded invalid!'

Tristan grinned at an opportunity to challenge him. 'Well big brother I am the weary traveller who rode relentlessly on through the alps to get here.'

'Yes.' Armand began. 'That was a feat of some —'

'But I' Sabatino cut in 'am the man who offered his service as your second for your challenge to meet the Wolf!'

Aurelie puckered to kiss him.

Armand began again. 'Yes. That was a favour of —'

'Tush!' said Aurelie, revelling in the power to command attention. '*All* our men are heroes.' She leaned to kiss Tristan, hugging him for sheer happiness to have him with her again. 'Don't you agree Ria?'

Ilaria pouted. 'Perhaps.' Her reply caused Tristan to spurt the contents of his beaker. 'What I mean to say Lee Lee' Ilaria ran on 'is that yes, they are heroic. But our *women* are heroic too.'

'Amen angel.' said Armand. 'That's the truth.'

Ilaria wandered from one to the next as she spoke.   'Aurelie's my heroine for becoming such a sincere friend in so little time.' She leaned to kiss her forehead. 'Sabatino's my hero for loving her and offering his unhesitating support to my wayward husband.' She leaned to kiss his forehead.

'However big brother' Aurelie had risen and sat upon the arm of Armand's broad chair '— wouldn't *you* agree that your own gorgeous wife is the *most* heroic of us all?'

'Amen!' he replied, looking well at ease.

'All this time' Aurelie continued 'while you required *constant* care she patiently suffered your antics in her condition. And she possessed the strength to refrain from telling any of us.'

'Why of course she —' Armand halted in confusion. 'But soft?' He glanced at Aurelie. 'Her *condition?*' His eyes leapt to Ilaria. 'Angel aren't you well?'

'Oh don't fret. It's really nothing at all.'

'But why haven't you told me if you're not well?'

Sipping from a gilded beaker, Ilaria lowered herself to hold him captive between Aurelie on one side and herself upon the other. Then in an attempt to confound the notion he was beginning to suggest, she looked at him earnestly.

'Oh Armand it's just a mere *trifle*. And ...' she frowned in mock concern 'well Maxine knows far more about it than I do. Perhaps you should ask *her* to explain it.'

To Armand's surprise, Ilaria hissed the last and to punctuate her mock mood, glanced *angrily* at Maxine. It triggered a suspicion in our victim that something sinister was wrong. I followed the growing deception with interest.

'Maxine?' He said sternly. 'Come here this instant.'

She shuffled in coquettishly to present herself, appearing to misunderstand. 'Yes Monsieur?'

'What do you know about my wife that can *only* be explained by you?'

Without warning she dropped to her knees.

'Oh Monsieur I *must* confess.' She clasped her hands. 'I've ... I've ... *stolen* a valuable token.'

'*You* have stolen a token?' he snapped in wonder. 'By thunder! Stolen it from *who*?'

'Dear mercy Monsieur, from my mistress.'

'From your ...? You've *stolen* a token!'

'Aye Monsieur.'

'Why cat have you gone MAD? What token was it?'

'Her *wedding* band Monsieur.' she shrieked.

'Her WEDDING band?' he spat with rising heat. 'Explain yourself!'

Oh my sweet friends, it was so intoxicating to see how completely enmeshed Armand was becoming.

'Before your strength began to return, you'll recall how madame tended you so closely each day?'

'Yes she did.'

'Every day and night against all interference.'

'I remember.'

'And while she did so Monsieur, she removed her wedding band and betrothal ring for *safekeeping*.'

'Did she?' he replied in confusion.

Thus far Maxine's performance was perfection. Ilaria and Aurelie began to feel the desperate need to restrain the corners of their mouths from creasing into smiles.

'Oh yes Monsieur. And you know how she hates to have either one off her fingers.'

'I hope so.'

'Oh she does. Particularly that gold band with its ruby for Capulet between the two sparkling emeralds that mimic her eyes.'

'What's that to the point?' he huffed impatiently.

'I'd sooner die than part with it.' Ilaria hissed again.

Armand glanced. She was clutching her hands. The signature betrothal ring, a rectangular diamond embedded in a golden casket — engraved on each side with a fleur-de-lis and ivy — was clearly visible. Yet missing from the left hand was her precious gold band with its ruby and emeralds.

Maxine ran on 'Yet Monsieur, dipping her hand in ointments so constantly while tending to you day and night wasn't good for the precious things.'

'I see.' he smiled fondly at Ilaria, kissing her hand.

Oh for the love of folly! That reaction nearly broke our will to watch more without bursting.

'Then when she removed the rings Monsieur, she kissed them lovingly and bid me to stow them in her casket, saying she wouldn't retrieve them until you were mended.'

'Well yes. But then why —?'

'Thereafter ...' Maxine dared interrupt 'when you slept and she left the chamber to converse with the Surgeon, I ... I *stole* the precious marriage band away.'

His eyes opened wide. His brows knit in delicious confusion. 'You stole her band?'

'Yes I *did* Monsieur!'

'But this makes no sense. Why steal a thing she'll so surely miss? Are you *addled*? What would compel you —'

'Oh yes I *was* compelled Monsieur.'

His eyes leapt open wider. 'By thunder tell me ALL! Who the DEVIL compelled you?'

'Devilish curiosity.'

Aurelie, Ilaria, Sabatino and Tristan were all holding fit to burst, attempting for all they were worth to put on hard frowns to mask their rising mirth.

'Can curiosity compel such *treachery?*' he growled.

Cupid's balls! He had swallowed all the bait. He was completely sidetracked by that antic ruse.

'Oh *please* forgive me Monsieur! I was so curious to *know* the answer.'

'The ANSWER?' he spat hotly in confusion. 'WHAT answer you devilish cat?'

'Please allow me to return it! Here it is!'

Suddenly the wily actress drew out the token from a hide safe in her skirts, tied upon a thin strand of golden silk.

'And please keep the pretty string ...'

'Mmm.' murmured Aurelie, leaning to inspect it. '*Such* a pretty string!'

Armand turned, staring in deeper confusion.

Ilaria screamed at Maxine. 'Thieving WENCH! That's MY ribbon too!'

Armand's head turned. Feigning indignation, Ilaria leaned to snatch away the band and leapt to her feet, glaring at the guilt-ridden thief with rare venom.

Oh it was PERFECTION!

Armand's eyes declared his bewilderment. 'The ribbon pilfered too?' he snapped. 'CAT! Why did you so desperately need to tie a ribbon to —' A light had sparked in his wide blue eyes. 'Your *curiosity?*'

'I've always been a curious person.' Maxine replied.

'Minx ... tell me the truth.'

'Of course Monsieur?'

'Why did you feel compelled to hang my wife's marriage upon a gilded string?'

In one gorgeous movement, Maxine's brows lifted cagily as her head tilted to one side, just as any cat might do when gazing upon a mouse caught between its paws.

'Oh Monsieur, my mistress knows *far* more about such things.

Perhaps you should ask *her* to explain it.'

Now Maxine's smile was matched by a mirror image upon Armand's lips. His frown was lifted, all heat was gone.

'Oh I think I see. So now the circuit has closed back upon myself. First I *must* question Maxine. Now I must question my *wife?*' He scanned about the company.

We were all fit to burst of course. Yet now we also looked guilty into the bargain.

'And now I see' Armand added 'more than just the hint of a smile on every Jack and Jill!' He turned to Ilaria quietly. 'Very well cat, I'll ask my heroic wife. But first I think I'll *kiss* her more deeply.'

Hoping to draw the moment out, Ilaria still attempted to evade him as Armand gripped her waist and spun her into his lap, she lifted her hands to rebuff him.

'NO! NO! NO! Not so fast!' Despite his beaming smile she held aloof, hoping to hold the gorgeous ruse aloft for just a moment longer. 'My heart, my handsome, don't you wish to *know* the answer to that mystery first?'

She let the ring drop to the end of its ribbon, dangling and turning. His smile softened. His eyes drank deeply.

'I'd like you to know how much I truly love you.'

'And now I hope ... you shall love me even more. For now my dear heart, there's more in me to love.'

Without forethought, her hand slid onto her belly.

Tears were misting in her eyes. Aurelie's eyes were filling with tears. Now that my fingers had stopped on the string, my own eyes welled with tears. Armand remained transfixed as all about the chamber hung upon his response.

'Maxine' he said softly, never straying his gaze from Ilaria 'tell me little witch, what does your sorcery foretell?'

'Well Monsieur. The band swayed upon the ribbon like a fisherman in a boat ...'

'A BOY!' I blurted, unable to hold a moment more. 'It *must* be a boy!' Yes sweetheart? The band professed a boy? Or ... was it a *girl?*' My eyes bulged with indecision, fearing I had misremembered.

'MARCEL!' squealed Maxine with exasperation.

Laughter burst open when I plucked a string to punctuate her pain! Then a burst erupted to hear every indictment she suddenly swore against my ignorance.

'BABOON!' *Pluck.* 'Yes it's a BOY!' *Pluck.* 'You KNOW IT!' *Pluck. Pluck. Pluck.*

Broadening smiles burst into peals of laughter.

'Ha!' I laughed nervously. 'Of course sweetheart. Yes a boy. For if it was a girl, surely the band would have ... surely it would ... um ...'

'AHH! Marcel you dullard! If it's a girl the band will turn a circuit *upon* itself!'

'That's just what I was *about* to say.'

'And I say ... if I be some kind of witch? Then you are NO kind of wizard!'

'I don't disagree sweetheart.'

'Oh you NINNY! Just PLAY something!'

'Quickly fool!' snapped Aurelie 'Or your sweetheart may pluck your bulging eyes from your empty head!'

A riot of laughter erupted.

I watched them all for a moment. Suddenly I noticed how much Aurelie's manner was so much like her brothers. She was pure charm to behold. Then Sabatino broke into fits of laughter to see her so happy, laughing among her *famille*.

'Oh yes sweetheart. I'll play!' I rolled my eyes. 'But first, just as our master bade our mistress, you must also kiss me deeply!' I puckered my lips.

Maxine smiled in jest, then made as if she'd slap my impertinent face. To see her do so, I shut my eyes, puckering harder against the threat. Then thinking the better of her impulse to scold me, she jabbed a peck on my pout, all to the sound of warm applause.

In that moment, I realised how much enjoyment our betters seemed to derive from watching our antics, as Maxine and I wrangled without restraint. The time ahead would reveal that our bickering and bantering *together* was often more entertaining than my *solitary* performances.

I had also perceived, perhaps a little jealously, that Maxine's antics drew more attention than mine. For a moment I stood to draw the attention back to myself, turning to Ilaria and Armand. They were kissing with abandon as only young lovers in young company may do.

'Voilà Monsieur and Madame!' I cried. 'For now *jubilation* has sprung from your *tribulation*.'

'Yes *great* jubilation!' Armand agreed. 'Yet dear Heaven. How in all my ignorance, during all that time, could I have failed to tell that my wife has a child!'

'Ignorance?' Tristan grinned. 'Yet I wager he was *knowing* enough when she encouraged him to conceive it.'

Hearty laughter lifted at the comment.

Ilaria's eyes opened wide.

'Meddler!' she snapped. 'Who says *I* did all the encouraging!'

Aurelie pointed an accusatory finger at Armand and caught Ilaria's eye. 'If I know our big brother he *demanded* you conceive it!'

Laughter burst out of all control.

Armand lifted and leapt for Aurelie, who shrieked and scrambled desperately to escape. Then, as if they were childhood urchins again, sweet bedlam swept through the chamber as they squealed and shouted and chased all about. Unable to resist, Tristan lifted in pursuit. An instant later, the exalted Capulets were a giddy, swirling mess of impropriety.

Maxine and I gazed in astonishment.

'Why sweetheart' I whispered 'our employers are serving the sauce to themselves and think we have none left to offer!'

'Oh don't be jealous my lovely fool.' She kissed my cheek. 'Play something festive.'

By the time a jaunty strum leapt from my lute, Ilaria had joined the mighty assault to wrestle the eldest Capulet to the floor. Amid the hurly burly, Armand cried to *have a care for his condition!* Yet of course, that just made her effort even more relentless.

She proved to be his most potent rival, tickling him in places only she could know the mighty warrior simply couldn't resist. Oh, the bundle of hands and feet was such a sight, with a pair of male and female Capulets wrangling upon the fur before the hearth. I tell you, by every saint who prays and every sweet angel that sings in Heaven, neither Maxine nor I will ever forget it.

Gasping for breath, laughing in fits, they wrestled with abandon as coiffured hair fell loose with abandon. Then suddenly — RIP! A great tearing sound announced a split to the side of Armand's hose which had caught on Aurelie's own dazzling ring — a twisted band studded with sapphires, blue and gold for the prima Donna of Corte-lanni. For an instant their mayhem suspended. Yet Tristan's guffaw rose at the sight of the damage! Pandemonium erupted once more as they set upon each other again.

'Bite my bare ass sweetheart!' I cried. 'The Capulets have gone to Hell in a haycart!'

Maxine smiled at me. For a moment the tumult began to settle, then lifted with gusto again until the persistent chime of a sharp edge against glass caught our ears.

TAP. TAP. TAP. Finally, it drew their childlike ardour down. Sabatino stood by, glass and stilleto in hand, smiling upon them.

Looking a little sheepish under the influence of his stern gaze, sighing and panting, the wild quartet hung off one another to give their attention to our well-mannered host. The great man was a decade older than Armand and older than his prima donna of course. But the primo don of Cortellani was also a soulful, intelligent man who appeared easy to like and easy to love.

At least to me, but I think to all who knew him, Sabatino seemed to possess a captivating charm that epitomised the very image of masculine Italianate grace.

'Well ... one and all.' He glanced at Aurelie. 'As our glamorous hostess appears to be indisposed ...' She huffed a gorgeous strand of dark hair from her cheek. 'allow me to take charge of this menagerie for a moment.' Even the servers were smiling. 'For I fear we have still not answered the query that set this conundrum in motion.'

'Dear Heaven he's right.' said Aurelie.

'The question was put as to *who* enticed *whom* toward the creation of this new life that we've already begun to celebrate so warmly.'

The lounging quartet glanced at each other.

'However' he ran on 'no matter which fond Capulet offered first enticement, let us hail the *result* by congratulating *both*.' Bodies began to stir. 'Nay, nay, nay, stay where you are. Stay. Stay. Rostand!'

The hovering maître d' snapped to attention.   'Si primo Don!'

'Serve the glamorous Capuleti upon the fur where they appear to be in such comfort.'

At Rostand's command, a pair of servers knelt with fresh beakers to offer.

'Mmm.' Sabatino's eyes were locked on Aurelie. 'Let's remain in comfort together mia cara.'

He lowered himself to lounge like a sultan, knee bent, leaning upon an arm.

'And now ' he held his beaker aloft 'let us drink to *his* safe coming in the ...?'

He paused for an answer, looking to Aurelie to suggest how long it would be.

So far as Ria and I may calculate darling, with the aid of our mystic Maxine, *he* was most likely conceived during the first *two* weeks of the marriage tour.'

Beakers clinked in reaction as smiling lips sipped.

'Therefore, somewhere beyond the turn of wintertide, perhaps between —' she looked to Maxine for assistance.

'Between the start and middle of January is when her blessed bundle should arrive.'

Sabatino lifted his brows in question to Ilaria.

'And so will he be another *Armand?*'

'Whatever name he may have, my husband's son will be a bold rascal.'

'Bold!' Sabatino replied. 'Then perhaps you should name him *Thibault*.'

'Our grandfather was Thibault!' said Tristan.

'He was bold by nature and name.' Armand grinned.

'Then perhaps fate is playing a hand.' said Sabatino.

Ilaria pouted and ran her fingers through Armand's thick dark hair. 'I love the name *Gabriel!*'

'Do you angel?'

'Yes I do. But for a son I know you may wish to to do the choosing. And that's all well as long as I may choose when we have a *girl.*'

'Oh darling' chirped Aurelie 'what would you call a lovely *girl?*'

'Mmm? Geneviève perhaps after maman? Yet there are so *many* lovely names to choose from.'

'You may have *need* of many!' Aurelie grinned.

'Oh my handsome husband would love to be surrounded by a tribe of doting young women!'

Laughter lifted again. Beakers tipped once more. But although Ilaria smiled, I thought for an instant as she glanced about, that the remark made her mindful of the women she already knew were looming as her own rivals. Yolanthe and Eloise both remained far away in Rome .

I mused as I watched her thinking — *perhaps this announcement had come in good time before their return.* With regard to their status as her potential rivals, I felt this news might set Ilaria's misgivings aside. Though what did I know. Perhaps for a woman, the coming of a child, may increase such misgivings rather than reduce them.

I've said before that Armand never offered any suggestion he would ever stray from her side. I already felt sure he had the purest heart Ilaria would ever find in any man to love her. I knew he doted on her. Certainly she doted on him. I hoped that she harboured no doubt upon the matter. I hoped she never would.

Yet as I continued to watch them, embracing and kissing, an adage my grandam used to say stalked quietly into my mind.

Doubt is a devil that doting may conjure.

We remained at Hazel Wood that evening.

Next day as we wound our way back to the Hill, all our celebration at the child's impending arrival, the apparent bliss of the Capulet's marriage, set me to wondering. What did fate have in store for my own life? All at once sweet friends, I found myself looking at Maxine rather differently.

Chapter 9 the Lure of Verona

Just as Maxine's mystic skills foretold, the babe was a boy. Then in the sunshine of a late winter's morning, some four weeks after the birth of little *Thibault*, the Capulets exited the gates of Sycamore Hill. It was Sunday. We were bound for the citadel. And it would be the first time they'd entered Verona since the trial was done. Ever since the duchess had departed — other than our dash to Venice, and even after Tristan arrived — they remained in the hills, venturing no further than Hazel Wood in the opposite direction.

Remaining close to Sabatino and Aurelie during that time had seemed the wisest course. That ensured the harvest was distributed and that preparations for the birth were attended to. But now Thibault had come and it was time to leave the security of their lofty nest upon the hill.

Well before that intended visit however — indeed the day after Armand discovered he was to be a father — I was riding home among our entourage and contemplating if I should sound Maxine out upon her interest to become my bride. For you see, that fickle woman had *also* announced she was with child. Oh yes. And Cupid's Balls were not to blame for it!

She had revealed it to Ilaria that morning. Ilaria revealed it to Armand. We had not even travelled half way back to the Hill when our entourage suddenly halted. I was summoned into their presence before a too large gathering of onlookers. I was told — in no uncertain terms — that I too was to become a father, and soon, as soon as the Capulets!

Now I say it to you. CUPID'S BALLS!

Oh yes, I proposed marriage. Of course I did. Well, my doubting friends, what do you take me for?

Yet Ilaria, claiming the right to decide upon that proposal for Maxine, temporarily forbade our match! Moreover she declared that

— for Maxine's sake — before a final decision would be announced I must prove myself to be as *reliable* and *mature* as a *father-to-be* ought to be! Well bite my bare ass on both sides sweet friends! You can imagine how I reacted to hear it. And what's more, I can't say the process thereafter went very well for me.

If you care to know every lively detail however, you may read about that portion of my own travails in a separate work I've entitled

—

Untold Morsels from the History of Capulet & Paris

Yet as painful as that short period was for me, thank Heaven we were finally married before our lovely daughter was born. Yes, a daughter. What's more than more, Ilaria also claimed the right to *name* her! That's a further — and rather juicy — tale told within the *Morsels*. But for now, at least you understand the most important fragments, that in less than three months I had married Maxine and we had welcomed our lovely little daughter *Figara* into our lives.

Indeed both Thibault and Figara entered our world just one week apart. And so it was agreed Maxine would serve as wet nurse to them both. Upon the Sunday now in question however — for the Capulet's return to the citadel — it was also to be Ilaria's first mass since the birth of Thibault.

For nearly a month before, she had been confined to the seclusion of her birthing chamber. And so by that time Ilaria yearned desperately for some social distraction. Her choice before then, to remain confined in the northern hills, had added to that feeling. Yet even for an elite woman, certain rites of passage must be adhered to. As you know, once a child is born, before re-entering the sanctuary of mass, a mother must first receive a blessing of *purification*.

No exceptions are made for premiere dames or prima donnas. Such a blessing, of course, also opens access to the social circuits that flow from her reappearance at mass. My *wife* Maxine — yes it took me some time to adjust to saying that sacred word — also required that special blessing. In my ignorance however, I had no idea that ritual was required.

What's more, when it was explained, I was confounded by it! For the Holy men and women tell us that the act of birth giving — despite its essence in *nature* — is considered *unclean* in the eyes of God! And so when the deed is done, until a mother has been *cleansed* of its taint, she's not welcome by our fucking Church to rejoin our fucking flock.

Apologies. I was upset to hear it explained that my lovely wife was held to be so unclean by those ... by them.

Moreover it was due to that fucking ... that rule that I wasn't allowed to witness the great moment when little Figara was born! Yes I wanted to see it! Thereafter Maxine told me that it was painful, very painful. My ears had heard that much for myself. She also said it was messy, very messy. Perhaps I'm glad I didn't see that much for myself.

But when I saw her next day, exhausted — though clean and smiling — and feeding our little girl upon her breast, I couldn't bring myself to accept Heaven must spurn her until some Holy halfwit officer may be allowed to mumble incant at her and fumigate her with incense.

That was the *second* time I ever thought to question the rules of our faith.

You may recall the first was back in Carentan, upon the matter of *fidelity* in the face of death. Yet now I digress and even regress.

And so, be all that as it may, in the months before Thibault and Figara arrived, Ilaria and Maxine found themselves far from home, yet in need of a spiritual guide to assist them. Then thanks to Aurelie's influence, to fulfil that need they made the acquaintance of *Friar Lorenzo.*

Yes, our tale's already introduced the friar to you. But to Ilaria at the time, Friar Lorenzo was the tall, engaging Franciscan that Esmeralda Montecchi had spoken so warmly about upon the ill-fated day she met her. We were reminded by Aurelie that Lorenzo was not merely a friar, but also an ordained priest. You already know the Franciscans are different from other orders, being able to refuse the directive of a superior if their conscience dictates.

However you may not yet understand that, to be a priest among the Franciscans is something of a rarity. For unlike the Franciscan sisters — who are private and monastic — the Franciscan brothers are a *mendicant* order. For any who know even less than I do, that means they're not locked away from the world, but may interact with it freely.

And like other mendicant orders, they're also allowed to serve as itinerant preachers, wandering about with no church roof to cover their heads. Under God's open sky — come rain or shine — they share his message by the roadsides or upon street corners, living off the offer of soft blessings or else hard labour, in return for meagre alms.

However as a priest, Friar Lorenzo also possessed the skill and rank — which set him apart from his brethren — to conduct mass, baptisms, marriages, last rites and burials, in addition to hearing confession. And so with that capability, wandering was never likely to become Friar Lorenzo's lot.

Yet for the sake of our continuing tale, most important to know about the friar is — because of that rank — he was assigned to mentor a parish along the northern riverbank that sat outside the citadel walls. Therefore his little church sat right at the foot of the northern hills. Yes, that sounds familiar, because Sycamore Hill and Hazel Wood were both located up in those hills.

In between that part of the riverbank and the northern hills sits a stout little mountain. Some insist it's too small to be a mountain! And so for the love of folly, it goes by *two* names. Some called it *Saint Peter's Hill*. Others called it *Rooster Mountain*. And though I feel it is more of a hill than a mountain, I prefer the latter name and shall use it.

Because that little monolith sits in between, to gain the best access from the north riverbank into the northern hills, one must ascend it before travelling on. Then when you reach the crest of Rooster Mountain, the entry to Sycamore Hill lies just half a mile further along. Two miles further is Hazel Wood, of course.

I hope it may now be easier for you to imagine that it takes us very little time — half an hour at speed, an hour at leisure — to descend from our villa, ride along to the crest of Rooster Mountain and descend to the north riverbank, before crossing the Adige over the old stone bridge to enter Verona's walls by its northern most gate. Yes, that was a long thought. No, I make no apology for it.

After we took possession of Sycamore Hill and became more orientated, we realised that two churches sat in closest proximity to it. One was large and audacious, one small and humble. Saint Peter's is the audacious church on top of Rooster Mountain. One passes by it on that journey to the citadel of course.

The more humble church sits down on the riverbank below it, literally in the shadow of Saint Peter's for the first half of every day. Therefore, on that same journey into Verona, one must pass by it too. Yet that church, nestled upon the bank just inside the grounds of the Holy Convent of Saint Clare, was Friar Lorenzo's. As you can imagine, the Franciscan Sisters also require a church to serve their need and a priest to serve their church. And so as fate would have it, thanks to his capability as a priest, Friar Lorenzo had been assigned to be their man — so to speak.

Yet as private as those humble sisters may be, they were also compelled to share the use of their church with local parishioners. Most in that district are very humble folk. Many make their living from the river, for the parish runs from the edge of the convent — along the northern riverbank for a time — then reaches away in the opposite direction toward the base of the foot hills.

Not unlike Lyon, Verona is a citadel fortress set by a river and surrounded by its walls. And so because the citadel sits in a broad bend of the river, its walls along the riverbank are shaped very much like a bell. Where the bell shape ends at one corner, a long battlement runs unbroken for quite a distance to create the flat bottom of the bell. That wall separates the open land beyond it from the enclosed citadel within, until it reaches the other corner.

Telling general direction in Verona is rather easy, because the top of that bell faces north, more or less. And the flat bottom of the bell faces south, more or less. Oh mercy, I'm not a cartographer.

More or less is good enough for me! As you can now imagine, the river running around the curve of the bell serves as a moat for Verona's security. I'm sure you can imagine that bridges are used to cross over it.

Indeed, along the curve of the bell, *seven* bridges offer access to seven stout gates. Three bridges cross over from the curve's eastern side. Three cross over from the western side. A final bridge — known as the *old stone bridge* to some, the *old north bridge* to others — crosses at the top of the bell. Its entrance sits near the corner of the convent. It's also the only bridge in Verona that has survived from its ancient Roman past. To my mind, perhaps for that reason, it appears more romantic than all the others do.

I'll never forget the first time we crossed it after the trial was done to exit the citadel and make our way back to Hazel Wood. You recall just one week before, we had ridden toward the citadel in the early morning darkness and crossed by that same bridge. But that first journey into Verona — by an odd circuitous route to avoid the Montecchi — had left Armand and Ilaria with little sense of orientation.

They hadn't comprehended that Rooster Mountain even existed. As we left that day along the old stone bridge — myself riding the she-ass beside the wagon — we saw it looming ahead of us with Saint Peter's on top of it. And though we passed by the convent at that time to reach the mountain's base and make our ascent, we hardly noticed it.

'Marcel' called Maxine as we approached 'what's the name of that mountain?'

'Is it a mountain?' asked Ilaria.

'Or is it a hill?' added Armand.

'Well Chevalier, Madame, it's confusing.'

'I'm sure even if it wasn't, you rascal, you'd make it sound so just to confound us.'

'In most cases Madame I confess that would be true. Yet in this case, the fault lies with the natives. For a gate guardian informed me that some call it *Saint Peter's Hill* but some call it *Rooster Mountain*.'

'Rooster Mountain sounds dramatic.' Ilaria declared. 'That's what I'll call it.'

'Coming or going Madame, I call it twenty minutes of leaning forward or back on this she-devil, who seems more compelled to fart when she's rising or falling.'

That afternoon our ascent took perhaps twenty minutes. An energetic youth scrambling straight up, rather than keeping to the path, could reach the top in less than ten minutes. And in some time to come, in the dead of night, a young lover will do just that, running on to linger in the Sycamore Grove at the base of our hill, awaiting a tryst with his paramour. She'll descend quietly from the Hill to meet him in that grove, accompanied by my own daughter Figara.

Yet that is to come.

For now, let's consider Friar Lorenzo a little more closely. He had found a happy home in the convent grounds, nestled on a riverbank full of waterbirds and fisherfolk with the Poor Clare's for company. The fast-flowing Adige offered them a bounty of fish, eels and more. And the mighty hill behind washed rich soil down to collect in the convent pastures, enabling them to grow vegetables and herbs, the latter being one of Lorenzo's great passions.

Some of the herbs Friar Lorenzo tended there were exotic. Some were very rare. Their healing properties were a matter of great importance to the friar, who held an interest in assisting those who practised healing arts. And a little way beyond those pastures, in the tradition of Saint Francis himself, the friar's modest cell was cut into the living rock of the mountain. There — in seclusion from the sisterhood — he ate and slept, offered counsel and even heard confession.

When he had arrived three seasons before us, his presence had drawn the interest of Esmeralda Montecchi. As that convent's most respected patron, she came every month bearing generous contributions — though she had never attended mass before in their little church. Then one day, accompanied by Aurelie, to humour the abbess, they agreed to join her and hear the newly arrived father conduct mass. And for their trouble both women were happily surprised.

The pair of prima donnas discovered a more entertaining priest than the bland cleric who served them at Saint Peter's. And the towering Franciscan's booming voice was far more charismatic than the whimpering tones of the archbishop in Verona Cathedral. Of course, word of Lorenzo's charm and sincerity quickly spread beyond his quiet catchment. Soon the humble church was bursting with the faithful, happy to stand whenever a lack of pews failed to seat them all.

Yet once Esmeralda and Aurelie had discovered him, the foremost pew was always given up for their use when they attended. For Esmeralda, that was whenever her brutal husband was absent on campaign or political business for weeks or months at a time. More often, she would attend with the Cortelannis. Yet even when they couldn't accompany Esmeralda, rather than show herself among the cathedral's elite, despite her rank, she would arrive at that humble church unescorted to hear her favourite.

On such occasions the abbess herself — not a shy woman despite her calling — would sit through the service with her most respected patron. Oh yes, a dozen Montecchi men-at-arms were always hard by to ensure their prima donna's safety. But they were Esmeralda's own retained men, answerable to none but herself. Each was able to take a secret to the grave and each needed to be able to.

For as you now know, after Esmeralda and Aurelie met the friar, both adopted him as their *confessor*. During Onorato's absences, Esmeralda's visits to Lorenzo's quiet cell to hear her confessions became longer — particularly when she arrived without the Cortelannis. As a result, she needed to trust those warriors who waited upon her leisure to be done, would relay a version of events to her volatile husband, that wouldn't arouse his interest.

Years later, during the time Lorenzo confessed his troubles to me about serving the inquisition, he also told of his first encounter with Esmeralda's senior man — a Portuguese stalwart who served her father — after she had departed his cell to return to her carriage.

Lorenzo's herb gardens sat between his cell, the convent and the river bank beyond.

'You like to grow herbs Friar?'

'Yes indeed Don Ramos. It's my great passion.'

'Do they need much care?'

'Yes and no. Some require special additions to the soil to ensure strong growth.'

'Such as?'

'Blood, bone, phosphor. Sometimes more unique nutrients for rarer species.'

'Interesting. I have little time for such things myself. Yet since the prima donna's alerted me that you're to be her preferred confessor ...' he paused.

'Yes, I was surprised at the request.'

'Hmm. I wasn't so greatly. But may I confess something to you?'

'Feel free to do so whenever you may need to.'

'Then let me say this, just once. If you give me any sliver of a reason to suspect you may be doing more in that quiet cell with my prima donna than hearing her confession, your herbs will suddenly have all the blood, bone, brains and Friar's balls they will need to thrive on.'

Completely taken by surprise, Lorenzo stared.

'Oh. Oh yes I ... I understand.'

'I hope you do.'

'I do. But may I say Don Ramos, I'm not sure all those additions would assist their growing.'

'They wouldn't assist your growing friar. I feel very sure of that.'

That was at the start of Esmeralda's relationship with Lorenzo as her confessor. Thereafter, as you know, her visits became more frequent. Yet since her wretched demise, she hadn't been seen at his church for service or his cell for confession, nor sighted any whereabouts in Verona. Indeed once the inquisition was done, it seemed to all the Black Witch of Verona had vanished entirely.

That was happily so for Ilaria to learn. For Aurelie had wanted to introduce herself and Maxine to the friar. Since Esmeralda's disappearance, no-one really expected her to re-appear any time soon. And by the time she may finally do so — if indeed she ever did — the Capulets may have decided to return to Lyon. That gave Ilaria the confidence to agree to Aurelie's suggestion to seek Lorenzo's guidance before Thibault was born.

And so, by that Sunday morning, when Ilaria departed for the citadel again, Friar Lorenzo had not only met Ilaria and Maxine, he had given them both the purification blessing, then christened Thibault and Figara thereafter. Both women were now ready to re-enter God's sacred house. Yet despite the friar's assistance to make them ready, it wasn't to his own humble church we travelled that morning, nor to Saint Peter's above it.

As a result of Ilaria's long confinement she had declared her wish to Armand that they seek more substantial distraction together. And so, as the Cortellani's guests in their new Germanic carriage, both set forth to attend mass in the citadel at Verona Cathedral.

That beautiful conveyance that arrived to fetch us had been purchased from the same maker who provided for the duchess. Indeed it was built in a town to the north, just through the alps, beyond the Bremmer Pass. Why should I care to mention that trifle? Hmm, perhaps no reason at all.

The Cortellani sat within, beaming smiles and beckoning the Capulets to enter. Maxine went along too, bearing the burden of nursing Thibault and Figara together. It was the first time Thibault would be seen in public. I sat by my wife's side attempting to keep both babes distracted. For the love of folly, it felt as if she had given birth to twins.

We descended the steep entry path, passed through the gate and turned right onto the sycamore lined road, heading south for the citadel. Aurelie, Sabatino and Tristan sat upon one side. Ilaria and Armand sat upon the other as they all began to chatter away. Approaching the crest of Rooster Mountain from behind, we saw the mountain-top fortress ahead with Saint Peter's beside it. Both edifices looked down upon the citadel below.

We halted at their clifftop piazza for a moment to enjoy the magnificent vista. Verona sat below us with the curve of the Adige sweeping around its nearest side, and to the south, a wide marshy plain stretched beyond the furthest wall. Oh sweet friends I've seen Lyon from the height of the hills that surround it. And yes, it is very pretty too. But nothings ever compared to the vision of beauty we saw that morning.

For I swear to you, by all the sweet angels who sing in Heaven, I'd never felt more inspired by the sight of a citadel than that sight of Verona, set against the bolt blue sky and warm winter sun which Heaven laid on for us. Nor to this day have I seen it's equal. No, it's not the largest citadel I've seen. Nor does it offer the grandest display of buildings, gardens and monuments. I've seen Paris, Milan and Rome. And yes, each was a magnificent spectacle to encounter.

Yet there is something about the perfection of Verona's composition that, taken all in all — particularly when seen from that dizzy height atop Rooster Mountain in Saint Peter's piazza — that makes it seem astonishing.

'Dear mercy my heart' Ilaria whispered 'we've never seen it like this. Oh Lee Lee what a sight.'

'Yes Ria it's very pretty. Sab brought me up here the first day I arrived. Remember?'

He pressed his lips to her forehead.

'Yes mia cara. After we had climbed the tower in Herb Market Square to look over the citadel.'

'I'll never forget that either. I fell in love with both in an instant.'

'But I thought you loved me *before* you arrived?'

Aurelie rolled her eyes with a sigh and a smile.

'Let's just say our breathless kiss in that tower helped me to make up my mind.'

Thereafter we ran along the little mountain's crest and began our descent toward the riverbank. As we neared the convent, Armand leaned out, turning back to consider the monolith again.

'It looks more imposing from below' he remarked 'with the sun rising beyond it.'

Aurelie caught his eye. 'Stay long enough big brother and you'll discover it has many moods.'

'Lee Lee there's the convent.' said Ilaria. 'Can you see Friar Lorenzo?'

'No darling. Yet he'll be there this morning. Ria did you know that it's rumoured, somewhere beneath the Poor Clare's convent, lie the remains of an ancient theatre?'

'Is that true?' asked Armand.

'The abbess used the word *rumour*.' Aurelia replied. Yet I felt she knew more than she revealed.'

'Ah!' I spurted with excitement. 'Imagine in ancient times, how many from the citadel must have left the safety of their walls to venture over the old bridge to that site to be enthralled by their plays and dance and music?'

'It's also said' Sabatino began 'the fortress on the hill next to Saint Peter's sits on the site of an ancient temple that once towered over all.'

My ears had pricked again. Any mention of ancient culture always put me into a passion. 'A Roman temple! Imagine how many more must have clambered up that path to pay homage at their vanished temple?'

Aurelie smirked, eyes full of mischief. 'Imagine what scandalous antics the pagans carried on with.'

Sabatino smiled. 'Indeed mia cara. Indeed I've often wondered which God that temple was dedicated to?'

'Or Goddess darling.' Aurelie corrected. 'They were all dedicated to one or another.'

'Often Madonna, they were dedicated to more than one divine being at a time.' I added.

'Some were austere and sober of course.' She smiled. 'But some were not quite so ... austere.'

'Or sober Madonna!' I blurted with a smile.

'Imbecile!' Maxine scolded. 'Be polite.'

'But sweetheart, the ancients had a God or a Goddess for every manner of thing.'

Armand drew back inside. 'Well our church raised Saint Peter's in its place.' he said. 'And so I suspect it may have been dedicated to *Saturn*.'

'Why to Saturn?' asked Ilaria.

'I recall his revels were held during winter. Now they're replaced at that same time of year by our celebration of Christ's birth.'

Tristan lifted his brows and nodded.

'That does makes some kind of sense big brother.'

Ilaria frowned.

'I'm afraid I'm a little sceptical of that notion.'

'Ilaria' Tristan scolded 'I managed to *agree* with my big brother. That's quite rare.'

Ilaria appealed to Aurelie. 'Bravo for your tolerance Tristan. But Lee Lee ... you must agree with me.'

'Agree to what darling?'

'That it wasn't a temple for Saturn. Why place a temple for *cold winter revels* atop such a high windy peak?'

Armand's eyes widened as he squeezed Ilaria.

'Angel that's a valid point.'

'I agree Ria.' said Aurelie. 'Perhaps it's festivals were for spring and summer?'

'That makes sense' Sabatino put in 'to celebrate the harvest. And in all that time since, our faith may have changed in Verona, but the impact of the seasons have not.'

Ilaria caught Sabatino's eye.

'Yes Sab that also makes sense. However —'

'Oh Armand.' Sabatino spat in mock frustration. 'Your wife's become more than just sceptical. I fear childbirth has caused her to become contrary.'

'Oh no Sab she's always been contrary.'

'Armand hush, I've never been contrary. However —'

'Yes agreeable one?' Armand smiled.

'What I mean to say is ... the *arena* is still standing.'

'Yes it is.'

Our cavalcade was approaching the bridge.

'And the Roman gates still stand in the citadel. And this ancient bridge is still here.'

'Yes angel. And so?'

'And so, for our church to feel such a need to erase all trace of the ruins above that hill and below it, if a theatre truly stood down upon the bank, then I feel the use above it may have been ... well something more —'

'Scandalous?' Aurelie cut in. 'Yes Ria of course. Why else would those petulant Holy men ...'

'Aurelie!' Sabatino warned mockingly.

'Oh Sab I'll have my say. A theatre below. And perhaps high above it sat —'

'A licentious temple of Bacchus?' I blurted.

Aurelie's eyes lit with more mischief. 'Yes skinny man I think that's it. An exalted seat for unbridled revelry.'

'Feasting and fornication!' I cried.

'Imbecile!' Maxine smacked me. 'Hush your bold mouth and tend to Figara.'

'Yes sweetheart.' I bleated.

A volley of laughter swept through the carriage. Aurelie reached to caress little Thibault.

'I may not have described it so precisely.' she ran on. 'But yes, a temple for the ancients to venerate what our rules now deem to be so sinful.'

'And now both precincts, above and below, are dedicated to our God.' Sabatino replied.

'It's true.' said Armand. 'Saint Peter has evicted the nymphs and satyrs above.'

'Yes Monsieur.' I said glancing cautiously at Maxine. 'And down below on the riverbank, where the poetry of Livius was once heard, the sisters pray and the friar preaches.' I feigned my despair.

'Well skinny man' Aurelie smiled 'you must dry your tears before the world sees them.'

Armand laughed and leaned to Ilaria.

'Our maman used to say that constantly.'

'She did.' Aurelie agreed. 'And Ria, although we won't hear anything in the cathedral this morning as lively as Livius, we shall still *see* something well worth our seeing.'

'Oh.' said Ilaria. 'What's that pray tell?'

Yet before Aurelie could answer Sabatino sighed.

'She means the mighty Prince Escalus of course.'

We soon discovered any chance for Aurelie to see the prince was reason enough for her to attend the cathedral. Ilaria had known nothing of his likely appearance when she chose it over the friar's humble church. For her, it had been the lure of a leisurely promenade along the streets between the cathedral and Herb Market Square which had made the difference. It would be a chance to gain more of a sense of what life in Verona citadel may really be like.

And Aurelie had insisted that social ritual was not to be missed. What's more she promised that, with her guidance, it would be much more enlivening. Aurelie hadn't mentioned any hope she held to see the prince again. Nor had she hinted at her playful obsession with the popular figurehead. Perhaps that was because, far more importantly, she felt this outing would be her first chance — perhaps her only chance — to help Ilaria solicit some enticing social connections in Verona.

By that time Aurelie understood that Armand and Ilaria were considering the prospect of staying. She wanted them to stay. And she felt certain that Ilaria's reaction to Verona may hold the key to that decision, particularly now she had her first child. But as we were waved on through the north gate, there was one element Aurelie hadn't counted upon, which may have accidentally aided her designs.

Oh yes, we understood their trial during the summer had made instant celebrities of the Capulets. But that knowledge didn't prepare us for how much their reappearance — with yet another handsome French stranger — would stir up such attention that morning among Verona's elite. Had we already returned to Lyon, perhaps none there would have ever given the exotic couple another thought.

Yet not only were they still in Verona, now rather dramatically, they were living on the infamous estate they had wrested away from the powerful Montecchi. Moreover they too — like Esmeralda — had disappeared from view for a time. At first rumours insisted they had fled to Venice. Then suddenly they were returned and said to be making love with abandon in the hinterland hills. Finally whispers abounded the elegant French prima donna had given birth to a child!

Then suddenly, without any warning at all, the eyes of all in Verona Cathedral's elite congregation were met by the sight of the feted foreigners gliding back into their midst again. Our arrival sparked an instant buzz of excited muttering and glances that swept through the assembly. Cupid's Balls! Although we had entered a cathedral, for a moment, if felt as if the court drama had erupted all over again. Yet this time, we very quickly realised that the mood was very, very different.

And chief among all those watching was Prince Escalus standing by the front pew with Princess Florentia. The chattering swell that lifted in the rear had drawn the eyes of all in their party, wondering whose entrance behind them had caused such a stir. Of course the last time such a hubbub was heard was when Esmeralda made her dramatic entrance. This entrance however, was entirely different.

Then as fate would have it, standing in conversation with Escalus and Florentia, was his Excellence Don Pasquale, the magistrate who presided over their trial and who accompanied our wild dash through the western borgo. As soon as he marked the Capulets following the Cortelannis in, a broad smile lit up his face. His wife Elettra lifted her brows to smile at Aurelie and Sabatino. Elettra whispered to her husband excitedly.

Then noted by all, the magistrate detached from his wife's side to walk the aisle's length to greet our party. For the first time he approached Armand and Ilaria with nothing but social intentions. There before all, Verona's well-loved magistrate embraced them, meeting Tristan too and assuring the Capulets how welcome they were. He turned with a broad smile to escort them forward, chatting with Sabatino and Aurelie who led the way with him.

Maxine and I could tell it made Ilaria feel greatly relieved to be so warmly received by such a well-respected officer. After the magistrate extended his welcome so clearly, a ripple of nods and solicitous glances was set in motion as they passed by each row of sumptuously dressed parishioners. All at once, glamorous watchers whose acquaintance they had not yet made were smiling — with what appeared to be genuine admiration — at Armand and Ilaria as they passed.

The Cortelannis ahead of them — as the social felicitators of the celebrity couple — were thrilled to have met with that unexpected swell of interest. Yes, they appeared composed. Sabatino and Aurelie were well-known and respected. Yet they were also ambitious to expand their influence among the more potent social players in Verona. The Prince and Princess, for example, were still relative newcomers from Venice. They had remained at a social distance from all but the Montecchi. Perhaps now, sooner than expected, that may change.

Yet perhaps more importantly for Aurelie, when she had married the much-admired Sabatino and arrived to take up residence as the Cortellani prima donna, she was alone. Now to have a feminine foil from her homeland by her side, even if it proved to be fleeting, was an extraordinary tonic. Ilaria was forthright, intelligent and gracious. And based on that mornings reaction, considered by all to be glamorous and intriguing.

Now Aurelie wanted Ilaria to stay more desperately than ever. Oh yes, it also seemed as if every woman in the cathedral felt compelled to stare at her big brother. Yes, she wanted Armand to stay. And indeed the sight of Tristan appeared to be stirring great interest too. Beyond all doubt, Aurelie wanted them all to stay and hoped that, not only this unexpected welcome, but the glittering sight of Verona's elite gathered in the cathedral, would stir Ilaria's interest.

She had warned Ilaria how richly apparelled that flock would be. And so both women ensured they and their husbands were dressed to match the showing of all — all save the Prince and Princess of course. For as you know, laws driven by the church exist to curb public displays of excess in couture and accompaniments. Certain furs, fabrics, colours and jewellery — tiaras for instance — are restricted for all but the nobility to wear.

That morning however, we discovered that despite the presence of their Highnesses, those rules were ignored more vigorously in Italy by the elite than we ever witnessed in France. This was particularly so in the cathedral, where the marshals responsible for monitoring infringements were forbidden to loiter. And so every Sunday morning, with none but the archbishop to dissuade the daring elite, Verona Cathedral became the primary vantage to witness a provocative display of *couture rebellion*.

Outside the cathedral, marshals ranged all about the citadel to monitor the restrictions. Particularly in precincts considered to be hotbeds of low brow attempts to transgress. A marshal could fine any man or woman, high or low, they dared to accuse of a transgression. Yet rarely would they accuse an elite man or woman unless paid a great deal by another elite man or woman to do so.

And so the major target — for the not very daring marshals — tended to be the more daring harlots who strayed from the cathouse when their shifts were done yet before they retired to rest for the day. Most hoped to attract a wealthy patron beyond the control of their minders. Such men were more like to linger in the haughtier piazzas or popular environments that fell under the restrictions.

And so after a long Saturday night upon Sunday morning, draped in forbidden fabrics the most daring would dangle themselves as bait, resting their forms in plain sight above scandalously elevated footwear. If challenged by a motivated marshal, their offending stilts and illicit garments may be confiscated on the spot and a hefty fine imposed.

The loss of their footwear would quite literally reduce the stature of a transgressor. Yet then they suffered the added indignity of having to make their way home in an antic state of disarray. Oh yes, you can imagine how often a Marshal might negotiate *alternate* payment with a victim. Little doubt that was the reason they were targeted so much.

Beyond such easy targets however, the middling class of aspiring men and women were the *next most* frequently held to account. Indeed many elite citizens were at pains themselves to ensure it. For in truth, the exalted cared little for the policing of harlots. But they expected any who occupied the mid social ranks — who had a mind to transgress — were kept within the boundary of their stations.

For unlike harlots — who hold no pretence to being elite — those middle ranked social pretenders offer more genuine offense to the notion of being elite. Oh yes, that sounded perverse to me. But it won't surprise you to hear that some among Verona's elite — the former prima donna of Montecchi for one — were well known for taking regular offence against social underlings whose display of attire seemed *overambitious*. Moreover, if a lawmaker failed to do so, some were willing to take matters into their own hands.

Indeed just two days before our arrival at the cathedral, Aurelie and Ilaria were lounging in the central courtyard at Sycamore Hill, listening to me play, drinking liberally and discussing what they may choose to wear, when one such lively episode was recounted.

'We were standing together in the Square of the Lords. Esmay was dripping in winter ermine herself, reserved for royalty, as you know.'

'Yes of course.'

'And so guilty of gross infringement herself, when she turned to the young woman beside us and tore away the front panel of her bodice.'

'Dear Heaven!'

'Her victim was a wine merchant's bride who had also dared to wear ermine.'

'Of course.'

'Yet it was merely a trim to frame her décolletage.'

'That seems a trifle.'

'Particularly given Esmay was wrapped in it. Yet what had enflamed her so greatly was that her young rival stood boasting about her *lovely garment* while the affront went unchecked by a marshal standing right next to her.'

'Oh gracious!'

'When he proved more intent on ogling the ermine-framed display of her breasts rather than breasting the affront of her display —'

'You've told this tale before.'

'Once or twice darling. Then Esmay decided to take matters into her own hands.'

'I can imagine.'

'Glaring with impatience to me, yet without any warning to her rival, she turned on the swaggerer, towering as she does against the stature of most women, and drove her fingers in behind the hem of the bodice!'

'Oh Lee Lee no!'

'Oh yes. Scraping soft breast with sharp nails as she went — and with great satisfaction I might add.'

'That doesn't surprise me.'

'Her wild-eyed victim was *very* surprised and screamed like a child as the fabric rent loudly. TUG! RIP! TUG! RIP! It took more than one effort to ensure the offending panel, and the undercovering below it —'

'Oh dear mercy.'

'Yes, was completely torn away.'

'Oh that poor girl!'

'All that commotion drew attention to Esmay's victim of course. The hapless girl was exposed from neck to waist and stood screaming as she attempted to cover herself.'

'What did the *marshal* do?'

'What *didn't* he do Ria! Confronted with a more revealing view he simply continued to stare.'

'Ah! Lecherous man.'

'He had little want to leer a moment later. Esmay spun on her heel and smacked him hard for his lack of attention to duty.'

'Dear mercy did she do that?'

'With Onorato standing by her she did. Yet I'm sure she'd have done so without him.'

'I believe that's right. At least I'll never see his lecherous face again.'

'That's certain. And in truth Ria, I feel it's most like that

Esmay's gone from Verona forever. Why would she ever return darling?'

Most of that wild story had made them smile to hear and tell it. Before that evening was over, both had chosen garments and accoutrements to wear. Next morning of course, they changed their minds completely. At least when we reached the cathedral, with both women dressed in the most elegant, yet daring couture, neither a marshal nor Esmeralda was to be found lurking outside or inside.

When we did arrive outside the cathedral, the cool air ensured that outer coverings remained in place momentarily, hiding from view, so many transgressions we'd soon discover were lurking just beneath. Yet even those outer coverings were intended to push boundaries. Right there in the cathedral piazza, as the Cortelannis and Capulets alighted from their impressive conveyance, the variations to be seen of fine velvets with exotic and forbidden furs upon heads, hands, collars and sleeves, was staggering to behold.

If restraint for the sake of attending their place of worship was meant to prick consciences that morning, it was not on display outside that mighty house of prayer or within. For once inside, as outer layers were peeled by serving staff to hold and fold, a decadent display — among men and women alike — began to reveal more flesh than one might see at a bathhouse. Ilaria's brows lifted. She leaned to whisper.

'Oh Aurelie you weren't exaggerating.'

'And you thought *we* would be too daring.'

'I did. Mercy but I never imagined this.'

'Welcome to Verona Premiere Dame Capulet.'

'Thank you Prima Donna Cortellani.' Ilaria grinned.

'Now darling don't stare. Smile just a little and breathe deeply.'

'Yes, yes, yes.'

Aurelie lifted her perfect brows in acknolwedgement of a couple at a short distance. 'If this start is any indication I have a feeling they'll all be short of breath this morning.'

The prima donna was right. Yet before the throng really knew the Capulets had arrived, the competition to be noticed seemed to be everywhere and most hungry to compete. Daring sights, gliding ahead of us, had already set brows lifting, whispers humming and eyes bulging. Maxine and I followed in awe as so many paraded with gusto under a thin veil of reverence.

It was clear that, even in their primary house of God, Verona's elite were practised in the art of offering reverence by their display of devotion whilst simultaneously offering offence in their display of attire. And it wasn't simply the women who were on daring display. Just as many muscular men raised reactions with revealing choices.

The sight of it all was a revelation to Ilaria. Oh yes, back in Lyon she had seen individuals parading like this before at events and social gatherings. Yet to see it in Verona Cathedral upon a Sunday morning, the notion of how both sexes appeared to use couture as a tool, not just for flirtation or to declare status but as a bold token of rebellion? It felt both theatrical and exciting.

Men in thin silken hose displayed firm buttocks and bulging thighs with codpieces stuffed for enhancement. And where no effort to accentuate was required, form fitting fabric to that portion left little to the imagination. More was revealed beneath short-waisted doublets of thick velvet brocade and damask with widely slashed sleeves. Broad, plunging necklines revealed shirts of the finest linen below which in turn revealed muscular necks, clavicles and chests.

Feminine counterparts revelled in their own displays of necks, clavicles, shoulders and backs. Below shoulder height, the modest or wanton swell of the chest was held behind sometimes square, sometimes circular, yet often plunging necklines. Hems to frame all were trimmed in fur, silk, lace or velvet. I tell you sweet friends, by all the saints who pray in Heaven — and were hiding their eyes to it all —the effect of it was startling, mesmerising and more.

My own eyes didn't know where to look. No direction felt safe as Maxine hissed in warning.

'Marcel stop gaping!'

'But sweetheart?'

'Eyes on the floor you imbecile!'

'Yes sweetheart. That may be safer.'

'Don't call *me* sweetheart you ... *gaping* man!'

'I'm gaping at the floor now. It's a very austere ... and cold looking ... floor.'

I glanced at her. She was looking elsewhere. I glanced where she was looking. 'You seem rather distracted by the sight of that man's ass?'

'Oh! she spat incredulously. 'Ninny I'm married!'

'Yes sweet. So am I.'

'Yet not nursing two babes! Eyes back on the floor.'

I did so for a moment. But as you can imagine I've never been able to keep my eyes still very long. And so for safety, I decided to gaze at less provocative members of the flock. Indeed some among them were dressed for the opposite effect, encased in austere black or grey or both colours styled together. After a few moments, I realised the sight of the demure simply made the sight of the daring appear more daring and more tempting to want to see.

And what I saw continued to mesmerise me.

All about us in the most exquisite ensembles — to ensure the shape and flow of all combined to give perfect results — their creators had employed a masterful painter's sense of composition. Every manner of contrasting fabric was used to draw admiring eyes towards the waist to begin, then lift to see more — midriffs, chests, clavicles, necks, chins, lips, cheeks, noses, eyes, brows and up to such elegant haute coiffures.

From a high —drawn waist to the peak of a headpiece, subtle composition released a vibrant sense of flow. It compelled the eye to follow, rising from the curve of a breast to the peak of a head, along the rise and fall of gorgeous hair, enmeshed in adornments, until the greater frame of each gown with its mingling of fabrics, in contrast and complement, smothered the eye with sartorial splendour.

Finally, all was accentuated by the finest jewelled, gold or silver adornments upon ears, necks and fingers. No elite woman sat among this ambitious flock who hadn't prepared the evening before and ensured she was roused by the crack of dawn to make ready. Even so early on Sunday morning, Verona's feminine elite had revelled in that chance to take and show their right to enjoy such licence.

For Armand and Ilaria, on their first social visitation to Verona citadel, the gathering that engulfed them appeared to be sparkling company. And it already seemed clear their decadent show was not just intended for the solemn atmosphere of the cathedral, but to enliven the social interplay that would follow outside. After the service, the promise of a promenade toward one of its many piazzas to mingle or drink or dine would lure them all. At least for a time. Yet for some it would last until sunset and beyond.

However, before such distraction could occur, all must first heed the most compelling call of their week — to honour God in his house. And some each Sunday morning may even suffer retribution for their daring before they departed. Some displays may draw a directed frown from the pulpit. Or during the sermon, the most daring rebels may draw a pointed rebuke. One might think the threat of such discomfort would cause the majority to display themselves with more modesty. Yet Aurelie informed us, in no uncertain terms, public censure appeared to have the opposite effect, making celebrities of such targets.

Fortunately, for once such as Ilaria — a woman who hoped to grow her fortune by creating couture to cover their bodies or reveal them — Verona's elite didn't react to censure with blind obedience but rebuked it with contrary reasoning.

> *Why gather wealth if it can't be spent for*
> *our indulgence and enjoyed publicly?*

For they all understood, as soon as the sermon was done and the cathedral doors opened, their gorgeous tide would be swept away to admire each other and indulge their lust for social engagement with little restraint. And so for the newlywed Capulets seated among them, unlike their life back in Lyon — where they still hadn't been introduced to elite society — in this foreign citadel they were already being treated like feted celebrities. For them, particularly for our merchant princess Ilaria, what may follow that cathedral service seemed to hold all manner of possibilities.

Of course, we knew there must be some sitting in that congregation who were Montecchi — or aligned to their powerful faction — that may bitterly resent the Capulet's presence. Yet Armand and Ilaria had arrived with the Cortelannis and were greeted by the magistrate and his wife. Maxine and I saw their faces lighting up together. That was something we hadn't really seen since we first arrived.

After their trouble during the summer, I felt it was a heady thing to see our elite young couple come forth, fresh from the birth of their first child. Suddenly it felt like a surge of status was enveloping their lives with the embraces, kisses, smiles and welcome words from Verona's elite. Now as I look back, I realise everything they saw, heard or that engaged them that morning — during that entire day — were like ingredients in an intoxicating potion. The glamour of the company; the beauty of the cathedral; Ilaria's release from the birthing chamber's isolation to be greeted by this impact of Verona at close range, all added to the intoxicating effect.

As Ilaria's final consideration was ignited around the pressing question of *whether to leave or stay*, she and Armand had no grim dramas to distract them any longer. What's more, now Thibault had been born, not in Lyon, but in Verona. Whilst Maxine and I continued to watch them closely, I felt that more than ever before, the lure of this tantalising citadel was drawing her in.

The pews we settled onto that stood near the fore were reserved for the Cortellani. Immersed in the distraction of it all, Ilaria sat next to Armand, considering so many elements that were swirling in her mind. Could they stay?

Last but not least to consider was one final factum. Two weeks into Ilaria's birthing confinement she had finally received a note from the Duchess. Yes, that enigmatic woman was still in Rome with Nobel and Eloise. But they had finally made contact with one of the two important men they sought to parley with, the mysterious *Count Orlandi*.

Perhaps to tease Ilaria, Yolanthe's tone was jubilant. To begin, she declared, she had managed to gain the Count's *unwavering* support to their enterprise. Though he held two estates in Rome — including the magnificent palazzo they currently sojourned in as his guests — Orlandi's roots were in Verona. He held vast assets inside that citadel and outside.

Yet perhaps most significantly, Orlandi was now the leader of the *Guelphs* in Verona. That meant he was now the Montecchi's major political rival. It also meant he had deep ties to the closest supporters of his Holiness in Rome. In particular, he had direct access to the man Yolanthe had mentioned with the musical name, Cardinal Piccolomini, who served up north in the Emperor's court. Orlandi had promised to arrange a meeting soon with that elusive man too. Yet so far he had divulged little more.

It seemed the young duchess was on a breathtaking adventure with Nobel and Eloise. It also seemed the circuit she was gliding through now was beyond tantalising. Moreover, in Yoli's excitement to discuss her outcomes there, she appeared too distracted in that note to attempt to press her ambitions with the Capulets any further. And that omission had caused Ilaria to fret.

Reading Yolanthe's glowing report, Ilaria began to wonder if her tactic of delaying so long may have caused her to risk losing — what appeared to be turning into — the merchant opportunity of a lifetime. She sat in Verona Cathedral with Armand, wondering even more deeply about those outcomes that had been reported. For as fate would have it, upon the day before they had ventured back into Verona, *a following* message arrived from the duchess.

It held more tantalising news of course, yet also had a disturbing edge to it. True to his word mysterious Count Orlandi had arranged a conference with the even more secretive Piccolomini. Yet the latter would only agree to meet with one member of their alliance, insisting it must be Yolanthe who represented the interest of the French Queen.

She agreed to that meeting of course. It was to be held there in Rome at Orlandi's palazzo. Piccolomini may be able to stay for a day, perhaps more, yet was uncertain. What's more he insisted, during that time of his possible arrival, all but the duchess must depart before he could attend. The nature of it all seemed highly unusual.

The fiery young duchess went on to divulge what she could about the man she was soon to meet, entirely alone. Yolanthe knew he was travelling from the Germanic court, where he had been serving the new Emperor Frederick for some time. At the start of his holy tenure, Cardinal Piccolomini had first become a priest in Germany. Then he was made a bishop before he became a diplomat – Cardinal – representing Rome's interest at the Emperor's court.

In his current task, he was helping to secure Emperor Frederick's marriage to the Portuguese princess, which would in turn enable Frederick's coronation as Emperor. Most interesting to note, despite the Cardinal's holiness, in Frederick's court *Enea* – as he was affectionately called by worldly confederates – had a long established reputation as a *musician*, a *poet* and was rumoured to be a *womaniser!* He was even said to have sired several children, each by different women!

Yet as far as Yolanthe could tell, while his musicianship and poetic bents were not denied – though still very unusual for a holy man to own as traits – she couldn't be certain that last reputed attribute wasn't a fabrication set about by rivals to unseat his influence with the Emperor.

Regardless of what the truth to that last may be, Cardinal Piccolomini was clearly a man who swirled in the kind of circuits most would never dream of gaining access to.

Finally, although the duchess hadn't said it in so many words, she seemed to cryptically imply that – although this creature appeared to serve the Emperor – his deepest allegiance may have been to his Holiness in Rome. Yet nothing seemed clear in that regard. And Yolanthe's own meaning on that point, seemed hazy at best.

Yet what was becoming less hazy to Ilaria – as she attempted to read *between the lines* as they say – was that this very potent player the adventurous duchess was soon to meet – so alone and so secretively – appeared to be some manner of *spy*. And he was not just any secretive political player, but one who appeared to play for both sides among the most powerful beings in our world. Cupid's Secret Balls!

Oh yes, that much was distracting enough for the Capulets to wonder at. But what else Yolanthe noted therein caused Ilaria to fret her decision even more. For also in that note, and rather bluntly, the wily woman went on to confess:

Now the Count is enlisted into our venture darling, and because he's a native of Verona, I no longer feel such an urgent need to forge alliances with other local asset holders in order to activate our plans for that citadel.

I watched Ilaria read that letter and I tell you bluntly, if she were a man, I would have said her mercenary new *friend* had managed to kick her hard in the balls with that remark. Wherever the volatile duchess was aiming, it seemed a calculated thing to call Ilaria *darling* at the start of a sentence, then unleash such a cutting remark before it was complete. Oh yes, she hoped to make her presence felt from afar. And by the way Ilaria's expression drained as she read it, that tactic had caused her to feel it.

Yet an instant *after* the wily seductress had kicked her new friend between the legs, she knelt to soothe the pain away. Oh yes, it's a ribald image, but suited to such ribald tactics. Cupid's Balls! For then she immediately went on to re-assure Armand and Ilaria that:

Now that we know a child is coming to you ...

Ilaria had sent word of her pregnancy.

Yet Yolanthe didn't know the child had come.

Nor that it was a boy.

And so not likely to wed her youngest brother.

... if you can make your final decision by the time you re-enter society after the birth ...

That sentence imposed a strict limit of time that would expire at the end of this very day.

... then Auguste and I would still be willing to embrace you both into our growing fold and extend the offer to the Cortelannis too if they remain disposed to go forward.

Finally it was declared — with no room for doubt — that beyond this final chance to agree, no further extensions of time would be granted for the Capulets to deliberate. Moreover, a clear warning was sounded at the end which made me imagine her mischievous smile as she dictated it.

> *Such is the danger, pretty people, of waiting*
> *overlong on important decisions.*

As you know, I'm not a merchant. But I've spent most of my life in the company of one of the very best. In that time I've learnt that a good merchant understands that the notion of *how much value* a thing may hold is often a matter of *timing*. To a livestock merchant, a healthy mare or stallion of fine stock may be worth a fortune for breeding. Yet if an accident or disease causes it to become impotent, suddenly that beast is worth nothing at all.

While Armand and Ilaria sat in the cathedral on that fateful morning, the time for them to decide was running out. For you see, the messenger who delivered that ultimatum had orders to enquire about the status of the recipients with respect to the issues at hand. He was to remain in Verona until the deadline passed, then leave for Rome immediately to report the result. Lodged at the apartments Yolanthe had purchased, he waited on a reply the Capulets had promised to deliver by the strike of nine upon Monday morning.

And so without further ado, they had to decide whether to join the alliance or risk losing the chance forever.

Chapter 10 Aurelie's obsession

The murmurs among the congregation had settled. Ilaria attempted to set all thoughts of the ultimatum to one side, yet it was difficult. She glanced at Armand, drawn momentarily by a whispered comment from Tristan. Just as she leaned to catch their attention, the glint of a jewel upon a headpiece drew her attention. Ilaria scanned again to consider her surroundings and assess their predicament.

She sat in a gorgeous cathedral in a captivating citadel beside her handsome husband. They were now Sieur and Dame Capulet. She glanced behind to smile at Thibault in Maxine's arms. And yes, they had a son. Now moreover, they seemed to be safely lodged among protective relations with the promise of new friends and ventures beckoning.

So much seemed to be appealing.

Yet the grave experience they had met so quickly at the hands of the Montecchi still troubled her. In truth, her fear of that faction still made the prospect of living in Verona foreboding, to remain within the reach of so many from that dark house. She glanced at Armand again, wondering what he may be thinking. I knew he had confided to her that very day.

'Put them from your mind angel. I don't fear the Montecchi any more than any famille we might accidentally lock horns with in any citadel in Italy or France.'

Perhaps that made sense. Perhaps if they did return to Lyon, they may just as quickly meet a local incarnation of that brutal faction and have to deal with them too. They may even fall foul of one that was more frightening. Then as they had continued to discuss their misgivings, I heard Ilaria utter a phrase that I fear fate itself may have whispered in her ear.

'And as they say my heart — *one may live more safely with the Devil they know.*'

Looking back now I wonder. How many lives — when a crucial

decision has been hanging in the balance — have been altered by their consideration of that ancient adage?

After their heartfelt conversation that day, Ilaria also understood that for Armand, it was her *own* feelings on the question that mattered most to him.

'Without your genuine desire to stay my love, the question of us lingering here is moot.'

Suddenly I realised that no one, certainly not Armand who was so in love with his angel, would insist we remain if her heart wasn't compelled to it. Though at first he had seemed to favour returning. Now he appeared to accept that the House of Capulet in Lyon may fare well without them.

Now seated in the cathedral, Ilaria knew that decision was hers to make. Vaguely she noticed a tall masculine figure ahead of us was rising to address the congregation.

'If you think him handsome to see darling? Wait 'til you *hear* him.'

The comment was purred into her ear by Aurelie. Ilaria felt a conspiratorial lean and squeeze of her hand as she spoke and saw Sabatino sigh, tilting his eyes to Heaven.

'Yes mia cara.' he whispered in mock reprimand. 'All Verona knows you're infatuated with Escalus. But please, reserve at least a modicum of passion for myself.'

'Tush Sab! A woman may long for a prince without offering offense to her husband.'

Sabatino pleaded for support.

'Ilaria is that what you think?'

'Oh Ria don't answer him. Sab knows I love him desperately.' She pouted to blow a conciliatory kiss, her signature offering at such moments.

Maxine and I smiled behind them. They seemed an endless source of entertaining, mock marital distress. In truth I felt he could never be angered by her in that or any mood.

'Sab is my *reality*. Along with three children.' Aurelie blinked playfully. 'Any longing for the attentions of a prince is merely my *day-dream*.'

'As long as you dream by day and still sleep in *my* arms by night mia cara, then all is well.'

'Mmm?' She purred again. 'Perhaps *more* than sleep tonight darling.'

That flirtatious promise took Ilaria by surprise. Aurelie's mood was clearly affected. Sabatino noticed Ilaria's reaction.

'Ilaria you'll discover that she's more scandalous in church than anywhere else.' He grazed a fingertip under Aurelie's jaw. 'Why *is* that my love?' He added as her eyes narrowed in mock defiance. 'Hopefully during your stay, Ilaria, you'll exert a more calming influence upon her.'

'Shhh!' she hissed excitedly. 'He's about to speak.'

'Heaven forbid I deprive you of *that* pleasure.'

'Tush. Once Ilaria hears him too, she'll stay forever.'

I was surprised by the suggestion someone other than the archbishop would be rising to address the congregation. But that holy officer hadn't yet made his entrance from behind us. And so it was Prince Escalus de Treviso who had risen to address us. As Podestà of Verona — assigned by Venice — he was their primary civic leader of course. That he was also a prince, made his authority feel more weighted.

Certainly it seemed to do so for Aurelie.

And what's more — to the prima donna's approval — though just above middling height, the prince was a muscular man with a fine head of thick dark hair. He also had broad lips, open soulful eyes, and to complete the regal picture, a slightly significant nose. Taken altogether, his features combined in a face and figure I'm sure most would admire as handsome, and that most would agree looked distinctively noble.

I'm sure you may have guessed that Prince Escalus was named after the ancient Greek poet of tragedy. No great wonder therefore, that his ancestral line was Greek — at least in part — and was linked to the mighty House of *Palaiologos*. Oh yes, try your best to pronounce that name. And that lineage was evidenced — for any who may recognise it — by a rampant, arrow tailed dragon, displayed on his familial crest.

At that time the gracious prince, perhaps thirty two or three years, was balding. Yet somehow his growing lack of hair — which Escalus did nothing to hide — didn't seem to diminish his allure at all. At least for Aurelie it didn't. It would be easy to imagine his likeness carved in marble with a contemplative look, perhaps with a laurel wreath wrapped about his balding head.

You may recall from history that even the great Julius Caesar, conscious of his baldness and wanting to mask it, had pressured the Roman Senate to allow him to wear a laurel wreath as part of his daily attire. Cupid's Balls! Can you imagine possessing enough power to force such a conceited wish into law? But I digress. Where was I?

Oh yes, Prince Escalus and conceit.

From the evidence I've seen since we've known the Prince, he has never seemed too preoccupied by vanity. Before that moment in the cathedral however, we hadn't yet seen him smile. Certainly during his attendance at the Ceremony of Disgrace — the only other time we laid eyes on him — he didn't smile at all. Perhaps that had left me with a more grave impression of the man. Yet at that moment, he was looking down upon his radiant wife, Princess Florentia, in the foremost pew and was smiling very warmly.

Escalus cleared his throat. Aurelie shut her eyes. Sabatino glanced and shook his head in resignation which made Ilaria smirk. Then to my surprise, the sonorous voice of Prince Escalus di Treviso drew the attention of all. When the much-admired man spoke and scanned that wealthy congregation, not unexpectedly, Aurelie began to swoon.

Yet as Ilaria listened, it was not the prince's hypnotic voice that caught her attention, but his purple velvet surcoat lined with winter ermine. Ilaria was little else, if not expert in the quality of all textiles, dyes and pigments. As you know she's also a maestra skilled in the design and creation of all elements of haute couture. Ever since her courtship, haute couture had become her special interest.

Spotless winter ermine, such as that worn by the prince, was a prestige trapping that only those of noble blood were allowed to wear. As was any purple hued fabric. She knew that dye was extracted from exotic molluscs usually found in Africa. She also knew that dye could be sourced direct from Africa through the nearby port of Venice. And so tantalising thought began to stir in her mind.

Along with other *sanctioned* elements of couture, ermine and purple were meant to be visible tokens that allowed all to instantly tell the members of an *elite* house from those of a truly *noble* house. And for noble factions to secure the supply of such elements, or to commission entire garments created from them in combination, the prices they were willing to pay could be exorbitant.

The exquisite dye required to stain that purple hue into his velvet surcoat and silken hose would fetch a living fortune for its provision. Moreover, the cloth and thread of gold in his garments, which dazzled her eyes, within the slashings to the upper chest and shoulder of his elegant houppelande, would likewise have cost a ransom.

Any who could provide such mighty patrons with a steady supply of such things, would be rewarded with steady and mighty profits. Indeed some of Ilaria's famille had specialised in that supply for generations. One of her uncles still held a rare patent passed on to him by her grandpapa. And it was one of only three that had been granted to supply wealthy houses of the French and Germanic nobility.

As Aurelie sat beside her and continued to gaze, Ilaria gained her first undistracted view of the prince in closer proximity. To sit among his peers and have the chance to observe him more at his ease, with a glow of friendly colour in his cheeks, was captivating. And given the potent question she knew she must answer that day, the merchant princess began to consider a new possibility.

If she remained in Verona, perhaps Ilaria could attract the attention of a patron like Escalus. Or, perhaps more importantly, his lovely wife Princess Florentia. While Ilaria watched and listened, it was impossible for her merchant blood to not begin to bubble. Perhaps a couple as exalted as the Trevisos would have the means to grant her a patent to supply such furnishings within their noble circuit?

She couldn't yet be certain such permission lay within the prince's power to grant. Yet even if she could secure their patronage for nothing more than the creation of their couture, their own faction stretched from Verona to Venice, perhaps all the way to Constantinople. Their *access* to those who *may* control such things might be considerable.

Ilaria turned to the handsome face of her husband. Armand appeared to be listening with interest. Her arm — clad in deep blue silk tinctured by Tolousian woad and studded with delicate pearls along the cuff — lifted to lay over his. She ran her fingertips over his hand. His brows lifted and she squeezed his hand gently.

A smile creased the corner of his lips as he turned to glance. He was stronger since taking his last injury. And now he was her child's father. Although she may have felt it an impossibility, in some enchanted fashion, for all they had endured in such a short time, Ilaria was certain she felt more in love with Armand on that day than ever before.

That Sunday in the cathedral was late in January. Ilaria knew that if they chose not to stay, at the very latest, they would need to depart for Lyon by early August. In that case, Verona would become nothing more than a summer escape, visited every other season perhaps or less often. There was still one day left to consider their fate — and ours.

Ilaria had promised Yolanthe's messenger he'd have their answer early next morning to send on to Rome. As Ilaria felt the touch of Armand's hand still, she was beginning to admit, despite any fear of the Montecchi, she felt summoned by this place and all its promise. Indeed, as she considered Escalus again and Florentia's smile, that feeling was palpable.

The thought made Ilaria smile. She glanced at Armand and leaned to kiss his cheek. Yet just as she did so, she spied a face across the aisle that gave her pause. All at once the broken beat of her heart ignited. It was the face of a man. His head had turned toward them for just a moment and his image from that view had triggered her recognition.

As instinct tends to force us to do in such moments, Ilaria glanced away for an instant then looked back again. Her pulse began to throb. There across the aisle, just ahead in the foremost pew, sat Aldobrando Montecchi, brother to the man Armand had slain, brother-in-law to the woman he had widowed. How could he have been so close and not drawn her attention before?

Suddenly Ilaria recognised the face next to him, his wife Donatella. Her mind flashed back to our confrontation in the burial yard by the river, the threats they had made, the treatment they'd tried to impose on the poor Grisantis. She remembered their new-born son Romeo, held in the arms of his wet nurse, and the irony of his following name — *Amicus*.

Brando and Donatella had become the undisputed primo don and prima donna of Montecchi. That was made clear during our confrontation in the western borgo. Seated together at that distance the couple seemed solemn and withdrawn. Perhaps their outlook had mellowed since that incident. Perhaps the gravity of recent events was tempering their deportment.

Then Ilaria realised, after all the commotion of her entrance with Armand, it was inconceivable that Brando and Donatella wouldn't know they were in attendance. Perhaps the knowledge that she and Armand had strutted into their cathedral, to be greeted like celebrities, had deepened the gravity of their deportment. Somehow that thought — that Ilaria's presence may be rankling their discomfort as she stared — troubled her even more.

Yet despite the chaotic feelings it stirred to have identified them so suddenly, something in that chance — to view them at a near distance, finally see them in a setting that lacked the adversarial heat of their recent past — began to still Ilaria's heart. Something in that chance to consider them this way made the threat of them seem less foreboding.

Her pulse began to slow, her breath began to settle, and then it happened. A terrible thought surged through her mind. She felt her heart stuttering again as she looked at the new prima donna and wondered if perhaps — her panic rose sharply at the thought — if perhaps scarface, the bitch herself, sat among them at that moment, lurking in their company!

Ilaria's pulse raced again. Feverishly she began to scan for any sign of that despicable woman, eyes narrowing, straining to see. Esmeralda was tall, statuesque. As a recent widow she would be clad all in black and veiled. If hiding among them, her silhouetted form would be easy to identify.

No. No. NO. Glancing up one row and down the other, then up and down again, she couldn't see a spectre like that seated anywhere among them. Her pulse began to slow. Her pounding heart began to calm again. Suddenly she realised just how much she still dreaded the portent of ever having to see Esmeralda again.

Yet from what Aurelie had said just two days before, the vile witch had indeed vanished. After her appearance at the trial, the Ceremony of Disgrace and her inquisition, that fallen prima donna wasn't expected to be bold enough to face her peers again. And one could only presume that if she ever did so, it would not be for a very, very, very long time.

Once imagined however, the image of that dread woman hung in Ilaria's mind. She recalled the story Aurelie had told her of how Esmeralda had confronted that young bride in the Square of the Lords. She imagined herself as the bride, cowering under Esmeralda's scorn. She saw the sharp fingernails reaching, her vile husband staring and gloating. Suddenly Ilaria's heart was pounding again. She felt sharp nails scraping into her breast, ripping her skin, tearing the panel of an ermine-lined bodice away.

And despite the story Aurelie had told, instead of lifting her hand to strike the marshal, Esmeralda lifted to form a claw with sharp lacquered nails that struck Ilaria's face, driving through to carve a scar through her left cheek. Suddenly Ilaria was staring into her looking glass. That mark was the image of the deep laceration Esmeralda now wore, the permanent token she received for her trouble on the day she attempted to murder Armand.

Ilaria's hand gripped Armand's. She felt him press in return. A hand lifted to her cheek to turn her eyes to him.

'Don't fret my love. Put her from your mind. We're together now and safe. Heaven is watching.'

How did he know? Yes, she understood that he had sensed her unsettledness. Yet how could he sense the nature of her thoughts so completely? Passionate green eyes poured their foreboding into the sanctuary of his calm expression. The calm in his eyes drove her stifling thoughts away. The warmth in his smile loosened the grip of her fear.

Armand's hand lifted to lay against Ilaria's opposing cheek, exactly where she imagined the scar was rent. He drew her head gently, leaning to kiss the corner of her forehead. She inhaled deeply and exhaled slowly. In the reassurance of his touch, the phantom scar had vanished. His eyes turned away. Her heart began to settle, as the deep tone of a masculine voice drew her back to attend to the Prince.

'Since that first celebration of Verona's great victory for independence, more than two hundred years ago, the *Palio del Drape Verde* — the race for the green cloth — has been an event that's open to all for the prize of a merchant's length of silk.

'A race?' whispered Ilaria. 'Is he talking about ...?'

'Hush darling.' Aurelie cut in. 'Listen to my prince.'

With the archbishop's permission, Prince Escalus had risen before mass began to conjure interest among the elite to compete in that popular event. Verona's *Race for the Green Silk* is a footrace. And this reminder from the prince was designed to ensure — for any who could be swayed — that there was still ample time to prepare.

'It's held each year in memoriam!' he continued. 'Today I speak to you formally as the master of Verona through the power of Venice.'

Aurelie leaned to Ilaria again. 'He can speak *informally* to me darling as *my* master!'

Ilaria felt the girlish jab from an elbow at her rib, followed by an excited wiggle in Aurelie's hips. It drew Ilaria in, and set a girlish grin on both their faces.

Escalus added. 'Yet no matter what power rules in Verona, that distinctive footrace held to celebrate your battle for independence so many years past, shall always go on!'

Maxine and I were listening too of course.

And though we didn't realise it at the time, as Escalus said that last, some among the Montecchi must have been cringing. For in that famous battle their ancestors had fought not *for* Verona's independence, but *against* it upon the side of the emperor's allies. Every year that footrace reminded one and all of that damning factum.

I glanced about. Every eye paid close attention when the great man spoke. His sensual voice, trained since youth to the task of public address, had drawn every listener in.

'Each year it's fitting that this great event helps us recall at what dear *cost* such blessings as peace and independence are purchased.'

'Viva Verona!' cried one from among the assembly.

'God bless the fallen!' cried another.

'Amen my dear friends. Amen. The lives of many foot soldiers were lost that day. And your footrace celebrates the sacrifice of those called upon by Verona to fight for its freedom. As you know, to the south of the citadel, where the race begins it course, is where your veterans and the untried flower of Verona's youth, high and low born together, took the field of battle.'

'God bless them all!' cried another.

'I know he does. They fought together and they died together. And so it's right that you should pay homage each year to the skill and bravery that secured that great victory and that you continue to be willing — high born and low born — to celebrate it together.'

Lips leaned to Ilaria's ear again. 'I'd be willing to celebrate with him!'

'Aurelie hush this instant.' Ilaria hissed. Her brows seemed fit to leap from her face, yet a tight-lipped smile betrayed her enjoyment.

The prince ran on. 'Moreover in addition to the *men's* footrace, I can confirm that the recent introduction by Venice of a *women's* footrace will continue this season.'

A murmur rippled and echoed about the cathedral.

'However —' he raised his hand. 'An alteration has been made to the allotment of prizes for both races. Rather than offering green silk for the men as we have in the past, a new prize of scarlet silk, the same as we offer for the elite mounted race, will now be offered to the men running afoot.'

'Scarlet's more sensual.' Aurelie purred.

'I'm very fond of green.' Ilaria whispered.

'Says the woman with gorgeous green eyes!'

'However ...' Escalus paused to scan 'green silk will remain in the prize allotment, but shall only be offered to the *women's* champion.' The murmur bubbled once more. Heads turned, whispers exchanged excitedly. 'Moreover this time, for the *first* offering of green silk to a women's champion, rather than being donated by the merchant's guild, it shall be donated by my beautiful wife Florentia.'

The murmur rose with even greater intensity.

'Ria that's her. Next to Gennaro. Oh she's *such* a lovely woman darling.'

'Of course' said Escalus 'as the women's sponsor Florentia will also present that prize to the victor in *person*.'

The stream of murmuring burst into babbling, causing the Prince to raise a hand to quell them.

'Ria that's almost incentive for me to run amok.'

'Have you done so before Lee Lee?'

'Of course not darling. Don't be absurd.'

Escalus lifted his eyes to scan again. 'Finally, and also at the urging of my beautiful Florentia, a *new* race will be held this season as a companion to our elite horserace.'

'Sab's won the horse race before Ria.' She stroked his beard. 'Haven't you darling?'

'Yes mia cara, now shush.' He inclined his head, rolling his eyes toward her as Escalus ran on.

'Unlike our exalted horserace however, this new race shall be open to *all* and won't require a saddle or any tack.'

'Interesting.' whispered Sabatino. 'Yet I fail to see —'

'You may ask how a humble man may *afford* to enter such a race?'

added Escalus.

Sabatino smiled. 'Indeed I was just about to.'

'Well my friends that's where Florentia's suggested a clever solution. To avoid the baleful cost of securing a horse, and for the sake of entertainment, the new race is open to men and women alike but can only be run aboard an ass!'

A burst of uncustomary laughter erupted, reverberating into the vaulted ceiling above us. Even Escalus beamed at the whimsical thought as Aurelie leaned to Ilaria.

'He may run *his* course upon *my* ...'

'Aurelie!' Ilaria hissed more sharply. She felt the poke of another jab. 'Gracious Sabatino? Perhaps I *must* stay, if only to reign in her *scandalous* sense of humour.'

'Ah Ilaria' Sabatino whispered 'now you understand what I have to contend with. I attend mass to seek forgiveness for *my* sins. Yet before I can manage to do so, I'm burdened to seek forgiveness for the sins that my wife commits during the service!'

As the congregations enjoyment subsided the cloak of their noise for Sabatino's commentary went with it.

All eyes returned to the prince.

'And finally, the *prize* for the foremost upon an ass?'

'Aurelie say nothing!' warned Ilaria clutching her arm 'or I may offer to help Sab wash your mouth with soap!'

Ilaria had heard the intake of Aurelie's breath in readiness to say more. That warning came just in time to hold her rampant tongue and set a grin of satisfaction upon Sabatino's benevolent face.

'A length of nine ells of silk will be awarded for the mule race. However it will not be green or scarlet but *pearl*.'

'Oh that sounds ... *ordinary*.' Aurelie muttered.

The prince scanned about and smiled broadly.

'I'll conclude by adding that I intend to enter the horserace again this season.' A volley of nods and murmurs of approval rose and fell. 'However I've also decided to run afoot against all comers. And of course I'll do so in the manner *prescribed* by your ancient traditions.' Another murmur erupted. Yet it was swelled by an undercurrent of giggling and guffaws. Ilaria frowned in confusion. 'I look forward to that contest my friends. I urge you all, high- and lowborn, to join the contest with me!'

Aurelie gripped Ilaria's arm tightly.

'Oh Ria Heaven help me!'

Ilaria's frowned turned to concern.

'Lee Lee what's the matter?'

'Gracious I'm going to faint. Sab Did you hear?'

Sabatino leaned into Ilaria and caught Armand's eye. 'Unfortunately, for both men and women, the *tradition* of our venerable footrace is to compete in the manner of our Etruscan ancestors.'

'Is that bad?' asked Armand.

'Well brother-in-law our ancestors ran *naked*.' Sabatino lifted his eyes to Heaven.

'Oh no!' whimpered Ilaria. 'Sab you *poor* thing.'

'Oh yes Ilaria. Heaven help her indeed.'

'Now Ria you *must* stay. At least long enough to see that. Imagine telling your famille in Lyon that you watched a prince running naked in the streets of Verona.'

'And' Tristan finally broke his silence 'from what his Highness announced, so must the women?'

'Darling' Aurelie lifted a single brow. 'if he announces by the power of Venice they've decided to run a *mixed* race afoot in that ancient tradition, I'll enter it myself! Then Ria I could tell my grandchildren that, at least *once* before I died, I had managed to get *naked* with a prince.'

Maxine and I smiled together.

Oh yes, Aurelie was being flippant.

Yet our day had only just begun and soon after mass was complete, the doors re-opened and that gorgeous tide swept into Cathedral Square to begin their grand promenade.

What awaited us upon that outing was to defy the expectations of the Capulets and Cortelannis.

Chapter 11   Rules of the Game

So far as the experience of my earlier years among the Capulets could tell, any who knew Ilaria then would say she always behaved with the manners of a saint in the guise of an angel. She was always polite, engaging and the soul of inclusion to all. Yet despite saying so I must confess that she also had fiery moments. Those moments tended to flare in my own company, and flared more frequently still after I married Maxine, and more so again when we had a child.

For as you will recall, when I first proposed marriage to Maxine after learning of her — of our — predicament, Ilaria forbade our match. She also forbade me from having more contact with Maxine until she had made *her* decision. However, once we were wed and my behaviour appeared errant, Ilaria could no longer impose separation from my wife upon me for punishment.

Nor could she make the accusation any longer — as she did in that previous time — that my irreverence would make me a poor father! For beyond even my own expectation, I was proving to be a doting father to our little Figara. Well bite my bare ass, yes I was. And don't be so surprised for I love little Figara, the light of my life. I'd do anything for her ... yet I digress.

And so at that time, whenever the urge to be flippant had me in its thrall — which was often — my company could prove a challenge for Ilaria's patience. I know it's not the case for ordinary folk, but in my own case I often feel the urge to be contrary just for the sake of it! Usually it rises during an attempt to entertain others and feels, at such times, like a delirious compulsion.

For some who find themselves on the receiving end of that mood, it can cause a level of ... *frustration*. Then if my mood's persistent, frustration may often transform into its more heated cousin ... *anger*.

I'm glad you now understand that about me. Perhaps for what follows, it may make you more sympathetic.

At any rate, by the time we left the cathedral that morning, I had only really known Ilaria for a single year. And only half that time was spent in closer company. The point to make here, is that both our lives were continuing to change and to change us. And so I was *still* learning to know the drift of her moods and navigate them more wisely.

Yet having known Ilaria for so long as I have now, I can attest that when she is moved to anger, there are *two* distinct variations. The first is most often encountered when a person of more intimate association — a member of her famille or a close server — makes a request that she feels compelled to *deny*. Thereafter, if those she denies feel compelled to challenge her denial, a playful, mocking manifestation of her anger rises.

We usually find this version entertaining. For when our stern mistress is in that mood, it always draws a smile from her before she grows dour. And when she's in that mood, if one attempts to test her resolve by challenging her a *second* time, that persistence invokes a frowning, yet *still* playful, reassertion that she still intends to deny them.

Then, if the twice-spurned petitioner looks ripe to persist, a high-toned promise to rid herself of the *pestering nuisance once and for all* is heard, wherein she promises to order the nearest lackey to fetch an *instrument of deterrent* — most often a dust smacker or riders crop — to use upon the rascal persistent petitioner if they fail to desist.

Presumably thereafter, with said instrument to hand our glamorous premiere dame would finally resort to that more physical manner of persuasion? Yet we discovered that even the most dire warnings she delivered in that humour, generally come to naught. Indeed I've come to call that version of her anger — *the premiere dame*.

More fearful however, is the other version of it which I christened *the prima donna*.

For in rarer moments, when Ilaria feels she's defending her own right or must stand as a champion for the rights of others, a more volatile mood lurches from her. Moreover, if she has assessed that a transgression by one has caused *injury* to an innocent, her tone doesn't rise but deepens instead. What's more, I discovered that change of tone was not a natural response at all, but a trick learned from her merchant mother who made her practice it for the sake of learning to haggle!

When I imagine her doing that, it makes me smile.

Yet her tone isn't the only change. In response to a volatile transgression, more ominous than her lowering of tone is hearing her voice also soften to a *whisper*. At such dire moments, in hushed throaty tones, her warning leaves one in no doubt, that Ilaria's burning with a fierce resolve. There's an unmistakable intimacy and venom to it. A firm intent fills her large green eyes, like a doe whose fawn stands threatened by a wolf.

I said before that when Ilaria chastises us in mirth, she calls for a punishment tool to escalate her warning. But when that other style of anger is unleashed, when we see the prima donna rise and she's truly disposed to vent her fury and is willing to strike in a fit of passion, Ilaria feels no need to call for a dust smacker whilst her open hand sits at the end of her outstretched arm!

And so it behove me to learn — as soon as possible — which version of Ilaria was rising before me. For it is woe to the fool who mistakes our prima donna for our premiere dame. And so yes, in the main, our angelic mistress behaved like a saint. And as we made our exit from the cathedral that morning, Ilaria and Aurelie agreed that our first destination must be Verona's melting pot — *Herb Market Square.*

But from the moment we left, I was in a rare fit of contrary compulsion. Maxine was nursing Thibault. And so with Figara in my own arms, I started to babble and became a greater and greater distraction, dancing nimbly back and forth over a thin line that separated one version of Ilaria's anger from the other. Oh yes, I noted her glances. Yet I felt sure that being so exposed to the public gaze would hold her mood in check that morning.

Aurelie walked arm in arm with Ilaria, pointing and chattering, though she was also observing my antics with more interest than I realised. In my defence I feel my mood was forgivable, for I had a gurgling daughter to entertain.

And since Figara's birth, I felt the urge to quip incessantly, babbling childlike nonsense, in the hope it would make my beautiful girl smile. Then whenever I was in the company of both children, I couldn't help behaving like a child myself.

I found Maxine usually compensated by behaving as if she were both parents. Indeed at that time, for the sake of my trade as an entertainer, my rising penchant for persistent knavery, was causing me to contemplate a new path. I began to consider if *buffoonery* should become my stock in trade.

Local fools were making a very good living by it. And I could still offer my services as a musician of course.

Yet between my music and my now constant fooling, it was becoming hard to tell which was my trade. And that change was already affecting my relationship with Ilaria. For my antics were becoming so relentless, she took to addressing me simply as *imbécile!* Then I made matters worse by appearing to embrace that disparaging title. And so, as fate would have it, as we continued to stroll on that lovely bright morning, I continued to babble.

In less than half an hour we heard the murmur of human traffic rising from Herb Market Square. Ilaria became rather excited. Upon any day of the week in Verona — but particularly a Sunday morning unless a festival claimed more interest — that sprawling piazza drew more people to it than any other. And for our choice of destination that day, Sabatino and Aurelie were agreed.

'Anything you wish to purvey or purchase lies in wait at Herb Market Square.' said Sabatino.

'Ria it's the prima place on Sunday morning to observe and to be observed.' Aurelie added.

As you know, Maxine and I had attended it before. Yet for fear of the Montecchi, we had never stayed long nor ventured in on a Sunday. By then I felt I knew the citadel rather well. And yes, there were many lovely piazzas to see in fair Verona. But as Herb Market Square lay at such a convenient distance between the cathedral and the old castle, it is by far the most favoured destination.

There's nothing quite like the atmosphere of that long sprawling market on a bright winter's day, with the sun warming your skin as you browse. Then in summer, when the gruelling heat beats down, the pretty central fountain, surmounted by its ancient statue, offers fresh water to slake a thirst or cool the blood.

But the most prominent feature is visible to all before one even enters — the civic bell tower with its mighty steeple. As we drew closer it lofted above the walls and roofs that hemmed us in, rising like a guiding beacon from the market's eastern corner. Our giant Caspar was leading our way for safety with young Fabrizio following him. They already knew the path, though as we moved along Caspar kept glancing aloft to keep sight of the tower.

After the Capulets decided to remain in the villa until spring, our giant warrior began venturing into the citadel more frequently on the pretence of helping to secure provisions. But his own presence with Fabrizio each time — for the sake of our safety against this very need — was to ensure they became acquainted with the streets and lanes.

Now he scouted ahead like a foreboding spectre with Fabrizio haunting his shadow. In reaction to the sight of Caspar, most on-comers parted to give him clear passage. Fabrizio enjoyed the same by default. Ilaria and Aurelie followed him, still arm in arm, as if they were childhood friends. Yet for all the world their gorgeous couture made them seem like a pair of princesses of the blood.

Maxine came next, nursing Thibault with myself close behind, cradling Figara. Armand had been behind, but drew next to me to smile at my daughter. He was making faces to her, just as I did. Behind us, Tristan and Sabatino dawdled in chatty conference, discussing the chevalier's recent experience in Milan during their civil war.

Last but not least, came our stalwart veterans Liberati and Boccolo. It was such a relief to have them back and know they guarded us in public again. Six of Tristan's men remained at the Hill. Six more waited beyond the old stone bridge to escort us back into the hills. All in all, I felt sure if the Montecchi decided to have at us this morning, we would give them a thrashing. And so I felt safe as we neared the northern end of the sprawling piazza.

The noise on the street had lifted of course. However, my own noise lifted to compete with it. The frolicking mood Ilaria had when we left the cathedral was steadily giving way to a quiver of impatience. But that was not only in reaction to my fooling. Ten minutes after we began our promenade, her impatience was triggered by an impetuous declaration Armand had made.

During the service Prince Escalus entreated every man seated, high and low, to take up his challenge to enter the footrace against him. And so, ten minutes after we departed the Holy sanctum, Armand announced his decision to do it! Yet to Ilaria's mind, he had barely begun to walk again since being so gravely hurt. Oh yes, perhaps that was an exaggeration. Yet I understand that's how she felt about it and, to a certain extent, I guessed that objection was simply a pretext to support greater fears she held at the thought.

And so she began to debate the wisdom of Armand undertaking the kind of gruelling regime that would prepare him in time to run such a distance? In truth it had been four months since the bitch shot him in the back. But Ilaria pleaded to Aurelie for support.

'And stark naked into the bargain!'

'Oh darling I've seen him naked before.'

'Lee Lee be serious! He's not yet fit to run around the villa without —'

'Angel ...'

'Hush you! How in Heaven is he expected to run the entire ...? Sabatino. How long is this ludicrous event?'

'In truth Ilaria it can vary each season. But it always starts a few miles south of the citadel.'

'Oh dear Heaven!'

'It starts out on the open plain, then runs the full length of the southern wall to enter through the harvest gate. And there's a broad circuit inside for a total distance of just four or five miles.'

'JUST four or five miles! Armand! Outside the safety of the walls!'

'Just at the start angel.'

'*Stupida!*' she snapped hotly.

'*Stupido.*' I corrected. '*Stupida* is the feminine.'

Aurelie smirked as Ilaria turned on me.

'Imbecile!' she spat with heat. '*Tais-toi!*'

That took me by surprise.

'Yes Madame.' I said pathetically. 'Apologies.'

'Oh Ria' Aurelie smiled 'I haven't heard anyone say that for such a long time!'

'Aurelie this is serious, we must talk sense into him!'

To Ilaria's chagrin, Aurelie's head tilted back as she laughed musically.

It made me laugh too. I've discovered long since that before demoiselles emerge into the social world, they're tutored to improve their laughing tone to make it more appealing. Aurelie's laugh was an intoxicating example. My own Maxine in comparison, not raised for refinement, had a laugh that was almost manly. Oh yes, I love her laugh. I find it infectious. Yet I wouldn't describe it as musical or elegant.

In time, the duchess would confide to me she had practiced a variation of her own laugh that she felt was more seductive and even the tones of her lovemaking to ensure her partners felt more satisfied. Cupid's Balls! That made me wonder if Maxine did that too? Then it made me wonder if I should do the same? More provocatively, that confession made me wonder if her use of the plural meant Yolanthe passed her affection from one lover to the next or gave it to more than one at a time? Yes, I kept that thought to myself.

In time however, both Ilaria and I would learn the provocative answer. Yet that is to come.

'Angel.' said Armand in a conciliatory tone.

'Armand Gabriel!' snapped Ilaria.

'Ilaria Eustadiola!' he retorted.

She turned on her heel to confront him.

'Do not use that *horrible* name for all to hear!'

'Yet you called *me* —'

'Perhaps buffoon is better? It suits you *STUPIDO!*'

'Don't curse me my love.'

'Aurelie? What's the Italic for *tais-toi?*'

'Mistress.' I offered with a quip at the ready.

'MARCEL!' she fumed. 'I did NOT ask you.'

'*Stai zitto?*' Aurelie answered her question.

Ilaria turned on Armand.

'Yes buffoon *STAI ZITTO!*'

'Angel please. I don't expect to *win* it of course.'

Her eyes bulged again. 'To WIN?'

'My entry will assist with our integration here. Cultivate more acceptance of —'

'Not MY acceptance! And I haven't decided to stay!'

'But I thought —' his response was cut short by her curt pirouette.

I spotted a basket of plums passing by at that moment and reached to pilfer one.

'Well I'd love to stay Madame. The plums here are much to my liking.'

Ilaria spun with a wild look in her eyes, it was clear she hung on the brink. '*TAIS-TOI* you imbecile!'

I dipped my head to bow extravagantly, flapping one hand while keeping Figara upright with the other as Ilaria turned on Armand.

'In the interim Armand 'til I decide on our future —'

'Until *we* decide my love.'

She halted, staring at him and melted just a little. 'Yes of course my heart.' She smiled thinly. 'Until then, I feel this race is too *unsafe* for you. Aurelie please tell him! This is such madness, with Montecchi all about us, to run in these streets —'

'Naked with the prince!' chirped Aurelie.

'Aurelie!' Ilaria scowled. 'With that ... that murderous bitch now at liberty ...'

Finally she had revealed her real fear for his participation. My eyes lit with inspiration.

'I'll enter also Madame' I cried 'to *protect* him!'

Ilaria's cringed and squinted in frustration.

'Beshrew my ears MARCEL!'

To my great surprise Ilaria's hand lifted. Maxine feared I'd pushed too far and to save my face, scolded me herself with a slap to the rear of my head!

'Dunderhead!' Maxine snapped.

Ilaria stormed up to me. My eyes lurched open as wide as a midnight owl. An instant later, her fingers clamped on my ear, making me grimace and bend. I was so tall to her.

'YOU will protect him?' she hissed. 'Imbecile you couldn't protect your own manhood from your own hand!'

I snapped my fingers over little Figara's ears.

Aurelie burst into song of musical laughter. I bit my lip hard to erase a rising smile. Maxine lifted fingers to her lips to stifle the same but Armand couldn't control his mirth. To hear that bawdy jibe leap from Ilaria's lips made him burst into a fit of laughter.

Worse than this for Ilaria, the market throng was pouring about us. No longer able to control myself, I let out a donkey-like guffaw that set the crowd staring! Her brows shot up then frowned hard as her upper lip pouted against the lower. She stabbed a fingernail at me in dire warning and spun on her heel with an audible huff, drawing Aurelie on.

I held still for a moment to increase our distance. Armand leaned next to me.

'She must be *very* angry' he whispered 'to use such language in public.'

'Oh Master she's in rare form!' I giggled excitedly. 'I *must* remember that curse for my own repertoire!'

Disastrously she heard that quip, turning to storm back at me.

'Daft imbecile TAIS-TOI!' Her eyes bulged. 'You have no leave to *speak* 'til the Devil dons fur underpants!'

An instant of silence prevailed. Yet that quip was too much for me. I burst into a fit of screaming laughter.

'Oh Madame, another rare morsel!' Ilaria glared in exasperation. 'I must remember that one too!' I glanced at Maxine. 'Sweetheart did you hear? The Devil in *fur* underpants!'

I was gasping for breath from laughing so hard.

Yet in sympathetic frustration, Maxine had pressed her lips, gripped Thibault to secure him, then with a scowl WHACK! In stout rebuke, her hand smacked the back of my head once again. Instantly then, just to settle little Thibault, her scowl returned to a smile.

Ilaria inhaled, swelling her chest as if it may burst, looking for all the world as if she would still strike me for good measure. But her open hand became a pointed finger.

'If I hear another sound behind me issue from any but *Figara* —'

The pretty little thing gurgled at the sound of her name. It broke Ilaria's concentration of course. She smiled on my little bundle, leaning to kiss her forehead, but then scowled at me again.

'Now *give* that babe to me.' She took Figara gingerly, yet hissed a final warning. 'Next time imbecile, you will not have Figara to *shield* you.'

Aurelie squinted over Ilaria's shoulder in mock scorn, or so I thought. Then Ilaria turned on her heel again to walk on, and both women began to gurgle at her new bundle.

As I watched them go I had an instinct to retort of course, yet I held my tongue. Ilaria had often threatened to strike me to impose order. Thus far, she hadn't been able to bring herself to do it.

A moment later, Casper halted with Fabrizio before the mouth of the bustling piazza. Ilaria and Aurelie were also halted but still doted on Figara. The giant stood scanning for trouble, though most passing in and out kept their distance at the sight of him. Some appeared to be attempting to discern who the monolith served.

I glanced ahead. Aurelie stood in deeper contemplation for a moment. She glanced at Ilaria. Ilaria turned to offer Figara to Maxine.

'Maxine please take Figara. Let me have my little Thibault. Lee Lee look at my little hero.' She smiled at Aurelie who remained sober-faced. 'I've been thinking perhaps I should feed him myself. The Church now looks *favourably* on it.'

Aurelie's eyes opened wide. Without a word, she reached and

drew Thibault from Ilaria, smiled at him, then handed him back to Maxine.

Ilaria's brows were knit in confusion.

'Armand!' Aurelie called. 'Before we go in, give me a moment with your lovely wife!'

'Be warned Armand!' said Sabatino. 'A *moment* to Aurelie will become an *age!*'

'Of course little sister.' Armand kissed her forehead. 'But I warn you both, my stomach is grumbling and so ...'

Aurelie squinted above a peevish smile and took Ilaria's arm to draw her aside.

'Ria will you summon Maxine and Marcel to us.'

'Oh. Yes of course if you wish.'

'Yet before you do darling, may I have your permission to chastise them.'

'To ...?'

'I would never do so without your permission.'

Ilaria hesitated. 'Lee Lee the last time I offered another woman that power ...'

'Yes I know. But Esme tricked you into giving it and sought to belittle you. I'm asking this time. And I think you know I only have your interest at heart.'

'Very well. But promise me —'

'No promises yet darling. But trust me. I hope you feel you can do so.

'I think you know I do.'

'Perfecto. Just a *tiny* but vital lesson for both in the performance of their duty.'

'I ... *very* well.'

'And just to confirm. At present you would say they are your two *closest* confidantes?

'Maxine certainly. Marcel? Of our men, other than Armand? Hmmm ... yes he is.'

'Even if he's not Ria, they're married now. And so what's said to *one* is said to *both*.'

'I'm sure that's true in their case.'

'Excluding one's husband darling, a prima donna needs two confidantes they can absolutely count on. One of either sex if possible. You have a matched pair who *may* do exceedingly well. However they still need some schooling. One in particular. Call them.'

'Marcel! Maxine!'

We approached innocently of course, expecting a banal request of further service. We were both surprised when Donna Cortellani began to address us.

'Maxine. Marcel. Ilaria's kindly given me her permission to *advise* you both.'

'Certainly Madame.' said Maxine with a smile.

'At your service Madame.' I bowed rather antically.

Aurelie's eyes began to simmer with intent. She turned to Maxine and the tone that responded was unexpectedly foreboding.

'Certainly *Madonna*.' Aurelie said quietly.

Maxine needed no more to sober her intent. Suddenly it felt as if the prima donna of Montecchi was looming before her again. That encounter had been a bitter lesson.

'Yes Madonna.' Maxine replied, lowering her eyes and dipping in a curtsy.

The prima donna turned her eyes on me.

'Madonna.' I said, dipping my own head to be cautious and bowing more sedately.

'That's better. Now Ilaria and I are going to talk *in* your presence. What we will say is *confidential.* But at present you are her closest *confidantes.*'

I was bewildered to hear her say so.

'Are we Madonna?' I asked cautiously.

'Yes, for the moment. Both of you. An elite woman needs confidantes she can utterly rely upon to stand as her witnesses to the interactions she transacts with all, private and public, personal and business, including her own *husband* or even a lover.'

Our eyes bulged to hear the last. Ilaria's did too.

'Does she?' I asked even more cautiously.

'She does. Moreover she needs a woman and man because in some settings, only *one* sex will be allowed to attend and in some situations only one confidante *available*.'

'Then perhaps there should be three?' I offered.

'Or more. Yet two is the minimum however. And we're starting with you both. And so from this moment, Ilaria and I will begin to observe you both and consider if, for the sake of her future, you will remain as her trusted duet. Do you both understand?'

With those words, it felt as if our entire future for continuing employment hung in the balance.

'Yes Madonna.' Maxine replied soberly.

'Yes Madonna.' I smiled.

Aurelie's brows furrowed. 'Does that sound *humorous* to you Marcel?'

'Ah ... no Madonna.' I stuttered. 'My smile's instinctive. Even when I'm fearful.'

'Then *wipe* it off your *face* man.' she hissed.

An open palm flashed to the right of my eyes. SMACK! It burst hard upon my cheek.

Maxine gasped and jolted, clutching Thibault and clamping her hand to her mouth. I stood in complete shock, staring dumbfounded at the woman who'd struck me.

'Take your eyes *off* me!' she spat.

Her bright blue eyes were blazing in anger.

Instantly my own eyes met the ground.

'I understand you're paid to entertain. I understand the need for you to *smile* frequently for that purpose. But now the premiere dame of Capulet needs far *more* from you. Do you understand me Marcel?'

'I ... I think so ... Madonna.'

'That won't be good enough from this moment forward man. Not if you wish to stay in her employ. And let me warn you. If one must go ... both will go.'

I glanced at Maxine. The look of dread in her eyes frightened me.

'Yes Madonna. I understand. I do.'

'That's better. Now ... as her entertainer, for much of the time when in company, she will expect you to be noisy and distracting. But there will be other moments when Ilaria will need you to be *sober* and attentive in a different way. This is *just* such a moment. Do you see?'

'Now I do Madonna. Yes.'

'She will expect you to show the ability to switch between both in an instant Marcel. To turn them *on* and *off* for her like a *tap* to a barrel. Is that clear?'

'Yes Madonna.'

'However, Ilaria is a fair woman. She may expect a lover to read her mind and mood without words. Yet Heaven knows *you* won't be capable of it. You'll need to share a *code* to know when to turn the tap one way or the other.'

I squinted in confusion yet dared not look up.

'A *code* Madonna?'

'Yes. Let me see.' She glanced at Ilaria. 'Yes I have it. If Ilaria refers to you with a smile as her *musician* or *fool* or *rascal* – you'll know you have permission to *act* like one. But if she refers to you soberly by name as *Marcel* you only have permission to be soberly attentive. Do you understand?

'Yes Madonna.'

'And now listen very closely. For if at any time Ilaria refers to you as Marcel, but you continue to play the fool or rascal *against* her need ... you will be severely *punished*.

'Oh I see.'

'You will soon Marcel. Because as we resume now, any punishment required to rein you in will not be imposed on *you*. It will be imposed upon your *wife*.'

'But Madonna –' I stuttered.

Her brows lifted high in mock surprise. 'But what, Marcel? That doesn't sound fair to you?'

'Well ... *no* Madonna.' I dared.

'Nor is the treatment I just witnessed you offering your *own* mistress in public.'

'Well I ...'

Suddenly the hand flashed again. SMACK! Foully and with far more spite, she smacked sweet Maxine hard against her cheek.

'Oh dear mercy!' I squealed '*Please* Madonna. Please *don't* hit her.'

'*Stai zitto* Marcel!' she hissed at me. 'You were about to challenge my resolve after I warned you what the consequence would be. I'm a prima donna. A prima donna says what she means and does what she says. Will you ever doubt that again?'

'No Madonna.'

'Oh no you impudent scoundrel. Now you'll address me as *prima donna*.'

'Yes Prima Donna.'

'And now that you understand, I'm sure you'll agree, Ilaria shouldn't need to *raise* her voice or repeat herself to gain your utmost attention?'

'No Prima Donna. No Madame. I'm so very sorry.'

'Does Maxine still need to fear your insatiable compulsion to ignore your mistress and talk back to her?'

'No Prima Donna. Not at all.'

'And so from this moment, when you hear Ilaria call you Marcel, or issue a directive for you to *shut your mouth?*'

'I'll shut my mouth ... Prima Donna. *Instantly.*'

She hung for a moment, looking unconvinced, perhaps just to punctuate her resolve.

'Marcel. Maxine. You're now man and wife. For better or worse, you must share everything. And so Marcel, at least for now, every transgression you make will be paid for by her.' Aurelie turned to Maxine and cupped her cheek. 'I'm sorry Maxine. I didn't want to hurt you darling. But I can see the manner of man he's becoming. That must be nipped in the bud. And until he's trained properly, I'm certain no other remedy will make an impression.'

'Yes Prima Donna.' Maxine said quietly.

'Do you *agree?*'

'Yes ... I agree Prima Donna.'

'Oh no you may call me Madonna. Only he may not.'

Ilaria was frowning with concern.

'Oh Ria don't fret. It seems a harsh method but it's very common here. Sab was subjected to it himself in his training as a squire.'

'I've heard Armand mention it. The transgression of one is paid for by all?'

'Precisely. And it works just as well for a pair as a posse. Now you two, we're going to enter that market. Yet before we do, Ilaria and I shall agree on a few important points of order. As her confidantes, who may be called at a later time to recall exactly what was discussed or agreed, you must both listen carefully.'

'Yes Madonna.'

'Yes Prima Donna.'

'You're about to learn a little of what she'll require of you from this moment forward. Thereafter, neither of you will have the excuse to say you've misunderstood.'

Aurelie turned with the sweetest of smiles and took Ilaria's hands. 'Now Ria, let's return to where we left off. You suggested feeding Thibault *yourself*.'

'Oh. Yes I did. Friar Lorenzo said —'

'I know darling.' Aurelie interrupted. 'You mentioned that the Church *advised*?'

'Well yes. He says it's now *encouraged* —'

'Yes one moment it's encouraged Ria, one moment it's not. Their advisements change like the wind. Now I know lanky Lorenzo is charming, but he lacks a vagina.'

Ilaria blinked in confusion. I wanted to smile.

'I expect that's true.'

'It is darling. And like all who lack a vagina, particularly men of the *cloth*, despite all their Holiness they're much too naïve in *certain* areas of a woman's life to dictate to you and I.'

'If you say so.'

'I do darling. Take it from me Ria, if a woman has the means, and you do, she doesn't want to damage her breasts for the sake of such *misguided* advisements offered by holy men. Why do you think we hire wet nurses?'

'Well ...'

'To spare the burden of tending and toting? Yes, that convenience is worth something darling, but it's not all there is to it. Isn't that right, Maxine?'

'Why ... yes Madonna.' Maxine was unexpectedly pressed to consider the notion more objectively.

'Thank Heaven we can afford the support to save us that effort. And yes he's a cute bambino. I know it's hard to resist that face. But Ria if you multiply the abuse of his little mouth sucking on each nipple by days, weeks and months.'

'But I really don't —'

'Then multiply that damage by two or three or seven children? Well Heavens darling, you're a merchant, calculate the benefit against the loss. Yes, I understand the urge with your first. I do. But you must resist it. Maxine will help to do so, won't you?'

'Yes Madonna?'

'But Aurelie, I *do* feel the urge to feed him.'

'I know Ria I felt the same. Alone among strangers at sixteen with a child in my arms, no close kin to guide me.'

'Oh that must have been *vexatious*.' Ilaria's eyes became distant. 'In truth, I expected to be back in Lyon for my first, with maman to guide me.'

Their eyes met. Tears began to well in Ilaria's eyes. Aurelie hugged her and drew a soft linen from her wrist.

'Ria you're my new little sister! I love you because my oafish brother loves you so completely and because you're so lovable.' They hugged impetuously. 'Oh it's so good to have Armand and Tristan here with you. They make me feel safe.'

'Lee Lee despite all that's happened, I'm so glad we came. I'm so glad I've met you.'

'Darling I won't lie. I desperately want you to *stay* in Verona. But that's a choice you must make for yourself. For the moment however, until you decide, let me be your guide for this and that.'

'Yes. Yes I would love that.'

I was glad to hear Ilaria sound so reassured of course. Yet, given the treatment Maxine and I had just met, it didn't sound as if we would love the manner of it quite so much.

'Oh I can't tell you darling. I'm just so happy to have a friend from home within reach. But let's continue. Now that you have a child to tote in public, let's agree on some clever rules before we enter the market.'

'Yes Lee Lee proceed.'

'While you're in public or engaged socially, ensure Maxine understands to keep Thibault in *her* care. She may *not* pass him to you unless you request it directly.'

Ilaria glanced at Maxine. 'You understand?'

'Yes Madonna.'

'Maxine. Marcel.' Aurelie continued. 'In public to your mistress it will be *yes Madame*. To citizens in Verona, she's still very exotic. That title increases her charisma. Help her to make good use of it.'

'Yes Madonna.' said Maxine. 'And yes Madame.'

'And Ria you must instruct Maxine ... oh fiddlesticks.' She turned to her directly. 'When in public, even if Thibault's not hungry, keep him at your breast.'

'Yes Madonna.'

Ilaria knit her brows in confusion.

'Ria you must make a *show* of being able to afford a wet nurse. You don't want those we meet to mistake her for a dry nurse. One's far more expensive than the other.'

'I'm glad you warned me. I don't think I'd have —'

'Trust me, you must. It's *all* for show but worth it. Like my fancy new carriage, our garments, jewels, nails and lips. Even your servants attire flaunting your crest, that *giant* henchman and *yes*, even this babbling musician or fool, or whatever he styles himself to be.'

I smiled again yet still didn't dare to look upward.

'They're all wonderful showpieces.'

'Yes. I agree.'

'Marcel look at me.' Aurelie ordered.

I lifted my eyes. She held my face with her hands.

'I like you despite your faults. Indeed I wish you were mine. So will many others. You're valuable to my new sister. But Ria you must use him — use *all* of them — more productively. Display them more appropriately.'

'You have suggestions?'

'I do. Just to get you started. Thereafter I'm sure your own instincts will guide you more securely than mine. But to begin. Here in the citadel Caspar must be seen in shining armour and fine leather. And Marcel must be *forbidden* to nurse his bambino.'

I opened my mouth to object but Ilaria saved me.

'Why that?'

'Darling you have a personal entertainer. He's a *very* great symbol of your status to show. Heaven knows *we* don't have one. I'm still not sure how you manage to keep him, but everyone we meet must know *why* he accompanies you *and* that he's yours!'

Ilaria glanced and rolled her eyes. 'Hmm. Yes I see.

'As we browse in this setting, to allow him to draw attention to yourself by drawing attention to himself, he must remain unencumbered. He should be singing, playing or juggling plums darling, cradling his lute not his daughter!'

Maxine felt hurt to hear her say so and showed it.

'Oh *yes* Maxine' Aurelie said soothingly 'I know she's adorable. And she has *your* beautiful eyes. Let's hope she doesn't have *his* mind.'

Maxine smirked. So did Aurelie. Even I smiled.

'Dear me.' said Ilaria soberly. 'I hadn't considered any of these things.'

'Consider them *now*. And Ria you *must* dress Marcel more richly and colourfully to fit him to his part. Just as our local *jongleurs* do. Well rogue? Would you like that?'

'I think I would ... Prima Donna.'

'Whether you would or not, you shall. Ria if he leaves the right impression, and I feel certain he will, many will invite you to social engagements just to have him perform in their circuit. He's a talented musician. And he's amusing when you're not too busy *scolding* him.'

Ilaria glanced around to consider it all.

'Yes. Yes I see.'

I was also beginning to see. The prima donna's tutorial was opening my eyes to my role in Ilaria's life.

'Now, after we enter this lively place we will meet many people who may help or hinder your path ... *our* path ahead.' That made Ilaria smile. 'They must see the Capulets as a couple who can play the game and know all its rules.'

'The game?'

'The *exalted* game darling. In Italy, just to be counted among its players at the very lowest level, a woman must either be a prima donna herself —'

'Or a premiere dame?'

'Yes. Or endear herself to a countess, duchess or queen or, if that's not possible, become the lover of —'

'A count, a duke or a king?'

'That last is not for us of course, but yes. And some will play it that way however, that strategy is fraught with great risk upon both sides.'

'Both sides?'

'A lover if his target spurns him.' Aurelie's brows lifted. 'A wife who doesn't know when to call an end.'

'Yet that won't be our folly to fear.'

'No darling. But we'll meet all manner of players, including such men and women, and need to deal with all. But first things are first. Our prima goal is to be noticed by those above us. The next is to ascend by acquaintance without, if humanly possible, giving offence as we go.'

'I see.'

'But Ria *patience* in the game, not *haste*, is the key. And I must warn you darling that here in Verona, it's played with more gusto and guile, than back in Lyon.'

'Lee Lee I must ask your opinion.'

'Yes what is it?'

'Need one ... play at all?'

'Darling no-one's obliged to. One may choose to remain aloof, keep to one's own.'

'However?'

'However a prima donna or premiere dame is expected to *grow* her faction's fortune. Great rewards aren't reaped by hiding in comfortable corners or cuddling on top of pretty hills for a lifetime.'

'It's peaceful on our pretty hill at present.'

'Ilaria de Capulet if that's who you want to be? Then darling so be it. Don't let me stop you. Don't let me start you. I am who I am. You need to decide who you will be.'

'I think I made that decision on the day we arrived when I encouraged Armand, so relentlessly, to approach the gates of Sycamore Hill.'

'Yes. I believe you did. And look what you've already gained from it. But Ria I warn you one last time, this game is not for the faint-hearted.'

Ilaria grinned. 'Ah but now, if I'm willing, I have an *experienced* player to guide me.'

'You do. And so. Shall we venture in together?'

'But shouldn't we conference with Armand before?'

'Tush Ria. I love my big brother but he's a *man*. It's our responsibility to prepare the elements needed to play. If he questions what we're doing, we simply demand these conditions as our prerogative. If he doesn't want Caspar to wear shining armour, you insist that he *must*. And no matter how resistant he may be Ria, *don't* relent until he complies.'

'But —' Ilaria began.

'Enough chatter Aurelie!' An impulsive arm drew Ilaria away. 'My stomach's not grumbling it's screaming!'

'Yes mighty Signore!' Aurelie mocked and curtsied. 'We come at your bidding, mighty Signore!' She lifted to reveal a petulant tongue poking between her lips.

Armand rolled his eyes with impatience.

Sabatino wagged his head in resignation. Aurelie's gesture reminded Ilaria of when she was a girl in the cathedral in Lyon exchanging a similar reaction to Armand as a grinning boy. The thought was endearing and caused her even more sincerely to count the blessing of having this new big sister by her side.

As Armand drew away, assuming they would follow, Aurelie unexpectedly cupped Ilaria's face in her hands and drew their heads together.

'One very last thing' she purred.

'Yes.'

'As for the Holy advisings of our church where this conference began?'

'Yes.'

'Just remember, such restrictions are preached to curb the excesses of the *many*.'

'Why yes and so?'

'And so Ilaria de Capulet ... you and I are *not* among the many. We're among the *few*.'

Her blue eyes blazed. She turned Ilaria's face.

'Look at your husband, your people. For pity's sake Ria look at yourself. Consider how all reacted to you in the cathedral this morning. Marcel, Maxine what did you hear?'

'It's true Madame.' I whispered. 'You and the master were on the lips of all.'

'Maxine?'

'Not a soul high or low in my hearing spoke of anything but the Capulets.'

'You must acknowledge who you *are* darling. And if you play the game right ...'

'The exalted game.'

'... who you may become.'

Aurelie could tell her effort was stirring the pot. She had intended this conference to be intimate and shocking, to stir Ilaria's blood and make her feel that in Verona, with her help, anything may be possible. I believe she feared she had little time left to do so and had decided to hold nothing back.

I couldn't help but notice how alike in some ways the prima

donna and duchess were beginning to sound. Yet they were not completely alike.

'Lee Lee it's been months since anyone has spoken to me this way.' Ilaria confided.

'You've been gone from Lyon since late last spring.'

'Before we married, I had Countess de Viviers and my maman to guide me. I realise now that I've wanted for such counsel since we left Lyon.'

'I know what that feels like.'

'Yes. Now I know that you do. After the trial Yolanthe spoke to me in a similar fashion. But as yet, I don't feel as if I can truly count on her as a friend.'

'No Ria not yet. But you have me now. And you'll always have me.'

'Oh I'm so glad to have you with me ... big sister.'

They embraced fondly.

Aurelie looped her arm and turned them together.

'And now for the first time since giving birth to her son and heir, the premiere dame of Capulet is about to re-enter the social fray.'

'Yes I am.'

'Are you ready to play little sister?'

'Lead the way big sister.'

'Let's see who fate has waiting for us inside.'

Chapter 12 Escalus & Florentia

Once reassembled, we stood ready to enter the bustling piazza. Armand signalled to Caspar and our guardians closed ranks, fore and aft, as our giant led us in. From the experience I had just endured, I felt sure that, if not this very day then sometime soon, something momentous would affect our lives. I won't say it was a premonition. That manner of mystic thing seemed to be the provenance of Ilaria's imagination. I will say however that a strong feeling of fated purpose was surging through me.

I glanced up. The civic tower's belfry hung high above the square. Incredibly at that moment, the sight of it caused me to recall a moment of premonition that Ilaria and I had shared after the Ceremony of Disgrace. You recall as we stood on the balcony together, how the Squire's foot broke through the ladder? He was hanging a wooden cross to replace the Montecchi trophies he removed from the wall.

Some scarlet and green ribbons had been hanging above it, remnants from Montecchi victories in the foot and horseraces. As the squire had tilted that cross, it unsettled those silken shards which fell and caught round the neck of the crucifix. Just at that moment, this same civic bell tower, heard by us in the distance, had chimed the strike of one.

And now, just moments after entering Herb Market Square I felt that surging sensation as I looked up and saw the tower and thought of that eerie moment. It unsettled me. It was not yet near the hour of one. Indeed, we hadn't yet heard the bell strike ten. And though Ilaria and I had both come to dread such portents, we had agreed that previous moment was an omen of future *success* rather than *strife*.

By now we all knew Ilaria had received her second message from the duchess, setting a time limit on her final decision. As we entered that piazza however, what no-one else realised, not even Armand, was that after Thibault was baptised a second message had also arrived for

Ilaria from Lyon. It came from her parents, a sequel to her own prior note to them declaring that their grandson had been born.

In her parent's earlier note, they had actually urged Ilaria to consider the prospect of *remaining* in Verona. This second message began by declaring their thirst for more news regarding the health of their grandson, yes, but it also carried a postscript. They requested Ilaria to discreetly — and as quickly as possible — to pursue an item of merchant interest in Verona citadel which had come to their attention.

What none of us yet realised was that her mother's call to action was the real reason Ilaria had insisted upon attending mass at the cathedral, rather than Friar Lorenzo's Church on the riverbank. Oh yes, she told Armand the letter had come. Yes, she divulged *most* of its gushing contents to him yet not *every* detail. She wanted the rest to be a surprise.

To the point of the matter, that *interesting prospect* they mentioned had been drawn to her parent's attention by a merchant from Verona who frequently visited Lyon. That reliable man divulged that a location in Verona citadel — which seemed well suited for the conduct of their trade — may now be available to *acquire*. In short, it was a prospective site for a fabric emporium that may be even larger than their current holding in Lyon. Cupid's Balls!

No, I didn't say that at the time because I didn't even know myself. Moreover, that reliable man had revealed that the site stood right in the heart of the citadel. And so, Ilaria's parents explained, no matter if she and Armand eventually decided to stay or return — given they now planned to remain a little longer — they would be pleased if Ilaria would enquire after the terms of its purchase — or lease — on behalf of their own interest or else for the interest of herself and Armand.

Oh no, the request didn't stop there. If their darling daughter assessed the prospect to be viable, could she then return a report as quickly as possible to allow them to act upon that interest in good time?

The note concluded by counselling Ilaria she should not consider the matter to be *urgent*. Nor should she behave in any way, to the location's representative, as if the matter *appeared* to be urgent.

Darling, if by the time you manage to make a fulsome enquiry, the chance to take advantage of the opportunity is found to be passed, consider it no matter at all. We may surely discover another prospective site at a later time, perhaps in a citadel much closer to Lyon.

Yet despite that reassurance they also intimated:

Pristine locations in markets such as Verona do present as something of a rarity. If the site in question appears sound and the chance were missed, to find another so well-suited and located may take some time to discover.

Hmm. When I heard about that letter — oh yes I sneaked a look at it — I felt their first insistence, that missing the chance *would be no matter*, followed so quickly by a warning that it may prove a *rarity not to be missed*, were two statements clearly at odds with each other. Indeed during my life I've discovered that, when people — even elite people — wish to buy or sell something of importance, they often struggle to make up their minds.

Finally, to explain why Ilaria was so secretive in the matter, her mother had suggested she should hold the matter close until she was in a position to know whether or not to secure it. And as fate would have it, that prospective site was located in Herb Market Square! And now the fearsome Donna Cortellani and the enterprising Dame Capulet had locked arms with their husbands to enter that location.

Ilaria knew full well it stood at the further end of the piazza. And by the time she found herself being drawn by the vitality swirling about them, she felt certain Armand's absurd notion of entering the footrace had been quashed.

Maxine and I were following in their wake, now under strict instructions how to behave in support of Ilaria's need.

And as harsh as that lesson had seemed, I began to respect how clever Aurelie was in her method. She had ensured that, beyond an insistence for our obedience, Maxine and I now felt as if we were far more important than mere servers. She explained something of the goals both women hoped to pursue for their futures. It was not *blind* obedience she asked of us, it was *sighted* obedience.

What wasn't in my sight or Maxine's however, was Ilaria's hidden agenda. And so with her new mentor following behind, in an effort to remain unsuspected, Ilaria took her time to enjoy the lively atmosphere. It was Sunday, after all. Her secretive goal could wait for an hour or two.

Perhaps more importantly, once in that square Ilaria hoped to show Aurelie just how well she could adapt to becoming a player in *the exalted game*. It was clear from their conference the thought of it sparked Aurelie greatly. The prima donna was hard but fair and undoubtedly ambitious to excel in her duty as matriarch to her faction.

I saw Ilaria glancing at Sabatino and Aurelie, who appeared so happy and in such command of their lives. I could tell she hoped her future could be like theirs and it made me consider Ilaria myself. On her wedding night Armand's parents had insisted she would need strength and ambition for the tasks that lay ahead. Clearly the duchess felt the same. Clearly that woman played the game with gusto and guile, marching without fear into Rome itself to pursue exalted connections for her faction to mine.

This morning was Ilaria's chance to make a true start of her own. With the prize of Sycamore Hill in their possession ,and an alliance with the duchess still able to be secured, Ilaria felt as if their play in the game had already begun. Now it was time — with Aurelie's firm guidance and perhaps Yolanthe's too — for Ilaria de Capulet to become a formidable player.

Indeed I was excited for my own future too. Oh yes, my cheek still smarted from the slap I'd received. Yes, Maxine still glared at me for the hurt she suffered on my account. Indeed as we entered, her face still wore the livid welt from that blow for all to see. I knew my own swarthy skin wouldn't show mine so obviously.

Yet I wondered if Aurelie had intended for that evidence on Maxine's face to be visible as we made entry. Any who saw that mark on her snow white cheek now — and realised she served the exotic French stranger — would instantly assume her own mistress put it there. Hmm?

I didn't wonder for long however, for the vision that met our eyes within the bustling piazza was a delirium of distracting colours, sounds and aromas. Fresh exotic herbs, spices and late winter fruit all lay before us, interspersed with flowers and food to sample. That melting pot had lured a throng of colourful people who seemed to populate every echelon of our world from the privileged to the privated.

Among the latter were a smattering of slaves. Since our experience in Venice I noticed slaves more acutely. And try as they might to remain unnoticed, the doleful looks of obedience many wore, like tragic drama masks, made me notice them even more. Now I felt as if I understood a little more of the hidden torment that lay behind such looks. No I can't say I understood much, but it was a beginning.

And now that sweet Verona was controlled by the mighty port of Venice, it was swelling with more slaves than one would ever see in a French citadel like Lyon. Most were light-skinned pagans of course — Celtic, Nordic, Slavic — the bounty of violent Christian conquests to the north-east and north. Some were darker skinned — Grecian, Arabic, African. Those were Moslem captives from martial conquests or else kidnapped by slavers from unprotected villages that lay along the southern shores of the Black Sea or Mediterranean.

All the slaves I noticed that day were either in service to merchants — selling, guarding, fetching, carrying — or following close to their masters to attend to the whims of the browsing elite. And despite the Church now imploring local donnas to feed from their own breast or use local women for that service, many of the wet nurses we saw were slaves. Suddenly I spied one young man, clearly a slave, who appeared so morose that it made me stare forlornly.

'Smarten up lively man!' hissed Maxine to me. 'You look much to dour to entertain anyone.'

'Yes sweetheart. It's just that, since Venice, the sight of slaves is very ... distracting.'

'*You* are meant to be distracting. Shall I have taken that punishment for naught?'

'Oh. Oh I'm so sorry.'

'Be less sorry and more entertaining. You know what she wants. You heard what's at stake now for both of us ... and for our daughter.'

'Yes. I know.

'Well then know this foolish man. That no matter what happens to us ... I love you.'

'Do you?'

'Oh *tais-toi* and get to it my love. Play or sing or pilfer some fruit and start juggling.'

I kissed Figara and Maxine, then left her side to forage for an opportunity. I felt whatever it was that I may do next should occur close enough to Ilaria to draw attention to her! She and Aurelie had separated from their husbands and were browsing together, finding great distraction among the faces, fashions and fare. Warm nuts and wine abounded for indulgence on a cool winter's day. I sidled past that distracted duet as they stopped at a seller's stall.

Browsing ahead, I halted for a moment to bask in a shard of warm winter sunshine. We had begun to appreciate that winter in Verona was less chilling than winter in Lyon. I glanced about to check on Maxine. In adherence to Aurelie's command, she kept Thibault at her breast to give the impression he fed. She also held close to Ilaria, who turned now and then to touch Thibault's cheek and ensure that all understood which mistress his wet nurse served.

All at once, it became like a game to me, an imposturous charade for the sake of decadent show. And to allow me to wander, poor Maxine also held Figara. Yet Fabrizio now followed her close in case she needed relief from toting a double burden. I wondered who insisted on his presence to do so. I guessed it was Ilaria. But the sight of my wife being so dutiful made me mindful of my own efforts.

I resolved to try harder. I must exercise my talent more vigorously to draw attention to myself and so to my employers. Hmm, gusto and guile? I had both to spare. And so I drew toward the centre of the long northern side of the market. I was hell-bent on doing something to make an impression, to please Ilaria. Yet she received more than a little shock to discover who fate had placed in my path to assist me — the Archbishop of Verona.

The venerable Holy man — now my target — was leaning over a bucket of fresh lilies which I assumed he was considering to purchase for the cathedral.

'Ah!' I all but screamed to interrupt him. 'Your Excellence!' His head turned, eyes blinking in confusion. 'Are you a *fool*?' I cried.

The exalted cleric straightened to glare at me.

'What say you fellow?' he whimpered.

He turned to a young Dominican attendant, who I discovered much later from Friar Lorenzo was the one I've previously referred to as *the shuffler*.

'Brother Simone who *is* this man? Do I know him?'

That stuttering brother struggled so greatly, I decided to save him from the effort.

'I'm Marcel Poquelin your Excellence. Though in exalted circles they call me *Marcel le Drole* and this morning I'm happily at your service.'

I bowed low and performed a tumbling trick with my hat. Exactly as I hoped, it set those around us gasping, ooh-ing and aah-ing.

'Moreover your Excellence, if you'll dare to allow it, I'm certain I can *prove* that you're a fool!'

Giggles and guffaws sounded about us. As our transaction began to bubble, Ilaria and Aurelie stood at the edge of the stall nearby, inspecting a tub that was brimmed with delphinium. Aurelie noticed me first. I was happy to note her smile of satisfaction as she gained Ilaria's attention. But as soon as Ilaria realised my predicament, she blinked and blanched to think how unwittingly she had unleashed her *imbecile* on such an important person.

Yet before she could move the archbishop responded.

'If I stay to hear more of your ranting fellow' he lisped 'you'll have proven me a fool!'

His rebuff to my challenge was music to my ears.

'Touche your Excellence!' I cried.

'Yes thank you, *shabby* man. Now move on.'

'It's *true* your Excellence.' My volume lifted to attract more attention. 'I'm *poor* in dress but *rich* in wit and I say you're a fool and can prove what I say!'

More giggling and muttering sounded at that.

In utter panic, Ilaria had turned in search of Armand and leapt to clutch his sleeve, insisting he rush in to call off *his* buffoon. Manly brows lifted and frowned. He drew forward in haste. Yet before he could arrive, and to Ilaria's great horror, an even more potent man emerged to intercede.

'Rascal!' snapped the archbishop. 'I was schooled in logic at the university in Bologna. If *we* match wits I shall *not* come off the worse. Now give *way* there vagabond.'

'Excellence are you *troubled?*' asked a deep manly voice right behind me.

The sound of him meant nothing to me. Yet as I turned, the sight of him meant a great deal. To my perverse delight, there stood Prince Escalus flanked by a brace of burly guardsman. Cupid's Balls! My eyes lit up. To have drawn such a valuable addition to my audience was beyond all expectation. Surely that hard slapping prima donna would be pleased with me now.

'Ah! Your Highness' I cried loudly hoping that declaration would draw more eyes. And so it did.

I bowed low and extravagantly, repeating my trick of rolling my headpiece along my arm. Yet this time, instead of returning it to my head, my catching hand flipped it over my back to catch with my head then I repeated the manoeuvre instantly along the other arm! Oh my sweet friends I swear, I was in rare form and ready for anything!

Loud oohs and aahs and commentary erupted.

'Your Highness!' I cried. 'I fear his Excellence is not so much *troubled.* Yet he does stand in *very grave* danger!'

The loaded comment caused the prince's brow to knit with alert. 'Danger man?' He glowered. 'Say what you know at *once!*'

Armand arrived to glower at me too.

'Very grave danger your Highness of allowing me here, before all and sundry, to prove he's an inveterate fool.'

Suddenly the concern on his princely face relaxed.

'And, exalted Prince, if you wish me to do so I'd be delighted to prove the very same of yourself!'

Open laughter lifted around us.

The prince tilted his eyes to Heaven and shook his mighty head then stared. 'Hmm. I think I may have more *potent* matters to attend.' He relaxed his frown and also his hand from the hilt of the shining dagger at his hip.

'Ah mighty prince' I ran on 'the *greater* a man's potence, the *more* foolish he may prove to be.'

Escalus pouted and frowned then looked about him. 'Who *is* this … man?' he demanded.

I opened my mouth to introduce myself again.

'Pardonnez-moi your Highness.' Armand pleaded.

'Ah. Chevalier Capulet yes?'

'Yes your Highness.'

'Well met Chevalier and buon giorno.'

Armand made to bow but Escalus offered his hand in a show of great deference.

From a short distance, greatly relieved to see him arrive to make amends for my folly, Ilaria and Aurelie closed in to watch. As they did so, Escalus flitted a glance to mark them with a warm, welcoming smile. All at once, beyond my wildest expectations, Aurelie and Ilaria were smiling at the Prince.

'What did I tell you!' whispered Aurelie. 'Let the knave run amok to do his work, already your husband is shaking hands with my secret lover.'

'*He*'s your lover?' Ilaria's eyes bulged.

'Oh, he just doesn't know it of course.'

Ilaria eyes rolled. She gripped Aurelie's hand and drove forward as our commotion drew the dawdling Sabatino and Tristan in to join us.

'Signore' bleated the Archbishop 'is this rascal in *your* service?'

His Highness, realising Armand and the archbishop had not been introduced, obliged.

'Chevalier Capulet, allow me to introduce his Excellence Matteo, Archbishop of Verona.'

The hand and ring of that Holy man were offered.

'Your Excellence.' He genuflected to kiss and rose. 'I am Armand de Capulet at your service. And yes this troublesome rogue is my ... *jongleur*.'

'Ah Chevalier Capulet! Of course I should have recognised you. And you have a jongleur? That's impressive. And so he sings?'

'Sings and plays virtually anything Excellence. Indeed he's very talented, if I may say so on his behalf.'

I smiled and bowed low.

'Chevalier may I officially bid you *welcome* to Verona. I'm so sorry your arrival sparked a series of ... unfortunate events. But now we may put those behind us.'

Escalus reached a hand for Armand's shoulder.

'I *saw* your giant stalking the piazza.'

Ilaria sidled in to take Armand by the arm as Aurelie, eyes glinting with interest, hung at her shoulder expectantly.

'Ah.' Aurelie whispered with a malicious smile. 'Both Caspar and Marcel drew in my lover's attention!'

Ilaria's eyes widened, yet she could hardly believe how right Aurelie had been.

'A *very* reliable man Highness.' Armand replied. 'Caspar is our trusty shadow.'

Escalus lifted a brow. 'And still a *reasonable* precaution. You're looking hale since your ... incident.'

'Thank you for saying so. I feel greatly recovered. Hearty and hale.' He turned toward Ilaria who waited expectantly. 'I don't believe you've met my wife Ilaria.'

'Sadly no, I've not yet met la bella Donna Capulet. I've seen her of course. We've all admired her from afar and Ilaria is such a lovely name. It's wonderful to meet you.'

I grinned a smile of pride to hear such a warm salutation offered by the Prince. Before Ilaria could even curtsy, the broad hands of Escalus extended to her shoulders.

'Ah no, no, no. Such a gracious woman must not be made to bow. Not even to a prince.'

He leaned to kiss her thrice. Ilaria was overwhelmed with the amicability of his greeting. Despite the gathering public gaze on their meeting, the ease of his manner put her at ease and made Aurelie behind her glow warm with envy.

'You flatter me your Highness.'

Ilaria's green eyes held the prince's gaze firmly as the archbishop's eyes lit up.

'Ah Highness do you *hear* it?' he asked. 'No matter whose tongue they speak, the French have such a lyrical tone. Handsome to see, beautiful to hear. You're *both* so very welcome to Verona.'

Since meeting the duchess, this was the second time I had heard Ilaria and Armand praised in such honeyed terms. I began to wonder if the licence to extend such bald flattery among the exalted was the norm in Italy. Or was it just the effect this unusual couple had among them?

Unseen by anyone else, a gently jabbing finger from Aurelie was probing Ilaria's lower back.

'Your Highness.' Ilaria turned, drawing her forward. 'May I introduce my sister-in-law Aurelie?'

'The bella prima donna of Cortellani? Though we've not met formally either Aurelie, I feel I know you already.'

Before she could curtsy Escalus put his hands to her shoulders also and kissed Aurelie thrice. I felt sure she would faint as she had promised to do if she saw him run naked. Yet somehow, she managed to save from buckling before he released her and raised his brows in recognition of Sabatino behind.

'However ... your *much* respected husband I have met before. Well met Sabatino. How are you man?'

Sabatino drew forward with a smile to embrace the prince warmly. Aurelie drew close in beside him.

The two men were of an age and similar in height. Sabatino was more lithe and Escalus more robust, both more than ten years senior to Armand's twenty-one and behaved with the ease of worldly men. Aurelie had married a far more mature man than Ilaria. As I watched the prince and Sabatino with her beside them, I wondered if Aurelie's match caused her to develop a preference for such company?

'And last but not least Highness' Armand continued 'may I introduce my brother?' Tristan stepped forward. 'Chevalier Tristan de Capulet.'

Escalus offered his hand once more.

'Another French horseman!' Tristan smiled. 'Ah yes, I see the resemblance. Verona is officially invaded by the House of Capulet. Welcome Chevalier.'

'Thank you Highness.' Tristan replied. 'Yet I'm sure it would take more than a brace of Capulets to warrant any concern for Verona's Podestà.'

'Hmm.' Escalus lifted yet another thoughtful brow. 'Judging by your brother's capability ... I'm *not* so sure.'

Armand pressed his lips and glanced at the ground.

'I assure your Highness. We all come in *peace*.'

'I hope so Chevalier.' Escalus put in. It seemed his instinct to protect Verona was rising a little. 'However the Captain of our Militia did wonder at the identity of a *foreign* cavaliere who was reported to him, mounted upon an extraordinary golden courser with a dozen men at his back.'

'My stallion *Ajax* Highness. He turns more heads than I manage to do without him.'

'I was told he's a magnificent beast. When you bypassed the walls and vanished into the hills, Captain Lanza assumed you had all travelled on.'

'Soon after my *injury* Highness' Armand began to explain 'given our predicament, I sent to Lyon for assistance as a precaution against ... reprisal.'

'That was a *wise* precaution. And remains so 'til you're safely turned for home.'

'Madonna Aurelie.' said the archbishop.

'Your Excellence. May I say your homily this morning was inspiring.'

'Yes you may, and thank you. Yet may I ask? To this duet of chevaliers ... you are ...?'

'Their *sister* your Excellence. And though I'm the eldest sister and elder than Tristan' she glared at him 'they *both* still call me their *little* sister.'

Aurelie curtsied with a smile, playfully thrusting a finger into her cheek.

'But now I recall it. You wed Sabatino in *Lyon?*'

'Our home. Yes your Excellence.'

'And oh that's right, his dear father died before he could attend your marriage.'

'I never had the chance to meet him.'

'That was a great pity. But here you are now, an admired prima donna with three children to swell our flock. And more to come of course.' He winked patronisingly. 'We encourage all elite women to hold nothing back.'

'If Heaven wills it Excellence. And Heaven knows, I rarely hold anything back.'

Ilaria wore a knowing smirk. If only the archbishop had attended their conference half an hour before.

'And so Chevalier' the archbishop turned to Armand.

'Your Excellence.'

'You're no longer a glamorous pair of tourists. Now you possess a local estate which, correct me if I'm wrong, *borders* that lovely estate of your little sister?'

'It does your Excellence.'

'And so now you hold not only a valuable local asset, but have direct ties in marriage and blood to our citadel?'

It seemed for a moment, a suggestion was being made, a tacit but volatile suggestion, that perhaps not all which had fallen out, in that regard, was *incidental.*

'Correct on all counts.' Armand said soberly.

Ilaria glanced nervously. Even Escalus appeared surprised by the comment. Sabatino and Aurelie certainly were. Yet it was difficult to tell if the archbishop meant to imply so much, or was simply misunderstood. Yet even a ninny like myself began to wonder if that holy man may be a sly Montecchi advocate, hoping to revisit their accusation of *impropriety* after Verona's court had laid it all to rest.

'Your Excellence.' Ilaria began soberly. 'I hope you understand that our possession of Sycamore Hill was not *at all* by our design. It was a wholly unexpected twist of fate.'

'Just so.' the archbishop replied candidly.

'And so your Excellence' I dared to interrupt, fearing the antic atmosphere I'd created might soon come undone. 'By that design of *fate!* The Capulets are now *feted!*'

The archbishop smiled. 'Touché impertinent rascal!'

'Marcel!' Armand shot as if warning a hound to heel.

I mimed the stitching of my lips together, which drew a smile, then antically curled my uppermost lip against the tug of an invisible needle. A ripple of giggling sounded. I turned to show the trick to Ilaria, but met her blunt stare, and instantly desisted. In response to her response, the entire company then burst into laughter, including the archbishop.

Unwittingly in that moment, she acted as the perfect blunt foil to my buffoonery, making my antics appear timed to perfection.

'Ah Donna Capulet' said Escalus with a smile 'he may be a fool but it's clear he *knows* who he mustn't trifle with. I'm glad to see that you have him on a tight leash.'

'I do your Highness.' She glanced at Aurelie. 'Oh I most *certainly* do.'

Quietly I thanked Heaven for Aurelie's scolding. Suddenly I felt as if all that time I'd spent thwarting Ilaria's control of me — for the sake wanting to rant and rave *off* the leash — was just pure folly. The world must see that Ilaria had me on her leash. The world must know I belonged to her and would shut my mouth if she so much as glanced.

'But it's true what the rascal said' the archbishop continued 'you've become the talk of Verona.' Ilaria glanced at Aurelie again. 'And please Chevalier, next time you and your lovely wife attend our cathedral, you must do me the great honour of extending a personal greeting. It will make me the envy of all.'

'Of course your Excellence.' Armand replied.

'Even a man of the cloth' added the archbishop 'can yearn for the pleasure of discourse with such elegant feminine company.'

Aurelie's fingers pinched Ilaria's waist.

She leaned to whisper. 'Did he say *intercourse?*'

Ilaria prodded her back with a fingertip to desist, supressing the urge to laugh herself as the archbishop ran on.

'I'm not always at leisure after mass to stroll through the market. Next time I'd sorely miss the pleasure if I couldn't extend my welcome to you both.'

He glanced from Armand to Ilaria and back again.

Ilaria showed him a deprecating smile, though I could tell she was growing agitated by — what had become — his fawning attention.

'Oh your Excellence, that pleasure would be *ours.*'

Ilaria lied and smiled falsely. In truth I was staggered to hear her say so, for that was the very first time I ever heard Ilaria de Capulet wittingly lie to anyone's face. There was no doubt experience was shaping the way she was deciding to respond to the world, at least with regard to certain people in certain moments.

'However your Excellence' Ilaria added 'next Sunday Aurelie has promised to take us to a pretty convent church at the foot of the little mountain.'

The archbishop's eyes narrowed for an instant.

'Ah no. No, no, no I insist that you, all of you, must attend at the cathedral again and offer me a chance to get to know you all better. My goodness Brother Lorenzo can wait just a *little.*'

I wondered if his reference to the friar — an ordained priest — merely as *Brother* had been calculated to reduce his stature in the Capulet's eyes. After that comment however, Ilaria became more discomfited by the man and sought to alter the topic. Glancing for inspiration, she found it upon the prince's hand.

'Oh your Highness what a beautiful ring!' She announced. 'Aurelie look there.'

Prince Escalus smiled as Aurelie shuffled to Ilaria's side. They leaned together to gaze on the prince's manicured hand. A mighty band of purest gold in a broad lozenge shape was wrapped about his finger. Set as a border within the lozenge was a thin annulet of shining silver. Inside that form sat a winged lion.

Escalus lifted his hand to allow closer inspection.

'Isn't it beautiful Aurelie?'

Of course the prima donna pounced on that rarefied excuse to reach and touch, while Sabatino rolled his eyes at the connivance. Even Armand suspected Ilaria of wily craft to create that excuse for Aurelie. He cast a knowing glance to Sabatino as both husbands watched on patiently together.

'My wedding band besides, this is Florentia's favourite.' said the prince.

'I'm sure it is!' said Aurelie as she lifted her eyes. 'Oh it's exquisite.'

Escalus held her gaze. Perhaps on the prince's behalf it was completely innocent, yet knowing of the prima donna's obsession, it was impossible not to feel that the connection of their eyes had generated a surge of interest. Certainly for Aurelie it seemed to be so.

'It's the token of my office.'

'As Podestà?' Ilaria enquired.

'Yes Donna Capulet. It's simple. The lion of St Mark is the potent symbol of Venice of course.'

'Very potent.' Aurelie echoed before she could stop herself. Ilaria gulped. 'I mean to say Highness, I recently accompanied Armand and Ilaria to see Venice for the first time and so ...'

'Yes your Highness.' Ilaria cut in. 'My own *famille* are textile merchants and so —'

'Indeed? Textiles? That's very interesting.' The prince's interest seemed genuine.

'For generations. And so, to a daughter of merchants, Venice is the most potent symbol of trade in Italy.'

'But now you're married, what shall replace that interest? What is to be the prima pursuit for your branch of the House of Capulet?'

'I have no intention of replacing that interest your Highness. Indeed we hope to expand it. Don't we my heart?'

'We do angel. Fabric is our future.'

The prince bent his brows with interest. 'I see.'

'We're also interested in the import of dyes. And a great penchant of my own is the creation of haute couture.'

'Highness' Aurelie put in 'these garments we wear, including our headpieces, were all designed by Ilaria.'

Escalus scanned them, lifting his brows in surprise and turning to Armand. 'Is that true Capulet?'

'Well yes your Highness but I must confess ...' Armand paused 'I had no hand in creating any part of it.'

A burst of laughter exploded. Everyone was smiling. The prince slapped Armand's shoulder as if they were soldiering allies. Finally, the tumult began to subside.

'Your Highness' Ilaria added 'thank-you for letting us inspect your lovely ring.'

'Yes' Aurelie agreed 'it's very beautiful.'

Escalus gazed at their admiring faces. They were elegant, attractive women and he seemed to be enjoying the unexpected flurry of attention his ring had drawn from both.

'I'll be proud to wear it for a time until Venice casts me aside for a successor.' he demurred.

'Your Highness we're still visitors to Verona.' Ilaria looped arms through Armand's. 'However in the time that we've remained, one thing has become very clear to us.'

'Hmm ...' the prince murmured 'that one should take care *not* to offer a visitation without *solicitation?*'

That quip was a reference to our now infamous visit to the Montecchi estate which had sparked Armand's duel and the tragedy that followed. Yet somehow, offered so lightly in the aftermath now by Escalus, his comment carried no hint of malice and made Ilaria smile.

'That's a *very* great lesson for all your Highness, but no. It's become clear that you're much loved here in Verona' Another jab poked Ilaria's waist. 'and greatly respected.'

'You're kind to say so.'

'I feel certain Venice will retain you here as Podestà for many years to come.'

A flurry of jabs erupted from Aurelie again as she demurred a smile

'My wife Florentia hopes that you're right. Indeed she lags amid the throng here ... somewhere.'

Ilaria's brows lifted. 'Her Highness is in the market?'

Aurelie lit with excitement.

'She is. And was following me with company.'

That news was bait Aurelie couldn't resist rising to.

'Indeed your Highness, when we saw you both in the cathedral' she blinked innocently 'Ilaria commented how much she would love to make her Highness's acquaintance.'

Escalus appeared as if struck with a wonderful idea.

'Why of course Donna Cortellani. I *must* introduce you both to Tia this morning. Her social circuit has grown rather selectively since we arrived. However she's *always* looking to enlarge it.'

Listening on, I knew Ilaria would be excited to hear the prince say so. I saw her hand lift to her heart and knew she had been affected enough to set it fluttering. Despite all the evidence we had before entering the market, Ilaria could not have imagined Aurelie would be so forward. Ilaria knew she would never have risked so much and so quickly by herself in the prince's presence. She was even more grateful to have Aurelie there to venture more boldly.

And truth be told, since the disaster of Ilaria's self-solicitation to visit the Montecchi estate on that fateful day, she had grown more hesitant in moments when she could have taken the initiative. She hadn't been so before then of course. Yet now, with Aurelie leading by example, the notion of soliciting a connection to the princess — a rare chance to cultivate a social relationship with such a high-ranking woman — was no longer beyond imagining.

Escalus tilted toward Armand. 'I confess Chevalier that since your first appearance at court, Florentia has rarely spoken a word without some reference as to how *beautifully styled* the couture of Donna Capulet appeared to be.' Aurelie jabbed again. 'Or how Donna Capulet's tasteful choice for this or that had set tongues wagging on this occasion or that.'

'As I always say your Highness ... *she* makes every gown look beautiful.'

'Ah man that's a *very* clever thing to say. I *must* remember it. No, your wife has a very great admirer in mine. I could count the days by Tia's waxing on the elan of Madonna ...' he paused to turn 'May I call you Ilaria? It's *such* a beautiful name.'

'I be delighted your Highness. Upon one *condition.*'

'A *negotiation?*' He glanced at Armand. 'By Heaven but she's bold Capulet!'

'She has her moments your Highness.'

The prince beamed. 'Very well *Ilaria.* What must I offer you in return?'

'You must *promise* to call my husband *Armand.*'

'Of course!' His eyes twinkled with fun.

'And to call my wonderful sister —'

'*Aurelie?* Yes of course. Well Armand. If I'm being *brutally* honest.'

'Hold nothing back on my account your Highness.'

'Then I further confess Ilaria...' he glanced at her 'not only is my wife a great admirer of yours. She also makes me rage with envy every time she sings your *husband's* praises.'

Armand's brows lifted in surprise.

Sabatino couldn't resist slapping his broad shoulder, laughing as Escalus and Tristan joined in. Armand hadn't expected such a comment, not even in jest. But for Ilaria, after all that morning's anxiety she finally had something to smile about in earnest. So much so that she laughed aloud and that reaction was infectious, causing the entire company to share in the mood together.

'Oh Highness.' Ilaria giggled when she saw Armand's face. 'My husband's a *fearsome* fighter but a very modest man. You've made him blush of course. And dear Heaven I love him for it. I admit your confession should have made me jealous, yet since we were wed, I've heard the same said *far* too often.'

'Say you *so?*'

'Oh yes. What's more I have it on recent report from the Duchess du Paris —'

'Oh no! That vixen! Don't tell me you're acquainted?'

'Yes we are!'

'Interesting. Yolanthe is young of course. And unpredictable. But my word she's a *considerable* woman.'

'She assures me that from Paris to Lyon, her Majesty commissioned musicians to sing of my husband's exploits.'

'Ah! That's very flattering.'

'Oh yes for him ... if he wasn't so *shy!*' Giggles and guffaws sounded around us. 'The unwitting result is that I find myself married to a man who is pined after by *every* woman that I'm *yet* to meet!'

A new volley of laughter erupted. For all the world, it felt like they had all spent years in company together. His highness tilted his head to look mischievously at Armand. He laid a weighty hand upon his shoulder.

'Armand I must hear one of these ballads for myself.'

That was my cue. 'Highness I know them all!' I declared with a bow. 'And from the sporting fields of Lyon, from Carentan to Formigny until our dire visit to Verona's ancient arena ... have been witness to all.'

'Very well then it's settled!' Escalus smiled. 'We must have your company at the castle next Sunday to dine, drink and hear a sampling of these ballads from your man. And thereafter ...' he shot a glance at me 'he may finally get his chance to convince me how much of a of *fool* I am!'

A ringing peal of laughter exploded. The prince's good humour infected so many who had gathered about to hang on his every word, including myself of course.

Cupid's Balls! I was so well pleased with my rather effortless result! And yes, I confess, I soaked up the attention. For the love of folly, I was bowing and scraping and twirling my hat. It seemed a fitting crescendo to our encounter had been reached. Any moment, I expected Aurelie to prompt a timely withdrawal.

Then suddenly a new voice entered the game.

'Ah your Excellence ... there you are.' A husky feminine voice had risen from the throng.

I looked. Bodies were parting to give way as the archbishop smiled and extended his arm.

'Mercy!' she added 'Now I've heard it all.' A feminine hand rested on the offered arm. 'Verona's mighty Podestà busying himself to fill up *my* social calendar.'

The hand that wore the ring of Saint Mark had reached for the hand of his own lovely princess. Her grey eyes glanced at the hovering forms of Ilaria and Aurelie.

'And I thought my husband would be far too distracted by politics for such trifles. Yet suddenly he's content to play my major-domo. It makes me wonder just what or *whom* ...' her eyes rested on Ilaria 'may have excited so much interest as to trigger such a turn in him.'

Oh sweet friends I tell you sincerely, those words were uttered by the most captivating woman — my own wife excluded of course — that I've ever stood in the presence of. To observe Princess Florentia di Treviso at a silent distance is one thing. Yet to stand in the presence of her feminine grace is another thing entirely.

Some people possess a single attribute of body, mind or spirit that — no matter how plain all their other parts may be — is enough to make them engaging. Armand always said Ilaria's smile never failed to melt his heart. For myself, I've never been able to resist Maxine's wilful sense of humour. For one person or another it may be one thing or another.

Yet for any who are fortunate enough to meet Princess Florentia, one part or another seems lost in an assembly of engaging parts that generate an overwhelming sense of calm and maternal care. Indeed there's something so kind and mindful in her manner that even the most jaded of frumps would feel the magnetism of her interest and be compelled to hang upon her every word.

And as introductions began to be exchanged, her words were all interest, all care and praise.

She praised Ilaria.

She praised Armand.

She praised her husband for being clever enough to make the acquaintance of Ilaria and Armand!

Even more so, the Princess praised her husband for having the sense to arrange that soiree for the following Sunday afternoon. Yet words are not nearly enough to describe how her presence made us feel that morning, as if we had stepped into the warm spreading aura of a living saint, where we would all remain protected by her kindness.

However a problem was posed for Ilaria by the arrival of this great woman. Because such people tend to hold the interest of all in the forefront of their minds, knowing where an individual may stand in relation to their interest, can be hard to determine. That was one challenge that now faced her. But as Princess Florentia continued to engage them, a very different kind of challenge arose which neither Ilaria nor Aurelie could have anticipated.

'Now that I've finally met you Chevalier' the princess ran on 'I hope you'll give my husband a run for his effort in the footrace.' She was beaming. 'He loves to be challenged at sport.'

Ilaria froze, yet Armand wore a grin that couldn't be wiped from his face.

'I would love to oblige him your Highness. However ... Ilaria has *grave* concerns and forbidden it.'

Florentia lifted her perfect brows. 'Oh *no* Ilaria! Grave *concerns?* You must allow him to run with Escalus.'

'Aye me, your Highness. I still fear for his recovery from the hurt he took last summer.'

'Oh I see.' She looked him over. 'Yet dear I must say he appears quite well. How do you feel Chevalier?'

'Ready to run to Olympus your Highness.'

'Ah that's the spirit! And dear really, for a recovering warrior, such preparations should aid his recovery not —'

'But your Highness —'

'And remember Ilaria, this is not a strict affair at all, but a festive and *charitable* event.'

'I know my fear sounds selfish. But I insisted and ... I love him for his care of my wishes.'

'Hmm. Care is a potent thing dear. Love's a potent thing. Yet I believe that trust is the *most* potent and often the hardest one to give. Would you agree?'

Ilaria attempted to mask her frustration.

'Yes. I suppose so.'

'I do understand dear. But I also feel it's a pity. Cal and I judge a great deal by how willingly those of privilege engage with the broad population. Don't we darling?'

'Yes Tia my love. Very much so.'

Ilaria felt the tug of Aurelie's finger against the edge of her palm. She glanced to see her gentle frown as if she held in mute agreement with all the princess was urging.

'I like to know what comforts an elite man or woman is willing to forego to show interest in the lives of those less fortunate.' the princess added. 'They look to such as we in an effort to gauge what should matter for themselves. Yes?'

'Why ... yes your Highness.'

'Agreed. And so Ilaria, should they see us prefer to prioritise our *own* comfort at such moments? Or witness the *denial* of our comfort in support of those less fortunate?'

'The latter of course.' Ilaria said stoically.

'Then we must set the example by showing that we care, by demonstrating our willingness to sacrifice some comfort for the greater good. Wouldn't you agree Ilaria?'

In the pause that ensued, it felt like every ear had bent in to hear Ilaria's reply.

'I ... I *hadn't* considered the event in that way.'

'Oh but Ilaria that's the *essence* of Verona's great footrace. And now, by the grace of Venice, *women* also have a chance to show their mettle just as much as the men.'

'Tia entered it last season herself.'

Escalus hugged her shoulders and kissed her cheek.

Ilaria blinked. I blinked. Ilaria blinked again.

'Forgive me your Highness.' she stammered. 'What did you say?'

The princess answered for him. 'Yes dear I ran, naked as an infant. This year as a sponsor the rules forbid it. Oh it was a thrilling experience. And greatly humbling. Yet that's just the point Ilaria. Offering alms for charity is one way an elite woman may show public care. And I encourage it. Yet what do you or I really *risk* of ourselves to do so?'

'Yes. I see your point.'

'I hope you do Ilaria. Imagine the effect upon an ordinary citizen, even a slave, to see an elite woman such as yourself caste aside her pride to play at sport with women of every station; to sweat and puff and jostle together; to know you won't be proven the better of another just by winning; to show all those watching, and every woman that runs with you, that you accept that you're mortal too? And then as you run under the eyes of Heaven together Ilaria, to show them that they — *every* last one of them — are your sisters too?'

A pause held expectantly. Ilaria looked utterly confronted until Escalus broke Florentia's bewitching spell.

'Tia you must leave poor Ilaria alone. As you can see Armand, I should have let her speak for me this morning. She's far more convincing.'

Armand turned to Ilaria and held her cheek.

'Angel let me run with his Highness. It'll be fun. And as her Highness —'

'Armand I insist you call me Florentia.'

'Ah no!' cried Escalus in mock despair. 'Now my wife will be lost to me forever!'

Smiles lifted on faces.

'Highness you're too gracious.' said Armand. 'But angel, as ... *Florentia* has suggested, this kind of regime will simply aid my recovery, not hinder it. I know it will.'

Ilaria's gorgeous headpiece swayed as she nodded in resignation. Her head bowed. 'Very well my heart. I won't protest any longer. Run if you must.'

'And Ilaria.' Florentia reached a hand to lift her chin. '*You* must run too.'

'I must? *Forgive* me, Highness, you *mean* ...?'

'And you must also call me *Florentia*.'

'Oh dear. Oh ... oh my goodness.' Ilaria's hand lifted to her heart again. 'Why ... yes of course ... *Florentia*. But are you suggesting that I should run –'

'Naked against the peasants, harlots and penitents? Of course dear. I did. And the harlots are *very* competitive. Bruising of course. I took quite a beating from one of them.'

'You took a ...? They *beat* you?'

'I beat some of them back for good measure. Escalus will tell you. He couldn't make love to me for a week.'

'The *longest* week of my life!'

'Oh liar! Stai zitto.' We smiled to hear her scold him. 'Yet earning that hurt for myself Ilaria, made me more mindful of how difficult it was for so many women to attempt to reap such a small reward for such a great effort.'

'A bolt of silk? Sitting as stock in our Emporium it would seem ... like nothing.'

'Yet to the proud winner it's everything. Some run for sport, some for penance. However most hope to gain a reward that could help their struggling kin. Some even used it to teach a woman like myself a rare lesson in humility.'

'She had a broken rib and black eye to prove it.'

'Oh dear mercy. Florentia that's awful.'

'Yes dear. But it was a lesson worth having. Do you have nothing like it in Lyon?'

'For men? Of course. For women? Nothing at all.'

'Well there you see? This chance may never come for you again. Take it with both hands.'

It was clear Ilaria's mind was reeling. She hung on a precipice wondering what to say. Suddenly an answer was given for her.

'Of course she will your Highness!' Aurelie put in. 'Because she won't need to concern herself with running against harlots. She'll be far too busy running against *me*.'

'Ah bravo prima Donna! You're entered?'

'Not at all!' Aurelie smiled. 'But I'm so inspired by your words, that I now feel I must.'

Sabatino and Armand shared a knowing look, as if Aurelie's announcement was in the wind from the moment the princess began to urge her case.

'I confess that I'm anxious at the thought. But it's also thrilling too. Ilaria and I will both run at your urging ... upon *one* condition.'

Escalus laughed. 'Tia I should have warned you. These Capulet women are very great hagglers.'

'A condition? Hmm. May I call you *Aurelie*?'

'I shall be very jealous if you don't.'

The princess laughed and embraced her warmly. I was staggered how effortlessly Aurelie seemed to wend her way into the good graces of that great woman.

'Then Aurelie darling you *must* call me Florentia. Name your condition.'

'That during our visit next Sunday, nudity will *not* be a requirement.'

'Oh but Aurelie ... I was going to *insist!*' Florentia smiled as laughter rippled again.

The wonderful woman showed us all that, despite her station, she could give as good as she was served. Finally, though a little awkwardly, Ilaria was smiling too.

The princess leaned to both women. 'In truth Ilaria, far from it. I expect you both to dress to impress. And I may even seek your advising on my choices *before* the event.'

'Oh yes your Highness ... Florentia. That would be my pleasure.'

When the train of Escalus and Florentia drew away toward the old castle, the archbishop and his Holy sycophant departed in the other direction. The crowd began to disperse, though some loiterers remained to exchange whispered commentary as they observed the glamorous strangers.

Aurelie and Ilaria seemed to relish that lingering interest but Armand's humility rose in reaction. Public attention always seemed discomfort him. As that thought crossed my mind I noticed a glint in Ilaria's eye, as if she had remembered something.

She turned unexpectedly and began to walk away in silence. Then her face turned, her voice lifted as a coy finger beckoned us all to follow. Yet Ilaria refused all pleading to divulge her destiny or intent.

The moment to decide, once and for all, had come.

Chapter 13 Phoenix

Until that morning I considered Ilaria to be a somewhat adventurous woman. I certainly didn't feel that, for the sake of pursuing an
ambition, she would seek much more than *private* attention. Yet
since being spurred on late last summer by the duchess, and now by
Aurelie upon the cusp of that spring, it seemed Ilaria could no
longer help being swept up by the whirl of public attention. It was
not unlike the effect that gripped her for a time, during their
courtship, when Armand's sporting success attracted attention,
before she became so fretful of where that may be leading him.

That thrall she was feeling in Verona however was quite different. It was an excitement for attention and adventure that Ilaria
could share in the company of other women who had begun to enter
her life, particularly Aurelie. Nor would that prima donna, despite
advising that *patience* was the key in the exalted game, hold Ilaria
back from that initial thrill if it might entice her to stay in Verona.

Moreover, just that morning, while they had wandered in the
market and before I drew attention to the archbishop, Aurelie had
confessed something more to Ilaria. It was something very secretive
which began to greatly affect Ilaria's view of her world.

As they leaned down to inspect the wares at a potter's stall, the
feisty prima donna announced in a cautious whisper that, because
she had three children already, and because she heard the duchess
declare the same, Aurelie had halted the progress of that obligation
for the moment.

'What obligation?'

Aurelie glanced about for caution and whispered.

'To spawn children relentlessly darling.'

By Maxine's later report to me, Ilaria was dumbstruck Aurelie
confess it.

'You mean to say ...' she stuttered 'but isn't that a ... are you
telling me that you and Sabatino are no longer —'

'Oh Ria don't be absurd. Sab and I haven't ceased being intimate darling. I just gained his agreement that, for the foreseeable future, our antics won't include the risk of my becoming pregnant again.'

'And he ... he agreed? Yet I thought he was very —'

'Oh Ria I didn't think he'd agree at all. But I was determined to sound him out and see if I could persuade him. After all darling, he's more mature. And I explained that I still want more, just not for the moment. And we have two strapping sons which made the negotiation —'

'The negotiation?'

'Ria you'll learn that marriage is full of vital little negotiations. But to my surprise ...' she glanced around again to be certain none but Maxine may possibly hear.

'Yes?' Ilaria whispered anxiously.

'Not only didn't he resist. Sab told me something that shocked me to the core and incensed me with anger.'

'You're angry with him?'

'Not with Sab darling, but the church. Our Church and it's ... *leaders* in Rome.'

'Lee Lee intercourse that evades conception is —'

'Denied by scripture? Yes darling, and so it's frowned upon by our Church. But so is spilling a man's seed outside a woman's sacred passage Ria or any use of the forbidden passage.'

'Aurelie! What does any of that have to do with it?'

'Because darling, though both are forbidden, I now know that many Holy men, particularly among the *elite*, use the forbidden passage with lovers to avoid conception.'

'Mercy mad woman. What are you suggesting?'

'I'm not suggesting. I know it to be true. And I've known for some time that male monastics do the very same thing to each other.'

'Aurelie!' Ilaria hissed.

'Oh they do Ria! To avoid the insanity of denying themselves. Heavens, for more than a thousand years they were all allowed to marry before our church suddenly forced them to vow celibacy. Scripture didn't insist upon it darling, elite holy men did so. And now I know the same holy men don't consider it necessary to apply that rule to themselves.'

'Aurelie! How could you know such things?'

'Darling I would have thought that by now you would have known about monastics. Yet I forget how young you are. You don't look your age.'

'Aurelie hush this instant.'

'But it gets even more sordid and double-faced Ria, which is what made me so livid.'

'Now you're just gossiping scandal to shock me.'

'I wish I were darling. But I'm not. For Sabatino swears he's seen a copy of an agreement drawn up in Rome.'

'Agreement? Mercy what kind of agreement?'

'One that offers permission to a travelling envoy, a cardinal no less, to continue to have — not to *have* mind you, but to *continue* to have — affairs with women as long as he doesn't deposit his ... seed inside any of their —'

'Aurelie hush, hush, hush! Mercy that can't be true.'

'It is!' she hissed. 'What's more they've agreed to allow this philander to continue so long as he confesses each transgression then submits to any penance prescribed for his unsanctioned — well now they're *sanctioned* — antics.'

'No Aurelie. No I can't believe it.'

'And I'm told even with *that* precaution this — man — now has *several* bastards to his credit.'

'Oh that's disgraceful. Why would they offer such a thing to anyone?'

'Sab says his influence up in the Emperor's court is said to be so indispensable that the powerbrokers in Rome allowed him to negotiate such scandalous terms!'

'Madonna!' Maxine hissed unable to contain herself. 'Can that really be true?'

'Now you see why I swore you to our confidence.'

'Oh yes Madonna. My lips are sealed.'

'I hope so Maxine. For if you breathe a word of it to a soul, I'll pluck out your eyes like Oedipus.'

'Didn't he pluck out his own eyes?'

Aurelie smiled. 'Darling I wouldn't rob myself of that satisfaction.'

'No Madonna.'

'Maxine hush.' Ilaria insisted.

'Yes Madame.'

'At any rate Ria, Sab's met the philanderer himself.'

'No.'

'Yes. He even discussed that extraordinary agreement with him and was shown a copy of the deed. The wicked creature carries it for his own safety!'

'Who is he?'

'Oh Sab won't say Ria. He sworn to secrecy too. It's driving me to distraction. I'm sure it's the only important thing he's ever kept from me.'

'Perhaps for your protection?'

'Yes. However I do know that he met the holy philanderer here last summer in the company of a powerful local patron.'

'Then who is the patron?

'Ah! He won't divulge that either. Perhaps I could seduce it out of him.'

'At least if you fail, you'll still have something for your effort.'

'It's true. Sab's an attentive lover. He never allows us to finish until I —'

'Lee Lee!'

'Oh don't be so naive Ria. And so darling, all this happened *before* you arrived. I told Esmay of course.'

'Was she just as mortified?'

'The opposite darling. Esmay didn't bat an eyelash. She told me I was naïve to be surprised. She confided Onorato knew of a cleric in the French court who had an agreement with the very same terms.'

'Mercy that's disgraceful. How many Holy men are swaggering about with these things?'

'Ria that's precisely my point. What's good for the goose must be good for the gander.'

'Lee Lee I …' Ilaria became lost for words. 'Oh I'm just *flabbergasted.*'

'Well I was more than flabbergasted. It made me furious. And now that I know, I certainly won't feel obliged to spawn children relentlessly at the insistence of Holy men who offer such agreements to each other.'

'Yes. I must confess it's very … disheartening.'

'If in doing so I must confess to my transgressions? Then so be it. If I must do strict penance for it? So be it.'

'What penance would they impose for such a thing?'

'Oh darling it's not harsh.'

'You mean you've already confessed and paid?'

'Since our last was born I've been doing as I wish.'

'Have you?'

'Yes darling. And each month I confess to Lorenzo.'

'Oh no. Poor Lorenzo.'

'Tush Ria. I think he's thrilled to hear of our antics. Yet he still prescribes punishment.'

'Severe?'

'No. He's as big as a bear but as soft as a kitten. My worst was a two hour of vigil on my knees with no cushion for comfort.'

'Oh. That's not too severe.'

'I told Sab. He insisted I serve it in our chamber so no-one else would see.'

'That's just as well. He's thoughtful.'

'Oh Ria that was purely selfish. He also suggested I served my penance naked.'

'Well … that's not … unheard of.'

'No. But after my first hour he stole in quietly and —'

'Mercy you're both scandalous.'

'Not as scandalous as confessing to Lorenzo in his cell that I sinned while serving the penance he prescribed!'

A burst of feminine laughter filled the stall as Aurelie, Ilaria and

Maxine exploded together. The trio drew away quickly with glances following them.

'Anyway darling my point is, I don't mind that inconvenience so long as I'm left free during this critical time of my life to get on and play at the *game*.'

'Oh yes. I see.'

'Well Ria I can't give it my full attention if I'm waddling about with another babe in my belly.'

'No. But you don't think I should follow suit?'

'Oh no darling, don't be absurd. Your bloodline just isn't' safe until you've had three or four.'

'That's what maman says.'

'For good reason Ria. Too many children fail to survive. You must play the odds until you know what fate has in store. But I just wanted you to understand that, if you do stay, for this season and the next, then I intend to be free to pursue every opportunity for us.'

'I'll take that under advisement Lee Lee. Thank you. Yet now I can't stop thinking about that scandalous man.'

'I know. But let's set scandal aside and see what *our* own men are — oh dear me.'

'Lee Lee what's the matter?'

'Don't look now darling but your fool has found a very ripe plum!'

Of course that was the moment when Ilaria first saw me accosting the archbishop and began to panic.

What Aurelie had confided to Ilaria was shocking. Yet it also opened her eyes to the fact that, even in deep matters of our faith, not all was as it appeared. How could such an undermining agreement — a dual standard — be supported so clearly? What's more, it didn't even appear as if elite men were at pains to keep that secret from each other. Indeed quite the opposite, it appeared to be an open secret.

And given Esmeralda's reaction to Aurelie, nor did it appear that elite women were unknowing. When Maxine told me her tale it made me wonder. How much of such matters did those like Prince Escalus and Princess Florentia know? I began to realise they must know it all. How could they not? Given how deeply political their lives were, they must know about such things. Moreover I felt, if that thought was occurring to a fool such as myself, it must be occurring to Ilaria and Aurelie.

One thing had now become clear. Even before Armand and Ilaria arrived in Verona, Aurelie had become intent on playing the game more vigorously. And with Ilaria looming as a potential ally to do so, Aurelie appeared to be reaching for any chance to draw them both in. Little wonder she had volunteered herself and Ilaria so quickly to accept the Princess Florentia's challenge.

If running naked among bruising peasants before all was to be the price of Aurelie's escalation? If that effort drew her into the ennobled company of Florentia and her potent husband? I felt sure it would be worth that discomfort to wiggle her way into a seat at their glamorous table. And the events of that morning were no less impacting for Ilaria. In less than an hour of browsing through Herb Market Square, one of her wildest imaginings — the chance to attract patrons like the prince and princess — now appeared to hang within her reach.

And just as Aurelie had predicted, more clever use of the tools at Ilaria's disposal — myself for one — had laid an opportunity at her feet that may help accelerate her budding ambitions. There it was again, that stirring and volatile word: *ambition*. Yes it seemed we had reached an exciting moment in Ilaria's life for the sake of her future prospects. Yet one thing I saw had begun to worry me.

I had witnessed Ilaria observe troubling behaviour from an associate, a kind of behaviour that had previously concerned her. Yet now she appeared to consider it *less* concerning. For once again she had watched as an elite peer — in this case it was Aurelie, before it was Yolanthe — used flirtation as a bait and flattery as a tactic to gain a result. Yet this time, not only had Ilaria *not* frowned upon it, she had *assisted.* What's more it was clear Aurelie's efforts — like those of the duchess — were being driven by a mercenary will to pursue ambitions like a hopeful, panting suitor.

Not only had Ilaria already observed the duchess do the same, but as far as one may tell from Yolanthe's correspondence, she appeared to be driving on from one success to another. Each goal she set appeared to be growing more ambitious. Each human target she set in her sights was growing in political stature. And for Yoli, the constant use of surprise as a tactic appeared to be paramount.

At that moment Ilaria knew she was in Rome pursing two potent new targets: the mysterious Count Orlandi and Cardinal Piccolo-mini. I felt certain in such company the fiery young duchess would hold nothing back. Even Prince Escalus had commented how much of an impact she already had upon himself and Florentia. I could only imagine — and felt by now Ilaria couldn't help but understand — Yolanthe de Paris would unleash every tactic in her arsenal upon both men to gain any result her faction may require.

Meanwhile in Verona, in the absence of that wily woman, Aure-lie leapt at the chance to take Ilaria under her own wing and guide her forward. I was relieved by that. Given the choice, I felt sure she'd be safer in Aurelie's firm hands than Yolanthe's teasing fingertips. And so sweet friends you may ask, why does all this appear to matter so much to me? Because now I have the benefit of hindsight.

Yes at that time it had begun to *concern* me. Yet looking back now I wish I had done so much more to stem the effect such influ-ences were having upon a young woman I'd begun to feel more responsible for. I feared Ilaria was beginning to accept that to play the exalted game one must be willing to agree seduction was an *accepted* and *expected* form of currency, used to purchase access into the potent world of the upper elite. Even more fearfully from what I had already witnessed for myself — from Esmeralda Montecchi, Aurelie Coretl-lani and Yolanthe de Paris — I felt that expectation to be true.

However a crucial question remained. No matter what those lively prima donnas or that volatile duchess may be *willing* to do what was Ilaria de Capulet *likely* to do?

As we followed her on through the sprawling market to an *undis-*

closed location, all those foreboding thoughts swirled in my mind. I trailed at the end of our entourage as the tide of humanity continued to flow about us. I glanced left and right, watching the exalted parties who had just left us as they vanished through the press in opposite directions.

Then all at once a thought struck me.

Cupid's Balls! I had been promised to perform for the prince and princess in just one week. That thought caused me to panic. I scurried forward to catch up with Maxine as they wandered through the middle of the market, appearing to be destined for the less crowded southern end. For my wife's poor sake I couldn't stop jabbering with excitement. When she shooed me away I jabbered to Figara. She took Figara and gave me Thibault so I jabbered to him.

After jabbering, all I wanted to do was return to our home away from home and prepare for that great event. Yet Ilaria hadn't exhausted her interest in Herb Market Square. On our way to wherever Ilaria was guiding us, she passed a fabric seller. Drawing myself and Aurelie aside they considered my withering attire and then scanned the fare, vowing that before we returned to the Hill, they'd gather a selection to transform my garb .

As distracted as Ilaria normally becomes when fabric stands before her, five minutes later we were quit of that seller's stall and moved on. At the base of the bell tower we halted to rest and allow Ilaria to assess our location. She glanced through the market in search of something at the further side. Then Ilaria's face lit up.

She reached out to Armand and drew him away quietly. Caspar and Fabrizio followed in an instant. Given her secretiveness, we were all watching closely of course and noticed them dawdling away. Aurelie stood and reached for Sabatino but then drew away teasingly. Sabatino followed her. Tristan looked set to follow him but then halted to glance about for safety and thought better of it.

He waited for Maxine and I to go ahead, linking behind us with Liberati and Boccolo to follow closely.

When we left Lyon the previous summer you may recall Armand had made it clear to all in our entourage — including myself and

Maxine — that Ilaria was the person who must be protected at any cost. Yet recently that instruction had changed. Now our primary charge for safety was little Thibault. Liberati and Boccolo had strict orders not to let the first son of Capulet out of their sight for an instant. Maxine and I were present when Armand issued his orders.

'If *anyone* attempts to approach without invitation to within a yard of Maxine, or whoever has charge of Thibault, no matter who they are or how official they look, take them down first and I'll ask questions later.'

'Yes Chevalier.' Caspar, Liberati, Boccolo and Fabrizio chanted in grim chorus.

I felt Maxine squeeze my hand as Armand glanced between Caspar and Liberati.

'If anyone attempts to lay an unwelcome hand on Thibault, do *whatever* you must.'

'Yes Chevalier.' they chanted quietly.

Armand glanced about to impress it upon us all.

'If my son is hurt, I expect it to be over the dead body of one or more or all of us.'

'So do we.' Liberati added soberly. 'So do we.'

Yet despite that stern conference, with our entourage still wondering what Ilaria may be up to, we had straggled apart as we followed her leading Armand across the width of the piazza toward the further side. Indeed we lost sight of them for a few fleeting moments as we wended through the press of the centre stalls. Maxine's eyes widened in fear as my own eyes narrowed to scan the path ahead and our hearts began to race. But then as we emerged through the other side of the stalls I caught sight of them and we both breathed a sigh of relief.

They were halted some distance from the edge of the stalls, standing in a more isolated part of the precinct upon the corner of a side street. Standing upon the opposite corner was a well-known structure. Moments later we were all staring at it in silence, like mourners at a stranger's burial. The building's upper housing displayed the distinct swallowtail crenellations that were visible above so many others in Verona. That design identified structures that were raised with funds donated by the Emperor, sourced by local members of his political faction – the Ghibellines. Even the battlements of the old castle, which housed the prince and princess at the time, displayed that same identifiable design.

Besides the main entry points north and south of the market, that side street was the only access point which offered entry into the piazza. The building we stood next to was the *Casa dei Mercanti* – the Hall of Merchants. Spread in a very pretty formation around its base was a hedge of Grecian laurel. Its pale-yellow flowers were beginning to show, warning that spring was all but upon us. That sight reminded me, it had been just one year since I followed my former master Toulon to war with Armand as his squire.

Armand seemed to pay little heed to that structure as Maxine and I halted. He was scanning about, then nodded to the watchful Caspar. Then the giant nodded to Fabrizio. They ventured into the mouth of the lane to sniff for lurking trouble. Other than poignards – strapped to their hips – none of our people wore any real weapons. Inside Verona's walls, war and hunting weapons of any description – including bows or crossbows – were forbidden for any but peacekeepers to tote. And so if we did meet trouble, with just hands and daggers, it would be a close and brutal affair.

'Shall we rest here angel before we start back?'

Ilaria plucked a leaf from the hedge to crush.

'Oh Armand smell the laurel. Isn't it fragrant?'

She lifted it as Aurelie and Sabatino halted.

'And significant.' Sabatino added. 'The Hall of Merchants sponsors the race festival. Every year that hedge provides the branches for each victory wreath.'

Aurelie stared tiredly, glancing about.

'Oh yes darling very interesting. But Ria, what are we doing here? This is *not* a lively corner for browsing.'

'I'll have you know it *is* lively. Nor have we come here to browse for trinkets.'

'That's well darling. Because there are no trinkets to browse on this *desolate* corner.'

'Agreed. However I've gathered us here upon a matter of *business*.'

Sabatino and Tristan were standing together again and exchanged a quizzical glance.

'Business new sister?' asked Tristan.

'Mercantile business new brother. Friday last my Papa and Maman sent me a note.'

'Yes angel.' Armand agreed. 'But you said all they discussed was Thibault? You didn't mention more.'

'Forgive me my heart. I wanted to surprise you with another matter they raised.'

'Then let me confess you have succeeded.'

'Moreover' Ilaria ran on 'before Yoli and Nobel manage to return, I hope to manage to surprise them too.'

'Angel how so?'

Quiet excitement was building in Ilaria's eyes.

'In their letter Papa and Maman requested —'

'Oh yes how are they?' Armand asked casually. 'We never had a chance to discuss them.'

That delay from his innocent question seemed to frustrate her a little.

'Oh ... oh yes my heart' Ilaria stuttered 'they are well. They send love and good wishes and wait upon news. However —'

'News of what angel?'

Ilaria squinted with rising impatience, yet attempted to maintain composure. 'Of their grandson of course.' She seemed to hope all questions were done. 'And so I —'

'Yes of course.' Armand interrupted again. 'And will they *visit* here perchance?'

Ilaria frowned. It began to be amusing but was impossible to tell if Armand was unwitting or teasing.

'No Armand.' Ilaria was at the edge of her patience. 'Not as yet. They await our decision. If we announce to stay, they will come. If not, they shall await our return.'

She smiled again, lips parted again, as did Armand's.

'Pardon me angel but what you just said made me mindful. Soon my *order* will call me to France to attend their roll call and offer my first report.'

Ilaria fell right into the trap of his meandering.

'Soon? Armand what do you mean? How soon?'

His brows knit in thought. 'Ah ... September. Late. I'm sure I explained that now as a chevalier —'

'You're obliged to attend every other year at least. Yes you did. Will you attend in *Carentan?*'

'Not Carentan, no. But Normandy, yes. On the *Isle of Mont San Michel.* If we return together we could time our journey to allow for that visit as a detour.'

Ilaria huffed and frowned. '*Must* you attend it?'

'Sabatino? Tristan? How must I answer?'

The cavaliere and chevalier both lifted their brows.

'If humanly possible Ilaria, yes.' said Sabatino.

'He must.' Tristan added.

Ilaria sighed in acceptance, yet seemed hopeful for a return to her topic, opening to speak just as Aurelie put in.

'Sab attends every *other* year darling. Thankfully in Venice however. Not on some deserted isle.'

'Saint Michel's not deserted ... I believe.' Armand smiled. 'I've never been of course. Yet angel, his Majesty will be in attendance. And so —'

'And so' Aurelie cut in. 'you may both enjoy the solitude of your drab isle with his Majesty while Sab and I enjoy the decadent distractions of Venice. After he confesses his sins or sings his own praises to his brotherhood, to allow them to pass judgement upon his exploits.'

'Is that what happens?' Ilaria asked despite herself.

'Yes angel something of that kind. And so come what may, I *must* be in Normandy by September. But now before we go, I must run the footrace here in Verona.'

'Naked with the prince!' chirped Aurelie.

'And you'll be running naked in Verona too angel!'

'So will my wife!' cried Sabatino. 'Just who, may I ask, is *not* running naked in Verona?'

'Well I'm not.' Tristan sounded emphatic. 'Unless the women invite me to run with them.'

That set us to laughing again. Even Ilaria smiled.

'And so angel, as for your parents coming or going? By September we will be returning with Thibault.' Armand frowned in thought. 'However before we depart, we must —'

'Make a *final* decision.' said Ilaria as silence descended. 'Do we return to Lyon with our son to *live* or ...'

She hesitated. Armand completed her thought.

'*Visit* Lyon with our son and return here to live?'

Aurelie lifted her hands in supplication with a smile. 'Oh Ria! Live here darling!' She released her train and twirled a demi-pirouette that set it swirling to entrap her. Sabatino glanced with a paternal frown. It reminded me of the distance between their ages.

'Leave Ilaria alone mia cara. She has an important decision to make which may depend on more important things than simply keeping *us* company.'

Aurelie frowned childishly. He drew her to him and she kissed him. Ilaria stood gazing at them in thought.

'More significantly' Ilaria said turning to Armand 'it may depend on *another* decision we need to make here at this unlively corner.' She was staring boldly into his eyes.

'I've seen that look. What is this other decision?'

Blue eyes met green in a collision of intent so engaging that it held all in silence for a ponderous moment.

'Ahem big brother!' muttered Aurelie. 'No more staring. And Ria no more teasing. Spit it out. '

'Yes very well. My parents have drawn my attention to their interest in *those* offices.'

She turned full about and motioned to the structure that stood on the opposite corner. Everyone turned to see. Armand's brows lifted. He drew in behind her to wrapp his massive arms about as he rested his cheek against her head.

'Hmm. Offices *for?*'

'Purchase *or* lease.'

He smiled. 'Ah yes. But *for?*'

Ilaria twirled from his embrace with a smile, raising her hands. 'Behold the *potential* site of — the *Grande Emporium of Marchand ... and Capulet!*'

All eyes beheld, but every mind questioned the sanity of that sug-gestion.

'Oh.' Armand replied quietly. 'The site of a *Grande Emporium?*'

'*Potential* site. Yes my love.' She tilted her head with an alluring smile.

'Oh ... so now it's *yes my love.* Not *yes buffoon* or *yes stupido?*'

'Armand.'

His brows knit in thought. 'Hmm. Of Marchand?'

'*And* Capulet. Yes my ... yes. Oh Armand I can see it in my mind so clearly. Tell me you see it too?' She slid a tentative arm about his waist.

'I see. The burnt out husk of a former ...?'

'House of Wax.'

Tristan slapped his thigh and laughed aloud.

'Of course it was!'

'Well I'm told a candle was left burning and *so ...*'

'Indeed? Well angel that's all very *illuminating.*'

Maxine giggled. Smiles curved on every face except that of our frowning mistress.

'Oh yes Armand, very droll. But say honestly now, what do you really think?'

He hugged her shoulders and turned his head. 'Sabatino? Tris-tan? What say you?'

'Aurelie will tell you I'm no merchant —'

'Yes I will.'

'Thank you *mia cara.* However Armand, it is a *prominent* corner.'

He glanced at Tristan who lifted his brows.

'Big brother I fear I'm *less* than no merchant. And I've known Ilaria for less than a season. However ... I think she has a *mind* ... no

I'd say a *gift* for this kind of thing.'

'Thank you Tristan. You're now my best brother!'

'What's more ...' he added 'her parents aren't fools and *they* seem to think it's of interest.'

Armand nodded soberly. 'Agreed little brother.'

Suddenly all appeared deep in thought. Ilaria laid an arm about Aurelie's shoulder. 'Lee Lee, my new big sister, *you* must cast the final vote. What say you?'

'Oh I say anything that ties you both to Verona is a magnificent idea. And let's face it darling, if you secure this curious corner you *must* stay to manage it.'

'I know you're right.' Ilaria replied soberly. '*Darling.*' she added with a grin.

'*Now* you're getting it Ria. To attract new peers you must call them all *darling* and flirt with a vengeance.'

'Aurelie.' Sabatino said warningly.

'Oh Sab you know it's true. They all expect it. Life's so full of grim reality. They want to rub shoulders with fun vivacious people. Dull frumps have no place in their world.'

'By the Devil mia cara you're a wicked influence.'

'Only if required.' She turned to Ilaria. 'Yet Ria, may I want to suggest one tiny alteration to your grandiose plan.'

'Hmm. What do you have in mind darling?'

Almost as one, Armand and Sabatino rolled their eyes in mock resignation.

'Well darling, let me just say that our parents are our parents and nothing will change that. Or them.'

Ilaria frowned in confusion. 'Yes and so?'

'But Ria you and I, Armand, Sab and Tristan are a *new* generation. We're leaders to our *familles* and *famiglia* but our world is changing every day.'

Sabatino sighed. 'Mia cara what are you driving at?'

With a mischievous grin, Aurelie reached for Armand and Ilaria. 'How would you both feel about raising a phoenix from those ashes that will embrace who we are now ... here ... together.'

'That sounds inviting.' Ilaria replied.

'Yes and so ... let's build a Grande Emporium of *Capulet and Cortellani* together!'

Ilaria took an instant to comprehend. Her eyes widened. 'Oh! Oh my yes! Lee Lee that would be wonderful. Sabatino? Armand?'

'Of course.' said Armand.

'By all means.' Sabatino concurred.

All at once, an infectious round of hugging, kissing and smiling broke out. Maxine and I stared at each other in wonder. For it seemed with that agreement, the fate of the Capulets, and therefore ourselves and our daughter too, was to become anchored in Verona.

Then suddenly, as if appearing from thin air, a quiet voice seemed to hail us from below.

'Olives pretty Madonna?'

A little urchin girl stood holding a wicker basket. And despite all appearances — for the sake of our future safety — the most important encounter in the Capulets' young lives so far was about to unfold.

Chapter 14 the Negotiators

Ilaria blinked in surprise as everyone stared upon the innocent face gazing up at her. Next to her stood a meek little girl — surely no more than eight or nine — with a wide shallow basket that hung from the crook of her arm. It was brimming with fare.

'Hello there. What do you have for me?'

'Cured olives Madonna. Handpicked *not* raked'

Ilaria's brows lifted. 'Oh is that better?'

'Yes pretty Madonna. Nonna says only a barbarian would use the rake.'

Sabatino smiled. 'She's right little one.'

'She always is Signore. And I have branches to sell for growing anew.'

His head tilted as he pouted. 'Hmm. Are your trees so special I should buy your cuttings?'

'Oh yes Signore. They're from the Domenico grove.'

'From the …? No child they can't be.' He glanced at Aurelie, who frowned in doubt.

'Pardon Signore but they are.'

Aurelie arched a stern brow in reproach.

'Then you're selling for a poacher girl?'

'No Madonna. I sell for my nonna.'

'Who is your nonna child?' Aurelie insisted.

'She was a Domenico. Grand-uncle Angelo's youngest sister.'

'Grand-uncle?' said Sabatino. 'Then you are …?'

'His great grand-niece Signore.'

'Dear Heaven girl you're not.' spat Aurelie.

Her innocent expression crinkled with defiance.

'Pardon me Madonna but I am. Heaven strike me at once if I'm not.'

'Hmm.' Aurelie held her eyes. 'Does Angelo know you're selling his cuttings for anyone to grow?'

'No Madonna. And though he forbids to sell them, these are from mamma's grove.'

'Heaven's girl! He'll flay you alive when he finds out. And your poor mother.'

The crinkle of defiance furrowed more firmly.

'He may do it after I sell them Madonna, not before.'

Every adult eye glanced about the circuit in wonder. Something seemed amiss.

'Pardon me little one?' Ilaria asked.

'Yes pretty Madonna.'

'*Pretty* Madonna.' Aurelie echoed in mock disdain.

'It sounds to me' Ilaria ran on 'as if selling these cuttings may bring you into strife.'

'It may. Yes it will.'

'Then why would you risk so much trouble? Has someone put you up to it?'

'Oh no Madonna. I can't blame Father Antony.'

'Father Antony child?' Sabatino frowned. 'What's he done to you?'

'He's done nought to me Signore. Yet I heard him speak wisely this morning.'

'Did he? Just what did he say this morning?'

'Well he ... Signore I don't think you understand.'

'Then perhaps you can help us to.' said Ilaria. 'Take your time little one.'

'Well pretty Madonna' Aurelie huffed with a roll of her eyes as Sabatino smiled 'my brother's fallen very ill.'

'Oh no little one.'

'Yes Madonna. The medicus says Luca needs a special remedy. But we're poor and the herbs he needs are rare and expensive. Great-uncle has enough to help. Yet he cares nothing for Luca.

'Oh no dear heart.' Ilaria frowned. 'I'm sure that's not true. Why do you think so?'

'It is true Madonna. Papa died in the war. Luca is his only son. If he doesn't get better ... if Luca ... if he's gone, grand-uncle will take our grove and give it to his grandson.'

Aurelie knelt too. 'Child who told you that?'

'My nonna did so.'

Aurelie and Sabatino exchanged a sober look. Aurelie glanced at Ilaria and Armand. 'If anyone knows the truth ... it will be her.'

'Pardon Madonna. But I don't care a fig for such things. I only have one brother. Luca must get better. This morning I prayed to the pretty Madonna in our chapel.'

'Oh *did* you?' Aurelie stared at Ilaria. 'Does she have dark hair like mine?'

'On no Madonna. Golden hair, just like this pretty Madonna. And then in his homily Father Antony declared ...'

'Ah!' said Sabatino. 'We come to him at last.'

'Yes Signore. He declared to all that God helps those who help themselves.'

Aurelie's brows lifted. 'Did he?'

'He did. Father Antony is very wise. And so I took some cuttings to sell with my olives and promised Luca to get his remedy. Then I knew God heard me when I saw —'

'This *pretty* Madonna appear in the market.'

'Yes Madonna. I'll confess to grand-uncle after I know Luca has his remedy.'

'Oh no little one.' Ilaria insisted.

'Yes, I will pretty Madonna. To grand-uncle first. Then to Father Antony.'

Sabatino turned to Armand and Tristan. 'Angelo's olives are famous of course. Their *famiglia* came from Greece many years ago. It's rumoured his trees came from the upper reaches of the Nile.'

Aurelie glanced at the basket. 'Taste one darling. You'll see.'

Ilaria looked in with a pout of interest.

'May I taste one?'

'Just one pretty Madonna. I must sell all I can.'

Ilaria reached in, chose a plump specimen then lifted it to taste. 'Oh my. Oh Armand. Oh you must taste this.'

She offered half to him as he wrinkled his nose.

'Angel you know I don't like ...' she popped it in to quiet his objections. He tasted. Brows lifted.

'Oh by thunder angel ... that's delicious.'

'I told you they're famous darling. However Angelo himself is rather *infamous*.'

'Yes unfortunately.' Sabatino murmured. 'I don't doubt her story Ilaria.'

Ilaria knelt again. 'Hmm. Tell me little one, how much for every olive in your basket?'

'*Every* olive Madonna?'

'Will that give you enough to purchase Luca's herbs for the medicus?'

'No Madonna. That's why I brought the branches. They'll fetch more.'

'I see. And so if I purchase *all* your cuttings too, will that pay for the herbs?'

'I ... I think so Madonna.'

'Then just to be sure, I'll have all your cuttings and every olive. The whole basket.'

'All of them all?'

'Upon one condition however.'

Her forehead crinkled again. 'Nonna says never to allow conditions.'

'Yes and she's very wise. But this is a special case for Luca's sake. Yes?'

'Yes pretty Madonna. What is your condition?'

'I shall give the cuttings back to your grand-uncle and you must accompany me so I may be with you when you confess to him.'

'And so will I.' Aurelie added sternly.

'And me.' Sabatino insisted.

Armand reached for another olive. 'I think we'd all like to meet Grand-uncle Angelo.' He added.

The girl looked about in confusion and back to Ilaria. 'That's very strange. He's not very popular. I don't really know if I should —'

'Come now don't be nervous. You want to sell enough, yes?

Think of Luca.'

'Yes, I must. Very well Madonna. Yet I also have a condition.'

'Oh. What is that?'

'I must be allowed to keep my basket.'

'It is a pretty basket. But its wearing out. Let me purchase that too and then you can ...'

Suddenly here little face was dark with foreboding. 'P a r d o n Madonna but no. Papa wove this for me. I'll never part with it.' She stared at her basket. 'Perhaps I was wrong. Perhaps you're not ... farewell.'

'No, no, no little one please wait a moment. Hmm. You say your *papa* made it?'

'Especially for me. My very first.'

'Yes now I see. No brave heart, you shouldn't be parted from it. Well ... you drive a hard bargain. But if you agree to all else, then I'll agree to forego the basket.'

A smile lifted on the little face.

'You'll spit on your hand?'

'Spit on my ...? Is that how you do it here?'

'I can't surrender such a large purchase to you Madonna if you won't spit on your hand.'

Ilaria stared wide-eyed at Aurelie and Sabatino.

Aurelie stared. 'Tradition pretty Madonna.'

'I see.' said Ilaria. 'Will you show me?'

The girl blinked in surprise and looked at Aurelie.

'Well little merchant' said Aurelie 'Show her how it's done in Verona.'

'Very well Madonna.' She faced Ilaria. 'First you must look me in the eye.'

'Oh yes.' Ilaria hung for a moment considering her ponderous garment. 'Wait just a moment.' She glanced around. 'Liberati. Boccolo. Please assist me.'

The stalwart guardians lumbered forward. The little girl clutched at her basket in suspicion as Ilaria whispered to them. Liberati arched a bushy grey eyebrow.

'Not again Madonna?'

'Yes Liberati. Now please do as I ask.'

He huffed in resignation. Aurelie glanced at Armand who turned his eyes to Heaven. Sabatino and Tristan wondered what was to do. Then with Liberati at one side and Boccolo at the other, Ilaria lowered to her knees to face the young negotiator who lit up in protest.

'Oh no pretty Madonna. Your beautiful gown ...'

'Save your breath little one.' Liberati grumbled. 'She's done it before.'

'Yes don't fret.' added Ilaria. 'They're used to my antics. Now little merchant ... what's your name?'

'Nicolette.'

Aurelie considered her again. 'Ah let me see ... Angelo's niece's daughter. And so you are an ... *Ambrosio*.'

'Yes Madonna.'

'Well then ... Nicolette Ambrosio' said Ilaria soberly 'where were we?'

Nicolette looked up to scan about, and made a solemn announcement. 'To be *fair* Madonna I shall place the basket *between* us.' She lowered it ceremoniously.

Aurelie rolled her eyes. 'Mercy child! Is she purchasing the jewels of an Empress?'

'Lee Lee hush. To be fair Nicolette ... that is well. And so what next?'

'Now look me in the eye Madonna.'

'Yes. Oh Nicolette you have beautiful eyes.'

'Grazie Madonna but please ... we must show no emotion when making a pact.'

Smiles rippled around the adult circuit.

Ilaria pouted apologetically.

'Ah, yes very well. But you must call me *Ilaria*.'

'Not yet Madonna.' Nicolette insisted. 'Perhaps when our deal is struck.'

'Hmm. Very well. And so?'

'When my sisters and brothers do it together, we spit upon each *other*'s hand.'

Maxine shuddered as if I had smacked her ass unexpectedly. 'No you will NOT spit on her hand!'

'Maxine hush! I must honour the tradition. What now Nicolette?'

'Offer your hand. I *spit*.' Nicolette spat with gusto. 'I offer my hand. Now *you* spit.'

Cupid's Balls! I had to hold my mouth to refrain from bursting with laughter. Then to make my predicament worse, Ilaria tried to summon her saliva with little result! And when she offered what she had, demure Nicolette, grown bold since the start, stared in utter dismay.

'Heavens Madonna! Spit!' Ilaria tried again. 'Spit like a PRIMA donna!'

'Nicolette Ambrosio!' Aurelie snapped. 'I'll have you know she *is* a prima donna.'

Nicolette's big eyes leapt wide. Her jaw fell open.   'No!   Oh no, are you really a prima donna?'

'Well yes, I suppose I am.'

'My apologies Prima Donna. I meant no disrespect.'

'It's my fault little merchant. I'm not used to so much ... spitting.'

Little brows furrowed in confusion.

'What kind of prima donna are you?'

'I'm a ... *French* prima donna.'

'Oh.' Her eyes lifted to Aurelie. 'That explains a great deal.'

'Yes I'm sorry.' said Ilaria. 'Let me try again. Is there a trick to summoning so much ... spittle?'

Nicolette thought for an instant and lifted an olive from the basket.

'Eat this Prima Donna.'

'Yes that should help. Oh Heaven it's so delicious.'

'Prima Donna please?'

'Hmmm. Mmm. Mmm ... yes just a moment.'

Ilaria gurgled and then spat with more result.

'Much better.' Nicolette declared. 'And shake.' Their eyes locked together. Hands slapped. 'Our pact is done.'

Ilaria's bright green eyes stared at Nicolette who seemed greatly relieved.

Then my blood ran cold as a harsh voice startled us.

'Make WAY!' it growled angrily.

Every eye lifted to see. A party of men-at-arms were driving toward us. Having fallen under Nicolette's spell that menacing posse had managed to close in without notice. I held little Figara as I stood by Maxine cradling Thibault. Armand hissed a quiet command.

'Caspar to Thibault.'

Our giant warrior's eyes grew dark. Without a sound he glided through like a stalking panther to stand ahead of Maxine and I. Tristan settled by his side. Suddenly Fabrizio was behind us. He had just turned thirteen, yet spent the last six months serving as Caspar's shadow. Now armed with a poignard at his hip, for the first time in my life as I clutched Figara I was glad our junior squire bolstered our ranks.

I glared at the menacing entourage. Four grim men-at-arms led their formation with a trio of elite followers behind and four more guardians marching at their back. On the chest of the minder who bellowed so gruffly sat the unmistakable sight of the Montecchi crest — upon a field of forest green sat a rampant black wolf clutching a castle icon, encircled by a white annulet studded with ten gold roses.

The image of it — vile and pretty all at once — had been burnt into my mind since the day we first saw it. Oh yes I know I've described it before. Yet every time I had seen it since that first foul day, it made me shudder.

Seeing it approach us so unexpectedly at that moment upon a late winter's morning, was no exception.

'Halt!' another commanded. 'Hold.'

I vaguely recognised that second voice. And even from where that man followed at their centre, he had sighted Caspar and recognised him instantly. Still hidden in their midst, his muffled words continued.

'Wait a moment darling. No, no, no don't fret. Make way forwards!

The leading quartet parted as a figure drew through them and scanned for a moment. I peered through the gap that opened in their column and squinted to see.

Cupid's Balls!

There before us stood their new primo don Aldobrando. Behind him at their centre was his wife Donatella with another woman behind her. As their column had approached us we were huddled about the kneeling forms of Ilaria and Nicolette, showing them our backs. By the time their man first hailed us, they still hadn't realised who was blocking their path. Yet now they certainly did.

Aldobrando glanced at the foremost man.

'Follow me close Gugino.'

I recognised him too, the blood cousin who served as sergeant-at-arms to their late primo don. It appeared he still held that office. He had been there last summer on the morning of the duel. Aldobrando served as Onorato's second and Gugino as his third. Both had born grim witness to their leader's defeat at Armand's hands. I feared this cousin may have been waiting for a moment to settle that score.

Armand lifted a wary hand in recognition as Liberati and Boccolo lifted Ilaria to her feet, then stepped forward to shield her and flank Armand. Watching the Montecchi come forward I suddenly realised, every man jack of them had a sword hanging from his hip, flouting the rules that forbade the carriage of weapons inside the citadel walls.

What's more the weapons looked unusual. I had never seen the like of them before. The blades didn't appear to have the heft of a war sword or hunting weapon or even a soldier's dagger. It had length yet also seemed narrow. Whatever it was, it meant each Montecchi had more than double the reach in his weapon against anything we carried.

Caspar saw it too. 'Do you see that chevalier?'

He quietly remarked to Tristan.

'I do. Have you seen it's like before?'

'No. It's thin, yet longer than our poignards.'

'Much longer.'

'Fabio?'

'Yes Caspar.'

'Without drawing attention, back out and glance around. Bring me something long enough to improve my reach but sturdy enough to beat those points aside.'

'An improvised polearm.' Tristan added.

Daring not to look behind, I heard Fabrizio's mumbled considering as he scanned about.

'Hmm. Ah. Each stall in the market has several staves under their canvas to prop up the covering.'

Caspar glanced. 'Yes I see them. Good man.'

'If I snatch just one, the covering shouldn't collapse.'

'Agreed. Now quietly but quickly, break off and gather one back to me.'

Suddenly a thought inspired me.

'No! No!' I hissed in a whisper. 'Let me do it. Fabrizio has a poignard and knows how to use it. It's safer for the children if he stays.'

Our giant's brows lifted. 'That's the first time I've ever heard you make sense.'

'I was never taught to fight with much skill. But I was taught to steal with dexterity. Sweetheart take Figara. I'll be back in just a moment.'

I was gone before Maxine could object. And if I do say so myself, in less time than it took for the Montecchi to advance to parley, I had deftly snatched a bracing stave from two separate stalls, without drawing attention, and delivered them to our party. And so, as if by magic, Caspar and Tristan suddenly stood armed with staves as long as any quarterstaff.

'Here.' Caspar turned to offer me his poignard. 'I won't need this with a polearm in my hands.' He glanced to Tristan. 'Chevalier perhaps —'

'Yes.' Tristan turned to Maxine to offer his dagger. 'Give your daughter to Marcel and take this. Better if you're *both* armed and to *separate* the children.'

'Yes Chevalier.' Maxine whispered. 'Marcel don't you let anything happen to our precious girl.'

Caspar glanced again. 'And if you must strike, this time don't hesitate and keep your fucking eyes *open*.'

That was a reference to the last miserable attempt I had made in defence. You recall how I smashed Armand's head with my mace for want of keeping my eyes open.

'Yes! Yes!' I hissed. 'But what do we aim at?'

'Below the chest. Fast in and out. As many times as you can. Kill those fuckers.'

'Dear God how can this be happening?'

Armand knew nothing of the drastic action we were taking and frantically whispered conversation. Having sighted Aldobrando and recognising Donatella, his eyes held to the front. When their ranks had parted, he saw them staring through the aisle at the image of Ilaria down upon her knees in our circuit, shaking hands with a young urchin.

When Ilaria realised who had halted before us, she lifted her hands. Liberati and Boccolo raised her to her feet and Aurelie swooped casually to dust her gorgeous garment.

'Give me a moment angel.' said Armand. 'Sab would you care to join me?'

'I'm coming with you Armand.' Ilaria put in.

'Would you stay if I insisted?'

'The danger of a war kept us apart once. I vowed to never let anything do that again.'

His eyes implored his sister. 'Aurelie please talk some sense into her'

'She made a vow. What do you want me to say? Her vow is less important than yours?'

Sabatino smiled. 'Then mia cara you must stay with the child.'

'I … must join the soiree.' She turned to Nicolette. 'Stay here little merchant.'

'Yes Prima Donna.'

'But listen to me. At the first sign of trouble, run as fast as you can and alert the tower guard.'

'Oh yes Prima Donna.'

One moment later the Capulets and Cortelannis went forward together. The sight of Ilaria and Aurelie spurred Donatella to follow suit, though it appeared her husband wasn't happy she had left the safety of their enclosure.

'Bonjour Don Montecchi.' said Armand.

'Buon giorno Sieur Capulet.'

Donatella arrived and linked arms with her husband.

'Bonjour Donna Montecchi.' said Ilaria.

'Buongirono Dame Capulet.'

'Brando, Donatella.' Sabatino greeted them casually.

'Sabatino. Aurelie.' Aldobrando replied.

'Homeward bound?' asked Armand.

'Yes.' said Aldobrando. 'We've had a refreshing walk but sampled too much fare.'

'You allowed me to call you Brando before. May I continue to do so?

'Perhaps we should —' he began frostily, then reconsidered. 'Well yes. Perhaps we should.'

'And do you mind Prima Donna if Ilaria and I still call you Donatella?'

'I'm not so sure …'

'Oh Donna' Aurelie cut in 'will it hurt us to be more civil to each other on a Sunday morning?'

'Hmm. Perhaps you're right Aurelie. Very well.'

Silence hung awkwardly for a moment.

'Forgive me for noticing' Armand began 'and please be assured Brando, that I mean no disrespect —'

'Then perhaps you should be cautious what you say.'

'Yes I will. It's just that, you have a formidable escort for a social stroll through the citadel, who appear to be heavily armed in spite of regulations.'

'That's ironic to hear you say so Armand.' Donatella replied accusingly.

'Is it Donatella?'

She opened to respond but Brando forestalled her.

'They're not weapons of war Armand, nor for hunting. And so the Captain of Militia has agreed they fall outside the restriction.'

'Interesting.' Armand replied. 'I've never seen such a sidearm before. I know it's not French. German?'

'Spanish. Made for *personal* defence in their citadels. It's sad to say they've become needed there.'

'Civic personal defence?'

'Since their own wars have ended, their towns are flooded with destitute soldiers who have turned to crime. Many Spanish citadels are altering their restrictions to deal with the crisis.'

'Perhaps now our war with the English is done, the same may happen in France.'

'I had hoped to never see such a thing required on the streets of Verona.'

'No darling.' agreed Donatella. 'Yet unfortunately times are changing, even in Verona.'

'And so yes Armand.' Brando ran on 'we're attempting to continue our Sunday tradition of enjoying a promenade after mass.'

'And so you should.' Armand agreed.

'Yes. But currently we feel the need to do so under escort Armand. And for your sake.'

Armand appeared genuinely confused. 'For mine? But why?'

'I'll tell you why —' huffed Donatella.

'Donna don't.'

'No Brando please.' Armand insisted. 'Let her speak her mind. Let's talk openly and honestly.'

'Oh I want to' she ran on passionately 'because in all honesty

Armand, until I know you're finally gone from here, I fear for the safety of my son.'

Armand was flabbergasted.

Ilaria frowned in disbelief. 'You fear for ... dear mercy Donatella. Is that really true?'

'Of course it's true. Why else would we take such ridiculous precautions on the streets of our own citadel?'

'Oh no.' Ilaria cried. 'Oh no this can't be. Mercy Donatella is little Romeo with you now?'

'He is.' Her eyes narrowed, her voice hissed in a whisper. 'And I warn you Armand, every Montecchi here will protect him with their lives.'

'Of course they would.' Armand agreed. 'Just as we would protect our son.'

'Yes.' Brando replied turning his attention to Ilaria. 'We heard tell you had a child.'

'I did. We did. His name is Thibault.'

'Then I trust that he's safe and well.'

'Yes so far. And he's here with us too.'

Donatella's brows knit. 'Then perhaps we can agree, at least for this moment, to be civil for both their sakes?'

Aurelie huffed. 'Oh Donna for the love of mercy!' Do you really think they'd harm him? A child? That Sab and I would ever allow such a thing to happen?'

'Please Donatella, Brando' Armand added 'don't fret over his safety for our sake. I swear before all and before Heaven, we would never lift a finger to hurt him. Never.'

'Do you say so Ilaria?' asked Donatella.

'I do Donatella, with all my heart.'

Brando glanced about. 'But Armand your entourage has just as many martial men as ours. And they appear to be armed with more potent weapons than these.'

He slapped his hand to the hilt of the Spanish sword. Armand turned in confusion.

'Our men are not ...' he began. 'Oh.' He tilted his eyes to

Heaven when he saw us. 'So they are.'

'We also heard' Brando added 'that a company of soldiers arrived from France to bolster your numbers.'

'Led by a vicious mercenary.' Donatella said coldly.

'A mercenary?' Armand appeared more confused.

She glared at Tristan. 'That man. Next to your giant.'

'Armand one of our men recognised him from the civil war in Milan.' said Brando. 'Are you still in a mood to be open and honest?'

Armand and Ilaria exchanged a frustrated look.

'Yes Brando I am. Now more than ever. Because they weren't armed like that before you appeared. And for months now, we've gone in fear of your faction's anger toward us, and now go in fear of their want to hurt us through our son.'

Brando and Donatella exchanged sober looks.

'Well ...' Brando frowned sympathetically 'given last season's events ... I suppose that's ... understandable.'

Ilaria leaned to whisper to Armand.

'Yes angel. Brando. Donatella. Please indulge me for a moment.' He turned toward our little band. 'Tristan! Come here. The dreaded mercenary is my younger brother.'

'Oh. Which means that he is Aurelie's ...'

'Brother too. Yes Donna. And I'll have you know he's a saint who wouldn't hurt a fly. Unless I insisted.'

'Allow me to introduce him.' Tristan approached, a stern look still showing on his face. 'Do you bring such a weapon and that grim expression to a diplomatic parley?'

Suddenly his brows lifted, his expression softened.

'Ah good people forgive my ignorance.' Tristan said charmingly. 'Then I won't require this.' He tossed the staff to Liberati. 'And I can smile. Indeed I prefer it.'

'Aldobrando and Donatella Montecchi, may I introduce my brother —'

'My favourite brother.' Aurelie hugged him.

'Chevalier Tristan de Capulet.'

'They fear you are a ruthless mercenary' said Aurelie 'come to

Verona to terrorise them.'

Fortunately for the sake of diplomacy, the reaction on Tristan's face made it clear that notion had surprised him. He nodded his head in genuine despair and looked Brando and Donatella in the eyes with sincerity.

'It's true that in Milan I served as senior squire to a mercenary knight. Yet that was my first martial engagement and I was elevated in the field. Now I am independent.'

'Congratulations Chevalier.' Brando said cautiously.

'Oh I was merely fortunate.'

'Knowing your brother's martial qualities Chevalier, I doubt that very much.'

'In truth Signore I'm glad to be quit of war and be at peace with the world. Had my fiancé survived the ordeal, by now I'd be bouncing my own son on my knee. Yet ...'

'Oh no.' said Donatella with unexpected sincerity. 'She was hurt in the war. Was she a local girl from Milan?'

'No Signora, Adelais was French, from Rouen. And so not hurt in the war, but after it had separated us.'

'That's a pretty name.'

'Yes. She fell very ill in my absence. And so Heaven took her before I could return.'

'Oh mercy no. Had you known each other for long?'

It was clear Tristan's reaction, that the unexpected need to share his intimate tale was affecting him. And by the expressions on Aurelie and Ilaria's faces, I suspected neither had heard this much detail about his tragic situation before.

'Betrothed for two years. Yet we only met for two weeks of courtship in the season that war erupted. Adelais was shy and ... well ... despite having had so little time to know each other, I must say that somehow her loss still haunts me deeply.'

'Oh that sounds ... so very sad.'

'It's kind of you to say so Signora. It *is* to me, yes. But now gentile Signora let's talk of happier things. Perhaps let's start with my confessing to you both that, unless we're aggressed upon, I have no intention of being an aggressor.'

'Oh truly Donna ...' Aurelie implored her . 'do you think this puppy would hurt your son?'

'Why would I want to?' Tristan saw Armand's brows lift. 'Ah I see, that's what you were discussing. And so Signora that's why you looked at me so ... cautiously. Yes?'

'Yes Chevalier. We don't want to be sad.'

'Nor do I wish for that Signore and Signora Montecchi ... Donatella?' he requested.

'Tristan?' she requested in turn.

Their mutual smiles confirmed agreement.

'That does sounds better. And I swear to you both by the soul of my sweet, departed Adelais — may she rest in peace for eternity and beyond — that I wasn't summoned here to act in anger. I was summoned to protect against it. Yes, the Capulets have always defended against aggression. But we do not initiate it. Indeed, the laws of our House forbid it.'

Ilaria stepped towards her rivals.

'Brando. Donatella. Please say you're satisfied we mean you no harm. We certainly mean no harm to sweet little Romeo.'

'And now you have a son Ilaria. *Thibault* you said?'

Yes.' said Armand coming closer. 'Named after our grandfather.'

'A strong name.' Brando put in. 'I assume you'll be returning home soon so your parents may see him? Perhaps, until then at least, for the sake of the children's safety we can all agree —'

'Brando.' Aurelie cut in. 'You should know that Armand and Ilaria are already home.'

His brows knit in confusion.

'Already home? What do you mean?'

'It's true.' said Armand. ' Brando. Donatella. We've decided to stay.'

'Stay in Verona?' said Donatella. 'For how long?'

'By *stay* we mean ... to live here in Verona.'

'You plan to remain permanently?'

The Montecchis exchanged a look of recognition that seemed to suggest they couldn't avoid the truth. Half measures would no longer solve anything. They must be all for war or all for peace. Both fell into deep thought for a lingering moment. Once more Armand broke their spell.

'And so we feel it to be in the best interest of *both* our houses, to see if we can't ...'

'Negotiate some kind of ...' added Ilaria.

'Truce or peace.' said Brando.

'A *lasting* peace.' added Donatella.

'Yes.' Ilaria agreed. 'But I still very much fear ... given what happened to Esmeralda ...'

'Esmeralda no longer lives in Verona.' Said Donatella candidly. 'She's gone Ilaria. Far away. Nor does she hold status here within our faction any longer.'

'It's true.' said Brando. 'You need not fear her authority any longer. We lead the Montecchi here now. Anything we say, agree upon or announce, becomes absolute for anyone here within our albergo or aligned to it.'

Gugino's eyes flinched. Armand saw it. Ilaria saw it too. Armand faced him squarely.

'Would you say that's true?'

If ever I saw a man wanting to speak his mind, but feeling he could not, it was in that moment.

'I would say ... I'd say ...'

'Gugino.' Brando warned.

'Brando if we hope to make this work' said Armand 'let's understand the truth of what we may be facing. I promise, if he's allowed to speak his mind, no matter what he feels the need to say, we will take no offence at all.'

'Alright then. Gugino. Say what you will.'

'Very well. I say that I was there the day you arrived, both of you.'

'You were.'

'Perhaps you came more in hope of purchasing the estate and less for the sake of genuine friendship. Yet I believe either way that you both came in peace.'

'Yes we truly did.' Ilaria pleaded.

'But you were not met with peace by our primo don ... nor even basic civility.'

'That's an understatement.' Ilaria hissed.

'Ilaria.' Armand pleaded calmly.

'Yes. My apology. Please continue. You have every right to say what you think.'

'I served Onorato for years Prima Donna. He saved my life more times than I can count. No one has more right to want his killer dead than I. Yet ... that day he was in the wrong, wrong from the start, from the moment he saw —'

'The crest on our wagon.'

'Somewhere along the way he became less of a warrior and more of a political creature. I know you didn't seek a quarrel. Your challenge to risk so much in a game of dice was bold but fair and he lost. In truth I admired how he seemed to take that loss in his stride at first. But then his challenge to you disappointed me. It was tainted from the start. You were clever to face him so quickly. I tell you honestly, he didn't expect that at all. As you intended?'

'Yes.'

'Despite his bluster the next morning, that tactic unnerved him greatly. He thought he had your measure until he heard your conditions. I'm sure it's why he instructed ... I won't say her name ... to lie in wait that morning. And truly Don Capulet, I had no notion she was there.'

'Nor did I.' Brando added with sincerity.

'I believe you both.'

'And so ...' Gugino added 'when you fought him fairly and had him beaten and then she ...'

Ilaria glared. 'Shot him in the back.'

'Yes. As much as it pains me to confess it ... they both disgraced our good name with their conduct. For the first time in my life, I felt ashamed to serve our house.'

Armand's frank gaze held on Gugino. 'I wouldn't like to have confessed that about my own mentor.'

'No. And Don Onorato left no legitimate ... no heirs. Now we have a new primo don and he has a fine son.' He glanced to Donatella. 'And forgive me for saying so Prima Donna, but we also know he'll be the *only* son and heir.'

'That's alright Gugino. It's true. And it matters.'

That confession took us by surprise. We didn't understand why, yet somehow Heaven had already ordained that Romeo Amicus Montecchi would not have a sibling.

'It makes him even more precious to us.' Donatella added quietly.

Gugino met Armand's gaze. 'And so Don Capulet, if our primo Don decrees we must have peace? I will abide it.'

'I believe you.'

'I can't promise all in our faction will feel the same. But if it appears that any are likely to transgress —'

'We shall deal with them.' Brando cut in. 'Harshly.'

'Then Brando' said Aurelie 'if what you say is true, if Esmeralda's sway in the matter of the Capulets no longer has to be an issue for those of your faction in Verona?'

'That is how it stands.' he reassured.

'And we both have new born sons?' said Ilaria.

'Then perhaps' said Donatella coming closer. 'We may all just ...'

'Agree between our factions to keep the peace?'

Armand had said that last as silence descended again and all contemplated enacting what none could have imagined just hour before.

'Maxine!' Ilaria called. 'Please bring Thibault here.'

'Yes Madame.' she replied.

Caspar began to move.

'No Caspar stay.' Ilaria insisted. 'Let her come to us alone. Donatella would you mind if I had a peek at Romeo again. He's such a beautiful little boy. I promise ...

'Yes Donna' said Aurelie 'I want to see him too.'

As Maxine approached with Thibault, Donatella glanced at her husband for guidance. He nodded agreement.

'Very well. Lucretia! Bring Romeo to me.'

We watched as the pair of children were carried toward each other in the middle of their gathering. There was Maxine holding little Thibault. There was Lucretia holding little Romeo. I couldn't help following and stopped at a short distance away, still holding Figara.

I crossed my fingers hoping for her sake that peace would be agreed. If we were to live in Verona I would feel more at ease for the safety of my family if the anger that separated these two houses was finally put behind us.

Donatella leaned to see. 'Oh he has his father's eyes. My word Ilaria but he's a striking child.'

'Thank you Donatella.'

'Call me Donna if you wish. May I hold him?'

'On one condition.' Ilaria glanced at Romeo in Lucretia's arms.

'Yes of course.'

Beyond all imagining, Maxine and I gazed in wonder as the prima donna of Montecchi cradled the heir to the House of Capulet, while the premiere dame of Capulet held young Romeo. Oh sweet Heaven I tell you, the hope of that image, the relief on their faces, the way both women glanced at each other and began to smile and giggle and then laugh. By all the angels who sing so sweetly in Heaven, I prayed the goodwill they managed to summon would be everlasting.

'Oh Donna, Romeo's such a sweet child. You must be very proud of him.'

'We are Ilaria. I hope he and your Thibault will grow to be the very best of friends.'

They held them closer together.

Armand caught Brando's eye.

'May I offer you my hand to declare peace between us once and for all?'

'When I see our children together Armand, I feel certain that for their sake ... Donna do you agree?'

'Yes we must think of their futures. If you're going to live in Verona ...'

'We are.' said Ilaria. 'It makes my heart flutter. But yes ... we are.'

'Then by all means' said Donatella 'let's declare lasting peace between us.'

'Armand give me your hand?'

'Of course.'

They began to reach.

'No!' came a panicked cry from below.

All eyes leapt to stare at the interloper! Nicolette's eyes were bulging as Brando's forehead creased in a frown.

'Girl what ails you?' he asked.

'Oh Brando forgive her.' said Ilaria. 'Nicolette's a skilled diplomat. Before you arrived she was advising me that in Verona, a pact is not sealed unless both parties spit on the other's hand.'

'That's right pretty Prima Donna.'

'Oh. You still call her *pretty* even though she's now a prima donna?'

'More so Madonna.'

'What about this prima donna? And I'll have you know that I'm a prima donna too.

'Three prima donnas!'

'Yes. What do you say to that little merchant?'

'I say' Ilaria cut in 'that before our men seal this pact, perhaps the prima donnas should lead by example.'

Ilaria turned to Donatella.

It was the first time I saw anything like a girlish glimmer light up in Donna Montecchi's eye. Both women drew their left arms under to free their right hands and secure their bundles more firmly. Ilaria repressed a mischievous smile as they swirled their right shoulders toward each other and lifted their hands.

'Prima Donna.' warned Nicolette. 'Don't forget to —'

'Look her in the eye. Yes brave heart.'

Their eyes met. Ilaria spat. Donatella spat.

Their hands clapped firmly together.

'That's better Prima Donnas.' Nicolette encouraged. 'But you didn't spit upon each *other's* hands.'

'Well Nicolette … we're not brothers and sisters. However —'

Donatella smiled. 'We're no longer enemies.'

'Amen Donatella. And thank Heaven.'

Breathing a sigh of relief, I held my daughter a little tighter as I drew alongside Maxine. She looked at Figara, offering a fingertip for her to grip. And perhaps for fear we might hex that blessed moment, neither of us said a word.

The following day the Capulets and Cortelannis called on the merchant who'd drawn the emporium site to the attention of Ilaria's parents. Acting as their agent, he initiated its purchase which was settled before noon. He also agreed, in return for a hefty commission, to offer his nomination to enlist both couples into the Merchants Guild.

Such nominations were very difficult to obtain and so worth a very great deal. But a second local nomination was also required to secure their entry. And despite that man's effort to assist, it seemed all others felt so threatened by the prospect of swelling their ranks with such formidable rivals, that no other was willing to second the nominations.

Moreover, the window of time for new nominations to be approved in that season, was closing fast. If a solution wasn't discovered quickly, even if the emporium could be built that season, it may lose more than half a year of trading to offset the cost of its creation. While they considered who else they may turn to for a nomination, Ilaria sent word of all that had transpired to Yolanthe de Paris. She hoped that Nobel, the master merchant, may suggest a solution.

Quite unexpectedly a swift reply followed.

It was delivered by a legal advocate who informed that the duchess, and Nobel were still in Rome but were finally on the verge of concluding their business. Yoli suggested that now Armand and Ilaria had decided to stay, if they and the Cortelannis would sign the trade pact, her advocate would return with it to Rome before she departed. That would allow her new ally, *Count Orlandi*, to become *their* new ally too. Most significantly for the sake of that current dilemma, as a member of Verona's Merchant Guild Orlandi would agree to second the nominations himself.

Oh yes, the wily young duchess understood that timing was everything. Yet somehow I believe that even before Ilaria's letter explaining what had come to pass managed to reach Yolanthe, she already knew the Capulets and Cortelannis were falling short of a merchant endorsement to secure that vital membership. And looking back now I have little doubt — though none suspected it at the time — that she and Nobel were somehow responsible for the local unwillingness to offer a second nomination.

Yes sweet friends, timing is critical. Particularly if one has the power to manipulate how timing may affect others for the sake of one's own powerful interests. In less than a week thereafter, copies of the executed agreement were delivered back to Verona from Rome, along with a declaration from the mysterious count to second the Capulet and Cortellani nominations to the Guild.

And so given that this man was now their sponsor, the Capulets attempted to learn more about him. Sabatino and Aurelie knew of him. Sabatino had even met him in person, yet only once, and otherwise *claimed* to know little. Then try as they might to learn more, Armand and Ilaria discovered that despite the great wealth Orlandi was rumoured to have amassed — with holdings in Verona, Venice and Rome — his life was shrouded in mystery.

I will confess to you now that in time, Ilaria will finally meet Count Orlandi. Yet the cost of her doing so would be … but that is to come.

Let's remain in the Capulet's present for now.

And so upon the day that executed agreement arrived back from Rome, Maxine and I found ourselves in the villa's central courtyard with the Capulets. They were sharing a quiet moment of reflection. I won't say it was a celebration. Yet with the scratching of ink on parchment, just as the pact that bound Armand to Ilaria some two decades before was finalised, a first decade of partnership between the Houses of Capulet, Cortellani, de Paris, Nobel and Orlandi had begun.

To any looking on, that powerful alliance appeared to be an instantly grown faction. Yet despite that perception, the wealth of assets it now represented in Verona alone, certainly rivalled those of the Montecchi. Moreover, thanks to Yolanthe and Nobel's efforts on their way east, before they arrived in Verona, the alliance now held assets in every major citadel along the silk road from Lyon to Venice.

And so now there we were, relaxing with Capulets after they signed the mighty document. Maxine was there with Thibault as Ilaria resisted the want to feed him herself yet again. Since our conference with Aurelie on that fateful Sunday morning, Ilaria and Armand had become used to the notion that anything they said together, could not only be said without reservation in front of Maxine and I, but that safety dictated, even during their most intimate conferences, it was better to have at least one. Certainly by that stage, both seemed comfortable to speak upon any matter in our presence. And given I had also been playing in their chamber so often when they became aroused, I felt they had reached that point with myself well before that time. Ilaria watched Maxine put Thibault to her breast. I could tell it made her envious. Maxine could too, and so she turned discreetly to wandered away a little.

Armand lowered the signed parchment to lift a beaker of wine from a salver and offer it to Ilaria.

'Do you regret feeling pressed to enter this alliance?'

'No my heart. Oh yes, Yoli's a handful. And yes, she wants to put her hands on my husband constantly. And the feminine company she keeps tends to make me feel —'

'Without cause.' he interrupted.

She lifted a fingertip to his lips. 'Insecure. However ... I do trust my husband. And we *both* want to stay.'

'Yes.'

'And I'm excited by this place.'

'So am I angel, as long as we're here together.'

'But without securing a guild entry, any decision to stay would have been hollow. I love Sycamore Hill. But it isn't a future for us as *farmers* that attracts me to Verona.'

'Nor I.'

'How do you feel my handsome? Can't wait to have another steamy session of negotiations in the bathhouse with our attractive allies?'

'Angel I do admit ... that was fun.'

'Oh do you?'

'Now I do, yes. But that was only fun because you were there. And I didn't think I'd ever say so, but I did enjoy seeing other women being jealous of my beautiful wife.'

That made Maxine and I smile.

Caught by surprise at his candour, Ilaria grinned.

'Armand de Capulet I would never have imagined hearing you say something like ... hmmm.' She purred in mock reprimand. 'Maxine, either my husband is changing, coming out of his shell, or —'

'All of those things at once Mistress.'

Armand glanced at the parchment, grazing it with his fingertips. 'In truth, now that this has arrived, I finally feel relaxed. Entering this alliance has relieved a major concern I had about staying.'

'Yes Maxine.' Ilaria purred again. 'He was fearful he may never see Yoli or Eloise back here again?'

I blurted out a laugh. Maxine smiled too.

Though Ilaria's look was more sober than I expected. She'd said she felt insecure. I sensed she was fishing for assurance. So did Armand and he offered it.

'Honestly angel I know you hoped that remark would sound flippant ...'

'Did I?'

She winked at Maxine then pretended to be distracted by Thibault to avoid looking at Armand but he swept her up into his arms. Their eyes met, blue blazing into green.

'I don't want you to doubt how much I love you.'

'Dear Heaven my heart I know I shouldn't. But I confess' She buried her head in his embrace 'that since having my first child, perhaps because he is a boy ... I did begin to fear ...'

'That it made me love you so much more and that you couldn't cope with so much love?'

'Imbecile.' She slapped his broad chest. 'Is that how you *really* feel?'

'Please don't mistake me for being flippant, but it is. I still love you with all my heart. Every time I look in our son's eyes, every time I look in your eyes or see you here or there, it reminds me of how lucky I am for us to be sharing our lives together.'

Maxine wandered back with Thibault. 'Mistress if you're really not sure how you feel, I'll happily swap husbands with you.'

'Sweetheart!' I frowned and pouted at Maxine.

'Max I'm sure you and Marcel will be very happy together.' Ilaria turned with a grin. 'And so you may wait in the line behind Yoli and Eloise and every other ...' Suddenly Ilaria hushed and her grin melted away.

I felt certain she had just experienced another one of her moments, a moment of inner sight, another premonition. She turned to Armand.

'But my heart you said ... you said you had a *fear* ... and now it's gone?'

Armand narrowed his eyes and began to shake his head in dissent. 'Well yes I did. But I meant to say ... as a result of this alliance, as to whether this peace with the Montecchi will manage to hold or not.'

'Why ever would it not?'

'Oh I'm sure that it shall. I simply meant that now, no matter what may come, supported by such a potent alliance it's hard to imagine anyone in their right mind — from their faction or any other for that matter — would dare lift a finger against any of our own.'

'Do you really think so?'

'Yes I do. Now I do. The count's nomination was vital. But the protection this agreement delivers is more so. I still recall Gugino's fear that some in his faction may not wish to accept our peace and may resist it. But now, with the backing of this local count, no matter how mysterious he may be, and a duchess besides?'

'Yes that should keep us safe. Thibault will be safe.'

Armand swept Ilaria into his arms again.

'Of course he will angel. We'll all be safe now. I promise to make sure of it.'

No more was said of their fears that day.

Nor did I press Ilaria upon the subject of whether she experienced a moment of premonition or not. And so sweet friends, we'll let that lie for a moment and press on.

Yet before we press on, I must explain something more. For you see, the Emporium site had been purchased in the names of Capulet and Cortellani, yes. But under the terms of that new alliance, the business that would be established there was to be a *joint enterprise* between all the partners. And it was further agreed — at Yolanthe's own suggestion no less — the establishment's name should imply the primacy of the Capulet's interest in it, and particularly imply Ilaria's participation. And so it was to be named —

Il Grande Emprorio della Seta di Madame Capuleti
Madame Capulet's Grand Silk Emporium

That name would establish respect for the Capulets as new members of Verona's elite society. Moreover it would reassure the most important patrons — wealthy women of Verona and every citadel within a week's transit — that the French *maestra*, already so revered for her grace and elan, held the reins.

In less than a month after those documents had been received, work began on demolishing the burnt-out House of Wax that had stood on the corner. The effort to replace it with a sparkling Emporium was planned to begin when the coming race festival ended. Before then, Armand and Ilaria both had a gruelling race to prepare for and run.

Years later, Ilaria confessed to me that Aurelie's guidance on that day, before she entered Herb Market Square for the first time, was instrumental in convincing her to stay. Regardless of the duchess, Nobel or anyone else, knowing she could count on her friendship and guidance had been the defining factor.

And if Ilaria had left Verona with Armand and Thibault for France instead, to deliver subsequent children into a life spent in Lyon? One of those would never be destined to meet Romeo Montecchi or become betrothed to the boy who would grow to be Count Astor de Paris.

You think you know who I mean to imply? Time will tell. And now time has passed, I look back and realise even more of course. For had the advice of that visiting merchant to Ilaria's parents in Lyon, never been passed on to Ilaria while she remained in Verona, the Capulet's lives may never have been set upon the path to remain in Verona.

Oh my sweet friends, we're told God's will is inscrutable. Yet we're also told there's a difference between *destiny* and *fate*. Destiny is meant to be the path one creates for oneself. Fate is meant to be the path we travel despite all our intentions and efforts. And by those definitions it would seem to follow that fate is just another word for *God's will*.

If that is so, if our *fates* are the result of divine will, then as I sit here writing this for you — recounting those fated steps that seem to have driven us on — I wish someone could explain how our world was made better by the suffering to come that would be felt by both factions. Perhaps, unravelling for you what came next for us, will help me unravel the dark sense of that.

For you see that *ill moment* which Ilaria experienced that day was like a tremor one feels before a cataclysmic quake. Sometimes such things are felt moments, hours, days or even a month before the event. I thought I saw her feel it.

Indeed she had but didn't confess it at the time. Another premonition did unsettle her and a cataclysm was coming.

CAPULET: AMBITION

It would be unlike anything we could imagine.

Chapter 15 Glamour & grime

The Capulet's trade agreement — delivered from Rome — had arrived on that Monday morning immediately after Armand and Ilaria were invited to the castle for the following Sunday. They were to bring me with them of course, to make music, sing and perhaps play the buffoon. We arrived with Aurelie and Tristan to be ushered into a spacious, luxuriant chamber. It's long gallery of tall windows overlooked the swirling Adige, its northerly aspect ensured the salon was lit with soft diffused light.

Don Sabatino did not come along. That disappointed me greatly. We were told, moments before their carriage departed to fetch us at Sycamore Hill, that he was called away upon urgent business. Yet as Aurelie attempted to explain the circumstances, I had the distinct impression it troubled her. I suspected — after how much we'd seen her tease Sabatino over her infatuation with Prince Escalus — it was one thing to endure her teasing while it had played out at a distance to that man. But now they were invited into his inner circuit, the thought of standing by while she caroused in his presence before others, would be too much to bear.

I felt sure however, Sabatino's absence wouldn't stop Aurelie from plunging into the social fray in pursuit of her goals. Indeed it may have spurred her to prove to Sabatino that the connection she sought would reap the kind of rewards she'd always promised for them, without generating any other result that could validate feelings of *insecurity*.

Yet that thought made me wonder. How many damaging infidelities may have begun in just that way?

Not that I thought such an outcome *must* become the result of this encounter. I felt Aurelie loved Sabatino deeply. But I could see the spectre of regret in her eyes as we departed for the citadel. I felt sure Ilaria did too, wondering if Aurelie feared her acceptance of this invitation was now a misstep, if she should have let Armand and

Ilaria attend alone and left the prince and princess off her own list of sought after connections.

I prayed the result wouldn't prove to be trouble for Aurelie and Sabatino. To my mind they were the soundest model of a happy and well-intentioned elite couple that we had met so far. I wanted the Capulets to have such models to guide them in this new life in Verona. And the Cortelannis were certainly more sound as mentors for them than whirling risk-takers like Yolanthe de Paris or Auguste Nobel – who may as well not have been married at all. Oh yes, that's enough ruminating Marcel. Get on with it.

Upon crossing the chamber threshold, the arriving quartet – Armand, Ilaria, Aurelie and Tristan – were introduced into the company of two dozen couples. Aurelie explained in an excited whisper that most were considered to be the very cream of Verona's upper elite.

'Oh now I am disappointed Sab's not with us. He's served with several of these men.'

'It's a shame he couldn't attend Lee Lee. Yet at least for Tristan's sake as your escort, given they are all couples, he won't be standing out all alone.'

'Yes that's true darling. Far less awkward.'

By now we knew Prince and Princess were linked to the Montecchis by marriage. Florentia's younger sister *Elisabetta* had married *Dante Montecchi* – Aldobrando's younger brother! Oh yes the familial web becomes confusing if one looks too deeply. Despite that connection however, that couple were absent to this event. Nor were any Montecchi relations introduced among the elite guests.

After introductions were done, I saw Ilaria breathe a sigh of relief to learn as much. And by a look I saw Escalus and Florentia share, I felt sure the absence of anyone linked to the Montecchi – other than themselves – had been intentional and for the Capulet's sake.

Armand and Ilaria were an instant success of course.

Oh yes, they loved me too. After my very first song, a flurry of vociferous offers to purchase my service agreement began to inundate my employers! As a veritable *auction* erupted, Aurelie smiled mischievously at Ilaria. Florentia stared with a smile then implored her rowdy guests to calm themselves.

'Darlings give our *guests of honour* time to finish a first liqueur!' Laughter rippled about. 'Or at least wait 'til Escalus and I manage to negotiate a deal ahead of you all.'

Aurelie couldn't help glancing and grinning. It was clear she considered the entire thing to be her own triumph. Indeed it was. And her unbridled satisfaction seemed to suggest Sabatino's absence was already forgotten. Oh and yes, I was glad to hear so much passionate praise for myself!

Yet sadly Maxine heard none of it. For after we arrived she was relegated to a chamber below with other nurses tending to children. And in case you may be wondering, no I did not attempt — as I had promised one week before — to prove the prince was a fool. Truth be told, my ego was so out of control with so much avid praise, that I decided to take much more licence than that.

For since I had gleaned so much information about both Escalus and Florentia from our first encounter, between my musical offerings I began to roast them a little. And when that cheeky effort summoned glamorous smiles, followed by glamorous laughter, I teased them a little more relentlessly until — I was roasting them both relentlessly! Cupid's Balls! It reminded me of the night in that alpine tavern when Maxine and I made so much fun of the Capulet's noisy lovemaking.

Now roasting our powerful hosts, Armand and Ilaria glanced nervous warnings at me. Yet somehow that egged me on! So did Aurelie who, drinking her fill in celebration, every time she saw either one frown at me, kept nodding encouragement to spite their efforts. As laughter continued to swirl and rise I decided to throw caution to the wind, boldly suggesting *his mighty Highness* only volunteered for the footrace in order to show off his massive member to every gaping citizen. Eyes popped as I ran on remorselessly.

'I'm sure he was hopeful the wondrous sight with his mighty balls swinging beneath would intimidate all Verona into cowering obedience. The secret weapon of Venice!'

Oh bite my bare ass! I wished you could have seen Armand and Ilaria's faces when I said so. In the deafening moment of silence that followed they were utterly mortified. Then an avalanche of laughter and raucous responses broke all around us! It was perfection.

By that time of course, every guest had imbibed so fitfully with wine and liqueur that lips were well loosened and so retorts leapt from all in their company. My work in Paris had taught me to gauge the readiness of a crowd for such moments. There in Verona, even in such elite company, that instinct hadn't failed me. Indeed other than the Capulets — the youngest couple present — not a single guest had batted a dissenting eyelash. Indeed it was quite the reverse, beginning with the Princess.

'Oh don't flatter him so much!' cried Florentia. 'I'll never hear the end of it!'

'But Tia is it true?' cried a glamorous woman.

'Let's see the evidence.' another suggested.

'I'm ready to be intimidated!' cried yet another.

Their jibes were relentless. And those was just a selection of course. I felt sure that last quip was Aurelie's, yet the chamber was so filled with shouts from all sides, I couldn't be certain. I did see Prince Escalus glance at her for an instant. Then he tossed his head back and laughed with gusto as Florentia laid her arm around his broad shoulders.

Oh the princess laughed so much I didn't wish to relent just to ensure she continued to enjoy herself, leaning her forehead into his cheek, their smiling faces lit up together. Indeed they were so willing to laugh at themselves, it was easy to see why they were so popular. Then I loudly announced my need to relieve myself, bowing with a flourish, rushing out antically as if desperate to find the ablution chamber. Giggles and guffaws rippled in my wake.

I found several ablution chambers ranged alongside each other in a sumptuous hall. Having pissed like a stallion in one, I made my exit to find Florentia and Ilaria together.

'It *is* a lovely castle Ilaria. And those views of the river are soothing. But it's a hundred years old now dear and feels ... old to me. If we weren't guests of Venice, I wouldn't prefer this location.'

'We saw very little of it the last time we were here.'

'Oh yes. That awful ritual. It's just that kind of event here that makes me wish we resided elsewhere. Hmm. Best to leave such things in the past.'

'I'm sure you're right. Yet I understand ... she was held here during the ...'

'Esmeralda?'

'Yes. During her ... other trial.'

'Her inquisition. She was. That was a ghastly week for all of us.'

'After seeing her in court, then here during the ritual, I tried to imagine what she must have gone through.'

'I'm afraid that would take some imagining.'

'I've wondered what it must have been like for her.'

'Oh don't do such things to yourself dear.'

'I can't seem to help it. To be confined here for a week to a single bedchamber.'

As she listened, the princess frowned and pouted in consideration.

'I feel that now' Ilaria ran on 'after my birthing confinement, I can sympathise a little.'

Florentia stared soberly, brows knitted in doubt.

'She *was* confined to a comfortable upper chamber Ilaria, yet only for a short time, a few hours on the first day.'

'Oh? Given her station I assumed ... May I ask what happened thereafter?'

Florentia thought for a moment. She flitted a glance at me then offered a little more.

'Once the inquisition convened, Esmeralda was taken down into the lower reaches.'

'The lower reaches? Below ground?'

'Yes dear. The interiors above us are comforting and sumptuous of course. Yet below ground ... well ... come now Ilaria. Let's rejoin the guests and forget such dark —'

'Please forgive my inquisitiveness Tia. But these lower reaches are ... a prison?'

'If you must know, yes. But it's a very grim prison. A dungeon built for purpose. When we arrived here, Escalus and I toured the castle together. I thought it was all rather beautiful. Then when Captain Lanza offered to take Cal *below* after I announced my intent to retire —'

'You insisted on seeing it with him.'

'I did. I don't believe an elite woman should shield herself from the brutal realities that surround her life, no matter how much others, particularly men, may attempt to shroud them in mystery. I knew as Podestà, that place would become part of Cal's working world.'

'So you wanted to see and know.'

'I love him Ilaria, rather desperately.'

'I can see you do.'

'Because I do, I wanted to see what he may have to deal with every day of our lives.'

'I understand that. I think that's wise.'

'Hmm. I'm not so sure any longer. Yet now come, let's return to the soiree and listen to this talented boy of yours again.'

She turned to go but Ilaria made no attempt to move.

'Florentia.' The princess halted and turned. 'May I impose on you to allow me to —'

'You want to see where she was kept. Don't you?'

'Somehow I feel —'

'No Ilaria. You're not responsible for Esmeralda's suffering. Onorato's actions are responsible. Her actions are responsible. No one else is to blame. Least of all yourself.'

'I understand. But still. To give me more peace of mind I feel —'

'Dear it may give you *less*.'

'Yet now that I'm here again. If it's at all possible Tia, it would mean a great deal —'

'I like you already dear, I do. But this? Oh very well. Yet upon one condition. You must ...'

The princess narrowed her eyes at me. I attempted to look trust-worthy. Ilaria laid a hand on Florentia's wrist.

'Marcel is sworn to keep my confidences. You can say anything in his presence.'

'A musician who keeps secrets? Dear I've never heard of such a thing.'

'I do love to chatter for entertainment. Yet for you elegant Princess I'd sooner die than betray a solemn trust.'

Her lovely grey eyes tilted to Heaven and back.

'I don't believe you. Yet that was so beautifully said ... perhaps I'm willing to risk it.'

'I will vouch for him.'

'Oh yes very well. In that case he'll attend as our mutual wit-ness.'

'I won't let you down.' I blurted with a gulp.

'If you do vagabond, that wife and daughter who came with you shall suddenly lack for a too talkative father.'

'Yes dread Princess.' I bowed ridiculously.

'Mercy Ilaria does this rake take anything seriously?'

'He can't resist a witty retort. But Marcel won't betray our confi-dence.'

'Hmm. We'll go down together. I haven't been below ground since we arrived. But we can't be long. Half an hour dear, no more.'

'Oh thank you Tia. But what will you tell Escalus?'

'I'll say we've taken a tour together. He'll entertain meanwhile. My absence will give him a chance to flirt. He's had his eye on your sister since we met in the market.'

'Oh? Aurelie?'

'Yes of course. It was clear she wanted to flirt with him. Oh don't look so shocked Ilaria. Cal's harmless but also handsome, vain and loves to know women still want him.'

That comment raised Ilaria's brows and mine. As the princess turned to the end of the hall, we glared at each other in disbelief. Flo-rentia curled a lacquered nail to a server hanging in wait. His brows lifted. He hastened in silence.

'Summon the keeper at once.'

'The *keeper* your Highness?'

'Yes man and do it quietly. Tell him not be observed. Then go to my husband and tell him I'm escorting Donna Capulet on a tour of the ... *upper* chambers.'

'The upper chambers? Yes your Highness.'

'Oh thank you Tia.'

'Don't thank me yet dear. The lower reaches are not for the faint-hearted. After he took charge, the inquisitor assigned a female warder to Esmay. However while she was kept below, the keeper that I've summoned remained on duty. And now before he comes ... my *condition*.'

'Yes Tia anything.'

'You must tell no-one of what you see or learn on this adventure. Not even Armand.'

'Oh.'

'You said you needed to do this for *yourself?*'

'Yes I feel I must.'

'Then it must remain with you. And Ilaria, no matter what you see or learn, when we return you must give all the impression that you're still having a *wonderful* time.'

'After touring ... the *upper* chambers.'

'That goes for you too rascal.'

'Yes my love. I mean — yes dread Princess.'

Her grey eyes leapt open. 'Heavens he's incorrigible. I can see why you like him. Now Ilaria do you still wish to go? Or shall we ... oh I can tell by that look in your eyes what the answer is.'

'I feel that I must.'

'The keeper will be here momentarily. He's too young and sensitive for his grim duty, and instantly recognised by the enormous ring of keys that jangle like —'

'A cow's bell?' I quipped.

'Like the bell of a cow led by the grim reaper.'

And so he arrived. And so he was. And so we went.

By the time we reached the chamber where Esmeralda was first deposited, Ilaria's demeanour had sobered considerably. To see that small cell with its stone slab, little window, and nothing but a small wooden bucket for ablutions, plunged us both into thought.

'As you can see dear, it's not glamorous.'

'Oh Tia ... it's ... its terrible. I can't imagine anyone being able to sleep here.'

'She didn't Madonna.' said the young guardian. 'Not straight away. Before sunset on the first day she was moved to a lower chamber. The prima donna came back here just once, to sleep for a very short spell after the ceremony of disgrace, that night after her civil trial had finally ended.'

'May we see the other chamber?'

'Well Madonna it's ... further below and very foul smelling and —'

'Please Tia. Now I've seen this, I must see it all.'

'Take us there man.'

Moments later we followed the jangling young man, surprised that we could only press on below by torchlight. The bare stone walls closed in against us, dripping with water as the cold, darkness and smells intensified. He stopped before a wooden door, fumbling with his ponderous ring of keys to unlock and open it.

He leaned his torch over the threshold. The princess frowned in recognition of having seen the like before, but Ilaria's eyes leapt open wide in the swallowing darkness.

'Oh dear mercy! Oh Tia no. Dear Heaven it looks utterly wretched.'

'Step in and hang your torch. I'll have a closer look.'

'Perhaps it would be better your Highness to remain at this distance.'

'I'm the wife of your Podestà, not a monastic. Do as your told man.'

'Yes your Highness. Then please, come in at your peril and excuse the foul smell.'

Hands leapt to mask our noses. The stench in that dark stone coffin was pungent.

'Heavens!' Ilaria cried. 'Oh mercy that's the rankest smell. Why is it so foul?'

'Unlike the upper chambers Madonna, no ablution buckets are allowed here. We clean after each inmate has been ... is gone. But of course —'

'Yes very well.' Ilaria interrupted. 'Ay me Tia this stench is intolerable. I think I'm going to retch.'

'If you must Madonna just purge on the floor and —'

Before he could finish Ilaria bent violently to retch. I leapt to catch her and bend her over far enough to ensure she didn't soil her gown.

'Oh dear ... oh I'm sorry ... I'm so very sorry.'

I drew out my linen, lifted it to Ilaria's mouth and glanced at the princess. She was stone-faced. As if she now felt the experience must be endured.

'Not at all dear. That's precisely why we're here isn't it? To purge your ... conscience. Come. Let's step outside.'

'Yes. Oh yes.' She staggered out on Florentia's arm. 'But Tia how could anyone stay in there? Sleep in that? There was no slab. Did they bring her a cradle?'

'Down here Madonna they have nothing. A handful of straw upon the ground.'

'In that thin wrap we saw her wearing in court? Laid on a layer of straw on that floor? Surely a blanket wouldn't keep the cold from her at all?'

'It didn't Madonna. She had no blanket.'

'What do you mean?'

'The inquisitor insisted. No light. No medication for her wound. No bucket to piss or shit in. Just water and bread, and that very sparingly. And until her time was ended, her female warder was forbidden to cleanse the chamber.'

'Dear mercy Tia how did she survive it?'

'It was very, very, very cruel. And what's more frightening to consider is ... Esmay is just one of many.'

'Never in my wildest imagining did I think ... oh dear mercy ... that a woman like Esmeralda would be treated in such a way. I simply can't believe it!'

'Unfortunately I can. A woman like her dear, or any other man or woman whose folly leads them into this place.'

'Oh Tia how frightening.'

I had said nothing so far. The grim reality that hung before us had left me speechless. I remembered the cell in Carentan where we found Caspar. It was like the first chamber we had visited, a slab and slit window letting light from the world filter in. But Esmeralda's dark, cold, foul stone hole in that underworld was a nightmarish sight.

'It is frightening.' said Florentia. 'Even our cheeky rake is lost for words.'

'Yes dread Princess I ... I certainly am. What can one say at the sight of such ... grime?'

'If you learn nothing else today Ilaria, you must realise that this *did* happen to Esmeralda. And it could happen to anyone. Myself, Escalus – anyone.'

'That is so very disturbing.'

'It's sobering dear. No matter what height a person thinks they may have reached, how powerful they think they've become, there are those further above who have more power to bring them down to earth and to drag them even further below.'

'Clearly that's true.'

'I didn't want to bring you yet ... perhaps it's been a lesson well learned. Never forget it.'

The key sounded in the lock. The keeper turned.   'Shall   I take you to the other chamber Highness? Or shall we return?'

'What other chamber man?'

'She was interrogated just down the hall. That's where she suffered the *ordeal*.'

The princess looked at Ilaria warily. 'Well Prima Donna, how's your stomach holding up?'

Ilaria glanced at the keeper. 'It's the last?'

'Yes. And has no stench like that bleak hole.'

'Very well man.' said Florentia. 'But we must return soon. Show us through quickly.'

Moments later we found ourselves standing together in that final chamber. It was perhaps four times the size of the cell we had just left, with a much higher ceiling. He described how the tables were arrayed for the inquisitor and captain at one end and the two scribes at the other.

'Captain Lanza?'

'Yes your Highness. He came in person to witness the final ordeal with the two scribes, a young Dominican brother and a tall Franciscan friar.'

'The tall Franciscan?' asked Ilaria. 'Friar Lorenzo?'

The keeper feared he had revealed too much.

'They're sworn to secrecy man.' The princess insisted. 'Tell Madonna Capulet what you know.'

'Yes it was him. During her time here he cried every day, quietly to himself after he left her, so she wouldn't see. I had the feeling they knew each other well.'

That was the first time I understood Friar Lorenzo, who had now become Ilaria's confessor, had anything to do with the inquisition.

'But when he came on the final evening, after the ceremony of disgrace ... when he saw the hooded henchman and their infernal machine set out upon the floor —'

'The machine?'

'It was hideous Madonna. Like a large child's seesaw, but with belts and buckles at each corner they used to strap her onto it.'

'Did they?'

'Yes. But first her warder was ordered to strip her naked. That's when the poor friar lost all control.'

'Mercy man. Why did they do that?'

'The inquisitor said that before an ordeal, he was obliged to strip every penitent bare to douse them in shame and purge them of pride.'

'I see. And ... after she was strapped down ... what did they do?'

Florentia's face grew dark as she watched the keeper fumble his words.

'They ... they began to — I can't say it Madonna. I just can't.'

'I can tell you.' Ilaria stared at Florentia in wonder. 'They drowned her.'

We both stood in shock to hear the grisly statement.

'You mean, Esmeralda is gone?' Ilaria muttered. 'She's dead?'

'No Ilaria. They just drowned her. Again and again and again.'

'I don't understand. How could they —'

'That's why it tilted like a seesaw. They tipped her head down, stuffed her mouth with fabric, filled a large ladle with water and spilt it onto her mouth.'

'Mercy no! Oh Tia that's hideous. I can't believe it!'

'It is hideous. Then just as Esmay looked certain to drown they tilted her back up, emptied her mouth and revived her. And then ...'

'They did it all over again.' I said quietly.

'Yes. I don't know if you realise ... but its considered an advantage that they can't —'

'Scream.' I muttered.

'Tia were you ...? Were you here?

'No dear. No of course not. Yet Cal told me everything. We share everything.'

'That must have been a hard report for him to hear.'

'He heard no report Ilaria. Cal was present. Indeed he called an early halt to it. He was certain the inquisitor had lost all control, that he'd kill Esmeralda. Finally he picked her up himself and carried her to our chamber. She lay there for two days before Aldobrando had her removed.'

'She recovered her health?'

'Oh Esmay was alive. Yet she was a babbling mess. Even when Brando came to take her. Honestly dear, I can't imagine her mind ever being right again.'

'Aldobrando said she's been taken far away.'

'She has. And now ... that's more than enough. Let's return to the air and the light and my guests. I need a great many more drinks to douse this experience.' She handed a coin to the keeper. 'Unless my husband asks directly, tell none we were here. Tell none of our conversation.'

'Yes your Highness. Thank you.'

Ten minutes later, we stepped back into the riverside chamber full of glamorous, laughing guests who hailed our arrival noisily, insisting I play for them at once. Just as Florentia had suspected, Escalus was in deep conversation with Aurelie. Without hesitation Florentia smiled as she approached them. She kissed Aurelie's cheek and fell into the prince's arms, kissing him as if the flirtation she witnessed meant nothing, as if — during her absence — nothing unusual had happened at all.

Ilaria watched on. Aurelie glanced at her and smiled as she stood and drifted away from them to mingle. Ilaria was held in a daze for a moment. I feared she may reveal her distraction and so I began to stroll as I played, then turned in front of her to catch her eye. She stared at me for a moment, then collected her thoughts. She caught sight of Armand. He was surrounded by several women of course and so Ilaria followed Florentia's example, wandering towards them before smiling and falling into his arms.

I thought he sensed something had changed in her mood. But in that convivial atmosphere, nothing was said. Nor did Ilaria tell anyone of our escapade thereafter, not Armand or Aurelie. Nor did I tell a soul, not even Maxine. That is, not until many years later, when I asked Friar Lorenzo to reveal all he knew about the inquisition.

The next day, when Ilaria and Armand had received the duchess's agreement and Ilaria experienced that jolting moment I observed, I learned that our dungeon tour with the princess had been the cause of it. After Armand left, I quietly asked her what had happened. She confessed she had seen a flash — a vision of Esmeralda being strapped to the device by the masked henchmen to be tilted, drowned and lifted again. But then the terrifying vision had transmuted.

A cackling voice had ordered the tormentors strap Ilaria to the board and tilted her down as the dripping form of Esmeralda loomed over her, stuffing her mouth with shards of fabric, hovering the ladle maliciously, then tilting it to trickle out water to drown her. As she poured, she screamed that Ilaria would pay for what she had done to her life and her House, before ordering her lifted back up to revive her. Grinning maliciously, the fallen prima donna then purred to her henchman to lower the board again, and the cycle of Ilaria's suffering repeated.

Then suddenly Ilaria's grisly vision shifted to the castle soiree. Escalus sat watching her with Tia upon one arm and Aurelie on the other. Yet while Florentia stood smiling, whispering to her husband and glancing at her rival, Aurelie watched them with terror in her eyes. And just as we had seen Esmeralda appear at the ceremony of disgrace, Ilaria's vision showed Aurelie standing in the same thin, dirty shift, barefoot and with her hair cut to shards.

With a jolt Ilaria had realised that, unlike the princess whose arms laid freely around her husband's broad shoulders, Aurelie's wrists were shackled, her nails cut back roughly. Ilaria stared into the Aurelie's blue eyes as Esmeralda suddenly appeared to whispered in Ilaria's ear.

Yes she's next you little French whore.

Given what we had experienced, how preoccupied Ilaria had become before we saw it, I wasn't surprised such a ghastly vision had sprung to her mind. For since we visited that grim underworld, the same kind of thoughts had haunted me too. I told her so. Somehow learning that seemed to calm her. She feared it may have been another view of our future. I told her I didn't consider it a mystic premonition, just a ghastly, yet understandable, imagining we both shared, triggered by the shocking truth that was revealed to us.

In that brief tour with Florentia we had learned how much more dangerous our world could become, even for an elite player as powerful as Esmeralda. Just as the princess had warned, the greater the power some were able to wield over others, and the greater damage those may be willing to inflict to display that power — to compel others to give them what they wanted or simply take it from them — had become truly frightening.

Before our tour, hearing rumours from a distance that such things may have happened in the silent shadows, made them seem less than real, and too difficult to imagine. But after our descent into the underworld, catching that rare grimy glimpse, the truth of it was undeniable and terrifying.

Gazing through the sunlit inner courtyard after experiencing that vision, Ilaria stared vacantly.

'What's most frightening Marcel' she whispered 'is that while she was kept below, suffering alone in that darkness, the elite were above her, just as we were. They caroused in that elegant chamber, drinking, eating, laughing and flirting, enjoying their lives as if her torment didn't exist in their world, or as if it shouldn't matter to them at all.'

That was Ilaria's first real insight into the reality of such power. It wasn't to be her last.

Chapter 16 Gods among the sycamores

While myself and Ilaria had been absent on our underworld tour with Florentia, and before Escalus had settled into a corner to flirt with Aurelie, he had discussed his preparations for the upcoming footrace with Armand. Indeed after making his announcement in the cathedral on the previous Sunday, he'd begun a rigorous schedule of training the very next day. And though the Capulets had been rath distracted since then — making peace with the Montecchi; purchasing curious corners; finalising agreements with Paris and Nobel — it jolted Armand to realise neither he, Ilaria nor Aurelie had yet made any attempt to prepare for that gruelling event.

What's more Tristan announced, that since Armand and Ilaria had decided to stay, he would remain long enough himself to enter the elite horse race which caused Armand to insist he must enter it too! And so upon the following Monday — with their alliance agreement finalised; the purchase of curious corners complete; a peace brokered with the Montecchi; an architect sourced to assist in the creation of an Emporium (as the Montecchi no longer blocked local artisans from interacting with the Capulets, and so, many showed great interest) — it was time to consider those upcoming events far more seriously.

Moreover, with all those things accomplished in such quick succession, we were now hopeful that the *Peace of the Bambinos* — as Sabatino had declared it — would be lasting.

Upon that Monday evening as the Capulets dined with the Cortelannis to celebrate their progress on all fronts, a decision was made to prioritise race preparations until the event was done. Not only did they devise a plan, but also decided it must begin the next morning.

All agreed to start early, very early.

What's more they agreed that, given the *unusual* nature of Verona's famous footraces, some unusual measures must be taken to prepare. Of course, to make ready for such a long meandering race afoot, an entrant must *run*. Yet it wouldn't suffice to run continuously around a short, predictable circuit. To be *fit-for-purpose*, a lengthy and less predictable training circuit was required.

The road below Sycamore Hill, along its two mile length to Hazel Wood, had been used before by Sabatino for the very same purpose. And so it was agreed that would serve as the training course. Yet having agreed on that choice, the matter of ensuring the protection of two elite women — who needed to run beyond the safety of our gates — had to be considered. Yes a peace had been struck with the Montecchi, but only one week before. And though the early signs had been promising, that pact couldn't yet be counted on as secure. There was also the matter of *privacy* — as much as it may be controlled on a common path without blocking access to others who must use it.

A schedule of training for the footraces first and horseraces thereafter was planned to begin one hour after sunrise. They would train every day — excepting the Sabbath of course — and all sessions would be completed by mid-morning. The footrace regimen would begin at the gate of Sycamore Hill, while the horses would be stabled at Hazel Wood and run the course from there in the opposite direction. Finishing there should allow all to rest and recuperate together in the luxurious comfort of that grand manor's chateau wing.

As a first measure for security upon that Tuesday morning, Liberati and Boccolo were posted to guard the gate at the base of the Hill. Just before sunrise on that first day, they trudged bleary-eyed down the steep entry path to relieve the night watch. Standing before that formidable gate, they spent the first hour yawning and staring. Then one hour after sunrise, both stood witness to a remarkable sight.

However, before either man *saw* anything, they *heard* feminine voices approaching in descent upon the hillside path. Just when they felt sure the newcomers would appear around the last bend, the grizzled warriors turned to face them, ready to incline their heads in respect. At the very first glimpse of a hand, they did so by instinct.

Then as they lifted their heads to hail them, bushy brows shot up in astonishment. Suddenly in a panic to avert their eyes, they glanced anywhere but towards the vision approaching them!

Two prima donnas were strolling towards them of course, yet their hair was uncovered, their shoulders and arms exposed, their bodies enwrapped, not in haute couture, but generous lengths of fine Egyptian linen, styled in the Ancient Greek fashion. The fabric was gathered up high on one hip to reveal one leg to the top of the thigh. And to complete the extraordinary image, bare feet were visible through sandals that wrapped fine leather strapping up to cross over and under beyond the ankles and calves — to be gathered below the knee and tied behind.

The two veterans stared at each other for an instant.

'In twenty-three years of service' Liberati muttered 'I've never seen such a sight.'

Following close behind, yet far less audibly, came two primo dons, similarly clad, yet barefoot instead. For all the world it appeared that somehow a quartet of Gods and Goddesses had descended from Olympus onto the crest of Sycamore Hill, then descended further again to revel in the sycamore grove among such mere mortals.

Now just four weeks and odd days remained for the quartet to make ready. Both Capulets were in attendance of course, yet so were both Cortelannis. For you see, upon that evening before, during their quiet celebrations, Sabatino had revealed that when they visited the citadel to register their entries, he decided, not only to enter the elite horse race as usual, but to enter the footrace again.

Now as is stood, Armand and Sabatino would be running together, as were Ilaria and Aurelie. And now the two brothers and their brother-in-law would be riding together. Sabatino was excited that he would finally race in company as a team player. He had won the elite race once before, yet had always entered alone. Yet he swore that the greatest competition each season came from those who raced as a team. And so the trio intended to do just that.

Indeed when my wife Maxine first realised Ilaria and Aurelie intended to enter the women's race, she had pleaded with Ilaria to allow her to run with them.

'Oh please let me run? As a barefoot girl in a large brood of brothers I was always running amok.'

'You're not a girl now Max. Now you have a babe to tend. Two babes.'

'Never fear that Mistress. I can still keep pace with the best of them, even with a babe at my breast if needed.'

'I'm sorry Max. But for the sake of your need to care for Thibault and upon Aurelie's advising, I must forbid you to enter. Perhaps next season.'

'Yes Madame.' Maxine replied with dour formality.

She was bitterly disappointed, of course. For there was no guarantee her circumstances would be different next season, or even the season thereafter. That would depend upon whether Thibault was made to wean after two seasons or three. And then, to make my wife yet more miserable, I made an announcement too. For upon a whim, yet partly for fear of Armand running so exposed in a race among so many, I had entered the footrace myself! Yet I also declared I had no intention of *preparing* at all!

No, that didn't appear to surprise anyone. Well given my lean physique and ability to talk incessantly without appearing to require breath, most felt that even without any preparation I would at least finish the course. Just where I may finish might be another matter. And so by that Tuesday morning, all entrants were ready to begin preparations.

While they had celebrated together on that evening before, the Cortelannis described in more detail, what Armand and Ilaria could expect to face on the great day.

'Oh darling a great number enter the footraces for both the men and women.'

'Really?' asked Ilaria.

'Yes.' Sabatino replied. 'In the men's race, many run to honour their ancestors. But for humble folk a bolt of fine silk is a very rich prize and attracts many contenders.'

Armand's brows lifted. 'I imagine it does.'

'And so' Sabatino ran on 'most entrants will be poor, very keen to win, and willing to deter all their rivals, regardless of rank, by making their presence felt.'

Armand grinned but Ilaria's eyes widened.

'Well that doesn't sound friendly at all.'

'No darling it's not.' Aurelie pouted. 'And for those who do win, the stature that comes with victory can lead to many benefits. Better employment for one —'

'Reaping the boon of free food, drink, attire and more.' Sabatino added.

'For an entire season.' Aurelie sipped. 'Or at least 'til the memory of their victory wears thin.'

Sabatino look at Armand and Ilaria. 'Needless to say, young novices, the less privileged entrants take the prospect of winning very seriously.'

'The main difference for those' said Aurelie 'is that compared to elite entrants, who have time to dedicate time to a daily regimen of practice —'

'Such as ourselves mia cara?'

'Such as we *plan* to do darling.' Aurelie corrected. 'But for humble competitors, unless they're sponsored by a patron, the only preparation they can afford is the grind of their daily work and life.'

Sabatino also explained he was sixteen when he ran the course for the first time. Since then he had competed more than a dozen times, but not in the previous five years. He had never won. Yet he often finished in the leading pack, so it was hoped his experience would be of great value.

Aurelie and Ilaria intended to remain together after each session. Then the *quintet* of competitors — with Tristan added to their number — would travel onto Hazel Wood. Once there, while the men began their circuits on horseback, the women hoped to recover and indulge.

Aurelie had retained a pair of masseurs from the *Pool of the Gods* to attend to them each day to oil, scrape and massage away their pain. Thereafter with morsels and wine, they intended to soak in her bathing tub built for two, filled with steaming herbal water. She had ordered the tub — handcrafted by their cooper — to be removed from the master chamber and placed upon the chateau's fore balcony. That vantage would offer our bathing goddesses a fulsome view of the entry avenue, its turning circuit and the road beyond where the horses would be running.

Aurelie had even ordered — from a rather notorious apothecary in Mantua — the same herbal remedy for muscular relief she purchased for Sabatino after he returned from his first martial campaign. And although Mantua was some distance to send to secure it, the prima donna swore that mystic woman knew her business more deeply than the ageing dolt who sold similar remedies in Verona.

Moreover she had discovered that Friar Lorenzo — who studied herbal lore deeply — swore by the skill of that mystic Mantuan but not the venerable Veronian. Finally, before retiring that night, both women had modestly declared that they had no ambition to *win* the footrace.

'Florentia challenged us. We simply hope to impress her by participating.' Ilaria declared humbly.

'Yes darling.' Aurelie agreed. 'However, for the sake of that impression and our pride, our *prima* goal must be to ensure that we *run* to the end without any need to walk or withdraw before time.'

'Agreed Lee Lee. We must accomplish that much.'

Yet after that declaration, I heard Sabatino confess to Armand that he felt sure, despite Aurelie saying so, she would not to be satisfied limiting herself to such a modest goal. That made me wonder, if the Capulet sister was anything like her brothers, Ilaria may find herself pushed well beyond the limits of her own humble ambitions.

Before they retired, Sabatino also suggested they make a solemn pact concerning their *commitment*. Though I hasten to add — after celebrating too much — it seemed a too simple matter for them to agree on that point!

'No matter how burdened anyone may feel from the effect of

daily practice –'

'Yes!' they all cried, giggling and guffawing.

'That unless injured in a manner that would *forego* safe participation ...'

'Yes!'

'Even if one is only fit to *walk* the course on any given day ...'

'Yes!'

'We must all participate *every* day without fail.'

'Here! Here! Here! Here!'

'Of course my beautiful handsome kissable darling!' Aurelie purred as she fell into his arms.

She plunged in to kiss him with a smile. I felt Aurelie may be hoping to assuage a sense of guilt after flirting so openly in his absence with the prince. I wondered how much he knew of how intimately his wife had shared a quiet corner with Escalus during Florentia's absence.

And so they were assembled together that next morning – all save Tristan – standing together beyond the Sycamore Hill gate. Ilaria and Aurelie gazed along the road in the direction of Hazel Wood. Maxine and I had arrived before them with both babes, one feeding upon the breast, the other gurgling in my arms. Sabatino's voice rose.

'The practice course is simplicity itself. Starting here each day we follow the road to the Hazel Wood gate.'

'Yes very simple.' said Ilaria. 'Or do I sound naïve?'

'Then ...' he smiled 'we continue along our entrance avenue 'til we reach the turning circuit before the chateau to complete half a circuit. That much spans a distance of –'

'A mile and a half?' Armand offered.

'Just so. Then without halting at all, we run the same path back again which will make one full circuit?

Aurelie calculated quickly. 'Ah, ah, ah, three miles.'

'Yes mia cara. And so, to ensure the full length we practise each time is valid for our purpose, we'll run that circuit twice for a total distance of?'

'Six miles!' I cried, rather happy with myself.

'Mercy Sab.' Ilaria bleated. 'That's not short.'

'No my sweet sister-in-law. But give or take a furlong, each year's allowance for the course ranges between four and a half miles at the least, to no more than six.'

'Why does it alter?' Armand enquired.

'Public works may block the prior path, natural catastrophes like a flood in the Adige, even an earthquake.'

'Earthquakes?'

'Yes. The very worst from Naples are often felt this far north quite intensely.'

'Oh don't fret Ria.' Aurelie lifted a mischievous brow. 'We haven't had a dangerous quake for many years.'

'That's right mia cara. Now, each season — once such things are taken into account — the Podestà has the final say on the length and direction.'

'Aurelie's new intimate friend!'

'Hush Ria don't make Sab jealous so early in the morning. He knows I'm just widening our circuit.'

Sabatino tilted his head toward Ilaria, pressing his lips in mock impatience. 'Is that what she calls it?'

Ilaria lifted a single brow in mimic of Aurelie.

'Oh Seb darling don't be ridiculous.'

That made us all smirk as Sabatino continued.

'Because Escalus is entered to run this season, most feel sure that as a respected man, no matter what route he announces, it's more like to be *longer* than *shorter*.'

'And so' Armand put in 'six miles would be our safest length to practice.'

All agreed, though the thought dismayed Ilaria.

'Now, depending upon whether its *dry* underfoot, each year the winning male usually completes six miles in just under an hour.' Sabatino continued.

'Or depending upon how many times the entrants slip, fall or are *encouraged* to fall!' Aurelie added wryly.

'*Encouraged* to fall?' Ilaria bleated.

'Both are common Ilaria.' said Sabatino. 'You'll be elite women running in humble company. And so before we're done, besides preparing yourselves to merely *finish* the course, you may wish to give some thought as to how you plan to *stay* on your feet.'

Ilaria glanced at Armand. Indeed he looked concerned. Staring soberly, Aurelie laid an arm about her.

'Darling the rules allow entrants a great deal of ... latitude. The whole reason they run naked is to ensure that one's rivals have very little to grip onto.'

'Oh dear mercy.' Ilaria muttered.

'Mercy will have little to do with the reception *we* receive. Yet ... it will be fun.'

Ilaria stared incredulously.

'Sab what manner of woman have you married?'

'Ilaria I ask myself that question every morning. Yet whatever she is ... I love her desperately.'

Finally it was agreed — upon Armand's enthusiastic suggestion — that when their second circuit was completing, rather than halt at the gate, they should attempt to climb to the crest of the hill and halt under the ancient sycamore! Comically, Ilaria glared at him in silence. And so it was *further* agreed — if needed during the early days of their practice — that portion could be *walked.*

'Yes my heart' Ilaria groaned sarcastically 'you can run up the terrifying hill to your soul's content. Yet I shall be *walking* up. Perhaps *crawling* up. Or instructing *Caspar* to carry me up!'

'Oh he can carry me Ria.' Aurelie purred. '*Before* I put my robe back on!'

Sabatino sighed. 'He's big enough to carry you both, naked or otherwise.' Aurelie

'Yes Ria! One under each arm!'

'Ah. You can giggle now.' Armand retorted. 'But when the end of the race falls in sight; when your thighs are drained and your lungs feel fit to burst —'

'Here he goes!' Ilaria tilted her eyes to Heaven.

'Pressed among rivals' Armand ran on 'the want to compete will suddenly rise in your breast —'

'Along with my nipples!' cried Aurelie.

Armand ignored her.

'And despite any effort you've given 'til that moment, your mind will implore you to endure one last bout, one final serving of sufferance to make a dash for the finish.'

'Dear God big brother! No wonder the English lost to the likes of you.' Ilaria pouted. 'Yes my heart that sounds stirring and romantic … yet also hideously painful!'

'My thoughts exactly Ria. You boys run for glory if you must. And yes, I'm up for my share of bruising and battering along the way, but otherwise, Ilaria and I shall merely run for our enjoyment.'

'And comfort.' Ilaria added with a smile.

'Yes darling for the first few days — perhaps the first week or more — we should have no greater goal than to complete the course without the need to walk or slow down.'

'I think that sounds reasonable Lee Lee.'

Sabatino bent a concerned look on them both, then suggested they may wish to set a less ambitious target in that short time to encourage more certain progress. They finally agreed their first goal would be, that by the end of the second week — no matter what their pace — neither would be walking or slowing for any portion of the course. No further mention was made of hoping to climb Sycamore Hill at the last. Yet despite that humble first goal, that spectre of climbing to the crest at anything faster than a breathless walk, would soon become an obsession for both women.

Both women were still young and healthy. What's more for Aurelie, the warrior blood of the Capulets ran in her veins. Like her brothers she had inherited a body that responded quickly to hard physical work. And so far for both women — just two years apart in age — the burden of pregnancy and birth had been forgiving.

For Ilaria, despite delivering Thibault in the late winter, in body at least, she appeared to have recovered strongly. It's true her weeks of greater solitude in the birthing chamber before and after his arrival had seemed to draw a cast of gloom about her for a time. It had concerned Maxine greatly, for she experienced the same pall herself with her first. And so she confided her fear of it to Aurelie.

It was then Aurelie suggested Ilaria should visit Friar Lorenzo at the Abbey, to begin her preparations to re-enter the flock and society. From the moment she left his cell that day, her heart had seemed lighter. After we attended the cathedral and Herb Market Square, where Ilaria had met so many enthralling people, gained agreement on the curious corner and made peace with the Montecchi, that darkness in her eyes seemed to have vanished entirely. As we left the square that day Maxine had breathed a great sigh of relief. So did Aurelie and yes, so did I.

Now as both goddesses turned to face Maxine and approached to see the children, a glimpse revealed both had decided to forego painting their faces, or to do any more than just bind their hair away from their necks against the threat of heat from the exertions to come. I knew they planned, after that first session ended to return to Hazel Wood — to be oiled, scraped, massaged and bathed together — then attend to their toilette in the care of Maxine and Aurelie's close servant Veronique. Thereafter the Goddesses would emerge resplendent to watch the men race their rounds on horseback.

As Ilaria leaned to stroke Thibault's cheek, my eye caught a glimpse of movement. Fabrizio appeared beyond the gate, acting more as a senior page than junior squire for the moment. Following in his wake were a pair of servers burdened with refreshments to offer. Behind these came eight veteran soldiers from Tristan's company. Jogging line abreast they were armed for trouble and swept past us all.

Turning hard left they continued along the road to populate the length of the course. Their attendance should ease any foreboding the participants may have for their security of course, particularly Ilaria and Aurelie. A sentinel would be stationed every quarter mile along the path, with instructions to retire back to Sycamore Hill whenever the trailing pair — whoever that may be — had passed on their return to complete a second circuit.

Then for the sake of added protection, the sound of iron-clad hoofs descending the path met our ears. Caspar appeared mounted upon Loki, his great painted battle horse. Our giant was to lead Ilaria and Aurelie — at a trot, walk or whatever may be required — around the circuit until they were done. As a last measure of safety — no doubt the least — I was instructed to follow Ilaria and Aurelie, leading an ass with Maxine aboard. My sweet wife toted a satchel of wisely chosen supplies against any urgent need that may arise.

Armand and Sabatino had trained for such events many times since they were squires. And so, planning to start first, expecting to complete ahead of their wives, as a very last precaution, once their circuits were complete they intended to retrace their steps until they caught up with Ilaria and Aurelie, then passing them by, fall in with Maxine and I to follow at a respectful distance.

With the soldiery dispersed, and libations now in hand to refresh the quartet, their company awaited Caspar's return. The giant hadn't waited at all but cantered on to confirm the course was secured all the way to the Hazel Wood gate. Every day until the day of the racing festival — excepting each Sabbath of course — this was to be our morning routine. If they could sustain it.

The athletes stood together in their Grecian finery as early spring sunshine peeked through the sycamore canopy. The servers hovered with salvers of silver beakers brimming with watered wine to slake their thirst and toast the start of their adventure. Two Gods and one Goddess smiled broadly.

'Aurelie.' Ilaria whimpered. 'I can't believe this madness! What have we agreed to?'

'Darling you're young and healthy. You'll survive it. As for myself, I know on this very first day I'll die out there somewhere upon the circuit.'

'Ah that's very sad.' Armand pouted and frowned. 'Will you mourn for her Sab?'

'Of course he will imbecile. Then I'll have to leave everything to

... well let's just agree that I'm about to die.'

'Lee Lee I feel so naked out of doors with no paint or lacquer or —'

'First of all Ria you look like a goddess. Second of all, none can see you?'

'Your definition of none?'

'Oh sooner or later all your people will see you at your best and worst. Don't dwell on it darling. They're not the ones we hope to impress with our showing in the world.'

'I'll take your word for it.'

'And don't forget, in less than two hours we'll be resting at Hazel Wood, pampered by strong hands and soaking our cares away. On competition day however, we'll arrive painted to impress and primped to perfection.'

'Boys' Ilaria began soberly 'you've trained for this manner of madness before.'

Sabatino smiled. 'Many times Ilaria.'

'As Armand knows Sab, I have a ritual of exertions that I learned as a demoiselle which I still perform daily.'

'Oh Ria I used to do that.' Aurelie replied. 'I don't know about yours but once we were married I realised mine were designed to prepare me for the rigours of the boudoir.'

Ilaria knit her brows in thought. 'Hmm. Lee Lee now that you say so —'

'Since then however' Aurelie cut in 'I decided the real thing counts for just as much.'

'Interesting.'

'And so now I do far less in the morning. However, darling, fucking is one thing —'

'Heavens Aurelie! It's morning.'

Sabatino and Armand lifted brows at each other.

'Oh Ria, morning or night I know this start today will be a disaster for me!'

'No.'

'Yes. With the exception of Sab chasing me about the boudoir, I haven't run a jot since I chased butterflies through our gardens with my children.'

I was standing by the mule with Maxine, listening and waiting. I still felt I knew little of Aurelie, but began to believe her protestations of inadequacy were offered to ensure Ilaria didn't feel threatened by her presence as a partner. Indeed — despite those rantings — I suspected the prima donna was more ready than she revealed. For since the day we knew they would compete, I felt sure Aurelie already appeared to be more trim and active.

I mentioned that quietly to Maxine. She agreed to my first assessment, yet felt the latter had been achieved by Aurelie, not in preparation for the race, but in anticipation of the soiree with Escalus two days before.

'I think I have those butterflies!' grumbled Ilaria. 'Gentleman. Suggestions?'

'Yes Sab' added Aurelie 'we hope to exert as little effort as possible for as much gain as possible?'

Armand turned to Sabatino. 'Hmm what do you think Sab. A request from our wives for an opinion?'

'Oh yes Armand perfecto!' he bleated in mock consternation. 'Push me off the cliff first? Oh very well I'll suggest something Ilaria. In all honesty my own physique is not really built for this kind of sport.'

'No Ria it's true. My husband's much better at another kind of sport!'

'Oh Lee Lee hush and pay attention.'

'Thank you Ilaria.' Sabatino continued. 'I confess that as a young squire, I found it difficult to make a good start with running. My mentor however, confessed the same to me and said he was mentored by an English knight who also suffered the same fate.'

'That all sounds promising. Lee Lee perhaps we won't make such a poor start? Sab what did he suggest to cure your shortcoming?'

'When I began he advised me to listen to my body.'

Ilaria frowned in mock confusion.

'Ria I think my husband's flirting with you!'

Sabatino rolled his eyes. 'What the man meant was that you mustn't make speed your first goal. Breathing must be your first priority, and I've found it's the absolute key.'

'Breathing?' snapped Aurelie. 'Splendid darling. I think I have that in order all ready.'

'I mean that to begin, don't run more vigorously than the breath your body offers you to support your first efforts.'

Aurelie caught his eye and laid her hand on his shoulder. She reached with the other and grazed a fingernail over the exposed portion of his chest.

'That's what he thinks about when we make love.'

All laughed, except Sabatino who smiled patiently, and Ilaria who listened intently.

'And ...' Sabatino added 'be sure to breathe in through the nose and out through the mouth.'

'Oh?'

'Yes that's important. And don't be afraid to puff rather loudly like a horse.'

'Puff?'

'Yes Ilaria. That helps a great deal. Feel free to puff as loudly as you like.'

'There you see Ria? He is flirting with you.'

We laughed again and Sabatino joined in.

He turned to Aurelie with a mocking frown.

'Mia cara —' She laid a fingertip to his lips.

'Yes lover I know. Go slow. Breathe through the nose and suck with the mouth.'

A volley of laughter exploded again. Now Ilaria was smiling too. Yet to my complete surprise, a raucous laugh had exploded from the gate as Boccolo lost control. Every eye turned to see, as all but Liberati beside him — who confined himself to a thin smile — laughed boisterously. Armand clapped Sabatino's shoulder.

'Now you see why I didn't offer advice!'

Sabatino glanced along the road and scanned us all.

'Now wayward people, settle down. Caspar will return in a

moment and I'll cease all my tutoring. But to summarise Ilaria.'

'Yes I'm listening.'

'Run as slowly as you wish to begin, for as long or as short as you wish, until you feel you must slow to a walk if that happens.'

'Yes thank you Sab.'

'However. Whatever distance you manage to trot for today, practice breathing as you go to ensure the flow of air remains continuous. Dealing with that first will reduce your fatigue more quickly than any other element.'

Ilaria grinned and rubbed his shoulder.

'That sounds very useful.'

'Yes darling wonderful.' Aurelie kissed his cheek. 'Now stop flirting with my brother's wife!'

'Ah, and one last thing.' said Sabatino ignoring her.

'Yes.' said Ilaria.

'If you feel you must slow down or walk, ensure you keep moving until the whole course is done. Unless genuinely injured, you must never halt completely.'

Aurelie frowned. 'But I know I'll get a stich from the start. That always happens.'

'I used to get them.' said Armand. 'When it starts, don't stop running, just concentrate on your breathing to distract you. That works wonders. Gone in an instant.'

'Like counting sheep.' said Ilaria.

'Yes darling that may work.' Aurelie agreed.

'I'll count my breaths.' Armand raised a knowing brow to Sabatino.

'Ah yes ladies, one important thing we both nearly forgot. Each day while you're still walking through the latter portion, add extra length to the portion you run to keep reducing the portion you walk. Your bodies will adjust much faster than you expect. Soon you'll be running from the start to the finish.'

'Thank you Sab.' Ilaria glanced at Armand. 'You've said very little my heart.'

'Oh angel I agree with Sab on all points. But I confess my own experience with running to begin with was quite different. I doubt it would be of any great help.'

'Different? How so?'

Armand hesitated for a moment. Ilaria's brows lifted in expectation. Aurelie's followed suit.

'Well in truth I found that I could run fast and didn't fatigue at all.'

Aurelie huffed and rolled her eyes in reprimand so emphatically that I couldn't help laughing. Ignoring my outburst she turned to Ilaria with a sober expression.

'In a moment when we disrobe darling, we'll have to avert our eyes because the sun will be shining so brightly from my brothers asshole —'

A broad hand clapped onto her mouth as Armand gripped her waist and lifted his sister under one arm to spin in a circuit, whirling her about. She screamed in mock protest under the cover of his hand. Cupid's Balls! It was priceless of course, and very much akin to their antics on the night Ilaria had announced she was carrying Thibault. When he finally placed her down, even Liberati had given himself up to laughter.

'Chevalier' called the old veteran 'if your parents could see you both! I haven't seen you do that together since you were children!'

'Aurelie indulge me for a moment.' said Armand. 'You may find my point is in fact humbling.'

'Humbling?' she teased. 'The big brother I remember was anything but humble!'

'Oh no Lee Lee.' Ilaria corrected her drily. 'Now he's very humble. Far too humble.'

Armand huffed. 'What I mean to say is that before I served as a squire I was fast. Very fast ...'

'Is that the *humble* portion?' Suddenly her mouth was restrained again.

'Nor did I fatigue at all but my mentor railed at me!'

He let her loose.

'For being so full of yourself!'

Ilaria frowned at her and hugged Armand with a consoling smile. He glared at Aurelie.

'No. Despite feeling pleased with myself he faulted my *balance*, said it was deplorable, working against me, wasting my energy and slowing me down!'

'And so my heart ... you were *very* fast but *slow*.' Aurelie leaned against Ilaria's shoulder as she giggled and pointed at Armand who rolled his eyes.

'He said my arms were swinging across my body as I ran, tilting me like a mad man.' He demonstrated for all.

'Oh yes!' spurted Aurelie. 'I remember that now. We called him the *mad baboon*.'

'With every step I was hefting my weight onto my heels. It wasted effort in my legs. The man forced me to alter my technique, to swing my hands by my sides and weigh each step into the front of my feet.'

'How curious.'

'At first it felt very awkward and I hated to do it. But then voila! Suddenly I began to run with less effort and faster than ever before.'

'Hmm?' Aurelie narrowed her eyes. 'I'm not sure the end of your tale doesn't still manage to brag —'

Ilaria scowled mockingly. 'Oh Lee Lee leave my poor speedy baboon alone!'

Cantering hoofbeats sounded upon the curve of the road. Every head turned.

'Here comes Caspar!' squealed Aurelie.

'Perfecto.' said Sabatino. 'And ladies one final suggestion since you plan to practice together.'

'Oh we must run together!' Ilaria insisted.

'Then ... until you can run the course all the way through, you must allow the slowest runner to set the pace.'

'Very well.' Aurelie agreed.

'And mia cara, now the most difficult advice of all.'

'Do not *talk* while you run!' cried Armand already bending and stretching.

'Oh but you can't be serious. No talking! I was looking forward to –'

Sabatino glared soberly. 'No talking mia cara. It will rob you of breath.'

'If you chatter little sister, you'll run no further than a pair of snails.'

Aurelie huffed and stared at him. 'Well I just don't believe it's possible, that's all.'

Armand pouted in thought. ' I do have a sure remedy for that problem if you're willing to allow it?'

Aurelie glanced at Ilaria. 'Ria that sounds ominous. What do you think?'

'We're in this far. Let him do his worst Lee Lee.'

'Really? Oh ... what the Devil! What is it?'

'Do you swear to abide by the rules of my remedy?'

'Oh yes, yes, yes, we swear!'

'Very well.' Armand turned on his heel. 'Marcel!'

I was standing nearby with Figara in my arms. Maxine was already mounted upon the mule and caring for Thibault. For once that beast hadn't farted at all, though I expected that to change as soon as it began to move. In haste at Armand's summons, I drew over to him.

'Sabatino?' he said. 'A word!'

The three of us drew together. Heads nodded in agreement. Then I returned quickly to whisper to Maxine. Her eyes opened wide. Aurelie and Ilaria both saw her do so. Suddenly both husbands were grinning maliciously.

'Well?' Aurelie lifted her brows.

'It's agreed.' said Armand.

'What pray tell?' said Ilaria warily.

'First let's disrobe angel.' He glanced at Aurelie. 'I think that will help clarify things.'

'Clarify?'

'Fabrizio!' Armand called with a smile.

'Yes Chevalier.'

'Collect our garments.'

The goddesses were about to regret offering their consent with so little debate.

Chapter 17 Discipline

One moment later shoulder brooches were unfastened and fine Egyptian linen was drawn away from bodies without the slightest compunction. Fabrizio's safe hands gathered up lengths of fabric as skin and muscles were revealed, taught and soft, bronzed from the sun, white from the lack of it, shoulders, backs, chests, nipples, midriffs, waists, buttocks, thighs and groin hair. Completing the panoply of flesh on display, a pair of masculine members were visible too. Neither man lacked endowment with balls to match.

Both women appeared to be whispering comparisons of their husbands' physiques. I glanced at Maxine. Yes, though Thibault still fed at her breast, her own eyes were distracted. I turned my attention to the gods and goddesses. Between the men, one looked more suited to run longer distances while the other seemed built for sprinting.

Armand was the latter of course, built for fast explosive power. His broad muscular chest displayed wide dark nipples and was covered in thick curling hair that ranged down his torso and groin to the tops of his thighs. Sabatino's upper form was muscular too, but lithe rather than broad and bulging. His nipples were smaller — boyish one might say — and from neck to waist, unlike Armand, his body was all but bereft of hair.

Both men had narrow waists. Yet Sabatino's physique was more straight from chest to thighs while Armand's broad upper form narrowed toward his waist, then bulged again through his muscular ass and broad thighs. No, my eyes didn't remain on them for more than a moment, for I quickly decided if Maxine could stare, then so could I.

My wife knew I'd seen Ilaria naked before. Not just in the bathhouse, or glimpses here and there, but given how often I played in their chamber during intimate moments I had seen her many times. Not so for Aurelie however. And yes, I had imagined what she may look like beneath her alluring couture. Oh well bite my bare ass, yes I had! And so as the goddesses stood side by side, divested of their garments, still staring and whispering, I also stared and made my own comparison.

Ilaria was taller, noticeable at that moment as both stood in sandals. Yet despite being taller her shoulders seemed delicate, while Aurelie's were more broad and firm. Although Ilaria's not buxom like the duchess, her breasts were larger than Aurelie's and her nipples were wide and pale. Aurelie's nipples were smaller and darker and appeared to be naturally protruded. It seems antic to say that they looked more alert, yet somehow they did.

Finally I noted Ilaria's hips were a little broader, yet neither had hips such as Maxine or the duchess possessed, the kind that accentuate how narrow the waist is in comparison. And with that last thought, I glanced at Maxine again. It occurred to me, a little frightfully, that other than my her lack of height and dark hair, Maxine's form was a compact version of the Duchess de Paris. At that moment, other than brown eyes compared to blue, the main difference between them appeared to be the duchess seemed to want to compliment and seduce me, while Maxine seemed to want to criticise and scold me.

Oh yes I know, I was lucky to have her. And yes, I loved her more than words can say. Yes, I'd better shut my mouth before I get into any more trouble upon that subject.

Finally let me observe about our feminine competitors that, taken all in all upon that morning at their start, Aurelie appeared more trim, firm and ready than Ilaria. Her back, belly, ass and thighs showed more muscular shape and seemed ready for the challenge ahead. Perhaps understandably, considering Ilaria's recent birthing confinement, she appeared softer all over. Indeed I was seeing her this way for the first time since Thibault's birth, and the form of her belly was different. I'm also not quite sure how, yet strangely I felt that her ass was ... flatter.

While the servers divested the group of their brooches and rope belts, refilled cups or gathered them, Fabrizio ranged about gathering and folding cloth, showing more interest in careful stowage than the sight of bodies to behold. Aurelie stepped over to Sabatino. Her eyes glanced down with a smile as her nail tip reached to the base of his penis and drew along it.

'Won't this wag relentlessly? It must be distracting?'

'It was at first mia cara.' He began to stretch. 'However one grows accustomed to it. I confess that your touching it is far more distracting.' He reached a fingertip to the top of her breast and grazed it down to circle her nipple. 'Won't these bounce relentlessly?''

'Hmm.' She glanced at herself. 'I was flatter when I chased butterflies. Yet I think I'll be fine. Ria has more to contend with.'

'If that causes you discomfort Madame' cried Maxine 'I have a remedy for it. My bust grew quickly when I was young yet it didn't stop me running wild with my brothers for very long.'

'We'll see Max,' said Ilaria. 'I expect some discomfort to begin. Let's wait and see.'

It was clear after disrobing both women had forgotten the conference Armand had with Sabatino and I before they disrobed. So had I! Armand lifted his brows to me and made a sign. I blinked in confusion, then nodded in comprehension, returning to the mule to gather something. Now I came forward. Ilaria and Aurelie realised something was different. I tilted my eyes to Heaven in mock innocence as Armand motioned for me to wait.

'Marcel will make the starting announcement to Sabatino and I first, then for you. Now remember, you swore to comply with my remedy to curb the temptation to chatter.'

'Oh yes we swore.' Aurelie sighed.

'This remedy was applied to myself as a squire. This time Marcel will act as marshal for it.'

'Marcel?' Ilaria protested.

'Yes angel. And the marshal's been instructed, any time a word is uttered by either of you before you reach the end of the second circuit, he has permission to *restore* quiet.'

'Does he?' said Aurelie defiantly. 'Just how does he intend to —'

Before Aurelie finished I drew a mule crop from behind my back and her eyes widened.

'He won't *dare!*' she insisted.

'He *will* dare, or Marcel will be sorely punished himself if he fails to carry out my instructions.'

Aurelie stared defiantly, blazing blue eyes met blazing blue eyes.

'Oh Lee Lee don't fret.' said Ilaria taking my own arm with a smile. 'When the men depart this rascal will be handsomely bribed to comply with *our* instructions!'

'You may attempt it angel. But Marcel's been warned that if any guard on the circuit reports his failure to me after we're done, he shall be banished.

'Banished? Don't be absurd. What do you mean?'

'Banished from keeping intimate company with his wife for six months.'

Aurelie and Ilaria stared at each other with concern.

'Merciful Heavens!' Ilaria shot.

'Oh yes' said Aurelie 'imagine that ribald rogue being banished from intimacy for six months.'

Ilaria frowned. 'He wouldn't bear it. I banished him for six weeks before they were married and —'

Armand smiled. 'In that time he was a *wreck.*'

'Lee Lee with a threat of six months' Ilaria pouted 'there'll be no stopping him.'

Aurelie scowled at me. 'What's more the knave appears as if he will *relish* the duty.'

Given the risk I now faced for failure, I refused to be intimidated and smiled in return.

'Oh Aurelie why did we swear to such nonsense?'

The prima donna glared at her husband who was still stretching but now smiling.

'Well Sab? Who gets to smack you both on the ass for talking?'

'I'll do it Madonna!' cried Maxine with a grin.

Sabatino smiled. 'Mia cara, whoever you can find to keep up with us, is welcome to try.'

Ilaria looked at me, hoping for hope. I knit my brows sternly to suggest there would be none.

'Armand no! I can't allow it. I *unswear* my vow!'

'Hmm. Unfortunately angel, once a vow is sworn it cannot be foresworn *so easily.*'

She pouted in frustration, appealing to Sabatino who remained sober-faced.

'Oh very well.' She turned on me. 'But I warn you, rascal! Tomorrow I'll bring my own crop to retaliate!'

My eyes opened wide as I stared at Armand, who smiled broadly. Aurelie grinned.

'Ah Ria that's clever!' she purred and glared at me. 'Well imbecile? Nothing about that in my brother's stupid rules! I shall bring mine too!'

'Now ladies ... it grows late.' said Armand.

'Yes.' Sabatino agreed. 'Let us begin.'

After that cascade of short delays, which seemed unavoidable to orientate them on that first morning, a few moments later the challenge began in earnest. Maxine and I watched two pairs of naked bodies, first the men and then — perhaps a minute later — the women, trotting away to complete their first circuit to Hazel Wood and back. Caspar rode between both pairs, leading the women by half a furlong. I reached for the she-mule's halter, drawing her to follow as Maxine ensured both babes were settled into the wide baskets we had suspended on either side of her.

And despite Ilaria's threat to me, though I managed to strike each bare ass at least once on that first morning — yes I enjoyed it — she and Aurelie quickly discovered they'd have no need to resort to retaliation thereafter. For in rather quick time, both athletes realised two things.

First, just as Sabatino had warned, attempting to speak while attempting to trot was difficult to do if one hoped to sustain their effort to continue. Second, despite my stern duty to smack their exalted backsides if they transgressed — and that wonderful excuse for me to keep watch upon said exalted backsides — I've never been able to maintain attention upon tasks of longish duration. And so, before we even reached the second sentry on the circuit, I had become too distracted by my need to help Maxine attend both babes, to maintain a close watch.

What's more, by the time we had reached the Hazel Wood gate on that first morning, both women had slowed to a walk and were chattering away. My duty only allowed me to chastise if their chatter interrupted their *trotting*. By then, at a walk, it did not. Ilaria and Aurelie finished their first two circuits by spurring back to a trot now and then — for shorter and shorter periods — until they reached our gate for the second time, then slowly climbed the final hill together.

Armand and Sabatino, having completed their run well in advance, doubled back as planned to follow them in company with Maxine and I. Neither Ilaria nor Aurelie had halted completely at any time. That goal was met. And their periods of trotting had set a first benchmark for them to gauge future effort by. As they halted under the shade of the ancient sycamore both women made a solemn pact.

'From this day on Lee Lee we can't fall below the benchmarks we've set.'

'Yes Ria. Every next day we must try to better it.'

'Agreed.'

Yes, they spat on their hands and shook to seal it.

Their start had begun.

After returning to Hazel Wood together with the men — including Tristan — who immediately began preparations to ride, Aurelie and Ilaria enjoyed the indulgence of a massage and hot soaking, perhaps more than ever before in their lives.

Maxine and I were happy to observe how much that adventure appeared to be uniting them already.

Next morning the social preamble that had prolonged the first start repeated once more, yet with less delay. By the third morning their preparatory ado had reduced to a briefer ritual. The couples began to exchange pleasantries more quickly, disrobe without commentary and make their start with little delay. By the fourth morning Ilaria and Aurelie seemed to be more mindful that, in four short weeks the princess would be watching. So would all in the citadel of course, including the new people they had met in Florentia's exalted circuit.

Bearing that in mind, their goal to ensure they ran to the end without any need to walk, took on a greater sense of importance. I felt that was because both could already sense they may accomplish that goal more readily than either had expected. On the first day both had fretted over whether they could achieve that modest benchmark before time was up.

Yet after surviving the first three days of gasping, sweating, sore thighs, calves, feet and all. After being laid on tables side by side to be oiled, scraped and massaged together while I played for their comfort. And after soaking in the decadent tub on that wide balcony with glasses in hand as they watched the horseman start their first run, both agreed they were ambitious enough to endure yet more.

'Cupid's Balls!' Maxine whispered in mimic of me. 'Given *such* soft treatment so would I.'

Maxine's sarcasm, of course, was due to her frustration at not being allowed to run with them.

As for Ilaria and Aurelie, they already felt certain.

'Come what may we'll impress the great woman.'

'Yes Lee Lee, I think we will.'

'We must darling. No one else that we could align ourselves to in Verona can offer as much support to our ambitions as Tia can.'

'And her charismatic husband?'

'Well yes darling. I haven't forgotten him.'

'I'm sure. And the value of that association is more potent now that we have secured our curious corner and the architect's begun to draw his plans.'

'Yes Ria it's very exciting. When we're done here tomorrow we should venture to the citadel to monitor his progress.' Her eyes lit. 'Perhaps send a note to Tia? See if she'd like to attend?'

'Oh that's a wonderful idea.' Ilaria smile.

'Perhaps ...' Aurelie added 'we could invite Tia *and* Escalus? Explain our plans to them both.'

Biting her own lip Ilaria looked at Aurelie thoughtfully. 'Hmm. Upon one condition Lee Lee.'

'Yes tempter?'

'This time seductress ... we must ensure Sabatino comes along. I want him to see that he has nothing to fear from our continuing contact with *either* of them.'

Aurelie became thoughtful for a moment, as if her first instinct was to resist.

'Yes darling you're right.' She frowned. 'I don't know why, but somehow this whole adventure arouses me. I quite enjoy taking risks.'

'Oh?' Ilaria lifted her brows. 'I hadn't noticed.'

'Perhaps ... I should be careful not to expose myself to quite so many at once.'

To hear her say so, Maxine and I exchanged a glance and breathed a sigh of relief.

Aurelie was beautiful and Escalus was handsome. The princess had told Ilaria he'd flirt with her harmlessly to satisfy his vanity. But since we came to Verona, we had heard that style of comment a great deal among the elite. It made me wonder, if the Capulets returned to Lyon, whether we'd hear much the same in elite circuits there? But we were in Verona. And they were discussing a prince who knew he wouldn't remain in his post there forever.

Sooner or later Venice would move Escalus and Florentia onto a new posting. Given that predicament, and how much wealth and power he had at his disposal to conduct an affair with discretion, I felt that, if given any more encouragement, the prince wouldn't be satisfied to restrict his interest to mere flirtation. What's more, it was now clear Ilaria didn't think so either. Nor did Aurelie.

Next morning their work continued, the first Saturday of their training. Perhaps for the best, they met with the architect thereafter, yet not with Florentia or Escalus. For the better part of a week, their mornings had been filled with fatigue and discomfort. But that effect already seemed to be fading and the challenge ahead was enlivening them both.

After the first rest on the Sabbath when their practise resumed at the start of their second week, half way around the first circuit Ilaria noted an increasing discomfort she felt from the motion of her breasts. Yet despite Aurelie's offer to halt, Ilaria refused to slow their progress. Hearing that complaint however — having anticipating the need — Maxine handed Thibault to my care and dismounted.

She drew two long strips of linen from the mule's off-side basket. Each strip was at least a yard in length and the width of a long finger. And so with Thibault in my arms and Figara gurgling in the near-side hamper, Maxine hurried forward to offer assistance. Yet despite all pleading Ilaria shunned her assistance, refusing to stop until Maxine assured her the remedy could applied as they trotted along together. She promised it would take just a moment, vowing it would work for Ilaria just as it had for herself.

Maxine ran to the fore, turning to face Ilaria and running on rearward! I was suitably impressed!

'Oh Maxine really ...'

'Just a moment Mistress! One moment.' She offered the middle of a length to Ilaria. 'Lay this flat and firmly against your nipples.'

Ilaria did so, then Maxine fell behind her to grasp the hanging ends and draw them toward her. She tied them firmly against Ilaria's back, ensuring the binding would hold still. She reached the other length forward.

'Take this one Mistress. Do the same again.'

Ilaria laid it over the first layer and held it in place again for an instant. Maxine repeated her part from behind, fumbling a little as she trotted along.

'Wiggle and adjust if you need. It's just for a start, yet that should do for the moment.'

'Yes.' Ilaria wiggled and adjusted. 'Yes Max that's better. Much better. Thank you.'

'Marcel has the children Mistress. May I stay for a moment to mention ...'

'Yes Max but quickly. We vowed not to chatter.'

'Yes. Yes. Yes. Expecting that discomfort might begin to haunt you —'

'It has been a little.'

'And so the other day, when you were visiting the architect in the citadel, I stole away to enquire about the race rules for women with regard to coverings on the body.'

Aurelie smiled. 'That was clever.'

'Thank you Madonna.'

'Max.' Ilaria huffed. 'To the point.'

'Yes Mistress. In the previous races, bustier women have been allowed to resort to that same measure without being accused of breaching the rules.'

'Yes.' Aurelie agreed. 'I recall one or two. Mercy, could you imagine the officials complaining?'

'Oh they did at first Madonna.'

'Of course. Once a year they want to see it all.'

'Well.' huffed Ilaria. 'The men show it all.'

'Yes Ria they do. And you have lovely nipples. Perhaps we'd be clever to show them off.'

'I think at this moment' Ilaria continued to huff '*comfort* is clever. Perhaps on the day ... oh I mustn't talk.'

'No don't talk Mistress. Breathe.'

'Nor you Max. Now retreat.'

'I will. But let me just add the official warned me such coverings are seen as a *danger* to the wearer not an *advantage* against their rivals.'

'Why?'

'If a rival grips it to help topple you, it's allowable.'

'Oh.'

'So is gripping hair or shoving with shoulders, elbows, hands, hips, heads, knees or feet!'

'Mercy. Yes I see.'

'So do I Ria. We'll have to give more thought to that part. Now Max —'

'Yes Madonna I'll go. I enjoyed running with you. I wish I —'

'Maxine go!'

'Yes Madame.'

Maxine fell back to me, pleased with the result of her assistance but still upset she couldn't run. During that day's session of recuperation at Hazel Wood, the information was discussed again. Aurelie felt they should both still run bare on the day of the event. But for now, both agreed the relief Ilaria felt from the improvised garment made it necessary.

When they resumed next morning — Tuesday — Ilaria's spirits seemed greatly lifted to know the work ahead would be much more tolerable. Moreover, since Maxine had warned about the danger of loose hair, Ilaria decided they must experiment with methods of tying it up so tightly it wouldn't easily fail if gripped at by a rival or pulled hard.

That day, after practise was done, our entourage of competitors decided to call upon the architect in the citadel. Quite by accident, their party encountered Escalus and Florentia in transit. Despite Sabatino's absence at the castle soiree — and our concerns as to why he was absent — he seemed to engage affably with the prince. Indeed both men seemed enjoy each other's company. It was curious to see, yet I felt sure neither man held a jot of resentment for the other. Was that because Sabatino trusted Aurelie implicitly? Or because he felt — with such a gap between their ages — it was inevitable that sooner or later she would take a lover?

I mentioned it to Maxine as she fiddled with my own lankish hair, attempting to solve the dilemma of how to tie Ilaria and Aurelie's more firmly.

'Don't be absurd. How do you think such things?'

'Well I only meant —'

'Don't forget, Don Sabatino's a soldier. He nearly died *twice* already.'

'What's that to the point of my —'

'Perhaps he wants her to understand, if fate should take him and leave her alone, he wouldn't expect Dona Aurelie to pine her life away or become a monastic.'

'You wouldn't pine for me?'

'Don't be ridiculous. You're not going to die in battle. Knowing your luck, you'll outlive us all.'

'I don't want to outlive you sweetheart.'

'Yes you do, thank you very much. I don't want to be left alone! I'll do the leaving first, if you don't mind.'

'Very well. Perhaps we'll manage to perish together.'

'Imbecile!'

'Well what's wrong with that?' I replied.

'Who'll remain for the children?'

'We only have one.' I bleated, yet Maxine glared in defiance. 'Oh yes alright then.' I groaned. 'I'll go second.'

Next morning Maxine styled Ilaria's hair differently, claiming she knew how to achieve the desired result. Plaits tied firmly in a bundle with strips of linen tucked into the folds were agreed as the final remedy. She had prepared mine as a model to show Aurelie's close server, Veronique, before it was attempted! Oh yes, all four women giggled uncontrollably at the antic sight.

By the middle of week two, steady progress was being made by both women. Aurelie's body had responded most to the effort so far, her torso and back beginning to ripple with muscle. Yet Ilaria also showed signs of transformation. She was becoming more lean, the effect of which was already visible in her face. And magically, even her ass seemed to be regaining its shape.

Perhaps for both, it was due in part to their stern agreement to follows Sabatino's advice.

'I know, because you're working so hard, it's tempting, but try not to eat any more than you would do if you *weren't* running. Indeed if it's possible, attempt to reduce your just intake a little.'

'Reduce it!' Aurelie shrieked. 'Mio dio!'

'Now mia cara I ask you, you're looking so healthy and strong, like the day you arrived here. Armand and I are both following the same routine. I know you can both do it.'

'Do you think I'm ... more beautiful than —'

'Excepting the days that each of our children were born. And the day that we wed of course.'

'Flatterer.'

'No Aurelie. You know I never flatter in that way.'

'Yes. I know you don't.'

Sabatino reached for his wife. 'My love I've never seen you more beautiful. You're glowing with health.'

I felt if Aurelie hadn't been motivated before, she certainly was after gaining that attention. By Thursday of that second week, Ilaria and Aurelie were running beyond the first circuit without reducing to a walk. No, as yet, neither could complete a second circuit without walking. Yet each day they crept closer to achieving that goal. And by then both had become hopeful of accomplishing it.

By the end of that week however, they had only *two* weeks left to do so, and still couldn't tell how long the rest may take achieve. Then, on the second morning of their third week — having followed Sabatino's advice to allow the slowest to set the pace until they could complete the entire circuit through — as they approached the last guard on their second circuit, with just a quarter mile left to finish it all, Ilaria hailed Aurelie and suggested they slow to a walk.

I was leading the mule and turned to Maxine who was squinting in a frown. She had been watching them intently. And although it was clear Ilaria was sorely fatigued, it was also clear Aurelie was fit to run on and reach the end. Sabatino and Armand were just behind us, having turned about some time before and run back to join us.

'Oh that's a shame.' Armand said quietly

'Yes.' Sabatino agreed. 'Perhaps tomorrow.'

I felt a tap on my shoulder. I turned to look into Maxine's eyes. She had a mischievous smile on her lips and glanced down. I followed her eyes. She held something in her hand. My own eyes leapt open, yet I took it and ran!

A moment later I was lurking behind Ilaria, protesting to Aurelie she was all but spent and would need to stop in a moment. Aurelie saw me. She saw what I held and rather than say a word, simply turned her eyes to the front.

SMACK! The crop leather slapped hard on her ass.

'AHHH!' Ilaria screamed wheeling in shock.

'No TALKING!' I bellowed. 'EYES FRONT!'

An ominous red welt painted her right cheek.

Ilaria wheeled and screamed.

'Marcel you DOG! AHHHHH!'

'TAIS-TOI!' I bellowed.

Her eyes bulged with anger and then ... I smacked her again! Harder!

Cupid's Balls! Somehow it felt very good to do so! Now she had a mark on each side.

'AHHHH! Oh you ... you ... FUCKER! How dare you smack me! I'll KILL you for that!'

We were all staggered to hear it. Never before had she cursed with such venom. Somehow, it sent me out of control and I cackled like a ranting witch.

'HA!' I cried. 'If you can catch me little BITCH!'

I ran a wild circuit around to turn Ilaria forward, then trotted on rearward, turning the crop, offering the handle. Her face was purple with rage. She needed no more encouragement, snatching it away with murder in her eyes.

'You CRETIN!' screamed Aurelie. 'Come on RIA! Let's make him PAY!'

For the love of Heaven pandemonium erupted!

Ilaria leapt like a wildcat as I spun on my heel to run for my life. In a very short time, as they chased me together, screaming vengeance on my head, both completed the final circuit without slowing to walk.

Oh sweet friends all that saved me from a thrashing was my ability to scramble over a firmly shut gate. Yet naked as she was, crop still in hand, Ilaria clambered over it too! Cupid's Balls! The look on Liberati's face as she did so was priceless! Taken all in all, that ending was one of the funniest sights I've ever witnessed. Armand and Sabatino were doubled over with laughter. Boccolo was scratching his head, staring as I raced up the hill and Ilaria bravely attempted to follow me.

But the feisty woman was not ready to manage such a feat. Her thighs were screaming, her lungs were bursting as she collapsed in a heaving, sweating, frowning heap upon the path for a moment. Then Aurelie arrived, followed by Armand and Sabatino, who helped bring Ilaria to her feet.

That was all I saw.

For when her angry eyes met mine, I ran up to the crest in a single breath — or so it felt — and straight into the stable to hide until she left for Hazel Wood to be pampered.

Chapter 18 Grit

By the time Ilaria returned from Hazel Wood that day I was forgiven, after she made me drop my pants and gave me as good as I had given! Oh yes, that was much to the amusement of herself and my wife. However, when I confessed to my punisher it was Maxine's idea from the start, she was also instructed to bare her ass and take her fair share. Yet that wasn't the best of it. For then, in the name of sweet justice, measure for measure, Ilaria offered me the crop, directing me to ensure that her mischievous close server felt the same intensity that she had suffered.

I must say, until that memorable day I felt that Aurelie had been the better performer. Perhaps that sounds obvious. In their effort from the start to allow Ilaria to take her time to increase her distance and speed slowly, Aurelie had been less fatigued. In truth, I felt she could have completed two circuits without halting long before that moment, yet didn't want to leave Ilaria to fend for herself. Now with every passing day, I began to like the prima donna of Coretallani more and more.

And when they finally achieved that great goal together upon that day, there was such elation as both wives and husbands smiled with delirious pride over the success. In a discussion the next day, Aurelie and Ilaria decided to delay their pampering until the men had finished their session, so they could languish on the tables together and take turns in the tub. But while they recuperated, drank deeply and considered the looming event, Aurelie confided a misgiving.

'Now that we know we can complete the course, I'm mindful of our second challenge.'

'Oh Lee Lee I haven't finished celebrating our defeat of the first!'

'Yes darling I know. Bravo to us. But remember what Tia said.'

'What did Tia say?' asked Sabatino.

'She said ...' Ilaria lifted her glass. 'the harlots and humbletons smacked her around.'

'Exactly Ria. Broke her rib. Blackened her eye.'

Ilaria went on grimly. 'Therefore if a princess is fair game for a beating? Ergo ...'

'Florentia has grit.' said Tristan, who rarely seemed to offer commentary on anyone. 'It's a sterling quality.'

'Well little brother, if that gains your attention then Ria and I must show we have it too.'

Sabatino pouted in sympathy. 'Don't fret mia cara. I'll disguise myself as a woman and run to protect you.'

'Yes darling, I'm sure your dangling manhood won't give you away at all.'

I couldn't help laughing at that saucy quip. Aurelie's sense of humour was proving to be akin to my own. I glanced at Ilaria who sipped as she gazed at Maxine.

'Hmm.' she murmured. 'I think I have a better idea.'

Quite unexpectedly she suggested a remedy that would — after a fashion — afford Maxine her wish to run. Now that both women were running without halt, Ilaria gave consent for Maxine to leave the children in my care and join them in earnest as they ran upon the course. But she would have a *task* to perform — to play the role of a rattling rival.

Maxine would still be on hand to attend to any domestic emergency, yet would otherwise be free to concentrate on her new task — abusing her betters. And so it was agreed that every quarter mile, my sweet wife was afforded unfettered licence to thwart Ilaria and Aurelie's progress in any manner she felt their rivals may attempt.

Of course some rules of engagement were discussed. The goddesses could retaliate against their new nemesis, yet for the sake of fair play, they agreed neither one could *initiate* any form of assault to gain an advantage — unless such occurred as an accidental result of *fair retaliation*.

All at once, the level of anticipation toward the next session of practice, became palpable.

Next morning when Maxine disrobed, her chest was tightly wrapped in like manner to Ilaria, yet she otherwise stood naked among them. Armand and Sabatino hadn't heard the *rules of engagement* until then.

Armand smiled to Sabatino. 'Surely a cat's being set loose among the pigeons.'

Then before the Gods ran on, now understanding what was to do, Sabatino suggested Maxine be allowed, for a day or two, to forego playing the nemesis and adjust herself to the effort required to run the course. She thanked him kindly for that suggestion. The goddesses agreed.

And so upon that first morning of Maxine's participation, she didn't attempt to launch assaults on her haughty rivals, nor did she do so on her second morning. Yet at the end of that session, she quietly confessed to me.

'I'm ready and chafing at the bit.' Her eyes narrowed as she considered her prey. 'I feel full of mischief.'

Cupid's Balls! I thought to myself.

I tilted my eyes to Heaven. *What could go wrong?*

Next morning, the men started first as usual.

Maxine hadn't announced she planned to begin that day, yet the expectation was in the air and so, from the very start, the tension was palpable.

The women lined up together for me to start them.

'Stand ready! Stay set! Go!'

As I watched three bare asses trot away together, I mounted the she-mule and crossed every appendage to summon luck for my wife's bold ambition. They trotted warily in silence together. Ilaria and Aurelie were glancing at each other as Maxine followed close in their wake and between them. Tension rose as they rounded a bend and the quarter mile sentinel fell in sight. Maxine had warned me that would be the cue for her rules of engagement to change.

Ilaria and Aurelie trotted for a moment, more warily still. Finally Ilaria couldn't resist the temptation to glance her eyes rearward between them. As soon as she did, a palm fell on her outside shoulder and hip, shoving her sideward.

'Uggghhh!'

She careered toward Aurelie.

'That's not *fair!*' Ilaria bleated.

'SHUT your mouth! CRY BABY!'

Aurelie smiled but then suddenly grimaced as her hair was gripped from behind!

'Maxine!'

'OUT of my way BITCH!'

Her head was yanked back then shoved forward hard. Aurelie stumbled and nearly tipped over. Expecting instant retaliation, my eyes were wide with fear. Yet none was forthcoming! Then just as Aurelie gained her balance, Maxine ran at Ilaria again.

And so it began. Assault by invitation!

When the men ran past on their return, they stared as a wet nurse manhandled their wives, shouting abuse and commands like a sergeant-at-arms to a junior squire.

'Keep your *wits* about you! WATCH for me coming!

BRACE yourself! Bend your knees or lose your balance. Ahhh that was too easy! Shunt away at the last moment! WATCH! DUCK! Too slow! Better! *Better!* BETTER!

Maxine was already tutor and abuser, schooling both women to anticipate, brace, avoid and fend off her assaults.

As they climbed the hill together at the end of that session, Maxine politely insisted that Aurelie must begin to wrap Ilaria's bust and I must do it for Maxine, in anticipation of the need upon race day that someone other than Maxine may need to do so for Ilaria.

Next morning Maxine confided to me she had planned something different, yet had no time to explain what she meant. My eyes were alert as I watched them begin. Then of course, from the moment we sighted the first guard, her assaults began and the shouting followed. Every quarter mile it repeated and repeated and repeated until they were halfway around the second circuit. Then for the very first time, to the surprise of all including Maxine, Ilaria surged forward to lead them on.

Maxine smiled and surged after her, lingering between Ilaria and Aurelie for a moment. Then suddenly she turned to face Aurelie, trotting rearward and lifted her brows high. Aurelie saw it. I saw it. Yet I knew it was a signal. Maxine spun on her heel and closed on Ilaria who was now more alert and saw her approach. She waited, and waited, and waited. Yet instead of attempting to shove, Maxine reached out and gripped hard on the rear of her linen wrap.

'Hey!' squealed Ilaria.

Maxine pulled hard. Ilaria tilted back.

'Ugghhh!'

Maxine pushed hard. Ilaria lurched forward. RIP!   The linen split apart with a great tearing rent.

Ilaria lurched forward, losing all balance, spilling hard against the road.

'ARRGHHH!'

Startled by her devious success and holding the evidence in her hand, Maxine blinked in surprise, then halted and instinctively rushed to help.

'No Max!' Ilaria cried. 'AWAY!'

In accordance with their agreement, Aurelie sailed past and offered no assistance. Instead she turned with a wry smile for both. Maxine's eyes filled with intent. She lifted in pursuit of her teasing target, yet not until after she had taken an instant to spin and blow a taunting kiss to her victim.

Getting to her feet, Ilaria checked herself for injuries as I passed by on the mule. Not only did I offer no comfort at all, but the she-devil under me let loose a significant fart. Oh it was priceless! Ilaria scrunched her face in anger. Despite the blood drawn from a grazing to her knees and elbows, she launched after the pair.

Ahead, in pursuit of Aurelie and nearly upon her, Maxine turned to check on Ilaria. Yet seeing her on her feet, she taunted her to come and have at her. Perversely however, she also shouted a warning Ilaria must ensure not to let her breath become erratic!

'*Anger* mustn't stop you regaining your composure!'

Ilaria's eyes narrowed. She shoved her bottom lip into her upper and pelted in pursuit. Maxine smiled, flicked her fingertips under her chi then beckoned with spider-like fingertips upon extended hands, daring her employer to attempt retaliation.

But Maxine appeared to misjudge the acceleration of her pursuer, for just as she spun upon her heel to surge and escape, Ilaria burst in to reach and gripped the rear of Maxine's wrap. To give as good as she got, Ilaria gripped hard and tugged. Yet the stubborn wrap wouldn't yield!

She yanked again wildly in a savage effort to tear the strapping away. Then again and again.

'AHHH!' she screamed in frustration.

Try as she might the hefty fabric not only proved hard to grasp, but was unmoving. Aurelie had turned to watch the tussle and drew in from the side, confounded with interest like a mischievous child. She reached and gripped to share the task. Even against both, the fabric – not linen but stout canvas – refused to give way.

Maxine turned and smiled, then halted to force them to run onward, only to turn to face their rear and launch another assault. Ilaria was shoved hard in the back. This time she kept her feet, though only by the merest blessing. Aurelie was distracted as she watched Ilaria steady herself when a mighty shove in her own back sent Aurelie sprawling forward for the very first time, tumbling down and horribly grazing the side of her body upon a patch of sharp stones.

Ilaria instantly halted to turn and render assistance. But Maxine gripped her arm and swung her about, screaming like a harpy.

'Get GOING!'

'She's hurt.'

'Do as your TOLD! None but officials may assist on the course.'

'We're not on the COURSE!'

'Yes you ARE! Get going or risk disqualification.'

'I'm staying right HERE.'

Maxine turned her frustration on Aurelie.

'Get UP Madonna! Get on your *feet* you ... prissy little BITCH!'

Aurelie's eyes darted, blazing with anger.

'MAXINE!' she screamed. 'Who do you think you're talking to?'

'You think you're a prima DONNA? You're nothing but a spoilt, whining BITCH! Get off your ass if you CAN!'

I was suddenly fearful for the mother of my child. 'Maxine!'

'MARCEL! TAIS-TOI!' She was out of control. 'This is between me and this little BITCH who loves to pretend she's such a POWERFUL woman!'

'Sweetheart' I bleated 'please think of —'

'I think she's not a PRIMA donna! I think she's a PRISSY donna!'

'MAXINE!' Ilaria shot. 'Apologise at once!'

Maxine was boiling. 'FUCK YOU MADAME!'

'Oh Madame!' I cried. 'She didn't mean it.'

'YES I did!' She glared at Aurelie. 'Well PRISSY Donna? Come and GET ME!'

Maxine began to walk rearward. I squinted in fear. She began to trot. Yet just like her, Aurelie had grown up among a band of brothers, all big enough to be warriors, who had taunted her remorselessly. The anger in her eyes was replaced with passion. Her grimace was replaced by a wicked smile. Aurelie stood. Ilaria hovered.

Aurelie began to trot.

'Aurelie remember —' Ilaria began.

'Oh yes Ria, I'll remember.'

Maxine was ahead, still taunting them to follow, yet as she watched the woman she had taunted so hotly, her brows began to lift. Aurelie's trot became a run. Maxine's eyes bulged. The run became a sprint. Passionate blue eyes blazed like an inferno, intent for retribution. Maxine feared she had incited more passion than she may be able to fend.

Following fast, Ilaria feared the same as Aurelie plunged on with terror in her eyes.

Ilaria cried. 'Lee Lee remember our promise to —'

'FUCK you Maxine!' Aurelie cried ignoring Ilaria completely.

'Aurelie we agreed —'

'FUCK that agreement!'

'We swore *not* to retaliate!'

'FUCK that!'

'Maxine has immunity!'

Maxine turned to escape. She broke into a sprint to save herself. Yet during the three weeks before, just like Ilaria, Aurelie had begun to revel in the challenge to be better and better and more skilled at this sport. Now she was leaner, faster and more enduring. Her midriff was rippling and hard, her hands thrust fast, drawing past her sides in perfect balance, like a prima athlete at the ancient games.

Just like her brothers Aurelie had discovered her body was built for hard exertion. Her breath chuffed loud and faster as she closed, like a sprinting she-wolf, hellbent on sinking her teeth into the rump of a challenging boar. As Aurelie surged toward her, eyes hellbent on her downfall, Maxine began to panic and flail.

'FUCK her immunity! I'm coming for you BITCH!'

Maxine's heart was in her mouth. I smacked the mule for all I was worth to catch them and save my only wife from imminent disaster. The beast began to bray wildly. I gulped in fear as Aurelie drew alongside the terrified servant. For the time one may count four, they ran side by side, stride for stride, panic bursting from Maxine's eyes.

'Oh sorry Prima Madonna!' she screamed. 'So sorry Prima Madonna! I didn't mean to —'

The next sound was a dull groan of pain.

Ilaria watched from behind as Aurelie, turning as she ran with venom in her eyes, lifted both hands to grip Maxine's thick hair and pulled with all her might. She dragged her victim sidewards. Maxine lurched and stumbled for balance, eyes leaping wide. With a final vicious tug, she flung Maxine headfirst into the hard ground.

Aurelie turned on her heel and halted, chest heaving, ribs expanding in and out. Glaring at her work, she stood and leaned to hover over her victim.

'Get UP!' Aurelie screamed emptying her lungs. 'Get up prissy BITCH! We're not DONE YET!' Now the prima donna was out of control. 'Get off your FUCKING ASS!'

Maxine turned in an attempt to sit and stand. Her eyes were dazed and a gash from a stone that had scored along her temple began to drip blood.

'AURELIE!' cried Ilaria as she halted. 'For shame!' She knelt to assist Maxine.

I yanked my beast to a stop yet dared not intervene.

'Poor thing!' soothed Ilaria. 'Max are you alright?'

She was a shuddering bundle of tears, cowering and convulsing in fear.

'Oh Aurelie! How could you do this?'

The prima donna's eyes flashed in recognition, realising her victim's terror was in earnest. Aurelie's threatening posture relaxed. She knelt and then shifted to cradle Maxine in her arms.

'No! No! Oh Maxine.' Aurelie hugged her warmly and drew Maxine's hair from her sweating face. 'Oh dear darling. No. No. No.' She hushed her gently as if she was one of her own children. Maxine's eyes opened slowly.

'Is he gone now?' she whispered. 'Is Dante safe?'

'Who Max?' Aurelie frowned in confusion. 'Is who gone darling? Who is Dante?'

'Oh ... Madonna? But where is ... where ...?'

Maxine fell quiet. Her eyes blinked, then stared forlornly. I knew who Dante was, Maxine's lost child. Ilaria knew of him too. My eyes filled with tears for my wife's deep sorrow. I didn't know what to say as she glanced about and then stared at Ilaria.

'Maxine ... do you know where you are?'

'Oh ... yes Mistress. Yes now I do. Oh. I must get up. We must continue —'

'Lie still for a moment.' said Aurelie. 'Lie still. Do you remember what happened?'

'I think I ... oh. Yes I remember. It was you running after me not ....'

'Yes darling. But I didn't mean it. You just got my blood running. I was just ... well Max ... you were doing your job so well.'

'I angered you terribly?' she sniffled.

'Why ... no. Not at all. Well, yes at first. Of course but I *loved* it. I love how you play your part for us so well.'

'You mean ... you won't have me punished? I won't be turned out?'

'Turned out? That's what you ...? Of course not. You were doing what you were told. And after all, I'm not your mistress. Why this is the most fun I've had since I was a child. This whole madcap adventure has become a ... thrilling experience.'

'You really feel that way Madonna?'

'Oh darling I wouldn't trade it for the world or change it for the world.'

'Then I may continue? You'll not take offence?'

'I'll take offence if you *don't* continue!'

'I'd like to. Yet I would also like ...'

'Yes Maxine' Ilaria urged 'what would you like?

'To run in the competition.'

Ilaria and Aurelie exchanged a glance.

'I see.' Ilaria murmured. 'Hmmm. Now come my brave heart, let's get you onto your feet first.'

The trio stood together slowly. I hovered in the near distance with a wrapped bambino in the crook of each arm.

'Ria what do you say? Why not let her run darling?'

'Look at us all.' Ilaria smiled. 'Blood. Bruises. Scrapes everywhere!' They smiled together. 'Well then Max ... you say you want to run?'

'I do Mistress.'

'If you want to run ... then try to catch me!' Without warning Ilaria shoved Aurelie and raced away. 'That's how you gain an advantage!' she cried over her shoulder.

'Ilaria Capulet!' Aurelie called and smiled. 'Come on Max. Let's get her!'

The pair began to trot, then lifted to a run.

Moments later they were hurtling on in hot pursuit. I was left in their wake staring after them, standing in a stupor next to the mule. I looked each babe in the eye. My daughter gurgled and I smiled at her.

'Surely little pea, the ways of women are more inscrutable than those of the Almighty.'

After the drama of that day, and given Maxine now had consent to compete, next morning she requested leave to investigate a new plan of action for their sessions of practice. Moreover, for the sake of that idea Maxine was entertaining, she sought permission to promise a payment of limited funds to a party — as yet undisclosed — for *services to be rendered*.

The goddesses were surprised. Maxine had never asked for such a thing before. Yet she claimed she would attempt to secure the assistance of a *different* style of tutor for them all, with regard to their needs for the race. No, she wouldn't tell me anything at all.

Both Aurelie and Ilaria tried to draw out the details. Yet Maxine held aloof, asking them to allow her to present the result — if it could be secured — as a *surprise*. Oh yes they agreed, but then questioned me to get to the bottom of it! However I truly knew nothing. I insisted they must trust her, and both finally agreed to let my wife have her way in the mysterious matter. Finally, by way of making amends for her assault on Maxine, Aurelie insisted any funds required to secure the *surprise* must come only from herself.

The next morning was Thursday and Maxine was absent. When she rejoined us on Friday my wife remained tight-lipped, yet seemed rather pleased with herself. She reported that she wouldn't know until Sunday if her plan would come to fruition. But if so, upon Monday morning, all would be revealed. Until then it was agreed they would run together without any need for Maxine to play the antagonist.

Then in her turn, Maxine was informed that, during her absence, something had changed. For the very first time at the end of the second circuit, Ilaria and Aurelie had attempted to storm up the hill together. What's more they had reached further than expected before slowing to a walk — perhaps a quarter of the distance. After that result they had made a new pact. No matter how fatigued they may feel, they would advance that result every day until the very end.

Now returned Maxine attempted it too and the rivalry of having a third seemed to spur them all on as, lungs bursting, thighs exploding, they neared the half way point to the crest before slowing. Ilaria now looked every inch as fit and fiery as Aurelie. Indeed, since the incident with Maxine — that very first time she had attempted to lead — she now led all the way and reached further up the hill than any other.

During the first two weeks — while they had still walked significant portions before reaching the gate at the base of Sycamore Hill — Ilaria and Aurelie had begun to attempt the final ascent at something more than just a walking pace. From the time that effort began, at each attempt they also increased the distance attempted, until they were able to walk briskly all the way to the very top.

With Maxine returned, and seeing that lift in their desire to conquer the Hill, Sabatino made another suggestion. He revealed that, as a squire, when his mentor discovered they were enlisted to fight in a siege, he taught Sabatino a trick for running up or down hills — short or long — that had greatly reduced his fatigue.

'Liar!' Aurelie huffed. 'What trick will put strength in our legs after we've exhausted them?'

'Not *after* mia cara ... *before*.'

'Oh now you're just trying to sound clever.'

'The trick is clever. It saves your strength as you go.'

'Yes, yes, yes Sab. Now spit it out.'

He lowered his voice secretively. 'When running uphill, your breath is more important than ever. But most importantly ... the trick is ...' he paused for effect.

'Yes, yes, yes.'

'Just as one begins to climb, *slow* down slightly.

'Slow down?'

'Yes and then concentrate on *lifting* your legs through the thigh, not *pushing* your feet against the ground.'

'Honestly Sab! If I don't push my feet —'

'Just try it mia cara. Once or twice.'

He attempted to demonstrate. I thought it looked comical. So did Aurelie.

'What's more if you do the same in descent, it avoids injury from over weighting your footfalls.'

Ilaria laid an arm around his waist and leaned to offer a reward to his cheek.

'It all makes sense to me clever man. I shall try it.'

'Thank you Ilaria. But I'm not the clever one. I will confess however, that since my mentor taught it, I've never turned my ankle. Yet before, I used to do so all the time.'

'That's true darlings. I've never heard him complain of hurting an ankle.'

'And finally —'

'There's more?'

'One small thing. As you run up, don't be tempted to gaze up ahead of you. Look straight ahead, *into* the hill.'

'But I always look up darling! It's natural. Looking into it sounds very ... dull.'

'I know. But staring up at the summit distracts you from the technique in your legs. And somehow it convinces your mind that the effort is much greater and so ...

Ilaria cut in. 'One will become disenchanted much more quickly?'

'Yes. And so mia cara please, don't look *up* the hill.'

Aurelie kissed his cheek softly and glared at Ilaria.

'I saw you kiss my husband.' She hissed in mock reprimand. 'I know what's going on here.'

Sabatino had offered that advice upon Sunday afternoon as we all returned from the citadel. Next day all three women were eager to put it into practice.

In truth, since the start, Ilaria and Aurelie had found the array of things they needed to consider as they ran — breath, poise, balance and now more — had become useful distractions. From the very start, turning their thoughts in a circuit to check each little thing had managed to turn their thoughts from fatigue. Then during their training, fatigue began to decrease as their speed had increased.

And finally to note, now they were no longer two competitors but three, Maxine was informed she would not only race but also enjoy being pampered at Hazel Wood. And so, until she reappeared in her working couture, Maxine was treated as an honorary member of the elite. When dressed thereafter, she resumed her duties on the balcony as Aurelie and Ilaria sat, sipped and watched at their leisure. Out on the course by that time — racing in reverse direction as agreed — the *boys* were lurching about at breakneck speed upon horseback.

The horse race would be held on the same path as the footrace. And so every day — excepting the Sabbath — they ran two circuits upon two different mounts each. That need to run a second mount was against the great possibility that one may run lame before the event. As mounted warriors with income, all were able to purchase and furnish more than one horse to ride into battle. Indeed, it was a requirement. As a local cavaliere Sabatino's estate housed many fine horses of course. Yet his favourite to race was a rust coloured Arabian which had three white socks that he called *Galante*.

Armand and Tristan each had a pair of battle horses, and each beast was formidable. To ride them into battle of course, they couldn't be anything less. Yet as you know, *Victoire* was Armand's pride and joy, his dappled dark grey courser with a black mane and tail. Gifted to him by King Charles at Queen Marie's request on the eve of the great battle of Formigny, I think you know by now, that stallion was much more than just a horse to him.

Tristan's premiere mount however was a spectacular stallion called *Ajax*. Yes I'd seen that bold beast before. And let me just say, that to see Ajax once, is to never forget him. Prince Escalus heard tell of the mythical creature before our meeting in Herb Market Square and felt the need to mention it then. Little wonder he did so, for Ajax has a shining pearl coloured coat with a chestnut mane and tail. I tell you sweet friends that stallion is a breathtaking sight.

Indeed every woman I saw who laid her eyes on the gorgeous creature seemed to fall instantly in love. The contrast of those extraordinary colours on his tall muscular form set eyes glowing in wonderment and triggered sighs of longing. After Tristan arrived and

Armand was finally well enough to ride again, the sight of Victoire and Ajax carrying them together was otherworldly. It were as if that pair of mythical beasts were meant to canter riderless among the clouds, rather than tread the firmament, tethered to the command of mere mortals.

Sabatino's mounts were also formidable creatures. Yet it was his skill as a horseman that was the most exceptional thing. As a page he had served in Spain, that legendary land of equestrian skill. And it's during that crucial time — as child warriors — they learn the essential skills of horsemanship before becoming more distracted, as squires, with learning to fight. And as we watched Sabatino running the course for pure speed — with no lance or armour to weigh him down — he ran among them like a man possessed. Though not as great as his passion for Aurelie, Sabatino seemed to lust after the thrill of lurching through twists and turns, and running the straight at relentless speed.

Interestingly, all three men had agreed to make a test of each other's mounts. Yet it never seemed to matter which horse Sabatino rode, under his seat every animal became infused with a will to fly faster than it knew it was able. And in the final stretch, Sabatino had a signature manner in the way he ran for home — leaning deep against the stirrups, his cheek wrested so far along the neck, each creature could hear his burning whispers of encouragement.

Whatever he said in those moments, made every horse want to fly like winged Pegasus. Not since we had seen that extraordinary display of horsemanship by Eloise du Marche in Carentan, had I witnessed such skill on a beast of war. Tristan swore he had never seen the like of it. But I knew he had never seen Eloise ride. And in my humble opinion, her skill was unmatchable. Yet now every day as the trio ran wildly against each other, the Capulet brothers' esteem for their sister's husband grew with each further display of his skill.

To see their stark white linen undershirts billowing against the wind, long hair trailing behind, snapping at their necks as if drawn by a rushing current of water, made for a rare spectacle. Aurelie jumped for joy every time to see Sabatino run first through the Hazel Wood gate. Tristan and Armand were always close behind, yet offered the victor credit with grace and encouragement. They slapped each other's shoulders, shouted their recall of every flashing corner and peril on the course, like street urchins celebrating victory against a rival band of boys.

Yes, the distraction wrought by the festival's approach had proven a tonic for us all. Now a single week before the event, few felt the experience of our preparations could become any more unique or hold any more surprises — then Maxine revealed the nature of her secretive plan.

Chapter 19 a week & Odd days

On the brisk Monday morning that followed, our quartet of immortals descended into the grove to face one final week and odd days of preparation. Since their routine had started, Armand and Sabatino had led the way down in an effort to prepare ahead of their wives and depart without much ado. Yet this time, as they neared the base of the hill both were alerted by the hum of unexpected chatter.

Close on their heels, Ilaria and Aurelie were laughing distractedly until they heard it too. They saw their husbands had halted and joined them. Not for the life of them could any suggest what so many voices may portend. Indeed it sounded as if a vociferous party had assembled in wait for them just beyond the gate.

Ilaria became agitated, voicing her concern. Not having anticipated a need to greet strangers, she and Aurelie were about to reveal themselves without paint to their faces, covered coiffures or appropriate couture, and to an audience which, by the tone of their voices, was mostly feminine. Cautiously they rounded the final curve to assess what lay ahead. As expected, beyond the gate stood our trusted sentinels Liberati and Boccolo. Yet both had very strange expressions on their faces. Beyond them, as expected, I stood by the mule, yet something appeared to be different.

'Goodness, where are the children?'

'Yes Ria you're right. Marcel's arms are empty yet so are the baskets.'

Yes my arms were empty. And I could tell they all wondered why. In reply — and perhaps to settle their obvious anxiety — I pushed my lower lip upward, lifted my brows and shrugged innocently. However something more noticeable was also different.

'Ria is that your wagon there under the trees?'

'Yes Lee Lee. It should be resting up by the stable.'

'And Armand' Sabatino said cooly glancing at him 'that team is still puffing.'

'And sweating.' Armand knit his brows in thought.

'With that much moisture so early' Sabatino added 'they must have come up from the citadel.'

Sabatino was correct.

And what's more, the rear board hung open and a suspended step casement was hanging from the rear corner. To all intents, it appeared as if passengers had recently disembarked from the conveyance. They wandered closer to the wagon to investigate and were greeted by a perplexing display of unkemptness within. Littering the floor was a rummage of cloth, mostly sheer fabrics and in fanciful colours. Aurelie turned to look back to the gate.

'And where's Maxine? For the last few mornings Ria she's followed behind us.'

'You're right. I'm not sure. Armand do you know what's going on?'

Armand turned back toward the gate. 'No angel however ... I intend to find out.'

In search of an explanation Armand glared at Liberati. To say the veteran's expression and that of Boccolo looked sheepish, was an understatement for the ages.

'Liberati!' spat Armand. 'Where is ...?'

Yet before he could utter another word, a giggling chorus erupted from a short distance and began to mimic his cry to the old soldier, yet in antic feminine portrayal of his deep booming tone.

'Liberati! I say Liberati! Get your hand off your pecker at once!'

A warbling chorus of giggles and chattering sounded.

Next to Liberati, Boccolo gulped. His eyes tilted up like a chaste urchin who seeks to avert closer inspection. Liberati himself — apparently incapable of speech — squinted with a pained expression. He pointed toward the nearest clump of trees from whence that chorus had arisen.

Every eye turned. Flashes of movement from behind the trunks became visible. The elite quartet exchanged confused glances.

'Maxine!' Armand called in frustration.

'Yes Monsieur! I come!'

All at once the giggling chorus of voices erupted again, this time in mimic of Maxine.

'*Yes Monsieur I come! Oh yes I'm coming! I think I'm coming Monsieur!*'

The banter bubbled and squeaked, as if every voice had sounded in reply to Armand's command. Maxine emerged from behind the fore pair of stout sycamores as the elite quartet raised eyebrows or lowered them in yet greater confusion. She appeared as if she was ready to run, naked except the canvas wrap I had applied to her bust — with increasing skill I might add.

However my wife also led a small tribe in her wake. Each follower was feminine. Each looked equally ready to run, lacking any cloth to cover them at all. At a glance they ranged in age from sixteen to twenty-six. Yes, that was difficult for me to gauge precisely. Yes, that was because it was difficult to concentrate. Yes, I need to shut up again.

Two sycamore nymphs were cradling and bouncing little Figara and Thibault. Their company chortled and smiled, giggling at the babes as they came on. Five in all followed their fearless leader — my wife — toward the imposing denizens who awaited them.

Ilaria leaned to Aurelie. 'Oh Lee Lee' she whispered. 'Oh no!'

'Oh yes.' Aurelie glanced at Sabatino with a smirk.

He look so amazed, palms turned outward, shoulders shrugged, as if to question how such an extraordinary sight could be possible.

'I take it this is her mysterious *surprise*.' said Ilaria.

'Marcel!' called Maxine. 'Come gather the babes!'

Another chorus erupted in mimic of her accent.

'*Marcel!*'

'*Oh Marcel!*'

'*I was a bambino once!*'

'*Come gather us all Marcel!*'

I wore an impish smile as I sauntered among them. Then when I attempted to draw the children away from their improvised carers, the tribe refused to set them free until each had squeezed or kissed their cheeks. Before I walked on, several offered me the same treatment! Oh yes, I tried to seem disinterested. Yet Maxine still pouted, rolling her eyes and glaring for good measure.

Finally I withdrew with a babe on each arm and an oafish grin upon my face. Maxine led them on to halt before the elite quartet at a respectful distance. She bowed her head to curtsy and her followers considered the gesture. They glanced at each other unsurely, then in a haphazard cascade, all attempted to mimic her.

Oh for the love of folly, it was an antic sight. Ilaria felt Aurelie's thumb jab into her lower back. Both women were now fighting to suppress smiles that threatened to grow more broadly. Armand arched a questioning brow. He lifted his chin and beckoned with a finger.

'Max.'

'Yes Chevalier Capulet.' she said with formality.

'Oooh' purred the one I assumed to be the eldest 'Chevalier!'

Maxine grimaced as giggles were stifled behind her. 'Hush girls! Please.'

'Max.' Armand stared. 'Who are these ... women?'

'I *hired* them Monsieur.'

'*You* hired them? To what purpose?'

Before Maxine could respond, a voice from behind her answered.

'*Any* purpose you may wish *Chevalier*.'

Snorts and guffaws erupted among them. That attempt of the eldest to mimic Maxine with such sultry intent set loose a new chorus of reaction. Aurelie jabbed Ilaria once more. Even Ilaria couldn't resist the temptation to smile, despite the fact that a comely naked woman had just offered herself so baldly to her husband.

From that reaction Armand had little doubt what the regular employment of the unruly entourage was. Aurelie and Ilaria had already presumed the same of course, yet still wondered what their purpose among the sycamores might be. I must add however, both women seemed to enjoy watching their husbands attempt to make sense of it all.

'They've been hired to assist *us* Chevalier.'

Emboldened by the eldest, the waif to her left slowly lifted her hand.

'Maxine pick *me* to assist the chevalier.'

To her left and right, eyes widened in panic.

'No me!'

'I want to!'

'He doesn't want you!'

'Maxine!'

Maxine turned sharply. 'Silence!' she hissed.

Quiet descended. Yet an instant later, a flurry of snorts and cackles erupted again. At that, Sabatino couldn't help but smile and did so openly. He slapped a hand on Armand's shoulder. Armand took a deep breath and narrowed his eyes at Maxine.

'Assist you with *what* pray tell?'

'To assist Madame and Madonna in their practice.'

Armand and Sabatino exchanged a glance.

'Oh?' said Sabatino. 'So they're *not* here to ...?'

'To ...? Why *no* Don Cortellani!'

'*Oooh girls!*' whispered the eldest. 'That's Don Cortellani!'

Aurelie snapped her hand to her mouth to stifle the urgent want to laugh.

'Hush there at once!' snapped Maxine. 'No Signore. Of course they're not.'

Another mimicking chorus lifted from behind her. Now every word uttered by Maxine, Armand or Sabatino seemed doomed to draw a mimic or teasing innuendo.

Armand looked relieved to hear her explanation.

'Cat ...' he said warningly.

A flurry of chatter interrupted his intent to run on.

'He called her *Cat*.'

'Isn't she *Maxine?*'

'Why is *she* Cat?'

'Should *we* call her Cat?'

Armand turned his eyes on them all. The chorus fell mute. He returned his attention to Maxine.

'I hope you know what you're doing.'

Sabatino lifted his fingertip. 'So if I may ... you've assembled this intriguing *sororitas* to ...'

Aurelie interjected. 'Darling I suspect they've been hired to give us a *difficult* run for our money.' She glanced at Maxine. 'And if I'm not mistaken ... it was *our* money that hired them?'

'Correct on both counts Madonna.'

'Hmmm mia cara, I confess that of all the investments we've made together ...'

Aurelie looped her arm over his but raised her brows in warning. 'Yes gorgeous man?'

'This one is the most ... intriguing.'

'I'm so glad you approve.' She pecked his cheek. 'Very well then.'

Aurelie turned to the tribe and without warning, released the fastening brooch at her shoulder. Her wrap fell unceremoniously. Standing in close attendance, Fabrizio widened his eyes in horror to see the delicate linen being sullied by the dirt. To the gaggle's surprise he scurried over and bent to scoop it up reverently.

Feminine heads turned back and forth, blinking or pouting in surprise.

'Pay attention to me!' came the brusque command.

Every eye snapped to Aurelie.

Suddenly, all seemed to understand a potent woman stood before them and five pairs of eyes glanced up and down her body in frank assessment.

'Come Ilaria.'

Another cascade began.

'Ilaria.

'Oooh, Ilaria.'

'Oh that's a—'

'Stai *zitto!*' Aurelie spat as her head snapped round to face them. 'Next to speak out of turn shall *regret* it.'

In an attempt to put his effort ahead of her need, Fabrizio stepped in to unfasten Ilaria's brooch. She held out her arms in response to his care. Five pairs of envious eyes looked on as her impromptu page averted his eyes respectfully. He drew the fabric down over her hips delicately as he kneeled, holding the garment at her feet to allow her to step away.

As he did so, Maxine lifted the front of Ilaria's new canvas wrap, laying it firmly against her chest and asking her politely to hold it, then stepped to Ilaria's rear to draw, tie and tuck the short ends in place. To finish, she walked a cautious circuit around her mistress, tugging to test the firmness. Finally she repeated the procedure on her braids and the wrapping to her hair.

'*Merci* Maxine.'

'My pleasure Madame.'

Among the watchers, more than one bottom lip was drawn back by upper teeth in reaction to see this quiet, elegant woman being treated with such care and respect by both servers. Aurelie observed them all with a wry smile as Ilaria came to her.

'Now darling ... let's inspect our people.'

The eldest dared speak. 'That chest wrap ...' Aurelie lifted a warning brow 'will be harder to grip if you smear it with oil.' Aurelie and Ilaria exchanged a glance. 'That's what we do ... *Madame*.'

Maxine wore a satisfied smile.

Despite the clear value of that unsolicited offering, Aurelie's smile turned to a scowl as she faced the entourage. She held in thought for a moment, pondering how best to approach her new charges. Making her decision, she stepped toward the eldest.

This one still wore the tinge of a smile from her victory in speaking after being warned to stay silent. Aurelie considered her soberly. Not only was she the eldest, she was also the tallest. The rebel stood sleepily with a hand rested on her hip, elbow cocked and knee bent. It was as if her posture which suggested seductive intent, was instinctive.

Aurelie moved closer and stared into her eyes. Speaking out of turn with valuable information was one thing. Having the audacity to coax her brother in front of his wife was entirely different. Just as that thought occurred to Aurelie, the rebel glanced at Armand again.

'Get your eyes *off* our men! You're *not* in the cat house now.

Stand up *straight!*'

Ilaria started at the sudden escalation. She held her breath, for the rebel towered over Aurelie and an impasse appeared to be rising. The bold prima donna stepped closer, tilting her chin to all but touch the tip of her rival's nose.

'Do it.' Her tone was venomous. 'NOW!'

For a moment longer the rebel held firm. Her instinct to defy such a challenge from any woman was clear. Yet it was also clear that in the presence of such elite company, an instinct for preservation was now fighting with it. Aurelie remained impassive, staring coldly. The rebel's compatriots glanced furtively, desperate to know the result.

The tall body began to straighten.

Ilaria was mesmerised to see Aurelie so quickly command compliance from such an imposing woman — her ability to know just what the limit of a challenger's potency may be. Then, along with Aurelie's victory over the leader, a cascade of compliance followed from the rest. Every hand lowered from every hip. Every knee and elbow straightened.

Now standing tall with her tangled mess of dun coloured hair, the rebel loomed two inches taller. Yet instead of lifting her chin further, Aurelie lowered it, tilting her eyes up to remain locked on her target. It was a trick her mother, Dame Margot, had taught her as a girl — having such constant need as she grew to confront the wilful demands of so many imposing brothers. Every Capulet son called Aurelie their little sister, yet only for the sake of her height not her age. None but Armand was actually older.

'Better!' Aurelie whispered.

Her one true older brother smiled as he watched Aurelie take charge of Maxine's rabble. For more than four years she had run her expansive household. And whenever Sabatino had been at war — which had been often and sometimes for many months — she had also run the estate and managed their other holdings without any assistance.

During that time, Sabatino had often been wounded upon his

return, requiring weeks or months to recuperate. And so, even after he had returned, her unimpeded management had often continued. All at Hazel Wood had become so used to her stature as their primary overlord, that even when their popular primo don was *in residence*, their staff approached the prima donna first and foremost to make important decisions or adjudicate any and all disputes.

Unlike some martial husbands, Sabatino seemed to have ceded that power graciously. Perhaps it was not hard to do since he had a partner of Aurelie's capability. She had proven beyond doubt that she could not only wield control, but astutely manage every aspect of the faction's livelihood. Watching on, I had no doubt that Aurelie had become the real power behind the respected House of Cortellani.

Some elite men simply couldn't cede so much power to their wives, either before they departed or any time after their return. And in truth, some wives couldn't be trusted with that authority. Yet most elite husbands seemed to withhold that power out of vanity or fear, hoarding it even while they remained absent, or else drawing it back as soon as they returned. It seemed to me that it wasn't love, or even respect, that bound such couples together.

Yet the Cortelannis were not such a couple.

And so, Aurelie had grown used to the responsibility of control and the burden of authority. Indeed, both seemed to fit her like a pair of fine leather gloves. To me it also seemed that, until that moment, Armand had never imagined his little sister to be such a leader.

Yet he was quickly discovering that just like himself, responsibility was a mantle Aurelie wore fitfully, and that male or female, to be born a Capulet was to be born to lead.

'You're here to *work* and so are we.' She turned to walk the line like a cavaliere mentor inspecting new squires. 'I'm Signora Cortellani. What do you say?'

Five pairs of eyes glanced at each other.

'Buon giorno mia Signora.' came the dribbled reply.

'Hmm.' Aurelie glanced at Ilaria and nodded her disapproval.

'Maxine!'

'Yes Madonna.'

'These sorry *sororitas* are *not* yet paid?'

'Correct Madonna.'

Squints of comprehension ran along the ragged line.

'And they will not *be* paid 'til the race is run?'

'Correct Madonna.'

A shifting unease began to ferment amongst them. Ilaria looked on wide-eyed, assessing the effect each comment wrought upon the motley band.

'Then ... let's try my introduction *again*.' She stood before the eldest. 'But this time understand that until the race is run, you all remain in *my* employ.'

Eyes among them glanced and shifted.

'Now allow me to introduce myself. I am prima donna of the House of Cortellani.'

Her tone had deepened and risen. Five pairs of eyes glanced again.

'Buon giorno Prima Donna.' came the sober reply.

Armand and Sabatino drifted forward to Ilaria.

'Sab *who* is that woman?' asked Armand.

Ilaria smiled at him, then glanced at Sabatino.

'Oh Ilaria. She was so shy when we met. Now even I wouldn't dare to cross her.'

Aurelie turned to walk the line again. 'I presume you all understand that, due to the unusual task we wish you to perform' muted giggles sounded 'not *that* kind of task. That while we're working together you will *not* be expected to show deference to our rank. Indeed quite the *opposite*.'

A wicked smile spread on the rebel's face.

Aurelie turned to face her again.

'Oh no.' whispered Sabatino.

'But each morning *before* our work begins, or during any discussions we conduct after it's complete, if addressed by me you will curtsy and *bow* your head in respect.'

'And if we do *not?*' The eldest stared ahead soberly.

Aurelie stepped up to her again. 'Then you'll be instantly dismissed to return on foot *without* payment. What's more you'll need to explain my rejection of your services to your employer, who will then be forced to remunerate *me* for *your* poor service.'

The heat in the eyes of the eldest was suddenly quenched. Aurelie stared impassively.

'Do you *all* understand?'

'Yes Prima Donna.' came a more earnest reply.

Aurelie approached Ilaria with a smile. She leaned in to kiss Sabatino's cheek.

'Now, once more to impress my doubting husband. I am Signora Cortellani.'

Almost as one, knees bent, heads tipped dutifully as they bleated together. 'Buon giorno mia Signora Cortellani.'

'Much better.' She escorted Ilaria to them. 'This is my sister. She is the premiere dame of the House of Capulet. You will afford her the same respect as me.'

Again all curtsied and bowed.

'Buon giorno mia Signora Capuleti.'

Despite herself, Ilaria smiled. Unlike Aurelie, she also dipped her forehead in polite reply. Her instinct to do so was not missed by the sororitas. Aurelie glanced at Maxine.

'That's title is not precisely correct yet ... it shall suffice for now. We're off to a *better* start and so ... you all deserve a reward.' Five smiles appeared. 'Therefore gentlemen, will you please reveal your beautiful bodies for their pleasure.' A ripple of giggles ran through the line. 'Then you may go. We'll be right *behind* you of course, watching your *behinds.*'

The sororitas smirked and snorted. The men glanced at each other and sighed in resignation, then grins lifted on their faces. I smiled too. For I realised Aurelie understood that, young or old, there was no more potent tool to temper discipline among hard people than for a leader — sparingly as occasion suited — to display a rowdy sense of humour.

The men tossed their garments to Fabrizio. Sabatino approached Aurelie and kissed her. Armand glanced at them all as he handed over his belt. In that moment, the eldest attempted to draw his attention again. Perhaps it was professional instinct, he was clearly a wealthy man. If she managed to lure him independently of her employer, the results may allow her own life to become more independent.

Yet such bold initiative carried risk. Drawing the anger of her employer was one thing. Drawing the anger of an elite wife was another. And both Ilaria and Aurelie had observed her second attempt in such a short time. I fully expected Aurelie to explode and dismiss her to make an example. Instead, in silent challenge to Ilaria, she soberly raised her brows.

Ilaria thought for an instant. Then as Armand came forward she stepped in to meet him, halting directly in front of the brazen culprit. The image of them together reminded me of the antics I witnessed a few months earlier, down in the bathhouse with the duchess and Eloise. For a second time, Ilaria stood naked with her husband before of a bevy of naked women who openly expressed their interest in him.

Cupid's Balls! How did such moments manage to keep occurring in the life of this couple?

I prayed to Heaven the handsome oaf understood the importance of that moment. So many times before I had feared Armand's reactions were too naïve, yet this time he surprised me. For you see, despite the distraction of their company, he looked into Ilaria's eyes as if no-one else in the world existed. Of course sweet friends, the truth for Armand in that moment was, that no-one else did exist.

However, Ilaria understood that others existed. So did Aurelie, who hadn't been present at the bathhouse. Ilaria also understood that Aurelie now expected to see her mark her territory, like a bitch pissing on a stump as she passes by. She turned her head to lock eyes with her rival, holding soberly for a moment, then slowly returned to her husband.

Stepping closer still, Ilaria laid her arms around Armand's neck and pressed her body against him. Bright green eyes blazed into blue. Although I knew he understood the prompt for her display, it didn't appear that he expected the intensity of the kiss that followed. Their passion was mesmerising. And standing at close range, the rebel watched on with smouldering eyes.

Finally their lips drew apart but their eyes did not. I was reminded that — although they were husband and wife and exposed to the gaze of us all — they were still young lovers who had only known the thrill of their carnal touch for little more than a year.

'But angel' Armand muttered 'now I feel tempted to *stay* with you.'

Every member in line, including her rival, sniggered, snickered and cackled. A smile creased Ilaria's lips. He couldn't have responded more perfectly.

'Present or absent my heart, you know I'm *never* without you. Tonight.'

Armand turned but her lingering fingertip grazed his cheek, neck, shoulder and back as he moved away.

'Marcel!' Armand called as he joined Sabatino.

Both men stood ready. From my place by the mule I had begun to tune my lute, yet straightened to offer the starting commands.

'Stand READY!' I cried, snapping a strum. 'Stay SET!' *Strum.* 'GO!' *Strum. Strum.*

Giggles sounded at each volley of strings, then without further ado both men trotted away.

Ilaria turned to consider her new compatriots. For all the need to challenge their discipline, the sight of them made her wonder. What must it be like to live without the security of wealth or the comforts of privilege she had enjoyed since birth? Yes, her conscience had been pricked by the question before, usually by the sight of the poor. Yet when faced with those five women, it seemed to resonate differently.

Aurelie appeared to be little moved by them. Yet it was the first time Ilaria had experienced a need to interact with such people. Already she was surprised that the youngest and eldest were just a few years from her own age. She was also surprised to see how they seemed to dote on the children, to hear them laugh together and, in a new way, had felt moved by their looks of envy and longing.

Until that morning, the notion of a harlot was more like an apparition to Ilaria, not flesh and blood young women who would appear to be anything like herself. She couldn't help but consider what it must be like to trade one's intimacy as a service every day to survive, while being looked down upon so potently by the rest of society.

She glanced at the rebel again. Perhaps it was little wonder she presented such a stubborn front at the thought of being controlled by Aurelie. Surely these women must think of Aurelie and herself as nothing more than a pampered pair of idle prima donnas. Indeed it made Ilaria question if that's what she really was. She didn't think so. She felt that she tried not to be.

Perhaps the chance to engage with such awkward bedfellows would put that notion to the test? Perhaps that was why the princess had urged her to take up this challenge. Certainly after her tour of the lower depths with Florentia she had been left feeling naïve, like a girl walking among women. Ilaria glanced at the youngest — surely not more than sixteen — and suddenly felt to be her junior, even her inferior.

She turned to Aurelie who remained so composed. Ilaria wasn't as practiced at command. Nor was she yet used to how relentlessly such people needed to be taken to task. She wondered if she'd ever prove to be the kind of woman Aurelie appeared to be. So despite the moment of rivalry Ilaria had experienced with the eldest, after considering what kind of life that young women found herself locked into, already her view of the tall rebel was softening.

I saw a thought rise in Ilaria's eyes. She motioned to Fabrizio. He hastened to her side and she whispered an instruction. A few moments later, to the feminine quintet's surprise, beakers of watered wine were being offered to all. I watched Ilaria watching then I began to grin. For you see, to her dismay those unruly young women all drained their cups with gusto and began reaching for more as if their work was already complete.

'Ladies!' she urged. 'Slowly. Slowly.' Already the eldest was putting her lips to the brim for a third time. 'No need to gulp. Just sip. Sip. There's plenty more —'

'Later darling.' Aurelie corrected. 'Not so much *before* they work!'

Maxine approached. 'Madonna. Madame. I think you should know that they're not merely hired to assist our practice. You may have observed that none of these are quite as buxom or curvaceous as one might expect from women of their ... profession.'

Aurelie and Ilaria glanced about.

'Now that you say so' said Aurelie 'yes I do notice.'

'That's because they've been chosen especially by their mistress to run this season.'

'Their mistress?' asked Aurelie.

'I struck the deal with a woman named *da Mosto*.'

'Ah' said Aurelie 'they're from *the Dragon?*'

'Yes Madonna. And though a man *runs* the establishment, Signora *da Mosto* appears to own it.

'Oh yes Max that's *Pruetta*.' said Ilaria.

Maxine blinked in surprise, so did Aurelie, to understand Ilaria could recall the forename of a brothel owner in Verona, or any brothel owner for that matter.

'Sergeant Nadalinus is her brother. We met her briefly last season, for just a fleeting moment.'

'Did you Madame? Where was I?'

'It was when we travelled through the borgo on the way to the burial ground. You were absent. I sent you off to inform Aurelie and Sabatino.'

'Oh yes that's right. I was surprised to learn she owned the Dragon. Her man said the laws of Venice no longer allow men to do so.'

'Is that true Lee Lee?' said Ilaria.

'Yes darling. But despite that law, their rival in the same street —'
'The *Wild Boar*.' Ilaria put in.

Aurelie widened her eyes. 'Yes darling — not that I want to know how you know that name also — yet the Boar still appears to be owned by —'

'A man, yes I recall his name too — *Luchinus*.'

'Luchinus *Montecchi*. It's clear that a faction with enough money and influence can bend anything to their will. Including rules that govern who can and can't own —'

Before Aurelie could say more a voice interrupted. The three women turned as five faces stared back at them.

Chapter 20 the Sororitas

'Prima Donna Cortellani?' came the tired voice.

The most middling in age of the feminine quintet, with curling chestnut hair, curtsied and dipped her head.

'Yes dear?' said Aurelie.

'Scusi Prima Donna. But we're the *late* shift and so ... we finished but an hour since.'

Aurelie and Ilaria exchanged a look of surprise.

'Oh?' Aurelie replied. 'Well then dear, you must be rather ... fatigued?'

The others gathered in as the eldest responded, shooting a frown at their complaining compatriot.

'We're not too tired Prima Donna. We'll make more in a week working for you than two months at the Dragon.'

Maxine raised her hands to gain attention.

'Now girls remember —' Figara chortled to hear her mother's voice.

Every newcomer sighed. Their reaction made Ilaria smile. I handed my little bundle over and they watched my sweet wife take a moment to shush her own bambino.

'Remember girls — oh yes *Figgie* hush hush hush. Remember that until next week, upon *Fat Thursday*, you all work for none but Donna Cortellani. We made a firm deal with the Viking.'

Ilaria's eyes lit up. 'Why do I recognise that name?'

Every ear bent to learn how the elegant woman could possibly know their bruising minder.

'He's Pruetta's man Madame. Last summer he served as marshal to the master's duel.'

A murmur ran among the sororitas. That mention sparked their comprehension. Armand and Ilaria were the infamous French couple they had all heard so much about. Suddenly they realised, the quiet man who seemed so in love with this polite woman, was the one who had slain the fearsome Black Wolf of Verona. Whatever was whispered among the sororitas now, all appeared to hold a very different level of consideration for the shy premiere dame who stood next to the haughty prima donna.

'Oh yes!' Ilaria glanced at the faces. 'But he looked so fearful.' The thought of these five being under his control fretted her. 'Yet in truth, his evidence at our trial was a very great help to us. I feel we owe him a considerable debt.'

'I believe' said Maxine 'that he and the owner are in a … romantic relationship. And that he ensures —'

'Gunter keeps us safe.' offered the youngest.

'Does he?' asked Ilaria.

'Oh yes Madonna. Whenever the patrons get —'

'Yes dear' Maxine interrupted 'we understand. But you must all understand Donna Cortellani has paid up *all* your earnings for the time you're with us. That means, until the race is done, you're excused from all other work.'

Ilaria smiled. 'And so you've *all* been chosen especially to run this season?'

'Yes and last season Madonna.' the eldest replied. 'All except *Falena* who was new. Yet now we know she's our fastest. This time she'll run and we'll run to protect her.'

'I don't need protection.' cried the next to youngest.

I presumed she must be Falena – *Moth*. I was used to the company of such women of course. And knowing a moth is considered a butterfly of the night, I assumed that name was her working sobriquet and that she worked the night shift rather than the day.

'Imbecile you do!' spat the eldest. 'Fat Luke has spies and will do anything to win. By now he knows who you are and how fast. He'll tell *Marietta* to take you out.'

Ilaria glared at Aurelie. 'Hmm. This Marietta doesn't sound very friendly.'

'Nor is Fat Luke Madonna.' added the eldest. 'He owns the Wild Boar.'

'Yes, I do know of him. I won't say we've met exactly. But I have

... encountered him briefly at a distance.'

'Any distance is too close to Fat Luke Madame.

'I tend to agree. And this woman Marietta is?'

The eldest looked vacantly. 'Luke's head girl.' Furtive glances shot from her compatriots. 'Let's just say that Marietta's ... a bit like me.'

A chorus of incredulous cackles sounded.

'Stai zitto you idiots!' she hissed. 'Every season, Luke and Pruetta have a wager.'

'I assume the *stakes* are substantial?' said Aurelie.

'Oh yes Madonna.' said the youngest. 'Four dozen barrels of Persian muscat.'

'That is substantial.' Ilaria agreed.

'They take it seriously. The Dragon's five fastest and scrappiest against the Boar's five best bitches.'

'Five against five.'

'More girls than us are entered Madonna' said Falena 'but not to run.'

'Oh? If they don't run in the race, what do they do?'

'Well yes, by the rules they must *run* Madonna. But those are the *new* girls.'

'Fatso enters his too.' said the eldest. 'To show off the new merchandise.'

'The merchandise?' Ilaria nodded in dismay.

'So they *must* run at the start. Yet as soon as they reach the south wall —'

'Where everyone can *see* them clearly.' Aurelie drawled sarcastically.

'Yes Madonna. Then they slow to a walk and start twirling and waving.'

'Walking, twirling and waving?' Ilaria asked just as comprehension lit in her eyes. 'Oh. Oh yes, I see.'

'Well we won't be twirling or walking!' Aurelie declared. 'And none of you will beat the Boar's best bitches by standing still. So my *Dragonesses* —'

All eyes in the entourage widened in surprise.

'How did you know that's what we call ourselves?' asked the eldest.

'I'm not just a pretty face.' Aurelie grinned. 'And I may have made a tidy sum on a wager of my own last season. Now ... give up your drinks.'

'Fabrizio.' called Ilaria.

The young man drew forward to collect their elegant beakers. Each dragoness did as they were told and turned on the hapless Fabrizio, frozen at the sight of so many naked women drawing towards him. The eldest reached him first and started an avalanche of teasing. She laid her glass upon the salver he held, but then in mimic of Ilaria's accent, purred his name softly and leaned to kiss his cheek.

Oh the look on his startled face was a sight to see!

What's more, for the love of folly, after he blushed at her attention — expecting it to be a singular incident — the next followed suit as did all the rest!

'Fabriziohh.' *Kiss*

'Fabriziohh.' *Kiss*

'Fabriziohh.' *Kiss*

'Fabriziohhhh.' *Kiss*.

So said the first four. Yet the last to come was the youngest, perhaps only one year older than our squire. She caught his eye as she offered her beaker. Then as his fingers closed to take it she held onto it firmly. By all that's Holy, his brows knit in confusion. It made her smile. Then unlike the rest who had planted their kiss on his cheek, she leaned to kiss his lips softly, holding for a tender moment.

The nymph drew away slightly, said his name again. Fabrizio's eyes, which had shut in fear, opened slowly and couldn't avoid being held in her frank gaze. I'm sure it was the first time our young man had experienced anything like it. Aurelie, Ilaria and Maxine were so taken by surprise, they couldn't help but stand in mute witness to the encounter.

As she turned to walk on, the poor fellow stood mesmerised until she stopped to glance over her shoulder. Then with the raise of a single brow and slow wink of her eye, she plunged his dull mind into a state of utter chaos.

'Oh no.' whispered Maxine.

'Dear Heaven.' said Ilaria. 'He'll *never* be the same.'

Aurelie sighed and clapped her hands for attention. ' C o m e along! No more antics! Now before we begin let's form a circuit. Ilaria with me. Max to this side. Close ranks.' she commanded. 'No I mean shoulder-to-shoulder!'

Those by Aurelie and Ilaria flinched at the thought of brushing against the elite duet.

'Come along. It's alright. Press in.' Aurelie insisted. They shuffled closer. 'Much better. Now hear me.'

A chorus of muttered acknowledgment sounded as sober heads nodded.

'From the moment this circuit is joined each morning, we're *no* longer your betters. We shall all treat each other as *equals*.'

The chestnut-haired waif rolled her eyes in reaction. Aurelie frowned in frustration.

'You? What's your name.'

Suddenly the waif wished she had kept still. 'Cunniza Prima Donna Cort —'

'Not prima donna. Not madonna or signora. For the next hour we're equals.'

'*Really* Madonna?' droned the eldest.

'Yes. That's an order.'

'Alright then my equal. What's your *fore* name?'

'Why?' Aurelie blinked in confusion.

Though confident to lead them, Aurelie wasn't used to offering such familiarity to women of their stature, particularly not when challenged so impertinently. Ilaria sensed an impasse rising again and played the diplomat.

'Her name ... is *Aurelie*. Mine is *Ilaria*.'

'Prima Donna.' The eldest glared at Aurelie. 'Do you really expect us to call you *Aurelie* and the nice one *Ilaria?*'

Her companions snickered. Somehow the extraordinary situation had managed to rob that brazen remark of its impertinence.

'Well …' Aurelie began then suddenly halted. 'Wait. Why is *she* the nice one?'

I smiled as I listened from a short distance, yet even Maxine couldn't help but smirk as Ilaria cut in.

'Aurelie let's focus upon our task.' She caught the eye of one. 'I suppose Cunniza is *not* your real name?'

'No.' the eldest answered for her bluntly. 'That's just some infamous old harlot.'

'Well, in point of fact that was the name of a *very* grand prima donna.'

'A prima donna *harlot*.' the elder insisted.

'The men like that sort of thing.' said Cunniza. 'It's usually a famous donna.'

'Or some old goddess.' said the youngest.

'Or else a stupid fucking name' Cunniza protested 'like Bunny or Ladybug or Sparrow.'

While Aurelie remained sober-faced, Ilaria was listening thoughtfully.

'I have an idea.' said Ilaria. 'While you're with us, we three can also have pet names. Perhaps I can be … let me see … Aphrodite?'

'I'm already Aphrodite!' cried the eldest.

Maxine smirked. Aurelie dropped her forehead to her fingertips in consternation, though Ilaria, as she always did, remained the personification of patience.

'Of *course* you are. Hmm. Perhaps you should tell us all your names first?'

'Yes.' said the eldest. She pointed to herself and the others in turn. 'Aphrodite. Cunniza. Theodora. Falena and Clotilda.'

'Clotilda?'

'It's Germanic Madonna.' said Clotilda. 'It means *loud in battle*. That's because I'm —'

'Oh!' squealed Ilaria. 'Well perhaps we don't need to disclose too much intimate information.'

'Gunter picks them. To keep our real names from customers

who aren't local.'

'I see.' Ilaria frowned. 'Hmm. Then I think I have a *better* idea. Just among us, we shall use your *real* names and have pet names for the three of us. I'll be ...'

'*Angel!*' said one.

'Oh you remembered.' Ilaria smiled. 'Yes that's easy. Maxine shall be —'

'*Cat?*' said another, recalling Armand's words.

'Yes very well. And Aurelie can be ...' Ilaria glanced at her '*Venus?* A Roman Aphrodite to lead us all.'

'Angel' the eldest began with a smirk — the rest grinned to hear her offer a pet name to such an elite woman 'you realise *Venus* is the patroness of harlots?'

'Oh?' Ilaria sputtered. 'Well that seems ... I'm mean we're all ... well it shows you have some education.' She scanned them all and held on the eldest again. 'Now it shall be our secret ... but what are your *real* names?'

'I'm *Brianna*. Then by age, Clotilda is *Vendramina*, Cunniza is *Greta*, Falena is *Teresa* and Theodora is *Fiametta*.

'Oh what beautiful names. Let me see if I have them. Brianna, Vendramina, Teresa?'

'No, Greta!'

'Pardon me Greta. Then Teresa and of course ... Fiametta?'

'Yes Madonna.'

The youngest smiled and glanced at Fabrizio again.

Heaven help the young rogue, suddenly he knew her name.

Aurelie huffed and took control. 'Alright now that's enough from the *nice* one.' She lifted her finger, tipping it to each as she spilt the names so fast it suggested a remarkable memory. 'Brianna! Vendramina! Greta! Teresa! Fiametta!' Every face in the circuit was grinning. 'Now you bitches' she whispered 'time to sweat!' Her voice lifted. 'Line up! Marcel!'

I jumped to attention. The dragonesses ambled onto the road and stood line abreast, facing the direction where the men disappeared. Venus, Angel and Cat followed them together as my wife leaned in to whisper a confession.

'Madonna I must tell you that when Gunter heard who required his assistance, he offered their services gratis.'

'You mean that I'm paying —'

'Nothing at all Madonna.' she replied as Ilaria blinked in surprise. 'I tried to insist yet he refused any payment, insisting upon carrying the cost himself.'

'Did he say why?'

'He feels guilty Madonna. As marshal to the fight, he allowed Donna Montecchi to gain access into the arena. Her attempt to kill the master still weighs heavily on him.'

'I see.' Aurelie muttered.

'And ... he may have mentioned that the sight of *Donna Capulet* crying over her brave husband, shot with an assassin's arrow, had melted his heart.'

'That sounds right.' Aurelie groaned with mock jealousy. 'The *nice* one.' She glared as they lined up.

That made Ilaria and Maxine smile.

By the time they were ready to start, so much time had been consumed that Armand and Sabatino could be seen in the distance, making their return. Leaning against the mule, I cleared my throat to call the starting announcement.

'Stand ready!' I cried. A light rose in Ilaria's eyes as she raised a hand to halt me.

'Wait Marcel *one* last thing! Ladies upon Thursday next week we shall race as rivals. Aurelie ... I meant to say *Venus* and I want *all* of you to run to win.'

Brianna knit her brows. 'Angel you understand that for the sake of Pruetta's wager, we only need to beat the bitches from the Boar, not win the whole race!'

'Oh I see. Yet, in the spirit of *encouragement* for you to achieve your utmost, I declare before you all that I will stake *four* golden ecus for any dragoness who wins outright.'

An excited murmur ran among them. *Venus* nodded her approval as *Cat* smiled broadly.

'Wonderful Angel!' bubbled Teresa. 'But what prize for the last?'

Ilaria blinked in confusion. 'For the last?'

'In Verona the last also wins a prize.' Greta added.

'Forget the last!' snapped Venus — *Aurelie*. 'Who's going to be first? Marcel!'

A few moments later I boarded the mule with a babe in each basket to follow an extraordinary sight — eight feminine posteriors were bounding away before me. A pair of masculine bodies ran toward us. Every dragoness gazed at their approach, some whistled like soldiers at the sight of a pretty woman, some turned upon their heels as they passed.

'Eyes front bitches!' Venus barked .

Instantly the wayward young women turned their heads about with grins upon their youthful faces. Then all at once, Brianna's eyes lit up with passion.

'Hey girls I just realised?' she cried. 'We don't have to take her orders anymore!'

'No!' squealed Fiametta suddenly comprehending. 'Not for the next hour!'

Brianna turned her head towards Aurelie.

'Then Venus I say ... FUCK your orders!'

Never had I heard such raucous laughter erupt among a band of women, exactly as I'd heard so often among soldiers in the war. Even Venus couldn't contain her mirth. They began to surge forward, running in an absolute mess, instantly leaning in upon each other. Venus reached with both hands and shoved Brianna hard. The challenge had been ignited. Suddenly a loud smack was heard from behind followed by a squeal of pain!

'Ahhh!' cried Ilaria.

'So sorry ANGEL!' mocked Greta, then ran on to escape retaliation, eyes gaping wide.

Indeed she smacked Ilaria so hard, right in the middle of her back, that a bright mark glowed in token of her effort.

All at once pandemonium broke loose.

'Don't you hurt Donna Capulet!' screamed Teresa hurtling in

pursuit.

'It's alright Teresa!' Ilaria cried. 'I'll GET her!'

Greta retorted. 'Angel's not a donna today! She's just my little BITCH!'

Just as Greta said so, the slight form of Teresa — crouched at a run — leapt at her waist with both arms wide.

'Arghhh!' groaned the victim.

They tumbled onto the hard road in a heap together. Yet in the twinkling of an eye, Teresa sprang to her feet, covered in grazes, yet running on with a smile. Moments later Angel couldn't help herself of course and slowed to assist her own tormentor.

'Allow me to help you ... *bitch.*' she said politely.

'Why thank you ... *bitch.*'

Grinning like siblings they ran on together.

The spell of their fear had been broken. All sense of regard for rank was obliterated. For a time — as their energy continued to unleash — the wild sororitas seemed more concerned with taunting and tussling than ensuring they reserved any strength to reach the end.

From that erratic start, my sweet friends, their week and odd days of practising together ran on. Every morning they met beneath the sycamores, making their start to push, shove, smack, scream and run together. It was a glorious week of panting, sweating and bruising competitiveness, as if a team of gladiatrices had arisen from ancient Rome to train in Verona's northern hills.

It was also an unrivalled time of sipping and gulping watered wine, pinching children's cheeks and of kissing Fabrizio until he no longer blushed. By Tuesday upon the following week — one day prior to their agreed day of rest before the event — the Dragoness's impact had also been felt more fitfully by Armand, Sabatino and Tristan.

For you see, from the day of their arrival, our routine of retiring to Hazel Wood to enjoy the spectacle of the men riding together, was no longer just a matter of Ilaria, Aurelie and Maxine doing so alone. For that week and odd days, the sororitas were also on hand to cheer the careering trio aboard their gorgeous mounts.

What's more, thanks to the hiring of more masseurs, each drag-oness enjoyed being oiled, scraped, massaged and fitted into much finer couture than they had worn when their week began. Given Aurelie had discovered she was paying nothing for their services, she and Ilaria felt it was worth the expense to pamper them so lavishly. I could tell from the looks upon their glowing faces just how grateful they were.

Ready, relaxed and ranged along the balcony rail, they leaned, leapt, shouted and celebrated as one cavaliere and two chevaliers raced like gods along the course together. During those sessions they had been surprised to see yet another handsome Capulet appear. And perhaps after each mounted practice was run — perhaps not unexpectedly — when the unwed Tristan entered to take refreshment among them, he received more congratulations for running second or third than the victor!

During that time however, none of his new admirers had laid eyes upon Ajax, his pearl-bodied beast with the chestnut mane and tail. While they watched Tristan in the hills he had been riding his alternate stallion. Each morning however, while Sabatino and Armand ran barefoot, he descended into the citadel where Ajax had been lodged. It allowed him to run the bold , as much as possible, over that portion of the course which sat outside the walls.

And though none among the Dragonesses had yet seen Ajax, they all fell in love with the sight of Victoire. Even though Armand rode the gallant beast, they never won while practicing upon the course. Though Victoire was fast, he was bred for the strength and trained to endure twists and turns in halting rhythms and the buffet-ing engagements of war, not to run flat out over enduring distances.

Yet to those who saw Victoire, the place in which the mighty beast finished had no effect on the esteem in which they held him. Even more moving to the doting young women, particularly Teresa, was the sight they beheld each day as they left Hazel Wood. Five pairs of eyes gazed through the rear of the wagon upon the sight of gallant Victoire — following at a gentle walk — with Armand and Ilaria on his bare back to return them safely home together.

Truly sweet friends it's no exaggeration to suggest the fond lovers appeared like a vision from a mythical tale. More impacting still was the sight of how Ilaria — fatigued from her labour each day — had adopted the lovely habit of linking her hands in front of Armand's waist, turning her head and leaning into his back to shut her eyes and rest. Before we even reached beyond the Hazel Wood gates, sighs and giggles sounded from the wagon as all looking on could tell that the *nice* one had already fallen fast asleep.

On the final Tuesday — when our wagon full of weary dragonesses was loaded for the last time — Maxine and I drove them down to return each one to their homes. Most resided outside the walls in the western borgo. As we drove along that day, Victoire carried Armand and Ilaria behind us once more until he turned toward the gate at Sycamore Hill. Ilaria was asleep. Armand smiled and waved as the gates opened ahead and he quietly coaxed the stallion through.

After we left them, Maxine and I heard our passengers musing upon how much in love the Capulets appeared to be, what an idyllic life they seemed to share and how lucky the sororitas were to have met them under such odd circumstances. Of course, had Aurelie not accepted Florentia's challenge to run on Ilaria's behalf, none of our passengers would have met any of us. Nor would we have ever met those fiery young Dragonesses.

I've told many people of the extraordinary preparations undertaken by the Capulets and Cortelannis for that race festival. And yes, I realise some elements may seem too extraordinary to believe. Yet sweet friends the truth of it was a far more extraordinary thing for me to behold. Recounting these memories never fails to make me wish I was there once more, able to enjoy it all over again with every participant.

I recall how Ilaria had dreaded the thought of having to endure the work to prepare for that footrace. And indeed it proved to be arduous beyond her most dire expectation. Yet by the time those preparations were finishing, I knew she felt it had been more fulfilling for Aurelie and herself than either one could have imagined. What's more their bond became fused, as if they were sisters of the blood. And Sabatino became as close to Armand and Tristan as a blood brother.

Moreover and finally, the Dragoness had agreed that, with such full preparations undertaken and such an incentive — four golden ecus — nothing would deter them from rising to Ilaria's challenge of winning the race outright. And it was well they all did so much to prepare.

For that year sweet friends, fate ordained that the races afoot and upon horseback for the green and scarlet silk prizes, would not only be more hotly contested than ever, but their results would also be bathed in cold blood.

Chapter 21 the Bell Tower

At the time of its inception — more than two hundred years before we arrived in Verona — the footrace for the green silk was only for male entrants. As Escalus had explained in the cathedral, it was run to honour the memory of humble foot soldiers. They had fought a great battle for Verona's independence against the Emperor's minions — including the Montecchis. And so the race had always been held as near as possible to the anniversary of that battle. Yes, that sounds admirable. No, not the Montecchi's treachery, the timing of the race and the gaining of Verona's independence.

And so, for the sole reason of that timing when it began, the race always fell within the *first week of Lent*. And yes my sweet friends, Lent is a very *worthy* period to hold a solemn race. Yet it's also a very *dull* period to hold a lively festival. Consider if you will that during Lent — none may eat meat and that makes people grumpish! None may sing or dance and that makes people more grumpish! What's more it robs talented entertainers of employment!

However since the race festival's inception, it was discovered Verona's independence wasn't enough to keep it safe from the ambition of the Emperor — or neighbours like Milan — to regain control and dominate it again. And so it became clear the only way for Verona to remain *lastingly* safe, was to give up it's hard fought independence in return for the protection of her mighty neighbour Venice. Hoorah!

Then once settled under that control, the leaders in Venice — who were *festively* minded — made a significant change to the footrace. They altered the date on which it was celebrated and also combined it with the annual horserace — originally held upon an entirely different date — to create a *racing* festival. Hoorah again!

Yes, the original date had *historical* significance.

Yet, as you now know it fell in the *dull* time of Lent.

And so, taking charge, Verona's new masters declared the date of celebration must instead fall one week *before* Lent upon Fat Thursday, a dizzy feasting day that sits within the main carnival season, one whole week before Lent even begins! Hoorah! Hoorah! Hoorah! After all sweet friends, what did Venice care for an ancestral date which celebrated the independence Verona had given over to them?

Thus, instead of running hungry athletes during a hungry season as hungry watchers looked on at a *single* foot race, now it fell on a day when watchers could have their fill of meat, drink, music and frivolity, all while enjoying the spectacle of more than one race in a *race day festival*. And to enliven it further, they announced the race for women. Then finally at this time, for the sake of broader enjoyment, Prince Escalus announced that race for all comers upon mules!

Oh yes, the Masters of Venice were clever to alter so much in Verona. Yet they were just as clever to leave one particular element *unaltered*: the compulsion for all who entered the footraces to run *in the manner of our Etruscan ancestors* remained unchanged. Clever.

Venice argued their want to retain that great tradition of running naked offered two sober benefits. First, though buffeting and tripping are allowed, naked sweating bodies are harder to grip and hold, which ensured more focus was placed on the challenge of *running* against a rival rather than vicious attempts to *bring rivals down*.

The other sober benefit, as Princess Florentia suggested, was the *social* victory which naked competition brought to the race festival. It was meant to celebrate the worth of humble foot soldiers, not elite warriors. And so every year in Verona, for at least one day, any person high or low who enters a footrace will appear to be equal in rank against any of their rivals. Ironically in this way, a runner's naked form and simplified coiffure could serve as a social mask, removing evidence of their rank from public sight.

Yet I believe that the masters of Venice — the world's greatest sellers of everything — understood *another* advantage to that condition which seems to go unsaid for the most part.

For after they moved the festival from a dull day to a lively day; then expanded the footrace to include women too while insisting all must adhere to that tradition of running naked; Verona's race festival seemed to offer a social spectacle that was capable of drawing a much larger attendance.

And from what the Cortelannis told us of the *before* and *after*, all at once multitudes began to pour in from other citadels — indeed other kingdoms — to witness the event. What's more, the elite horserace gained such great esteem by the festivals new found popularity, it began to attract riders from the furthest corners of Christendom and beyond.

Oh and finally, did I explain that before the changes were made, Venice had discovered the original footrace cost Verona a very great sum to stage during Lent each year? Yes it did! Yet in that original form it returned nothing at all and ran at a grievous *loss* for the citadel. And so sweet friends, for the sake of moving the date by a mere fraction — just one week — it suddenly became the most popular and profitable festival on Verona's calendar. Hoo-fucking-rah!

As I began to perceive that for myself, Venetian cleverness got me to thinking. As you know, I had entered the footrace too. And like the rest I'd be racing without a stitch to cover me. Yet I had entered the mule race too. And so for that entry I also planned — secretively — to race without a stitch to cover me. Perhaps I might wear a headpiece.

After all, if the beast I rode must be naked, then so should I.

I reasoned that in a festival which celebrates the equality of all under Heaven, the she-beast and I should appear equal too. Indeed the notion first came to me when I heard Brianna explain how the Boar and Dragon always entered some women with no intention to run the full course. They were there to be seen for the sake of *promotion*. As an entertainer, I appreciated the value of such a plan.

Moreover I felt certain — given my calling — that I could benefit by ensuring my efforts during the festival drew as much attention as possible. Well bite my bare ass, yes I did! If Venice, Verona, the Boar and Dragon were doing their utmost to profit their utmost? Well then so should I. For though we hadn't attended the festival before, Aurelie assured us that of all such events in Verona's festive season, the race carnival attracted the greatest attendance by far.

'Ria every citizen high and low moves Heaven and earth to ensure their attendance.'

Ilaria and Aurelie had wandered into the dove house with Maxine and I. Ilaria wanted to choose four plump doves as a reward for the last place getter among the Dragonesses.

'They fill the entire length of the southern wall' Aurelie ran on 'tussling to gain the best vantage for watching the outer course. The rest line the streets within, all the way to finish.'

'Lee Lee where should *we* watch from?'

'Don't worry darling. We have a plan that allows us to see the best from both sides. Most of the elite will be gather upon the wall to admire or critique the form of newcomers and veterans alike. Now both male *and* female.

'I'm sure they'll critique every inch of our bodies.'

'Or envy us or dote on us. Tush it's unavoidable.'

'I suppose it's just one hour to endure. And we'll be moving constantly. None will manage to stare for too long.'

'Oh Ria I say let them stare. Let them gossip too.'

'Gossip?' Ilaria blanched.

'Of course darling. Mercy, gossip is the great motivator for so much attendance. The most lasting threads for our year are fuelled by what's seen in a single day. Imagine being a wretch who has to admit they didn't attend!'

'I hadn't considered that our participation would —'

'Oh don't fret Ria. Every year until now, I've enjoyed the gossip myself.'

Ilaria whispered. 'What kind of things do they say?'

'Oh what else? Envious sniping, promiscuous innuendos, praise and admiration. Who cares Ria? As long as their interest in *one* person hangs upon the lips of *many*.'

I was following them with Figara in my arms. Given my own plans for the festival, my mind bubbled with interest as I listened to Aurelie.

'Well ...' Ilaria bleated 'I think *I* care.'

'Care that no matter *what* they say darling, it can do nothing more than *add* to our mystique.'

'Are you certain? You don't care what any may *say*?'

'You can't control what they *say* Ria. However you can control what they *see*.'

'Lee Lee I already fear what they'll see.'

'They'll see two elite women, strong enough to risk their gaze and opinions, when most know they'd never have the spine to attempt such an audacious thing.'

'I suppose ... that *could* be true.'

'Of course it is darling. Florentia was right. As elite women, no matter the outcome, merely by entering this race we can't fail to gain from the effort.'

'Lee Lee I'm still not so sure. Yet I'm certain that, thanks to yourself and Max, I'm as ready as I could ever be.'

'So am I?' I blurted.

'Oh imbecile!' snapped Maxine. 'What did you do but held bambinos and flirted with young women!'

'Ah yes.' Ilaria smiled. 'I also owe a great deal to our wild Dragonesses.'

'I think they feel the reverse is true Madame.' Maxine glanced at Aurelie. 'And to you Madonna.'

'It's alright Maxine.' Aurelie mused. 'I know they simply fear me, yet worship the lovely *Donna Capulet*.'

'Oh no Lee Lee.' Ilaria insisted. 'They love you and respect you. They all want to be just like you.'

'Tush Ria. They like my bawdy sense of humour. Yet I must say ... I've come to respect them all.'

'Yes so have I. I'm glad we've had this time to share with them. Hmm. I'll be sad to part company with them.'

'So will I Ria. But we can hardly continue to socialise with them after the festival is done.'

'I know it's true. Yet somehow ... I'd still like to.'

'Oh keeping their company in the seclusion of these hills for a week is one thing darling. Or confining our antics thereafter to Hazel Wood. But down there in the citadel Ria, beyond that one day of the festival? You know those in our world wouldn't stand for it.'

'Yes I understand. But now we've met them all it … it just … well it seems a shame.'

Aurelie knitted her brows. 'Perhaps we can sponsor them next season? I don't mean compete ourselves, but make their training up here a regular event.'

'That's a wonderful thought. Yes we must suggest it. Now let's pick four plump doves to reward the last.'

That final comment made me curious at how the festival was said to award prizes for the last. At first, we thought it mere fancy. Then we discovered it was true, which inspired a notion for the races I had entered. Perhaps … I should attempt to secure a prize by coming last. Yet I needed more knowledge of the rules to be sure, and so ventured down to the citadel in search of intelligence.

What's more, as fate would have it, I also required a string for my lute. As you know, the merchant's guild which sponsors the race festival sat in Herb Market Square opposite the new Emporium site. That was my destination. Several times before, Maxine and I had browsed a musical sellers stall in the sprawling piazza. It was manned by a Jewish merchant called *Noam*. I felt certain the amicable man was a long-standing citizen, and hoped he would not only supply my string, but may know what I wished to learn about the races.

And indeed he did. Noam explained that after the final race was run, an hour or so before sunset, if any last place getters wished to claim their prize — the leg of a pig or a live rooster — then before they could take it away they must walk afoot, or ride their horse or mule at a walk, through a rowdy gauntlet of spectators, all of whom were permitted by the rules, to make every attempt to snatch said prizes away!

'The gauntlet they walk' Noam began to explain 'starts from the finish line at Saint Fermo Square, then runs a tight circuit through the streets to return to Saint Fermo. Each prize is tethered to a thin leash. The pig leg is hung about the neck of the losing horse or mule. For each footrace loser, a tether is attached to one ankle of their rooster.'

'Bite my bare ass!'

'Yes some may attempt to do that!' Noam quipped. 'And so as the gauntlet's walked by them all, any spectator may approach with a knife to cut a cock free or the hanging piece of pork or just attempt to cut off a portion.'

'Cupid's Balls! They go at them with knives?'

'Most of them. Yet because the horserace is an elite affair, the cavaliere that carries it usually let's it go with a good grace. However, the man and woman leading their roosters upon a leash, are usually humble folk.'

'More desperate to keep their prize?'

'Precisely. And so any who dare approach them will have a tussle on their hands. Sooner or later of course, someone manages to cut the leash and set the cock free. Then pandemonium erupts as every Jack and Jill runs amok to catch it.'

Finally Noam explained that once a rooster was cut free, any loser hoping to keep their prize must recapture it against all other efforts! At that point, many losers resign themselves to simply *giving them the bird*, as they say. Yet for the benefit of their poor family, some stout athletes fight fiercely to regain it.

After hearing Noam's tale I felt strangely drawn by the notion of it all. I knew that in one race or the other, I must attempt to finish last. My own goal however was not to *keep* the prize but to be *seen*! And so I decided, if I was to run that gauntlet among such a wild throng, I would stand out more if I was naked upon a mule rather than walking upon the street! I must come last in the mule race.

I had that discussion with Noam upon Tuesday, two days before the race. The following day was our *potential* day of rest which became our *declared* day of rest. And so no practice was run in the hills upon Wednesday morning. Yet by noon upon Wednesday I was in Herb Market Square once more, this time attending with our elite competitors.

Led by Sabatino, we were high above the market, gazing down from the dizzy height of the civic bell tower. Acting as our race mentor, Sabatino had gained permission for us all to ascend. Just one dragoness accompanied us however, their prima competitor, young

Teresa. Unlike the rest of her sororitas, she hadn't run before. And so Ilaria suggested Teresa join their party for a *strategic* briefing.

Once ascended, it took a moment for most to regather themselves. For all, save the young dragoness, the climb to the summit proved to be literally breathtaking. Halted upon the belfry walkway, most were panting and perspiring, at least a little. Yet we also recovered quickly and began to lift our chins to gaze over the citadel. And sweet friends, the images we saw in every direction, were also breathtaking.

Suspended just beneath us were two great bells. The smaller bell which marks the clock is called the *Marangona*. The larger bell is the mighty *Rengo*, whose unmistakable chime is used to warn the citadel in moments of danger.

Of course, our visit to the belfry was nostalgic for the Cortelannis. As you recall, on the day Aurelie arrived in Verona, before visiting any other place, Sabatino halted there to ascend the tower with his shy new bride. He wanted the sight of his beloved citadel to be impacting. They had climbed the narrow winding stair together, stood panting in each other's arms, then shared that famous kiss which Aurelie swears marked the romantic moment she fell in love.

The purpose for our ascent on this day however was not romantic. Yet that didn't stop Ilaria from declaring it was still a very romantic moment to share. She kissed Armand, turning to lean as they gazed over the citadel. Teresa gazed at them. I'd noticed whenever they stood together, the young dragoness rarely took her eyes off them. It was clear in the short time Teresa spent with us, the loving couple, and Ilaria in particular, had left a great impression on her.

On the day before our visit to the tower, Prince Escalus declared the course would remain unchanged from last season. With that news Sabatino planned our touring agenda. After a survey of the circuit from that lofty height, we'd travel outside the walls to the starting point. It lay to the south-east through the open marshland. From there we would trace the racing path back to the citadel. Then he planned to complete our investigation by following the inner circuit to the finishing post, already erected at Saint Fermo.

Sabatino pointed from our perch to the starting place — three to four miles distant from the walls southern corner — near the edge of the hallowed battlefield. On the following day, under the watchful eyes of a starting marshal, one corps of competitors after another, would assemble at that location and sally forth.

'As much as the numbers will allow' Sabatino began 'each group will begin their race as one body. Wardens are set at intervals along the open course to oversee progress 'til we enter inside. Once through the gate, they'll still mark the course but be harder to see among the press lining the way.'

Glancing at Ilaria, Aurelie lifted her brows.

'Ria I'm getting goose bumps already.'

'Yes so am I.'

As Sabatino described the beginning, the image of it all began to spring to life. Each pack of racers — mounted or afoot — would surge north from the start to run through the open plain and approach the citadel. Yet well before any reached the looming battlement walls, those racing at the fore would cause the pack to stretch into a lengthening line.

'You'll reach the wall at the south-east corner.'

'Shall we enter through that gate?'

'No Ilaria. Everyone must wheel left there and run the southern wall, for nearly its full length, and enter through the Harvest Gate.'

'Isn't that gate always locked out of season.'

'Yes darling.' Aurelie agreed. 'Yet they open it during this festival to allow us to enter through there.'

'Entering there means the wall's full length can be used to give more watchers a chance to see the action.'

'Clever.' Ilaria replied. 'It enhances the spectacle.'

'Above the *centre* gate darling is the favoured position for most to view the outer course.'

'Oh? Not the Harvest Gate?'

'From the centre you gain the longest view of faces and chests and torsos running towards you ... then backs and thighs and asses running away from you.'

'Do you mia cara?'

'Oh ... so I'm told darling.'

'Teresa.' Ilaria smiled at her. 'What do you think? That looks like a good stretch of the legs for us!'

'Yes Madonna. It rises up slightly all the way. Yet for us, that will be no problem at all.'

'Now' Sabatino put in 'turning hard right all your asses will disappear through the Harvest Gate ...'

'I may be *dragging* my ass through darling.'

'From there you'll charge straight ahead through the citadel, past the castle' Sabatino pointed 'and on through the double arches of Jupiter's Gate.' He pointed again.

'Yes they look beautiful.' said Ilaria.

'In ancient times it was Verona's main entry point.'

'Was it?' Ilaria replied. 'How interesting.'

'Oh yes, but darling please get on with it! This height is beginning to make me giddy.'

'Yes mia cara. Then ... you'll race past the north entrance of Herb Market Square.'

'I love Herb Market Square.'

Aurelie rolled her eyes. 'Hush Ria let him finish.'

Teresa giggled. Ilaria smiled at her warmly.

'At that point' every eye traced Sabatino's finger, 'you'll hear a special chime from the *Rengo*.'

'Will he be standing at the entrance?' asked Ilaria as

Teresa giggled again. 'Well why is that funny?'

'Madonna Rengo is the name of the great bell below us. The alarm bell.'

We looked into the abyss. I felt giddy too.

'Rengo will alert every runner on the course that the leader has reached that vital point.'

'I know who that will be!' Ilaria glanced at Teresa who blushed deeply as a cascade of smiles agreed.

'Then ...' Sabatino pressed on 'as each of you reach the point ... even you little dragoness, and even if you do find yourself in the lead, be careful not to push too soon.'

'Yes Don Cortellani. I'll be cautious.'

Sabatino shifted along to follow his own finger.

'Now ... just after passing the market, you enter a short run of turns — left, right, left, right — and must take care. Men ...' he glanced at Tristan and Armand 'if you enter there in company on horseback, slip inside your rivals at the second turning or else run behind. But on that hard surface don't get caught outside them in the second and last corner.'

'Yes.' said Armand and Tristan nearly as one.

'Run fast, lean hard, but be careful. For those afoot, no matter how tired you feel going in, keep your wits about you. It's the final place for those running in teams to halt and turn on the blind side of a corner in an effort to ambush their rivals, particularly on that last corner.'

'Oh that's diabolical.' Aurelie hissed.

'Yes mia cara and the women do it to, so be careful. Once out of there, you'll quickly reach Saint Anastasia.'

'Near the end Signore?' Teresa asked excitedly.

Sabatino smiled with a twinkle in his eye.

'Very much so little rabbit. The basilica is the beginning of the end. You'll run a broad circuit around it to the right to meet the river-side promenade facing south.'

'Right not left?' asked Ilaria.

'Yes. If you see the old stone bridge ...'

'Then darling you're an imbecile who's gone the wrong way!'

A burst of laughter rang out. Sabatino tilted his eyes to Heaven and turned to lean on the rail and face us all.

'My friends, that run along the bank of the Adige is your final burst. It follows the river downstream and so ...'

'It's *downhill* hill all the way.' Tristan smiled.

'Yes slightly my friend. And so, if you're a larger burden on horseback take care —'

'Not to lean too far forward?' Armand put in.

'To save our mount's feet' Tristan added 'and lighten their tread for that final burst.'

'Precisely.' Sabatino agreed. 'As for those afoot, that run will take us all on to the winners post at Saint Fermo.'

'It sounds so exciting Madame!' squeaked Teresa.

'Are you going to win?' asked Armand with a smile. Teresa looked stupefied.

'I'll try my best Signore for Donna Capulet.'

'Please call me Armand.'

'Oh no Don Capulet. I ... no I couldn't. You're far too ... I'm far too ... I ...'

'What's your name?'

'I'm called ... that is ... my name's Teresa.'

'At least we're talking at last. Why do I feel you avoid me Teresa?' Armand said a little too earnestly.

'I'm sorry Signore.' Teresa stuttered. 'It's just that you're —' Suddenly she was quiet.

'Armand stop pestering our champion.' Ilaria said sympathetically. 'It's alright Teresa. He won't bite. He's really rather nice.'

'Oh yes I know Madonna. All the girls say —' she gulped and fell quiet again.

Aurelie's brows lifted with interest.

'Yes Teresa? What do *all* the girls say?'

Teresa blushed deeply in utter panic. 'Oh Madonna forgive me. I shouldn't have said anything.'

'Teresa!' Aurelie snapped in mock-warning. 'Until tomorrow you still work for me. Now tell me this instant. What do they say?'

'Oh Madonna they ... they love *Victoire* of course.'

'The *horse!*' Sabatino grinned. He clapped a hand on Armand's shoulder.

'Indeed Signore. They all say he's *such* a beautiful creature. Yet they also say ...'

'Yes Teresa?' coaxed Aurelie.

'The horse is *nearly* as beautiful as it's master.' Suddenly Teresa's cheeks turned every shade known to the pallor of human skin.

'Devil's balls!' hissed Aurelie in frustration. 'Is there no end to it?'

'What's the matter mia cara?' Sabatino pouted in mock sympathy.

'I've lived in Verona for years and struggled to earn every shard of respect. My brother stays for just one season and every woman, from the whores — sorry dear — to her Highness fall in love with him at a single glance. Honestly Ria! How do you put up with it?'

'Oh.' She smiled at Teresa. 'I manage to suffer through it.' Teresa grinned as Sabatino pressed on.

'Now if the women in this tower could refrain from complimenting every man in this tower *except* myself —'

'Oh hush darling. You're the most handsome man alive. Isn't he Teresa?'

'Oh yes Madonna very handsome. Much more handsome than his horse!'

I doubt it was a regular occurrence, yet for any so far below us who may have been able to hear, instead of bells, peals of laughter sounded from high above them.

'I'm glad my horse didn't hear that. And now, to the order of events.'

He explained the day would begin with the horserace. The mule race would follow and the women's race thereafter. Last of all, the footrace for men which began the tradition so many years ago, would close the events. Thereafter in Saint Fermo Square, prizes for winners and losers would be awarded by the sponsors, including her Highness. Then before sunset — in an effort to retain their prizes — the last place getters would run the wild gauntlet.

'Without summer heat to contend with, the horses will start at midday.'

'Scusi Don Capulet.' Teresa glanced at Armand. 'Will you ride Victoire or the other one?'

'I'll ride Victoire. But don't expect him to win Teresa. He's not really built for such a race.'

'But he's very beautiful.'

'He is. But you haven't seen my brother's mount. He's beautiful too. And I'm afraid when your friends see Tristan's favourite, they may fall in love with another.'

'Yes. The girls are very fond of Signore Tristan.'

'I meant his *horse* Teresa.' said Armand.

'Well my heart' Ilaria put in 'at least you finally seem to have a rival.'

'Sabatino how long between events?' asked Tristan hoping to alter the subject.

'Half an hour between the horse and mule — if all goes to plan. An hour between the footraces. The prize presentation is set for just after the strike of five.'

Ilaria gazed south across the open plain.

'Sab how quickly will they run it?'

'Six miles for the men? A little less than an hour. Some factors will affect it, rain with slipping and tumbles, how much they tussle. Either one can slow the pace down.'

'For women?'

'Their race is still quite new. And so —'

'If I recall' Aurelie put in 'the women's victor last season finished in *less* than an hour.'

'Oh that seems fast.' Ilaria threw an arm about Teresa's shoulder. 'We may have our work cut out for us.'

'Discounting the women who just run to be *seen* ...' Sabatino resumed.

'*I'm* running to be seen!' I blurted.

'Discounting such women and *Marcel* ...'

'The imbecile!' cried Maxine.

'I've noticed in the last few years, that those running in earnest seem to finish in just a little more than an hour.'

'Ah!' chirped Aurelie. 'Then based on our results Ria we shall *not* run last. And may even finish among the fore.'

'Splendid.' said Ilaria glancing at Sabatino. 'I imagine there's far more tussling among the men.'

Aurelie's brows lifted.

'You may wish to *reimagine* that darling.'

'There's often more at the start Ilaria.' Sabatino warned calmly. 'But as you begin, I urge you to be less mindful of tussling and concentrate on *pacing* yourself. It's over three miles to the south-east corner of the walls.'

'More than half the whole distance.' Ilaria added.

'Yes.' Sabatino pointed again. 'Then along the wall to the Harvest Gate, *two-thirds* of a mile more.'

We followed with our eyes.

'Once inside, how long is the rest?' asked Armand.

'From that gate to the basilica' said Sabatino 'it rises slightly for three quarters of a mile.'

'Then downhill for the riverbank run.' Tristan added.

'More or less half a mile in that dash to the finish.'

Aurelie was gazing soberly.

'As you said darling, we must pace ourselves.'

Tristan frowned in thought. 'You also said there's a place where some tend to push too *soon?*'

'Herb Market Square. The crowd there is always large and excited. Particularly if they hear horses coming. Yet mounted or afoot, don't let them spur you too soon.'

'Hmm. Point taken. Any other dangers?'

'No Tristan. I think that may be —'

'Darling don't forget *Jupiter's Gate?*'

'Oh yes mia cara. How could I forget?'

'What goes wrong at the beautiful gate?' said Ilaria.

'Unfortunately it has an infamous history. So keep your wits about you. There are wardens in the citadel but as you approach it, glance about to see if any rivals are close.'

'Look from here darling.' Aurelie pointed at the gate. 'you can see how the frame forms two portals side by side, with a *column* in between?'

'Yes.' said Ilaria. 'That's what makes it so lovely.'

Aurelie lifted her brows. 'And makes it a treacherous spot to shove a rival into the frame from either side or from either side of that column in between.'

'Or to grab their hair' Sabatino added 'and smash a head straight onto the stone.'

'Ohhh Teresa.' Ilaria groaned. 'Just hearing that gives me a headache.'

'Tell them what happened last year darling.'

'Someone was hurt badly?' Armand asked.

'I'm afraid so. A foreigner in the men's footrace. Two others worked in concert. One pushed, one tripped. His head crashed into the centre column.'

Ilaria winced. 'Oh that sounds hideous.'

'More than you know Ilaria.' Sabatino replied. 'He didn't live to tell the tale.'

Every eye widened.

'Heavens that's dreadful!'

'Never fear Madonna.' whispered Teresa. 'I'll be watching from behind.'

'No little rabbit. You'll be winning from in front. Don't stay back for me.'

'Yes Teresa.' Aurelie agreed. 'If any of those bitches — girls — from the Boar are ahead of us by then, you must stop for nothing.'

'Bitches from the Boar?' Sabatino lifted his brows.

'The Dragon and Boar darling have —'

'What are you doing at the Dragon *or* the Boar?'

'Oh yes Sab, *hilarious*. The proprietors have a wager for the winner each season. Just among themselves.'

Armand's eyes widened. 'Ah then Tristan. Sabatino. Perhaps we should investigate this wager. Teresa?'

'Yes Don Capulet.'

'Are any of your girls *likely* to win the wager?'

'In truth, it's hit or miss Signore. Brianna brags that she'll pummel every sow to be sure one of us wins by default. Yet I'm sure our rivals boast the same. Fiametta's fast. She won for us last year. And this time Greta swears that she has a potion to make her run faster.'

'A potion?'

'Yes Madonna. Yet please God Signore and without meaning to boast ... I think I may stand some chance.'

'The others seem to agree.' Armand said quietly. 'What makes them so sure? Do *you* have potion too?'

'Oh no Don Capulet. Potions are *expensive*.'

Not expecting to hear Teresa say such a thing, we all burst into a fit of fond laughter.

'Then what's your secret Teresa?' asked Ilaria.

'No secret Madonna. I only started at the Dragon last summer. I stay with the girls in the borgo now, yet my nonna raised me and lives just beyond the starting point in Tomba.'

'How does that help you?'

'Every other day after our night shift, I run back to visit my nonna.'

Ilaria blinked with surprise. 'You run all the way?'

'So we may break our fast together. I eat a little; sleep a lot; stay as long as I can — at least until five. Yet our shift starts at six. So I run back to be sure I'm never late.'

'No wonder Pruetta put you in.' said Aurelie.

'And speaking of the starting point' Sabatino said politely 'I think it's time we descended to venture out there. Come along good people.'

'But Sab you didn't say how long it takes the horses.'

'Oh yes Ilaria, just quickly. From the starting post to the corner of the wall is a quarter hour.'

'Just over three miles? That's not at a gallop.'

'No Armand. To spare our mounts, we'll start at a canter. Without saddles or stirrups through that open stretch, the trick will be to keep our seats against the early heckling. The gallop begins as we turn to run along the wall. Then once we enter through Harvest Gate, the pace will rise until we reach the basilica —'

'And then?' said Tristan.

'Then my young chevalier, if it hasn't already, all Hell may break loose.'

'That's ironic darling!' giggled Aurelie.

'What is mia cara?'

'As you reach God's house, all Hell's breaking loose' she patted his cheek.

Teresa smiled to see the fearful prima donna behaving so flippantly.

'Hmm.' He rolled his eyes. 'As for time, from the corner of the wall where the pace begins to rise, to the post at Saint Fermo can be run in *three* minutes!'

'Oh that's fast!' Tristan grinned. 'And so if a rider doesn't fall, he may run the full course in —' he wagged his head in calculation '— less than *twenty* minutes.'

'What if you *do* fall darling?' asked Aurelie.

'We're not squires anymore little sister.' Armand replied. 'This is no longer sport but practice for war.'

'Yes mai cara. Any fallen cavaliere is easy prey.'

'Any horseman that falls in a fight must get up fast,' added Tristan. 'Get up and fight for his life. I'd rather die in an effort to rise to my feet than die on my back.'

'Well said brother.' Armand offered stoically.

'Very well said.' echoed Sabatino.

'You hear that Teresa?' Aurelie offered her a challenging look. 'If we fall?'

'We must rise Prima Donna. Rise to our feet and fight to the end.'

'Heavens!' Ilaria sighed. 'I just want to reach the end ... and put my clothes back on.'

Laughter echoed in the daunting stairwell as we entered together to descend. It had been revealing to watch Teresa during our lofty conference. As I had recently learnt, she was just one year younger than Ilaria. Yet to see them together in that setting, one had so much and the other had so little. One behaved as if the other were ten years her senior when in fact they were nearly the same age.

And despite the more hardened path Teresa's life had taken to that moment, as she made that brave declaration and glanced at her makeshift employer, behind her eyes was a tremor of uncertainty. I've found some men and women are hardened by life against the threat of their fears, while some are made more fearful of life by its hardships.

Yet that doesn't seem to make the first more like to be brave and the others less so. Not at all. Indeed it has always seemed to me that to be the latter kind — one who has fear but is still willing to expose themselves to danger for the safety of another or a moral principle — is to possess a very particular kind of courage. I saw it in Teresa that day. Some of Teresa's age and in her predicament, already carry a hard-bitten look about them. Yet she did not.

Teresa appeared to have the kind of courage that may tremble in fear just before her strength was summoned in spite of any fear. Ilaria did too. Of course there are those, good and bad alike, who possess a more brash kind of courage. I know some of those will see the trembling fortitude of one like Teresa and mistake it for cowardice.

However I've learned when those two opposites clash together, it's often the moment that fate turns the world of each upon their head. The bald strength of one will underestimate the veiled strength of the other. I saw it that day when Armand faced the threat of Onorato Montecchi.

I had hoped to never see the like of it again.

Chapter 22 Gossip & Whispers

As we made our exit from the base of the tower into the bustling piazza, Caspar and Fabrizio stood waiting for us though Liberati and Boccolo did not. Since the Capulets brokered peace with the Montecchis, we no longer browsed the citadel with the same amount of protection, nor did they. Indeed every now and then, usually at a distance, we even caught glances of Aldobrando and Donatella. A polite nod of heads and smiles would be exchanged, more often by the women. However no more attempt was made to interact with them beyond those mute, civil acknowledgments.

From where we assembled, the site for the new Emporium was diagonally across the market space. Purely by chance, the architect Ilaria had engaged stood close by, lingering in a stall. He sighted our party, approached and urged them to digress for a moment and consider the progress he'd made on the site. The former building's burnt-out husk had been entirely removed. Now the clever man was ready to mark out the site for what was to replace it.

While they followed the ancient thinker through the stalls, I dawdled along at the rear. By chance, we passed within eyeshot of Noam's musical stall again. Having purchased my lute string there the day before, I recalled the same need for my battered Irish harp. I glanced ahead. Convinced that our party looked fit to loiter for more than a moment, I diverted with every intention to return quickly.

Arriving at Noam's stall I found him occupied with a patron. I spied the style of string I required and drew one out for inspection. Yet hard by the stall — and within earshot — a young donna was chatting to her companion. Oh yes, I usually eavesdrop on any conversation I can hear. This was no exception. And this discussion quickly revealed something of interest.

They were discussing a last-minute entrant in the women's race — not an ordinary woman but an exalted one — who apparently registered on that very morning. I leaned to learn more just as Noam hailed me with a greeting, and so became diverted. I greeted him back, explaining my need for haste, and so purchased in haste, and departed in haste.

By the time I returned all were set to depart. And so with a flourish of excitement, I blurted out my tasty morsel of gossip. It set Ilaria and Aurelie wondering if the princess had decided to run after all. Or perhaps she had managed to persuade an exalted associate. Armand stood nearby with Maxine, tickling little Thibault. He was also intrigued to hear that news. So much so that it caused him to stop tickling and think for a lingering moment. A wary look rose in his eyes that troubled Maxine.

He glanced around as if he expected to see something, yet apparently did not. I saw him glance at Caspar. Then to my surprise, he drew us both aside.

'Two elite ladies you say?'

'Yes Chevalier. Both married and young. One had a striking gold headpiece. They seemed settled to browse and may be there still. Is everything alright?'

Armand knit his brows. 'I'm sure it is. But that's an odd piece of news and ... Max do you know this stall?'

'Yes Master. It's very close.'

'Hmm. Then just before we move on, give Thibault to Marcel and go quickly. Don't stay long Cat. Try not to arouse suspicion of course, yet see if you can learn more. Risk a direct question if you must.'

'I can do it.' I offered.

'Yes rogue. But a woman engaging them to share gossip will be less conspicuous.'

'Master, a talking elephant would be less conspicuous than my husband.'

Oh yes, I thought that was very funny.

And so Maxine hastened to see if she could glean more information than myself or an elephant! Yet by the time she arrived, the duet had moved on. Yet before she turned to depart, noticing Noam was unoccupied, she reasoned if I had heard so much, perhaps he had too.

They hadn't yet met directly. And so Maxine pretended to browse before engaging him in conversation. Yes Noam heard tell of a new entrant. And in his affable, and perhaps too charming way, he informed her that entrant — if gossip may be believed — was genuinely exalted. *No less than a countess* they'd said, yet unknown to any in Verona.

'Countess von Bremmer?' Maxine echoed.

'Yes. So they said. The Bremmer Pass is up in the alps on our northern border.'

'The border to Germany?'

'The same. I assume that she, or at least her husband, is Germanic. It's cold there. I suspect they've come for the warmth of our festival. It attracts so many these days.'

Mindful of her need for haste, she thanked Noam and made an attempt to retreat with those extra morsels. Yet he sought to hold her interest for a moment more and confessed, that from recent sight of her in the market, he felt sure she was employed by the *French* couple. She confessed she did. Then quiet unexpectedly, Noam glanced about, and lowered his voice to a whisper.

'I've heard of another entrant who may be of interest to the man who slew Don Montecchi last summer.'

Maxine's eyes lit with caution. 'I see.'

'A last minute entrant to the men's race.'

'What's the man's name?' She expected to hear an exalted family name.

'Silvius.' said Noam quietly.

As he talked, he polished the brass neck of a Nordic lur, as if making ready to display it. Yet all the while he glanced to ensure they weren't overheard.

'Just *Silvius?*'

'Aye. Just Silvius.'

'What's he to my master? Who is this Silvius?'

'He's an iron smith by trade. Villainous strong. All smiths are strong. Yet this one's tall and broad to boot. Some say he's the very image of ... Onorato Montecchi.'

'Say you so?'

'I do. Yet unlike the dead man, Silvius has light skin, blue eyes and carotene hair.'

'Carotene? What a strange ...'

'Your master may also be interested to know, that some years ago ... perhaps *eighteen*, when the primo don lost his only child at birth —'

'I never knew they had a child.'

'Aye they did. For a very short time. Very few mention it. Yet to my point, a slave was purchased at that time to be wet nurse to their babe. An Irish slave.'

'Irish? With light skin? '

'And blue eyes. Very comely, with carotene hair.'

'I see.'

'After their child died, the prima donna tried to sell the woman. But her husband —'

'Insisted that she remain?'

'He did. I understand the prima donna of ... I should say ... *former* prima donna of Montecchi — who discovered she could bear no more after the death of their son — was not fond of the attention her husband began to show that slave.'

'Yes. I can imagine.'

'The story goes that she beat the slave savagely, and threatened to sell her to a cousin who runs the Boar.'

'A fat cousin?'

'You know Luchinus?

'Thankfully no. But I've heard tell.'

'Hmm. Since the primo don was slain last summer and his wife ... well, all Verona knows what happened to her. As for the slave ...' he trailed off.

'Yes what of her?' Maxine leaned with interest.

'Well, despite all that she suffered at the prima donna's hands, and despite the prima donna's recent undoing, I'm told that — quite remarkably — the slave has *remained* in her service. Curious isn't it?'

Maxine's mind was racing feverishly.

'Perhaps, *not* so curious.'

'No. Perhaps not.'

Her eyebrows knit in confusion as her suspicion began to swell. 'Why did you tell me this? I only asked for news of the other.'

'In truth sweet woman, I have no *love* for the Montecchi. My son served afoot in the Wolf's last campaign. They raided a village but discovered it was an ambush. My Ezra was trapped. To save himself, Don Montecchi withdrew and made no attempt to save his men.'

'Oh I see. I'm so *very* sorry for you and your wife.'

'Thank you. That dog abandoned our boy. Left him to die. Any enemy of the Montecchi is a friend of mine. Offer your master my compliments. Besides ...' He halted his polishing and met her eyes with interest. 'I *like* you. My name's Noam. I have a good business here. I know you're married to that skinny fool —'

'Marcel. Yes I am. My name's Maxine.'

'Ah that's a lovely name. And so Maxine, if you ever decide to leave your husband ...'

'What of your wife bold man?'

'Sadly, soon after my Sarah heard that our Ezra had perished, she took her own life.'

'Oh Noam. Oh no. Truly I'm very, very sorry.'

'Thank you again. And don't mistake me. Your man seems a nice fellow. I like him. But he also seems ... childish. I believe you have a child?'

'Yes. A daughter.'

'How lovely. But I wonder if you already feel as if you have two children?'

'That's none of your ...' Maxine halted. 'No I confess, that thought does cross my mind occasionally.'

'I'm not happy to hear it. I think love's a beautiful thing Maxine. Yet a time may come when a woman like you may prefer to share her life with a man. No offense.'

'None taken Noam ... for now.' She turned to go, then returned. 'If you hear more?'

'Maxine, music is the food of love and the elite. Many that work in Verona's great houses visit me every day. I hear a great deal from their gossip. If that's to be my excuse for summoning you, it will be my pleasure to send word at once.' He finished his polishing and blew the horn for good measure.

Oh yes, if you must know, she *smiled* at her seducer! Cupid's Balls! Must I give every description? Apologies. Telling this portion is difficult for me. I'll attempt to continue with less ... something. And so as Noam hung up his gleaming lur, Maxine scurried along with a backward glance and a smile! She understood that by treating him *kindly*, she had made a valuable ally for the Capulets.

When she reported to Armand, even in my hearing, she told us all. We had sworn to keep no secrets from each other. And so she didn't. I understood why she didn't wish to risk the value of his continuing help for the sake of offering him a frosty rebuttal. Yet I still felt jealous, knowing how bluntly Noam had offered his interest, despite knowing Maxine was married with a child!

'And besides' she quipped 'Noam has a very charming way about him.'

'Oh does he?'

'Yes. And he seems much more settled than my *childlike* husband.'

I confess at that time, even though she kissed me for it, I took the jest frostily. Perversely however, I must also confess, that evening she made love more passionately than we had done for some time! Well bite my bare ass! Yes she did! And indeed, she bit my bare ass! Yet I digress.

Far more important than my insecure reaction to Maxine's report, was Armand's response. She told him this man Silvius had entered the race and that Noam suspected he was Onorato's son. She also told us what more she learned about the mystery woman, reported to be a German Countess von Bremmer. He decided to share one morsel with Ilaria and Aurelie, but not the other.

'For the moment Cat' he warned 'the spectre of that man and his *possible* pedigree is not to be shared beyond us.'

She hesitated for a moment. We were both sworn to share all we knew with Ilaria. 'Very well Master.'

He moved on to join Sabatino and Tristan who were already mounted. The three prima racing mounts — Victoire, Ajax and Galante — stood together. Sabatino intended the rest of us should follow in the wagon to the starting post. Yet the day was so desperately blue and clear that Aurelie and Ilaria insisted it was too lovely to remain inside the wagon.

And so, with time still on our side, as we reached the Cortellani apartments, we halted to gather a pair of mounts for them. Fabrizio assisted the ostler to secure two shining black palfreys which Aurelie called Gemini and Gemina. Shining brown side-saddles were fitted to the pair. To lift herself into the saddle, Aurelie laid her booted foot upon Fabrizio's interlaced hands.

Our junior squire flitted about to check the girth's fastenings. Having eschewed the temptation to don a riding habit, Aurelie drew back the fall of her silken train to offer the squire access. Fabio hefted the stout leather through the wide buckle, once, twice, then attempted a third yet was satisfied with just two.

'I wonder if Florentia is acquainted with the Von Bremmers?' said Aurelie.

'A count and countess?' Ilaria replied. 'Possibly.'

'If not Ria, at least as entrants, we'll now have a chance to make the acquaintance of another potent woman.'

'Yes. She'll be more competition.'

'Oh tush. I say we're ready for anyone. Let the German come.'

'I'm sure that like ourselves, she simply hopes to reach the end. She may be very pleasant.'

'Yes darling. Or she may try to smash our heads against Jupiter's gate.'

'Not if we approach *before* the hostilities begin and invite her to enjoy a pleasant soiree *after* we've done battle?'

While the women remained distracted, the men stood together. Armand quietly summoned Maxine and I to recount our untold portion of gossip to Sabatino and Tristan.

'That's interesting.' Sabatino said thoughtfully. 'You did very well Maxine.'

'Perhaps more than just interesting.' added Tristan.

'Yes.' Armand agreed. 'But it may still amount to *nothing*. Sab, have you heard of this fellow? Do you know if he entered last year?'

As he searched his mind, Sabatino breathed deeply and pushed a pout sidewards.

'I *do* know the man. Yet I don't recall him running last year. And once you see him Armand, you'll realise he would not have been easy to overlook.'

'He's big?' asked Armand.

'He's big and tall. But with a shock of red hair.'

'He sounds like my old mentor Toulon.'

'I know he's a capable smith. But this is the first I've heard of him being Onorato's bastard. However, now that's been suggested, and my mind considers it? If I dismiss the colour of his eyes and hair? I must confess, by his face and build, he's a fair match for Onorato. Not that I've ever considered it before ... but yes, now I *do* see it.'

'To judge by the tale of this merchant —' said Tristan.

'Noam.' Maxine interrupted, which made me squint.

'Yes.' Tristan smiled. 'It may well be *true*. If that story of the death of his *son* is true —'

'Ezram.' Maxine interrupted again.

Tristan lifted his brows. 'Yes. Then the man would have no reason to lie for the Montecchi's sake.'

'Do you believe him Cat?' asked Armand.

'I do master.' She frowned. 'Very much so.'

'Sab if this man is a smith ...' Tristan said quietly 'what's his specialty?'

'Weapons I'm afraid.'

'Perfect!' he spat with rising anger. 'Now I wish I had entered the footrace.'

'Perhaps.' Armand smiled. 'Yet it's hard to imagine that with all Verona watching as we run alongside the prince, anyone would dare to pose a significant threat. And besides Sab, you say he's a hefty giant?'

'Yes I'd describe him that way. Not like Caspar of course, but in the image of Onorato.'

'Then over six miles he's like to be slow and may not even *reach* the end.'

Tristan laid a hand on Armand's shoulder.

'Big brother he may have no plan to see an end to the *race* ... just an end to *you*.'

'He's right Armand. If Silvius shows to start, we'll have to err on the side of caution. If all the merchant says is correct, he's the son of the man you're known for killing.'

'The bastard son ... *perhaps*. And technically, I defeated Onorato, but the Marshall's men killed him.'

'I'm sure that distinction means little to Silvius. And now at the last moment, he's entered to race against *you*.'

'Or simply to win himself a valuable prize.'

'At the very *last* moment? This slow, massive man, who may not reach the end?'

The look on Armand's face made it clear there was little he could say to refute that conclusion.

'Oh!' Maxine blurted in fear. 'The mistress will be sick with worry to hear —'

'*No* she won't Cat.' Armand warned quietly. 'Now more than ever, we mustn't disclose any of this as yet, to Ilaria or Aurelie. They have too much to vex them already. At sunset tomorrow, when all the races are run, we can tell them that we know. Hopefully by then, more than just whispers and gossip will have come to light.'

I had remained silent. Yet I could see that Maxine was thinking precisely what I was thinking.

'Perhaps Chevalier' I began quietly 'you should withdraw for the sake of caution. Say your injury has flared from your preparations and so —'

Armand frowned. 'Rogue even if I wished to do so, which I do not, the code we're all sworn to won't allow it.'

'Yet —'

'It's true skinny man.' Tristan interrupted me. 'Once a challenge such as this is revealed, it must *not* be evaded.'

I saw a tear rising in Maxine's eye. I glanced up at the three men seated high on their horses.

'Oh what a ridiculous rule!' I hissed to their amazement. 'Why by that *perfidious* logic, it would be a *challenge* for me to attempt to kill myself! Then once I had the notion to do it, I must also *attempt* to do it!'

'Perhaps you *should* skinny man.' Tristan replied. 'Mmm. Let us know how that turns out.' Sabatino.

I tossed into a tantrum. 'Oh yes Signories! Hilarious! You're three very exalted ... very impish ... very ...'

'Marcel.' I felt Armand's hand upon my shoulder.

I knew he was serious whenever he called me by my name. That troubled me more.

'I know you're concerned for my safety.'

'Concerned?' I huffed. 'By all the sweet angels who sing in Heaven! I've watched enough men try to kill you for one lifetime. I thank God every day that madame wasn't with us in that arena. But tomorrow I don't want her to —'

'Yes. Yes I know. And I thank you for your care. And there may be *no* challenge here at all. But now that we know there *may* be ... I know you understand that I *cannot* shrink from such a thing.'

'Agreed.'

'Agreed.'

The echoes sounded from Sabatino and Tristan.

'Even the vague whisper of that threat *must* be faced and this time ... I won't be facing it alone.'

'I'll be with you.' I muttered.

He smiled. 'Yes you will. And Sab and I are running together. He's a more experienced soldier than I.'

'Which urges me to suggest ...' Sabatino put in.

'Yes.' said Armand.

'If Silvius *is* Onorato's bastard. And if he *is* running to make mischief against you.'

'Yes.'

'Then given the reputation you already have here for being able to defend yourself Armand, the man may have enlisted a few allies to assist him.'

Tristan frowned. 'That makes sense. And the Montecchi don't lack for money or means to enlist them.'

Armand frowned thoughtfully.

'I don't disagree. Yet having this news on such short notice, we'll have to risk that much.' He glanced at Maxine. 'But thanks to you Max, at least we do *know* this much.'

'Forewarned is forearmed.' she muttered.

'Precisely.' He glanced at me. 'Now rogue, by your leave, in the spirit of my wife, I'm going to kiss your wife.' He leaned to kiss her forehead. 'I'm in your debt clever one. Now the prima donnas are waiting. Both of you into the wagon. And smile.'

Maxine smiled thinly as we turned to walk together.

Then I began to feel a very great foreboding.

CUPID'S BALLS! What was beginning to happen?

NOTHING was as it SHOULD be!

Armand was calling me *Marcel*!

My wife was becoming a *spy*!

All at once he was kissing her forehead!

An amicable merchant we barely knew was coaxing her to leave me for him!

My mind cast back to the fisherwoman Ilaria and I met upon the shore of Lake Garda, almost exactly one year to that day. She had appeared in our path — as if by accident — presenting herself like a soothsayer that could cast light through the future's darkness. It made me wish I had the power of such sight. That woman seemed certain the Ilaria shared the power too.

Then I recalled that image which had affected us both at the Ceremony of Disgrace — a tilted cross; green and scarlet ribbons falling upon it; the bell which chimed in the distance thereafter. My mind was racing as that image loomed large again. I glanced at Maxine walking beside me. Despite that feeble attempt to smile her eyes now revealed how uneasy she also felt.

Maxine whispered to me. 'Not since the day we arrived at Sycamore Hill, when the disaster first unfolded, when he drew me aside to quietly urge me to climb aboard Victoire and ride like a bat out of hell to raise the alarm, have I been an accomplice to such a dire conference.'

'Yes sweet. I remember.'

'Now it's happened again. Perhaps not precisely the same.' She gulped. 'Yet I can't help but feel —'

'So do I sweetheart. And after that conference, just one day later, a man lay dead.'

The portent of harm now loomed large in both our minds. And Maxine's exaltation to have been permitted to run, the excitement that drew her to this moment, had evaporated into a mental mist of deep foreboding.

'How can I fail to warn our mistress?'

'No you mustn't. We promised.'

'We promised her *too!*'

'It's just one day. Telling her now will only make her fret. And as he said, there may still be *nothing* to it.'

'Do you believe that?'

'No! But it's a threat to him sweetheart, not to her. And now he knows. So we must trust he'll be watchful and avoid danger. I wouldn't like to be those villains, hoping to surprise him, when he's already alerted to their coming.'

'No. Perhaps not.'

'We know he's a warm kind man, yet he's also a cold-blooded killer.'

'Yes you're right. Very well, I'll keep my lips sealed. And now the mistress is watching us. Smile.'

Soon we were on our way to the starting point. As we passed through the south-eastern gate and onto the open plain, I looked to the heavens in disbelief. Even the sky, so impossibly blue before, was beginning to darken. Clouds were massing together in mischief.

When we reached our destination and turned to face the citadel, it looked as if the darkness of Hell had settled above Verona. Then Heaven's wrath unleashed a frightful torrent that soaked us to the core.

Yet despite the deluge — having no thunder or lightning to scare the beasts — neither Ilaria nor Aurelie sought refuge in the wagon to avoid it's effect. Remarkably, before we finished scouting the outer portions of the course, as we made our return, the downpour ceased and the clouds simply scattered. Even before we passed on through the Harvest Gate, that ill omen of clouds and rain had vanished. Despite being soaked to the skin, every rider was smiling.

As we passed back in however, though the sun had reappeared; though the image of doom that met us as we held at the starting point to gaze upon the citadel was gone; it still hung in my troubled mind. I wondered what the fisherwoman would make of it all? I felt desperate to share my new thoughts with Ilaria, to tell her the secret of the Montecchi bastard. I wondered if now, like myself, she felt that sudden jolting storm had been another grave portent.

Yet her smile said no.

Normally I would have scoffed at such notions. Since becoming acquainted with Ilaria however, I no longer felt certain of such things. I promised Armand I wouldn't tell. I'm sure you know by now, I wasn't good at keeping secrets or even promises. Yet by that time, I felt that any promise I had made to Armand or Ilaria, was sacrosanct. Moreover, by accident, I also kept another new scrap of information secret.

For as we entered through the Harvest Gate, before we drew on to Jupiter's Gate, we halted to set Teresa down at the mouth of Castle Bridge. Unlike the Capulets she knew the streets well and insisted on her wish to stretch her legs and walk home into the western borgo. And though she objected shyly, Armand insisted that for her safety, Caspar must accompany her. To the end of my days, that sight of them walking on together, our towering giant escorting that lithe young woman, is an image I'll never forget.

Yet while everyone else was distracted by Teresa's parting, watching the odd pair go, I also happened to glance to my left. There at a distance, passing through the central entry gate into the citadel, went the cavalcade of a potent party. I turned my head more fully to see. By the time I saw plainly, they had vanished beyond the ancient arena. It was only a flash of recognition, but I was certain. I knew that party were meant to be allies. Yet now their proximity to the Capulets made me uneasy.

As if enough portents weren't brewing in my mind already? I made a mental note to tell Armand as soon as we were quit of investigating the course. Yet, not only am I not good at keeping secrets, I'm worse at remembering scraps of information. In truth I became so distracted thereafter that, though I felt the information to be valuable when noticed, before we were done, it had completely slipped my mind.

After Teresa departed with Caspar we pressed on through the streets until we reached the basilica. The party dismounted. With smiling faces, despite their soaked state, they chattered as they walked along the final stretch to the finishing post. Already erected at Saint Fermo Square, it stood aloft to encourage them forward. And despite my foreboding, I smiled at the image of their serenity.

To see Ilaria and Aurelie, drenched and arm in arm, smiling together as they went along that riverbank path, gabbing as Aurelie pointed out every scrap of interest which Ilaria hadn't yet seen. Somehow the drubbing of rain they received had only managed to bolster their spirits.

I thought to myself — *I must stop fretting at shadows. Surely with men like Armand, Caspar, Tristan and Sabatino in our company, life among the Capulets would remain safe?*

So far at least — no matter all else — it was proving to be the greatest adventure of my lifetime.

The sun was low.

The gates all about the walls were closing.

That night there would be no return to the hills.

The Cortellani's citadel apartments were large and luxurious.

We would remain there that evening to ensure ease of access to all in the morning upon Fat Thursday morning. And as we made our way to that destination, due to the great carnival atmosphere at that time, the darkening streets were more alive and festive than usual.

Yet sweet friends, despite that carnival atmosphere as we walked on, we knew every member of our entourage — the bambinos excepted — were entered in some manner of event for the following day. And so for us all, that festive evening may as well have been the dour start of Lent.

From that evening — until our races were run — all had promised to withhold from the indulgence of food or wine. Maxine and I finally managed to lay down for the night. It was hard to close our eyes. Before we did so we prayed that at days end tomorrow, all would still be safe and smiling.

Chapter 23 Mythical Beasts

The afternoon deluge had resumed during the night while we slept. Next morning however Apollo's fiery chariot ascended into a fair sky over Verona. Fat Thursday had come and it appeared Heaven wished to bless the race festival with warming expectation. Yet as a result of that rain during the night, the outer course — from the starting place to the south-east corner of the walls and onto Harvest Gate — had become mired and would be full of mischief for any competitor afoot or ahorse. We hoped that by noon, when the racing began, it may have dried significantly.

On the prior day we drank and ate our fill before sundown. Yet because of our pact to fast from then until every event was run, Fat Thursday began with no more than watered wine and fresh air. Welcoming that morning's slight chill, we left the apartments to attend early mass and seek Heaven's blessing for our efforts to come.

The Prince and Princess were also in attendance. They welcomed the Capulets and Cortelannis warmly. In Florentia's presence, Aurelie fawned in silence over *her* prince. Yet the archbishop fawned with full voice at first sight of Ilaria and Armand. As promised, they approached him after the service, to offer a personal greeting.

The exalted Holy man promised to spur on their athletic efforts from a central vantage upon the south wall. A special place was being held for his attendance. And he boasted that perch was secured every season for the exclusive use of his own elite party.

Aurelie whispered to Ilaria, that was indeed the vantage she had mentioned, chosen to obtain the most prolonged sight of bodies — front and rear — as they ran the length of the battlement wall. And though I knew she loved to scathe that boorish man, since travelling the course we understood what she had said about the location was correct.

The moment we returned from the cathedral, our preparations began in earnest. Sabatino and Armand kissed their wives, then withdrew to the stable with Tristan. Aurelie and Ilaria entered within to prepare, yet before they did so, quite unexpected, Maxine excused herself. As an entrant, Ilaria had permitted my wife to forego her duties until sunset. And so, claiming herself to be prepared already, Maxine declared her need to depart upon an urgent *errand*.

She handed Figara over to *Micola*, the vintner's wife, who Ilaria had asked to care for both babes until sunset. She pecked my cheek — no not Micola, Maxine — promising to return soon, and then scurried away. I blinked in surprise at Micola, then ascended the lovely marble casement of stairs.

'No' I said vaguely to Micola 'I have no idea what she's up to. What would your husband say if you ran off into the citadel without explanation?'

'He'd say "bring back something nice to eat." '

That made us both smile and thereafter it seemed, that in no time at all the Civic Bell was chiming our approach to midday. It irked me that Maxine still had not returned. Yet in that intervening time, working together, the Cortellani and Capulet ostlers and stable-boys had readied three muscular beasts for our first competition. I heard their hoofbeats exiting the stable. My pulse began to rise.

Soon our entourage would separate.

The women and I would make for the gate at the walls south-eastern corner. No, not the central gate of course, where we would have needed to withstand the archbishop's company. Aurelie preferred an alternate perch — above the corner gate — for its closer proximity to the finish at Saint Fermo that stood just four blocks to the north.

'From the corner position, we'll see the starters approaching through the open plain.' she explained. 'After they pass, we'll follow their backs along the wall 'til they vanish through Harvest Gate. Then darling, at that critical moment, we'll run hell for leather down onto the street, and over to the finishing post to cheer them on in the final dash!'

The horses would start at noon, with just a half an hour until the start of the mules. I was entered for the latter, yet discovered I wouldn't need to make my way to the start alone. Because the women's race would follow mine, not wishing to arrive late themselves, or feel rushed at all, they decided to accompany me for the start of the mules.

Oh yes, they would have the distinct privilege of watching me set out. Yet they knew nothing of my antic plan to attract as much attention as possible. As you know, I already had one trick up my sleeve for that. Yet I'd hit on another clever notion too that I felt would ensure my result. However, after we had returned from the cathedral, Armand announced a last moment alteration to our starting plans.

'Ladies I'm sure it's *unnecessary*' he began as Aurelie interrupted.

'Then darling why does it sound as if something is about to *become* necessary?'

'Seeing the citadel is already teeming with strangers' he ran on 'I've assigned Caspar, Liberati, Boccolo and Fabrizio to accompany you all to the start.'

'But Armand.' Ilaria protested. 'The start will be populated with dozens of naked women.'

'All the more reason to be cautious.' he insisted.

'Oh very well. But when we arrive they must set us down at a respectful distance and stand-off at a distance.'

'And big brother ...' Aurelie added.

'Yes little sister.'

'We anticipate there may be some rough and tumble treatment among us. And so ...'

'Oh yes.' Ilaria put in. 'And so my heart, no matter what happens, our escort must promise *not* to interfere.'

'But angel if —'

'If you can't swear they will comply? Then we will transit without them.'

Armand tilted his eyes to Heaven. 'Very well.' He turned to our giant. 'Caspar you understand?'

'If naked women make trouble among themselves' he boomed quietly 'we'll keep our hands off them.'

I blurted a laugh and everyone stared. The thought of his mon-strous hands, groping about among so many naked women, was too much for me to suppress.

'After our race angel, we'll make our way to the south-eastern gate to watch you run.'

'Don't forget to run to the finish and see the end.'

'Of course.' Armand promised. 'Then I have a full hour to regain the start before my race with Escalus.'

When that last event started, the women planned to repeat that same hasty circuit. At last Aurelie would have the chance to watch *her* prince run naked before her upon the streets of Verona. She would live to tell that lively tale to her grandchildren. No other changes were made beyond that last. And our plans should ensure that day — as we flitted back and forth — we'd be kept on a constant merry-go-round of competing and watching and cheering.

I guessed that an undisclosed part of Armand's change, was to deposit our men at the start with the women, but with orders to linger until his own arrival. Then if the Montecchi bastard showed and did intend trouble, I felt it more like to erupt *before* the race began than *after* the start. If so, this Silvius and his cronies would have more Capulets to contend with than they would otherwise be expecting.

Perhaps more cleverly, the women would reach their start more safely, yes. But they wouldn't suspect our men were lingering for the sake of potential trouble we'd been warned against. Yet that was all to come.

At that moment, I was outside the apartments again, standing at the base of the stairs, awaiting the appearance of all in our party. From the direction of the stable I heard hoofbeats clopping towards me. From the entry dais above I heard the approaching chatter of our two prima donnas. Any moment they'd appear to descend and greet their husbands.

One way or another, our plans were laid and ready.

I felt warmth upon my face and gazed upward. Apollo watched

down from his fiery chariot as it lifted into a blazing blue sky. The ancients say he hovers at noon to pass judgement over all he surveys, then metes out rewards or punishment to the deserving. Despite feelings of renewed assurance since the morning, that thought gave me pause.

I scanned about. Maxine had still not returned.

Where the Devil could she be?

I glanced in every direction. The citadel was bustling with fever and festivity. The sounds of revelry and smells of Fat Thursday were expanding in the air as Armand, Sabatino and Tristan appeared, leading their mounts into the street. Dear Heaven it was a sight I'll never forget, when those three mythical beasts appeared for the first time together upon the streets of Verona.

Despite the rising warmth, each horseman wore hefty woollen hose, light leather ankle boots — without spurs — and billowing undershirts of the finest Egyptian linen. Wrapped across each chest was a broad silken sash that mimicked the colours of their houses. It was tied at the hip in a lavish knot and pinned to the upper right shoulder with a large golden brooch in the form of each man's personal seal.

For the moment their long hair hung free. For the footrace thereafter, for safety, Armand and Sabatino intended to tie it back firmly.

'There they are!' Ilaria cried excitedly. 'Oh Lee Lee don't they look magnificent?'

Appearing in readiness for their own race, the women appeared on the wide marble stair dressed in a far more decadent version of their Grecian couture. Despite Ilaria's enthusiasm, both descended elegantly. Their hair was plaited and woven in a mimic of each other, drawn tightly, yet veiled under silken wraps so fine they were translucent.

Unlike our mornings spent among the sycamores, now their faces were painted, lips glossed, brows tinted and cheeks rouged. It were as if a pair of high priestesses had arrived at a temple ready to offer a potent sacrifice. Armand and Sabatino grinned at their approach and the sight of the silken favours each held dangling from their hands.

It was clear the looming start of the first race was charging them all with excitement. I scoured again in search of Maxine, still not returned from her *errand*, which began to make me fret. I didn't want her to miss these moments. And her absence kept nagging at me with a sinking feeling.

Suddenly all eyes turned and lifted as mighty Rengo chimed out a warning. The first assembly of entrants was being summoned. Any in the citadel – particularly those in the northern reaches – who intended to race, must make their way to the start or risk running out of time to reach it.

'Friends ...' Sabatino began with smile 'it's the hour to be mounted. Time to be away.'

Though each beast was a tall battle horse, any horseman worth his salt could vault fully armoured into the height of a war saddle. This time, with such light accoutrements and nothing but a bridle, reins and girded cloth upon their mounts, all three leapt lightly onto the backs of their coursers.

The moment Armand settled on mighty Victoire his wide nostrils flared, head tossed and near hoof stamped with spirited impatience. The stallion wouldn't step until bidden. Yet the moment he felt that weight rest upon him, the fire in his belly to demonstrate his strength was charged.

Sabatino sat aboard his gorgeous red Arabian, Galante. Of the three, his beast was more built for pure speed. Aurelie stepped to his side. For a moment she draped the favour about her neck, tugging at the thin girth that held the soft blanket while Sabatino adjusted the buckle to suit her satisfaction.

'Fussy.' He smiled. 'I'll look for you mia cara.'

'Above the south-east corner darling. Just as last time. We'll watch the pack run by. Then rush to Saint Fermo and cheer your finale.'

'Last time I won. Yet today ...' he glanced at Armand and Tristan with a grin 'I have more competition.'

'Last time you crossed the line with a blackened eye and a broken nose!'

'You know winning has its price.'

'Yes I do. And I love it when you win. But ... oh just return safe! And ... be *nice*.'

Sabatino's brows lifted. 'Be *nice*! Ilaria look at the effect you're having on my wife!'

Ilaria, Armand and Tristan all smiled and stared.

'Oh yes, very drole. Sab give them *Hell*.'

'Ah. That's more like it. And ...?' he waited.

'And you're our primo Signore! Don't let them *fuck* with you!'

Ilaria rolled her eyes. 'There she is! Spoken like the prima donna I love and fear.'

Sabatino leant with a smile to receive Aurelie's golden favour. She wrapped it thrice above his elbow, tied it with a bow and tied again.

As you know sweet friends, a favour is offered in token of a giver's want for its wearer to return safely. In war, perchance it may be the last parting a couple may share, and unless love has been lost between them, that transaction is always sealed with a lingering kiss. And so they kissed.

I glanced at Tristan, sole bachelor among them, whose betrothed had died while he was at war in Milan. He sat patiently above his own mythical beast to watch the ritual. I knew he expected no favour today. Nor had I seen him wear one as yet. However I felt sure that somewhere among the women of the world, he'd find another match.

Perhaps she may appear when he returned to Lyon, perhaps in Verona before or somewhere else entirely. Surely fate would reveal her in good time. I understood he was a lively warrior, yes. Yet over the last few months he had also proven himself to be a patient and quiet man.

Ilaria approached Armand as he leant to offer his arm. I saw her lift that familiar ruby silken favour, the very same token she offered him on the day we rode away to fight the English in Normandy. Then he was still a squire to our old master Toulon. He returned gravely wounded, no longer a squire but a chevalier, and our brave master was gone.

Oh yes, she knew he wasn't riding to war. But I could tell a lump had caught in Ilaria's throat as her eyes held his, bright green blazing into blue, pouring her love into his heart. She lifted the favour to wind it, yet before she could ravel it, a pleading shout rose at the corner nearby!

'Oh *wait* Monsieurs! *Please* wait Monsieurs!'

It was Maxine. And the chorus that followed her own cry to wait was unmistakeable. For then, like a fabled mirage, five breathless, barefoot, Grecian-clad nymphs appeared with my wife at their head, spilling around the corner together and skittering toward us. Each trailed in their hand, or had tied to their hair or wrist, an entwined pair of favours, one black, one silver — the colours of the Dragon.

Brianna arriving foremost, laid a bold hand upon the rein of Tristan's mount as they gathered to his side in a cascade of fond oohs and aahs. None of them had seen mighty Ajax before with his shining pearl coat and chestnut mane and tail. All at once a flutter of impulsive sighs and a flurry of compulsive petting began.

Oh sweet friends for the love of dear folly! I had never seen anything like it. Despite their excitement the mythic beast stood impassive, unlike his master whose brows were lifted in surprise, lips pressed, gazing down in wonder from his lofty seat.

'Monsieur Tristan!' declared Brianna. 'Today you ride for the Dragon!'

In blushing confusion he glanced at Ilaria and Aurelie. Yet both merely smirked, rolled their eyes and nodded their heads together in disbelief.

'Of *course* I do.' He smiled as five grins beamed up at him. 'How did I manage to *forget* such an honour?'

Fiametta tapped upon his boot. 'Don Tristan! Your horse is so *very* beautiful. What's his name?'

'Ajax.'

'Oh I like that name!' Fiametta replied, unleashing a cascade of agreement.

'So do I!'

'Me too.'

'And me!'

'Yes it suits him.'

'Sabatino rides Galante.' Tristan added. 'And Armand rides Victoire, given to him by the King of France.'

A volley of replies followed so fast it was hard to tell who spoke which.

'The King!'

'Victoire's beautiful.'

'We didn't know he was from the King!'

'Monsieur's beautiful too!'

'Shut up *stupida!*'

'Galante is handsome too!'

The married pairs gulped in amusement to see their favourite bachelor gushed over by so many young women. Suddenly I recalled their impact on Fabrizio the day we met. Yet Tristan was not a demure young squire. He was a quiet man, yes. He was a gentle man, yes. But he was also a skilled chevalier, blooded by war.

'Don Capulet?' said Teresa bravely.

'Yes Teresa.'

'How does he know *your* name?' hissed Brianna.

A chorus of disapproval erupted. 'He doesn't know mine! I like him too! How did that ...'

'Hush you all!' spat Teresa. 'Don Capulet asked me yesterday when we surveyed the course with Donna Capulet! Now HUSH!'

'Oh! He asked yesterday! They were together in a group. That's not so bad! No not at all!'

'Girls!' Maxine interrupted. 'The bell has rung. Their time is short!'

Another burst of replies cascaded.

'Yes.'

'Oh yes!'

'Teresa stupida ... ask him now!'

'Oh yes!' snapped Teresa. 'Don Tristan —'

'*Monsieur* Tristan!' Brianna corrected as Teresa huffed and rolled her eyes.

'Monsieur Tristan. Will you accept our favours?'

'Will I ...? *All* of them?'

A cascade of agreement bubbled in reply.

'It was Cat's ... *Maxine's* idea.'

He glanced at Maxine who pouted with guilt.

'I see. Yet Teresa, to accept a favour, we're meant to be on more ... *intimate* terms.'

'I wish to be intimate!'

'So do I!'

'And me!'

'Yes we all do.'

Aurelie smirked, squeezing Sabatino's hand, turning to avert her desperate want to laugh out loud.

'Devil's Balls!' she hissed. 'Sab it's too much! I'm going to burst! It's just too much!'

Sabatino chuckled at Armand's incredulous stare.

'Then Teresa ...' he smiled patiently 'you must call me *Tristan*.'

Teresa's eyes went wide. Suddenly Greta was jostling against her.

'Tristan' she said boldly '*please* accept our favours?'

'Of course. Who shall be first? And offer your names so I can remember each.'

'Girls!' snapped Maxine. 'Youngest to oldest.'

The gaggle lined up — Fiametta, Teresa, Greta, Vendramina and finally Brianna.

Tristan leaned down to receive the first. Fiametta wavered an instant, then saw Ilaria still held her own favour.

'Scusi Madonna Capulet. But how should I ...?'

'Watch Fiametta. Just as I do.'

Five heads leaned to observe the tutorial. Ilaria wrapped her favour thrice and tied it just as Aurelie had done. Five heads nodded comprehension.

'Oh yes I see!' said Fiametta excitedly. She wrapped the favour thrice. She tied it gently. Then with a demure smile she repeated her name and made to draw away.

'Non non non!' Ilaria insisted looking along the line. 'A woman's favour is offered in token of wishing a safe return. It's a solemn pact. A pact must be sealed. And so one last thing is required to seal it.'

'But Angel ... scusi ... Madonna Capulet. How can we seal our pact?'

A sly smile broadened on Ilaria's face.

'There's only one way I'm afraid.'

Ilaria turned her head and raised her chin to look into her husband's eyes. Armand bent low. Elegant hands and painted nails wrapped his neck and cheek. Then, to a rising chorus of ribald feminine encouragement, their lips met in a lingering kiss.

Tristan blushed. Suddenly the part he may have to play next was stealing him of breath. Ilaria released her husband, patted his thigh and turned to Fiametta.

'However Fiametta ... the very *first* kiss one shares should be *less* ... intimate.'

'That's my cue!' cried Sabatino. 'Well brother-in-law?' He looked to Armand. 'We already have our kisses.'

'Indeed. Shall we away?'

Galante and Victoire swirled to the touch of their master's reins and a tap of their heel. The pair came about together and cantered along the street.

'Hurry on little brother!' called Armand.

'Quickly girls! Quickly!' cried Maxine.

Fiametta wrapped her favour. Tristan leaned to receive her puckered kiss. Then in complete mimic of Ilaria, she also tapped his thigh. Then came Teresa — tie, kiss, tap. Greta — tie, kiss, tap. Vendramina — tie, kiss, tap. As the age of each rose, each kiss lingered longer and our bachelor's shyness appeared to wither. Then Brianna stood before him.

She struggled with her bow a little. Tristan glanced to see Armand and Sabatino cantering beyond the curve. Despite his rising concern for haste, Brianna was the eldest. She knew an opportunity that may not come again when she saw it. If she had failed to lure Armand on her first day, perhaps on her last day she may lure the next best thing.

As he lowered to receive one final kiss, the temptress laid her hands about his neck softly and drew his lips to hers. The kiss that followed might have *shamed a harlot* as they say, but not Brianna. Nor, to Ilaria's great surprise, did it appear to shame her quiet brother-in-law.

Somehow the swirl and fuss of five dragonesses had managed to draw Tristan's interest out from its cocoon. They hung there kissing for the time one may count three. Then after a moment more, he slowly straightened and smiled.

'I'll dedicate my ride to the Dragon and .... its five fiery dragonesses!'

A chorus erupted in reply. *'Bona Fortuna Tristan!'*

And so, with the feeling of Brianna's warm lips on his mind, the young man and his mythical beast, who had lured the favour of five dragonesses, cantered away. Tristan smiled and waved with a backward glance. To all that he passed, the chevalier offered the extraordinary sight of a rider with five favours streaming from his arm.

Before he turned the corner to disappear, Ajax halted, lifted and spun on his hoofs to pirouette in the street. His raised forelegs hung high in the air as Tristan saluted us all with a smile. Then he was gone. None but myself understood how reminiscent that was, of an unmatched display of skill I had seen with Armand during the war. You'll recall it was given in Carentan by Eloise du Marche, when she rode out on her monstrous white mare, disguised as a herald, to parley with the English leader.

On that stirring day Eloise rode out alone, prancing and dancing her muscular beast to deliver that brave town's bold message of defiance ... Cupid's Balls! That thought suddenly reminded me of what I'd seen the day before — that party arriving through the central southern gate — which I intended to warn Armand about but had entirely forgotten. Just as I recalled it, was minded to tell again, I was distracted again by a scathing comment that passed by in the street.

'How can five women agree to offer favours to the very same rogue!' questioned one aghast woman to another. 'Surely after the first ... well ... do the rest have no shame?'

'Shut your mouth stupid hag!' hissed Brianna. 'And mind your own business!'

The woman took one look at our growling Amazon and the four young scowls, hovering over her shoulder, then wisely decided to shut her mouth and move on.

Moments later, I was wandering behind that feminine cavalcade, headed for the south-east corner to find our perch. As we arrived, eight Cortellani followers were standing patiently to hold our placements. They vacated with dutiful bows to their prima donna, then hurried to Saint Fermo Square to do the same again in readiness of our coming.

Including myself however, I noticed we were nine not eight. We managed to squeeze. No, I didn't mind being locked in that press of feminine company. The bambinos were safe in the Cortellani apartments, cared for by Micola. And so, unencumbered as it were, Maxine and I were free to enjoy the day together, a rare opportunity since both babes had been born.

For a moment, in the anonymity of the throng, I felt her hand rest upon my thigh. I lowered my own to grasp it, ran my fingers between hers, gaining that comfortable feeling. I lifted to kiss it tenderly as I turned to smile, yet Brianna's coaxing eyes met mine instead of Maxine's!

In a fit of surprise I drove our hands down to release them, fearing we may have been seen. I glanced about like a frighted marmot. Thankfully my inadvertent fondness to another woman seemed to have gone unnoticed. Without a word the vixen pouted and offered me a coy smile.

It made me realise that in less than four hours, Brianna's work for Aurelie would be done. Before that time expired, it appeared she may be determined to lure the interest of any man of our company that may prove lasting. Now she had been introduced to our circuit, perhaps she felt willing to do anything to ensure she remained linked to it.

I glanced again. Our eyes met again. Strangely she seemed more sincere than malicious. I couldn't blame Brianna's want to make such an attempt. Perhaps she hoped to escape her life by remaining among us. Perhaps she just hoped to enrich the tone of her clientele? I dared not ask to know, yet felt sure if I had been in her place, I would have done the very same thing.

Sadly however, with the first race not yet begun, the little incident made me wonder if we would see them again when the day was done. I jumped a little when the clock bell shattered my thoughts.

CLANG! CLANG! CLANG! CLANG!
CLANG! CLANG! CLANG! CLANG!
CLANG! CLANG! CLANG! CLANG!

Midday had come.
The excitement was palpable.
The race would start at any moment.

Brianna's eyes were gone from me.
My concern for her life had vanished in an instant.

Ilaria, Aurelie, Maxine and all gazed southward in anticipation yet I glanced upward. Apollo hung there, risen to his full height. Little did any of us understand by the time his chariot fell from the sky and rose again, fate would wrench two lives from our embrace.

Chapter 24 the Flight of Pegasus

Away to the south, a thin breasting line was strung tight across the road, holding all at the starting point. It was watched by a wide-eyed pair of wardens. Behind it and twitching impatiently, an avalanche of horseflesh and riders hung in wait. Those aboard, local and foreign, numbering thirty in all — more or less — were elite cavalrymen or senior squires. Every man sat above a prime warrior's mount, whose muscular shoulders and thighs, exposed for lack of armour or cloth, rippled and bristled and strained for a start.

The width of that southern road allowed for nine beasts to stand abreast, while the rest ranged two and three deep behind. Next to the whispering Race Marshal stood the Master Crier. Sabatino recognised the latter, known for his deep booming voice of course. The loud officer was positioned by a post that had a bell mounted at shoulder height. As he waited upon the marshal's sign — a four fingered tap upon his shoulder — he wiped sweat away from his upper lip with the back of a trembling hand.

Two tall posts stood to either side of the road with a starting line stretched between them. Standing by each post were a senior and junior warden. Each gripped an iron ring attached to a pin that ran through their post and protruded out the other side. At the top of each post, the end of the line was fed through a shackle and anchored to a hefty, free-hanging weight.

From its anchorage to that weight, the line ran through the shackle, down the post to slip under the pin and stretched across the road before running under the farther pin, up the far post and through the other shackle, where it was tied to the other weight in the very same manner.

Nought but the pull of those weights kept the line in place against the hold of those pins. The crier knew it. The wardens knew it.

In just a moment when the marshal felt satisfied all at the fore stood ready, he'd tap the crier's shoulder, signalling him to bark out the *holding* commands, before tapping again to signal the crier to signal the wardens to pull their pins as he rang the bell! Yet with horseman ready to jump, that last was a matter of strict timing. The crier's final signal to the wardens must occur a split second before he rang the bell.

Upon that silent command — nodded *not* shouted so as not to set the horses off too soon — both wardens would lock eyes. Then to ensure precise timing, on that nod from the crier the senior warden would lift his chin to the junior, and as he dipped, they'd pull their pins free at the very same moment. In the instant those pins are pulled out, the weights plummet down to whip the line up and offer free passage, before the crier yanks at the bell to signal their start.

Sabatino, Armand and Tristan sat line abreast together but were not at the fore. Given the length of that course they were content to start from the rear. And so they had settled among the senior squires, held back in deference to the elite cavalieres who waited impatiently before them.

Next to Armand however sat an accoladed veteran, a Spanish caballero with an open, friendly face. He was mounted on a pure white stallion. Every cavalryman knew Spanish mounts were formidable and Spanish masters even more so. Indeed that affable man, Senor Ernesto Alonso, was whispered among the talkative to be the rider to beat.

That begged a ripe question of course. Did the Spaniard's choice to start at the rear indicate *modesty* or *strategy*? A matter of moments would reveal the answer. And so as snorts, stamps and slaps upon backs sounded all about, Armand leaned to engage him in conversation.

'You've come a long way Caballero?'

'Just north of Cadiz. A sleepy little place called Jerez de la Frontera.'

Armand smiled. So did Sabatino and Tristan, now listening with interest.

'Sleepy yet famed for fine horsemanship.' Armand replied. 'And quite a journey.'

'I came by sea from Cadiz to Pisa — not quite as far as it seems. And you *Chevalier?*'

'My accent betrays me. I hail from Lyon. Yet recently my wife and I have decided to settle in Verona.'

'Ah then, I wish you both well. I hope you share a long and happy life together.'

'Perhaps after the race you'll be our guest to dine?'

'Let's see if your offer stands after you know the result Chevalier.'

'Win lose or draw it'll still stand with a warm welcome to you and yours Caballero.'

Smiling together both men looked ahead.

The mounts of the haughty cavalieres at the fore jostled, twitched and bucked in excitement. Front and centre among them all stood a massive black courser. Aboard that bold beast sat Aldobrando Montecchi.

That stallion's name was *Trionfo*. Yes, the very same that had belonged to Aldobrando's slain brother. One season before it stood before all during that infamous Ceremony of Disgrace. Then a gruesome effigy of the former primo don of Montecchi sat above him. Now before all, Trionfo would carry their new leader. And he seemed to know it. For the mighty black stallion was stamping and snorting and tossing his head like an animal possessed.

Ranged about him sat the most noted horsemen from the most venerated Houses of Verona and beyond, including a masked rider at the very edge of their line. Yet that entrant was not the only one whose identity was veiled. Two others had shunned the lure of renown, competing for no more than a sense of accomplishment. If one such emerged as the victor, more often than not they'd relinquish their prize to a charitable need without revealing their identity at all.

However that masked entrant at the forefront had arrived late the day before in a train of luxuriant Germanic carriages. Then at the very last moment — by an order of Prince Escalus himself that morning — the latecomer had gained entry. Moreover, along with the

Spaniard next to Armand, that mystery entrant was the only other rider mounted upon a pure white beast.

Indeed when Tristan was making his way to the rear, as he passed that fellow he complimented him on his mount. He also enquired politely if the man rode for a sponsor or himself. The masked entrant had little to say yet did claim, in a rasping voice, to be riding for the *House of Paris*.

A warning ratchet lifted in the Marshal's hand.

WHIRR! WHIRR! WHIRR! WHIRR! WHIRR!
All aboard braced, bursting with intent.
The Race Marshal cast his eyes all about.
Horses, sashes and favours showed a riot of colour and energy that surged against the man's stoic restraint.
The Master Crier lifted a hand to grip a rope that hung from the ringer. The Race Marshal's eyes narrowed. Waiting to feel the first rap, the crier licked his lips.
The marshal scanned once more. Again. Again.
The crier gulped deeply and then ... SNAP!
Four tense fingers rapped on his shoulder.
'Stand READY!'
The booming voice startled every man and beast.
The marshal scanned again. SNAP!
'HOLD your mounts!'
Scan. Scan. SNAP!
'HOLD for the bell!'
Scan. Scan. SNAP!
The crier's head lifted and fell!
The warden's locked eyes as each pulled his pin!
Hauling weights fell! The barrier leapt upward, squealing in ascent. Then for all he was worth, the hefty man SMASHED the blunt bell ringer back and forth!
CLANG! CLUNG! CLANG! CLUNG!
CLANG! CLUNG! CLANG! CLUNG!

Thirty warlike beasts leapt upon the start to the shout of their Household cries — Montecchi! Querini! Gonzago! Paris! Barozzi! O'Rourke! d'Armano! Visconti! Kozlov! Spira! Alonso! Huntington! Pasquale! Von Bremmer! Diego! Foscari! Onifacio! Ziliolo! Nobel! Grassi! Loredan! Hartvigsen! Della Scalla! Nani! Antelini! Tiepolo! Cortellani! Orlandi! Capulet!

Back in the citadel, in answer to the clang of that distant bell, mighty Rengo boomed from its belfry as a rising cheer woke in celebration on the battlement wall. Their ovation rippled through the citadel streets along the path of the course. Every eye strained southward to see as a damp thunder of cantering hoofbeats drew on. Every man, woman, child and beast in Verona knew the bold riders were coming.

Ilaria, Aurelie, Maxine and five dragonesses leaned in excitement to stare at the pack racing toward us, hoping to discover who led or followed in pursuit. By instinct at the jump, Brando's wild black stallion raised his head with an open maw, then drove a snapping bite on the bare neck of the beast next to him. The bitten creature leapt and careered, driving three apart. All were forced to shunt and then wheel to rejoin, as the shouting primo don burst away before all.

In a blink and a flit that gap was filled by a spilling tide of muscular horse shoulders, all surging to catch the wild black beast of Montecchi. With few exceptions, the racer's mounts were made for combat. Shoulder-to-shoulder among friends, drew one manner of conduct. Shoulder-to-shoulder among foes, drew something else entirely. Now every rider at the fore left their mounts in no doubt as to what manner of conduct was expected today!

Necks wrenched, teeth snapped, shoulders smashed, flanks buffeted, hoofs — fore and rear — lifted and snapped, striking out savagely. Every mount was a stallion. Every stallion behaved as if every rival vied for the pleasure of a single mare running in heat before them all.

Yet such wild energy spent at the start would come at a cost. Keeping it up would never do for such a long and tiring gallop. So despite every rampant instinct of those huddling beasts to fight, as the half mile warden drew in sight, the instinct of each racer to last the distance, began to assert more control. The buffeting rabble set their eyes on then settled into a firm canter.

Quietly behind them all — bringing on the men of Capulet and Cortellani — Galante, Victoire and Ajax began to drive and sift their way forward. Riding at their head, Sabatino met the first assault. To his offside an indignant squire sat atop a surly painted mount, bucking its rump as Galante's red face surged alongside. On came Galante. The growling squire launched a thumping fist that shot too high. Sabatino ducked beneath it with a smile and poured on.

Following fast, Tristan drew abreast of the same laggard. The heated squire lifted his paw to strike again, driving into Tristan's shoulder. The blow hit hard, shunting him in his seat. An unintended push of Tristan's heel, to steady his weight, signalled Ajax to veer. Yet that opened a gap that brought the massive form of Victoire surging into it.

Rankled to see a third rival, the frustrated novice lifted and held, then launched a backhand blow straight at Armand's face. Yet that moment he took to hold displayed poor skill and gave Armand warning. Trusting Victoire implicitly, he had already dropped the rein and touched his near-side heel and toe to command the dappled dark grey beast to drive in fast and shorten the squire's reach.

The attacker's eyes opened wide as he felt the snap of a palm on his forearm as broad fingers gripped hard. He was stuck with his arm outstretched. Then before he could blink, another hand reached to lock behind his shoulder. Armand gripped through his thighs to firm his seat, then slid his forward hand down the wrist to enwrap the knuckles.

Yet everything happened so fast!

GRIP! SLIDE! GRAB!

Armand shoved against the front of the captured hand. The purchase he gained to push, locked the squire's shoulder HARD into its socket! That force was compelling. Armand's lips pressed hard. He hefted forward at a sharp angle. Not enough to toss the lad but enough to tip him, sending the hapless squire hard to the offside!

That awkward shuffle in the squire's feet signalled his mount to veer. Off ran the painted beast, careering away. Then Victoire, seeing open space with rivals running ahead, shook his mighty head and stirred onward.

Armand drew alongside Sabatino and Tristan as the one-mile warden appeared – waving wildly to ensure recognition – then was gone in a flash. All eyes ahead, now they were hot on the heels of a half dozen more, holding in wait for their moment behind the midfield pack. Yet waiting is one thing, winning another.

All at once a lane opened wide among the waiters. Beyond them our trio saw the Spaniard driving through the midfield bunch toward the gap that separated all from Aldobrando at the fore. That was enough to coax Sabatino.

To free his hands, he secured the rein under his thigh. Tucking his right thumb, he pointed four fingers to himself and thrust his hand forward. Then with a hand for each, he pointed to Armand and Tristan, followed by arcing gestures – left and right. The Capulet brothers nodded their assent. Sabatino gathered his rein as they began their move together.

By design, Galante plunged through the centre to alert their rivals to his threat. Heads turned, angry eyes darted as the pack swung in from both sides to close ranks, hoping to block the racing red stallion. Unwittingly however they offered clear passage upon each side. And before the laggards could close the centre lane completely – as if executing a parade manoeuvre with Ajax and Victoire streaming around the sides – with a burst of speed Galante dashed through to rejoin the brothers ahead of the waiters.

Tristan turned in his seat to see the aftermath. Having surged so desperately to stop Sabatino, their cantering mass had collided. That set the rivals heckling each other. Tristan grinned from ear-to-ear and set his eyes forward. The trio surged on, intent to catch the streaming tails of the midfield pack. Between that group and the fore, a further gap awaited.

'One thing at a time.' said Sabatino.

Sleeves billowing, hair flying back, line abreast, the trio cantered on nose for nose as the sight of the two mile warden loomed ahead. Sabatino hailed their attention again.

'At the second mile, nothing rash, but we must drive firmly through that middle clump or risk losing touch with the forward pack.'

'Agreed!' cried Tristan.

'Aye strategos!' called Armand.

His use of that ancient title for a general set broad grins upon their faces. Sabatino was eldest of course. He'd run that race many times. He'd fallen twice. He'd won twice. Only once had he failed to finish.

'Let me take the centre!' cried Tristan. 'No flanking this time. Let's all have at them!'

'Lead on Chevalier!' cried Sabatino.

Then mighty Ajax, his pearl coat gleaming, plunged on as Galante gave way to the left. A moment later the racing red stallion swung back to hang upon the left flank. Armand drew in from the right. Victoire hung close as the three mighty beasts formed into an arrowhead. And with a familiar hand signal from Tristan, to lift the canter firmly and drive through, each man braced for a hail of resistance.

Ajax pushed in, head, neck, chest ploughing between two rumps at the centre. To the midfield racers, the sight of one challenger would have triggered a volatile response. Here came three in formation together. A flurry of feet and a hail of fists began to fly in bitter resistance. For the time one may count ten, a wild free-for-all erupted. Tristan first, then all three together, bore the brunt of a relentless assault.

Before the race had started, our trio agreed that *retaliation* was sporting but *initiation* was not. Once among the desperate midfielders however, they had no need to pick and choose. Rivals from every direction flailed desperately to unseat the insurgents. All three dropped their reins to free hands and fend off blows or launch counterstrikes, urging with knees and heels to drive their mounts through and beyond the melee.

In mistrust of their skill, all but one rival held tight to their reins, limiting the sting of their fiery assaults. For those, feet became the weapon of choice. Yet a man mounted bareback in a fight who prefers a foot to a fist must relinquish the grip in their seat. What's more, to make any kick worth the effort — to shove against the hip or higher — the foot must lifted above the thigh.

Expecting this, Armand prepared to use a trick taught him by his old mentor. Waiting for an attacker to lift the knee, Armand leaned back and let the foot come, then thrust his hand under the ankle. The face of his rival set alight with comprehension as the wretch felt the error of his effort. Then raising the back of his hand, Armand dropped his shoulder and rolled his wrist to face the palm under. With a driving slide up to grip the meat of the man's calf, the victim's eyes bulged as he felt his hip lifting from his seat.

Suddenly lacking any purchase to secure his captured thigh, the hapless lout made that guttural, sighing shout of the unwitting who have lost all sense of balance. As his body tipped, instinctively the desperate man dropped his reins to reach for the craning neck of his beast, wrapping his arms, clinging on for all his worth. That beast running beneath him — better trained than its master — sensed all control was lost, slowed and vanished.

At the very moment of execution, Armand had touched both heels to Victoire's flanks causing him to surge. When his offside assailant caught sight of that hapless rival — so easily tilted and diverted — it was enough to give the man pause. That rival hesitated and thought. He thought again, then gave way to the dappled dark grey and his master.

Riding clear Armand scanned ahead, then left and right to assess if Tristan or Sabatino required assistance. Both had dispatched their rivals with some effort. Both now stared with broadening smiles.

'Devil's Balls big brother!' cried Tristan. 'That was a handy trick!'

'Just something I *picked up* little brother!'

The pun set them laughing like rampant boys as another waving warden came on and swept by.

'Three miles!' shouted Tristan.

'Men!' called Sabatino. 'Before we turn to run along the wall, we must gain the last of the forward pack!'

'Agreed!' cried Tristan.

'Then by the time we reach Harvest Gate ... we must be among the fore.'

The Capulet brothers nodded.

Armand scanned ahead to consider the length of the course. His brows knit. He listened to Victoire's breath for a moment, then drove three fingertips through his coat to feel the warmth and moisture of his skin.

'Once through the gate ...' he called 'you'll *both* be faster for a final dash! And so for what's to do now, let me take the lead. Line astern 'til we reach Harvest Gate.'

'Armand!' shot Tristan, rising to object.

'Once we're through little brother, if all's well, then it's every bastard for himself!'

It was a noble gesture, typical of Armand of course. Yet in truth Victoire was the heaviest, built for barrelling strength and leaping obstacles of war. After having raced together for a month, there was little doubt the suggestion made sense. To spare Galante and Ajax for that run through the citadel, the mightiest mount would plough a path through to deliver their fastest to take on the foremost.

Reluctance was written on Sabatino and Tristan's faces. Yet they felt like a team. And if — as Tristan said in the tower on the day before — this was to be treated as practice for war, then his offer was precisely the style of sacrifice that a dire moment in battle might demand from any of them.

'Agreed big brother but ... you're a *big* dickhead!' Tristan grinned.

'Sabatino?' Armand cried.

'I agree Armand. You are a dickhead!' He smiled. 'But a generous one! Lead on Chevalier!'

Armand pressed a smile and set his eyes ahead.

Just as his master Toulon had done during the charge that took his life in Carentan, Armand made a knife of his left hand and drove his fingertips forward to signal the advance. Victoire surged again but held at a fast canter, just beneath a gallop. Galante's red nose chased the black tail tip, the pearl nose of Ajax was chasing the red.

They drove on.

A moment later Victoire's flaring nostrils sounded in warning behind a pair of riders trailing the foremost pack.

Both glanced rearward to scan the looming threat. To one side sat a Germanic horseman that Armand recognised. It was the Viking himself – Gunter von Hartvigson – the dragoness's protector. To the other side ran a local cavaliere. Gunter was a giant, nearly as imposing as Caspar, yet both rivals loomed large for the bulk of both rider and beast.

Ahead of that pair ran a bunching, impenetrable wall of horseflesh, thrashing and spitting up turf, mud and stones into the path of any who dared to follow. In a matter of seconds Armand's hair and face, chest and sleeves were drenched and darkened by a spattering flurry, kicked up to greet him. He felt the thrill rise and took a moment to set.

The reins fell loose as Armand pressed his offside knee and Victoire's massive shoulders set to work.

DRIVE! And PRESS against the left flank.

DRIVE! And PRESS against the right.

DRIVE! PRESS left. DRIVE! PRESS right.

LEFT! RIGHT! LEFT!

Victoire's surge summoned a smashing hail of protest to rain down upon his rider. Though the Viking refused to strike, that local cavaliere gave his all in defiance. And Armand knew the riders ahead would be less kind. Yet despite that onset, unwilling to risk retaliation that may slow his progress, he lifted his arms to brace, ducked his head and allowed his hefty forearms, neck and shoulders to bear the brunt from right and left. Armand knew that wending, thrusting surge would compel a path to open, as Victoire's massive grey shoulders shoved left and right.

Hot on Armand's heels, surging through the lane he carved came Sabatino and Tristan. Scanning as he went, Armand glanced left and right under his arms, then ahead. Clearing through the next pair would deliver him into a gap which led to the tails of the foremost riders.

Peering again at the rearmost of the leading pack, he spied two flashes of white side by side. One was the mystery entrant who rode for Paris — now his ally not his rival. The other was the Spaniard. Both white mounts were speeding towards the four-mile warden who now lay in sight.

All at once, a mighty sound erupted ahead of him! Like a dam bursting its bank a cheering cascade spilt from the crowd on the battlement walls. It rose in a frenzy as the first frantic rider reached that four-mile man. On they came in a charging pack together, racing for the turn at the south-east corner, hard by the bank of the fast-flowing Adige.

Armand pressed his lips and narrowed his eyes. Despite the sound of that rousing flourish, their plan insisted a pace must be held until the corner was turned — not before. Mighty Victoire still beat his shoes rhythmically, neck arched, head down and gaining, gaining, gaining on the rear of the foremost pack.

Suddenly the rumps of his next rivals were there.

Once more, the battle horse set to work, pushing, shoving and carving a lane through that hurtling mob.

PUSH! DRIVE! PUSH! DRIVE! PUSH! DRIVE!

Victoire burst into open space once more. Armand turned, urging the duet to follow him fast. The heads of Galante and Ajax thrust alongside Victoire's. The team were clear and running abreast. Beyond the final gap — now shortening every moment — snapped the tails of the leaders that were hurtling ahead of them.

Just half a length from the tip of Victoire's nose, the majestic white of Alonso's stallion raced beside a hulking bay brute. Sabatino knew the bay's rider by sight but not by name, a Montecchi associate, certainly an ally of the man racing ahead of them all aboard black Trionfo.

The wall's southern corner loomed larger than ever. With its cheering hoards leaning, leaping and waving so emphatically, Armand feared the mayhem would spur the leaders on. After that blunt tussle Victoire just endured, perhaps he could deliver another burst up to Harvest Gate. Yet that would drain him too much to stand any chance of finishing among the fore at Saint Fermo Square.

Armand narrowed his eyes to look beyond. Leading the pack by more than a length, Brando aboard his wild stallion plunged on to turn the corner first. And yes, the Capulets and Montecchi may be at peace, but the sight of the primo don of Montecchi leading that pack was more than enough to rouse the young premiere sieur of Capulet.

The stakes were rising. Armand set his eyes on the Spaniard and the Montecchi man. In his pledge of sacrifice to aid the faster pair – Sabatino and Tristan – this would be Armand's final push. A thought flashed in his mind. His eyes lifted, risking a glance to see if he could see Ilaria upon the wall ahead. Too far. He glanced again. Too many and now ... too much at stake. His eyes set forward.

SNAP! He flicked the reins, then pressed his heels to urge on the muscular battle horse thundering beneath him. Victoire began to drive his chest between the flanks of the formidable pair. The mighty head tossed. Driving hard, Victoire shoved against the Montecchi mount. Armand braced a forearm in readiness to fend off an assault.

A flash of silver caught Armand's eye. The Montecchi had dropped his reins to draw a steel gauntlet from his billowing shirt. The cretin shoved it onto his left paw, gathering the rein with his right. He leaned, snarled and SMASHED a steel-clad fist at Armand's temple. Blood streamed across his face as the dastard lifted to strike again.

Just as he did so the Spaniard surged on and the crowd cried encouragement. The Montecchi miscreant spat, turned and spurred to give chase. As Armand had feared, the massive bay broke into a fiery gallop. Now it was clear that henchman was placed to keep challengers off Brando's tail. Galante and Ajax drew abreast of Victoire. All three men's eyes followed the galloping bay for a moment.

That speeding burst had brought the Montecchi man hard

against the neck of Alonso's gorgeous white stallion. In a flashing moment more, the henchman's shoulder leaned in to the bobbing white head. Then employing a trick Armand recognised as lethal in a fight, the cretin's steel fist THUMPED the creature's nose to distract it, then gripped the bit and SHOVED down HARD with all his might, driving the head of the racing white beast under!

The massive animal buckled into a hurtling somersault. Instantly a thousand pounds of white horse flesh SLAMMED down with a sickening CRASH! The crowd erupted, gasping and screaming as the lurching thrust drove the stricken Alonso SMASHING to the ground ahead of the racing form of Victoire. Instinctively the battle horse stuttered in his stride, then upon a swift command to execute a *courbette*, Victoire leapt high and clear with his hind legs lowered to touch down, then instantly leapt again to avoid stamping on the wreckage of man or beast.

Galante and Ajax, hurtling on in Victoire's wake, had a demi-second more to respond. The pair swung apart wildly to avoid the twisting white mass below, as grim-faced wardens swarmed in with gusto to assist. Yet now, without waiting to confer, Armand pressed his lips and narrowed his eyes. From all but a standing start, mighty Victoire burst into a gallop to chase down the vile culprit.

Armand knew it was the kind of desperate move that could easily unseat the man who launched it. That wouldn't be risked in a sporting match except to settle a personal score or if it was ordered by one who stood to gain by the crime — perhaps for the sake of a hefty wager. He also knew the friendly caballero may be dead, or if injured may be stricken for life. Perhaps by Heaven's grace he was safe.

No matter the outcome, Armand's code as an accoladed chevalier wouldn't allow him to watch such rank dishonour run on without answer. The cost to that craven lackey must be swift and severe. As he galloped toward our watching group, Armand's eyes lifted to the sky.

You know I had seen him do so before, first from the walls of Carentan; then on the day he rode away to fight at Formigny; finally last summer upon the morning of the duel. I knew what he was thinking.

'Heaven is watching.' I whispered.

Ilaria heard me say it. She gripped my hand. Beside us Aurelie filled her lungs and leaned against the parapet, screaming in fury as she pointed at the criminal.

'ARMAND! GET that disgraceful fucker!'

Despite her livid description — perhaps because of it — an instant chorus of agreement burst all around us and lurched along the wall.

'Viva Capulet!' she called as many took up the cry.

The rat looked behind him to see retribution now racing towards him. Ominously Armand sign a cruciform. Then his voice lifted in a call to action.

'Victoire!' He commanded. 'Charge boy! Charge!'

From where we watched, every heart leapt to see Armand give chase. All at once the leaders were forgotten. Nothing mattered but justice. The rat racing before him turned in his seat with a malicious grin, only to meet the glare of hot blue eyes running him down in cold pursuit.

Hot on Armand's own heels, Sabatino and Tristan had burst forward together.

The brute turned back to face us, panic etched upon his foul face. The battlements loomed. Like a stone from a catapult he shot through the corner before us. Yet every watcher on the wall, witness to his brutality, hurled their abuse, then cheered to see dark grey vengeance race past in pursuit. Perhaps the cretin hoped to outrun his pursuer, make Harvest Gate and then vanish in the citadel.

Yet like a thunder cloud driven on the wind, Victoire closed menacingly behind him. His black mane and tail whipped and snapped as Armand's mud-strewn shirt and broad sleeves, flapped and smacked in anger. He drew alongside the Montecchi man. All at once they were racing neck and neck. Menace leapt from the villain's eyes. He knew all those taunts following along the wall were for none but the vile miscreant that had driven the Spaniard down.

'FUCK you Frenchman!' he bellowed. 'What can you do? Fucking GUELPH! WHAT!'

He flicked the steel fingers of his gauntlet under his chin. A steely gaze met the taunt. A heartbeat passed between them. As they neared to pass the central gate where Escalus, Florentia and the arch-bishop stood watching with every exalted guest of the festival, the boastful cretin heard the cold command.

'Victoire! Drive right!'

The mighty battle horse drew to the right. The henchman scowled in defiance, leaning to pump and thrash, hoping to dislodge the avenger. Yet Armand's massive thighs held tight. Hard blue eyes stared into black.

SMASH! THUMP! SMACK! A flurry of panicked strikes were launched by the cretin to no effect. His avenger seemed to be made of marble. The flurry of strikes halted! Like a sharp toothed mackerel that's bitten onto the hook, a flailing fist was suddenly snagged, caught in a grip of his avenger's clutching hand.

SNAP! A lightning flick of Armand's palm slipped under the wrist to catch it from behind. The cretin's eyes bulged in fear. He wrenched his shoulder and bucked wildly to draw himself free. Yet the fearsome grip had snapped even tighter.

'What have you caught there brother?'

Tristan galloped along the offside.

'A crawling snake!' Sabatino raced on the other side.

'FUCK you Cortellani! Fuck you ALL!'

'Victoire!' Armand commanded. 'Drive left!'

I've learned there are subtle ways to command a mighty battle horse without using a single utterance. A touch of the heel is one, then the toe, the rein or the spur. Yet that firm vocal command — as if given during a salon parade — ensured that vile cur understood, the will that had pursued him was inexorable. As Victoire drew left, the tip of Armand's right boot pushed in firm encouragement, for the opposing beast to separate.

The black-hearted devil aboard began to tip and flail. He even dropped his rein to strike down in desperation against the grip that still held his hand captive. For an instant, that effort had firmed up his poise, even coaxed him to strike again in vain hope. Yet he had already reached the tipping point.

For just a half breath more, the only thing that held his descent was the avenger's grip. Both coursers were galloping at breakneck speed. The ground ran under them like a torrent through its bed. Armand's grip released. The miscreant tumbled into the hell below as his unburdened mount bucked and ran off toward the battlements.

Without so much as backward glance Victoire, Galante and Ajax ran on. Eyes forward once more they saw three riders ahead, racing along the last section before Harvest Gate. Brando Montecchi was one, now challenged by just two, including the other flash of white. Armand, Sabatino and Tristan galloped on in pursuit.

But Victoire's effort to grind the path before and then chase the henchman down, had taken a heavy toll. Now the stoic courser was labouring just to keep up the pace.

'Victoire will never catch them. Go boys! Run them down! Go!'

'Viva Cortellani!' cried Sabatino.

'Capulet and the Dragon!' cried Tristan.

On they raced to catch the leaders. Forced to watch them spur forward, Victoire shook his head with impatience. Yet despite that want, his heart could only manage to follow them in withering pursuit. Still ahead of them all, including Galante and Ajax, the foremost trio flashing brown, white and black, wheeled to face Harvest Gate.

The smashing pad of hoofs on sodden turf was transformed into the clang of shoes on stones, bricks and mortar, still dangerously moist from the prior night's rain.

Above Harvest Gate another cheer erupted. The crowd watched the racers vanish underneath, then swung across wildly to cram the inner balustrade and watch them re-emerge. Sounding to the other side in a volley of hoofbeats, craning necks and straining eyes followed the flashing trio inside — BROWN! BLACK! WHITE!

Now bystanders along both sides of the street took up the duty to urge the racers on, screaming and stamping and hooting. They pumped palms and feet against anything to generate more sound than their cries and caterwauling.

Moments later pearl and red coats flashed through the citadel gate as Galante and Ajax raced on in pursuit. When they passed by the castle both were closing fast on the trio ahead, riding like men possessed, straight for the beckoning arches at Jupiter's Gate.

A chestnut of Foscari led the black of Montecchi and white mount of Paris by barely half a length. Two portals raced towards them. Foscari veered left but Montecchi surged to block him. Foscari veered right, shoving Paris right as they careered for the right portal together. With no room or time to adjust course, the masked rider's leg was on course to collide with the stone façade.

Yet beyond all belief, just before impact that rider's right heel swept back and up and over the white rump to avoiding the collision and kept going! Then in a breathtaking show of acrobatic skill, for just the split of a second the masked rider dismounted, facing rearward in full flight!

As both feet seemed to barely touch the ground, both knees bent in a flash to vault him back up and catapult him high to remount at full gallop and run on!

CUPID'S BALLS ON FIRE!

Closing from behind Sabatino and Tristan saw the remarkable feat and stared at each other. Four lengths back, Armand saw it too, yet the sight made him furrow his brows in suspicion. Montecchi saw nothing. He raced for Herb Market Square in a bid to be first to enter the snaking turns beyond it. That twisting, turning way would draw them west but further north too, almost to the corner of the Basilica of Saint Anastasia. Once there, two final turnings — wide left and hard right — led to the river path and the dash to the post.

If Brando held the inside track going in, he could block the trailers all the way through until the run for home. And crowded followers at such sudden turnings were more like to meet catastrophe than any rider at the fore. Yet despite any hope Montecchi may have, Sabatino was closing fast. He knew Galante's speed, knew the will of his wild red racer to run through hard turns without fear would be to his advantage. But a fearless mount is one thing. It's rider must be fearless too and willing to let the horse have its head as they entered such a snaking path.

Sabatino plunged on, pouring like quicklime through Jupiter's gate as Galante and Ajax raced to catch the leaders. A mighty CLANG burst from above. Rengo boomed in warning to all. The leader had reached Herb Market Square. In one blistering minute the race would be decided.

Seconds behind the forward quintet, Armand galloped through the twin portals alone as twenty raging riders surged through Harvest Gate behind him. Each was boiling with intent to finish before the last. With Rengo clanging to stir every pulse, Montecchi, Foscari and Paris galloped past the mouth of Herb Market Square.

The crowd screamed wildly to spur them on. One instant later Galante and Ajax raced by, shortening the gap with every stride. Sabatino leaned against the stirrups then lay his chest on Galante's straining neck to whisper hot encouragement. In a blink, a breath and a heartbeat the flashing red racer shrunk four lengths to three, two and then one as the black beast of Montecchi led Paris and Foscari into the first corner.

Brando snapped his head back to glance behind, grinning to know the inside track was his. Yet his eyes leapt at the sight of Galante and Ajax hurtling in behind. He knew Sabatino. He had lost to him before. He leaned and kicked and laid the rein hard against Trionfo's neck. The stallion shunted his massive chest to the left, then right, then left.

One more right would face him toward the Basilica!

Brando risked another turn in his seat yet couldn't believe his eyes. Galante's red nose was nudging the tail of Paris, whose nose sat hard on his own tail. The breathtaking speed of Galante through the rocking, twisting turns had drawn Sabatino through to catch Foscari and slip inside him.

Head to tail the new leaders broke into the open street, plunging toward the Basilica.

Three horses flashed by the watchers.

BLACK! WHITE! RED!

Foscari leaned hard at the last snaking turn to block the pearl stallion now hot on his heels. Yet the eyes of both horse and rider leapt open as the chestnut floundered for grip on a slippery patch of stone. Foscari yanked the rein. His chestnut swung the other way, lurching wide with skittering steps. In a diabolical dance, and to the gasping cries of bystanders, the beast staggered and stomped, then swirled a pirouette in an effort to stay on his feet.

To avoid a blunt collision, Ajax instinctively stuttered a step. But his hoof stomped the slippery patch too. His knee began to buckle. Thinking fast Tristan signalled the mythical beast to *croupade*. Before his weight could drive down, Ajax dropped his rump to lift his fore legs as hind knees bent to launch in a demi leap. After landing again the hind knees bent and braced then leapt again, bursting them clear and launching Ajax straight into a gallop.

Running the short straight for the basilica corner, black, white and red horses ran nose to tail as Ajax poured on from behind. The second last curve loomed ahead. Sabatino surged alongside the masked rider. Red and white noses chased a black tail as both plunged on together.

Emerging from the snaking pass, just in time to see them vanish and chase the recovered Foscari, came bold Victoire still running for all he was worth. Three seconds after the dark dappled grey raced on in pursuit, a cacophony of clattering rose up at the exit of the last snaking turn. All at once an avalanche of riders poured round the corner behind Armand in pursuit of them all.

One heartbeat more and to Sabatino's surprise, the pearl nose of Ajax bobbed at the red tail of Galante. The masked rider glanced past them back to Victoire. A flash of interest lit up their eyes as Montecchi ahead, leaned left for the next to last turning. Knowing that wide curve led to a sharp right that would turn them about for Saint Fermo, Sabatino took a chance and let the masked rider surge on.

Once past, Sabatino plunged straight after them, pushing heels to spur and then — after watching, watching, watching — he pressed the rein to drive hard right. His heart leapt to his mouth. While one may count two Sabatino stared in anticipation. Black and white both drew wide before him.

NOW! NOW! NOW!

Sabatino pressed his heels again, surging past the muscular white beast as the red head and shoulder drew alongside the puffing black stallion. Brando's head turned.

'Have at you Cortellani!' he shouted with a smile.

'Have at you Montecchi!' he cried in reply.

Turning onto the river road at last, the leading quartet burst on in close staggered pairs. Each beautiful monster felt the relief of a falling path as it rose up beneath them.

The Adige flashed by upon their left. A massing crowd lined the last stretch from Saint Anastasia to Saint Fermo, cheering, waving, stomping and leaping like antic clowns as the four horsemen of Verona unleashed with all their might, screaming their battle cries.

'Montecchi!'

'Cortellani!'

'Paris!'

'Capulet and the Dragon!'

Just half a mile stood between victory and defeat.

Nostrils flared. Iron shoes smashed against stone. The mighty hearts of four battle horses pounded in massive chests. A driving zephyr rushed against them all, streaming the locks of riders and beasts as sleeves, sashes and silken favours snapped fanatically.

The white stallion galloped like fury to challenge the noses of Trionfo and Galante. Ajax poured after in pursuit.

The river course jinked right.

The leading trio swerved.

Three ran abreast together with the head of mighty Ajax on the tails of them all.

The river course jinked left.

The leading trio swerved and straightened into the final stretch that led past the mouth of Saint Fermo bridge and the victory post beyond!

In the near distance at the corner of that bridge stood five anxious young women with lips pressed, brows knit, and hearts pounding wildly. Thundering like gods the trio came storming to the finish, immersed in a blur of excess that only horse and rider can know, when the teetering balance of speed and control engulfs all sensibility, summoning an irresistible urge to want to fly like Pegasus.

Headlong they plunged, noses level. It seemed nothing could separate them. Fate seemed determined that all three must win together. Then a voice lifted from behind.

'CHARGE Ajax! FLY for me boy! CHARGE!'

Like a mythical beast summoned by the spirit of ancient gods, the muscular pearl shoulders surged with the power of an avalanche. As if leading a host to battle, Tristan thrust his arm forward. Five favours streamed wildly! Five screaming young women at the mouth of Saint Fermo bridge lost every ounce of control!

'Capulet and the Dragon!'

That was the cry which led at the finish.

Tristan de Capulet won the mounted race by half a neck against that formidable trio of Montecchi, Cortellani and a masked rider for Paris. And despite being level nose-for-nose-for-nose, those three had appeared unbeatable and inseparable until the very last.

Chapter 25 Revelation

Their wild rantings were uncontrollable. Each dragoness hugged and kissed one another and screamed for joy. They hugged and kissed Maxine and screamed for joy. They raced to the finish post and hugged and kissed beautiful Ajax and screamed for joy. When Tristan dismounted — dumbfounded to see the rider for Paris had been a woman — they hugged and kissed Tristan and screamed for joy.

Armand finished fourth, happy to have played his part in the victory but was apparently perturbed. I assumed it was for the Spaniard's sake. Yet once dismounted, he glanced in the direction of the white stallion. Oh yes, the rider had revealed herself. Yes Armand recognised her but didn't appear surprised. None of us in transit from the wall to San Fermo had witnessed her acrobatic display at Jupiter's gate. Yet once he witnessed that daring manoeuvre, Armand felt sure the rider for Paris could be no other.

Despite her gaze, which held him fast, and a mischievous smile, he turned with an intention to go to Tristan and congratulate him first and foremost. As he did so, Ilaria and Aurelie approached in the company of the Duchess de Paris and Nobel. Their arrival had been the information I forgot to relay on the previous day.

Of course we had no notion that Eloise du Marche was racing. Aurelie and Ilaria had met Yolanthe and Auguste in transit as we rushed from our perch upon the wall to watch the ending at Saint Fermo. When we encountered that pair, they were chatting happily with the prince and princess in the company of the archbishop.

Armand felt a rap of fingertips upon his arm. He glanced at Maxine who was lifting a wet cloth to wipe blood from his temple as the duchess arrived.

'Oh I can do that darling.' Yolanthe drew the cloth from Maxine with a smile.

'So can I ... darling.' Ilaria reclaimed the cloth from Yolanthe with a smile.

Yolanthe huffed and rolled her eyes as Ilaria dabbed the spot and kissed Armand in congratulations.

'Well at least let him kiss me in *greeting*?'

'Very well but I'm watching you ... already.'

Armand embraced her cautiously and kissed her thrice. She held his eyes.

'It's a pleasure to see you Yolanthe.'

'Just to hear you say my name again Adonis makes it a pleasure to be here.' She glanced at Ilaria and leaned to kiss his cheek. 'Oh Ria that one was for winning.'

'He didn't win Yoli.'

'I beg to differ. You saw what he did to that cretin.'

'Yes. That was frightening.'

'And thrilling. He won it all as far as I'm concerned.'

'What brings you to the festival?' asked Armand.

'I heard it was a racing event. Yet when I met your wife and sister presenting as ancient goddesses, I thought it must be a costume carnival. And imagine my shock to discover a feminine entourage in mimic of them ...' She glanced at the dragonesses. 'following in their wake.'

'Yes. And they're all racing together.'

'So is your beautiful sister I'm told. And so are you?'

'It's true.'

'And Escalus too!' Yolanthe stared at the prince.

'We're running as rivals.'

'Tia there must be something in the water in Verona.'

The princess smiled. 'Perhaps it's in the air Yoli. Public spirit.'

'No I'm sure some witch has poured a potion in the fountain which compels the elite to disrobe and run amok.'

'That's another possibility of course.'

'I confess I arrived here with little expectation to find anything new of interest. Yet on this extraordinary day, I discovered both the men I pine for have pledged to run naked in the streets together.'

'Ah Florentia.' Ilaria kissed the princess and embraced her. 'I'm happy to see she doesn't flirt exclusively with my husband in his wife's presence.'

'No Ria she also counts me among her cuckolds.' Florentia turned her eyes to Heaven. 'Though I believe she singles us out for more emphatic treatment.'

'Oh no lovely friends. I promise you I don't!'

'By the Devil but she's brazen Ilaria.'

The duchess pushed her pout to one side, shrugging bare shoulders in her signature fashion.

'Heaven help our men Tia if anything happens to either of us.'

'Exactly darlings!' countered the duchess. 'I've offered you both fair warning. Stay alive. Stay married and keep them happy. Otherwise I'll claim one for myself.'

Held at the edges of the gathering, arm fondly about her own husband, Aurelie stood smiling politely. It seemed that in the duchess she had discovered a rival for the prince's interest. I wondered how much she saw herself reflected in Yolanthe's rampant chattering.

'And now Adonis.' Yolanthe smiled. 'I'm also told you have a brother in Verona?' She glanced at Tristan.

'Younger brother.'

'Well darling when his entourage are done fawning over him, you must introduce me. Dear Heaven Tia! How many women can one man attract?'

Florentia frowned playfully. 'Yes Ilaria I thought you said Tristan was shy? He appears very popular.'

The prince also frowned and leaned to the princess. 'U n l i k e somebody else, I'm afraid.'

'Escalus who do you mean?' purred the duchess. 'Oh yes. My *surprise* entrant.'

Eloise had arrived holding the ribbon attached to her discarded mask. With the covering now removed, her face showed the evidence of how brutal their contest had been.

'Eloise! Who did that to your eye?'

'One whose eye is now a match for my own I hope.'

She lifted to unravel a tie that held the manly cue which had helped to disguise her. He chestnut locks shook free as Yolanthe caught her chin to inspect the damage.

'Point the villain out to Escalus so he can be flogged for his trouble.'

'Yoli don't be so dramatic. The fellow didn't know I was a woman.'

'The only woman to enter Verona's elite horserace. And you nearly won it.'

'If they held a horserace for women of course' Eloise glanced at Escalus. 'I could leave the men to their devices. But I thank your Highness for allowing my late entry.'

'I must confess Eloise that when Yoli requested a last-minute placement, had I known I was allowing you to ride among the Cavalieri? I would have refused.'

Florentia knitted her brows. 'Cal I fear some of those she has beaten may take it very ill.'

'Yes Tia.' Escalus agreed. 'Some of them look ... rather unhappy.'

Their comments caused me to glance. I saw Aldobrando standing with a clutch of local riders. He appeared at ease. Yet it seemed he was listening to a chorus of discontent from the rest and attempting to calm them.

'I wish you had remained incognito 'til they dispersed.' Escalus shot a withering glance at Yolanthe.

'Well I don't disagree darling.' Yolanthe pleaded. 'That was our plan Eloise. Why *did* you unveil?'

'Because she can't help herself.' Armand replied.

Though Eloise demurred, there was no mistaking the shine in her eyes as she heard him say so, nor the glint of envy in Ilaria's eyes to hear him say so.

'Marcel and I remember your antics in Carentan..'

Any mention of myself was always a cue to ensure I continued to be noticed.

'None would have suspected' I began in a sage voice 'that beneath the billowing linen of a heroic horse*man* was the soft breast and stout heart of a heroic horse*woman*.'

'None would suspect' Eloise countered 'that rising beneath that same linen, are dozens of bruises to remind me of the cost of this adventure.' She pecked my cheek impulsively and turned. 'Oh Armand! Ilaria! It's so good to see you both again.'

She hugged and kissed them with such fervour and so innocently it was hard to hold her in admonishment. Ilaria opened to speak but Armand had become impulsive.

'Well Eloise I must say that I'm *fearful* to see you. And Escalus is correct. You should have kept that covering on 'til those riders were dispersed.'

'But Armand I —'

'This is *not* Normandy. To dangle the ruse as a herald before the English was a remarkable thing.'

'Did you do that?' shot the princess in amazement.

'She did Florentia.' Armand ran on. 'But we were at war. And so her daring won the hearts of all.'

'As did yours.' Eloise rejoined. 'Remember Chevalier?'

Ilaria pressed her lips at the reminder that, during his absence last year before they wed, Armand had shared such an important experience with this vibrant woman.

'That's nothing to the point Eloise.' Armand said cooly. 'To reveal yourself so baldly to these men after defeating some of their most venerated cavalieres —'

'Armand?' she pleaded. 'I defeated you too but you don't seem to mind?'

'It's not the same. I know you. I respect your skill. Yet just now as I left them. Many were grumbling —'

'Tush and be still. It was all in fun. They'll drink and dine and forget I was ever —'

Armand glowered at Yolanthe. 'I fear the opposite. Yolanthe she must take care in this. In Carentan she had her Majesty's protection. Here —'

'I'm protected by the mighty House of Paris.'

Eloise wrapped an arm around Yolanthe's waist who leaned to kiss her forehead. 'Yes you do wayward girl.'

'Armand' Eloise added 'I promise to be *cautious*.'

'If she is ...' Yolanthe put in 'it shall be the first time since I've known her.'

'Oh enough of *me*.' Eloise smiled. 'I'm told you're running today. And *you* Ilaria?'

'Yes I am.' Ilaria replied. 'Please tell me you don't plan to disguise yourself as a naked man?'

'In truth I considered it when I heard Armand was entered.' Finally a titter of laughter arose. 'Yet I confess the challenge of how to do so has stumped me.'

'Just as well.' Ilaria replied. 'Why not run with the women? Aurelie and I are both entered.'

Eloise's eyes lit up. 'How extraordinary. Oh I wish I had known! I certainly would —'

'We may still be able to enter you.' Ilaria glanced at the distracted duchess. 'Perhaps even —'

Yolanthe took a moment to comprehend then her brows lifted. 'No Ria certainly not!'

'Yes Yoli.'

Smiles lifted on every face expect Yolanthe's. Even Nobel was grinning like a cat.

'Ilaria de Capulet NO! I have no intention of running naked in the *daylight* in front of —'

'Yoli we shall all be naked.'

'Perhaps in the dark ... with candles and shadows ... and a beautiful man.'

'Come now Yolanthe.' the princess replied soberly. 'Join these bold women.'

'No darling. No, no, no. Eloise should do it. She's still on the market.'

'But I only prepared for a horserace.' Eloise glanced at the prince. 'However ... if I was allowed to enter the women's race too Highness, I would run on *one* condition —'

Escalus glanced at Florentia and rubbed his chin in thought 'Well ... if she ran with the women, it may dampen the sting of this entry as a singular display. A condition?'

'Yoli must run too.' She stared defiantly. 'Come along loud-mouth. I *challenge* you.'

Yolanthe's brows lifted. 'No! No don't do that! You know that I can't —'

'We don't have to win, just drag our bare asses past that post before sundown. Ilaria's doing it. So is Aurelie.'

Yolanthe stared at both women. 'Auguste and I *only* stopped in Verona to check on the progress of you two laggards!' she spat in exasperation. 'And to meet Ren and Astor. Indeed they should have arrived by now.'

'Your husband is coming here?' asked Ilaria.

'And my little brother who I'm desperate for yourself and Armand to meet. Otherwise we'd have met them in Brescia last night. I certainly didn't come here to run through the streets like a harlot chasing a delinquent client.'

'Hmm. But I still want you to run with us and —' Ilaria glanced to Eloise. 'I sensed a nerve when you challenged her?' She stared back at the duchess.

'No you didn't.' Yolanthe spat emphatically.

'Yes you did.' Eloise corrected.

'Ah. Then I challenge you too. So does Aurelie.'

'Do I?'

'Yes you do. So does Florentia.'

The princess lifted her brows. 'I do? Oh yes. Run if you dare duchess. Or ... stand with the *timid* and watch.'

Yolanthe narrowed her eyes in frustration. It was clear — perhaps because of the status of her challenger — that affected her.

'Yoli she's right.' Eloise added. 'Come on! What's one more bare ass among friends?'

'Ria how long do we have?' asked Yolanthe.

'The mules are next and so ... an hour. More or less.'

'Then in an hour — more or less — you'll have my final answer. After I consult with ... whatever potent refreshment is left in my carriage.'

The Saint Fermo bell rang out above us, it's chime far sweeter than Rengo. And because of that difference it was being used to warn all entrants to make for the starting point. The mule race was next. I had to collect my beast. With a kiss from Maxine, I hurried away. If all went well, we'd meet again at the Southern gate to go on together.

For regardless of Yolanthe and Eloise, our plan still held. To have time in excess to prepare, Ilaria, Aurelie and Maxine would accompany me to the start. But with the bordellos' wager being decided that day, the dragonesses had fallen back under Pruetta's control. She was taking no chances before the race began. For safety when travelling beyond the walls, she instructed they stay together and meet the Viking at the Arena where he'd escort them to the start.

Yolanthe also agreed that — one way or another — she would make her own way to the start with Eloise, either to start with them or to watch them start. She had still made no promise for either as yet. At that moment however, she remained interested in the Capulet brother she still hadn't met. So did Eloise. Both women glanced in his direction.

Tristan remained occupied with his admirers as announced to the Dragonesses he had entered the footrace too. That news met with firm approval. He didn't reveal it of course, yet after considering that new threat of the Montecchi bastard, Tristan decided the only way to offer Armand security was to be on the course with him.

With little time to spare before they must depart, Ilaria decided to accompany Armand to introduce Yoli and Eloise to Tristan. If her husband must remain in their company for a little longer, she preferred to remain with him for as long as possible. Aurelie and Sabatino followed behind, yet they could barely approach for the bevy of young women now gathered about the younger Capulet.

Yet now, more signorinas than the Dragonesses had gathered in hope of meeting the handsome winner. But when the bell rang to summon our girls who would be racing soon, he allowed each one to draw their favour from his arm. Fiametta went first but was hesitating as Ilaria approached.

'Donna Capulet?'

'Now your favour's ready to be returned Fiametta —'

'He must kiss me again?'

'*Both* kiss to signify that, with your reunion, both your hearts still feel the same.'

The duchess stared at Ilaria lifting her brows with a smirk in response to the extraordinary display.

'Oh yes my heart feels the same Madonna. Yet —'

'Fiametta?' asked Ilaria. 'What's the matter?'

'My heart feels the *same* ... for Fabrizio.'

A chorus of giggles erupted.

'Fabrizio?' said Yolanthe. 'Mercy Ria how many men serve this harem?'

'That may take some explaining.' Ilaria smiled. 'Fiametta I'm sure Fabio will be glad to know it. And he won't be offended if you retrieve your favour and just kiss the cheek politely.'

'Hurry up Metta!' snapped Brianna. 'We're waiting.'

Yolanthe leaned to Iaria again. 'Does this brother always command this sort of attention?'

'Much more so recently.'

Then one after another, five favours were reclaimed. By Maxine's report to me later, Brianna attempted to repeat her passionate kiss. Yet Ilaria persuaded her because they were exposed to so much more scrutiny, she must be more discreet. Yes, apparently that rankled her more than a little.

Armand suggested Ilaria introduce the duchess and Eloise. As Yolanthe came forward the Dragonesses gave way but glared with suspicion. Yes, they heard Yolanthe's intimidating title but seemed more awestruck to learn that the woman next to her — still dressed in a man's riding habit — was a ward of the French Queen.

Despite all intimidation the Dragonesses hung close to their champion. And the darkening shade to Eloise's eye threw them into more confusion. It seemed the royal ward had recently been clouted by someone! Brianna wondered just what manner of woman the Capulets were keeping company with. Certainly this one — ward of a

Queen or not — looked more like something they'd see in the cat house by night, not in elite company on the streets of Verona by day.

'Had I known' Tristan pleaded 'I wouldn't have smacked you in the eye!'

'You're the brute who hit her!' spat the duchess.

The Dragonesses tittered in amusement.

'Yoli to be fair, when I felt him closing on the corner? I smacked him first'

'You did Mademoiselle. And it was very well run. A masterful ride.'

'I think you mean *mistressful*.' she quipped. 'I truth Chevalier I thought I *had* you for a moment.'

Yolanthe sighed 'For a moment darling we thought you had them *all*!'

Tristan shrugged his shoulders. 'Honestly I didn't think I could win. Yet I had to call my boy to action and try.'

Suddenly his entourage erupted.

'Ajax!'

'Hoorah for Ajax.'

'We love you Ajax.'

'So beautiful.'

'We love him.'

'Mercy they're besotted!' shot Yolanthe. 'Is all that passion for the horse or the rider?

'For both Prima Donna!' declared Brianna.

'I'm more than a prima donna my girl. Yet that will suffice for now.'

Yoli patted the charger's muscular neck. 'Heavens he is a beautiful creature. They're both beautiful creatures.'

Five pairs of eyes stared back in romantic defiance. Brianna stepped closer with a challenging look.

'Don Capulet and Ajax raced for the Dragon.'

The duchess turned to Ilaria and leaned on her hand. 'Clearly there's something about Capulet men that seems to set women alight.'

'I wasn't sure if I should push him further.' Tristan added. 'Yet something just —'

'Takes you?' Eloise smiled.

She rested a hand on his forearm.

The lower lip of every dragoness thrust into the upper. Brows furrowed in dismay.

'Precisely Mademoiselle. And as they say ...'

'Nothing ventured? Well Chevalier if I had to *lose* —'

'Lose?' Tristan smiled. 'Mademoiselle in a field of more than thirty over six miles you came second by a head.'

'Shit!' Greta cried. 'That's impressive for a woman!'

'Impressive for *anyone*.' Tristan corrected. 'And you didn't even see what we witnessed at Jupiter's gate.'

Yolanthe's brows lifted in surprise. 'What happened at Jupiter's gate darling?'

Armand glanced about. 'I think we should discuss that later at our leisure.' he suggested quietly.

'I agreed.' Eloise replied. 'For now let's just say that ... I felt inspired by the Maid of Orlean's spirit.'

'You know that our father fought in her company?'

'No!' Eloise spat incredulously. 'No I did not.' She turned to Armand, eyes wide in disbelief.

'It's true. He fought with her from Orlean to Patay. France is forever in her debt. But when our enemies captured her, they made her pay dearly for that show of spirit.'

Eloise frowned. 'Are we still discussing —'

'I fear this show of spirit may have earned you some enemies too Eloise. You saw what they did to the Spaniard?'

The faces of all listening grew dark.

All listening had seen it, even the duchess.

'No.' Eloise glanced about. 'Who was the Spaniard? What happened to him?'

'The rider on the other white mount?'

'Oh yes.' she turned to the marshalling area and realised his mount wasn't among the finishers. 'Where is he? Did he fall? As we ran for the gate I heard a commotion yet kept my mind on the race.'

'He was close behind you and —' The warning bell sounded again. 'No matter. Let's discuss it later. But until you depart safely tomorrow Eloise you must take care.'

'Oh yes. I'll take care.' She turned to Tristan. 'May I call you Tristan?'

'Of course you may.'

'Tristan if I had to lose, I'm glad it was to such a divine horse as Ajax. And to a Capulet.'

Her words seemed acceptable to the Dragonesses but the fond look she offered him was less well received. Ilaria and Aurelie had observed it with interest, perhaps even approval. Anticipating the same reaction, Maxine glanced at the duchess but it appeared Armand's warning had begun to weigh on her mind. The disgruntled cavalieres appeared to be gone but she was gazing distractedly where they had stood muttering together, casting hostile glances at Eloise.

With the bell now rung twice, Ilaria, Aurelie and Maxine hastily took their leave to meet me at the southern gate. The men led their mounts back to the Cortellani stable and then ventured on to the wall. The Dragonesses did as Pruetta had instructed, walking on together, chattering and laughing toward the Arena to meet the Viking.

The bubble and froth of the horserace dispersed. Now the notion of fun the mule race may bring began to infect the citadel. Every little beast that could stand upright appeared to be making its way. Soon they were cramming the course heading south, mounted by men and women, old, young, fat, thin, pretty or plain, including myself.

And I tell you sweet friends, the first running of that race was ribald fun from its antic start to its zany finish. Perhaps not in small part to the nature of my own appearance. For the brilliant notion I had hit upon — that I felt would ensure my winning of the losing prize — was not only to ride naked, which I shared with you before, but to run my beast *rearward*! And so over the previous four weeks I had tutored the she-ass to do so over lengthy distances.

Therefore as I emerged from the cover of a large tree — behind which I had doffed my attire — to line up with all comers for the start, all stared in amusement, hooting and bellowing and guffawing. And so, save for an antic headpiece I found in the market that very morning, as I came forth upon that she-beast, both of us were completely naked!

However I had not shared *every* part of my plan with my wife. Indeed until she stood waiting for me to appear Maxine knew nothing of the two most important details! When she saw me approaching naked as the day I was born, facing forward while my beast faced rearward, Maxine shrieked in dismay!

'Marcel Jacques Poquelin! DUNDERHEAD! How could you SHAME me so! How could you shame our DAUGHTER so! Even that farting BEAST is ashamed! You're NO husband of MINE!'

'I LOVE you sweetheart!' I cried.

Not since I had left my home in the slums of Paris to venture into the world had any woman called my entire name in public. Then it was my sweet maman warning me to take care. To hear Maxine, reminded me of that moment. I had felt so aggrieved to leave Maman alone with Grandam. I wondered what they would think of me now.

I knew what Aurelie thought. She was laughing out loud and pronounced it pure madness. The merchant-minded Ilaria declared she could see the logic to my antic choice, yet only the duchess agreed with her. And before Yolanthe had arrived at the starting line — in the privacy of her luxuriant carriage, the exalted woman also agreed on something else.

When the duchess had peaked beneath Eloise's blouse to more closely inspect the damage she'd taken from the race, she declared the demoiselle was far too bruised to bare her body in public. Yolanthe accepted the challenge to run. But on her way to the start, she ordered her conveyance to halt at *Piscinia Degli Dei*, the exclusive bathhouse she and Nobel had lured the Capulets into the day after they met.

Upon her arrival with Eloise that day, before the duchess drove on alone, she ensured that her ward was delivered into the caring hands of Linus and Penelope Kazan. The hosts were overjoyed to see the duchess of course, and despite the crush of the festival, agreed to make room for Eloise at once and take very special care of her.

What's more they agreed to Yolanthe's request, just to be safe, to summon a medicus. He would inspect her injuries more closely before allowing the masseur to oil and scrape her skin or push and ply her aching muscles. As the duchess drove on, Eloise was ushered into a sumptuous private chamber. It was not unlike the one we had used, yet was built for a couple, and so was more intimate, with a smaller tub for bathing.

The medicus came and went followed by the masseur. From the moment he was done, Eloise was handed into the care of a young private valet. He offered drink and some morsels to eat. He tested the steaming water, adding herbs to infuse it precisely, ensuring it was ready for his elegant patron to lay back and soak in to take her rest.

After her revival was complete, Eloise planned to dress elegantly and rejoin the festivities. She was eager to watch the footraces among friends and meet Yolanthe's husband and brother again. She had only met them once – for a few hours – and so couldn't say that she knew them at all. After sunset they would all dine together in the company of the Capulets and Cortelannis.

Next morning they planned to depart for Paris and return Eloise to the care of Queen Marie. It would be the end of her great adventure abroad. Yes Yolanthe had urged her to stay. But for the sake of her own heart, Eloise had also decided that, remaining so near to Armand and Ilaria, was not the way forward for her life. Not even the interest of a new Capulet brother could turn her from that decision.

Just before Eloise sank her head beneath the steaming water to soak her cares away, the first warning peal of Saint Fermo sounded, calling the women to the start of their race. That gave her just enough time to enjoy another blissful moment alone. Eloise submerged her chin, her lips, her nose. Then she shut her eyes and slid under the surface.

Chapter 26 Diabolical

Away at the starting point, the line was drawn tight again by the junior and senior wardens. Competitors approached to mass behind it. Both men struggled to know where to cast their eyes. Suddenly the *ground* was of very great interest. The entrants were tall, short and middling in height. Some wore sandals yet most were barefoot. Some had their chests wrapped in linen or canvas yet most did not. Many bodies were lathered in oil from neck to knee. And married or not, the hair of most was revealed for the event but tightly bound to hold against the jolt of their motion, the wind or the threat of a tug from their rivals.

Behind the starting point, an antic collection of carts and small wagons trailed away upon either side of the road. Upon the offside at a near distance stood a selection of elite covered wagons and carriages with footmen and servers idling in and out of them. All displayed emblems of powerful houses or wealthy establishments. The Cortellani's conveyance was there, having already disgorged its occupants. Aurelie, Ilaria and Maxine however had not yet joined the start but stood waiting for another.

The opulent carriage of the Duchess de Paris stood nearby. True to her word Yolanthe had arrived but remained inside, waiting for the last moment to emerge. As you know she was expecting the arrival of her husband Reynard and little brother Astor. Yoli said she longed to see Astor again and introduce him to Armand who she hoped would agree to mentor him. For the sake of that hope — and Astor's potential as a match for a future daughter of Capulet — she needed Ilaria to like him too.

Yet I know from later confidences that I shared with the enigmatic duchess, that after the better part of a year apart from her husband, the prospect of being reunited with Reynard was unsettling her. He and Astor were due to arrive by noon. Indeed by that time, both would not only have arrived, but be standing on the wall with the prince and princess to watch what was left of the festival.

Yoli had gone to the start with every intention of participating. Indeed she had pledged to do it. And as Eloise knew, the fiery young duchess felt obliged — to the point of obsession — to accept any challenge offered by another elite woman. This dare had been issued by several, and in the presence of elite men, two of whom she felt desperate to impress with her willingness. Yet after being separated from *Ren* for so long, she hadn't planned for his first sight of her to be her running naked through the streets of Verona.

More potently, Yolanthe had left Reynard fuming in a marital rage on the eve of his return to the war. Indeed he was so angered by her antics in public that night — when she announced the great merchant venture to her faction — that he left before time. What's more he had left despite her promise of a night of unbridled passion together. It was very unlike him to forego such pleasure. Indeed at that time, it was more unlike herself, to forego it with him.

But that night Yolanthe's perspective on her own sense of destiny had begun to change. And since departing with Nobel in Eloise's close company, since meeting the Capulets, since visiting Rome to form an alliance with two men whose combined wealth and power was breathtaking, now she considered her future with the irresistible duke to be ... uncertain.

When she had departed the next morning her greatest concern was for leaving her brother in the Duke's care. After Astor's chivalric mentor had died in the war he was temporarily reassigned to Duke Reynard as his junior squire. Yet after that angry separation, Yoli feared he may take his frustration out on her little brother, and so was greatly relieved to learn Astor was still safe. And now the war between France and England was done once and for all, both had enough leisure to travel abroad to be reunited with her.

And so in the next hour, one way or another, she would greet them. And she had decided that, one way or another, even if she decided to find a way to extricate herself from her marriage, she wouldn't do so until after they had all returned to Paris. Until then Yolanthe knew they would fuck each other like rabbits — her phrase not mine — every day as if that outcome wasn't a possibility at all.

For no matter what Yolanthe's appetite for the future of their match may be, her appetite for that handsome elder husband remained insatiable. And, she assured herself, the fact he was there at all had signalled he still felt the same. Moreover, the last time they met, Yoli had promised Ren that the next time they met, Eloise would be ready to *join* them. And by that time, Yoli knew that she was.

Demoiselle du Marche had departed Paris a virgin. Yet even before Eloise left Lyon she became another lover of the Duchess de Paris. Shortly thereafter, Nobel had joined their bed. Then while in Rome, both women were introduced to a hedonistic world that utterly defied description. Yes Eloise was ready. And before they reached France, the mercenary duchess hoped to pass the Queen's ward onto the seductive duke, in return for his agreement to let Yoli go.

The fact that Eloise had agreed to return to Paris, yet didn't hope to return to Verona, indicated she was ready to move on. Yoli knew her heart would be heavy at letting the fantasy of Armand go. But for a handsome seducer like Duke Reynard de Paris — particularly if his wife colluded to ensure it — Eloise would be ripe for his picking. And if Eloise shared their bed all the way back to Paris — felt comfortable in his intimacy before that final proposal was suggested — the result of their match together, after Yolanthe's own freedom was finally secured, seemed inevitable to the duchess.

I believe at that time Yolanthe may even have been in love with Eloise. Yet from what I learnt from the duchess years later, from the moment she met Eloise by accident in the queen's company, and her Majesty unwittingly suggested Yoli take the brooding demoiselle abroad, her mercenary intention was to groom the relationship to gain advantage.

At that time she had no notion how much she may dare to create and deepen that relationship. Nor did she know what type of advantage may emerge for her to reap a benefit. She assumed it would be as a broker of marriage to someone for Eloise. She never suspected she may wish to negotiate that match to her own husband.

Now one year later her bond with Eloise was enmeshed. The potential of its full value had come to light. And if the task of securing that bond had provided the duchess with valued companionship and intimate pleasure, so much the better. Moreover Yolanthe understood that an attractive, wealthy and powerful woman such as herself, could attract both men and women like bees to honey. Then once drawn into her closer company, once Yoli understood what a newcomer desperately lacked, she convinced them to embrace an *alternative* she had at her disposal to supply.

And when a target embraces that solution, like Eloise accepting her offer of love as a substitute for what she lacked so desperately, the duchess found that — with little more than the patience required to outlast lingering doubts and resistance — she could easily bend their will to her own.

I know my sober friends, it sounds diabolical. Yet I swear to you that during a moment in our dark future together, the young duchess will candidly confess all such thoughts to me.

'People in need want it to be filled. People in pain want it to end. I sift to reveal which they require. Then I offer the solution and claim our fee.'

'*Our* fee?'

'Everything I do is for the sake of my faction.'

'What is your fee grave woman?'

'They must fulfil my need to my satisfaction or extinguish my pain to my satisfaction. And they must do so until I agree they no longer need to.'

'That sounds like slavery.'

'Not at all. The beauty of my method is that by the time I'm served, those who offer me service *want* to please me and are happy to do so.'

'What about Armand?'

'You know none of that applies to him.'

'Why?'

'I ... well clearly he ... Oh I don't know why. I can't seem to explain it.'

'Love?'

'I'm not sure if I believe in — yes. It's love. Though I prefer to think of it as *obsession*.'

'What would your faction say if they heard you talking like this?'

'They must never hear it.'

'And if I told them?'

'I'd cut out your tongue and shove it down your throat 'til you suffocate.'

'That sounds severe.'

'Then skinny man don't tell and save me the trouble.'

And so as a result of that education the duchess had gained over the previous year, her notion of how the love of any one person may matter to her life, had changed significantly. Oh yes, as you heard there was one *exception*. One man she encountered still made her feel as if she wanted to give all she had just to mean something to him. In the matter of that man, and the woman who stood between them, Yoli was ready to play a long game to get what she wanted.

And no longer did the fact that Armand was married seem like an obstacle to her, merely a challenge. Nor did the fact that he seemed so in love with Ilaria or that Ilaria was so in love with him. Indeed Yoli had dared *herself* to overcome each obstacle, as well as the only obstacle she feared may keep Armand from her once he was ready to be hers — her own marriage to the Duke.

If there was any way Yolanthe could keep Ilaria in the picture, perhaps share Armand with her, even enjoy them together, she may be satisfied to do it. Yet in truth, unlike the pliable Eloise, she couldn't feel sure Ilaria could ever be groomed to accept such a situation. She hoped she may. Yet she feared the premiere dame of Capulet was too much like herself. At that time Yoli felt Ilaria didn't yet understand just how alike they were. But she was already certain that, in all the ways that truly mattered, they were almost identical.

And now if all went well on that Fat Thursday, not only would Yoli, Ren and Eloise enjoy an intimate trip that would end in Yolanthe's ultimate freedom, but Astor would remain with the Capulets.

His welfare was everything to her, but his future was everything to her plan. In time, just as she had promised when she first dangled the lure of his betrothal to the Capulets, Astor would rise to become a count.

Yet to become a true count, one must also become a mercenary leader of hard-bitten soldiers. Yoli felt sure her blonde-haired boy could do that, rise to be a man of cold reputation. Indeed in our future, thanks to the devotion of his sister, Count Astor de Paris would loom large in the Capulet's life, particularly in the lives of two daughters of the rising generation.

But upon that Fat Thursday in Verona, Astor was still a junior squire of thirteen years. Nor was he standing, as Yoli expected, with the prince and princess. Instead the forward thinking Nobel had taken Duke Reynard and Astor to meet Armand, Tristan and Sabatino. And so all the men stood together atop the south-eastern gate. Astor waited to see his big sister, who was apparently about to race naked among a crowd of *ordinaries*. Just why that was happening, he couldn't possibly fathom.

Chapter 27 Countess von Bremmer

Away at the start Yolanthe de Paris was still sulking in her gorgeous carriage, thinking too much and sipping too much. Not far from her conveyance was another elite wagon that displayed the lurid image of a *Rampant Boar*. Having finished my own race I rushed back to the start on my beast — forward this time — to see the runners off and follow them along to the first corner. Thereafter I planned to rush to Saint Fermo and cheer Maxine on when she raced to the finish.

As I halted to hitch my mule I saw the Boar's wagon. The sight of it made me wonder what its team and proprietor may be like. For to say the least, the image that represented them was unmistakeable. Like most such icons — based upon a notion of raging animalistic intent — the boar looked aggressive to the point of viciousness and lecherous to boot.

Below its snout, the head of the beast showed a pair of sharp-ened tusks. And each tusk thrust to either side of a massive lancing tongue! From its head to its ass ran a cropped mane of hair that gave one the sense it was standing on end. Then, to increase its sense of animosity, its reaching hoofs were sharpened too!

Yet if all that were not enough for an observer to recognise its malicious intent, below its waist jutted a hostile erection above a size-able pair of balls. If this boar was rampant the only question seemed to be — was it rampaging in *anger* or *lust* or *both* at once?

And of course next to that wagon, leaning and slouching for all the world like menacing vagrants, stood the five entrants that would oppose our Dragonesses along with a collection of ... others. And there with his *sows* stood their master Luchinus Pugliano Montecchi. Yes, we encountered him once before, during our perilous jaunt through the Western Borgo. A disgraced former cavaliere, Luchinus was considered to be the lost black sheep of the Montecchi flock.

On that occasion he stood at the centre of a line of Montecchi henchman attempting to block our way to the riverside burial ground. Then he was armoured up and dressed for conflict, looking far more warlike. This time Luchinus was dressed for ... well whatever he was dressed for, it was the opposite of war.

And beyond all expectation *Fat Luke* — as so many called him — actually appeared fetching in a boyish way, with deep dimples upon his cheeks. Yes his form was hefty. Yet while he was overfed, once I was able to see so much more of him, I had to admit that he *held his bulk well.* Indeed at this second sight of the man, I had to remind myself he was an infamously harsh and lascivious bordello patriarch.

As you can imagine, the chance to observe such people at close range in daylight and in public, is not a frequent occurrence. And so while I'm sure I should have displayed my open disgust for the sight of them all, I fear that — like so many others standing by — I simply gazed in wonder as the diabolical man ranged among his women, issuing instructions and *helping them prepare.*

For the sake of the latter, Luchinus ran his oiled hands over anyone in reach to ensure his team were as slippery for the course as he appeared to be in life. All the while he scanned about suspiciously. And though exposed to the scrutiny of all watching his display, no body part of any team member was spared from his casual, brazen attention.

I felt sure the presence of a predominantly female audience — including more than a dozen exalted women — seemed to spur on the mongrel in Luchinus to perform. I was told it had been five years since his fall from grace. And so it seemed he was already used to being thought of as a social outcast. What's more he seemed to revel in his pimpish reputation, and loved this yearly wager against Pruetta and the Viking for his Sows to do battle against the Dragonesses.

Our own team confided to Maxine and I that, in the main, Luke didn't appear to care if he won or lost. The entire affair was good for business for all, not just for a week or two thereafter, but for months. Of course he wanted to win if he could. Yet win or lose the wager itself, he wanted the *cost* to his competition — *the damage to their goods that his team could inflict before the end* — to be noteworthy. That's what he would brag about from one race until the next.

However ... this season would be different.

Though we knew nothing of it, this time the Sows had a special task ahead of them. A formidable patron had offered Luke enough incentive to ensure another outcome. This time there was far more to gain than the result of the wager or any damage to the Dragonesses. And so this time, Luchinus paid more attention than usual to the five entrants he chose to run the race in earnest.

As with our Dragonesses, Luke's five were less buxom and more slender through the hips. *Built better for running and fighting than fucking* — Brianna had scoffed. Three other entrants for the Boar hung close by, their newest recruits, entered solely to boost patron interest. By the time they neared the south wall they had instructions to slow to a walk and smile and wave and twirl as they progressed.

That trio wouldn't finish the course or even enter the citadel, but were under orders to skirt the wall and cross into the borgo by the Saint Zeno bridge. And though they'd be walking back naked through those streets, as Montecchi employees with their employer's mark visible for all to see on their person, none would dare harass them in the daylight.

For you see, all the Boar's women carried Luke's brand where only a client would normally see it, burnt upon the left cheek of each ass like the branding of a slave. Luke apparently carried a similar mark himself, not a brand but a birthmark, upon the left cheek of his ass. That mark had inspired his dark notion to display something like it on the rump of his harlots.

That highly illegal measure was a testament to his cruelty of course. Yet it was also evidence of how successfully his powerful faction had managed to keep Luke's foul antics beyond the reach of the law in Verona. And indeed, until I saw one of those marks for myself, having had some interaction with cathouses and the women that worked in them, I didn't expect to find the sight of them or himself disturbing. Yet as I stood observing and each in turn laid hands on the wagon side to offer their backs as he rubbed the oil on, once I realised what that mark really was and guessed how they had received it, my sense of just how dangerous Fat Luke was leapt beyond all comprehension.

And in the cold light of day, still dressed in their Grecian finery, Ilaria, Aurelie and Maxine also watched on. Eight posteriors declared their harsh allegiance to that volatile man as he smeared them with oil. He patted their rumps and smirked, staring at any who dared to glare in protest. All three women stared coldly. Luke leaned into one of his own and whispered. She glanced at our trio and whispered back. Luke's eyes hung upon Ilaria for a moment.

Just as that exchange occurred, my eye was distracted by the sight of a wagon drawing alongside the Cortellani carriage. Clearly displayed upon its leathern coverlets was the sign of the Dragon. And up on the high seat, drawing the team to a halt was the enormous man they called the Viking. For an instant I thought I saw him staring at Ilaria. One instant later I knew that I had.

'Get your eyes off our people Luchinus.' He growled. Or I'll pluck them out to feed to my team!'

'I wasn't looking at your people Gunter!'

'Shut your fat mouth! Anyone in the direction of my people are my people! So little turd, mind your own business if you know what's good for you.'

Cupid's Balls!

It were as if Heaven had sent the Viking just at that moment to put the disgusting lech in his place. Ilaria looked up at the enormous man with a thankful smile as the Dragonesses spilled from the rear, looking ready to do battle.

Next to Gunter sat the Dragon's proprietor Pruetta da Mosto. We'd also only seen her once before very briefly, on the same day we first saw Luchinus. Then she had stood upon a balcony at a distance, taking charge of the rabble in the street, ordering them to let us pass. However no direct conversation had occurred between Ilaria and herself. And so this was the first time they had a genuine chance to meet.

The Viking leapt down with far more agility than any might expect from such a towering man, dwarfing every man or woman in sight. He offered his hand to his employer, the raven-haired daughter of a cooper from Milan. Yet despite Pruetta's humble beginnings and now questionable trade, she was rich. And she dressed to remind all she met that Pruetta da Mosto no longer needed to present a humble façade.

Though not her husband, Gunter was her man. They shared ownership of the business, yet not equally. Pruetta held seventy percent to his thirty. But it seemed the Viking wished for nothing more than Pruetta's love. He protected the Dragon and all connected to it as if they were his own. Pruetta had seen Ilaria just that once, and assumed the woman beside her now was the one who had offered to fund Maxine's madcap idea.

Aurelie's brows lifted as she approached.

'The famous Pruetta I presume?'

'The infamous Donna Cortellani?' Both women smiled. 'It's a pleasure to meet you at last. My girls tell me you're the only woman other than myself who's ever managed to put the fear of God into them.'

'May I call you Pruetta?'

'You may call me Pru. Most people do unless I say they may not.'

'Perfect. This is my sister Ilaria.'

'Of course. The *nice* one.' All three laughed heartily. 'Donna Capulet.'

'Please call me Ilaria. And Ridder von Hartvigson, good afternoon to you.'

Pruetta's eyes opened wide, her lips pressed into a smile. It was rare she stood in his company when any elite person addressed Gunter as befitted his hard-earned knightly rank. To most he was the Viking, the Dragon's gigantic bruiser. It seemed that sobriquet was all she ever heard. It was even more rare to hear anyone use the correct Nordic title to address him, let alone watch on as he received formal kisses in welcome from any elite woman, let alone two.

'Please call me Gunter Madame. Madonna.'

'Yes Gunter but you must call me Ilaria. It's been too long since I saw you last. However I feat that I was very distressed upon the day we met.'

'You had grave cause to be. And I remain deeply ashamed that I allowed —'

'Tush! I won't hear you say a word against yourself. You were without fault. Yet Gunter I have no excuse for not showing you more courtesy *after* the trial. Armand and I owe you a very great debt for your help on that dark day. And for your testimony thereafter. We shall *never* forget it.'

'Oh you are the nice one.' Pruetta grinned.

'As a marshal Ilaria I was just doing my duty. Then in court I told the truth as I'm sworn to do. Yet despite your kind words, since that day I've felt great shame for allowing the chevalier to be ambushed by that woman on my watch.'

'I can attest to that Ilaria. It's haunted him deeply.'

'Oh no Gunter! Please don't say so.'

'It has. But I hope, as a small token of recompense, the girls have been of some assistance.'

'Yes they have. And we love them all. You're both so generous to offer them as you did.'

'Well I intended to charge a hefty sum!' spat Pruetta. 'But this *man* insisted —'

'I would have paid a hefty sum.' Ilaria insisted.

The womanly trio smiled together, as if already fast friends, while the towering Gunter looked comically abashed by his tiny paramour.

'I'm impressed to see you both running. Our team is impressed too.'

'Pruetta if I may, I did want to ask something?'

'Yes Ilaria?'

'The one they call *Falena*.'

'Oh ... Teresa? We have three Falana's. Yes she's a very sweet girl.'

'She is.' Aurelie agreed. 'And we got to know her a little better yesterday.'

'I didn't want to suggest it to *her* until I had a chance to discuss with yourself.' Ilaria added 'However I would be interested in purchasing her contract from you.'

'Indeed?' Pruetta and Gunter blinked their surprise.

'Yes. If yourself — and Teresa of course — are willing. I'd like to offer her work at Sycamore Hill. Or perhaps in our mercantile emporium when it's ready.'

'Ah! You're the one opening an emporium?'

'In partnership with the infamous Donna Cortellani.'

'Aurelie?' said Pruetta. 'Is the nice one going to manage to run an *estate* and an *emporium?*'

'Pru I confess that she shows some potential to be more than just *nice.*'

'I'm in great need of assistance to manage both.'

Pruetta knit her brows. 'Hmm. As for Teresa, Gunter speaks for thirty percent. What do you say vita mia?'

'I say ... Ilaria may have my thirty percent gratis.'

'Gratis!' Pruetta's brows lifted. 'Aurelie does she have this effect on all who negotiate with her?'

'Strangely Pru I'm discovering she does.'

'Well Ilaria if I throw my share in ... *gratis*' Pruetta cast a warning glance at Gunter 'will you consider my errant knight to have paid for his shame in full?'

'He's never been my debtor. But yes. Of course.'

'Then after the race is run, if Teresa agrees, we can draw up a deed.' said Pruetta.

Gunter offered a rare smile and glanced to the start.

'But for now ... you *all* have a race to run.'

'Yes.' Ilaria agreed. 'Yet I'm curious to meet the mystery entrant.'

'If she shows.' quipped Aurelie.

'This *Countess von Bremmer* does seem a mystery.'

'Well by my calculation' Gunter replied 'she has little time left to show her face. But I believe that' he pointed a massive finger 'is her conveyance.'

Every eye glanced toward the sight of a darkly lavish carriage that stood near Fat Luke's wagon.

Every opening was shut tight.

'Oh. It's been there all this time.' said Ilaria. 'Yet without a peep of movement.'

The warning ratchet of the race marshal sounded. Every competitor who hadn't yet approached the starting place, began to do so. Ilaria glanced toward an entirely different carriage and touched Aurelie's arm.

'Please excuse us. We have one last entry to solicit.'

A moment later Ilaria and Aurelie rapped upon the carriage's window frame. The leathern coverlet rose to reveal Yolanthe de Paris sipping wine from an exquisite silver beaker. She looked them up and down in their Grecian finery and raised her sceptical brows.

'I'm naked in here darlings and my nipples are hard as nails. I hoped a wash of stiff wine might relax them.' She glanced at her chest. 'Hmm. Not as yet.'

'But you *are* running with us?'

'Oh ... yes I am. But I won't emerge from here until you're both naked out there.'

Ilaria signalled for Fabrizio. He arrived in haste. A moment later, she and Aurelie unfastened their wraps and he received them with great care.

'Who's that young man?'

'Armand's junior squire Fabrizio.'

'Ah! The infamous *Fabrizio*! Lover of young harlots. Well junior Adonis, when I emerge you must tell me how ravishing I am.'

Fabrizio glanced at Ilaria who nodded slightly.

'Of course your Grace.'

Yolanthe handed her beaker to him through the window. The door swung open. Her own equerry hurried in to lower the folding step, offering a dutiful hand as the naked form of Yolanthe de Paris made a grand exit, then reached for her beaker again. And sweet friends I must confess, each time I saw her this way made me feel I had stepped into a maestro's studio while a model for Venus took a moment to relax from her posing.

Her blazing carotene hair was coiffured as if for a grand ball rather than an athletic event. She had no oil on her skin nor sandals on her feet. Yes I've described her before, yet it won't tire me to do it again. She isn't what one may call muscular but the duchess is tall, buxom yet somewhat lithe. Some people have a gift of tending to slenderness no matter how much they consume or how little they ask of their bodies. That gift seemed to run in her family.

Yolanthe was the great grandchild of a crusader who married a hard living, barefooted shepherdess. Now her own bare feet — with immaculately glossed toenails — felt the sodden turf beneath them. Unlike her hard-muscled ancestress however, not since Yoli was a demoiselle had she indulged in stern physical toil for an extended period of time — except to dance, hunt or make love of course. Indeed she felt that strolling, dancing, hunting and lovemaking should be an elite woman's sole sources of exertion.

'Your Grace.' said Fabrizio gazing.

'Yes young Adonis?'

'You are indeed a vision of beauty.'

'Hmm? Liar.'

'Fabrizio's sworn never to lie.' said Ilaria 'You know Armand would never allow it.'

Yolanthe's brows lifted. 'Interesting. I like him.'

'Oh everyone loves Fabio.' Ilaria smiled. 'But where is Eloise?'

'Alas I had to insist she forego this adventure.'

'Oh?'

'Yes darling. I sent her to recuperate at the bathhouse. You remember it.'

'Oh the same? Yes it was very elegant and inviting.'

'She was so badly marked from that encounter with the men. And not just her eye darling, Eloise was covered in bruises. I was so shocked to see the toll she paid that I insisted the Kazans fetch a medicus to be sure nothing was too damaged. I never should have encouraged her to do that. Yet by now, she's in a pool of sweet-smelling hot water.'

'Now I think I envy her.'

'Yes Ria. Next time we see our tomboy she'll be dressed like a princess, posing on the wall with Ren and Astor, smiling wickedly as we scamper by naked.'

'We can look for her there Yoli. Come along.'

'If I make it that far!' She turned to Fabrizio. 'Well little Adonis, one last gulp for courage.' She took the beaker and drained it. 'Ah yes. That's better my darling.'

Aurelie smiled. 'Isn't this exciting?'

'Exciting?' Yolanthe brows lifted. 'Ria is she sincere? Why darlings this is total fucking *madness!*'

Aurelie burst into laughter. She linked an arm with one of Yolanthe's while Ilaria linked with the other.

'Come along mighty duchess.' said Ilaria.

'Yes girls. Lead me on.'

They wandered toward the line.

Maxine approached with the Dragonesses in tow who had received final instructions from Pruetta. Maxine was not of her employ, she ran for herself that day. Yet as their go between and part mentor, my wife also felt responsible for the quality of their showing.

Now the eyes of many who stood amassed at the start, including Ilaria and Aurelie, couldn't resist glancing at the only elite conveyance that was yet to reveal a passenger. The mysterious Countess von Bremmer's carriage remained shut. Not unlike the Paris and Cortellani carriages, it was also Germanic, yet larger and appeared even more luxuriant.

'ONE minute!' came the crier's booming voice. 'The marshal insists all who would run MUST take their places!'

With that brusque final call, every wandering eye turned upon the course.

Nerves fluttered. Maxine hung with a jar of oil, still anxiously lathering patches on any body part she felt was too dry. Ilaria's bust was wrapped in tough canvas like Maxine's, now lathered inside and out to resist the chafing she had begun to feel from the stouter fabric.

'Maxine give the duchess a lathering.' said Aurelie.

'Maxine touch me with that and I'll break your fucking hands.'

Giggling erupted around them as many glanced at the tall elegant woman. She appeared more ready to plunge into a bath than run a barefoot race through the muddy marsh.

'My skin can't abide thick oils. I'll be fine. After all, who's going to lay their hands on a duchess?'

'I will sweetheart if you get in my way.' growled a menacing rival behind her.

Yolanthe turned to glare and opened her mouth to respond but was halted.

'Make way there for her Excellence! Make way for Countess von Bremmer.'

All eyes turned. The door of the sumptuous carriage was hanging open. A serving woman with flawless light skin, blue eyes and carotene hair — the image of an elder sister to Yolanthe — drove a path from the rear.

'Stand aside.' she urged in a Gallic accent. 'Make way for the Count and Countess.'

Being drawn by the hand of a tall foreboding man of rank, presumably Count von Bremmer, came his wife. Some men come by such titles through sycophantic favour or hereditary succession, without earning it as a military leader. One glance at this man however left no doubt which type was approaching us. His face and hands were littered with the scars of battle. And his sumptuous couture couldn't hide the muscular frame that filled it.

The Gallic server ducked under the breasting line, turning to face them. The count did the same as his countess came forward. The woman was as tall as Yolanthe but lean and hard. Like an ancient gladiatrix, her olive toned torso and thighs rippled with muscle. Yet her face was covered with a sheer veil that reached to the base of her nose. It hung, in the style of an Egyptian Priestess, from a wide silver band in the centre of her forehead, beneath the line of her tightly tied, raven-coloured hair.

And despite the festival's theme that every entrant be treated as equals, led by such a foreboding and exalted man, no-one had dared to block the woman's approach as she came on to stand wherever she chose. Then, by way of allowing her husband to take his leave, the mystery woman dipped under the line and straightened to kiss him. The moment revealed a back flexing with muscle that rippled at the slightest movement. She lifted both hands to caress his scarred cheeks, tilting her head as their lips met softly.

Anyone watching could be forgiven for feeling they must have been enamoured of each other for some time. In truth as I watched from a distance, there was a lingering moment when I felt she was loathe to leave the safety of his company. Nevertheless she turned, bobbed under the line and turned again. He pressed his fingertips to his lips.

'I'll see you at the end my soul. We'll leave as soon as its done.'

'Yes darling I can't wait.' she purred. 'Thank you.'

To my ear there was something in that voice.

The Count stalked away without a backward glance. The server stepped forward to lift the delicate veil up and over the countess's head, tucking it firmly into the folds of her tied hair. She retreated a half-step to assess, yet before she turned upon her heel to follow the Count, she seemed to catch the eye of someone who stood just behind her mistress.

Ilaria could no longer resist her need to know.

She leaned slightly, turning her head to see past Yolanthe who stood beside her and between herself and the stranger. Then her eyes leapt wide in stark recognition. It was the bitch herself. Somehow Esmeralda Montecchi had become resurrected as Countess von Bremmer.

A shining new band on her finger attested to the fact Esmeralda was no longer a widow. And the evidence of that kiss declared that, less than a year since her foul former husband died in disgrace, Esmeralda had moved on from any need to suggest she still held any vestige of passion for him. Not than any who ever knew Onorato would wonder at that.

Ilaria's heart was already racing. Aurelie blinked in surprise. Yolanthe however, who only knew Esmeralda by sight from the trial, seemed to find the drama of her entrance amusing. As that exalted final entrant took her time to settle, the marshal watched with care, almost as if he anticipated the need to wait. Now all four women, Ilaria, Yolanthe, Esmeralda and Aurelie stood side by side. Suddenly the front rank had become filled with incredibly potent women.

The marshal gulped. The previous year he had dealt with a princess alone among the common entrants. She was very much loved and that proved to be less worrisome than he anticipated. This year he understood that two prima donnas had entered. Yet he hadn't expected to deal with a Germanic Countess, let alone a French Duchess who now appeared tipsy too boot.

Esmeralda's head turned slowly to the right. Her dark eyes rested on Ilaria. The erratic rhythm of Ilaria's heart began to skip and pound. I saw her instinct to lift her hand to allay it. Yet she pushed it back down, not wanting the bitch to see she was affected. Aurelie saw it too.

'And so Esmay ... you're the mystery countess?'

Esmeralda's head turned to face front.

'A mystery no longer Aurelie.'

'You vanished completely. All Verona thought you were gone for all time. Yet here you are.'

'Here I am.'

'It appears since your recent ... misfortunes ... you've found fortune again.'

'I have. Thanks to my *famiglia* and the emperor's sincere interest.'

'The emperor? Interesting. Well, however you came by it, I'm glad to see that you're safe.'

'Are you?'

'So am I Esmeralda.' Ilaria offered contritely.

Though she managed to say so, Ilaria continued to reel, not only from the shock of seeing the phantom again, but the imposition being in such close proximity.

Aurelie smiled. 'You remember Ilaria of course.'

'Of course.' she replied, staring straight ahead.

'Oh and allow me to introduce our dear friend, her Grace Duchess de Paris.'

Esmeralda didn't look surprised. Nor did she seem impressed by the title. Yet despite that. And despite Yolanthe being ten years her junior, for the sake of caution Esmeralda couldn't risk failing to acknowledge her. She turned slightly to note the more exalted woman.

'Your Grace. I recall you from the castle. You were standing with that *Jew*.'

Intending to deride Nobel and rankle the duchess, she let the word linger on her lips. But Yolanthe was already used to fending off taunts aimed at her ally. She caught Esmeralda's eyes, pale blue gazing into black, and smiled seductively. Yoli was affected by wine and knew it. Moreover one glance at this hard-bodied countess suggested she wouldn't keep pace with her on the course. This would be the only chance she would have to rankle Esmeralda in return before watching her tight ass run away before her.

'You're referring to my business partner Sieur August Nobel? He *is* memorable Countess ... for being the richest merchant from Venice to Paris. I consider him exalted company. Yet look what exalted company I'm managing to keep right here, barefoot and naked in a marshy field to the south of Verona.'

'Life's full of surprises Duchess.'

'It is Countess. And if memory serves, last time I saw you I was *very* surprised at your appearance before all, barefoot in rags, hair shorn like a hapless sheep however ...' Yoli leaned as if to inspect her 'now I see it's grown a little. Oh and that nasty wound has finally healed into a ... rather noticeable scar.'

As Yolanthe responded, rather than confront her detractor Esmeralda turned slowly to stare at Ilaria — her expression a grim mask of intent.

'Healed Duchess?' she hissed. 'Not at all. Some wounds will never heal.' Esmeralda turned to Yolanthe.

At the Race Marshal's urging, hoping to halt their chatter the Master Crier cleared his throat.

'However Duchess ... I didn't come her to talk.'

'Mmm?' Aurelie put in. 'Which begs the question Esmay. Why did you come? Von Bremmer's not only Germanic but geographic. Have you retired up into the alps for a life of solitude?'

'He has — *we* have a castle on the northern border.' she purred in reply. 'I returned here to purchase a palazzo for us and to fulfil two promises.' Ilaria's heart sunk to hear it. 'Brother Eustace made it a final condition of my penance to run. And so here I am.'

'The other promise?'

A louder clearance of phlegm sounded.

'I'm afraid the marshal waits upon our pleasure. So do these good women. And ...' she smiled 'I have no more stomach for talking to French whores.'

Yolanthe's brows lifted. She glanced at the marshal with a wan smile.

'Yes poor man. He does look nervous or excited.' Yolanthe purred. 'I fear it's hard to tell with so many whores about. Yet now you've joined us, perhaps it's the latter. I heard he has a penchant for soiled Portuguese pussy.'

Ilaria gulped in shock. Aurelie grinned. In a flashing moment Esmeralda's hand lifted, nails arching to strike. Yet before she could strike the tipsy duchess, a mighty shove from behind sent Yoli sprawling onto the wet muddy road.

'I warned you!' screamed the rival from behind who I now recognised as an entrant from the Boar.

She hovered in menace as Ilaria and Aurelie helped Yolanthe to her feet. Her face, front and gorgeous hair were spattered in slush as she drew herself to stand. She glared at her assailant, who glared back with intent.

'You're not a fancy woman here sweetheart. Shut your trap so we can get on with it.'

A second sow stood menacingly at her shoulder.

'And show some RESPECT to widow Montecchi' spat the second 'or ELSE!'

With that it became apparent that Fat Luke's team had known Esmeralda's identity before she was unveiled. Unknown to us — since his own fall from grace — Luchinus Montecchi had become deeply indebted to the former primo don and prima donna. And was still her loyal henchman.

'Madonnas! Madonnas please!' The emphatic marshal bustled

over to face them. 'I beg you to stay poised for the start.' He glanced at Yoli. '*Scusi* Madonna Duchess?'

'Yes nervous man.'

'We're very late your Grace. May I *please* proceed? I've never started late before!'

Yolanthe smiled, turning on her abuser. 'You see *sweetheart*. He asks *my* permission to proceed. Your world is much bigger than this little gathering. And your life may be much longer than this little race.'

The tall sow lifted her hand in anger. Her partner wrenched an arm over her elbow.

'Marietta!' she hissed.

'Fuck off Priscilla she asked for it.' spat the Amazon.

'*She's* not the one.' Prisicilla said. '*Stick* to the plan!'

The elder glanced venomously. Her junior had said too much, making Ilaria, Aurelie and Maxine suspect deeper trouble was afoot which Yoli's provocation had drawn to the surface. Suspicion rose further when a warning glance from Esmeralda drove the mouthy pair back.

Although brief, those loose remarks had been heard and begged two glaring questions.

What *was* the plan?

Who was the one?

Yolanthe smiled at the Race Marshal.

'*Monsieur Maréchal* ... you may proceed.'

The gruff marshal smiled despite himself. He drew a cuff across his brow to wipe away the sweat, bowed and returned to his post.

Somehow it was simpler to bring a host of elite men to heel. Most were soldiers, used to heeding athletic commands. Yet since the introduction of the women's race — particularly when exalted women attended — he struggled to balance his authority against an instinct to pay deference to such potent members of the opposite sex.

His hand lifted.

The ratchet whirred!

'Stand ready!' boomed the crier startling every woman in sight.

The marshal scanned again.

'Hold to your marks! Hold for the bell!'

The crier's head snapped at the warden's once more. The barrier leapt up.

The crier yanked at the bell, launching a passionate stampede of women onto the gruelling course.

It was a great relief for the marshal, crier and wardens to literally see the backs of them all.

Yet every man gazed in wonder, and for as long as possible, at the extraordinary sight that ran on before them.

But for some in that frantic throng, racing ahead of them, it only took a matter of moments for suspicion to become recognition. For just as Esmeralda's muscular back, ass and legs drew forward, five posteriors bearing the Boar's scorched brand drew in behind her.

From the very beginning, a wall of defence was formed around Countess von Bremmer as she strode on like a goddess, water splashing underfoot at every bound. Not only did the Sows intend to defeat the Dragonesses, they seemed to have orders to ensure their reborn patron remained at the fore, free from the hinderance of rivals.

Yet now the race was on.

The course was full of rivals.

And our team had their orders too.

Chapter 28 Battle Cry

Five Dragonesses ran on together with the Sows in their sights. And despite the unlikelihood that Yolanthe would manage to keep pace with the fore, Ilaria, Aurelie and Maxine had no intention of running among the rearmost. They had trained hard and didn't expect to win, yet they didn't plan to sit back timidly either. Indeed Maxine started next to Brianna and found herself running at their head with the amazon while Ilaria and Aurelie ran hard on their heels. Brianna extended her right arm to her side, raised a knife edge hand from the elbow and lowered it forward.

The Dragonesses began to surge.

As the rest of the field drew out behind them, Yolanthe found herself trotting in the company of the Boar's three special envoys. Unlike their team mates racing ahead, it seemed that trio — like the sobering duchess — were in no great hurry. It began to appear to Yolanthe those three were on a very different style of errand. She began to suspect more trouble for herself. Perhaps since causing them so much grief at the start, they were told to loiter and repay a portion of it?

She noticed them whispering and glancing. She braced for an approach. The effect of their presence behind sobered her more quickly. Then to her surprise first one, then another and the third trotted alongside, breathlessly introducing themselves as they ran. Thanks to the Race Marshal it was no secret that the tall siren was a French duchess.

Yes, the trio were Fat Luke's newest recruits. Yet despite the torturous branding they had received — indeed because of it — they felt no allegiance to their vicious pimp. And now he too was already far ahead of them, gone in their wagon to collect the others at the finish. And so until they reached the wall, they had all agreed to see if they could benefit from a show of amity to the potent foreign visitor.

It wasn't the first time the young duchess had attracted hopeful sycophants. Yet under these circumstances — the shove she received from their fellow at the start, the sight of their brands the trio were at pains to display to her — made Yolanthe more responsive than usual.

'Run in front of me girl.' Yolanthe leaned to see. 'Tits of Venus! That must have hurt?'

'I cried for hours.' said sycophant one.

'That fucker! It hurt for days!' said sycophant two.

'He doesn't care!' said sycophant three.

'Save us from him!' one pleaded again.

'We're trapped prima Madonna!' echoed two.

'We want to work for you!' three pleaded.

'You *all* want my protection?'

'Yes Madonna Duchess.'

'Please help us escape him.'

'Take us away with you.'

'Hmm. First you must protect *me*. Then after the race, if I'm satisfied with your efforts ... I'll consider it.'

The desperate trio exchanged furtive glances then nodded emphatically. Yolanthe de Paris had struck yet another agreement in Verona. While ahead at the fore, the first mile warden waved on the lone figure of Countess von Bremmer.

Close behind, with the one they called *Marietta* at their head, Esmeralda's line of defence ran firmly. Their leader scanned left and right, then spun a pirouette without breaking stride.

Led by Brianna and Maxine the Dragonesses were closing the gap with every stride. Yet hovering closer to Marietta's team were three independent rivals who would clearly be first to challenge their line. One was a young laundress from the western borgo, stoutish and shortish but bursting with speed. Pressing on their heels boldly, she was eyeing a gap between the outer pair on their right wing. As Marietta flashed by the warden, his waving distracted her for a moment and the laundress surged for the gap.

Marietta glanced back and screamed a blunt command.

'Show that bitch OUT!'

Four rampant sows showed massive grins. Marietta's call had

mimicked the command Fat Luke loved to bellow at his henchman to set them upon a wayward patron. Her underlings glanced for an instant to assess their danger.

SMASH! The back of a curled fist pounded into the intruder's face. The head of the laundress snapped back. She swayed and shunted then lifted a hand to launch in retaliation. Yet before she could do it an elbow thumped HARD from the opposite side straight into her torso! The laundress curled in pain and cursed but wasn't done. SHOVING hard to her right, she forced the flanking sows apart.

Swinging left, the laundress spurred on and then, hot with rage, SMASHED the back of her right fist into the cheek of another. It drove her victim back but drew the scowling form of Marietta across to bear down on her mercilessly. In a bursting effort to evade their grim leader, the laundress faltered on a rut beneath her flashing feet!

She teetered for an instant. In that moment Marietta swooped without hesitation, laying an open hand on the back of the laundress's head. Then surging in an unexpected sprint, Marietta drove her victim beyond her own pace and THRUST down! An unseen foot smacked the victim's ankle from the other side. The laundress stumbled. Despicable teamwork had executed diabolical tactics to perfection. Marietta grinned as her victim spilt forward and SMACKED face forward into the muddy ground.

Ahead of them all Esmeralda strode on in comfort without a backward glance or any modicum of response. It were as if Diana herself ran alone through the woods upon the hunt. The five harlots behind her howled with delight. That first melee was their warning to all. Indeed the other two challengers had slackened their pace to fall back for a moment, far more hesitant to try their luck.

For an instant Marietta spun upon her heel to face the coming threat. She bared her teeth as she ran, spreading her arms open wide, motioning with her fingertips like the walking legs of two tarantulas.

'Come on you little BITCHES! Come and GET some!'

Again she channelled her employer's lurid spirit and by the time she shouted that challenge her right wing had reformed. Yet during

Marietta's tussle with the laundress, behind her at the head of the dragonesses, Brianna had been busy. Having watched on with interest like a general upon a battlefield, she now signalled her own quartet to reassemble their line. Brianna directed each to form up behind the sow that appeared to be the most fit match for their purpose.

Brianna placed herself behind the bragging Marietta. As the two-mile warden — too distracted to wave his hands — watched Esmeralda approach and run past him unmolested, Brianna called her Dragonesses into the attack.

'Charge Dragonesses! Fly for me girls!' she cried in mimic of Tristan.

'Cortellani and the Dragon!' they shouted in reply.

Their Cortellani cry urged Esmeralda to risk a backward glance. Every dragoness had stirred to the call. Knowing every other runner would attempt to conserve their energy for the distance to come, Brianna led them on.

As the rivals closed in upon each other pandemonium erupted as all went to Hell in a haycart!

Fists, feet and elbows swung hard into cheeks, chins, torsos and ribs. Nails dug into oiled skin, scraping and slipping. One nose broke, bleeding profusely, then another. But though that season's melee had finally erupted, Brianna sensed that something was different. By that point, they should be sprawled upon the ground in pairs, bashing and biting like wildcats. In a moment of clarity she realised the Sows were trapped by new orders to protect a patron who ran on with no hint of acknowledgment. And to fulfill that unexpected task, they must all stay on their feet and keep moving.

But her own girls were trapped by a need to give chase and bring them down. Brianna knew the surest way to win Pruetta's wager was to disable their competition. The surest way to disable the Sows was to bring them to ground and smash them all. But for nearly a mile more as they ran on, Marietta's bitches lunged and struck, then ran clear to evade, not daring to be drawn into the kind of tangle that would allow a Dragoness to take any down.

Brianna knew she must try something more drastic. Every year their battle had erupted further back on the course, far enough from the citadel for the wardens not to care and leave them to their sport. Yet in one more mile the south-east corner would be looming. Then their antics would be witnessed by all and scrutinised more grimly.

Brianna surged at Marietta and struck again. The fiery rival fended the blow from behind and scanned about desperately. Marietta's eyes widened in panic to realise that during all the push and shove among pairs of rivals, gaps along their line had opened. Maxine and Aurelie, now running together, were closing in fast, aiming for a gap as they jostled with other rivals at their shoulders. All were threatening to spill through Marietta's line and throw the competition wide open against her fearful new patron.

The widest gap was open upon the left. Unseen behind Maxine and Aurelie, Ilaria swerved past them to surge for that gap, followed by the plucky laundress, blood still streaming from her brow and covered in grime from head to foot. And despite all Marietta's tussling and evasion with Brianna, she kept her eyes scanning feverishly. The face of every rival in sight seemed to sense it was time to start closing the gap to the fore or risk giving up too great a lead to claw it back later.

Brianna hung close the Sow's leader, considering her chance of leaping in to tackle Marietta, of bringing her down now to force the issue. Then to Brianna's surprise, as that flurry of rivals pressed hard at her enemy's line, Marietta's real instructions were suddenly revealed when a look of horror rose on her face. Brianna's head turned to see what had caused Marietta's reaction.

Upon the Sow's left wing *the one* was breaking through. Scowling like gargoyle, Marietta suddenly veered. Brianna reached desperately to grab her. But Marietta SMASHED down hard, swerving left, screaming as she went.

'To ME! To ME! Get that blonde BITCH!'

Every Sow heeded her call. Left and right they ran in together as Marietta ducked and RAMMED her shoulder straight into Ilaria's waist.

'URRGGGHHH!' A grunting gasp exhaled.

They hit the ground in a tumbling scraping heap.

Completely unaware, Maxine and Aurelie ran on in pursuit of Esmeralda. One moment later, they were snapping at her heels. Maxine scanned around, expecting to see a following smile on Ilaria's face. Instead brutal chaos had erupted behind her. She gripped Aurelie's arm in panic. Both heads turned and their eyes leapt at the sight.

On the ground behind them, as her bitches swarmed in, a rampant Marietta had straddled Ilaria's chest, thighs locked tight, she SMASHED furiously with both fists. Ilaria tried desperately to cover her face until a cackling sow dropped down at her head, grappling for her wrists. Ilaria flailed and wrenched to keep her hands free. She felt extra hands shoving. Marietta had halted for an instant to aid her accomplice. Suddenly Ilaria's hands were hauled above her head and pinned hard against the ground.

Marietta screamed with delight! Ilaria turned her face away. A hand gripped hard to wrench it back. Marietta glared like a demon.

'Pretty face little bitch!'

Marietta's free hand leapt out and SWUNG back hard, SMACK-ING for all she was worth AGAIN and AGAI

'UGGGHHHH.' Ilaria groaned as one hand released and the other gripped her face, to unleash a flurry of furious blows exchanging from left to right. Like a pair of thrashing sticks, the fists of each arm smashed IN and OUT. Ilaria gasped for breath, twisting desperately in an attempt to wrench a hand free again to protect herself. Her lips were split, her nose was broken, her eye socket was expanding. Fingernails raked the skin under her arms. Then in helpless horror Ilaria felt someone, hidden behind Marietta's back, grip tight on her right ankle. Her leg lifted up to a cackling chorus of delight.

A kick SMASHED into Ilaria's thigh. 'AGGGHHHH.'

The searing pain caused a BURST of resistance to explode within her. Ilaria shunted savagely to free her foot and fend off the unseen assault. Yet before she could free herself a flurry of kicks poured in brutal retaliation, THUMPING into her leg and ass. Then despite the beating to Ilaria's face, her eyes jumped wide in horror.

Another unseen hand GRIPPED her left ankle. Snorts of ribald laughter exploded as her legs spread apart. Then the voice of Priscilla, the one who had all but revealed their plan at the start, suddenly filled her with terror.

'Now I'll give her something to remember!'

Ilaria braced hard, hips bucking in terror when the flash of a bare foot passed before her. Suddenly the weight of Marietta on her chest was wrenched aside. Confusion wracked her mind for an instant. The Dragonesses wore sandals. Who was her saviour? There standing over Ilaria, puffing like a spent charger, yet looking supremely satisfied with herself was Yolanthe de Paris.

In the instant Marietta had tumbled, Ilaria's hands and feet had been released. While Yolanthe helped her damaged ally to her feet, Ilaria scanned about groggily. Each Dragoness was wrestling savagely with whatever Sow they had managed to lay hands on. Then from the ground right beside them, Marietta rose to her feet with murder in her eyes for Yolanthe. She exploded in a RAGE reaching and lurching. Ilaria shunted to shield her friend but with no warning at all Brianna's HURTLING form SLAMMED shoulder-first into Marietta's waist. Their blunt collision, more sickening than Ilaria's own downfall moments before, had forced the same exhaling grunt from its unwitting victim.

The largest pair of rivals SMACKED into the ground, wrestling like wildcats, bucking and squirming. Yet in the time one may count three, in a fit of blistering speed Brianna had shunted herself about to clamber over Marietta and pin her onto her back.

'FUCK you BRIANNA!' Marietta bellowed.

A relentless flurry of blows from Brianna pelted Marietta's face in reply. The Sow tucked her fists and elbows hard against each other to shield from that onslaught as Maxine and Aurelie arrived.

'Ria are you hurt? Mercy your nose! Your lip!'

'I'm hurt but...' She stared at Brianna. 'I can run.'

'Then we must go quickly!' Aurelie urged.

'Mistress if we stay any more than a moment —'

'Yes ...' Ilaria muttered still gazing in wonder.

Despite her peaceful nature — despite the violent beating Brianna was unleashing at her feet — Ilaria's sense of pity for Marietta had been shattered. Now she felt a disturbing reaction. Having just experienced that horror herself at Marietta's hands, for the first time a lack of sympathy was surging through her. It was driven by a burning need to see her abuser taught a lesson she would never forget, though Ilaria wasn't sure that would be the result in Marietta's case.

Yet also in that brief moment, as Ilaria felt compelled to watch on, she realised there was something more. Unlike herself when attacked, the hard woman's instinct to shield herself in that way wasn't an instinct that Ilaria shared. What's more Ilaria realised, that if this was the manner of danger a woman may be exposed to — living away from the shelter of a life lived near her parents — then she had very little skill to deal with such threats.

Imagining the ability to defend oneself was one thing. Having the ability and the mind to activate it was another. Even Yolanthe, in an effort to defend a stricken ally, hadn't wavered for an instant when she drove the ball of her foot through Marietta's face. It seemed the House of Paris had prepared their own premiere dame rather differently.

Unwittingly, as the Dragon's head harlot bashed the Boar's hardest bitch into submission, she offered the *nice one* a tutorial on just how violently inflicted some of life's lessons may be. As Ilaria watched on, all that flashed through her mind in just a fleeting matter of moments. Now Brianna's face, blood streaming from her own broken nose taken before she managed to arrive, had become a dread mask of intent.

She reached her left hand over the barrier of Marietta's forearms, gripped the furthest wrist hard and wrenched the covering arms to her left. That first tug was resisted stoutly. Brianna's lips pressed, eyes squinting, the muscles on her stomach flexed hard as she tightened to wrench the arm again. That second wrench gained purchase and Brianna leaned, shifted and shoved her weight down through her left arm, pinning the forearms aside.

Brianna's free hand lifted a merciless fist. With that protection gone, Marietta turned her face to compress it, just as Ilaria had done, just as a child might do.

THUMP! Brianna smashed the unprotected cheek. THUMP! THUMP!

The third blow smacked down, resisted by hysteric tension in Marietta's neck and face. THUMP! The nose broke to a grunt of satisfaction. THUMP! THUMP! Marietta's cheek was shattered. Her energy faltered. Each thumping fist rose back higher. Each fell more heavily. Each blow drew a grunt of pain. Each grunt had less voice and breath until Marietta's body fell limp in surrender.

Brianna heard appeals, felt hands drawing her off. She stood and blinked at Aurelie, Yolanthe and Ilaria.

'One down.' she muttered. Scanning about she saw every Dragoness was embroiled with a rival. Brianna scanned ahead. In the matter of moments it had taken for the battle to erupt and reach that climax, Esmeralda had spun upon her heel to trot rearward as she watched with some interest, expanding the distance.

Brianna met her eyes.

Esmeralda smiled, turned and ran on.

'BITCH!' spat Brianna. 'She'll win without a fight.'

'Perhaps not.' said Ilaria. 'It's still a long run. If anyone can catch her it's Teresa and Fiametta. Yoli and Max, help me with Teresa. You two get Fiametta.'

A moment later three pairs of hands drew Teresa from her rival, kicking and screaming as Fiametta was rescued from a mismatched brawl that threatened to hurt her badly. Her incensed rival broke free in a mad daze. Then seeing herself outnumbered, burst away to escape in the wrong direction.

'Come on ladies!' Ilaria called taking flight. 'Catch up and run together.'

The pack converged at a faster trot with Ilaria at their head. Aurelie smiled to see her taking charge.

'They won't risk lifting their pace' Ilaria cried 'until they reach Herb Market Square!'

'Teresa! You and Metta must run on together.'

'No!' cried Teresa.

'Yes! But you must take care and protect each other.'

'But Angel —'

'Teresa GO! Take Fiametta and run that bitch down!'

Both girls grinned. They'd heard Ilaria curse in fun. Yet neither expected to hear the *nice one* curse in anger.

'Yes Madonna!' cried Fiametta.

Fiametta grabbed the still-reluctant Teresa by the arm They ran on together. Once they were a short distance away, Teresa spun on her heel, running rearward, staring at Ilaria.

'But Angel we must stay to protect *you*.'

Aurelie shouted. 'Until this is over Teresa you still work for ME! And I say GO!'

'GO Teresa!' Ilaria pleaded. 'I'm surrounded by help. Remember your promise on the tower! Rise and FIGHT!'

The sight of a freed sow slipping past Teresa was finally enough to spur her on. It was Priscilla, the loudmouth who warned them all to show respect to widow Montecchi and who bragged she was going to kick Ilaria so hard that she'd never forget it. Teresa scowled and turned to give chase.

In their wake, our team followed at a rising trot while Brianna, all but spent from her exertions in the melee, began to trail behind them. Further back, where Marietta still lay, the trio who had followed Yolanthe too slowly to aid her against their own team, ambled towards the limp form of their leader.

Marietta was groaning and writhing, perhaps in an attempt to revive herself. The trio knelt to rouse her as a gaggle of the slowest contenders, puffing and panting, trickled past them. Two other sows who had managed to escape the onslaught also returned to aid Marietta, lifting her to sit, then onto her feet.

They assisted Marietta to walk gingerly. After just a few steps she shoved them aside in a rage. Grimacing and cursing, then broke into a slow painful trot.

'Don't just stand there!' She screamed at the duet. 'Catch up with the others!'

Both minions hovered for a moment, expecting her to fall.

Somehow she remained on her feet and her scowl spurred them on. However the sensual trio, still hovering, spent a moment wondering if they were also meant to run ahead. Yet the effort to do so was clearly beyond, if not their bodies, at least their will. Instead they trotted on quietly with Marietta, far too frightened to utter a sound. Unexpectedly Marietta slowed and began to walk, then limp, upon her left leg.

'Help me you fucking imbeciles.'

Eyes widened in fear. The three new recruits scurried in to assist, one lowering under each arm to offer support. Now running last they came on together as Marietta lifted her head. Her gut wrenched to see the form of Brianna trotting back toward them. The trio quaked as Marietta braced for another assault. Then to their utter confusion, as Brianna came abreast she turned upon her heel to walk alongside.

Marietta glared savagely. 'FUCK you Brianna!'

'Calm down tough bitch. Truce.'

'FUCK your truce!'

'Really? Fatso's gone to the finish. Neither of *us* will catch up. You three!'

'Us?' the trio quailed in tandem.

'Who else! Rietta and me are finishing together so you three can fuck off.'

The trio spurred on in fear.

'Stupid bitches!' hissed Brianna. 'Get back behind us!' The trio halted. 'We're not coming last!'

'That's for fucking sure.' Marietta agreed. 'But we're not walking in either.'

Brietta lifted her brows. 'You can run?'

'No thanks to you bitch.'

Brietta pouted. 'Alright then. Slow.' They began to trot together. 'I've had enough of this shit for one year.'

By the time Esmeralda reached the four-mile warden under the eyes all upon the wall, Fiametta and Teresa had caught up with the foremost still lagging behind her. Yet she had gained such an advantage from Marietta's assault, that a hundred-yard gap still lay open between herself and the next challenger. That lead shielded Esmeralda from any urgent need to drain her own energy, so she ran on at her leisure.

The audience she approached had no knowledge Esmeralda was entered of course. Nor did they have any notion of what had transpired in the distance which had set the running order as it now appeared before them. And so in ignorance — most failing to recognise the fallen prima donna — they cheered wildly at the sight of the leader to spur her on.

Among our party of men however — though it took a moment to be sure — Armand and Sabatino recognised her. They dreaded to think how mortified Ilaria must have been to have encountered Esmeralda at the start. And the very fact, after all which had occurred, that she was here in this way, made Armand wonder what else she may be capable of.

All at once the warnings of a rumoured Montecchi bastard entering the men's race took on more significance. Even from the height of the wall, the livid scar where the crossbow bolt had scored Esmeralda's cheek was now visible. The sight of it tossed his mind back to that grisly moment. Armand never saw Esmeralda being struck. By then her foul husband had dropped to his knees, a wound gaping at the back of his thigh where, in a cold moment to cut him down or be killed himself, Armand's dagger had sliced it through.

Intent on mercy Armand had stepped behind Onorato to offer him a chance to yield, not knowing Esmeralda was hidden high up in the arena terraces, armed with a bow. Yet he felt the massive thud as her arrow hit his back. Thereafter Armand fell to Onorato's side and remembered nothing more but had since been told. In the despicable sequel Onorato had raised his dagger to strike Armand when the Viking, as marshal, ordered his men to fire.

Every arrow, save one, had struck the primo don. Yet one bowman turned in the direction of his phantom prima donna and struck her through the cheek. Now less than a year later, Esmeralda was running free before her victim, cheered by the watchers on Verona's walls as if she was a heroine. Sabatino's hand upon

Armand's shoulder woke him from his reverie. He scanned for Ilaria, frowning as he considered how fretful she must have been to see her.

Sabatino and Armand both scanned among the pack following Esmeralda. Neither Aurelie, Ilaria or Maxine appeared among them, nor any Dragoness. Then a wave of relief swept Armand's mind as he recognised Teresa and Fiametta surging through the gaggle in pursuit. Half a minute more passed in anxious wait. Sabatino's hand snapped again.

'There's *my* troublemaker! Ah and yours! And the duchess further back.'

'Look Astor.' said the duke beside them. 'Here comes your sister.'

'Yoli!' cried the junior squire.

His call was enough for the three running below to gain their bearings on an adoring audience. Aurelie, Ilaria, Yolanthe and Maxine waved and smiled as they pushed on. Their backs drew forward toward Harvest Gate as the party on the wall withdrew in haste, intent to make their way to watch them finish at Saint Fermo Square.

It seemed clear none of their loved ones would win the race. Yet by look of the stragglers that ambled after them, they wouldn't run last. For last of all came two battered athletes, side by side, with three dawdling behind them.

Down upon the course Ilaria, Aurelie and Maxine spied Esmeralda ahead, still running comfortably yet nearing Harvest Gate. Despite their setback Teresa and Fiametta appeared to be catching the leaders. But so was the mouthy Priscilla who was bound to cause trouble.

'Fuck!' spat Vendramina. 'Look at those two!'

Every eye scanned right.

The two sows Marietta had ordered forward in support — who had no need to heed the rules — were running an aggressive short cut across the corner. Though they leapt antically through that wetter, muddier section, the straight line they struck directly at Harvest Gate would see them meet the leaders just ahead or behind Teresa and Fiametta.

Ilaria made a decision and ordered them to separate. She would slow for Yolanthe and they would finish together. One had begun the event ill-prepared. The other was battered beyond expectation. Both knew they could finish but had no chance of catching the leaders. With the risk of another assault now looming, Aurelie, Maxine, Vendramina and Greta must run forward in support. Moments before they parted Aurelie warned them all.

'The path rises from here to the basilica. Last year many fell out from spurring too soon. If we lift our pace and hold, then lift again at the square, we may catch the leaders!'

They raced off together.

Ilaria slowed to fall back with Yolanthe as both shared a stoic smile. The sight of Ilaria made the young duchess realise that so far, the cost of their fucking madness to herself, was as nothing compared to what she had gained to entrench her alliance with Ilaria. Now after saving her at the height of the violence, it would be hard for their relationship to hover at a distance. Moreover, the satisfaction Yolanthe felt from smashing her foot into the face of that bitch who had pushed her at the start ... was exquisite.

Chapter 29 the little Harlot

The racing quartet of Aurelie, Maxine, Vendramina and Greta ran forward together. They also spied those two sneaking rivals cut a short path over the marsh to run through Harvest Gate just behind Teresa and Fiametta. The cackling Priscilla now had close support to help her wreak more mischief. That felt like a setback to our racing quartet but they soon felt relief. Moments later as they followed through the gate, to Aurelie's surprise she found they wouldn't have to wait until reaching Herb Market Square to catch up with the laggards. Trailers who had spurred too soon were now labouring just ahead of them.

That sight lifted the spirits of our quartet. When they had separated from Ilaria, not counting two cheats, eleven racers stood between themselves and Esmeralda. Now as they raced by the castle, three slipped behind them to reveal four more floundering ahead.

'Merciful Heaven!' cried Maxine. 'Look there!'

Beyond the four strugglers, indeed just in front of them, ran the foremost quintet with Esmeralda at their head, and all were now racing for Jupiter's Gate. Not only was the scar-faced countess now close enough to see, more incredibly, the four that ran in her wake were so hot upon Esmeralda's heels that every spirit lifted in hope that she wouldn't reach the end uncontested.

At the head of those chasers ran the plucky laundress with Priscilla hanging close off her shoulder. Fiametta and Teresa ran a distance behind yet were gaining with every stride. Every runner ahead was lifting to catch the leader. But against the now rising path, even Esmeralda began to slow in an effort to conserve strength for a surge at the end.

Unlike our own Teresa and Fiametta however, Priscilla and the laundress hadn't been hardened by the discipline of running each day, nor by the challenge of a gruelling climb at the last, like Sycamore Hill, to harden their will and deepen their endurance. Yet it soon became clear, Priscilla had little thought for conserving her energy to reach the end at all. She ran for a single purpose — to thwart any rival who threatened her powerful new patron.

Ahead of them all was Jupiter's Gate. Esmeralda raced through the left side of the twin portals as waves, shouts and cries of excitement, lifted upon both sides. Just seconds behind her, neck and neck came Priscilla and the laundress, racing at it together. Priscilla glared at her battered rival. The laundress risked a glance in return and then locked her eyes straight ahead.

They appeared the same age and stood the same height, matching each other, stride for stride. The white portals loomed. Teresa and Metta ran ten yards behind yet Priscilla was so locked upon her rival that she had no notion they were closing so fast. The laundress veered left. Priscilla drew right. In a moment they'd flash through together upon separate sides.

Then just before entering Priscilla braced and LAUNCHED herself sideways like a startled cat, reaching with both claws! One claw SHOVED at the shoulder! The other claw SHOVED at the laundress's cheek! Under the weight of such hurtling momentum, the hapless girl staggered, then sprawled and SMASHED her head into the stark white stone!

Priscilla spun in a racing pirouette to glance and gloat. The laundress careered, mind utterly gone, hung groggily for an instant then sprawled in a heap on the street.

Onlookers swarmed to the crumpled woman. They were shaking fists, screaming and shouting FOUL PLAY, angrily plucking the backs of fingertips under their chins at the smiling assassin who now ran free and clear. Priscilla smiled at the impotent threats, half-turned to offer her ass, then smacked her branded cheek and howled in triumph.

'Don't mess with the Rampant Boar's bitches!'

She spun to scan forward. Her patron was running free. They were so near the end it appeared that Priscilla was anticipating her work to be all but done. She spun a final demi-pirouette to face the scene of her carnage and blow her victim a mocking farewell kiss. Still running away rearward, Priscilla shut her eyes for an instant and pouted her lips.

As her eyes reopened, like a pair of avenging angels, Fiametta and Teresa came charging through Jupiter's Gate. Priscilla's eyes leapt! She spun about wildly, cursing to Heaven with her claws in the air. She cursed her stupidity at taking that moment to gloat. Like a thief spotted in the market, panic seized Priscilla as she burst into a flat sprint.

But this bitch of the Boar had spent all her energy catching a hapless victim. Prisicilla was gasping for air, chest heaving, thighs screaming as her feet pounded yet seemed to go nowhere. Her arms swung wildly, tossing her about, mocking her effort to escape. That manic surge brought her closer to her patron. But Priscilla knew a pair of rivals were coming and now she was the last line of defence.

Ironically, though Priscilla hadn't seen them, running seconds behind her pursuers, were the two sneaky sows. Yet as they approached Jupiter's Gate, a bystander recognised one as a compatriot of the villain who had hurt the laundress. The bystander pointed a finger, shouted in recognition. Another pointed at the telltale brand on their rumps. Without the nerve to risk going forward, the gulping duet spun on their heels and ran back in the opposite direction.

Unwittingly Priscilla's taunt had cost her that chance of support in her most dire moment. She glanced back again. She knew she'd be caught in a moment. She glanced ahead and filled her lungs. Unused to her patron's new title, Priscilla screamed in warning.

'RUN Donna Montecchi! RUN! RUN! RUN!'

Hearing the tone of sheer panic, Esmeralda risked a backward glance, revealing her vivid scar and a startled look in her eyes. Even her pursuers saw the perfect blend of shock and anger written plainly on her face.

CLANG! CLANG! CLANG! CLANG! CLANG!

Mighty Rengo exploded in announcement to all.

The race leader – Esmeralda – was passing by the mouth of Herb Market Square. Wild ranting and cheering erupted. Yet before

Esmeralda could turn to run on, more anger rose at the sight of Aurelie as she hurtled through Jupiter's Gate alongside Maxine.

Aurelie's heart had leapt at the sound of the bell, then leapt again to see Esmeralda so close. And perhaps, just as Sabatino had warned, the startling spur of that clanging and cheering at Herb Market Square might now lure the leaders into pushing too soon. Three quarters of a mile lay ahead. All at once Aurelie felt the chance to win was very real. If her old friend panicked now, she might still catch her before the finish! Aurelie felt as if the Hill loomed ahead of her one final time yet now she was more ready than ever to climb it.

Priscilla continued to fall behind her patron, puffing and gulping like a drowning woman. She watched her vanish into the snaking turns beyond. Then as Priscilla entered the first turn herself, she could hear Fiametta and Teresa in her wake, running her down. They could sense her desperation, smell her guilt as she twisted through one turn, then another.

'Priscilla FUCKING BITCH!' screamed Fiametta.

'We SAW you!' Teresa shouted.

A howling laugh rose ahead of them.

'Fuck BOTH of you!' She tilted her head and laughed aloud, cackling in defiance.

Fiametta realised her own breath was labouring. Her eyes were stinging with sweat, thighs and calves burnt in the grip of tension. The hard pace from the south-east corner was taking a heavy toll. She glanced to check her teammate, then blinked and looked again.

Like a wild mare in an open field Teresa was running effortlessly. Her eyes were bright. Her breath was strong. In an instant Fiametta knew what she must do. Yes she was fast. But she no longer had a chance to win. In a moment they'd catch up to the cackling bitch who glanced back before every turn to check on her pursuers. That would be her chance.

They were hot on Priscilla's heels as she approached the exit turn. The Sow glanced back and cackled. Yet as she looked forward to mount the final turn, Fiametta burst ahead of Teresa to vanish around the corner. A SCREAM erupted. An instant later Teresa hurtled through and collided with the tangled pair. Priscilla and Fiametta were SMASHING at each other for all they were worth. Teresa spun to gain her balance and began to slow.

But just before she did so, there in plain sight Teresa had seen Esmeralda — much closer than she had expected — racing on for the basilica. The river path to the winning post lay beyond it. Teresa was wavering as Fiametta punched wildly yet the wildcat took an instant to glance and see. She glared in hot anger at Teresa.

'Don't you DARE STOP! I've got this fucking BITCH! GO Teresa! GO!'

Off raced Teresa to run the leader down.

Grappling together in a frenzy, Fiametta reached with her digging fingers. She felt firm purchase as her nails dug deep into the bun of Priscilla's hair. She took a deep breath and wrenched the cackling head down in an arc, stepping in to tip her balance at the same moment.

Arms flailing wide Priscilla SWUNG forward.

Just as she did so Fiametta lifted the captured head up FAST to expose the belly. Priscilla's eyes leapt! Instinctively she knew but her hands plunged far too late to protect herself as Fiametta's curled fist swung HARD and SMASHED into her.

An explosion of air mixed with a bursting groan. Priscilla was engulfed in misery and now at the mercy of an attacker who could take an instant to assess. Their eyes met. HATE defied PITY. With no shred of mercy the Dragoness repeated the manoeuvre. PUSH! LIFT! SMASH!

Fiametta thumped the belly harder, then shoved the crumpling form of her rival to the ground. Her feminine employer had ensured that the Viking taught her girls not only how to fight but how to finish. Fiametta always remembered his grim warning.

I have many dead friends who, for mercy's sake, walked away before the job was done. If the enemy have at you then have at them harder. If you bring them down don't leave them with the capacity to rise and follow you.

Just as Fiametta heard those harsh words in her mind, Aurelie and Maxine burst round the corner to be greeted by a grisly sight.

Fiametta had straddled Priscilla, two hands gripping the hair above her temples, drawing the head toward her. Although both women glanced as they ran past, neither faltered in their stride, even as a whimpering plea rose behind them.

'No ... no ... Metta PLEASE!'

The back of Priscilla's head thumped against the street. Fiametta's angry eyes scanned about. She heard runners entering the snaking corners. Aurelie and Maxine were racing on as Teresa now ran hot on Esmeralda's heels. They vanished around the northern side of the basilica. Fiametta stood and glared down at her victim.

'Zita does *our* laundry. She'd better be alright. Or the Viking will be pissed.'

A horrible awareness filled Priscilla's eyes. She feared the Viking even more than her own wicked employer. She rolled onto her side, curling like a child as the back of Fiametta's fingertips flicked under her chin. She hung for a moment, wondering where Brianna had got to. Then Fiametta ran on, intent to see it through to the finish. She would arrive with a satisfied smile and a lively report.

After the mayhem of watchers who had lined the way from Harvest Gate to Herb Market Square, the next section of turns and the stretch beyond to the final turn at the basilica, was always an isolated portion of the course. But from that point on, the battlement walls following the river that ran through to the finish, would be teeming with expectant watchers.

And so when Esmeralda burst into sight beyond that last corner, a wave of welcoming cheers rose up and surged along the battlement walls ahead of her. Now in such close proximity she was more easily recognised. None knew her new title but most knew her old title. Wildly excited to see that muscled warrioress striding alone in the centre of the course, a chant began to rise in their throats for *Montecchi*.

For Esmeralda it must have seemed like a dream.

Then like a clap of thunder that bursts from a darkening sky, a *second* cheer erupted. Esmeralda's brows knit with foreboding. Willing herself not to glance back she kept her eyes forward, but the temptation to know rose like a spectre. Then another wild cheer burst from behind and the urge to know overcame her. Esmeralda turned to look over her right shoulder. As if emerging from a fog in her dream, Aurelie and Maxine had turned onto the final path.

At two hundred yards, they were coming on like demons yet somehow, the little harlot who had been so hot on Esmeralda's heels seemed to have vanished completely.

With less than half a mile to run, she allowed herself to smile. Her eyes scanned front but then jumped in horror. There upon her left was Teresa. I stood at the finishing post with the men watching them come.

Cupid's Balls! The sight of both was confounding, like a panther and gazelle running side by side. And unlike the rising path both had climbed to finally meet the river, deliciously now, Teresa could feel the ground falling away. Her muscles were filling with fire as her feet sprouted wings.

Maxine and Aurelie felt it too and lifted to a sprint still hoping to catch Esmeralda. But a gasp rose from the wall. The panther launched a paw in exasperation and flung it hard against the gazelle, shoving her towards the wall. Teresa floundered and steadied but Esmeralda gained a yard.

'Run TERESA!' screamed Aurelie.

Many watching on who were suddenly incensed now had a name for the gazelle. A rival chant rose to challenge the chant for Montecchi. Teresa's name lifted on their lips, spreading along the riverbank like a windswept fire along, racing ahead of them. Teresa spurred again and a mighty cheer erupted!

To Esmeralda's chagrin the little harlot had become their favourite!

Again Teresa ran abreast of Esmeralda. Black eyes glared angrily as another hand launched to strike not to push. It smashed Teresa's cheek. Howls of derision leapt from the wall. Esmeralda was desperate to taunt the little harlot but couldn't afford to slow. She lashed out again and again. With each burst of effort the pace of both racers, stuttered for an instant, then burst on.

Suddenly a cheer rose behind. Esmeralda risked a desperate glance. Her assaults had cost her pace and energy. Her panic escalated. Not twenty yards behind, Aurelie and Maxine were storming toward her. The finishing post loomed ahead. Teresa surged, her nose reached the front as a wild cheer carrying her name boomed its encouragement.

The exalted name of Montecchi was gone, banished from their lips in favour of a tramp from Verona's streets. Hot anger coursed through Esmeralda's muscular body. In an explosion of rage her entire form was pulsing with energy as she burst forward to retake the lead. Teresa spurred again. For a heart stopping instant they ran side by side.

With less than a quarter mile to run, panic rose on the scar-torn face. Esmeralda's mind, racing faster than her feet made a desperate decision. She drew her left fist across her belly to the right. She lifted it high. Then with all her might she SWUNG it like a flail, intent on SMASHING the little trollop's face. A gasp erupted as it flew!

Accusing fingers pointed!

Passionate hands leapt in protest!

Yet after being stung twice already, Teresa was no fool. As that clenched fist SWUNG hard to assure Esmeralda of victory, in the simplest motion imaginable, the little harlot ducked! The angry fist hit nothing but air! Raucous laughter poured in from every side. Then as Teresa leapt into a fiery sprint for the finish, the weight from Esmeralda's shoulder — driven behind the blow to ensure she would hurt her victim — had pulled her to the left with no support.

The overreaching Countess von Bremmer swayed, teetered, then crashed into the battlement wall as another mighty cheer erupted to see her pay for that treachery. Against the pain in Esmeralda's shoulder, she glanced off the wall in a stumbling pirouette, regathered her poise and ran on. I felt sure that sight of Teresa running to the finish must have broken her black heart and filled her with rage. Yet far worse for Esmeralda, the thunderous reaction from all that celebrated her failure, must have crushed every last vestige of her pride.

In the time it had taken for Esmeralda to right herself, Teresa drew a dozen more yards ahead. Stonily the newly minted countess stared after the little harlot. There was no more for her to do, so she lifted her chin and ran through to the finish as the second place getter.

'That should be enough penance for you Esmay?' suggested Aurelie as she halted. Maxine and herself had finished just a hair's breadth behind and were puffing and panting, almost by her side. Esmeralda glared venomously.

'Don't presume to call me that anymore.'

It was clear to Maxine that Esmeralda's anger over that result was very raw.

'Please don't blame Teresa Madon ... Countess!' Maxine pleaded. 'Heaven was watching us all.'

Aurelie expected a hot rejoinder but Esmeralda pressed her lips and smouldered in silence.

'Nothing to say to a pair of French whores?' Aurelie offered glibly. 'Well then ... Esmeralda ... go in peace.'

An instant later Esmeralda's flame-haired serving woman hovered at her side to lower her veil back down and drape her body in fine linen. Countess von Bremmer stalked away toward the beckoning hand of her younger husband. The dangerous looking man stood at the open door of their sumptuous carriage. Maxine, fearful for Teresa at the hands of Esmeralda's animosity, spurred to follow but Aurelie gripped her arm.

'Let her go Max. She's had enough for one day. Hopefully for a lifetime.'

My wife turned to scan back along the course for a moment. 'Oh Madonna. Here comes trouble.' she quipped.

Aurelie turned expecting to see a final surge by some rampant Sows. Instead she saw a trail of independents streaming towards the finish. Among them was Yolanthe alongside the battered form of Ilaria. And before Aurelie's approaching husband could arrive to congratulate her, she grinned at Maxine and both ran back along the course.

They reached the lagging pair and slowed to a trot. The quartet formed up. Line abreast trotting behind them, smiling and chattering, were the remaining dragonesses — Vendramina, Greta, Fiametta — without their fearless leader.

'Lee Lee who won?' asked Ilaria.

'Who do you think?' she said coyly.

'The bitch?'

'Was beaten!' cried Maxine with a grin.

Aurelie lifted her brows. 'By a bold little harlot who ran for the Dragon.'

A cheers rang out from the trio behind them.

'Teresa!' Ilaria was beaming. 'Oh that's wonderful.'

'Sister-in-law you look ghastly. I'm so proud of you.'

'Oh Lee Lee I'm so proud of us all. Even Yoli!'

The duchess tilted her blue eyes to Heaven. 'Well yes darling but don't be so emotional.'

'Oh hush. And I'm so, so, so proud of Teresa.'

Aurelie frowned and pouted. 'How do *you* feel Ria? Perhaps we should get you to a —'

'In truth ...' Ilaria interrupted 'I feel better than I think I may appear. A medicus can wait. We have time. Give me a moment to catch my breath and see and ... and we still have to watch the men.'

Maxine glanced behind them. 'Where's Brianna?'

Vendramina lifted her brows. 'I saw her. She and Marietta were headed for the Saint Eufemia bridge.'

'That big one from the Boar?' Ilaria replied.

'Yes Angel ... scusi *Madonna*. The one who smashed up your face.'

'You mean to say' Yolanthe glared 'your bruiser went off with the tall hussy who pushed me at the start?'

'Yes Prima Donna ... scusi *Duchess*. The one that you kicked so hard in the head.'

A snickering chorus of blunt compliments erupted.

'You got her good.'

'She had it coming.'

'Ugly bitches all had it coming!' spat Fiametta.

Vendramina rolled her eyes. 'They were headed for the borgo together.'

Aurelie huffed. 'Her keeper may not take that well?'

'They're rivals Madonna' Greta put in 'but they've known each other for a very long time. And now Marietta's too battered for Luke to claim that she didn't give her all.'

'Yes.' Ilaria agreed. 'Brianna hurt her badly.'

'She had to give her more than what Marietta gave you. And enough to satisfy Luke when she doesn't show.'

'But now they'll get drunk.' mused Vendramina.

'Marietta and Luke?' asked Maxine.

'Marietta and Brianna ...' Vendramina replied. 'And then sleep it off together for days.'

The comment raised a cackle. Greta grinned at the look of confusion on Ilaria's face.

'They used to be lovers.' Greta offered bluntly wondering if it may raise a brow.

'Lovers? Oh I see.' Ilaria, Maxine and Aurelie betrayed their surprise though Yolanthe had none to betray.

'We fuck men for a living' Greta declared. 'But men are fuckers!'

Fiametta flicked the back of her nails in agreement.

'It's hard to *love* any man when you have to deal with them as we do.'

'Maybe later.' Vendramina added. 'When we're free of this life.'

'I see.' Ilaria replied contritely. 'Hmm. Now ladies let's all smile and congratulate the winner.'

They halted beyond the finish together. Teresa came running and smacked into their embrace. They hugged her hard and smothered each other with kisses in celebration and relief as the men's entourage approached.

'Well ...' Ilaria began 'whether your leader has left us to love our enemy or returns in time to —'

'You're our leader now Madonna Capulet.'

Vendramina had said so but every Dragoness smiled.

Ilaria blushed. 'For a moment today, I did feel like it. And that was wonderful.' Her bright green eyes gleamed at the victor. 'However … Teresa is our shining star today.' Everyone patted their new heroine. 'And nothing will ever take that from her.'

Ilaria listened fondly to all their candid banter, knowing after that day, she may have very little chance to interact with them again. It relieved her to know that before the sun set, she would at least have the chance to offer Teresa an opportunity to extract herself from that life.

Before the men dared to impose upon their celebration, Fabrizio appeared with an armful of silver satin wraps to offer our competitors, now including Yolanthe and much to her own interest. Beginning with each elite woman, the duchess first of course, he laid the shimmering folds over each pair of shoulders with a dutiful inclination of the head then assisted to ensure it was draped to perfection.

No, Maxine couldn't help herself but to assist him.

'Tits of Venus.' Yolanthe whispered. 'You say he's Armand's squire?'

'Junior squire.' Ilaria replied.

Fabrizio tied each wrap at the waist with a silken pearl cord, weighted upon each end with an elegant tassel, to ensure it hung and held. The Dragonesses came next, sighing over the beautiful fabric. Fabrizio treated each as if they were elite signorinas, then received what had become a traditional kiss upon his cheek and smile of appreciation.

And despite what Fiametta had said before about the life they led, the youngest had clearly grown fond of Fabio. Knowing there would be no practice tomorrow, she looked very loathe to leave his company. Every Dragoness stared at her in sympathy as they watched Fabrizio tie her waist, perhaps more reluctantly than any other. She kissed his cheek. She offered a wan smile but looked for all the world as if she'd rather cry. His eyes held her for a moment.

Impulsively Fiametta grabbed his shirt and pulled him to her. She kissed him hard, burst into tears and smacked his chest, turning fast to fall into Greta's embrace as the other young women tried to soothe her. Yolanthe leaned to Ilaria and Aurelie.

'I've never seen a server offered such affection.'

'I told you everyone loves Fabio.'

'Some perhaps too fondly.' Aurelie added.

'Fabrizio.' Yolanthe's command brought him to her.

'How do I look now darling?'

'Your Grace is ...' he glanced at Fiametta 'even more beautiful than before.'

'Hmm. I feel more hideous than *ever* before. Yet now ... I actually believe you.'

Ilaria summoned the entourage together. She informed them the wraps were a keepsake of their time together. She and Aurelie both thanked them for their great service. Aurelie promised that she and Pruetta had agreed they would all receive their payment before sunset.

'And Teresa.' Ilaria smiled. 'For safety the golden ecus you earned for winning will be lodged into the mercantile bank. If you come to see me tomorrow, we'll go there together and arrange a note of credit in your name.'

Suddenly a large pair of arms wrapped around Ilaria from behind. Eyes lifted and smiles curved to see Armand in their company. Already I had my own arms around Maxine, congratulating her and asking forgiveness for my antics in the mule race. When Ilaria turned to kiss Armand of course, he was angered to see how battered she had become at the hands of the entrants.

'Never fear Don Capulet.' said Fiametta. 'Her attackers fared far worse.'

'We saw to it!' spat Vendramina.

'Did you?' Armand frowned. 'I hope so.'

'We did Signore.' said Vendramina. 'And Madonna Capulet was brave!'

Armand pouted in thought. 'Indeed?'

'Yes. And the prima donna duchess can't run at all but she scraps like a wildcat!'

Armand turned the her lifting a brow.

'Somehow that doesn't surprise me at all.'

That made the Duchess grin with great satisfaction.

'And what a tongue she has!' Greta cried. 'She called the countess a soiled —'

'Girls!' cried Aurelie. 'I fear it's time for the men to prepare for their own contest and you must report to Pruetta. Vendramina. 'Til Brianna reappears you're in charge. Stay together and be safe.'

'Yes Prima Donna.'

The Dragonesses closed ranks and fell to chattering as they began to wander away. Armand inspected Ilaria's face with renewed concern. She protested however that she would survive and was eager to regain their perch upon the wall to watch his own race. A chorus of agreement from Aurelie, Yolanthe and Maxine seemed to calm his anxiety.

For a moment thereafter, while the Dragonesses remained in sight, I saw Ilaria held in thought as she watched them go. In truth, the experience of seeing them deal so savagely with their rivals set her to wondering. And by the time she and Yoli had emerged from the snaking turns on the course, they were not too late to see the finale of young Fiametta's brutal treatment of Priscilla, the one who bragged how badly she would hurt Ilaria before she was done.

Last but not least, the admiring comments the girls had for Yolanthe's pluck, made Ilaria wonder how important it may be — even for an elite woman — to consider the notion of her self-protection. Since she had been married a year before, the world kept revealing itself to be a more dangerous place. More than ever before the race preparations had taught Ilaria to revel in the athletic use of her body.

And after watching the Dragonesses during the race, with regard to her own safety Ilaria now felt she understood, that her own reactions — intuitive or tutored — could make the difference between how well she fared through such violent encounters. Indeed had it not been for the girls presence on the course — the result of Maxine's care not her own — Ilaria feared that she may have more literally been left for dead.

Perhaps more importantly after this experience — because Ilaria now understood so much more of what happened to Esmeralda in the castle — knowing she was behind that effort to hurt Ilaria on the course, she felt she could no longer harbour any illusions about how dire the outcome may have been, had she not enjoyed the protection of five loyal Dragonesses.

Despite Ilaria's attempts to convince Armand that she felt hale, he was slow to appease. He frowned and fretted until Yolanthe — seeming to enjoy the oddness of an occasion that condoned her to parade in public dressed in nothing but a silken wrap — drew towards them. Ilaria watched her come and could see the mischief in her bright blue eyes. She watched Yoli draw her arm through Armand's and pat his broad shoulder with a smile. Then she brazenly snuggled against him, declaring that he mustn't fret.

'Adonis her hurt is nothing that great volumes of wine won't soon put an end to.'

In reply, just as Ilaria had done on the first day Brianna flirted with Armand, even with Yoli still attached to his arm, Ilaria stood before him, lifted her hands to his face and raised upon her toes to kiss him deeply. She knew Yoli would make no attempt to detach herself or even avert her gaze. Yet in truth, she no longer felt threatened by it.

Indeed, after the adventure they had shared Yoli's bald flirtations no longer seemed to bait her. Of course, that acceptance was one sign of progress which the duchess had hoped to see from her efforts. Then Ilaria urged her frowning husband to accept that, between blackened eyes, bloodied noses, scrapes, bruises and mud-strewn bodies, no woman in the race had escaped the event unscathed.

'Yes my heart, I'm sore and tired and thirsting. Yet when earned in such good company, I wouldn't exchange a single bruise or welt I have for any comfort under Heaven.'

'I feel the same Adonis.' Yoli agreed. 'However, given I had no time at all to prepare for this madness, I confess at this moment to being envious of Eloise for taking the chance, when it offered, to soak her pains away in a hot scented tub.'

Ilaria frowned. 'Yoli do you really?'

'No Ria of course not.'

Broad smiles lifted on their faces. To Armand, and to any who could see them, it was clear both women were well satisfied. Ilaria also confessed, perhaps just to allay Armand's lingering fears, that somehow even confronting the spectre of Esmeralda had released a heavy burden.

'I can understand that.' he replied quietly.

The warning bell chimed to call the men away.

'But for now' Ilaria smiled 'I want nothing more than to take my place on the wall and watch my husband run naked with the prince.'

'Oh yes darling I need to see that too.'

'So do I.' Aurelie added kissing her husband. 'No off you go Sab. And look after my brother.'

Only one race remained. The presentation of victors and last place getters would follow. Thereafter the walking of the gauntlet would end the festivities. And then quiet and peace could return to the streets of Verona.

Chapter 30 Debt & Dishonour

Away at the starting place just half an hour later, the assembly of male entrants was the largest the Race Marshal had seen. Nearly one hundred in all stood a dozen abreast and eight or nine deep from the line. Some exalted men stood among the fore with a sea of naked, hard-muscled commoners ranged behind them. They varied greatly in height, shape and muscularity. Yet no matter if lean, stout or otherwise, all standing ready knew that — with or without preparation — they could run the gruelling course to the end without halt.

Unlike the bodies of the women that had run before them, the men's wide necks, shoulders, biceps and forearms bulged with muscles. Male endowments of every size hung for all to see, above large, middling or smaller parcels below. Some were planted in a mass of wiry hair while others were so bald as to appear shaven, which indeed some were. To ensure against any suggestion of effeminacy, with the exception of one, none had footwear of any description.

Prince Escalus stood among the fore. Yes he was naked with a few local notables ranged to either side of him, , including Armand and Sabatino. Most had divested adornments from their fingers, wrists and necks. Yet for the sake of his rank as Podestà Escalus still wore his ring of office. Back among the rearmost, as yet unseen by our party, was the man we received the grim warning to beware.

With a little time left before the ratchet warning sounded, and while many stood challenging each other to wager upon the finish, Escalus agreed to hold the place beside him for Armand who slipped away quietly before the time to do so was lost. To all intents he was heading to the road's edge to relieve himself. Neither Sabatino nor Tristan, positioned near the prince, assumed he would mislead them.

I had taken up a place in the centre of the third rank and watched as he slipped away. As Armand had announced, he did stop to relieve himself. No I won't describe that event — pay attention. Yet when that was done he didn't turn back the way he'd come but wandered to the rear to seek the man in question. From the description we had heard the fellow shouldn't be hard to recognise.

As an accoladed chevalier now in possession of knowledge regarding a threat against him, Armand felt compelled to face it openly. His code wouldn't allow him to cower in wait. You know his great spiritual guide in such matters was the venerated author Geoffroi de Charny. His writings were clear on such points. And Armand's late mentor Toulon taught him to learn as much as possible about a threat before it has a chance to assail you.

"Many a man's perished for the lack of gathering timely intelligence." Toulon would say. "Yet many have survived for the sake of gathering it before time."

Armand didn't need to search for long. The man's shock of red hair made him easy to sight. The sandals on his feet were another signature trait. It seemed he was the only man running whose vanity didn't compel him to go barefoot. Spying the man standing in conversation at the very last rank, facing away from him, Armand approached and tapped lightly upon his muscular shoulder.

The tall broad man turned with a smile that vanished when he saw who sought his attention. His light blue eyes darkened. Even from the distance where I stood — having followed Armand — I could see the man was a foreboding mountain of muscular form. The sight of him made me dread the thought of anyone tangling with him. I slipped in among the runners and edged closer, each step made him appear more formidable.

Just as Onorato Montecchi had stood three inches clear of Armand when we first met him, this stranger towered before him. Their eyes held each other's for a moment, blue and blue. Armand seemed calm and sober. The stranger seemed to smoulder with a calm kind of hostility.

'I'm told you're a smith? Weapons are your specialty?'

'I am.' he grunted. 'They are.'

The absence of any attempt to offer a deferential title to Armand, felt like an ominous start. Yes they may be naked, and so bereft of any signs of rank, yet from the look on the brute's face when he turned, I had little doubt that he recognised the man who hailed him.

'I'm told your name's *Silvius*.'

'Then you're told too much for my comfort when I have no knowledge of you. Move on.'

'I am —'

'I know who you are.' He stepped from the line to distance their conference.

Armand turned cautiously to face him.

'Hmm. No knowledge of me yet you know who I am.'

'Perhaps I should have said I have no *acquaintance*. Indeed I crave none.'

'What say I came to your forge as a *patron?*'

'I'd say I was busy.'

'And if I offered you a generous commission to —'

'I'd still be busy.'

'I see. I mean you no trouble Silvius. I certainly don't mean to offend.'

'Yet this approach is becoming offensive.'

Their eyes narrowed at each other.

'I'm told you may be some manner of relation to the late Don Montecchi.'

'The man you *swindled*.'

'In the face of blunt proof the law here declared the reverse to be true.'

'The man you *killed*.'

'The Marshal's ordered ended Onorato's life. I faced him in a fair fight which I also did my utmost to avoid.'

'The man whose actions caused his widow to be tortured by the inquisition.'

'She also brought that upon herself when she tried to assassinate me from the shadows.'

'You're a high and mighty chevalier. I'm the son of a slave who was bedded by her master. Now he's dead but his widow kept my mother in service. More recently that widow requested a service from me ... for a price.'

'Whatever the price is —'

'The price *was* her slave's freedom.'

'I see.'

'What you do not see ... is that her slave is now *free*.'

'Which means you've agreed to render this service.'

'I have.'

'And have already gained by your agreement.'

'I have. Then when the service is rendered, my mother and I will both gain by it, for then we'll *both* be free.'

'Hmm. That sounds like a difficult agreement to extract yourself from.'

'It is. For until then, my own freedom remains in her possession. And now I stand in her debt for the sake of my mother's freedom.'

'You understand Silvius that I now have a firm pact with the Montecchi. Aldobrando will never —'

'Don Aldobrando controls the faction in Verona. My owner no longer lives in Verona. And after a recent marriage, she ceased to be a Montecchi. I assume that today you discovered she's now *von Bremmer* and a countess to boot.'

'Yes. That was a surprise.'

'She intended it to be, even for Don Aldobrando. Her new husband's every bit as lethal as her former, yet on more intimate terms with the emperor. And so now, my owner has even more power to get what she wants. She tells me she answers to none but the count and the emperor himself.'

Armand looked at him thoughtfully for a moment. The marshal's rachet sounded.

'Time to return to where you're welcome.'

'Yes. Life waits for no man.'

'And death chases them all.'

'Touche. But what say Silvius, if I offered to purchase your freedom from Esmeralda at any price ... then offered it back to you gratis?'

'I say I'd accept. But do you really think she would sell my freedom to you?'

'Given what you've explained? No. No I feel certain she wouldn't. I'm sure she has just one price in mind.'

'I'm sure that's correct.'

'I'll leave you to the race and wish you the best in your efforts today. As I said, I came with no intention to offend, just to ensure you understood I seek no quarrel with you.'

'I *seek* no quarrel either. But I've made an agreement. I'm just a dumb smith, not a fine chevalier. I must see the world as it is and live in it as I must.'

'That's pragmatic.'

'And you should know. It's agreed that even if I fail in the attempt to offer my service, any validated effort will ensure my mother's freedom. And so one way or another ...'

'You must make a valid attempt. Mmm.' Armand turned to leave but then turned back again. 'You say you're not a chevalier Silvius. Yet you had the grace to warn me on several counts. That was well done.'

'For a lowly dumb smith?'

'For any man. I hope someday we may be friends. Yet I fear that may not —'

'Don't approach me again.'

'I won't do so intentionally Silvius. Yet if fate draws us together again and you fail to address me with the respect due to my rank ... I will be *obliged* to cite you for the fault.'

'You hope for another duel? A fair combat?'

'It would count for you as a *valid* attempt.'

'It would. But I warn you ... I'm no chevalier.'

'That's a pity to hear you say so. I believe you may have the heart of a fine man.'

Without another word Armand departed.

Moments later he rejoined the Prince at the fore.

'While you were gone I felt the need to go myself.' said Escalus. 'When I didn't see you I wandered a little and saw you in discussion with the smith.'

'Ah yes. I made his acquaintance.'

'Be careful Armand. You know who he is?'

'I was advised. I wanted to meet him and see if he may be willing to do me a service.'

'Success?'

'He has been offered a valuable new commission to keep him distracted.'

'By yourself?'

'By another.'

'From what I know of the man, he'll not only see it done but the result will be worth it.'

Armand lifted his brows. 'He's reliable?'

'So I'm told.' Escalus agreed. 'And though young, he's already considered a very skilled artisan.'

'I suspect that's true.' Armand replied.

Shortly thereafter, with much less ado than the women afforded him, the venerable Race Marshal stood ready to start the final race. Before the Master Crier bellowed at the start, the men jostled and bumped. Some even farted in ribald rivalry. For the last time that day the breasting line shot up, the weights fell fast and the entrants ran off.

Over the first two miles many bumped and shoved at the prince in good humour. And Escalus gave as much as he received with a fulsome spirit. Yet unlike the treatment of elite entrants in the women's race, unless a rival genuinely challenged him for his place among the fore, none dared to seriously assault Verona's lord of order and justice.

Armand was fit and ready of course. So was the Prince. They ran together like titans who had been promised the hand of a goddess in victory. Sabatino held just behind them. Tristan however, who had entered only for Armand's security ran at the rear with me. He appeared to be unknown to Silvius and followed the hulking brute like a shadow.

By the time Armand, Escalus and Sabatino reached the southeast corner of the battlements together, they were still in the leading pack, yet well behind the leaders. Princess Florentia, Ilaria, Aurelie and the duchess all stood together, drinking, waving and smiling. As the men raced along below the wall, they blew kisses to their wives while racers, more fleet of foot and more needful of the prize, strode past them.

By that moment Ilaria and Aurelie still knew nothing of the presence of Onorato's bastard running among us. Nor did they seem to glance at Silvius when he appeared, even though Tristan and I ran no more than ten yards behind him. We both held steadily with no apparent wish to accelerate.

However Maxine was the source of our intelligence about Silvius and stood with them. As the brute loped towards them under his shock of red hair, her eyes latched onto his unmistakable form. The only other who seemed to take note of him was the duchess. I presume any man with the same-coloured hair always attracted her attention. He seemed to loom toward the wall before turning to pass by. Perhaps he was considering a halt at the corner gate.

Silvius was tall and wide with frightening muscularity. But he was a smith not a warrior. By the time he reached that corner he was labouring. The notion he might somehow keep the pace in such a race began to loom as the absurdity it was. By that time, whatever danger Silvius may have in store for Armand, it no longer seemed credible it would occur during that event. That was the thought Tristan shared to me.

'I think Escalus's attendance is too much for his comfort. He and Armand have run together from the start. That oaf doesn't have the stamina to keep up with them.'

I puffed in reply. 'I tend to agree. Yet I fear he entered here for a reason that has something to do with his plan.'

'I'm sure you're right. Perhaps it was a chance to observe his quarry at closer quarters in a way that wouldn't arouse suspicion. That's what a genuine predator would do.'

'That sounds concerning.'

'What concerns me most is, if that's what he was doing here, if he was planning to strike today but felt intimidated by the prince —

then he stayed to observe. That means he's patient. A patient predator is far more dangerous.'

Indeed the men's event completed without great incident as far
as we were concerned. And though I was relieved at that outcome,
Tristan's conclusions had scared the living lights out of me. The first
and last were recorded for posterity. After the finish I heard it noted
by some of the most ancient bystanders, that running of the men's
footrace was the most harmless they had ever witnessed!

When the victors for every race were assembled together to
receive their precious lengths of silk in order of the events, Tristan
came first. He held the scarlet prize aloft to the cheers and squeals of
the Dragonesses. By then even Brianna had returned and stood
among them to see their exalted hero again.

The mule race victor came next and was a woman — daughter of
a fishmonger whose beast ran baskets of fish up Rooster Mountain
every day. The third victor to be presented was for the women's
footrace. Up rose young Teresa to shyly receive her bolt of green silk
from the hands of the princess. The final victor presented was for the
men's footrace of course, a cooper's son who finished well ahead of
us all.

Then in their turn the last place getters, including myself for the
mule race, were assembled and presented with pig legs and roosters. I
revelled at the chance to ride the gauntlet with my prize. Yet Maxine
chastised me for stripping again to ride the farting she-devil through
the throng. Cupid's Balls! That antic ride was utter bedlam. All that
was left of my pig leg was the bone!

As our quartet of last place getters re-entered Saint Fermo
Square, the church bells rang clear and were answered one final time
by mighty Rengo to announce the festival's closing. The sun was lowering. The extraordinary day was ending. Shadows began to reach
through the citadel.

Under the heavy influence of having drunk so deeply in celebration, the Dragonesses took their final leave of us. They walked on
together toward Castle Bridge. From there they crossed, a little too
boisterously, into the western borgo.

Ilaria, Armand, Aurelie, Sabatino and Tristan also drank deeply as they caroused with the duchess, her husband Duke Reynard, little brother Astor and Nobel.

The potent duke and duchess invited all to revel on at the sumptuous apartments Yolanthe had purchased. As they wandered back together, Caspar once more leading us all for safety, Eloise hadn't yet joined them. Nor had she returned to watch the men's race. The intoxicated duchess felt sure we'd find her returned to their abode, ready to greet us.

Her glamorous husband Reynard led her on as we followed them together. Just as Yolanthe had always boasted the Duke was handsome, perhaps twenty years her senior, and seemed affable and charming. As they walked together like smitten lovers it was plain to see why, despite her many flirtations in his absence, she spoke so fondly of him.

Astor walked alongside Yoli with Auguste Nobel while the Capulets and Cortelannis followed closely. Wandering together through the streets of Verona they were a distinguished group, laughing and embracing and toasting Tristan's success. It arose in their conversation that Esmeralda had vanished again after the end of the women's race. No sign of her new husband or any trace of their conveyance was reported thereafter. Most were convinced that in her anguish, and true to his promise not to linger, they must have quit the citadel in haste to return to the northern alps.

Esmeralda had said she intended to purchase a palazzo during their visit. That evening its whereabouts remained as much a mystery as the countess had been before her extraordinary re-appearance. Then Esmeralda was forgotten entirely as the exalted company passed through the distraction of Herb Market Square. The duke and duchess's apartments lay just beyond.

Before they made a final push to move on, Ilaria held them for a moment outside the site of the new emporium. She announced the architect had completed the foundation. Construction would begin on the following week. The intoxicated party cheered and hugged each other. Tristan declared the Emporium's first offering must be a gown made from his silken prize.

Ilaria added solemnly 'On this site an emporium will rise that shall bind our efforts together.'

Yolanthe replied 'More importantly darling a new faction has already risen and now binds us together.'

'Yes.' Ilaria smiled. 'Paris. Nobel. Capulet. Cortellani.'

'Then as the man who lays claim to initiating this giddy venture' Nobel put in 'I suggest that before the sun sets we retire in to celebrate together until the sun rises again!'

In that shadowy hour the citadel still bustled with carts offering wine, food and favours of all description. Despite that, our group's sense of festival celebration was withering save for the banquet they now planned to share. After the boisterous party entered the elegant apartments, now barely conscious of any need to dine, they drank even more. That caused every comment to become a target for the amusement of all.

All the day's fervour appeared to be stilled.

All the day's pain and threats seemed to be forgotten.

As darkness fell outside Verona's gates shut firmly. Within its walls, life upon the streets appeared to relax in a blur of safety and security. Yet not so among the guests of Duchess de Paris who began to realise something was amiss.

Where was Eloise?

Our Story Continues:

Capulet
Book 5: Retribution

Capulet
Book 6: Folly

www.ingramcontent.com/pod-product-compliance
Lightning Source LLC
Chambersburg PA
CBHW061608210726
48287CB00001B/42